WILD CARD

WILD CARD

Lora Leigh

St. Martin's Griffin
New York

This is a work of fiction. All of the characters, organizations, and events portrayed in this novel are either products of the author's imagination or are used fictitiously.

www.stmartins.com

ISBN 978-1-250-03106-8 (trade paperback)

First St. Martin's Griffin Edition: August 2012

10 9 8 7 6 5 4 3 2 1

I once knew a girl who claimed to be Irish. Whether the story she told me of Wild Irish Eyes is true or not (she wouldn't admit either way ☺), it still in part inspired the idea for this book.

So thanks to her and other Internet friends. Stories told, hours of laughter, What Ifs, and precious memories. The world is open to us now, as are stories true or imagined, and laughter with those across the seas, across the nation, or across the street is but a click away.

ACKNOWLEDGMENTS

Special thanks to Natalie, Jennifer, Melissa, Kelli—the best sis a writer could have—Roni, Janine and Annmarie, Chris and Jess. For the hours of reading, your comments, and your suggestions. I couldn't do it without you.

And special thanks to my editor Monique. Who doesn't mind to snap the whip, or listen to the ideas.

And to my family. Who put up with me when I'm on tight deadlines. My husband Tony who makes certain I eat, my son Bret who makes my coffee, and my daughter Holly who listens to me gripe when I get behind.

I couldn't do it without you.

WILD CARD

PROLOGUE I

Nathan sat beside his grandfather, Rory Malone, on the crude front porch of the shack he lived in. Nathan was only ten, but he knew exactly why Grandpop didn't live with him and his parents. Because Nathan's father, Grant, was ashamed of him.

"He's too fucking Irish," Grant would rage for hours after visiting with his father. "He uses that brogue like it's something to be proud of."

And God forbid that Nathan should let a hint of that brogue free, though he practiced it as often as he could away from his father.

Nathan's father didn't like being Irish. He didn't like people knowing he was Irish. If he could ship Grandpop off somewhere, then Nathan sometimes thought that his father would do it. But Grant Malone couldn't make Rory Malone do anything. The old man was as wise as the mountains and the cliffs around them, and just as stubborn.

"Nathan, my boy, look at that sunset." Rory pointed out the majestic colors that washed over the mountains. "Almost as pretty as Ireland, she is. Almost." And Nathan heard a whisper of homesickness in his grandpop's voice.

"Why don't you go back?" Nathan asked. "Dad says you have enough money to live anywhere."

He looked at his grandfather's weathered face. The bright

blue eyes, just like Nathan's, brighter than Nathan's father's and without the hints of green his father's had.

Grandpop smiled. A strange, sad little smile.

"Because my Erin is here." He pointed to the small grave-yard.

There, Nathan's grandma, Erin Malone, was buried. On one side of her were buried the two sons they lost in Vietnam, his uncles, Riordan and Rory Jr., and the daughter that had died of a fever, Nathan's aunt Edan.

"Grandma wouldn't want you to leave?" Nathan frowned. His grandma was dead, what would she care?

"Oh, now my Erin, she'd smile down on me no matter where I walked." Grandpop smiled that little smile again. "But I'd be separated from her, and I'd feel that separation in my soul, you see?"

Nathan shook his head.

Grandpop sighed. "You have the Irish eyes, boy. One of these days, you'll see from eyes, not your own, feel with a heart outside your chest. Wild Irish eyes, Nathan. When you love, love well and love true, and take care, lad, because those Irish eyes are windows into not just your own soul, but the soul of the one you love." Grandpop looked out at his Erin's grave. "And when you lose that heart, you can't leave the places where your memories are the best. And if I left her, I'd not be buried beside her."

Grandpop stared back at him then, and Nathan felt his chest grow tight at the thought of ever burying his grandpop in the hard, bleak soil.

"Wild Irish eyes," his grandpop murmured then. "My father gave me the same warning I give you now, boy. Don't lose the one you love. You lose a part of your soul when you do. The legacy of those eyes will ensure it."

Nathan frowned. That didn't make much sense, but maybe he'd ask his uncle Jordan about it later. Uncle Jordan still remembered his mother. He had been five when she died, just before Nathan's birth. But Uncle Jordan was in Houston right now on summer break with Nathan's older uncle Doran and his family.

"So my eyes are bad?" Nathan finally asked.

"Not bad." His grandpop sighed. "Not bad at all, boy. You'll see one of these days. One of these days, you'll see. Wild Irish eyes see what they shouldn't see, but even more." His grandfather stared down at him sadly. "The one who holds your soul, who holds your heart." He thumped Nathan's chest. "They see through you as well."

"Dad doesn't have Irish eyes then?" Grant's eyes had flecks of green. He always frowned. He always growled.

Worry flickered over Grandpop's face. "Your dad is a good man." He repeated what he always said.

"Is he, Grandpop?" Nathan thought about the baby sleeping in the house. The tiny baby that Grandpop said was his brother. The baby Grant Malone denied. "Little Rory should have a dad too."

Grandpop touched his head gently and said softly, "Nothing is as we think, boy. There are always layers, and layers, shades of gray and shades of black or white. You gotta find why, not see what."

"Because he doesn't love us," Nathan whispered, accepting it as only a child can.

And Grandpop shook his head. "Layers, son. Remember that. There's always what you don't know and what you don't see. And love doesn't always do what we think it should. Just remember that, and you'll do fine."

And he grew. He looked for layers, he looked for shades of gray. Nathan Malone matured, became a SEAL, and the layers drifted from his mind. But they were there. Always shifting, always moving. Until the day he saw hell. And from the ashes of hell, he learned there were layers he never knew existed.

PROLOGUE II
Sixteen years later

Nathan Malone sat at his desk in the office of the garage/service center he owned and watched the young woman talking to one of his mechanics.

She didn't look happy. She looked frustrated. Sun-streaked blond hair fell to her shoulders, a beautiful swath of waves that glistened in the sunlight. Nicely rounded, not too slender. She had a butt to die for beneath the black skirt she was wearing, and breasts that rose temptingly beneath a maroon blouse.

Slender heels completed the outfit. He wondered if those were hose or stockings she was wearing. She looked like a stocking woman.

Finally, she threw her hands up, looked around, and her gaze caught his. Her nostrils flared in determination and she moved quickly past the protesting mechanic to the door of his office.

He watched as the most amazing vision stalked across the floor and planted her hands on his desk, glaring at him.

"Look, all I need is a wrench," she said forcefully. "Just loan me one. Sell me one. I don't care. But if I have to go much farther in my car, I'm going to find myself hitchhiking. Do I look like I want to be hitchhiking today?" She spread her arms out from her body as she straightened, her pretty gray eyes cloudy, distressed, her pink lips tight as the mechanic moved in behind her.

"No, ma'am, you don't." Nathan shook his head, his gaze moving over her appreciatively before he looked around her at the mechanic. "Is there a reason why we're not looking at her car?" he asked the other man.

Sammy's eyes narrowed. "Garage bays are full, boss, I told her that."

"A wrench," she ground out between her teeth. "Just loan me the blasted wrench."

She was frustrated. Perspiration clung to her forehead, glistened at her cheeks. Then her expression smoothed with obvious control.

"Look, really." Her voice softened and he was enchanted. Right there, to the sound of a sweet Southern belle, Nathan Malone lost his heart. "I really just need a little bit of help here. I swear. My job interview isn't going to wait for me. I promise, I won't take long."

She smiled, and he felt his world tilt on its axis. A sweet curve of her lips, a hint of nervousness, frustration, and worry lingered in the soft curve. But she smiled at him. Hell, he felt like a teenager again.

He moved around the desk and held out his hand to the door. "Show me the car. We'll get you back on the road."

"Boss, we're packed," Sammy protested.

Nathan ignored him as the young woman turned and preceded him to the door. He was watching her ass as she walked and it was the damnedest view. His hands itched to touch her. Itched to cup those curves and feel them flex beneath his hands.

"I'm Sabella." She flashed him a smile over her shoulder. "I really appreciate this."

That Georgia accent was going to make him come in his jeans. No way was he going to hold it back if she kept talking to him.

This one was his.

"It's going to cost you," he drawled as he popped open the hood to her little sporty sedan.

"It always does." She sighed. "How much do you think?" She looked worried. She was definitely a woman with a goal and intent on getting there. Pretty polished nails, just enough makeup to highlight her features, and pretty soft lips.

"Dinner." He grinned back at her, catching the surprise in her eyes.

"Dinner?" Wariness filled her voice.

"Just dinner," he promised. For now. "Tonight."

She stared back at him for long seconds, those gray eyes seeming to sink inside him, to search, to warm places inside him he didn't know existed. Let alone knew they were cold.

Finally, her lips tipped into a charming, flirtatious grin.

"The bad boy of Alpine is asking me out to dinner?" she said mischievously. "I believe I just might swoon."

"That's not me. That's Sammy." He pointed to the mechanic. "I'm just a poor mechanic and Navy SEAL." The girls loved SEALs. Anything to impress her.

"Nathan Malone, the SEAL with the wild blue eyes and the heartbreaking grin," she stated. "I know who you are."

"But I don't know who you are," he stated somberly. "I'd love to find out."

That look again. Intense, probing. "Dinner," she finally agreed softly. "I'll meet you."

Whatever he could get. "Piedmont's." He named the most expensive restaurant in town, which wasn't saying much. "Seven."

"Seven it is. But I'll never make it if you don't fix my car."

Sabella kept a knowing smile to herself. She had a feeling if she just told him what was wrong with it, he'd never believe her anyway. She let him piddle around, find the loose hose, and tighten it. There, just like she said, all she needed was a wrench. Her daddy had taught her how to work on her own car a long time ago. Unfortunately, her own wrench was missing.

So she let him fix it. She played helpless. Because she liked the way he looked at her, the way his wild blue eyes darkened just a bit, seemed more neon in his tanned face.

"Seven," he reminded her as he closed the hood and stared down at her. "I'll be waiting on you."

"And I'll be there," she promised. Because there was no

way she was going to miss this. She'd seen him in town often enough, she'd even fantasized about him a time or two after glimpsing him.

The hot SEAL. The bad boy of Alpine. Every woman she knew at the college lusted after him. And Sabella decided, in that moment, Nathan was going to be hers.

Two years later

"Oh my God, Bella, what have you done?"

Bella jumped as she turned to face Nathan, seeing his wild eyes, his pale features, his hard, buff body stalking across the front yard, his chest slick with sweat, bits of the grass he had been cutting sticking to his jeans as he strode furiously to where her car met the back of his truck.

"It's just a little dent, Nathan. I promise . . ." Her heart was in her throat. Not in fear. He would never hurt her. But he sure knew how to pout when he wanted to.

"A little dent." He gripped her shoulders, moving her aside as he stared down at the crumpled fender as it sank into the bumper of his truck.

It was an accident. It was all his fault. If he hadn't been wearing those butt-snug jeans and boots with no shirt as he cut the lawn, it would have never happened.

"You hit my truck." Male pride and offended dignity filled his voice. "That's my truck, Bella."

Yes. It was. And he was very proud of the powerful, black four-by-four he babied worse than any woman would a child. She would be jealous if it weren't for the fact that he couldn't actually bring it into the house.

"I'm really sorry, Nathan." Her accent thickened as she stared up at him, biting her lip nervously as she wondered how much he would pout.

Nathan could go all quiet, somber, and answer her in monosyllables that drove her insane. He would glare at her.

He would watch ball games. He would come to bed late. Late. After she went to sleep. And wouldn't give her any until the next morning. It really wasn't fair.

"Nathan, please don't be mad at me . . ."

"How did you hit my truck? How? It was sitting in plain view. Plain view, Sabella." He was getting angry. He only said her full name when he was really getting angry or really, really horny. And he was not horny. Okay, this wasn't good. She could do without for days. But she didn't like it.

She stomped her foot, glaring back at him in irritation. "If it weren't for you, I would have never hit it."

"Me?" He stepped back, shaking his head fiercely. "How the hell was this my fault?"

"Because you were cutting the grass, with no shirt, in sexy jeans and boots, and seeing your tight ass striding across the lawn made me horny. You distracted me. It's all your fault. If you would dress properly things like this just would not happen, Nathan . . ."

He kissed her. It wasn't a gentle, easy kiss. It was rough and ready and smack full of lust as he jerked her against him, pressing his cock into her belly as she gasped in pleasure.

"You are so spanked." He picked her up, striding across the lawn, leaving her car door open, his truck abused. "Spanked, Sabella. I'm going to watch every inch of that pretty ass turn red."

He slammed the door behind him, locking it quickly before heading for the stairs.

"Oh, spank me, Nathan," she breathed teasingly into his ear. "Make me beg."

He shuddered against her, threw her on the bed and proceeded to make her beg.

One week later

"I'll be home in a week." He was dressed in jeans and a T-shirt. He didn't look like a badass Navy SEAL, he looked like her husband, going off on a business trip. Not a big deal.

She was good at fooling herself.

"The truck will be out of the shop tomorrow." She nodded as she watched him pull the duffel bag from the closet and turn to her. "I'll have it in the garage, all nice and pretty for you."

She grinned back at him cheekily as she brushed the long strands of her hair back from her face. "You owe me though. I had to flash some leg to get it done so fast. Your mechanics are so easy, Nathan."

He owned the garage and auto service station just at the edge of town. A thriving little business she knew he loved.

He grunted, his gaze going to her bare legs as she leaned back on the bed, her shorts riding up her thighs.

"Witch," he growled. "My ride is waiting downstairs and you know it."

She drew her shirt off and released her shorts, letting them fall down her legs. Watching him, she slid her fingers over the bare, wet folds between her thighs then lifted them to his lips.

Nathan groaned. She loved that sound. His lips parted and his eyes went wild as he tasted her.

"So make it a quickie," she whispered, desperate to have him, just one last time, before he left. She straightened on the bed as he neared, her fingers going to his belt, working it loose quickly. "I dare you. Fuck me like you mean it . . ."

He turned her, pushed her over the edge of the bed, and within seconds he was filling her. Hard and throbbing, stroking, penetrating, burying inside her in rapid hard strokes until she felt pure white-hot sensation wash over her.

"Nathan. Nathan, I love you," she cried out as he came over her, holding her in place as his hips jerked against her, his hands gripping her, fingers burning into her flesh.

And then he whispered the words. The lyrical flow of sound, Gaelic. He whispered his love for her in a language his grandfather had taught him, and she felt it in her soul.

"Always," she whispered, turning her head to him, taking his kiss. "Forever, Nathan."

One week later

Bella opened the door, and she froze. Nathan's uncle Jordan was standing beside the chaplain. She knew he was the chaplain by his dark uniform. Jordan was in his dress whites, his Navy hat in his hand, medals shining on his chest, and she felt the collapse of her spirit.

"Nathan's due home any day," she whispered, her lips numbing as she stared back at Jordan and saw his grief, his sorrow. "You're early, Jordan. He's not here yet."

She was crying. She could feel the tears, hot, blistering her skin as she pressed her fists tight to her stomach and felt her knees weakening.

"Bella." His voice was thick, unshed tears glittering in his eyes. "I'm sorry."

He was sorry? Sorry? He was tearing her soul right out of her chest and he was sorry?

She shook her head. "Please don't say it, Jordan. Please don't say it."

"Bella." He swallowed tightly. "You know I have to."

He had to. He had to destroy her.

"Mrs. Malone." The chaplain spoke for him. "Ma'am, it is my greatest regret to inform you—"

"No. No!" She screamed the words as Jordan caught her, dragging her into his arms and helping her into the house as the screams poured from her. They ripped from her chest, like a knife, brutal, merciless. The pain dragged her into a pit of such deep, stark despair that she didn't think she could survive.

"Nathan!" She cried out his name, screamed his name, she begged him. He swore he would always know when she needed him, even in death. Because he had that gift. It was the eyes, he had said, and she had laughed at him, and now she wished it were true. Because she needed Nathan, her Wild Irish eyes. "Oh God, Nathan!"

Six months later

Bella came awake to her own sobs, her chest heaving as she searched the bed, her hands reaching across the distance, clawing at the sheets, the pillow, desperate to find him.

He was bleeding. She could see the blood on his hands as though she were staring through his eyes. She could feel his agony, gut wrenching, desperate, a ragged gaping soul of unvarnished agony howling around her.

It had to be a dream. Sobs tore from her throat as she ripped at the blankets, a guttural cry of raw agony tearing from her heart.

"Nathan!" She screamed his name, her voice hoarse, raw from her tears, from the past horrific months.

The funeral . . . They hadn't even let her see him.

She fell forward, her tears dropping to the bed as she remembered, remembered and knew it wasn't a dream. Nathan was really gone. Forever.

They had closed his coffin to her. She hadn't been allowed to touch him, to kiss his beloved face, to whisper goodbye. There was nothing to hold on to, nothing to ease the agony breaking over her.

There was only the emptiness. The emptiness of her bed. Her life. There was only the horrible, aching hollow in her soul. It ate at her, burned into her mind and reminded her every second, every day, that Nathan was gone.

Nathan was gone.

Forever.

Except in her nightmares. Where he cried out her name. Where he touched her then backed away from her. Where he stared back at her with hollow grief. Or when she felt the pain that tore through him. Unending, agonizing, so much pain.

Then as quickly as they began, as fast as she realized it was Nathan's pain, the dreams would shift, change.

"I'll love you forever, witch." He leaned over her, naked, *his chest gleaming, golden flesh blocking out the sun as his brilliant, neon eyes watched her intently. "Feel my soul touch yours, Sabella. Feel me love you, baby . . ."*

An agonized cry rasped her throat as she clutched at air, the insubstantial memory drifting away, gone. Just as Nathan was gone.

"Oh God. Oh God. Nathan . . ."

She clutched his pillow to her breast, rocking herself as her head fell back and a scream ripped from her soul.

"Damn you, Nathan . . ."

CHAPTER ONE
Nine months later

Nathan Malone stood in the clinical white office he had been brought to. He was six months past the most horrific nightmare he could have imagined enduring. Six months. He knew how many days, how many hours, how many minutes and seconds had passed since he had "died."

Since the day he walked out his front door and headed into hell. The mission was supposed to be simple. Rescue three young girls from a cartel drug lord in Colombia and allow himself to be captured just long enough to draw out the government spy working with the cartel lord, Diego Fuentes.

There had been an electronic tracker in his heel that he could activate the moment he saw the spy. Unfortunately, the spy had known that. His heel had been sliced open before the spy ever appeared. Before Nathan could realize the danger he was in, he had been strapped to a hardwood table and the first of a series of synthetic drugs pumped into him.

Whore's dust. A powerful, blinding aphrodisiac. Hell. Because there had been no relief. Because Nathan, enraged, crazed, animalistic, had been unable to break the vows he had made to his wife. No matter the amount of drugs. No matter the provocation.

He stared back now at the small group of men who had rescued him from Diego Fuentes's hell. Three doctors, an admiral, some scowling bastard in a suit, supposedly a JAG representative, and his uncle Jordan Malone.

Jordan wasn't in uniform. That was telling enough. His resignation from the SEALs three months before had surprised Nathan when he'd heard about it. Of course, there wasn't much left to do but listen to rumor in the highly secured, specialized private clinic he had been recovering in.

Surgery after surgery to repair his body and his face. They'd fixed what had been damaged. They'd rebuilt what couldn't be reset. But his mind still felt broken. The man he had once been was no more than a dream.

He was still a SEAL. He hadn't resigned. But he had a feeling he wouldn't be one for long.

"Lieutenant Malone." The admiral nodded back at him, his lined, weathered face drawn in worry and concern. "You're doing well."

Like hell he was.

He stood to attention, but this was fucking shit. He felt like he was being stretched on a rack of fire.

The three doctors watched silently. The psychologist assigned to him made a few notes. Damned bastard was always making notes.

"Thank you, sir," he finally managed to say. Hell, he just wanted to get back to the exercises he'd been doing. The ones that pushed his body to exhaustion, that made the hellacious arousal that still cursed him lessen.

The admiral frowned back at him.

"Are you in pain, son?" he asked him.

Nathan forced patience. Forced patience didn't sit well right now.

"Yes, sir, I am." He wasn't going to lie about it either.

The admiral nodded. "That explains your borderline disrespect. Maybe."

Nathan gritted his teeth. "Sorry, sir, protocol isn't my strong suit these days."

He expected a snap in the admiral's reply; he didn't expect the old man's face to smooth out or the understanding that lit his gaze.

Admiral Holloran had once been not just his superior officer, but a man he respected.

"Sit down, Nathan." The admiral nodded to the chair behind him before taking his own seat.

Nathan glanced at Jordan. His uncle was sitting, all protocol pretty much abolished where he was concerned. But it wasn't disrespect, it was an arrogance, a confidence that had only been thinly veiled until now.

Nathan sat down gingerly. He was still having trouble with one leg, but it was strengthening. As were the muscles in his back that he had worked to rebuild.

The admiral finally sighed as silence filled the room.

"I attended your funeral," he stated then. "I grieved, Nathan. Seeing you now"—he shook his head—"makes me wonder sometimes at the decisions that are made behind my back. I wouldn't have approved that mission."

"I agreed to it."

Simple. It was supposed to have been so simple. He still had the hole in his heel to prove it hadn't been.

"We'll discuss that another day," the admiral growled. "We're facing another problem."

"Has my wife been informed I'm alive yet?" The words felt torn from his ruined vocal chords.

His voice was rougher, darker than it had been, but hell, at least he could talk.

"Not yet," the admiral answered.

"I still prefer she not be told."

Nathan stared straight ahead now. He was aware of the bandages that still covered his face, the wounds that were still healing on his body. But even more, he was very much aware of the effects of that fucking whore's dust those bastards Fuentes and Jansen Clay had pumped into his body.

Eighteen months of it. He had been the guinea pig. The SEAL to break with the black evil they forced into him. But he hadn't broken. He'd become a monster instead.

"Sabella's been grieving, Nathan," Jordan said then. "She's still grieving. She still cries for you."

"She'll stop crying. Sabella's tough." He shrugged as

though it didn't matter and glimpsed the admiral and Jordan's exchanged look from his periphery.

He was lying. His Bella wasn't tough. She was soft and sweet and he swore he heard her cries in his dreams, in his nightmares. The ragged wound that was his soul would never heal, because he couldn't get the sounds of her screams out of his head.

How much worse would her screams be if she saw him now? His gentle little Bella had loved his body. When he had walked out the door that last day he had been strong, powerful, but even more, he'd been a man who knew how to be gentle. That man didn't exist anymore. There was nothing gentle in the dark, twisted dreams he had now. Dreams of death. And dreams of Bella. And a hunger he knew he would never restrain if she came to him.

"I'm dead," he told them, his voice cold as he thought of the consequences of trying to return to her. "I'll stay dead."

The psychologist was scribbling furiously on his pad. Nathan's gaze jerked to him. As though he could feel the spikes of fury aimed his way, the balding little man lifted his head.

His shoulders shifted beneath his ill-fitting suit jacket, and behind his plain glasses, his brown eyes flickered nervously.

Nathan's eyes jerked back to the admiral. "Would you get him the hell out of my sight, sir."

Admiral Holloran stared back at him for long seconds before nodding to the doctors and jerking his head to the door. They all filed out quickly. None of them were comfortable in his presence. They never had been. Of course, they'd had to deal with an animal for the first three months that he had been under their care.

Admiral Holloran sighed wearily and stared back at him.

"Last chance, son," he said softly. "Let us call your wife. Send someone for her."

He bared his teeth in fury. "No, sir." The "sir" was habitual, the growling rage in his voice wasn't. It was pumping through him, numbing his mind, filling his senses with the echoed images of his nightmares.

"Enough." Jordan spoke into the silence. "I warned you he wouldn't change his mind."

"Your respect has gone to hell, Jordan," Holloran snapped.

"So has my patience," Jordan bit out. "I was given complete control of this unit, Admiral, and that supersedes even your rank."

"If he changes his mind then he can't go back," the admiral argued. "Is that what you want for your nephew, Jordan?"

"If he changes his mind then that decision is mine to make, not yours or anyone else's." There was a hardness to Jordan, a bleak anger Nathan had never seen in him before. "He'll be transferred to the command center tomorrow and the doctors there will work him with the others."

"You haven't even asked him if he's willing!" The admiral was in Jordan's face now. The two men nose to nose, two incredible wills clashing. It would have been amusing if Nathan had been in the mood for it.

He wasn't.

He rose to his feet and headed to the door.

"Nathan."

Nathan paused before turning back to face his uncle. Jordan had once been not just family, but a superior officer, when they had both been SEALs, when Nathan had been a man rather than the animal he had turned into.

He stared back at Jordan. "Make it quick. I have exercises to finish this evening."

Jordan got to his feet. "There are other options than the SEALs."

"Oh yeah?" Nathan arched his brows. "What's better than the SEALs, *Uncle*? Hell? Been there, still take trips."

Jordan nodded slowly. His brilliant blue eyes, wild Irish eyes, his grandpop had called them, stared back at him. "There are other options, Nathan."

"Really?" Nathan stared between Jordan and the admiral.

"Yeah." Jordan nodded. "You walk out of here as a SEAL and you walk out as Nathan Malone. You walk out with me, and Nathan Malone ceases to exist."

The admiral moved from his chair with a jerky movement and paced to the other side of the room.

"You leave with him and the SEALs won't exist for you anymore, Nathan. The only men you'll have contact with are those in your old team under Commander Chavez, to retrain. You'll be dead forever. Nathan Malone will no longer exist. Not for you. And not for your wife."

Nathan stared back at him, but it was Bella he saw. She hated a broken nail, she worried about wrinkles. How would she handle a husband who was little more than a monster?

He turned to Jordan. "So where do I sign up?"

Three years later

Jordan Malone stood in his office and stared through the privacy glass at the exercise room. His hands were shoved in the pockets of his jeans, a scowl on his face as he watched his nephew.

Nathan, now known as Noah Blake to the world, was only five years younger than he was. Jordan had been a surprise to his parents, a shock to his older siblings. And he had been more like a brother to the man pouring with sweat beneath the weights in the other room. The change in Nathan over the past years was nothing short of miraculous. Hell, the first six months, the very fact that he had survived had been miraculous. It had been the first three years that had been the hardest though. The nightmares and effects of the whore's dust in his system had nearly driven Noah insane.

But had he survived? Sometimes, Jordan wondered if the man who had taken that final SEAL assignment was the same one he was staring at now.

His face was different. The plastic surgery had made it leaner, the bone and muscle more defined. Fuentes had done a job on Nathan's face while he was a captive. Bones had been shattered, the repairs had been extensive. The change drastic. No one who knew Nathan Malone before would guess at his identity now. His build was different. His body was leaner but more powerful, rock hard, and his will was steel. He was a cold, icy-eyed killer.

He wasn't Nathan Malone anymore. He was truly Noah Blake, because Noah had made certain nothing of Nathan existed.

Noah's training with Reno Chavez's unit in the past years had worried Jordan. Where once the Navy SEAL Nathan Malone had pulled his punches and killed only when he had to, now . . . Jordan shook his head. Noah killed with deadly, silent efficiency.

Jordan remembered the night they had rescued the man who had been Nathan from Fuentes's hold. Nearly every bone in his body had been broken at some point. He had been wasted away, nearly starved, and pumped so high on whore's dust his eyes had glowed like a demon's. And he had fought. He had fought not to rape the girl locked in the cell with him, he had fought to protect her. And he had fought to walk out rather than be carried out.

Jordan had been certain his nephew would never survive the withdrawal of the drug and the effects to his brain. He'd never imagined Nathan would come back, stronger than ever rather than broken. Darker than ever, and so different that his identity change rarely blipped Jordan's radar anymore.

"He's never going to be the same, is he?" Lieutenant Ian Richards said somberly, admitting what none of them had dared say aloud over the years. Ian was part of that SEAL team, had stood with the other men who had spent the past years with the man they called Noah.

It had been harder on Ian in some ways, because he had been closer to Nathan than even Jordan had been. Nathan had only been ten when he heard young Ian's screams echoing through the desert landscape of their ranch. He had awakened his father, harassed that mean-assed Grant Malone out of the house, and found the young boy whose mother was dying in his arms.

Grant, in a surprising display of compassion, had helped the young woman and her child. Grant had his moments, Jordan thought, they were just few and far between.

"No, he's never going to be same." He admitted the truth to Ian, as well as to himself. "This man isn't Nathan Malone anymore, Ian. He's truly Noah Blake. We may as well accept that."

"He's a machine now," Ian stated heavily, his expression saddened as he watched Nathan work out. "He's the best, damned killer I've ever laid my eyes on. Silent as a thought."

Jordan turned to Reno Chavez, the commander of the group.

Reno shook his black head. "He's not a SEAL any longer. He questions orders continuously, lays in backup plans out the ass, and always has a plan if that one goes bad. If he feels he needs to deviate, then he deviates. He's not insubordinate, but he's a leader now. He won't follow easily unless he's assured the plan is the only way to go. He's a wild card, Jordan, but he's a damned efficient one. Like a shark. Cold-blooded. Focused. And deadly."

Jordan nodded. "Thank you, Reno. I appreciate the report."

"You have my written report as well." Reno nodded to the file that had been laid on Jordan's desk.

The monthly reports hadn't deviated in years. Nathan was barely a man any longer. He often reminded Jordan of a robot, little more.

"Jordan, he's not going to survive like this," Ian said quietly, turning back to the window, watching the man that had once been his friend. "He'll self-destruct. One of these days, he'll put a bullet in his own head."

As though Noah had heard him, sensed him, he sat up on the weight bench and grabbed a towel. His gaze sliced past the two-way mirror and stared back at them. His eyes were darker, wilder than Nathan Malone's had been. Searing navy blue in a dark, sharply defined face. His black hair was thick, long, nearly to his shoulders now. He refused to cut it. As he turned his back Jordan glimpsed the black sun pierced by a red sword that had been tattooed on the left shoulder blade of Noah's back.

The emblem of the Elite Operational Unit was another reminder of how Noah had shed his past as Nathan Malone. He had signed his life over to a unit that at times could be little more than a suicide mission.

"He'll survive." Jordan kept his response cool, but what he felt inside was anything but cool. "He's not finished yet. He just thinks he is." Nathan hadn't returned to his wife yet, and Noah, the man he was, hadn't forgotten that woman. He wouldn't find himself until he did.

Jordan had pulled his nephew into this unit because he knew the man he loved like a brother would have never survived intact if he'd had to face the world after his release from the clinic. Or if he'd had to face his wife.

The psychologist had agreed. Nathan would have taken a walk one day and just never returned. He hadn't been ready. Noah might still not be ready either. But Jordan was going to end up testing him anyway.

Three years later

"It won't be easy to get him to agree to it," Ian Richards warned Jordan as they watched the six-man unit of the Elite Ops working out in the gym through the two-way mirror that looked into it.

Noah was stronger than ever. Lean. Powerful. Cold.

"He'll go," Jordan said softly. "He'll not let her remain in danger."

Ian blew out a hard breath as they stared at the man they all knew as Noah now.

"Would she want him back like this?" he asked.

Jordan had questioned that one himself. For six years Sabella Malone had been without her husband. In the past three years, she had finally begun living again. Dating again. There was a chance Noah could lose the wife he never admitted he had, very soon, to another man's arms.

"We'll find out, won't we," Jordan mused.

"We'll be your backup in the Alpine mission," Reno told him then. This small group of men had been assigned to the

Elite Ops; partly privately funded, partly government backed, the unit was a test unit, a group of dead men, of rogues. In the past years they had become a highly advanced, specialized unit dealing in operations that other agencies couldn't touch either because of political sensitivity, or the level of danger involved.

Jordan nodded slowly before watching Noah once more.

"We'll meet up at the command center set up in Big Bend National Park," he told them. "You'll receive your orders within the next day or so."

Ian and Reno nodded and left quickly, heading out to prepare for the coming operation. All that was left was getting Noah Blake to go along with it.

Jordan sat down at his desk, picked up the file he had on the mission, and called Noah into his office.

Noah made him wait. When he walked into Jordan's office, his hair was still damp from his shower, his blue eyes cold, no emotion, no life flickering within them.

"Are we ready?" Noah took the seat in front of the desk that Jordan indicated.

"Almost." Jordan nodded. "Command center will be broken down tonight and flown to the new location. We should be set up within forty-eight hours."

Noah didn't say anything, he just stared back at Jordan, waiting. His patience was seemingly endless now. But when he erupted into action there was no one faster. No one deadlier.

"You're delaying," Noah finally drawled, that ruined voice scraping.

That voice had once been flowing, deep. Now, it was guttural, almost raw.

"First mission is in Texas," Jordan stated.

Noah didn't respond. His gaze didn't even flicker. As though nothing in Texas concerned him. No family, no grandfather, brother, or father. No wife.

"Command center will based forty miles out of Alpine."

"No." Noah's tone was icy.

Jordan lifted the file and slapped it down in front of him. "Read the file. You don't want the mission, then the hell with it. You can head to Siberia for all I give a damn and babysit that scientist they had us kidnap last month, in the cold. But you will read the file first."

Jordan stomped from the office, slammed the door behind him, and left Noah to the information they had gathered.

Noah, he never thought of himself as Nathan anymore, stared at the file as though it were a rattler. He didn't want to read it. He didn't want to know. Siberia suited him just fine. Hell, that scientist was a quiet little thing, she just liked working on her projects, she didn't like company. She would do.

He got to his feet, then stopped. He stared at the file and almost turned away. Almost. A picture had slid from just inside the file, and he knew that chin.

He picked it up slowly. The center of his chest was a hard, searing knot of agony as he pulled the picture free and frowned.

And there it was. That familiar curve of the brow, those pretty, soft gray eyes. But he'd be damned if he knew the woman they belonged to.

She looked like Sabella. *His Sabella*. It was his Sabella. But she was so different.

Her sun-streaked blond tresses were darker, almost brown in some places. And her hair was longer now. Well past her shoulders, thick and heavy. Her face was thinner, her expression was quieter.

There was no smile on her lips.

Unless she was angry, Nathan had never seen Sabella without a smile. The thought of her smiles, her laughter, her joy, followed him into his dreams sometimes. Sometimes, they held the nightmares at bay. What would he hold on to now that he saw that smile was gone?

He held the picture in one hand, staring at her. He had refused to read any of the reports he knew Jordan kept on her. Refused to hear anything about her in the past six years.

He had only two questions if her name came up.

Was she alive?

Was she safe?

Jordan had always nodded, and Noah had always walked away.

He opened the mission file.

It didn't take long to read it. Even less time for him to have to fight the howl of pure rage that burned in his throat.

Sabella was smack in the middle of an operation that had already killed three FBI agents and the wife of a prominent politician.

Son of a bitch. He'd asked his father for one thing in his entire life. If anything ever happened to him, to watch out for Sabella, and that lying bastard had sworn he would. But he hadn't. Sabella was undefended.

Only his bastard half brother was trying to help at this point.

The mission file was peppered with information on Sabella, his half brother, Rory, his grandfather, Riordan, and the father he could feel himself beginning to hate now.

And it was filled with danger. That danger could touch Sabella. He could see it. He could see the threads that, if pulled just the right way, would tighten around his wife's neck and put her in harm's way.

Nathan's wife, he reminded himself bitterly, not Noah's. Noah Blake had no wife. But he couldn't erase the past that had once belonged to him, or the dreams of a wife that had been his, no matter how hard he tried.

And now she was in danger.

Because he hadn't watched out for her.

He sat down and stared at the picture. It was bad enough the man she had loved had died, but the haunted shell that was left hadn't even been able to watch out for her.

He ran his finger over the picture, down the curve of her cheek, as he closed his eyes and remembered her smile. Remembered touching her. As he let himself remember, outside his dreams, of loving her.

"Go síoraí," he whispered, breathing in the scent of those memories. "Forever, Sabella. I'll love you forever."

And the first crack in Noah Blake's shell appeared.

Nathan." His name was breathed into the darkness as Sabella came awake. As though the past six years had never happened, as though she had never lost him. She heard his voice in the darkness. Those words. The ones she had never asked the meaning of. Go síoraí.

She stared into the dimly lit room. No Nathan. Nathan wasn't there. Dry eyed, aching, she lay back down and closed her eyes. "Goodbye, Nathan," she whispered back, wishing she could still cry. Wishing the pain could be shed so easily. "I miss you."

CHAPTER TWO

The little shack that sat in the middle of the sprawling Rocking M Ranch looked just as weathered, just as faded and familiar, as it ever had even in the dark, beneath a bleak, black night.

Noah moved through the darkness like a wraith. He jumped the little wrought-iron fence and moved to his grandmother's grave.

Erin Malone. Go síoraí. Forever. They were the only words on her granite tombstone. His grandfather had chiseled them in himself.

Kneeling by the tombstone, Noah stretched out his left hand, touched the stone, and lowered his head. His grandfather had always paid homage to their grandmother in this fashion. All her children had except Grant Malone. And Noah did now. He wondered if his brother Rory did as well.

He lifted his head and stared at the shack. It was dark, shadowed, but he knew his half brother was there.

He eased back from the grave then and bounded back over the fence before moving to the cabin.

Rory was quick. He was suspicious. He had known throughout the day that someone was watching the cabin, but Noah hadn't tried to hide it.

He moved around the shack on silent feet. He flowed with

the shadows, became a part of them, used them to his advantage until he stood at the end of the back porch and stared at the young man who sat in the aged rocker.

Rory was twenty-five, a man grown, and he looked too much like Nathan had at that age. He was broader in the shoulders and his muscles were heavier, but not as effective.

Rory sat silently, his rifle resting across his thighs, his body tense.

"I know you're here," his brother muttered. "If I haven't scoped you by now, I'm not going to. You might as well take the shot." Disgust lined his voice, filled his expression as his head lifted.

Rory thought he was dead, just as everyone else did. And Noah needed to ensure no one else suspected. Except Rory. Nathan would need his help.

As silent as moonlight he was over the banister of the porch, the rifle pulled from Rory's grip, the barrel across his brother's neck as the rocker tilted back to the wall.

It wasn't a harsh grip, it was a warning one. He didn't want to wake the old man. He didn't want to add to Rory's grief, or to his own shame.

"Stay silent," Noah hissed in Rory's dark face. "I'm not here to hurt you."

Rory's expression was frankly disbelieving. But Noah would have been surprised if he'd reacted any other way.

"You have one chance to know what I know about your brother," Noah warned him quietly. "One chance. Blow it, and it will never return."

Rory's eyes narrowed. Startling blue eyes, true Malone eyes.

"My brother's dead," he bit out quietly. "What could you tell me about him that my uncle couldn't?"

Noah leaned closer. "Bràthair, what could I tell you that you want to know?"

Then Noah leaned back again slowly. Rory was shaking. His dark face, Gaelic dark, paled as he stared back at the shadow hovering in front of his vision.

Noah moved back slowly, still gripping the rifle. "Come

with me." He jerked his head to the shed at the edge of the house yard. "Does he still keep the shed lit?"

There was no answer, but Rory was following. They stepped into the shed and Noah closed the door carefully before flipping the light on.

Rory collapsed on the old chair in the corner and stared back at him. His gaze was dark with pain, anger.

"I thought you were my brother," he whispered. "Hell, I hoped you were."

Noah watched as his brother rubbed his hands over his face and shook his black head.

Noah removed the night vision glasses he wore. A new toy the unit was playing with. One he had taken advantage of. He stared back at Rory, realizing the color of the eyes he saw every morning in the mirror was wilder, bleaker, much darker and more dangerous than his brother's.

Rory blinked.

"Do you still sneak in here to smoke?" Noah asked, remembering how his brother used to slip a cigarette when he thought no one would catch him.

Only he and Rory had known that.

Rory's hand shook. He gripped the arms of the old chair and stared at Noah as though he could force himself to see what he needed to see.

"Who are you?" Rory finally breathed out painfully, his voice filled with more disappointment than Noah had expected. "And what the hell do you want?"

Noah shook his head. "I don't have time for games, Rory."

"You're not Nathan," Rory whispered.

"I'm not the Nathan you remember." He moved to the wardrobe in the back of the shed, opened the small door in the bottom and extracted the bottle of whiskey he knew his grandfather kept there.

He hid his spirits from his Erin, he would always grin when he slipped a sip. Even though his Erin was dead, his grandfather continued the tradition.

Uncorking the fine imported Irish spirit, he tipped the bottle to his lips and took a healthy drink. He didn't grimace as it went down, he savored it. Recapping it, he returned it to the drawer and turned back to Rory.

The boy was staring at him now as though he had seen a ghost.

"No one knows about Grandpop's stash," he whispered.

Noah nodded shortly. "You knew. I knew. Grant never knew."

Rory breathed out roughly. "You stopped calling Grant dad after you found out about me."

Noah lifted his shoulders in a shrug. "He couldn't be your dad, then he was no dad of mine."

Rory shook his head as though to shake the confusion clear. Nathan almost felt sorry for him. He didn't have time for pity though.

He grabbed an old wooden chair and pulled it to him. Straddling it, he stared back at his brother.

"You're not making sense," Rory said, his voice forceful. "You're not Nathan, but you know the things only he knew." The younger man's gaze looked him over desperately. "Who are you?"

"Nathan's ghost." He sighed. "I'm Noah Blake, Rory, and you can't ever forget that. From this second on, believe Nathan is dead, because that man is long gone. Only Noah exists."

And still Rory was trying to find Nathan within him. Noah watched the desperation in his brother's gaze, felt it lashing at his soul.

"I need your help, Rory."

"My help?" Rory shook his head again. "Hell, I don't even know who you are."

"You wouldn't have known me even five years ago," he told him. "Hell happened. Death happened."

"Sabella?"

"Doesn't know." Noah's voice hardened. "And no one's telling her. I wasn't joking, kid. Nathan Malone stays dead."

Rory stared everywhere but at him for long, tense moments.

"Damn you!" The boy got to his feet, anger churning in

his face now. "You son of a bitch! You're not Nathan. And you know how I know you're not Nathan?"

Noah stared back at him remotely. Pushing the emotion back was the killer. Hell, he'd thought it would be easier than this. He had told Jordan, a walk in the park. This wasn't the park, it was a bleak nightmare.

"I'll tell you," Rory snarled. "You're not Nathan because Nathan wouldn't be here." He stabbed his finger at the floor of the shed. "He wouldn't be here with me right now, he'd be taking care of his wife before someone else decided to do the job for him."

Before Noah realized the lack of control festering inside him, before Rory could guess his intent, Noah lifted him by the throat from the chair and threw him against the wall. Pinning him there he snarled back in Rory's face.

Rory looked as Nathan had once looked. He was built as Nathan had once been built. Or as Noah had. They could have been twins at one time. They could have been born of the same mother and father, rather than different mothers.

Rory was a younger Nathan. And Noah bet he remembered how to laugh.

"Have you touched her?" Ice seeped inside him. It filled his voice, filled his soul. "Did you comfort her?"

His hands tightened around Rory's throat. He could see it. Rory touching her, holding her, as Sabella whispered Nathan's name, whispered forever. His hold became tighter.

His Sabella. Sweet, soft, warm. Forever whispering in his ear. She had promised him forever. Was she giving it to Rory instead?

"Nathan?" Rory was choking as he stared back at him in shock.

Tears filled the boy's eyes, darkened them. "Nathan," he wheezed. "Oh God. Oh God. You're alive. You bastard!"

Noah deflected the kick, the fists to the kidneys, and the younger man's choked curses. He released the hold on his neck, twisted his arm behind his back and flattened his face to the table next to the wall.

"Did. You. Touch. *My wife?*"

"I should have," Rory cried, half sob, half enraged bellow. "I should have. You son of a bitch. You son of a bitch. You're just like him. Just like that heartless little bastard that made you."

Rory laid his head on the table as Noah released him and his shoulders shook. He kept his forehead pressed into the wood, and a sob tore from his throat.

Noah flexed his hand, staring at it, his jaw tightening until he felt it would crack as he stretched his fingers and realized, they had been wrapped around his brother's throat.

"Get out of here!" Rory straightened, keeping his back to him. "Get out."

"I can't do that, Rory."

He turned furiously, his eyes blazing as he sneered back at Nathan. "Granddad cries when he talks about you. When he sees Sabella struggling with that fucking garage. Trying to survive. He tried to help her and that son of a bitch father of yours took damned near everything he had. And here you are." He flipped his hand back to Nathan, fury filling his face. "The big tough warrior the old man had such pride in. Six years, Nathan. Six years and where the hell have you been?"

Noah lashed out, pushing him back in the chair as he glared back at him. "Watch it, boy," he bit out. "Keep pushing and you'll get more than you want."

"I got more than I wanted when I felt you watching the place this afternoon," he snarled, anger pushing past fear.

"I'm back, that's all that matters." Noah rubbed his hand over his short beard. "This isn't as simple as why I didn't come back. It's not even as simple as having the option to come back for a damned long time. I'm here now, and I need information."

"That's what they make computers for." Rory was three seconds from attacking him again and Noah knew it. The boy had that damned Irish pride and temper.

"Listen to me, you little shit!" He moved over him vengefully. "Look at my face. My body. Do you think this shit happened because I wanted to be someone else? Because I wanted my life fucked up the ass and back? Look, Rory. Look at the scars. You want to see my back? How about my legs? You want to see the hole they cut in my foot? Will that help?"

He jerked back, furious, enraged. So much for control. He hadn't let his control snap in more than five years.

He inhaled roughly. He wasn't going to let it snap now, not any further than it had already.

He turned back to his brother and pushed back the emotion. The horror in his brother's eyes wasn't what he'd wanted to see.

"Belle's not the same without you," Rory whispered. "She's sad all the time. All she does is work. All she does is close herself off. She's not even the same girl anymore. Any more than you're the same man."

Noah clenched his jaw, his fists. He couldn't talk about Sabella. Not now. Not yet.

"Tell me about the Black Collar Militia."

Rory blinked. "BC?" He snorted. "I stay outta that shit. I remember the whipping you gave me before you left, okay?"

"I didn't ask if you were still stupid," he growled. "Tell me what you've heard."

Rory licked his lips and looked away for a second. "Two of Belle's mechanics are BC. Low level mostly. No one knows what's high level. The little twits like to brag sometimes. Mostly they run errands, crap like that."

Noah straddled the chair again. "When did they start working for Sabella?"

Rory narrowed his eyes at him. "You always called her Bella, Nate."

"Rory, don't piss me off again." He sighed. "Answer my questions. And you call me by that name again and I'll bust your head. My name is Noah Blake."

Rory flinched before tensing and shaking his head.

"Hell." He breathed out roughly. "A year or so ago maybe. All the guys working for you left that first year. Belle was in bad shape for a long time. When she finally came out of it, she was on the verge of losing the house and the garage. I couldn't keep it running." His expression twisted painfully as he stared back at Noah. "I tried," he whispered. "But I couldn't keep it going." He shrugged. "And Belle, she's a hell of a mechanic, but she doesn't have good people skills, ya know? Getting things back up and running has taken all our time."

Sabella, a mechanic? Noah held back his total disbelief. That one he would have to see to believe. And no people skills? Who had kidnapped his wife and replaced her?

"Just tell me about the militia," Noah growled.

Rory pushed his fingers through his hair. "I simply don't know much." He shook his head. "I'm pretty sure Mike Conrad associates with them. I know he's hot for the garage since news came you were dead. He's made Belle an offer a few times, but she refuses to sell. Sometimes Mike gets a little drunk, and when he does, he'll run his mouth, but he hasn't spouted off about anything dangerous yet. Sheriff is a badass, he could be in it, but with him who the hell knows. There's rumors the BC are involved in some of those deaths in the National Park, but, like I said, rumors. Hell, Noah, I've been so damned busy just trying to keep the wolves away from Belle that I don't have time for that crap."

Noah nodded. He hadn't expected Rory to know a lot.

"You're giving me a job at the garage. You hired me tonight. You met me last month when you were at that bar in Odessa."

Rory gave him a surprised look. "You know about the bar?"

"And the barmaid," Noah grunted. "I showed up this afternoon, found you heading back here and stopped. We chatted. You offered me a job."

Rory stared back at him confusion. "And Belle?"

"Won't know who I am," he told Rory quietly. "And if you tell her, Rory, if you even hint it to her, you'll disappear until all this is over, you understand me?"

He stared back at his brother. There was no anger now, no emotion. The ice was falling back into place.

"But Bella's your wife," Rory whispered painfully. "You almost stayed away too long, man."

"I'll take care of Sabella, my way." He rose from the chair, staring down at Rory with hard eyes. "Do you understand me, Rory? My way."

Rory nodded hesitantly.

"Stay here tomorrow. Sleep off that drunk you're going to tie on tonight. Don't show up until you can get a handle on this."

Rory grunted. "Then I guess I'll see you next lifetime."

Noah stared back at him silently for long moments.

"Fine. Day or two." His brother shrugged.

"And you don't tell Grandpop either," Noah warned him.

Rory shrugged. "I won't tell, doesn't mean he won't know. You know Granddad."

Unfortunately he did. Riordan Malone always seemed to just know things. It had been creepy as hell when he was a kid, comforting as he grew older. And now, now it was just worrisome.

"Why Noah?" Rory asked the question Noah couldn't answer. "Why the name, and why are you back here for the BC and not your family?"

Bitterness filled his brother's voice, his expression, and Nathan was damned if he could blame him.

"I'm back because the BC threatens my family," he stated, his grating voice harsher, darker than it should have been. "As for the name." His lips quirked. "It's Irish. Now keep your eyes and ears open. I'll tell you more as I can."

Rory gave him a mocking sneer. "Fuck you, man. You know, you're right, Belle doesn't need to know who you are. She has a second chance now; maybe this time, she'll get a man that will stay home a while."

Noah froze, he didn't even blink. "Meaning?"

"You should have checked things out a little before you came back and accused me of touching what's yours. It's not me you have to worry about, *Noah*. Try worrying about your good friend Duncan Sykes. She's been seeing him since his divorce a year ago." Rory's smile was mocking. "If I were a betting man, I'd bet she'll be letting him drive your truck soon."

Noah pushed back the demon rising inside him. Long of

fang, sharp of claw, it tore at his brain, threatened his control, his ability to think.

Duncan Sykes.

No. It hadn't happened. Bella hadn't been with another man. No other man had touched her. No other man would dare. Because he would kill him. And he would have known.

Noah slipped back into the night as silently as he had come in. He made his way back around the house, moving quickly, staying in the shadows until he reached the canyon where he'd left the Harley, more than a mile away.

He was aware of Rory trying to track him, but the kid wasn't experienced enough. He'd lost sight of Nathan seconds after he left.

But there were other eyes, old eyes, tear-filled eyes, that watched every stride he took with pride, love, and fierce exultant joy.

Dawn wasn't far way, but rather than returning to the command center to catch a few hours' sleep and report to Jordan, Noah pointed the Harley home instead.

He couldn't get it out of his head. Sabella was seeing someone? Was she sleeping with his old friend Duncan Sykes? He had to know. He had to see her for himself, feel her, know she belonged to him even though he knew he couldn't have her.

Six years. He couldn't be reborn. Nathan Malone was dead in more than just name. The man he had been was dead. The man Sabella had loved was dead. Had she found someone to replace him?

He couldn't consider it. Over six years without her touch, without the soft scent of her. He couldn't take another woman. He couldn't bear the thought of it. His vows held him. Sabella's soul held him. He couldn't have her, but he couldn't have anyone else either. Could he bear to know she was in another man's arms?

He turned down an old back road and pulled the Harley into a shelter of trees, turned the ignition key, and swung off. He began the short hike that would take him to the back of the house. The two-story brick house sat at the edge of town. There were no neighbors close enough to see him if he came in on the lower edge of the property. He just wanted to stay a minute, he told himself as he moved through the predawn light, keeping to the shelter of trees that bordered the back- yard.

He had nearly stepped into the yard before he stopped. Came to a hard, freezing stop and just stared at the vision that stepped out on the back porch.

His reaction was like a fist to the gut, threatening to dou- ble him up. It was the immediate, violent erection in his jeans. It was his heart rate increasing, the blood rushing through his veins hard and fast. His breathing felt restricted, locked in his throat. His fingers curled against his palms, forming fists so tight the bones ached.

He stared at the woman, the man's long white shirt falling past her thighs, gaping open to reveal the white tank top and boyshort panties she wore beneath. She lifted a cup of coffee, the steam curling against her face as dawn edged in, lighting the yard, the porch, and the woman with gold and violet rays.

"Sabella." He whispered her name.

Rory had noticed his slip. He had always called her Bella, unless he wanted her. Unless the need to be buried inside the velvet-soft, rich warmth of her body had been overwhelm- ing. And it had never been as overwhelming as it was now.

He imagined he could smell her scent in the air, a blend of honeysuckle and feminine warmth. Against his palm he imagined he felt the heat of her flesh, silken and giving, lift- ing to him, her lips whispering his name.

He remembered several times, many in fact, that he had taken her on that back porch. He'd lifted her astride him as he sat on that swing. He'd bent her over the railing and buried into her from behind.

Agony pierced his chest and bit into his soul like an ani- mal's fangs. And that was how he wanted to bite her. He wanted to grip her neck between his teeth and hold her in place like an animal. He wanted to pound inside her and hear her scream for more.

But her screams would be far different than when she cried for more, he thought. The man he was now, the dark hungers that filled him, would terrify her.

But still, he watched her. Watched as she enjoyed that first cup of coffee. The almost sensual pleasure in her face as the heated liquid passed her lips, and he let himself remember when that sensuality had once flowed over him as well.

He remembered her laughter and her smile. He remembered touching her, holding her, and he had to restrain the need to remember sharing dreams with her. Once, they had had such dreams. Simple dreams. A dog and a kid. Maybe a pool in the backyard.

And now here he was, hidden from view, watching as his wife's too somber face lifted to the dawn, and he swore he felt her whisper his name.

A few more hours, he thought. He would check in with Jordan, shower, and change clothes before heading to the garage.

When he had first gone back to Texas with the other members of the Elite Operational Unit he had joined, Noah had told himself he would do the job and leave. That simple. As he stood staring at his wife, he had a feeling it wasn't going to be that simple at all.

Today, he would step back into her life as another man. A man whose hungers were so dark, ran so deep, that sometimes they made him pause. A renegade. A wild card. He would come to her, not as Nathan Malone, but as Noah Blake. And he would come into her life as nothing she could ever imagine.

CHAPTER THREE

"Hey, Belle, Mike Conrad just called about his car and that damned motor hasn't come in yet. He's on his way here and he sounds drunk again. There's some badass waiting in your office for Rory, who called in drunk this morning, and you're making me crazy having to talk to your legs. Get the hell out from under that car."

This wasn't good. Her receptionist/gopher was sounding less than pleased and more irritated and harried than first thing in the morning should be calling for. She stared up at the innards of the vehicle she was working on: grease and grime and years of neglect met her inspection. It almost reminded her of her own life, she thought with a grimace.

"Answer me sometime today, Belle." Toby was sounding more harried by the minute. "Look, this dude is a major badass. He's going to crush my head and shove it in my pocket like a damned baseball if you don't talk to him."

Her lips almost twitched. Toby, with his gangly, too tall body and intensity sometimes reminded her of Nathan's brother Rory when she had first met him. And he could be just as melodramatic as Rory had once been.

Sabella pushed tiredly against the underside of the motor, sending the creeper rolling across the cement until her head was free, leaving her to stare up at Toby, the young man she had hired to take care of the office.

His shoulder-length light brown hair was pulled back in a low ponytail, his brown eyes filled with anxiousness as his forehead creased into a frown.

Dammit, she didn't have time for this.

"I told Mike the motor would be ready tomorrow, not today." She heaved herself upright, sitting with her jean-clad legs spread over the narrow hard plastic device used to maneuver beneath the vehicles as she lay back to work beneath them. She propped her arms on her knees, staring up at him in exasperation.

She wiped her grimy fingers negligently against the side of her jeans before brushing the loose strands of her dark brown and blond-streaked hair back from her face.

"We're not hiring, and Rory will be here when he gets here. That's all I know. Now take care of it." She moved to lie back down, determined to finish the final tuneup of the sedan that the mechanics had neglected to inform her was sitting out back. Mike Conrad wasn't the only one waiting on his vehicle.

"Oh, no you don't." He shook his head fiercely as she moved to push herself back under the car. "I can't handle this dude, Belle. He's like the Grim Reaper's cousin or something. He's not part of my job description, ya know? You deal with him."

Sabella pushed back the anger, drawn more from her own impatience than Toby's attitude. The boy was normally pretty stable and dealt with aggravated customers with a flair she envied.

"Just tell him to come back in the morning. Rory will be here . . ." She hung her head as he began shaking his head violently. "Fine."

She struggled to her feet, picking up the creeper and propping it against the side of the garage wall as she grabbed a stained towel and began trying to rub the oil from her hands. After a few seconds, she tossed the rag back to the bench and stalked through the four-car holding bay to the office beyond.

They couldn't afford a new mechanic, no matter how much she needed one to keep the garage profitable. She was going to lose her ass here, and she knew it. If she didn't manage to straighten up the mess she had allowed to develop in those first horrific three years after her husband's death, she was going to lose the garage, and her home. The benefits she had received just weren't enough to save it all.

She couldn't lose the home she and Nathan had shared. She'd worked three years to rebuild it. She couldn't lose it.

God, she couldn't lose that last connection to him. It was all she had left.

"Tell Danny I want that car finished and out of here this afternoon," she ordered Toby as they neared the office. "Tell him we can finish the Carltons' truck later this evening, but Jennie needs her car to get to work and it took too long to get those parts as it is. I have everything ready, it just needs going over and testing."

"On my way." Toby nodded before turning and loping over to the far side of the garage.

"And don't run," she muttered, knowing he wouldn't pay attention to that order if he did hear her. He was like a puppy. All gangly legs and nervous energy.

And she hadn't even asked him the employee wannabe's name. She shook her head, pushing her fingers through her hair before jerking the office door open and coming to a hard, cold stop.

Arrogance shimmered off him. Dark blue eyes seared into her brain, glowing from a face that was sun bronzed and savagely hard. Flat cheekbones, a nose that was just a little off center, lips that were sensual but just a tad thin. A dark, short black beard covered his face, closely cropped and giving him a dangerous appearance. Long black hair was pulled back from his face and secured at his nape.

A shiver raced over her skin, a primal warning of danger, as she stared at him. He was lean and tall, but she bet the muscles beneath that black leather jacket, T-shirt, jeans, and riding chaps were like steel. Heavy boots covered big feet, and he stood staring her from beneath thick, too thick, silky black lashes.

This man was a predator. It was her first thought. Long,

lean, and dangerous, the kind of man Sabella had learned to steer well clear of after her husband's death. Once bitten, twice shy. She had learned her lesson about that air of danger, and she had no desire to revisit it.

He leaned casually against the desk, his palms flat on the surface as he watched her with predatory intent. For a moment, just a moment, she went back in time, to that day she had first pulled into the lot, her car overheating, her nerves frazzled because she was late for a job interview. It was hot, she was sweating in the late-summer Texas sun, cursing her move from Georgia and the Texas heat that seemed to take forever to get used to.

And standing in just that position had been Nathan Malone, the owner, and later her husband. His eyes had raked over her slowly, a smile tilting his sexy lips as his eyes, Irish eyes, brilliant, seductive, stole her heart.

She felt her mouth go painfully dry. Her hands were shaking, her stomach cramping, as she stared back at the stranger. She didn't know this man, she didn't want to know this man, but for a moment, just a moment, she glimpsed the past with him. A bittersweet, painful knowledge of love and loss and everything fate had denied her.

"There are no openings. Please leave."

Okay, so that was really rude, but she was really busy too. And she didn't need the headache she knew would come with this man.

"Rory assured me there was an opening for a mechanic."

Oh God, that voice.

His voice was deep, raspy, almost guttural. It raked over her nerve endings and sent an edge of dark response. Damn, damn, damn. She didn't need this. She didn't need her body awakening now after so many years in a deep freeze. She sure as hell didn't need it awakening for a man more dangerous and likely a hell of a lot harder than any other man she had ever known.

His voice was cool and filled with purpose, but the undercurrents were dark, hungry. She had never heard that in her husband's voice, had never seen it in his eyes.

She turned back slowly, forcing herself to stare at his chin, the short clipped beard and mustache blurring his features. Were those scars?

No, she didn't want to know. She didn't care.

"Rory isn't here." She had to force herself to speak, nearly wincing at the raw sound of her voice. "And he doesn't run the place. I do. There are no openings."

He shifted. As though fascinated, Sabella glanced down, seeing the powerful lean thighs covered in faded denim and leather, the hard abs beneath the thin cotton shirt he wore. Boots covered big feet, a sturdy base for at least six feet four inches of hard male.

As her gaze moved back to his face, she watched as his eyes moved to the wide windows that looked out on the gas bays and parking lot. Several cars sat deserted beneath the hot, midday sun, awaiting attention. The gas pumps were empty, the blacktopped lot cracked and sporting several lumps of hearty grass. Yeah, so the place wasn't looking so good, she thought, pushing back her frustration, her pain. But she was doing her best. And it looked a hell of a lot better than it had three years ago when she had dragged herself out of her grief enough to realize what she was losing.

"You're doing a good job here, but if you want to survive, you need someone willing to do the job right, and to get the best out of the men working under you." His gaze swung back to her, the blue of his eyes threatening to steal her breath again.

His voice was quiet, reasonable, but it sent a flare of fury racing through her system. How dare he be here, ruining the fragile balance she had found in her life with his blue eyes, his raspy voice. She lifted her chin defiantly, hating it, hating his eyes, and the weariness that seemed to fill them. And she refused to let herself care.

"I'm doing just fine, all by my lonesome, mister," she assured him mockingly. She drew herself stiffly erect. "You're a stranger here—"

"Ma'am, I'm stating a fact."

Oh God . . . She wanted to scream at him, to beat at him for stealing her peace, for taking the fragile calm she had finally managed to build around herself with the unexplained response she could feel roiling inside her. "All I need is the job Rory promised." He flashed a hard smile. "He is your partner, isn't he?"

"That's not the point," she snapped. "Look, mister—"

"Noah. Noah Blake."

Noah. Irish. *Go síoraí, I'll love you forever.* For a moment, the slightest wish whispered through her mind and she thought of Nathan.

He hadn't loved her forever though. His need for danger, for the adrenaline rush and excitement, had carried him away from her, and he'd found death instead. Leaving her alone. Leaving her to survive without him for six heart-breaking years.

Now another Irish wildman was stepping into her life, trying to take it over? She shook her head. No, never again. No man would ever fill her, ever own her as her husband had. It wasn't possible. And she wasn't going to give this one the chance.

She opened her eyes, lifted her head, and stared back at him as the old, driving fury consumed her once again. She straightened her shoulders and lifted her chin defiantly.

"I said no. Now leave. I have work to do and I just don't have time for you." She turned on her heel and stalked back into the garage, stemming the hollow pain that beat at her throat and moistened her eyes.

She was finally forgetting, she didn't need to be reminded of Irish eyes, soul-stealing kisses, or promises broken.

Her husband was gone. He was dead, his body sealed in a government casket and lowered into a dark, open hole. She had watched them cover it, watched each shovelful of dirt as it sealed a reality she had fought to reject.

God, how she had loved him. His laughter, his voice, his big body and his temper.

She forced herself to breathe through the memories, to

place one foot in front of the other and to walk away from her response to the man who uncovered those memories within her.

"Belle Malone." A furious male voice sliced through her thoughts as she headed for the sedan she had been working on earlier, bringing her to a stop as she turned slowly toward the open garage doors and bit back a curse.

Ladies didn't cuss, she reminded herself. No matter the provocation. And she was being provoked. God, why hadn't she just stayed in bed this morning? Mike Conrad was a bull of a man. He'd been one of her husband's friends, but now he was becoming a pain in her ass.

"Mike, we're working on it." She lifted her hand in greeting, praying he hadn't been drinking. "I'll have it ready in the morning."

"That's what that little bastard Rory has said for two weeks." He stalked into the bay, ignoring the sign that warned customers to stay behind the dingy yellow line. "You said two weeks, no more."

Sabella bit her tongue and reminded herself she couldn't afford to piss him off too much. His bank held the note on the garage and on the house, and he had threatened more than once to make sure they foreclosed if she missed so much as the first payment.

Thinning blond hair was cut short, almost buzzed. Weak brown eyes were watering and bloodshot from liquor and his bloated, reddened face was twisted in rage. Great. She needed this like she needed the behemoth standing in her office right now.

"I still have today, Mike." She pulled on patience she didn't have. She couldn't afford to piss him off; he could make paying off that loan incredibly difficult. Besides, he had been Nathan's friend.

Kinda.

"Like hell." His voice was surly, his broad, pitted face flushed ruddy red, as he neared her and the smell of liquor hit her in the face. "You finish that truck now, bitch, or you can kiss this business goodbye, you hear me? Wouldn't Nathan be

damned proud of your sassy little ass then? This garage was
his pride and joy."

Mike had definitely been drinking and his mood was as
foul as any she had ever seen.

"Nathan is gone, Mike," she reminded him, fighting for the
calm she swore she wouldn't lose. Mike had always seemed to
blame her for Nathan's death, for some reason. "How he
would feel is beside the point."

She drew herself stiffly erect, knowing her diminutive
five-five frame had nothing on his six feet. He was stocky,
his paunch had grown over the years, but the man Nathan
had once called a friend had let the bottle and his own fail-
ures destroy him faster than her own pain had nearly destroyed the garage.

"Nathan should have kicked your ass out and put his
place in dependable hands before he screwed up and got his
ass blown away." The cruel words struck at her heart, no
matter how she fought to ignore them. "He should have
known better than to trust a flaky little blonde to hold on to
anything."

Dammit to hell. She hated the thought of having Toby
call the sheriff. There would be questions and paperwork
and she didn't have time for this crap.

"But he didn't, Mike. And this flaky blonde is working as
fast as she can." She was aware of the mechanics gathering
behind her and wanted to groan in frustration. She didn't
need this. "I'll have your truck first thing in the morning. I
have tonight, according to the contract. I'll be on time." She
couldn't afford not to be.

His bloodshot brown eyes raked over her insultingly. "He
married him a piece of flashy pussy, I have to give him that."

Sabella's eyes narrowed as she tensed and ground her
teeth to hold back a retort. This was going to be bad enough
once gossip circulated. She didn't need to make it worse, she
reminded herself.

"Mr. Conrad, Ms. Malone said in the morning." Toby
stepped to her side, his voice vibrating with anger at the insult.
"It will be ready."

Mike's gaze whipped to the boy as his lips titled in a snide little smile.

"You fuckin' her too, kid? Piece of prime pussy like that needs a—" He never finished what he had to say, and not because Toby jumped for him.

Before the younger man could cover the three feet of distance a shadowed blur moved past them. Mike Conrad was jerked off his feet and literally thrown from the garage.

Sabella stared in shock at the stranger, Noah, seeing the fury pulsing in his face as he picked Mike up from the blacktop only to toss him against the convertible BMW he had driven into the lot.

One big hand latched around Mike's bulging neck and, icy cold, murderously, Noah Blake began to squeeze.

"Stop." Sabella forced herself to move, to run to the pair, her hands locking around Noah's wrist as she stared into those cold, merciless eyes in horror. "You'll kill him. He's just drunk. Damn you, I said stop!"

Rage glittered in the dark blue depths, the promise of death shadowing and darkening the unusual color as his fingers tightened further, his lips twisting into a snarling grimace.

"Have you lost your mind?" She jerked at his wrist, screaming at him, desperate now as she heard Mike strangling behind her.

Sabella glared up at the stranger, seeing the predatory promise of death in his eyes as he stared down at Mike Conrad.

"Touch her again." His voice was a gravelly sound of rage as he stared into Mike's eyes. "And I'll kill you."

She felt his wrist relax as she saw the rage darken the brilliance of his gaze as it locked with hers. A muscle pounded heavily at his jaw as his lips flattened, his eyes flicking over her shoulder as Mike groaned heavily. The sound of Mike collapsing in the car was easily heard in the silence of the parking lot.

"Rory said the apartment over the garage was available." His voice was guttural, low. "I'll store my gear and finish this bastard's truck myself or I can kill him now. Your choice."

And he meant it.

Sabella shook her head in confusion as the BMW started up behind her, the tires screaming on its exit from the lot.

"Why?" she finally whispered, her voice hoarse as she tried to make sense of it all. Why this, why now? Why had fate thrown someone in her path guaranteed to destroy her, just when she was finally rebuilding her life?

"Choose."

She released his wrist, realizing she was still gripping it with a strength she hadn't known she was capable of.

Finger by finger, she forced herself to let him go. She couldn't answer him, she couldn't choose, but when she got her hands on Rory she was going to kill him.

Ignoring the shocked and surprised faces around her, she turned and moved slowly back to the garage. She had a job to do, she couldn't, she wouldn't, let this interfere.

She didn't need this.

She sat back down on the creeper and let it roll her back beneath the car she had been working on. A few more little tweaks and it should be finished. Just a little bit more.

She picked up the wrench on the cement floor beside her and went to work. If tears rolled from the corners of her eyes and into her hair, then she ignored them. If the pain tightened her chest until it felt as though her heart were being ripped apart, then she ignored it.

Today, there was work to be done. When everyone else was gone, she'd pay Noah Blake for the day and send him on his way. It would hurt. She needed the money and the bank payment was due next week. If she had to, if there was no other choice, then she would sell some more of the jewelry her mother had left her to cover the rest of the payment.

One thing was for sure. Noah was going to have to go. She couldn't handle this. She couldn't handle her instant response to him, and she couldn't handle the conflicting emotions that raged through her at the sight of him. There was something familiar and yet something too dangerous about him for her to get a handle on. Something about him that had made her feel again. Something more than the regret she had resigned herself to three years before. She had finished grieving three years ago; sometimes, now, she just regretted.

She didn't notice the sob that tore from her chest at the thought, but the man standing by the car heard it. Heard it, and hated it.

Noah could still feel the rage coursing through him, burning through his mind like a haze of red. The sight of Mike, the sound of him, the vicious words that had poured from his lips when he spoke to Sabella. Noah had lost his mind. Even now, he wanted the other man dead. A lifetime of history, of friendship, was over that quickly. As far Noah was concerned, Mike was living on borrowed time.

He glanced down at the ground, and the sight of Sabella's legs bent, feet braced on the floor, knees raised against the fender of the car, sent another sort of fury surging through him.

She had no business under there. No matter how damned sexy she looked with her jeans stained with oil and a smear of it on her chin and her cheek.

She was killing herself. Noah hadn't missed the dark circles under her eyes, the weight she had lost, the haunted depths of her misty gray eyes. This wasn't the woman he had left behind. There was no makeup on her surprisingly youthful face, her once honey-streaked light blond hair was a mix of burnished golds and dark blond now. He hadn't even known she colored it. How had he not known that his wife dyed her hair?

He brought to mind the memory of her naked body. How he had loved her body, curvy and warm, fitting against him perfectly. The bare soft flesh between her thighs had been devoid of curls, so he'd had no idea what the natural color should be.

And God, she looked young. The makeup she had worn had made her look older, more experienced. He knew she had been eighteen when they married, and he was suddenly desperately aware of how young she had really been.

At twenty-six, she still looked like a kid without the shield of cosmetics to add maturity to her still unlined face. But the grief was there. It was thick and dark in her eyes, in the tightly controlled line of her lips, the stiff set of her shoulders before she disappeared beneath the car.

He drew in a deep hard breath as the mechanics stared back at him, watching him as Sabella disappeared beneath the car. Their expressions were wary, part relief, part concern. They weren't the same men who had worked here when he left, they were unknowns and unknowns were always the enemy. And he would never forget that only one, the youngest, had stepped forward to protect Sabella while the others stood back.

"She's not alone anymore," he growled, knowing the fury that roughened his voice now. "Get your asses in there and finish the work now, or get your stuff and get out. I want every vehicle in that damned bay finished before any of you go home tonight, or the only one I want to see in the morning is this one." He stabbed his finger imperiously toward Toby. "And your ass belongs in the office, if I'm not mistaken."

Toby swallowed tightly, his brown eyes flickering in indecision toward the garage where Sabella had disappeared. It was obvious he was more concerned about leaving her undefended than he was about his job.

"Go, boy," he snarled. "We'll discuss details later." His gaze swung to the other men, watching as they shifted nervously, their oil-streaked expressions and wary eyes staying trained on him.

"Make your choice now," he snapped. "And make sure you make the right one."

He didn't wait for their decisions. He made for the garage, striding straight to the line of clipboards on the workstation and grabbing the first one. It was time to get to work.

He wasn't fooling himself; after the others had left, Sabella would let that temper he knew she had, erupt. He'd only seen it once before in their marriage. The day he had made the mistake of telling her she couldn't do something.

She had taught him fast and hard exactly what happened when he tried to control her.

Control came naturally to SEALs. It was a part of who they were and what made them so efficient. So it wasn't unexpected that the night she had arranged to meet some of her girlfriends for drinks and dinner, he had told her she couldn't go. He wanted her home with him. He'd been horny, and he wanted his wife. He didn't want her at the local watering hole together with a bunch of women and the men there lusting after her.

She'd stared back at him silently for long moments then continued to inform him where she would be and when she would be home.

Dammit, Bella, you can stay home tonight. With me.

He'd barely ducked in time to miss the salt shaker that had been aimed a little too close to his head. Then his sweet, soft-spoken little Southern angel had erupted.

Flushed, furious, she had proceeded to lay down the law regarding their relationship, and by time she stalked out of the house, ass twitching beneath her jeans like an enraged little hen, he'd had his tail tucked between his legs despite the fact that he had informed her to just stay the night with her damned friends. He'd be fine without her.

Two o'clock that morning, he'd driven around town until he found her car, parked at the house of one of those friends. He'd carried his tipsy little wife out of the house, put her in his truck, and driven her home. And he'd never made that mistake again.

And now, after hearing that muted, smothered little sound from beneath the car, coming from the woman he wondered if he had even known as his wife, he realized that there was a chance Sabella had held as much back from him as he had held back from her.

Because he hadn't had nearly enough of her before he had "died." He hadn't touched her in the ways he'd wanted to, even then. The darkness that filled him had always been waiting for an outlet, he realized. And now it was focused on one, tiny, too independent little woman. A woman who deserved far better than she was about to get.

CHAPTER FOUR

It was closing on seven that evening, the brilliance of the sun was fading and easing over the mountains as the mechanics left, staring back at Noah, as though afraid to leave her there with him.

At least the sheriff hadn't shown up, which meant Mike wasn't pressing charges. Yet. His truck had been delivered to the bank while he was still there, and if luck was on her side, she wouldn't have to deal with him again for a while.

Noah Blake, on the other hand, she was more than ready to deal with. The blood had pumped furiously through her veins all day, leaving her nerves heightened, a feeling almost like excitement digging sharp claws into her chest.

He had worked hard, steadily, and kept the other men working faster. But she didn't need him there. She didn't want him there. She didn't need him interfering with the structured, ordered existence she had created for herself. And she didn't want the excitement or the feeling of tension she could feel tightening inside her.

The men working for her would accept taking orders from her eventually or she would do as she had done the past three years. Fire their asses and hire others. She'd fired plenty of them since taking over, another here and there didn't make a difference to her.

Toby delayed as long as he could until Sabella had to push

him out the door before turning to face Noah. She jerked the
money bag from the desk and shoved it in her purse before
slinging the leather bag over her shoulder and glaring back at
him.

This was it. He could get the hell right back out of her life
now and she could stop feeling so *alive.*

"When you see Rory, tell him I want to talk to him. Immediately," she snapped. "And if he isn't back to work tomorrow, then as far as I'm concerned he doesn't have a job
any more than you have one. I won't have a maniac working
in my garage and attacking my customers." She held a hand
up as he started to speak. "Whether they deserve it or not."

He stared back at her, his eyes raging, wild, twisting with
color in an expression that could have been carved from
stone.

His gaze flicked over her body and she flushed. She could
feel her own hardened nipples beneath her shirt and bra. She
could feel the flesh between her thighs tingling and she hated
it. She hated feeling that and she hated him for making her
feel it.

Her gaze flickered to the parking lot as a vehicle pulled up
and she almost grimaced. She'd forgotten about Duncan.
Nice, safe, easygoing Duncan Sykes with his dark blond hair,
brown eyes, and steady smile. He wasn't dangerous. He didn't
have the power to destroy her sanity or her self-control.

"I'll be here in the morning." His lips thinned at the
sound of a car door closing. "With Rory."

Sabella smiled at the thought of getting her hands on
Rory. Oh, her brother-in-law was in some serious trouble.

"You do that," she told him softly as Duncan approached
the door, a frown on his face. "And be ready to ride out the
same way you rode in. Now, thanks to you, I'm late, and I'm
not ready for my date. You deserve to be fired for that alone."

She put a smile on her face as the door opened and Duncan stepped in. And of course, she compared the two men.
Not that there was much comparison. Noah was hands down
harder, tougher, sexier, more vibrant and imposing than Duncan would ever be.

"You're not ready." Duncan grinned, amusement dancing in his eyes despite the curious glance he flicked to the other man. "Why did I have a feeling you'd forget our date if things got busy?"

"Because you know me." She grinned back, aware that her amusement was more faked than she would have liked.

Her gaze flicked back to Noah.

"New employee?" Duncan asked, turning to Noah as though he weren't a rabid maniac on the loose and holding out his hand. "I'm Duncan Sykes. I own the electronics store in town."

A shiver of foreboding raced through Sabella at Noah's smile. It was the chill in his eyes, the flash of teeth, that warned her he wasn't nearly as friendly he was pretending to be.

"Noah Blake," he introduced himself.

Duncan glanced back at Sabella.

"It's good to meet you." Duncan nodded then smiled back at Sabella. "We're going to be late if you don't hurry and get dressed. Do you need me to lock up?"

Oh, she really didn't think so.

"Everything's ready, I just have to lock the door behind us." She turned to Noah, her eyes narrowing as he continued to stare at Duncan. "Noah, I need to lock up."

A flash of dread raced up her spine as he turned back to her. His eyes were flat and cold, his lips unsmiling, his expression too still. Too calm.

"Have a nice night," he told her quietly before leaving the office and moving to the black, wicked Harley parked outside the garage.

Sabella was barely aware of the breath she had been holding until it released silently and she turned back to Duncan. "You'll have to enjoy a glass of wine while I get ready. Time got away from me today."

"You're always worth waiting on," he told her as they stepped from the office and she locked the doors. "Besides, we've been seeing each other long enough, Belle, that I know to build in time when I make reservations."

Sabella grimaced. She was always late. She had never been late for anything until her husband's death. It seemed as though she had been running late ever since. Trying somehow to go back rather than forward.

As she slid into the passenger seat of Duncan's car for the ride up to the house, she couldn't help but notice that Noah was still there. He was bent next to the Harley, fiddling with something, no doubt being nosy, because his gaze wasn't on the bike, it was on them.

"I'm going to assume Rory hired him," Duncan stated as they drove past the Harley.

"You assume right," she breathed out roughly.

Rory was always pulling in strays. Thankfully, they never seemed to stay long. She had a feeling she was going to have trouble getting rid of this one though.

Nothing else was said as they pulled into the driveway in front of her house.

"Come on in." She moved quickly from the car, house keys in hand. "You know where the wine is, go ahead and get a glass, I'll get showered and be down in half an hour."

She opened the door and rushed in, making for the stairs at a quick pace.

"I'm timing you," he said, laughing. "Twenty bucks says it will take an hour."

"You're on." She threw him a quick smile, but ducked her head, knowing that smile wouldn't reach her eyes.

She couldn't stop the feeling that somehow, some way, she was being unfaithful to the husband who had died more than six years ago. She had fought that feeling for a year, ever since the first date she had accepted with Duncan. The first time she had promised herself she was going to get over Nathan's death.

Each time she and Duncan left the house she had shared with Nathan, she had felt the queasy, sick feeling that she was betraying the man she loved. The man who had loved her.

It was insane. She had to assure herself daily that Nathan would have wanted her to be happy, that he wasn't staring down from heaven, feeling hurt and angry because she had turned her back on what they had shared.

She hadn't turned her back, she told herself as she stepped beneath the shower. He had been a warrior, and he hadn't returned home. He was dead and gone, and she was still alive. Wasn't she?

Noah had a meeting to go to, an operational briefing that he knew he should already be heading to. Instead, he was standing in the tree line outside the home he used to share with Sabella, a pair of military binoculars in his hands, staring at the house.

No matter how much he had bitched while they were married, Sabella still left the blinds and curtains open until dark. They were open now.

Duncan Sykes was in the kitchen and, be damned, but he was opening a bottle of wine. His lips tightened. That was his wine, no matter who he was or wasn't. He'd spent years building his collection of wines, rarely opening a bottle, enjoying the sight of the little wine cellar in the basement as it filled up.

Now that son of a bitch was opening one of his best bottles and pouring a glass. By God, if he caught that bastard in his bed, with his wife, there would be murder.

He blew out a hard breath. Wasn't his business, he reminded himself.

The hell it wasn't. Jagged, forked spikes of pure fury buried themselves in his brain as he felt the control he had built over the past years beginning to crack. If Noah saw Duncan touch her, he wouldn't be able to control the rage.

Noah was aware of Rory coming up behind him, following the order Noah had given him when he called from the garage. His brother wasn't happy. And that was just too damned bad, because Noah had never in his life been further from "happy."

"How long has this shit been going on?" he bit out, keeping his eyes on the house rather than glancing at Rory.

"What shit?" Rory eyed him warily.

Noah flicked his hand at the house. "Sykes."

"'Bout a year." Rory flopped down at the base of a tree and yawned as though he were safe.

Noah flicked a look down at him. "And you didn't stop it, why?"

Rory looked up at him in surprise before scratching his cheek thoughtfully. "Hell, probably because he's the only one of the men she's gone out with that I actually like."

Noah's jaw clenched. "How many have there been?"

Other men. Not just one man. Other men had gone out with his wife. Stared at her smile, lusted after her. He couldn't imagine one of them touching her, or he'd have to kill them all.

"Just a few." Rory shrugged as though it didn't matter. "They never last long. A few dates here and there. Then she'll get all guilty feeling, wear her wedding band for a while, and bury up here in the house when she's not working before she forces herself to try again. She hasn't worn her wedding band in over a year now though."

Rory picked at a blade of grass as Noah went back to watching the house.

Sykes was still in the kitchen, probing around, looking through drawers. The bastard straightened a cup on a hook and paced to the far window to look down on the garage. There was a look of pending ownership on Sykes's face, as if he were already imagining exactly what he intended to change in Bella's life.

Yeah, Noah knew him, well. Duncan hid his strong will from most people, but he was no one's fool. He'd been seeing Sabella for a year, then he was serious about it. He had every intention of owning everything Noah had once possessed as Nathan Malone.

"You left her," Rory stated with a hint of anger. "It wouldn't be any of your business if she had fucked half the town, anyway."

He didn't say anything, because Rory was right. He had left her. He had taken that mission knowing there was a chance of failure. He had failed and he hadn't come back.

"What happened with Grant?" he asked Rory. "He tried to take the garage and the house after promising he would take care of her if anything happened to me. Why?"

"Same reason he ended up with Grandpop's stuff, I guess." Rory sighed. "Because that's just how he is. Grandpop still excuses him. Says Grant is doing what he thinks will protect her. Grandpop always excuses him though. Calls it layers."

Layers upon layers, he had always told Noah a lifetime ago. Nothing is as it seems. With Grant, Noah couldn't imagine how it could be anything less than total selfishness.

"And Mike Conrad?"

Rory snorted. "That pig. He's pissed off because Sabella wouldn't screw him or sell him the garage. He seemed to want both. He chased after her for over a year until she had to threaten to sue him for harassment. Then he started getting ugly. He wanted the garage worse than he wanted her though. Tried to turn the town against her for a while, but that didn't work out too well. You had too many friends. Once she pulled her ass out of grieving for a man that just didn't want to come home, she threw herself into the business and pulled it back up. She does good now."

"Keep sniping at me, Rory, and you're not going to be able to walk for a while."

Rory snorted. He was quiet for long minutes before saying, "Grandpop went to your grave today. Usually he just walks out and talks to Grandma. But today, he went to your headstone and just stood looking down at it."

Noah didn't want to hear this. He pushed the rage and pain back inside himself and continued to watch Duncan prowl the kitchen.

"Strange thing about Grandpop, I just never figured it out until now."

"He didn't grieve," Noah answered for him.

Hell, he should have known better than to think he could fool the old man. Jordan should have known better. Grandpop had always known what was going on before it ever happened.

"That's true." Rory nodded. "Not even once. And not like Sabella did. I used to stay up at the house some. She would wake me up every night screaming your name, swearing there was blood on her hands, or swearing you were hurt. Begging me to save you."

Rory jumped to his feet. "Screw this. I'm going home."

"She was right."

He felt Rory still.

"What?" his brother asked carefully.

"She was right. I was hurt, Rory. Damned bad. And by the time I was rescued, I was barely alive." He watched Sabella walk into the room and smile at Duncan.

The other man finished his wine, kissed her cheek, and they headed for the door. Duncan's hand was at the small of her back, touching her, leading her. Damn, Noah was going to enjoy killing him.

He pulled the binoculars away from his face and stared at the house silently for long minutes before turning back to Rory.

"Grandpop should have grieved," he told him, his voice low. "Because the man I was died in a cell in a rotting jungle. Her husband, your brother. Son and grandson. It all died inside me, Rory. I'm not the man I was, and I never will be."

Rory gazed back at him for long moments. "That's not what happened," he finally said. "All of you didn't die, Noah. Trust me. All that stupid, testosterone-driven, arrogant-bastard pride of yours that you always hid from Sabella is still alive and breathing." Rory shot him a scornful look. "That part survived just fine."

Noah's lips quirked at that. Maybe, in a way, Rory was right there. He'd always hid parts of himself from those he loved, but Rory was a Malone, he knew that side of himself just as he knew the side Nathan had held back. Until now. That dark inner core, the dominant arrogance and powerful will had always been kept hidden, toned down. He had been civilized. Noah wasn't civilized.

"Follow them," he ordered Rory.

"Do what?" Rory exclaimed, outraged shock in his eyes. "What, you want her to kill me or something?"

"Do you want me to kill you?" Noah was in his face, his voice low, demanding. "Which one of us can hurt you more?"

He wouldn't really hurt Rory. Hell, that was his kid brother. He almost grinned at the man his brother had grown into. He felt affection. Fondness. Where Noah had felt next to nothing emotionally, for years, he now felt flooded with emotions. Emotions that tore at his control, that made a mockery of the years behind him.

Rory shook his head, his hands propped on his hips, as he lifted his gaze to the heavens. "I pray. I go to mass. I even remember to respect my elders and help little old ladies across the street. What the hell did I do to deserve this?"

Noah clapped his hand on the younger man's shoulder. "You breathe, Rory. Remember that. When Malones breathe, shit happens. It's cosmic. It's their fate."

"You suck, man." Rory grimaced. "Bella's gonna kill me."

"Beats me killing you," Noah grunted. "I can make it hurt worse."

Rory glared at him. "Man, you are so clueless. You don't know Belle at all, do you?" Then he grinned rakishly. Noah remembered that smile. A smile he had once had himself and it didn't bode well for Noah. "You are in for such a surprise."

Jordan watched as Noah stalked into the briefing room, nearly half an hour late, but the vision that met Jordan's gaze had his eyes narrowing.

Dangerous. Powerful. Like a big jungle cat, all smooth moves and predatory awareness. This wasn't a cold-blooded shark. His eyes weren't icy. They would never again be that Malone blue, laser surgery had darkened the color to a navy blue rather than that neon sapphire blue they had once been. The color of Jordan's, and his brother Rory's.

Those eyes had been hard, cold for five years now. Until tonight. Tonight, they were wild, fierce, as Noah paused and stared back at him.

"We need to talk." There was a snarl, an animal quality to the tone that had Jordan's brow lifting.

"Hey there, wild card." Tehya chose that moment to move behind Noah and pat his butt.

Jordan knew what the other woman had done, but he didn't expect Noah's reaction. Tehya had been patting Noah's ass for years, mostly to piss Jordan himself off, and Noah always ignored her. This time, he caught her wrist, loosely, and stared down at her.

"Don't." He said the word softly, gently enough, that Jordan came slowly to his feet.

Tehya's impudent smile was enough to make a man grind his teeth.

"Oh, all that testosterone." She pretended to shiver. "Watch it, Noah, I'll start thinking you're claimed or something."

Or something. Jordan sat down as the minx carried the stack of files to the briefing table and winked back at him. "The others will be up in a few minutes. Ian and Kira were running late as well."

As she moved through the door, Noah turned, closed it softly and locked it as Jordan leaned back in his chair, propped his elbows on the arms and steepled his fingers in front of him.

"You have a problem, wild card?" Jordan asked.

Noah turned back slowly and those eyes raged.

"You knew she was dating," Noah stated.

Jordan contained his smile as he nodded. "It was in the report I give you every month. You know, the one you toss in the trash can after simply asking me if she's safe and if she's alive?"

Noah paced closer. Danger surrounded him, fury pulsed inside him.

"She's dating." His lips pulled back from his teeth furiously.

Jordan tilted his head and stared back at him. "And this is your business how? Nathan Malone is dead, wild card. Remember?"

Noah flinched. He jerked back as though stung, his expression instantly closing.

"Unlock the door," Jordan ordered him coolly. "We have a briefing and a mission to complete." He turned his attention to the files Tehya had brought in. "Noah." Jordan lifted his head, staring back into those furious blue eyes. "Her husband didn't want her. Did you think she'd wait on him forever?"

Perhaps that was exactly what a part of him had believed.

Noah took his seat slowly, forcing back emotion, forcing back the rage. He'd worked too many years at putting his past behind him, but somehow, in all those years, he'd never imagined Sabella allowing another man to touch her. Likely because Noah had never been able to touch another woman.

He had sworn himself to her. Heart, body, soul. All he was, all he could ever be, belonged to that woman.

The man that had been born from the ashes of hell in no way resembled Nathan Malone. He had known that the day he found some clarity in his mind, months after his rescue. He was no longer the man Sabella had married. But the man he had become still claimed that one part of Nathan Malone's life. Noah Blake claimed Nathan's wife.

As the others filtered into the room, Noah stared at Jordan Malone. He'd even forced himself to forget the fact that this was his uncle. That Rory was his brother, that Grandpop had been his base all his life. He'd let go of everything but the wife.

"Okay, here's what we have." The lights dimmed as Tehya passed out the files and Ian and Kira Richards stood to the side of the large-screened LCD monitor that hung on the wall across from the briefing table.

Five dead men, American, Russian, Israeli, Australian, and English. They were the Elite Operational Unit, codenamed, marked by the sign of rebirth and of death. A black sun and a scarlet sword. Dead men. They had signed their lives away for the chance at vengeance.

Jordan and Ian commanded the group. The rest of Durango team, Reno, Kell, and Macey, were their backup. They knew who he was, what he was, what he had walked away from.

"The Black Collar Militia." The first of the photos began to flash.

"Angelina Rodriguez, the wife of a Mexican-American Texas Senate hopeful, killed, their brand on her hip. 'BCM' was indeed branded on her slender hip. Emilio Rodriguez dropped out of the senatorial race when his wife's body was found and a message indicating that his twin daughters would be next. The FBI covered the murder to allow an investigation into the BCM. Stated cause of death was accidental, due to the fact that she was found in her vehicle, in the bottom of a ravine not far out of Odessa where she had been visiting."

The photos glared back at them from the screen. The woman was pretty. Long black hair, dark brown eyes. A generous smile in life, a grimace in death.

"Added to her death." More photos, these of illegal Mexican aliens found throughout Texas and New Mexico. Victims, Noah knew, of illegal hunts. The BCM brand was buried on the flesh of their backs, some on the buttocks.

"We have a dozen hunts and deaths," Jordan stated. "We have three dead FBI agents sent to investigate the information that BCM is based in Alpine. Two men, one female. Their bodies were mutilated beyond recognition, teeth pulled, fingers removed. DNA identified the bodies."

The photos were horrifying. Burned, hacked, faces beaten until the features were obliterated.

"The Black Collar Militia is being coined a white supremacy group; they're actually closer to a homeland terrorist organization." Ian stepped forward at that point. "You have all the information in your files. Black Collar is centralized in Texas, but it's moving swiftly into neighboring states. Rodriguez was only the most public figure they've targeted. Several so-called accidents at plants and manufacturing firms that use legal as well as illegal aliens have occurred. Owners have been kidnapped, tortured, their family members have had a variety of suspicious accidents, some fatal, some not."

"And no one has identified the members?" Travis Caine, formerly British Secret Service, spoke up then, his light blue-gray eyes narrowed as he stared back at Ian, then Jordan. "Isn't that a bit unusual?"

"Each investigation focusing on them has ended in cases abruptly closed, or agents dying. This group has at least one highly placed government informant, perhaps more."

"Public support of immigration laws is growing," Nikolas Steele, formerly Russian Special Forces, said then.

"Nothing's perfect," Jordan breathed out roughly. "But this." He pointed to the image of the dead agents. "Has to stop. Our job is to identify and interrogate the commander of the group located here, in Alpine. All signs lead here."

"We have an Israeli, an Irish immigrant, and a Russian," Noah said. "We should be able to target interest."

"We also have this," Jordan stated, and the screen flipped a satellite view of the garage Rory and Sabella owned.

Noah stared at it silently, aware of the looks directed his way.

"We keep her out of it," he grated out.

"That's not possible, Noah." Jordan sighed. "Her name is already in it, as you know. The garage itself is a target. Profitable, a central point for gossip, and in the past months showing a measure of growth. The last report those field agents sent in was that Malone Service and Repair was a target. Owned by Rory and Sabella Malone. That report stated there were plans to either incorporate Sabella Malone into a marriage with one of the central figures or kill her and Rory. We can't overlook that report, and we can't just keep Sabella Malone out of this."

"Why target a gas station?" the Israeli Mossad, hard-core ice, Micah Sloane, asked the next question. "It's not busting millions. Why not open their own station and use it for whatever they need Malone's for?"

"Malone's is established," Noah answered the question. "Started by Nathan Malone, a man most people in that town either respected or feared. It would be above suspicion for the movement of arms or the laundering of funds."

"Bingo." Ian stared back at him coolly. "Several suspected BCM members have tried establishing relationships with her. The only one to have shown progress is this man."

Duncan Sykes's picture showed up on the screen.

"Duncan Sykes. Owner of a profitable electronics business in town. Never hires aliens, illegal or otherwise. Known to have been a close, personal friend of Nathan Malone's before his death. Sykes as well as Mike Conrad, another friend of Malone's, were mentioned in that final report, which, I should point out, disappeared within days of transmission to the D.C. office, just before the agents' disappearance."

"High level," John Vincent murmured. Code-named Heat Seeker, the Australian Special Forces soldier had pissed off the wrong group in Australia.

"Very high level." Jordan nodded. "Alpine is a central base, we bust it, gather their head generals, and we can backtrack it straight to D.C. and our leaks. That's our mission, gentlemen."

"Nik and I will be in the garage," Noah stated, still staring at the aerial view of the garage. "Initial information is that two of the mechanics are BCM. If Malone's is one of their primary targets, and Sykes is a general, then we'll see how they like being screwed back."

Sykes was gone. Noah would make certain there wasn't a chance in hell that Sabella would continue that little friendship.

"First phase, information only," Jordan ordered them. "We'll meet back here in a week, see what we have and then go from there. Travis will be at the college as a professor of English history. John, you and Micah will cover. You're just drifters out for a good time. Target the bars, the college hangouts where they recruit from, and you'll also be backup."

Micah and John nodded to that. They made damned good shadows. All of them did, but Micah was a master at it.

"Durango team is in place to provide backup as well if we encounter trouble. Other than that, we're on our own," Ian told them. "We have six weeks to complete this mission, because in six weeks, we have this."

The screen changed again. The letter was simple, to the

point. Addressed to the owner of a manufacturing firm in Dallas that hired legal aliens from around the world. The message was clear. He had six weeks to ensure his firm hired naturally born Americans only, or he'd pay the price.

"The owner of this firm is who?" Micah asked.

"The owner of this firm just happens to be a financial supporter of Helping Hands, an organization that encourages multinational growth and harmony." Jordan smiled tightly. "Boys, meet one of your employers."

CHAPTER FIVE

Three days later, Noah forced himself away from the garage as he watched Sabella roll herself beneath another vehicle. One of the vehicles he'd completed. She was going over his work as though he hadn't spent the better part of thirty-five years working on vehicles.

Top to bottom, she was spending the day going over every move he made.

He grimaced as he shoved a wrench in his back pocket, threw another look at her over his shoulder, and pushed into the office.

And stopped.

"Excuse me." He turned to walk right back out.

"Ah, Noah Blake." Grandpop Malone rose up from where he had been sitting next to the desk he'd had Rory blocked in at. "Don't leave so soon, son. I hear we have something in common."

Noah grimaced, gritted his teeth, then turned back and let the door reclose behind him and faced the man who had been the base of his entire life.

Grandpop. He was wrinkled, stooped, his dark face was still imposing, his eyes were still that bright sapphire blue that Noah had opted to have changed.

"We have something in common?" he asked, glancing at Rory's shuttered expression.

"Irish, son." Grandpop's smile had Noah pausing. The old bastard knew, and Noah knew it. "We're both Irish."

He couldn't deny it. He was fully prepared to lie to the old man. Knew he'd eventually meet up with him. But now that the moment had arrived, he couldn't do it.

"A bit," Noah answered carefully.

Grandpop had sat back down and now he shifted in his chair. His long body was weaker than last time Noah had seen him, checked on him. His hair was completely gray now, there was barely a hint of the black it had once been.

"Rory, I'll be heading out for a while," Noah tried.

"Running away?" Grandpop lost his smile. "Irishmen don't run away."

Noah's brow lifted. "Should I be running away?"

Grandpop stared back at him. That knowing, certain look as Noah looked at Rory once again. He'd kill the little shit if he'd spilled his guts.

Rory gave his head a subtle shake, but he grimaced. As he'd been warning Noah, hiding things from Grandpop wasn't easy.

"I wanted to meet you." Grandpop rose to his feet and Rory followed him. "Wanted to see this new man that had my little girl in there so upset. No one's upset my girl since her husband left."

"I hear he died," Noah pointed out.

Grandpop nodded slowly. "Yeah, that's what they tell us," he said. "I argued that death with my son. He was a SEAL, you know. For a lot of years." Grandpop shook his head. "I didn't believe him." He stared back at Noah now. "I eventually changed my mind though."

Noah, Nathan. Husband. Grandson. Brother. He felt all those parts of himself reaching out to the old man that knew the truth without being told. He'd disappointed the old man.

"My grandson was a hero, you know that?" Grandpop stated as he headed to the door.

"That's what Rory tells me," he finally said quietly.

His grandpop, treasured, revered, stopped again and stared back at him for long, tense moments.

"The boy always did what he had to do. What was right. What was responsible." He blinked back tears and Noah felt grief swamp him. "He died," Grandpop said. "Before I could tell him I understood why he let go."

He stepped from the office then. Noah heard the message, the careful phrasing, the message behind the words as Rory rushed to the door and followed behind the old man.

Fuck! He didn't need this.

"Grandpop left? What did you do to him?" Sabella rushed in behind him, threw him a glare then followed Rory and Grandpop to the parking lot.

Hell, he didn't need this.

"Grandpop," Sabella called out as the old man pulled himself behind the wheel of his pickup truck and watched as she approached. "Is everything okay?"

He bestowed one of his smiles on her. Fondness. Affection. She could feel it wrapping around her as she moved behind the door and gave him a quick hug. "You didn't wait to say hi to me."

Grandpop always said hello to her before he left.

"Just stopping by to meet your new man." Grandpop smiled back at her. "Us Irish have to stick together, you know."

"He's not my new man," she muttered. "He's Rory's." She glared at her brother-in-law, because Rory refused to fire him.

Three days she had fought him. Argued with him, and now he was talking about hiring another mechanic. Some big blond biker that she knew had to be associated with the arrogant bastard trying to take over her garage.

And he was standing firm, refusing to back down. Of course, in the last three days there had been more business, but only, she suspected, because everyone was curious about the new mechanic.

Grandpop just smiled back at her in that patient, wise way of his then patted her shoulder with his gnarled hand. "Irish boys will keep your blood hot at night," he told her with a rascally wink.

"I've had my wild Irish boy," she told him softly. "No other can replace him, Grandpop."

Nathan had been her soul, and in too many ways, he was still so much a part of her heart that she compared every other man against him. Unfortunately, there were times she forgot to do that when Noah was around.

"Follow your heart. Not your head, child," Grandpop told her gently. He'd always told her that. "And come see me soon. I miss you."

She moved back as he closed the door and seconds later watched as he drove away.

"Rory, what are you up to?" She turned to her brother-in-law as Grandpop pulled into traffic.

Rory's expression was too innocent, and reminded her too much of when Nathan had hidden things from her. Same expression, the same set of his broad body.

"You're too suspicious, Belle," he sighed.

"You're not hiring that Viking," she told him.

Rory's jaw clenched and his blue eyes fired. "Should I leave, Belle?" he asked.

That hint of anger in his voice had her eyes narrowing.

"No, you shouldn't leave." She frowned back. "You should discuss hirings with me."

"Like you've discussed with me?" He rolled his eyes. "Three years, Belle. You walked in and took over three years after Nathan died, and I let you, because I didn't know what the hell I was doing. But I know more now. It's time I pulled my weight. And the mechanics we have now aren't efficient."

She couldn't argue that, but she hated him pointing it out.

"I don't like Noah Blake. Fire him and hire the Viking. Then we'll discuss the others."

"Come on, Belle." Frustration filled his voice now. "You don't like him because he knows what he's doing and be-cause he doesn't mind telling you that. No one's done that since Nathan and you can't handle it," he accused her.

Sabella flinched. She could feel the ache she kept hidden, buried beneath the reality of Nathan's death, snap hot and sharp inside her chest.

"Nathan didn't arbitrarily argue with me," she bit out.

"No he didn't," he said roughly. "Because you never let him know who you were or how much that damned garage meant to you. Well, someone knows now. Give *him* hell instead of me."

With that, he stomped off, his hands buried in the pockets of his work pants, as Noah stepped outside the garage bay doors.

Those dark, dark blue eyes were locked on her. Lean, hungry, powerful. His body drew her gaze whenever he was around whether she liked it or not. And dammit, she didn't like it. She didn't want another dangerous man. But she also didn't want a man who agreed with her, and she didn't want a man who was safe. For the first time in the three years since she had taken her wedding band off she admitted in her head what her heart already knew. Safe wasn't going to do it. Duncan didn't do it for her. Unfortunately, though, Noah Blake did do it for her. "It" being that sexual curiosity, that pounding heart, that surge of excitement. Something she had never felt with another man— only her husband. And that fact had the power to make the hurt, the anger, and the animosity toward this one man run deeper.

Right now, she hated Noah Blake clear to the bottom of her soul. Because he was forcing something no one else had ever been able to do. He was forcing her to feel things she had only ever felt for her husband.

And to Sabella, that betrayal to Nathan's memory was worse than any other she could have committed.

She couldn't forget that. As the day went on, she dealt with vehicle computers that didn't want to cooperate, and the mechanic from hell that didn't seem to be able to do anything but draw her eye.

At one point she lifted her head from the interior of the pickup she was working on to watch, fascinated, as he glared into the guts of another vehicle, slowly twirling a wrench between his fingers.

There was an oddly familiar frown on his face. A way

he had of glaring at the engine as he flipped that tool, finger to finger, and considered whatever it was he was considering.

It was sexy. Impossibly sexy. Dressed in dark gray work pants and a matching short-sleeved shirt, he conveyed an image of raw, powerful male that she couldn't help but notice.

"Hey, Noah," Rory called, interrupting her musings. Noah turned and frowned back at Rory in the office. "I need you in here."

"In a minute," Noah called before turning back to the engine.

"Now!" Rory's voice held a snap.

Noah's expression became still, dangerous, but he shoved the wrench in his back pocket and walked to the office. Prowled to the office maybe. There was something dangerously predatory and pissed off about him now.

The door closed quietly behind him as Rory lowered the shades to the windows that looked out to the garage. Sabella's eyes narrowed. She dragged the oily rag from her back pocket and wiped her hands before moving to the office. Gripping the doorknob, she tried to turn it, only to find it locked.

Locked out of her own office? My, how interesting. She could feel her face flushing with anger as she jerked the keys out of her pocket. She was set to unlock it as the door jerked open.

"Guy talk." Rory's grin was stiff, his blue eyes brighter, though more with concern than anger.

"Guy talk, your ass!" She smiled tightly as she stepped into the office to see Noah standing by her desk, his arms crossed over his chest as he stared at Rory with a flat, hard gaze. "What did he do?"

"Sabella, can you please let me handle this one little thing?" he said impatiently. "Really. I promise. I can manage some stuff on my own."

Rory sounded a shade put out. Okay, so she was a little territorial with the garage, maybe too much so. But over the years she had let it become her husband and her baby and everything in between. Rory knew that. So why was he becoming so angry now?

"I was just curious." She shoved her hands into her pockets and gave Noah what she hoped was a sweet smile. "Just tell me what he did and I'll leave. Are you going to fire him? Can I watch?"

"Fine." Rory didn't look happy, that was odd enough. He looked angry at her, and he was never angry with her. And his smile. It was tight. All teeth. When had he turned into a full-grown man on her? He wasn't a kid brother any longer. "He was staring at your ass! Now you deal with it."

He turned and slammed out of the office, leaving her to stare at him in shock before she turned to meet Noah's amused gaze.

"He was lying to me," she said.

He grinned. Noah was absolutely entranced. Once again, he had to ask, though, what had happened to the Sabella he had known six years before. The one who never chipped a nail, and would have never, under any circumstances, butted into a male/male confrontation.

"You have a fine ass," he stated, and knew she wasn't buying it.

Her eyes narrowed. "And you're not going to tell me what he was chewing *your* ass over?"

Noah had to chuckle. "It was more in the way of a warning."

He was treading a fine line. Nathan wasn't as dead as Noah might wish; he still had habits that had once been ingrained. One of those habits? Twirling that damned wrench as he tried to figure out a particular problem beneath the hood of a vehicle.

She sniffed at his response. "Piss him off too far and I'll convince him to finally fire you."

He had to grin at that one as he sauntered to the door. Before passing her, he stopped, lowered his head, and whispered, "And I caught you looking at my ass too. Maybe I should tell Rory on *you.*"

She caught his arm as he moved to open the door, staring

up at him soberly. "You're messing up my life," she told him quietly. "And I don't like it."

Noah sobered. He could see an edge of pain, of knowledge, in her eyes. For the past three days they had been circling each other like combatants, edging forward and back, trying to make the other force the confrontation they both knew was coming.

"How am I messing up your life, Sabella?" Once, long ago, he would have known. He would have known the woman standing before him and could have sworn he could anticipate her every thought and move. He was learning, though, and hated it, but he was learning there had been so little that he had known about her.

Nathan's wife would have never barged into the office. Hell, she would have never been working on a car or staring him down now. The woman that had belonged to Nathan had hidden from him, just as Nathan had hidden from her.

But *this* woman was going to belong to Noah.

"You think you can take over, don't you?" she asked him softly. "Walk right in here, and everything you want is going to fall into place."

He narrowed his eyes on her. He'd had that thought, maybe. She was disabusing him of that notion quickly.

"I just needed a job." He forced a grin and watched as her gaze examined his face.

"You just need something to control," she told him as she eased away from him and moved to her desk. "You need someone to control. Your world has to be under your thumb, following your rules."

He turned and watched her closely as she leaned against the desk.

Her hair was pulled up in a ponytail, her face streaked with oil. There was a smudge on her neck and her jeans were stained with it. And she was the damnedest sight he had ever seen. All woman, confident, almost imposing, and the snap of lust that shot past his control nearly sent a shudder tearing through his body.

"I won't deny wanting you," he told her.

Her eyes widened. "I didn't ask if you wanted me."

"I'm tired of tiptoeing around the subject," he growled. "We're playing a game here and it's starting to irritate me, Sabella."

A mocking smile crossed her lips. "I don't need you, Noah. If you didn't notice several days ago, I have one relationship to keep me busy. I don't need another."

"You don't sleep with him." He moved to her then.

Anger lit the depths of her gray eyes then. "And you know this how?"

"Because your nipples are hard right now," he bit out, glancing down at the hard little points pressing against her bra. "Because you're doing everything you can to piss me off and get close to me at the same time. Because you feel the heat between us just as much as I do."

Sabella inhaled sharply. She wished she hadn't, because beneath the scent of oil was the scent of the man. Sweat dampened, lustful, determined. It was there in his eyes, in the tension that filled his body, whipped around her, reminded her how damned long it had been since she had been with a man. Since Nathan had touched her, she reminded herself desperately.

"This conversation is over." She pushed herself from the desk and moved for the door, only to find his larger body suddenly in her path.

"Ignoring it doesn't make it go away," he said softly, catching her shoulders, holding her still in front of him as her head snapped back to stare up at him.

"I don't have to ignore what isn't going to happen and what doesn't exist," she retorted desperately.

"It's going to happen."

She stood still. She should be fighting him, running, screaming, or something. Anything but standing here, feeling her knees weaken, as his head lowered, his gaze holding hers, his lips coming closer.

"Don't," she whispered when his lips were but a breath away from hers. "Don't turn this into a war."

"It's already a war," he warned her, his voice grating, so

rough. Unnaturally so, she realized as she let herself see the scars beneath the rasp of beard. "Give me your kiss, Sabella. You want to. You know we both need to."

He spoke against her lips, and they parted helplessly. Her hands gripped his wrists, something inside her clenched in longing, in desperation.

"Enough." She jerked away, but he pulled her forward.

Before Sabella could react, before she could escape, pleasure swamped her.

His lips were on hers. They covered hers. Slanted over them, parted them, and she was lost. The kiss rocked her in places she didn't know she could be rocked. It was dark, forceful, dominant.

Within seconds he had her against the door, lifting her against him and pushing his tongue inside her mouth as Sabella heard her own, half-frightened, half-shocked cry of pleasure.

"That's what you want," he accused as his head jerked back, lust flaming in his eyes and burning in her veins. "You want it, Sabella. Just as hot and just as wild as I do. Be careful, sweetheart, very damned careful, or you just might get it before you're ready for it."

Sabella felt pinned before him in shock. Pleasure was coursing through her; the dark, dominant power of that kiss had awakened something she knew she didn't want to face. Something she wasn't ready for.

She pulled back slowly. "Tell Rory I'll see him at closing."

"Running?" he growled as she turned and headed for the entrance to the door that led outside.

Sabella turned back, her gaze flickering over him, seeing the bulge in those pants, the hunger in his eyes.

"Stay away from me, Noah," she told him bleakly. "I don't need you. I don't want you. All I want is for you to be gone."

Lies. All lies and she knew it as she pushed through the door and almost ran the distance between the garage and the house on the hill. The house she had shared with the only man capable of doing what Noah had just done. The only man who had ever awakened a desire she couldn't control, one she couldn't combat. If she didn't get away from him, and get away from him now, then Sabella knew, she was looking at nothing but more pain, more loss. Noah wasn't the staying kind. He wasn't the loving kind. He wasn't her husband.

CHAPTER SIX

Sabella managed to avoid Noah the next day, and the day after that. She could feel his gaze on her as she worked in the office. When he came into the office, she escaped to the convenience store. If she worked in the garage, she worked far enough away from him that she could almost ignore the rough rasp of his voice.

Something had happened to his voice. It grated too deep, it was too rough, too gravelly. The scars on his face, the fine web of them beneath the hairs on his muscular arms, made her wonder at the hint of them that she had seen peeking beneath the collar on his shirt. What had happened to him? It would take a lot to scar a man that powerful, in such a horrible way.

No matter where she moved, she could feel his gaze on her though, and she could feel that kiss that had burned through her and left her shaking and weak for hours.

She could feel the tension ratcheting up the next evening in the garage. Each time he tried to speak to her, each move he made in her direction, she went the other way. She didn't want to deal with this. Her life was fine without him in it. She was fine alone. A date every now and then was okay. And though Duncan was pushing for more, it hadn't yet reached the point where she was going to have to break the relationship off. She enjoyed the companionship. She enjoyed his laughter. And she feared Noah's intensity.

She almost escaped him one more day, until closing. Rory left and the others followed close on his heels, closing down the garage and leaving Sabella alone in the office as Noah entered.

"We need to talk," he told her as she shoved the money bag in her purse and felt her heart rate accelerate.

"No time," she told him. "I have a date tonight. That means I need to get out of here on time."

"The hell you do."

He stomped to the door, twisted the locks with a snap of motion that had her flinching at the savagery in it. Then before she could evade him he snagged her wrist and pulled her to the stairs that led to the apartment above.

"What the hell—"

"Stop cussin' at me, Sabella," he growled, pulling her up the stairs. "We're finishing this. Here and now."

"Finishing what?" She jerked at his hold as he pushed her ahead of him and into the apartment she had once shared with Nathan.

She should be screaming, she should be trying to kick him, punch him, not let him drag her, with only minimal struggle, into the large apartment.

A leather duffel bag had been tossed on the couch. There was a box on the cabinet, evidently some groceries. He was moving right in, taking right over, she realized. Here, where she and Nathan had first made love, where he had proposed to her, made love to her that first time. Suddenly, the thought of another man here was intolerable.

"Move right back out." She turned on him, shaking at the sight of another man's possessions in Nathan's space. "Now. Get out now!"

A haze of heat was flooding her. Fury. She told herself it was fury and nothing more.

He snorted at that. "Rory was nice enough to stock me up with groceries while I was working my ass off on those cars downstairs," he said. "The hell I'm leaving."

"I don't want you here. Get out before I call the sheriff." She was furious. He was staring back at her as though he owned the apartment, the garage, and her. He was staring at her as if she were pushing him too far.

But she wasn't backing off. She wanted him out of her life now, before it was too late.

"And you think I'm going to let the sheriff run me off?" he asked her, his ruined voice sending shivers up her spine.

Sabella stopped and stared back at him. He looked dangerous, the tension surrounding him was dangerous, so why wasn't she frightened? Where had she managed to lose all the common sense she had once possessed?

"Why are you here?" She stared back at him, the anger and disbelief coalescing inside her. "What the hell makes you think you can just walk into my life and take over like this?"

He turned away from her a second, obviously hiding something or fighting to control his temper, she wasn't certain which. When he turned back to her, she took an instinctive step away from him.

"You're running from yourself, Sabella. Why?"

In a sudden moment of insight, Sabella knew he wasn't going anywhere, and his expression assured her that she couldn't force it. Rory had hired him, and he owned half of the business. He had as much right to loan out the apartment as she did. And he could hire anyone he wanted to hire.

She and Nathan had agreed to that before they ever married. Should anything ever happen to him, then half of the business that he had built would go to Rory, because he knew their father would never leave the other man anything.

She was stuck with Noah until he decided on his own that it was time for him to leave, and that was all there was to it.

"I'm not running from anything except a man that's taking too damned much for granted. You're not a Malone, Mr. Blake. You're nothing here and you never will be." She turned and took the first step to the door. One step, and in the next second she found herself against the door, firmly, if gently, held in place by the big, hard body suddenly pressing her into it.

Her breath caught. She felt surrounded, suddenly hot and weak. His head was beside hers, his cheek rubbing against her hair, his hands holding her in place as the feel of his erection pressed into her lower back.

"Why are you so frightened of this?" he whispered then. "Or are you just too frightened to live again?"

"Live for you?" she scoffed. "You don't measure a tenth of what my husband was, and I didn't need him to live. I sure as hell don't need you to do it."

"And does Sykes make you feel alive?" he asked her. "Does he tell you how perfect you are? Touch you like you'll break and whisper roses and candy?" He sneered. "Is that really what you need, Sabella?"

"You bastard!" She fought him.

She twisted around, her knee slamming up, only to find Noah lifting her, parting her thighs until the thick, hard length of his erection was pressed against her and his lips were slamming down over hers.

The rasp of his beard and mustache was unfamiliar. His lips were hard, hungry. They took hers, he didn't ask, he didn't hesitate. As though he knew a need inside her that she didn't know herself.

It wasn't a gentle kiss. It was ravenous. It was laced with such hunger and elemental lust that it struck a flame to some hidden spark inside her own body.

Her body suddenly had a mind of its own. Her arms latched around his neck, her fingers dug into the thick, wild mane of his hair, and she was dragging him closer.

It had been so long. So long since a man had touched her body, since the need for touch, other than Nathan's, had even been a thought in her mind. And now, it was exploding inside her.

A sharp, furious cry tore from her throat as his tongue pierced the seam of her lips, licking at hers before drawing back. She pulled at his hair harder, nipped his lower lip, bit at it. Within a breath she was flattened between the door and his body and it was all over but the hunger and the want driving inside her.

One hard hand tangled in her hair, jerked her head back.

He wasn't easy, and she didn't want easy. She wanted the burn and the force and the impossible demand rising between them.

Her knees tightened on powerful lean flanks, her hips moved, writhed against his, driving his cock harder against her through the layers of denim separating them.

She heard him growl something, groan something. His hand tightened in her hair and he dragged her head back farther, his lips at her chin, her jaw, nipping and licking.

"Ride me," he snarled at her ear, his beard rough against the lobe as she twisted against him. "This is what I want, Sabella. Right here." One hand gripped her butt, holding her closer as she ground herself on his erection.

The seam of her jeans bit into her clit, the spike of sensation making her crazy for more. She was wet and growing wetter. She could feel her clit swelling, her sex heating and growing slick, saturated with her need.

"Ride me, Sabella," he bit out again. "Oh yeah, baby, rub against me." He was rubbing against her, his hips thrusting against her, digging his flesh harder between her thighs.

She lowered her hands and gripped the material of his T-shirt, dragging it up his back. She had to touch. She had to feel his flesh beneath her hands. She whimpered as his lips came back to hers, as she pulled and jerked at the material until he suddenly shifted, drawing his upper body back just enough to tear the shirt over his head before he was back to her. Kissing her. One hand in her hair, the other kneading her ass.

Oh yes. This was what she needed. The heat of his body seemed to sink into hers. She could feel him burning against her palms as she let them stroke over his shoulders. She could feel a crisscrossed roughness, the scars she had known marked his body. Her nails scraped over his flesh before he nipped at her lips again and she dug her nails into his flesh with a cry and held on.

Because they were moving. The world was twisting, tilting, until she felt her back meet the leather of the couch and heard the thump of his duffel bag as he pushed it to the floor and came over her.

His lips never left hers. He didn't give her a chance to think and she didn't want one. His hands gripped her shirt, tore it out of her jeans, and before she could process the action he had it and her bra above her breasts.

A hard, peaked nipple felt his beard first. It scraped over the tip, drawing her back into a arch a second before his lips brushed it, then his mouth took it.

His hips pressed harder into the vee of her thighs. He rode her mercilessly, taking her despite the material separating them, driving her closer to a brink she hadn't known in years. Her hips lifted to him, writhing back, rubbing into him as her head dug into the cushions of the couch and her fingers dug into his shoulders, holding him closer.

It was so good. So hot and liquid. Little starbursts were exploding before her eyes, sensations ripping across her nerve endings.

"Now." He jerked back, grabbed her head roughly and lowered his chest to her. "Touch me, damn you. Touch me, Sabella."

She bit him. Her teeth buried into hard, thick muscle before the wildness of the act took over. She nipped at the hard flat discs of his male nipples, licked at them, sucked at one. Her hands roamed over his back, only dimly acknowledging the scars there.

His hips jerked against her, ground against her. And she wanted those jeans off. Wanted hers off. She wanted the thick, heavy length she could feel tearing into her. Thrusting and driving her past the point of pleasure or pain.

The blood was rushing through her body, pounding through her head. She was close. So close. She bit at his chest again, feeling him stiffen, hearing his curse.

Then he was pulling away from her, jerking back, his savage gaze slicing to the back door of the apartment as he jerked her bra and T-shirt over her breasts.

And still, she heard the pounding.

"Belle? Belle Malone? It's Sheriff Grayson. Belle. Open the door or I'm going to open it myself."

Noah raised her to a sitting position as she tried to pull her shattered senses back into some semblance of order. She watched as, still shirtless, Noah stomped across the apartment, into the kitchen, to the door that led to the side of the garage and the deck.

The scarring on his back wasn't atrocious, but it was painful to see. On his left shoulder was a tattoo, a black sun pierced by a scarlet sword. It looked as tough and sexy as the rest of him. And just as dangerous.

She could feel a chill washing over her now. Icy reality flooding her system as Rick Grayson stepped into the kitchen, his brown gaze finding her immediately as he kept a careful distance between himself and Noah.

"You okay, Belle?" His eyes were narrowed, his hand resting carefully on the butt of his gun as Noah closed the door carefully.

Sabella stared at Noah. His eyes were wilder than before, almost lighter, terrifying, lit with an inner fire that had her heart racing in excitement and in panic.

"Belle? Why don't you come on outside with me, talk to me for a bit." Rick's eyes hadn't left Noah.

Sabella shook her head before pushing her fingers through her hair and giving a hard, mocking laugh. Rick had talked to her like that at the funeral.

Just let me and Sienna hold you here, Belle. He and his wife had stood on each side of her as she swayed next to Nathan's casket. *It's gonna be just fine here, Belle. See. It's all good, honey. We're just gonna stand here a minute and then it will be over with.*

Rick was her best friend's husband. Sienna had stood with her, cried with her, hurt with her. And Rick had talked to her just like that. Like a child that needed a careful hand.

"Rick, meet Noah Blake." She waved her hand to Noah as he stood against the kitchen counter, his arms crossed against his bare chest, his back turned away from her. "Rory hired him."

Rick watched her carefully as she forced herself to her feet. She didn't want to move. She wanted to curl herself into a ball and rock away the pain rising inside her.

"Belle, honey, your chin looks bruised," Rick stated. "You come outside with me for a minute now, okay."

Belle rubbed at her chin and frowned before moving to the mirror hanging on the wall. She brushed her fingers over the little bruise, then to her neck where the faint redness and another mark was now showing.

"He has his own bruises then," she said, turning to Rick. "He bit me. And I bit him back."

Rick's eyes narrowed on her. She felt as though she were going to shatter as she picked up her purse and moved to the door.

"We don't need to talk, Rick," she told him.

"I think we do, Belle." Rick moved between her and Noah. A buffer? She looked at Noah, saw his eyes, the warning in them. No, no one would ever get between them and survive unless he allowed it.

For now, he was just standing there, watching, waiting.

She turned back to Rick. "You interrupted a hell of a make-out session and I appreciate it." Her smile was brittle, shaky. "But it wasn't his fault. I think I might have bit him first. But you can ask his opinion if you like. Personally, I'm going home."

"Belle, someone called in a report that you were being harassed by this man." Rick caught her arm as she moved to pass him. "I have my deputies outside that door. You're protected here, honey, you know that. Do you want me to make this man leave?"

She stared back at him in shock. "You what?"

"You heard him, Sabella," Noah drawled. "He thinks I'm harassing you and wants to toss my ass in jail for it. Do you want to give him the chance?"

"Shut up." Rick rounded on him, his expression tightening angrily. "Mister, I don't know you, all I know is you've

already caused trouble with one citizen of this town. And I
don't care who you are. But you won't be harassing Belle."

"He's not harassing anyone or anything but my patience,"
Sabella snapped. "For God's sake, Rick, use your eyes instead
of your suspicions. Look at his shoulders." She gripped the
doorknob and shot Noah a cold, hard look. "Arrest me for the
bloody scratches there, but he hasn't done anything you need
to know about."

This was between the two of them. Her and Noah. She
knew that. She wouldn't make the mistake of drawing others
into it. Not now.

A s the door closed behind her Noah turned to the sheriff
and wanted to smile mockingly. Rick Grayson was a
damned good man. Former marine. He believed in the law.
Believed in the county he worked to protect. But that didn't
mean he wasn't on Noah's list to check out, or that he trusted
the other man now. Noah had learned all about broken trust a
lifetime ago.

"You have any identification?" Rick was glaring at him.

Noah lowered his hand, ignoring the careful manner in
which Rick gripped the butt of his gun. He pulled his wallet
free of his back pocket and opened it before extending it to
the sheriff.

Rick took the identification, looked it over, and handed it
back to him slowly.

"Belle's a friend, Mr. Blake." It was a warning. "We look
after our friends here."

"Do you really?" Noah arched his brow mockingly. He
hadn't seen much taking care where Sabella was concerned.
"Well, Sheriff Grayson, that's real nice to know. I'm sure it
comforts Sabella at every turn."

Rick stared back at him coolly. "Don't hurt her, or you'll
deal with me," he finally stated before heading to the door.
Once there, he paused and turned back to Noah, staring at
him hard. "Be careful, Mr. Blake, I'm a bad enemy to make.
And playing games here would definitely make an enemy
of me."

Rick opened the door then and left. The door closed behind him softly, but the effects left in the wake were clashing.

Noah stared down at his hands. Scarred hands. He'd held
on to Sabella as though she weren't as fragile, or delicate, as
he knew she was. He had bruised her, and in their entire relationship, he had always been careful to never mark her soft
flesh.

He rubbed at the back of his shoulder, then glimpsed the
smear of blood on his finger. He felt the sensitivity of his
lower lip, the mark she had left on his chest. She had made
him wild. They had made each other wild. As though a carefully sealed lid had been released on both their lusts.

He would make certain it was released again.

Sabella slammed into the house. The heavy oak door
echoed with the violence of the act and pierced her nerve
endings with a shattering surge of electric tension. She could
feel the electrical sensations racing over her flesh from the
back of her head, sizzling through her brain and creating an
overwhelming surge of panic.

Oh God. What had she done?

She dropped her purse to the floor and raced upstairs. She
tore the greasy clothes from her body, dumped them in the
trash can, and adjusted the shower water as hot as she could
stand it before stepping beneath the spray and scrubbing at
her hair, her skin.

She wanted the feel of him off her body. The smell of him
out of her pores. She could still smell him. She could still
feel him.

She leaned her head against the shower wall and breathed
in roughly, a sob tightening at her chest. Another man had
touched her. His hands had cupped her breasts, his lips
had sucked at her nipples, and his cock had rubbed, hard and
heavy, against her clit, and she had been on the verge of begging for more.

"Nathan." She pressed her face into the shower wall and
let the cry free.

Guilt seared her heart. It burned into her soul like a conflagration she couldn't quench. She ached. She ached inside for the man she had never imagined being without, and she ached on the outside for the touch she had been denied for so long.

She slid to the floor of the tub, pulling her knees to her chest, and lowered her head, the sobs tearing through her as she rocked herself.

My witch. Go síoraí. Love me, Sabella. Love me forever.

His voice drifted through her memories and the cries came harder. She loved. She loved until she couldn't understand how she drew a breath, second by second, without his presence in her life. Without his touch, his kiss.

Six years. She sobbed at the thought, her head falling back to the shower wall as the water pounded around her. Hot as her tears. But neither eased the blistering guilt burning inside her. Her husband had been dead for six years, and still the vows they had shared held her, tormented her.

The tears left her hurting more, because the tears didn't help. She could cry an ocean of them and Nathan wouldn't suddenly be there, pulling her into his arms and easing the grief that sometimes seemed to eat her alive.

And now, the guilt.

She picked up the washcloth and soap and she washed again. She scrubbed until she felt raw, and still, another man's touch was on her flesh, and still, she was swollen, aching for release.

"You left me, Nathan," she finally sobbed into the steam gathering around her. "You promised, Nathan. You promised you would never leave me."

He had sworn he would always hold her, always surround her. He wasn't holding her. For over six years he hadn't held her and still the pain could rip inside her, as though it had been yesterday. As though he had betrayed her and just not returned to her. As though he still breathed, and didn't touch her.

And the tears poured, like rain, like sorrow. Like the need for the touch, the kiss, and the release from another man.

When no more tears could be shed, when the water grew cold and she knew she had to move, Sabella dragged herself from the floor of the shower. She wrapped a towel around her and stepped onto the thick fluffy rug that covered the floor.

She moved to the mirror and looked into it. She saw then why Rick had stared so hard at her face. The reddened rasp on her skin from Noah's beard. There was the faintest hint of blue where he had bit her. The thought of that bite sent a surge of sensation pouring into her womb, into her sex. She licked her swollen lips and stared at her neck and her knees weakened. She carried his marks down her neck to her breasts. Faintly red, little brands from his touch, his kiss, his nips.

She hadn't wanted gentle, she had wanted hard. She had wanted to loosen the dark, furious need she hadn't even known had been building inside her. She had wanted it free, and he had freed it.

It was more than obvious she was canceling her date with Duncan tonight. There was no way she could face him like this. No way she could let him see this. And it was even more obvious that she wouldn't be seeing him again.

Shaking her head, she dried her hair, dropped the towels to the floor, and tugged on her robe before going back downstairs and making the call to Duncan.

He wasn't pleased. It was short notice, and he was irritated with that. Duncan liked to stay on schedule, and she had just messed up his little schedule. When she hung up the phone she sighed wearily at the thought of the frustration in his voice. She would have to break things off soon. Companionship was no reason to keep him hanging on. And companionship wasn't enough anymore. She had tasted hunger again, and she wanted more.

She craved more.

Sabella wandered around the dimly lit house, finally finding herself in the living room, in front of the large window, where the long table held her and Nathan's wedding photos.

How handsome he had been. She picked up the picture of them together. Her in the long white gown he had bought for her. Her head was against his chest, his dress uniform stiffly starched beneath her cheek. His hands gripped her bare shoulders and he stared down at her as though he had found something in her that he had never found anywhere else.

She had been his Bella. His Southern Bella he used to call her because of that Southern drawl she had never even tried to get rid of.

His eyes had been brilliant. So blue. So filled with life. She touched those eyes through the glass, slid her thumb down his face, then lifted her gaze to the window.

The throttled purr of the Harley could be heard from the garage that sat within sight of the house. She watched as the single light pierced the darkness and the motorcycle headed to the main road.

Noah was just a shadow, as was the cycle as it gained in power and disappeared from view. She watched the taillights until she couldn't see them any longer then looked down at Nathan's smiling face once again.

A tear splashed on the glass covering his face.

"You left me," she whispered again. "What am I supposed to do, Nathan? Tell me." Her breathing hitched as her stomach cramped with the pain of loss. "Tell me, what am I supposed to do now?"

CHAPTER SEVEN

Noah pulled the Harley into the hidden bay that housed the individual vehicles of the Elite Ops Unit, turned off the ignition and pulled in a hard, deep breath. Damn, he hadn't wanted to leave. He'd wanted to stomp straight up the hill to that house and spend the night sparring with the wife who made him hotter than a fire in winter and mesmerized him now, more than she had six years ago. He shook his head. Getting to know her again, seeing all the things she had hidden from him when they were married, only reinforced the fear that he had made the mistake of his life when he believed Sabella couldn't handle the horror of what had happened to him.

They were waiting on him, and he was late. Late because he'd stomped around that damned apartment, swearing he could feel Sabella. Sworn, he would have sworn it on a stack of Bibles that he heard her whisper his name. But it wouldn't have been the first time. It had happened too often over the past years.

Nineteen brutal months of hell with Fuentes. He swore at times that his Sabella was with him. Wiping his brow, her eyes confused, her voice agonized as she begged him to let her help him. Then he would touch her, and he would see his own hands, bloodied from his attempts to escape or the guards he tried to kill. And she would cry. In those ragged nightmares she always cried.

He tightened his jaw at the memory of that as he stepped into the briefing room and closed the door behind him.

"'Bout time." Jordan stood from his chair and darkened the glass with a flip of a switch as Noah took his chair. "We have intel on the names we've pulled in over the past week of suspected BCM members."

Jordan wasted his time asking why he was late.

"We have Mike Conrad, manager of the town's largest bank, also the bank that we've managed to identify as possibly a central location for the laundering of large funds to support the BCM."

Mike was on the LCD screen hanging on the wall.

"I knew him," Noah said quietly. "Mike would fit the paramilitary profile. Even when I lived here, Mike was very vocal about immigration laws and the nation's inability to pass the right ones, or to enforce the ones they have. He was a proponent of stricter laws and militias to enforce them."

"And the two of you were friends?" Micah asked curiously.

Noah shrugged. "We grew up together. I didn't have to agree with him to like the man he was at the time. That was over six years ago. Evidently, he found a way to follow his vision."

"They all do, mate," John Vincent grunted, his rugged features concerned as they flipped open the files Tehya was passing out.

"As you read, you'll see that two of the mechanics working at the Malone Garage, Timmy Dorian and Vince Steppton, are both suspected lower-level members of this militia." Their pictures came on screen. "We've been tracking them," Jordan continued. "They make frequent trips to Gaylen Patrick's ranch as well as Mike Conrad's home outside of town. We've also been tracking Conrad and his contacts." Several pictures came up; one of them was Duncan Sykes.

"I tried to hack Conrad's computer the other night." Tehya stepped in at Jordan's nod. "Spectacular work," she said, sighing. "Someone has attached a very advanced system to his connection. Sykes has the ability and the knowledge for such security. When I couldn't get in without tripping his security I tried Patrick's. We have the same setup there. We need some-one on-site to upload the program I've written that will let me bypass the security entirely."

"I can get that done." Noah nodded. "I helped Mike build his house. He made an addition to the plans he bought that no one but the two of us knew about. A small escape tunnel and entrance into his study. He wouldn't have changed it af-ter my 'death.' He'd feel more secure than ever."

"Good." Jordan nodded before breathing out wearily. "We have a report of another hunt that took place in the past week as well. Border Patrol found the bodies last night."

Those bodies were on the monitor now. A young man and woman, blank eyes, expressions twisted into lines of horror as they stared sightlessly from ravaged faces.

"A young Mexican family. Illegals slipping across the border, we believe." The picture of the young couple was horrifying. The young woman had obviously been raped, tortured. Her husband had been sliced open in so many places he looked like a patchwork quilt. "The baby that the relatives claim the family had with them is missing. We have no pictures. Three months old, a birthmark on its left hip. That's all we know."

"We have reports these murders are taking place during il-legal hunts," Jordan stated. "Several couples, legal and ille-gal, that have gone missing between Dallas, Houston, and the surrounding area have turned up here, in Big Bend National Park, showing signs of flight, and of having fought their at-tackers. As you'll recall from our last meeting, the Federal agents that were killed received a tip of a hunt taking place the night they disappeared."

"Border Patrol involved?" Micah Sloane, the former Mossad agent, asked Jordan, his black eyes cool, calm. The Israeli was one of the deadliest men of the group. The train-ing maneuvers he had taught the rest of them had only added to the strength of the unit overall.

"Not that we can substantiate. Various bodies have been found over the past two years by Border Patrol, Park Patrol, ranchers, hikers, and a few cowboys. Never in the same area twice. They spread them out," Jordan informed him. "Do we have anything new to add?" He looked around at the others.

"I begin mechanics duties tomorrow." Nikolai grinned as he leaned back in his chair. "It would seem Rory Malone has finally managed to get his coowner to agree to a trial period of work."

Noah snorted at that. Rory had fought Sabella tooth and nail for it. That boy was more stubborn than Noah had suspected.

"I've stayed pretty much to the shadows," Micah informed them. "There's a lot of rumor. I put that in my report. A lot of talk, but nothing conclusive yet."

"No shit, mate," the Australian quipped. John Vincent could be a sarcastic bastard. "Those bars and hangouts I've made my way through are a waste of my friggin' time. Nothing but a bunch of too curious little girls and too drunk cowboys. From what I've seen of the few I suspect myself, they meet, then leave to discuss whatever they have going."

"Watch the accent and the attitude, John," Jordan told him coolly. "Micah, stay in the shadows, see if you can't follow some of those walking conversations. We need to determine who our main points of interest are and who are just lower-level glory soldiers."

"Those hunts are professional," Nikolai said. "Those aren't glory soldiers. My guess would be those soldiers may know of them, but they aren't high enough for involvement."

"A lot of those glory soldiers as well as Duncan Sykes make a habit of showing up at the garage and finding time to talk to both Timmy and Vince, the BCM mechanics we have there," Noah told them. "You're blond and look American enough they might talk to you."

Nikolai grunted at that.

"Have you made many contacts?" Jordan asked Nik.

The big Russian shook his head. "First name as Nik only. A few drinks, no heavy conversations with anyone. My American accent seems to be working well enough."

But, Noah knew, Nikolai had had practice with that accent a long time before he came into Elite Ops.

"Nikolai, you'll be going by Nikolas Steele, you're a California native," Jordan informed him before turning to Tehya. "Get his papers together. Do a family tree back to the frickin *Mayflower*. Let's give them an impoverished blue blood son of America."

Tehya grinned as she winked at Nik. "I'll have it before you leave, Nicky."

He grimaced at the playful nickname.

Jordan looked back at Noah sharply. "Are there any other issues at the garage?"

"None I didn't anticipate." He shrugged. "I intend to have Rory fire the mechanic Timmy just to shake things up some."

The mechanic was ineffectual, and even worse, he didn't know a wrench from jack. Why the hell Rory or Sabella had hired him Noah hadn't figured out yet.

Jordan nodded at that. "Our mission parameters are simple. Identify, capture if possible. Contain if captured until they can be extracted by the bureau and taken care of. If all else fails, we eliminate. That's a worst-case scenario only. We need information on this one, we need top-level names and organization leaders. This militia is spreading and we need it contained. To contain it, we need information. See if you can find a way in and get what we need. Let's take care of it."

The files were opened. Another two hours were spent going over scenarios and ideas. Jordan sat back, listened, and commented when he needed to. The group worked well together. Noah was confident this mission would proceed just as the others had in the previous years. Dangerous. Bloody.

They were trained to work alone until they had to work together. Trained to disassociate or come together as needed. In this case, disassociation would work best with the exception of Nik in the garage.

There was no doubt in Noah's mind that someone was trying to sabotage Sabella and Rory's business. Rory had admitted the previous night that before Sabella took over, vehicles were going out not quite finished. Sometimes dangerously so. She had taken to going over the finished repairs herself and checking for any anomalies before signing them out.

Noah's neck itched whenever he thought of the problems she'd had with the garage. He couldn't help it. It had been itching ever since Mike Conrad had shown up. Drunk, insulting, violent. He hadn't seen Mike like that since they were teenagers, and the fact he had abused Sabella with it had shocked him.

But Sabella had never liked Mike. He should have trusted her instincts rather than the lifetime he had spent being pushed in Mike's direction by his father.

The Conrads were friends of the Malones. Mike and Nathan were the same age, had been raised together. They had hunted together, fished together. Noah had always thought that they would raise their families together as well. He'd have to ask Rory if Mike's father and Grant Malone were still friends.

"Tehya and Macey are running communications and electronics here at the bunker. I'll be at the Malone ranch for a while today and part of tomorrow. I'm hoping I can get some information there. Keep your cell phones secured. Micah and John, you'll stay on backup. Right now we have Durango team, except for Macey, in the park watching things there. They're last resort only," Jordan stated.

The Elite Operations Unit was specially designed and trained to run bare-bones. The fewer who knew who they were and what they were doing, the less likely the leaks. The better the chance they remained "dead."

The lights came back on as the meeting drew to a close. Noah didn't waste time. Sabella had claimed to have a date tonight, and he intended to make certain she got home without getting pawed by that bastard Duncan.

"Noah." Jordan caught him as he was swinging his leg over the Harley, his fingers on the key, ready to turn it.

Noah watched his uncle approach, wondering, not for the first time, why Jordan had chosen him specifically for this unit.

"I had a call today," Jordan announced.

"Yeah?"

"Rick Grayson, the sheriff."

Noah stared back at him.

"Grant gave him my number. He said there's a stranger in town." Jordan's lips quirked. "Working at the garage. He said that stranger was manhandling Belle and he thought someone from the family should check him out."

Noah twisted the key in the Harley slowly, never breaking eye contact with Jordan as he kicked it in neutral and eased the cycle back until he could turn around, kick it back into gear, and ease it from the parking bay into the little canyon that ran for over a mile in two directions.

Big Bend National Park was filled with canyons, gullies, cliffs, and mountains. He kept the headlight off; the brake lights were set in a switch that allowed him to ride, totally dark, as long as he needed to.

Once he reached the main road, he flipped the lights on and headed back to the garage. The house that sat on the rise above it was dark and shadowed. There were no lights, nothing to indicate life. But Sabella wasn't sleeping. She was watching. He could feel her. And Duncan's car wasn't there, that meant Sykes had obviously not been asked in for a drink.

He parked the bike, swung off it, and stared up at the bedroom window. Their bedroom. Their window. She would still sleep in their bed, he knew. Did she still hug his pillow to her? Or had she laid it aside?

Shaking his head, he moved up the steps of his apartment, knowing even before he turned off the cycle who waited for him at the top.

"You're already causing trouble," Rory accused him as he stepped to the deck.

His brother shifted in the plastic chair that sat next door, rising and staring back at Noah with a scowl as he unlocked the door and stepped inside cautiously.

It was silent, empty. Just as it should have been. The cobweb-thin string was still stretched between the door frame and at the other door he caught the faintest hint of the piece of toothpick that still stuck from the door lock there.

He eased inside carefully anyway, feeling Rory move in

behind him silently. They checked the apartment out before meeting back in the kitchen.

"Damn, I need more than a beer." Rory sighed as he pulled two from the fridge and tossed Noah one. "Duncan Sykes called. He's blaming me because you're somehow responsible for Belle breaking their date tonight."

Noah let a satisfied grin curl at the edges of his lips.

"I'll take care of her." He twisted the cap from the bottle and tossed it to the garbage can before taking a long, cold drink.

"That's what you said the other night," Rory bit out, his blue eyes firing in ire. "Dammit, I had to watch her cry every time she saw me for almost two years. She couldn't stand to look at me. And now just when she was starting to get her life back together, you have to show up, and instead of telling her who you are, mess her life up worse."

"Don't piss me off, Rory." Noah didn't want to hear it. "What the hell are you doing here tonight?"

Rory snorted. "Granddad threw me out for pacing the floor. When I went outside to pace he told me he was going to shoot me."

Noah almost grinned. That sounded like Grandpop.

"Use the spare room." Noah shrugged. "By the way, you're firing Timmy in the morning. Take care of it first thing."

Rory stared back at him, the irritation growing in his eyes. "Come on, Noah. Timmy's helping support his mother."

"No he's not, he's smoking junk behind the garage when no one's looking and he's reporting everything Sabella does to Mike Conrad the minute she tips her head in a different direction. Get him out of there."

"Hell. Belle hired him. She's gonna go off on me again."

"She doesn't bite." Noah shrugged again.

No, she didn't bite, but she could make a man's balls draw up in fear anyway when she got mad enough. When she was mad and hurt. When tears sparkled in her eyes and she started throwing things, then it was time to head for the hills until she cooled off. Way the hell off. She wasn't violent, but damn if she couldn't make a man miserable with just a look.

"She might not bite, but she throws a mean-assed punch when she wants to," Rory said. "The first time I tried to drag her away from one of those cars and put her ass back in the office, she popped my jaw like it was a balloon."

Noah didn't show his surprise, or his shock. Sabella had never hit anything while they had been together. She hadn't even punched her pillow when she was pissed.

"Get some sleep." He nodded back to the bedroom. "I need to go out again."

"I could go with you." Rory shifted on his feet. "I know how to cover you. You taught me how."

Yeah, he had. A lifetime ago.

"Not tonight." Noah shook his head. Where he was going, he wanted no witnesses, no shadows, no tails. And he sure as hell didn't want Rory dragged into this crap. "Get some sleep. You have to deal with Sabella in the morning."

"You suck," Rory said as he grimaced. "She's gonna hit me again."

"She has a short swing. Stay a few feet away from her." Noah moved back to the door, opened it, and slid back into the night.

Mike Conrad didn't live far away. Tehya had slipped him the program she needed installed in Mike's computer before he left. Hopefully, getting into it wouldn't be too difficult.

An hour later, Noah made his way through Mike's underground tunnel and cracked open the panel that led into the office. He checked for audio and video security, read the readout on the electronic device he brought with him and shook his head. The office was wired but deactivated. Keeping the unit he carried turned on to ensure it stayed that way, Noah moved into the office.

Mike had always been an arrogant son of a bitch, but Noah had never thought he was stupid. Attacking Sabella had been stupid, and perhaps not as out of character as Noah had believed if Mike was indeed a part of BCM.

If Noah remembered correctly, when Sabella had worked at the bank, before their marriage, Mike had always been a little too friendly and Mike's wife had always been a little too cool to Sabella. It made sense why now, when at the time, Noah had tried to push back the warnings with the excuse that he was a suspicious man. Mike wasn't the cheating type, he'd thought. Maybe he had been wrong.

He moved to the office desk first and the laptop that sat on top of it. He slid the flashdrive Tehya had sent into the USB port, then quietly powered up the computer. The program on the drive would slide into bootup according to Tehya and take care of all their problems.

He watched as it powered up, as security protocols were bypassed, password was automatically logged and added to the drive Noah had inserted before the program itself quickly uploaded.

When it finished, the laptop powered down, turned off, and Noah slid the drive free before tucking it into the zippered pocket of his mission pants. He looked around the office, eyes narrowing as he began checking the room.

Silent in the darkness, he paused after picking the lock on the bottom desk door and stared inside coldly.

There, with an extra handgun, ammo clips, and a black hood, were three black scarves. There had been black scarves tied around the necks of all the victims that had been hunted and killed in the past months.

Noah closed the drawer, relocked it, and slipped back through the panel. After securing it, he made his way through the tunnel again, careful to clear his tracks from the dusty floor. It didn't appear that the passage was ever used.

One thing was certain, a Black Collar Militia member was now on the short list.

CHAPTER EIGHT

What had made Sabella think she could hide from Duncan that night with the lame excuse she had given him, she wasn't certain. Maybe it was because Duncan had never argued when she had to cancel before, maybe it was the fact that the more she thought about it, the more she realized herself how the relationship they had had was so platonic as to be laughable.

It was late when she heard his car pull into the driveway. Sitting in the living room finishing the bottle of wine Duncan had opened days before, Sabella stared at the window where the lights were reflected and realized several things at once.

One, for some reason, men thought she was a pushover. Nathan had seen her as the helpless little wife he had to protect. Duncan often patronized her over her "hobby" at the garage. And even Rory seemed to question every move she made lately. And now, she couldn't even break a date without someone thinking they needed to question her decision.

She rose from the couch, straightened the loose T-shirt she wore over silky shorts, and then, wine glass in hand, moved to the door. Pulling it open she stared at Duncan's handsome though irritated expression as he lifted his knuckles to rap at the door.

He was dressed as precisely and unwrinkled as ever. A

white short-sleeved polo shirt and tan slacks and black loafers. He was always clean-cut and perfectly groomed and now was no exception.

His gaze took in the wine glass, then her face, before he focussed on her chin and neck. Yeah, she knew those marks were still there. One on her jaw, one on her neck. Tiny bite marks, and the thought of the pleasure they had given her was curling her stomach with guilt. And hunger.

"Can I come in?" he asked, his smooth voice suddenly at odds with her senses.

He sounded patient, warm, but she saw anger in his eyes.

"Sure." Sabella stepped back as she sipped at her wine and he entered. "It's midnight. Isn't it late for you to be out?"

"I don't have a curfew." That vein of anger wasn't as hidden as it had been moments before.

Sabella pushed her fingers through her loose hair before heading back into the living room. This was her sanctuary, a room Duncan rarely liked coming into. He preferred the kitchen. He had never made it upstairs.

He followed her though, stopping just inside the doorway across from the fireplace and staring at the mantel as Sabella sat down in one of the chairs, curling her legs beneath her.

There was a hint of discomfort on his face, a quiet, flash of hurt that made her chest ache. He had been a good friend over the years, he would have made a good lover or husband. If her body, her heart, had been willing to accept him.

"You keep his pictures out like he's coming home," he said quietly. "As though you think he's just going to walk in the door any day with open arms."

Sabella glanced over at the mantel, then to the long table beneath the window where other pictures sat. She probably should have put them away a long time ago; she just hadn't been able to do it.

"Letting him go hasn't been easy." She finally shrugged uncomfortably. "But I'm sure you didn't show up here at midnight to discuss whether or not my husband is coming home."

"Nathan's dead, Belle," he said roughly, impatiently.

"You've never accepted that. It's why our relationship never worked, isn't it? Because you can't accept he's gone."

It had taken her three years to accept that Nathan was indeed forever gone. That long for her to get past the horrific nightmares she lived through for over three years. First the ones full of blood, then those full of pain and fury. Sabella had been convinced he was alive, in pain, and in those nightmares he begged her to come to him. And then they stopped. One night, they were just gone, and Nathan had left her entirely.

"Yeah." She finally nodded. "I've accepted that, Duncan. And I warned you when we started seeing each other, I'm not looking for love."

His lips thinned angrily.

"Or sex," he bit out. "You barely let me kiss you, yet apparently the rumors that you're sleeping with your new mechanic are true." He flicked a finger toward her. "I know a hickey when I see one."

"I'm not sleeping with Noah Blake." She had to bite back her frustration, her irritation. "No matter what the gossips are saying."

"You're sure as hell not sleeping with me," he argued, moving farther into the room. "Tell me, Belle, do all these pictures keep you warm at night?" He lifted his arm to indicate the mantel, the table. "Will they give you children? Will they hold you when you cry for him?"

His voice rose, the anger building inside him. Duncan was finally realizing that the warnings she had given him over the past months had been sincere. She didn't want anything more than his friendship.

"Do you want to hold me while I cry for him?" she asked in frustration, jerking from her seat and grabbing the wine bottle and her glass before moving to leave the living room. "Is that what you want, Duncan?"

She set her glass and the wine on the L-shaped kitchen counter that doubled as a bar before turning to face him.

"And when Noah's marking your face and your neck, are you crying for Nathan then?" Duncan sneered hatefully, shockingly, as he followed her into the kitchen.

"Stop, Duncan." She threw him a wary look over her shoulder as she entered the brightly lit kitchen and moved to the counter. Where she felt safer.

She had never seen Duncan upset. Actually, she had never heard of Duncan becoming angry much at all. But it was obvious he was just a little pissed off right now.

She stared at him across the counter, seeing the edge of growing anger in his face as well as his eyes. His lips were thin, his expression flushed

"Do you think I don't know why that mechanic made it this far, and I haven't?" he accused furiously. "You're fooling yourself, Belle. You know you are. And you're making a mistake."

"It's midnight, Duncan," Sabella argued back. "I don't want to discuss this with you tonight or I would have asked you over. You're not in a position to make any type of decision for me, or to question the decisions I make."

"He's like Nathan." He glared back at her. "That's why you want him. That's why your skin is marked by him, because he reminds you of Nathan. And he's not Nathan."

Sabella stared back at him in shock. "He's nothing like Nathan," she informed him, beginning to grow angry herself now. "Nathan was nothing like him. Nathan loved me, Duncan."

"He loved you so much that he wouldn't even consider leaving the SEALs." Duncan said, sneering. "Do you have any idea how often I told him he was going to end up dead? That he'd leave you alone suffering. Did he care?"

Nathan had just been Nathan. A man and a SEAL. He would have expected her to go on, and it was that simple.

"You could end up dead climbing those damned cliffs you enjoy so much," she shot back. "Nathan was a SEAL, Duncan. It wasn't a job choice for him. It was who he was."

"And you were the helpless little Southern belle to pamper his ego whenever he was home. That used to make me so sick I could barely stand it." Disgust laced his voice, his expression, as she stared back at him in surprise.

"I was his wife," she said, confused now by the direction

of his fury. "I gave him what he needed, just as he gave me what I needed, Duncan. That was none of your business, nor was it your place to judge it."

" 'Oh Nathan, the oil in the car needs changing'," Duncan mimicked in a high-pitched, furious voice. " 'Oh Nathan, could you check my tires?' You'd bat your lashes and act like you didn't know shit. Then he died and you walked right into that garage and hit those cars like a professional. Hell, Belle, didn't you feel just a little guilty, lying to your husband like that?"

She hadn't. Nathan had needed to take care of her while he was with her. She had needed that single-minded focus he had given her between missions. Would it have changed as their marriage progressed? She had no doubt it would have. But the two years they had been together, it hadn't mattered. Working on cars wasn't her life's work. She might have enjoyed it, but she enjoyed Nathan more. While he was on missions, she tinkered on her own car, sometimes she tinkered with his precious truck.

"I never lied to my husband," she answered him quietly. "And I never lied to you about how I felt. I told you I didn't want what you obviously wanted from me. I told you that a year ago and I've repeated it, several times."

"But you do want it from that shiftless son of a bitch that stinks of oil and grease?" he snarled.

Sabella stared back at him, her own anger rising now. "I think we've both pretty much accepted the fact that's one of my favorite scents."

"No shit," he snarled. "You stink of it continually. Maybe I'm sick of smelling the stuff while I'm trying to eat my dinner."

She had never seen this side of Duncan, had never suspected it existed.

"You thought you were getting Nathan's wife." A bitter smile curled her lips. "The little woman that sat at home and, you thought, did as she was told." Sabella shook her head. "You didn't live in this house, Duncan. You have no idea how little I did that Nathan tried to order me to do. And it's more than obvious that you never cared to see beyond the surface."

He flicked her a furious look before turning and pacing to the window.

"Get rid of him!" He turned back to her, his voice strengthening, turning hard and cold. "Fire him, Sabella."

Her brows arched. "Rory hired him, I can't fire him. But I wouldn't now simply because I don't follow anyone's orders, Duncan, least of all yours."

"Get rid of that bastard or you'll end up regretting it." His expression twisted into lines of bitter fury. "He's dangerous. You can see it in his face and in his eyes. That's the only reason you want him and you don't have the good sense to see it. He's just as dangerous as Nathan was."

"Leave." Sabella straightened slowly, edging closer to the phone as Duncan glared at her. "I want you to leave right now, Duncan."

"Because you can't handle the truth?"

Suddenly, he wasn't nearly as handsome as she had once thought he was, not that handsome was one of her requirements. But Duncan had always appeared sophisticated, possessing an almost male elegance that was now marred by a severe temper tantrum.

"Because you're out of hand." She picked up the phone and stared back at him. "Leave."

He glanced at the phone. "Go ahead and call the son of a bitch," he told her. "Go on, Belle, I dare you. How much you want to bet he's not even there. He's out screwing someone else because you're not woman enough to hold a man at the house. Not a man like Nathan and sure as hell not a drifter like Noah Blake."

That should have hurt, Sabella admitted. It should have, but she knew better. She had married a SEAL, not an accountant. She had known when she married her SEAL what she was getting. There were no guarantees and she had lost early in the game.

"Then you won't mind walking out, will you?" she told him coldly.

"Like hell!" He surprised her when he moved for her. When she finally realized Duncan was more furious than she thought, it was too late.

She had hit the first digit of 911 when the phone went flying from her hand. She threw herself back, trying to evade the hand that attempted to latch on to her wrist.

Just as his fingers curled around her flesh, she heard a furious growl, and a larger, broader, darker hand latched onto Duncan's wrist and, before Sabella's shocked gaze, bent his wrist back and twisted it so that Duncan went to his knees with an almost girlish cry.

Noah was icy. Sabella stared at him in shock, taking in the T-shirt and leather vest, the faded jeans and black chaps. The motorcycle boots and the chiseled, emotionless expression.

If she didn't do something, then Duncan was a dead man. The icy rage went deeper this time than when Noah had had his hand around Mike Conrad's neck.

"Noah. I'm getting tired of you manhandling men around me," she told him firmly, no anger, just a simple observation. "I could have hit him myself, you know?"

His gaze turned to her as Duncan gasped at his feet.

"Let him go." She wrinkled her nose at him as she had done with Nathan the few times she had seen him really pissed. "He's not worth getting blood on my floors. That would really make me angry."

"I know how to get rid of the body," he told her, his gaze flicking over the T-shirt and shorts she wore. "It wouldn't be hard to do."

"Yeah, but then I'd have to feel guilty and I'd have to tell Rory. Of course." She shrugged as though it didn't matter. "I could use it as an excuse to get Rory to fire you."

"He'd help me," Noah promised her, but there was the barest hint of a crack in the ice. "And you're playing games to get me to let him go. What do you really want to say, Sabella?"

"That you're being a damned moron and I want you to let him go before I have to kick both of you out of my house and call the sheriff," she yelled back at him, letting the mad show, because she was sick of dealing with thick-headed males.

His brow lifted.

"Let him go, dammit." She picked up the phone then hung up again as she shot both of them a disgusted look. At least Noah's grip on Duncan had eased. "He's going to puke if you don't and I don't want to clean it up."

Duncan had that look on his face. Of course, the pressure on his wrist had to be agonizing, and Noah was holding it there as though it were no effort at all.

He let him go slowly.

"Get the fuck out." Noah stepped back as Duncan struggled to his feet.

Duncan's shirt was wrinkled now, his slacks might even have been a little damp at the crotch, but she didn't bother to look.

She felt as though she were going to throw up herself as Duncan rushed from the house. Noah followed him as far as the door, slammed it closed then stalked back into the kitchen.

Hands propped on the counter, Sabella lowered her head and fought the hurt and anger churning inside her. Damn. She'd liked Duncan. And she could have sworn she had discussed all those irritating little subjects like love and sex and her reasons why she wasn't ready.

"You should have never let him in the house." Noah stopped in front of the counter. "For God's sake, Sabella, I thought you would know better than to confront that son of a bitch while you're carrying my mark."

She kept her head down. How many times had she laughed at Nathan when he had said something similar? When he had been irritated with her, or was just being a man.

She should have known better than to go four-wheeling with Sienna that first year they were married, without him, because when she wrecked, she wrenched her ankle and he hadn't been there to make sure she was okay. She should have known better than to try to fix a busted pipe in the basement on her own, because she'd ended up drenched and the basement had gotten wet. So many instances. And she should have always known better.

She lifted her head. "Now you can leave. You should know better than to piss off an already angry woman."

She should have known better than to give Rory a say in the hiring.

"Sabella, sweetheart, look at me." His voice roughened. "If he had hurt you, I would have had to kill him. I would have enjoyed killing him."

"And it would have been my fault." She nodded with a bitter smile. "Sure, I understand."

"No, it would been his fault for being stupid enough to touch you. But haven't you figured out yet that men aren't always smart enough to keep their hands off things that don't belong to them?"

Her head jerked up in surprise. "So you think I belong to you now?"

She didn't flinch when he reached out to touch her. Over the years, she had always had to suppress a flinch when another man tried to stroke her, kiss her.

"You don't belong to him," he told her, his fingertip stroking over the rasp of his beard that he had left on her jaw. "Testosterone is a dangerous thing sometimes. You should have waited to talk to him."

At least Noah sounded reasonable, and he was right. She knew he was right. She had thought Duncan understood. She had imagined he had accepted that she couldn't give him the things he wanted.

"He'll get over it," she finally breathed out roughly. "But I really think you should leave now too. I'm tired."

She moved around the counter to lead him to the front door, only to feel his arm curling around her, pulling her against his hard body as she stared up at him in surprise.

"You ran from him," he told her. "You know you're safe with me. Admit it."

"I was safe with him," she told him quietly. "I'm not a moron, Noah. I know how to protect myself. And I will, when I have to."

"Then prove it." That gravelly, rough voice was a dark croon. "Try to get away from me, Sabella."

She almost laughed at the challenge. She would have, except something inside her was burning, begging, pressing closer to him as he lifted her against him.

"You want me," he stated roughly.

"I don't want to want you," she whispered back painfully. "Because he was right about one thing. You're dangerous. Too dangerous and too dark for what I need. If I had a brain in my head, I'd have made certain you were gone a week ago."

"You have plenty of brains." His head lowered, his lips feathered against hers. "Enough brains to know whose arms you belong in. Enough to know where you're safe."

Noah wasn't fighting it. He knew now wasn't the time to take her. Her common sense would kick back in, she would blame them both when morning came, but the adrenaline was racing through him. The mix of whore's dust and lust was torturing his cock, filling it with blood as his balls felt tortured between his thighs.

It had been over six years since he had taken his wife, since he had known the tight grip of her hot, sweet pussy. Since he had devoured her, licked her from head to toe, and heard her screams for more echoing in his head.

All he knew now was the hunger. A hunger that clawed at him, that had him lifting her into his arms as he claimed her lips. Slanting his against them, his tongue pushing inside, tasting her, the sweet, delicate taste of passion and woman and the wine.

He wanted to pour that wine over her body and lick it off her. He wanted to watch it stream over her pussy and bury his lips between her thighs to consume it. He wanted to be drunk on her, drunk on the lust and the need and a pleasure he had never been able to forget. Never been able to escape.

"God, the taste of you," he groaned, sipping at her lips as her head fell back, her hands pressing to the back of his head, tunneling into his hair.

Oh, he knew what she wanted. A hard smile tugged at his lips as he let his beard rake over her neck, felt her shudder as he lifted her.

Noah set her on the counter before moving between her

thighs. The thin shorts did nothing to protect her from the hard, denim-covered length of his cock. Pressing against her, he swore he felt the heat and dampness of her. Remembered how tight her grip was, how that sweet sheath rippled and hugged him.

Her moans were like fuel poured to the fire raging inside him. He tasted her neck with his tongue, gave her the caress of the rasp of his beard and felt her grinding against him.

No sheriff to stop them now.

His hands lowered to her top. She wasn't wearing a bra beneath the loose T-shirt. Her pretty breasts were unbound, nipples hard and hot. And he wanted to taste. Needed to taste.

Sabella moaned, cried out at the sensations racing through her body. They were wicked, carnal, so intense she couldn't think, didn't want to think. The rasp of his beard was a dark pleasure, his kiss like a potent wine. He made her head spin, sent her senses reeling and her heart hammering in her chest.

And she needed more. She needed his touch. As his hands slid beneath her T-shirt she pressed closer, begging silently for his callused palms against her nipples, because she needed now as she never had. As she had only needed with one man, and the need now was brighter, stronger, and dug its claws deeper inside her.

She wanted Noah Blake more than she could ever remember needing her own husband.

Fear sliced through her. Shock. Fury. Fury at herself as well as Noah.

It took everything she had, every measure of inner strength, to jerk back and force him to release her, to jump from the counter and stumble away from him.

"This is what I should know not to do." She placed several feet between them. "This is exactly what I don't need. Now, please, just get the hell away from me. Just go, before I end up doing something we'll both end up regretting."

Noah stared back at her for long moments. He could have her, so easily. Touch her, hold her, ease some of that pain in her eyes. And he wanted to, needed to.

God help him, what had he done to his wife? She was standing before him, staring at him as though he were her destruction rather than a man she ached for, longed for. And he could see the guilt in her. The guilt that another man could make her respond, that another man could touch her as only he, her husband, had done.

And added to that was his own damned jealousy. The parts of him that had been Nathan hadn't died as thoroughly as he had thought they had. The man that was Noah, darker, more dominant, more arrogant, hated the man he had been as Nathan. Because it was Nathan she ached for. And it was Noah who was left living to hunger for her.

"I'll see you at the garage in the morning," he finally told her, shaking his head at his own thoughts as he turned and left the house.

Tortured. His dick was pounding and the pulse of lust in his blood was like fire in his veins.

CHAPTER NINE

Sabella dragged herself out of the bed and stumbled to the shower the next morning. By the time she made it to the kitchen and the pot of coffee waiting on her, thanks to the timer, she wondered if she would ever force her eyes open enough to actually make the breakfast date she had arranged last night with Sienna Grayson, the sheriff's wife, and Kira Richards.

Ian Richards had been Nathan's best friend. His marriage several years before to socialite Kira Porter had been a surprise to the small community. The fact that they still returned each summer to the house Ian had kept since he lived in Alpine with his mother was even more surprising.

They'd become friends over the years, though only in the past year had Sienna been able to join their breakfast dates. Sienna did not like getting up early.

This morning, Sabella well understood the feeling.

She felt flayed by the dreams that had tormented her the night before. Duncan's accusation, Nathan's wild blue eyes staring at her in love, in pain. And Noah, reaching out for her, but he had Nathan's eyes, and Nathan's voice. They were more vivid, more terrifying, than the past dreams had been. Or perhaps they just seemed more vivid because of the short break she had been given.

As she pulled her car into the Richardses' driveway, she

breathed out a hard breath as she glimpsed Ian's tan-colored Jeep sitting in the driveway. The Richardses lived in a sprawling single-story ranch in the National Park area. Surrounded by cliffs and pine, this area's stark, desolate beauty always managed to steal her breath.

Sienna pulled in behind her.

"It should be illegal to get up this early, Sabella," Sienna stated as they got out of their vehicles. "I should have Rick arrest you."

Sabella stared at her friend closely. Despite the perfect makeup, Sienna had dark circles under hazel-green eyes and an edge of worry at her brow.

"I have to work this afternoon," Sabella told her. "Morning is the only time I could get away." She frowned as she gave her friend a quick hug and felt that Sienna had lost weight in the past weeks. "Are you doing okay?"

"Me?" Sienna gave her tired smile. "I'm fine. Rick's been busy and you know how grouchy he gets when he can't solve a case. Those deaths a few months back are driving him crazy."

"The Black Collar Militia," Sabella muttered. "Bastards. I knew that girl they killed."

"She was an FBI agent." Sienna sighed as they walked to the house. "I couldn't believe it when I read that in the newspaper. Of course, Rick had known, but he hadn't told me."

Sabella knew Sienna had raged at Rick for years because he refused to tell her about the cases he worked, or when he was close to breaking a case. There were times Sabella knew it strained their relationship.

"He's not allowed to tell you, Sienna," Sabella pointed out gently. "Just as Nathan couldn't tell me about his missions."

"Yeah, but you didn't have to live with Nathan while he was on a mission." Sienna snorted. "Some nights, he doesn't even come home," she said softly, sadly. "I hate it when he does that."

There was nothing Sabella could say. She could see Rick's point of view. Although Sabella had understood that Nathan was a SEAL, Sienna had never been able to understand Rick's dedication to being a sheriff.

"Rick didn't even tell me about the trouble you had with your new mechanic," Sienna pouted as they approached the door and Sabella tapped on it lightly. "I had to hear through gossip."

Sabella rolled her eyes and tried to control her flush.

"They sure weren't wrong about that beard burn though." Sienna craned her head around to look, snickering back at Sabella. "The man knows how to do it right."

"Good morning, ladies." Kira chose that moment to open the door and invite them in. "Breakfast will be ready in a few. I just have to finish the tortillas and we'll be good to go." She paused and stared at Sabella, her eyes widening before a teasing smile curled her pert, pouting lips. "Wow, Sabella, gossip is right, that new mechanic of yours knows how to give beard burn the right way, doesn't he?"

Sabella narrowed her eyes at her friend. "We're not talking about the new mechanic."

"The new mechanic?" Ian chose that moment to walk into the room. "Belle, could you let him know I have to bring the Jeep in." He stopped, stared at her jaw and neck, lifted his brows and stared back at Kira.

Kira smirked. "The new mechanic."

Great. "You guys act like you've never seen beard burn," she muttered.

"Have you looked in the mirror?" Sienna laughed, though the sound was tense. "Or did you do what you normally do and just ignore what you don't want to see?"

Sabella turned back to her, her lips tightening. "Meaning?"

"Meaning it's not just beard burn." Sienna laughed. "Sweetie, your mechanic left a hickey, and he did a damned good job with that one little bite while he was there." She reached out, touched the area just under Sabella's jaw, and shook her head. "We should all be so lucky."

Sabella walked into the garage late that afternoon. There were more than half a dozen vehicles lined up in the garage waiting area. Toby was pumping gas and there were several college students in the convenience section of the station.

Rory was taking care of the register as Sabella moved into the office and closed the door behind her. She went to the coffeepot as the wide door into the garage bay opened and Noah stepped in.

She was caught by his eyes. She was always caught by his eyes.

"You're late. Everything okay?" He entered the office and closed the door.

"I stayed longer than I should have at a friend's for breakfast." She shrugged as she poured her coffee and headed to her desk.

She pulled the overshirt she wore tighter around her. It had been one of Nathan's shirts. Stained with oil, and she imagined she could smell him on it, though she knew the scent had long since faded. It was a comfort shirt. It was a warning to other men. Today, she needed something to hold Noah back, and she had prayed it would work.

She watched as his eyes moved to the pocket patch. Nathan's name was emblazoned there. When his gaze came back to hers she caught a hint of anger.

"Still holding on to him?" he asked her softly, his rough voice darker than normal.

"Always." Let him make of that what he wanted to. She had stopped holding on to the hope he would come home three years before, but hadn't forgotten what they had shared. No matter how hard she tried.

"It's been six years." He poured his own coffee then sat on the corner of the spare desk. "Long time to be a frozen widow, don't you think?"

"So Duncan informed me last night," she snapped. "I don't need you reiterating the message."

Noah could see the pain that flashed in her eyes and it enraged him. The knowledge that he was fighting his own memory pissed him off even further.

He hadn't expected her to do this to herself. To put her life in such a deep freeze that no one else could touch her, hold her. Like an animal, she had burrowed into a hole to lick her wounds, but the wounds were still ragged and pain filled.

But he couldn't blame her for it. He'd done the same thing. Closed off everything, concentrated on the here and now, and the battles that came along. At least he had, until he returned home and learned nothing was as he had thought it should be.

"I think you need to live a little." He had never wanted her to be alone if something happened to him. But, just as he had done, Sabella had continued to hold on to that bond that stretched between them. The one Nathan had tried to break between them, but never could.

"What I think is that it isn't any of your business. You didn't know him and you don't know me."

He grunted at that, sipped his coffee, and stared at her bent head as she went over the accounting book. He'd gone over it himself, several times. It was in perfect order. Once she had returned and knocked the garage back into shape, she had managed, miraculously, to hold on to it. Mostly because, according to Rory, she had refused to sleep and had practically lived at the garage.

"I don't have to know him," he told her, as he rested his wrist on his knee while holding his coffee and staring back at her. "I've had him shoved down my throat every day I've been here. Every one I've met loved 'Irish.' " He nearly spat out the word. He was so sick of hearing about himself he could barely tolerate it.

When the hell had people in this town decided he was larger than life and no other man was going to compare?

"Nathan had a lot of friends." She shrugged, her fingers picking at the edge of the accounting book, her expression tight.

"Friends that let his widow suffer," he reminded her. "What happened, Sabella? Who finally told you the garage was going to hell? According to Rory, you hid in that house on the hill and wouldn't even answer the door some days. How did you figure out the Malones were trying to destroy you?"

Her lips tightened.

"Yeah, old Nate, he was well loved." He sneered. "So well that his widow was deserted and nearly lost her ass while she was grieving. What the hell happened with that one, Sabella?"

"Again, none of your business." But her voice was tighter, the edge of hurt flaying his guts.

He knew what had happened. His family had turned against her. Mike Conrad, it was rumored, had offered to help her out if she would be so kind as to let him fuck her. Noah had to force the violence down. And once the Malones and the bank had turned against her, then finding anyone willing to help hadn't been easy. Only the fact that Nathan Malone had indeed had friends who were still willing to use the garage had saved her. Friends who didn't have power, and there were too many of them for Grant Malone, or Mike Conrad, to be able to strike out at effectively.

He knew what Mike Conrad had wanted. The garage was the perfect setup for laundering money and was centrally located for the militia members to congregate. With the apartment upstairs, the reputation of the garage, and Nathan Malone's good name to fall back on, it would have worked.

The sheriff and his wife had stood by her, though it was rumored the friends Mike Conrad had in the local government were pressuring the sheriff to choose sides. Mike's or Sabella's. Noah knew Rick Grayson, if he wasn't part of the BCM, was at least a suspect. Hopefully, the program Noah had slipped into Mike's laptop would give them the proof they needed to bring that bastard down. Him and his friends.

The mayor, one of Grant Malone's boyhood friends, had taken the city's contract from the garage, illegally. Rory was checking with a lawyer in Odessa about suing for that one. What they had done to Sabella was unconscionable and wouldn't be tolerated any longer.

The gossip and rumors that filled small-town life were there for anyone willing to listen. And Noah listened each time a customer got nosy enough to question him regarding the talk now circulating that he was taking the place of the man they had nicknamed "Irish." He listened, picked through the gossip to find the truth, and the truth only managed to piss him off more.

"I'm making it my business," he finally warned her.

The battle he faced would have been amusing if it were anyone else. He was going to have to steal his wife's heart back from his own memory. Hell of a position for him to find himself in.

He watched as her gaze lifted, just her eyes, and she stared up at him, and he could have sworn he felt his balls twitch in warning. He had only seen that look one time in the two years they had been together.

Her lips parted as the door from the convenience store opened and Rory stepped in.

Noah's gaze sliced to him, his demand to leave clear. Rory grinned back then his gaze moved to her neck. She was getting sick of that. The surprise, the look of shock that a man had marked her neck. What, did everyone suddenly think she really wasn't woman enough to draw a man's passion?

She curled her lip angrily before getting to her feet, moving around the desk, and jerking open the door to the garage. She stepped into the garage bay and slammed the door closed behind her.

"Asshole," Rory muttered as Noah stared at the door she had gone through.

Noah turned to look at him. "Take care of that firing you've been putting off today. Your new mechanic is showing up tomorrow."

Rory grimaced. "Yeah, just get her all pissed off at me now."

"Do it," he growled, before rising to his feet and making for the door to the garage. "And stay the hell out of my way for the next little bit."

He pushed through the door and found Sabella standing next to the mechanics' counter, going over the roster. She was frowning, then she glanced in the direction of the mechanic Rory was about to fire.

Before she could say anything he surprised her, and everyone else, by pulling the clipboard from her hand, slapping it to the table, and pulling her back to the office.

"Have you lost your mind!" she yelled as the door closed behind them. "Why isn't Timmy's name on the roster? He's standing out there twiddling his damned thumbs on my time and I want to know why."

"Rory took him off." He took the easy way out. "He's firing him."

Her eyes narrowed. "Did Rory know he was doing this before you told him to?" Sweet Southern rage brewed in her voice.

Noah crossed his arms over his chest and glared down at her.

"Rory agreed he's not doing his job and made the decision." Sort of.

"The hell he did." She was in his face, her gray eyes dark and thunderous, her face flushed, her little fists clenched at her side. "My garage. My employees. My decisions."

Her jaw was so tight he was afraid it was going to crack. Her lips tightened, moved, he could see the fury burning hot and wild inside her. Fury and arousal. It burned in him too. It set a spark to the darkness he tried to keep under control, to the hunger he fought not to reveal to her too quickly.

"Rory has never done anything without asking me first," she bit out. "You made him do this."

Noah shrugged. "I merely made the suggestion."

"You bastard!"

"Call me another name, Sabella, and you're going to regret it," he warned her.

She had never cursed him during their marriage. She had rarely cursed.

She bared her teeth at him. "You arrogant damned misfit."

That was it.

He dipped his shoulder, threw her over it, and turned for the stairs that led to the apartment.

He ignored the little fists beating at his back, the shrieks of rage, her attempts to kick out of his hold.

Sabella didn't curse. She had never cursed. She had given

him that haughty little good girl look every time he said "damn" and asked him if he really wanted their future children to hear that dirty word coming out of his mouth.

She had nearly broken him from cursing in two years. Now, if she wanted to handle the cursing she could deal with the consequences. Because it made him hornier than he had been to begin with and made him wonder what else he could convince her to say if he used just the right persuasion.

He slammed the apartment door behind them, locked it, then let her slide to her feet. He caught her fist as it slammed toward his face, then caught the other one and glared down at her.

"Enough!"

Something flickered in her gaze, some shred of trepidation as he released her wrists and stepped away from her.

"You are not firing Timmy." She jerked that damned shirt around her like a shield.

"Rory is firing Timmy and as of today you'll be back in the office where you belong," he snapped, turning back to her in time to catch the sudden, overwhelming hurt that flashed in her face.

"No, I won't be." She squared her shoulders and faced him with a defiant lift of her chin and rage burning in her eyes. "Neither you nor Rory can enforce that one, Noah. I'll burn this garage to the ground before I'll let you take me out of it."

Her expression was fierce, furious, and reminded him of the night he tried to force her to stay home rather than go out with her friends.

He frowned back at her. "Dammit, Sabella, you're killing yourself out there. It's hard, damned dirty work. There's no sense in your having to labor like that. You could go to the spa. Get your nails done. Wouldn't that be nice?"

Sabella fought to hold back the fury strangling her. She wanted to hit him. She wanted to scream at him and slap that arrogant, condescending expression off his face. At that moment, she could see where Duncan got the impression that Noah was just like Nathan. Superior. Certain of his own strength and determined to have his way. Nathan had gotten away with it simply because she hadn't matured enough in their marriage to put her foot down while he was home. She had matured now. And this wasn't Nathan. Noah wasn't a SEAL who could be called out at any minute on a mission, and he wasn't the man who had once claimed her soul, so he could go to hell as far as she was concerned.

"If I wanted a manicure then I would have one. If I wanted to sit back and play receptionist all day then that's what the hell I would do. If I wanted another man to decide how I should act, dress, or present myself then I'd have one. That is not a part of your job description, Mr. Blake, and if you think you can make it happen then you can take a flying leap into hell."

Noah stared back at her, shocked.

"Your husband dictated those things for you?" he asked her, feeling his guts ice over, because he knew he hadn't.

She paused. He watched her expression soften, sadden. Her gray eyes flashed with arousal, and suddenly, her slender body seemed softer, sexier with whatever memories poured through her.

"No," she finally admitted. "I dictated it, because it was what I thought he wanted. He liked his painted-up little wife. The nail polish and the pretty clothes and the helplessness." She shook her head as he felt his chest clench at her sorrow. "He used to call me his little Southern Bella. He died before he ever learned what a complete imposter I was. Before he ever knew that I was just as knowledgeable about cars as any of his mechanics were. I loved Nathan. He was my heart and I gave him what he needed while I had him with me." She flicked him a searing glance then. "But you're not Nathan. And I don't give a damn if you have what you need or not."

Did she think he had given a damn about the frigging nail polish? Anger tore through him, not rage, not fury, but pure unbridled offense and male pride. Damn her, what pleased her had pleased him, but had she thought he had needed her to be something she wasn't?

He tensed at the sexual, dominant surge of heat that filled

his body. Before he could stop himself he was stalking toward her, jerking her to him.

"And did you get what you needed from him?" he rasped. "You've eaten me alive every time we've touched, Sabella. Did he fuck you like you needed or did you play the pretty little doll for him then too?"

"He gave me everything I needed," she snarled back.

But he saw it. A little lie, just a little one. And he remembered the nights that she had tossed restlessly in their bed beside him. How he had felt, sometimes, that his Sabella needed something harder, something darker, than he had given her, but then thinking that it was only his own fantasies and needs that drove him to sense that.

It wasn't. He saw it in her eyes. He recalled the torrential lust of last week when she had marked his shoulders with her sharp little nails, then his memories of their life together before hell, and he knew. He knew Sabella had longed for a hell of a lot more than he had allowed himself to give her. Pure lust.

A tight, hard smile twisted his lips as her gaze finally flickered in awareness of the animal she had just let loose inside him.

"You're a liar," he breathed, knowledge searing him, dominance rising inside him. "Tell me, Sabella. Did you ache? Did you dream of being taken hard and rough? Of getting wild and dirty with your husband? Were you too afraid to be the little wildcat you wanted to be?"

There was the truth. The flush leached from her face, her eyes darkened. He could see the lust filling her, pure, unbridled, but tinged with an emotion that tightened the heart in his chest.

Sabella wanted more than just sex. She wanted more than just the wild loving. She wanted everything he had ever dreamed of giving her. And he was going to give it to her right now.

She'd hidden things from him; well, there were damned sure things he had hidden from her as well. And the need to hear his sweet Southern Bella get nasty had been an all-consuming need.

"You can get wild with me, baby." He jerked her harder against him, let her feel the erection pounding beneath his jeans. "Come on, I dare you. I'm a stranger, Sabella. Nothing to you. Nothing to that paragon of a husband you knew. Get wild with me. And I'll show you how I can get wild right back."

CHAPTER TEN

Get wild with him? Pour everything into him that she had fantasized about pouring into Nathan? She stared up at Noah, her body so sensitive, so highly excited, she couldn't deny her need.

She could barely breathe for it. It was tearing through her veins, the temptation burning through her sex.

"You want to be taken hard and wild, Sabella." His voice deepened, darkened, as his hands speared into her hair, fingers clenching, pulling at it.

Sabella felt the shocking sensations unravel inside her. Her lashes fluttered, her knees weakened.

"You want to pull my hair, baby? Come on, Sabella, I dare you. You don't have to give me anything he had. Give me what he didn't have."

She jerked against him as she felt his lips on hers, whispering over them. Her eyes opened, and wild dark blue eyes held her trapped.

"I carried your scratches last week like other men carry a medal," he growled, then nipped her lips. "I jacked off remembering how hot you were in my arms. And then I imagined your mouth. Watching your eyes. Seeing how hungry you could get."

He tapped into her fantasy.

Sabella licked her lips, unconsciously imagining it. Feeling his hands in her hair, imagining him holding her in place, straining against her, demanding she take him, suck him.

Noah watched her eyes, saw the need, and his cock felt tighter, harder, thicker than it ever had.

Keeping one hand in her hair, he used the other to jerk his shirt off her shoulders. She wore his clothes like a defense against the world. He wasn't going to allow her a defense against him any longer.

Below it was the sleeveless T-shirt she wore tucked into her jeans.

"I don't think—"

"Don't think," he urged her, keeping his voice low, his eyes on her. "Unless you want to think about me fucking your mouth. I'm going to do that, Sabella. I'm going to watch those pretty pink lips open, watch my cock sink inside your mouth."

She'd gone down on him before. She'd teased, licked, sucked playfully, she'd even taken his release and licked her lips like a little cat. But that wasn't what she wanted now, it wasn't what she needed.

"Take the boots off." He held her gaze as he moved her and pushed her onto the couch. "Take them off now, Sabella, or you'll be wearing your jeans around your ankles while I slide deep and hard inside you. Wouldn't you rather use those pretty legs around my back, holding me inside you?"

She licked her lips again as he moved back and sat on the heavy coffee table to untie his own boots. He got them untied, then looked up when she moved.

But she didn't move to take off her boots. She came over to him. Noah went back on the table, catching her, his hand burying in her hair again as her lips were on his, a cry of need and hunger filling the air.

"Ah hell. Yes!" She flowed over him, straddled his hips. Her hands buried in his hair as he shoved his tongue in her mouth and fought to dominate the kiss.

She was wild. As she writhed above him, her back arched, her pussy bore down on the thick erection beneath his jeans and her hands tore at his shirt.

He managed to get it off. Managed to get her shirt and bra above her breasts while she sucked and bit at his neck, leaving a mark he knew the world would see and he didn't give a damn.

And it wasn't the only mark she would leave. Her lips moved to his chest, his hard, male nipples.

She had never done that before. Sucked and licked at the flat, hard discs, and it made him wilder than he swore even the whore's dust had.

"Damn you, yes," he growled as she moved lower, her hands falling to his jeans, jerking his belt loose, scrambling to loosen his jeans. "Take it, Sabella. You little wildcat. I'm going to fuck your mouth until you're begging for me to come. Begging to taste it. To feel it. To fuck me with every breath in your body."

He was snarling the words. Hands in her hair, controlling her, pushing her down until she straddled his bent knee and pulled the fully erect, throbbing shaft of his dick from the parted material of his jeans.

She looked up at him and the expression on her face was one he knew he would remember forever. Pure, undiluted hunger.

Her hand tried to wrap around the width, but her fingers didn't quite meet. She stroked up, over the violently sensitive head, and stared back at him with drowsy lust as she breathed in and out, each panting breath lifting those hard, flushed breasts.

"Make me," she whispered then.

The demand seared his brain, his imagination, his fantasies.

He gripped the shaft of his cock with one hand, and with the other he forced her head down, his eyes locked with hers, watching as her lips flowered open over the bulging crest.

Sabella was lost in the lust. She ground her sex against his knee, feeling the exquisite sensations of cloth rasping against her swollen clit as the heat and hardness of his cock head pushed inside her mouth.

God, his taste. It was hot and male. Earthy and filled with

lust. She licked over the blunted crest, feeling the iron hardness, the silky flesh, the throb of lust beneath.

She looked up at him, saw his wild eyes, like an unearthly glow, and dark, primitive need slashed through her. She needed to taste, needed to torment.

She licked beneath the head, rubbing her tongue over that spot that her Nathan had once loved her to caress so well. Noah tightened, the muscles of his thighs bulging, his hips arching, burying his cock deeper inside her mouth.

"Suck it, Sabella." There was an odd, lyrical quality to his rough, dark voice. "Take me."

She took him. His hands clenched in her hair, pulled at the strands as he moved her head, fucked into her mouth, and filled her with the heated hard crest of his erection.

She was needy, hungry for him. She could feel that hunger raging inside her as she cupped her own breast, her fingers plucking at her nipple, creating another burn, losing herself in the pleasure.

"I'm going to come, baby." He was moving between her lips, fast, hard, almost bruising as he strained beneath her, and she loved it.

He was wild. He was dark and earthy and she needed it.

She sucked him harder, deeper. She pulled at her nipple, tugged at it, cupped her breast and felt the fever raging, building in her clit.

"Yes! There!" he growled.

Her tongue was tucked against the underside of his cock head, rubbing and caressing, rasping against it as he moved over it, stroking past her lips, his hard flesh tightening further as she felt his release building.

She stared up at him. Saw it moving in his face. The way it tightened, turning stark, forbidden. Then she felt his release.

The first spurt exploded inside her mouth, the second had her moaning, her clit exploding as she rubbed herself against his knee.

"Ah hell, yes, you little witch," he groaned.

Sabella froze. She felt, tasted, she existed. But she stared into his eyes and dropped back in time.

Suck me, you little witch. My sweet, beautiful little witch.
When his hands eased in her hair, she moved back. She
stared at him, shaking. Horror and guilt rose inside her, flaying her soul with the consequences, the truth of what she had
just done.

She could still taste him in her mouth. He was staring at
her, dawning realization darkening his eyes further as she
jerked her bra and shirt down with trembling hands.

Noah sat up slowly, watching as she stumbled to the door.

"Don't you leave here, Sabella," he ordered her roughly.

She shook her head. "I can't do this."

"The hell you can't." He rose to his feet, tucking his still
stiff flesh back into his jeans and zipping them carefully.
"You're not leaving like this."

She gripped the doorknob. As fast as he knew he was, as
powerful, she was still out that door and running down the
steps before he could get to her.

Cursing, he jerked his shirt from the floor, dragging it
over his head as he raced down the stairs after her, nearly
tripping on the dragging strings of his boots.

"Damn it, Sabella," he yelled as he burst into the office to
see her racing out of the garage.

Rory stared at him in shock, Toby's face tightened in
anger. That damned kid was too protective of Sabella by far.

Noah sat down, quickly tied his boots, and headed out of
the garage to watch her running up the hill to the house. She
wasn't going far, he told himself, forcing back the lust, the
demand that he race after her, that he force her to acknowledge everything she was running from.

His hands clenched at his sides as he stared at the house.
His home. His woman.

He forced himself to turn and stalk back to the garage.
Forced himself to jerk up the roster and go to work. He forced
himself to concentrate. He knew how to do that. He had spent
six years doing just that. He could wait just a little bit longer.
Just a little bit. And then she would learn she was his. She had
been his before, and now, she would be his again.

An hour later, he looked up from the engine he was tuning, twirling the wrench he held absently as he watched Sabella's car pull out of the driveway and head into town.

His eyes narrowed, his lips thinned. She was running, and he hated that.

His gaze slid to his side as Rory moved in carefully then reached up and took the wrench.

"Told you once, the funny thing about this wrench," Rory said softly, making sure no one heard but Noah. "My brother used to do the same thing." He slapped the wrench back in Noah's hand and moved away again.

Sabella was pissed. Rory was pissed. And that was just too damned bad, because Noah was home now, and he was set to reclaim everything he thought he had lost. Just as soon as he cleared the garbage out of his town, and away from his wife.

Sabella had had enough. She pulled her car into Kira's driveway again that day and drew in a deep, hard breath. Sienna was still there, which was unusual. Sienna didn't normally hang around with Kira after Sabella left. Sometimes, she wondered if Sienna even liked Kira.

"Belle. Come on in." Kira's attractive face was lit with a smile as she opened the door and waved her in.

She tugged at the hem of her T-shirt. She should have changed clothes. She tugged her braid over her shoulder. Maybe she should have done something with her hair.

"Sienna's still here?" It was nearly three in the afternoon.

"She just showed up again perhaps an hour ago." Kira smiled. "We pulled out a bottle of wine and decided to trash men for the day."

Uh-oh. Obviously Sienna and Rick had had another fight after the other woman returned home.

She inhaled slowly and walked up to the porch where Kira stepped out and welcomed her into the house again.

Dressed in jeans and a gaily striped shirt, her dark hair piled carelessly on her head, Sienna looked like an overgrown teenager. In comparison, Kira Richards looked dark and mysterious. With her black hair and friendly gray eyes.

Dressed in silk capris and a camisole, Kira looked cool, sophisticated, and yet still managed to convey compassion.

"The planets are out of alignment," Kira said softly. "Let me guess, your Noah was acting like a man too?"

"Tell me that Ian at least is pretending to have some common sense." Sabella sighed as she collapsed into a chair across from Sienna and glanced up at Kira.

"Ian is a man, darlin'. What do you think?" Kira laughed.

The wine was on the table. Kira detoured to the kitchen and a few seconds later returned, another glass in hand, as Sabella glanced back up at her.

"Rick's pissed because I took the baby to his sister's again this morning." Sienna sighed. "Kent loves his aunt."

And Sienna loved her social life. Sabella agreed with Rick, Sienna needed more time with Kent, but the aunt was possessive as well. Sabella could only imagine how difficult the situation was.

"Sabella, I hate to tell you this, but the beard burn is worse on your chin. You need to have a talk with that mechanic of yours," Kira said, laughing.

"Talking doesn't work," Sabella muttered.

"I think she likes it," Sienna accused with a laugh. "She hasn't been gone more than three or four hours and already she's back after he got another taste of her. She's hiding from him."

Sabella bit her lip and looked back at Sienna.

"I heard Rick had to respond to a call of harassment because of him?" Kira said then. "Was he harassing you?" She leaned forward and stared back at Sabella curiously. "I talked to Ian after you left. He seems to think he's a very odd man. Maybe you should fire him."

Sabella looked from Kira to Sienna with a frown.

"He's not odd," she finally muttered as Kira sat down slowly, filled Sabella's wine glass, and pushed it to her with a faintly apologetic look.

Kira stared at the two women. As Ian's wife, and an operative herself, she knew the truth. She would have been amused if she didn't feel so damned sorry for the widow who wasn't a widow. She didn't like the fact that Nathan Malone hadn't come clean with his wife. She sure as hell didn't like the fact that the girl looked so bewildered and lost. And the friendship they had developed over the years had only increased Kira's worry. Sabella had never let go of her husband, and now he was back again, tormenting her in another way.

"Ian's worried about you after this morning," she told Sabella, giving her a quiet, almost gentle smile. "He loved Nathan like a brother." And he still did. Though Kira would have preferred to kick the other man's ass.

"I know he did." Sabella sighed then took a healthy drink of the wine and Kira watched as her jaw clenched in anger.

Kira wasn't having any part of being pushed out of this particular conversation.

Sabella had been faithful to her dead husband for over six years. The memory of the love she felt for him had tormented her. And for half that time, Nathan could have eased her pain.

Sabella licked her lips. She pressed her knees together and seemed to be trying to hold in emotions that were only festering inside her.

"He's making me crazy," she muttered. "He just takes over everything, as though it's his right."

"But you still want him."

Silence descended.

"She doesn't need him," Sienna finally stated. "He's not the staying kind and she knows it."

"That's not what it is. I know the expression of a woman steeped in guilt and fear because she's finally met a man threatening her husband's place in her heart," Kira stated gently. "This has nothing to do with whether or not he's the staying kind. It has to do with Sabella letting Nathan go."

Kira was nothing if not forward. Sabella had learned herself, long ago, that the worst thing a woman can do is hide from herself.

"Yeah, well, that doesn't mean I have to do anything about it." Sabella frowned.

Kira leaned back in her chair and watched Sabella for

long, sober moments. "No, it doesn't." She shook her head.
"Ian loved Nathan like a brother." She stared back at Sabella
then. "When they told him Nathan was dead, he took it very
hard, he told me. We've become good friends, Sabella. I've
watched you the last few years. You laugh, you go out with
friends, sometimes you date. But you haven't had a lover
since Nathan died. Have you?"

"I've been fine." Sabella shook her head. "I'd be better if
men would stop getting in my way and acting as though I
need someone to tell me what to do."

"Get a little drunk," Kira advised her, her brow wrinkling
at the pain she could see in Sabella's eyes. "Get pissed off.
Tell us what an asshole Nathan was because he left you."

"Kira!" Sienna snapped, anger brightening her green
eyes then. "That's enough."

"And each time she's stepped away from Nathan's memory you've reminded her of the man she lost, rather than the
fact that there are other men out there, haven't you, Sienna?"
Kira said softly. "I've known the two of you for years now,
and I've seen it. I'm just a neutral bystander with too much
gossip under my belt and married to the man who was the
asshole's best friend."

"Nathan wasn't an asshole," Sabella snapped.

"He was a SEAL, sweetheart. I'm married to one. They're
so dominant, fierce, and certain of their own abilities and
opinions that they can't help themselves," she stated, amused.
"So in the kindest vein, yes, that's exactly what Nathan was.
But he's gone. He doesn't exist any longer, but here you are,
years later, from all accounts incredibly attracted to another
man and fighting that attraction because of your guilt about
your husband's memory."

"I don't have to just jump into bed with every man I
meet," Sabella snapped.

"But neither were you buried when they told you your
husband was dead."

Sabella stared back at her, seeing in the other woman's
eyes sympathy, without the history she had with Sienna.
Without the memories of Nathan she and her friend shared.

And she was right. Sabella didn't have to like it, but she did have to acknowledge it.

"Duncan says he's like Nathan," she whispered. "And maybe in ways, he's right. He's taking over," she said harshly. "He's walked into my life and he's just taking over."

Kira leaned forward a bit more. "And he's darker and more dangerous than your husband was, despite Nathan having been a SEAL. Ian says this man is harsher, more commanding. And you're not the proper little SEAL wife any longer, are you?"

"What do you mean by that?" Sabella frowned.

"He went off to war and refused to let you cry when he left. Refused to let you worry while he was gone. And because you didn't want him to worry, you held it all in. When he was home, it was whatever Nathan wanted; you cherished him. But those days are gone now, aren't they, Sabella? Because Nathan's gone. He went away, and you found out all kinds of interesting things about yourself, didn't you? You found your independence and, despite your grief, you grew up. And now, this man who would take over as Nathan once did doesn't have a chance of pushing past that independence. Does he?"

"I found out being without Nathan was hell," she raged. "I want him back. I don't want that." She jumped to her feet and flung her hand at the door, indicating the world outside. "I want my husband."

And she didn't. Nathan was gone and she knew it, but she had no other excuse for the emotions tearing through her, the rage building inside her. Noah Blake was twisting her world around. He wasn't safe. He wasn't easy to handle and he wanted more than she was comfortable giving any man now. He wanted all of her. And her own independence had held parts of herself back from her husband. The parts that tormented her. The parts that would have given him her entire soul. The sexuality she had never been comfortable with, the need to be wild, to be nasty, to eat him up and make him take her hard, fast, rough, and desperate.

"And your husband is gone. And you've very nearly had

sex with another man. And you liked it." Kira came slowly to
her feet.

She had been waiting for this for weeks. She had placed
herself in Sienna's and Sabella's paths years before, made
friends with Sabella, knowing this chance would come.
Nathan Malone had made a mistake in hiding from his wife,
and as Kira had known all along, his wife was the one paying
the highest cost.

"Damn, Kira," Sienna muttered, poured more wine and
drank it. "That's harsh."

Sabella turned back to her other friend, looking at her as
though for reinforcement and watched as Sienna stared back
at her with compassion, although she clearly agreed with
Kira.

"This is none of your business." Sabella groaned. "Why do
people suddenly think they can butt their noses in my business?"

"Because we got tired of watching you try to die with
Nathan," Sienna retorted painfully. "Sit down, Sabella. Let's
just get drunk like we used to. We can rip into Noah and
Rick, talk about how arrogant they are, and you can go home
and live again," she whispered tearfully. "I don't care if
Noah is a Martian alien hiding horns. I haven't seen you like
this in too long. Almost alive. And I could kiss his cheek for
making your eyes sparkle like that."

Sabella collapsed on the couch and stared back at the other
two in bemusement. "You don't understand. Nathan . . ." She
grimaced. "He still holds a part of me. I dream of him. And
he's still so much a part of me."

Kira resumed her seat and poured Sabella more wine.
"Don't let him go if you can't, Sabella. But don't feel guilty
because you're a woman. Because you need to be touched or
you need to be held. Take what Noah Blake has to offer." She
leaned back in her seat as both Sienna and Sabella drained
their glasses and refilled them.

"He's taking it all over," Sabella snapped. "The garage.
Me. As though he thinks everything Nathan had should be
his."

"He could just be dominating." Kira waved the truth of Sabella's statement away. "Hell, ride him for a while, get him out of your system, then send him on his way. Things are never so complicated as they are in the middle of a sexual crisis. Get the sex out of the way, and the problems tend to solve themselves."

Sabella stared back at Kira.

Sienna didn't speak. She sipped her wine and watched Sabella instead.

"Are we going to get drunk? If I have to have this conversation, then I at least want an excuse for being blunt, if you don't mind? Otherwise, Rick is going to be pissed I stuck my nose in this. And you know, I tend to do without sex myself when he's pissed."

Sabella emptied her glass and held it out for more. Kira watched them both in amusement.

They drank that glass and started on another when Sabella suddenly sighed heavily.

"I gave him a blow job."

Kira jumped as Sienna's wine spurted across the table. The sheriff's wife choked, covered her mouth, and turned to Sabella.

"You did what?"

Sabella finished her wine, amused that her friend was so shocked. "I told you what I did."

"Was it good?" Kira drawled.

Oh, Kira could not wait until Ian came home. This was going to be so much fun. Better yet, she couldn't wait until she saw Noah again.

"It was so good." Sabella was tipsy. She hadn't been tipsy in years. "So good. More excellent than I imagined it could be."

"And did he at least return the favor?" Sienna sighed. "I'm going to get in so much trouble here. You two know this. Right? Rick will just worry."

"You're going to tell him I gave Noah a blow job?" Sabella whispered. Horrified. "You wouldn't?"

"I'll be drunk," Sienna moaned. "And we have a bet."

"A bet?" Sabella was outraged. "What kind of bet?"

"He bet me you would throw him out." Sienna glared at her. "I bet him you would pull his ears off."

Sabella blinked uncertainly. "Why would I do that?"

Sienna rolled her eyes. "You know, sweetie. Grab his ears and pull when you come." She wagged her brows. "'Cause it's good."

Sabella turned to Kira as she snorted, nearly choking on her wine.

"We know better than to let her get drunk," Sabella reminded Kira. "She gets naughty. Remember?"

"Yeah, like that night Nathan had to come get you from the house." Sienna laughed. "Do you remember, Sabella? I told him we were going to buy you an electric blanket and a vibrator?"

Sabella had to laugh. "I don't know if he was fascinated or outraged."

"He was definitely thinking about the vibrator," Sienna said, laughing even more.

Sabella smiled. It was a good memory. He had carried her out of Sienna's house and taken her home. And he had loved her.

"I miss him," she said softly, finishing another glass of wine.

"But he's gone." Sienna said, her voice quiet.

"Yeah," Sabella breathed out, watching as Sienna refilled her glass as well. "He's gone."

And now Noah was invading her life.

"What do I do now?" She looked at the two women.

"I'm all for you pulling his ears off," Sienna said.

"Nathan left you, Sabella," Kira told her gently. "Do you think he would berate you?"

Sabella was quiet for long moments before she whispered, "I promised him forever."

"Forever with him. Is he here now?" Kira pointed out gently. "You don't have to give Noah forever, Bella. Give him a night. Get over the sex and take your life back."

"I'm not cheating," Sabella said, her gaze meeting Kira's.

Something inside her loosened. Something fell into place, but she was just too damned tipsy to realize what it was. "Am I?"

"Oh dear, trust me." Kira smiled back at her. "The last thing you're doing is cheating. You can take that one to the bank."

Glasses clinked, refilled, and the three women sat back and proceeded to get outrageously tipsy. Well, Sabella thought several hours later as Ian walked in and stared at them in shock, maybe they were a little bit drunk.

CHAPTER ELEVEN

"Oh hell!" Rory groaned as he hung the phone up then covered his face with his hands.

Noah turned from where he was watching the driveway through the windows of the office and glanced at his brother with a frown.

"What?"

Rory had that look. One of trepidation. Warning. Male amusement.

"Belle's drunk."

Noah froze. There it went. His balls drew up in fear. Pure, unadulterated male fear. Because Sabella did not pull her punches when she was drunk.

"Tell me she's not at Sienna Grayson's?"

"That was Ian Richards. She's at his house." Rory sighed. "The sheriff is there to pick up Sienna. He's threatening to lock Belle, his wife, and Ian Richards's wife up for the night if I don't come get her. Evidently, they're trash-talking men in general and having a hell of a lot of fun doing it. I think I heard something about a sexual crisis in the background, and Ian is cracking the hell up with laughter."

Yeah, that was fear pinching his balls.

"Call him back," Noah breathed out roughly as he grabbed his jacket from the wall peg and grabbed the keys to Rory's truck from his desk. "Tell him we're coming after her."

The garage was already closed and everything locked up for the night. They had just been waiting for Sabella to return.

"Should I wish you luck or order roses for your new gravesite?"

"Just call Ian and tell him we're coming," he growled and headed out the door. "I'll pull the truck around and pick you up."

He should have known when he saw her drive off. Hell, he had known. A part of him was well aware that his wife was pissed off and would head to Sienna's. He hadn't expected Kira. He knew they'd connected as friends, but not to this extent. There would be hell to pay now, and not just from Sabella, but Kira as well.

He and Rory arrived at the house, pulling in behind Kira's small sports car, and Noah shook his head. He knew Kira. She was a troublemaker. A former Homeland Security agent with too damned much time on her hands now. She had driven Ian insane until he married her in what Nathan swore was an attempt at some peace.

The door opened as he neared it, and Rick Grayson stared at him with narrow-eyed displeasure from across the room as Ian stepped back and allowed Noah to enter the house. Amusement glittered in his commander's eyes and tugged at his lips. Damn. Noah didn't need this.

And there they were. Sabella was sprawled out on one end of the couch, Sienna on the other. Kira was reclining on the love seat. They all stared at him.

"Oh Sabella," Kira drawled mockingly. "I disagree, he looks like a very shady character." She looked at Sienna. "Has your husband run his background check yet? I bet he has a record."

"Twice. He's clean," Sienna announced blithely, peeking over the back of the couch as Noah winced. "You know who he reminds me of?"

"A thief?" Kira answered quickly.

"No." Sienna frowned. "You know . . ."

"Do you think his ears are big enough to pull?" Sabella

peeked over the back of the couch, narrowed her eyes, and stared at his ears consideringly.

The three women erupted into gales of laughter.

"I should arrest you," Rick muttered to Noah. "This has to be your fault."

Noah grunted, strode across the room, and picked his wife up gently from the couch.

She stared at him in surprise, but she didn't fight him.

"I can walk," she assured him.

"Of course you can." He nodded seriously. "But Rory has a date, so we're in a hurry."

She thought that was funny. But as she laughed she laid her head against his chest and her little hand rested over his heart.

"Night, Rick. Ian. I've had fun," she called out as they passed the two men.

"Stay out of trouble, Belle," Rick grunted before shaking his head as Noah passed.

"Everyone thinks you're very sexy, you know?" Sabella piped up as he carried her to the truck.

"Really?" He glanced down at her. She was watching him, drowsy, a little too tipsy.

"Really." She sighed. "Do you know Gaelic, Noah?" she suddenly asked.

His heart clenched. It actually hurt, as though spikes of steel had been dug into it.

"Should I?" he asked her, moving to Rory's truck as his brother headed around to Sabella's car. Thankfully, there had been a spare key to the car at the garage.

"Maybe not," she mumbled as he opened the truck door and slid her across the seat before getting into the truck, sliding it into gear, and heading home.

She was silent then, staring out the window as though she were interested in what they passed. As he pulled into her driveway, she stared at the house silently, her expression somber.

"Sometimes, I'm very lonely here," she suddenly said as he cut the motor and clenched the steering wheel furiously.

"You didn't have to stay alone," he told her hoarsely.

"Yeah, that's what Kira and Sienna seem to think." She sighed deeply, still staring at the house, as Noah winced.

"Why did you stay after he died?" he asked.

She didn't turn to look at him, just stared at her home, the grief on her face twisting his soul, wringing it dry.

Finally, she said, "It's home."

Shaking his head, he got out of the truck and strode to the door she was pushing open. He lifted her from the truck, steadied her, and helped her to the house.

"You can't come in," she told him.

"Sabella, this is the wrong damned time to push me." He'd just about had enough. He'd had enough of the hollow grief raging inside him, and the hunger ripping him apart.

"I'm drunk. Are you going to take advantage of me?" she asked him blithely as he unlocked the door and led her inside.

"Not tonight. Maybe I'll take advantage of you tomorrow night instead."

He caught the little pout on her lips as she gave him a glare.

"You're being very mean to me, Nathan. I think you should know that."

He almost flinched as she used his real name in her tipsy state. She couldn't know what she was saying. A slip of the tongue, he reminded himself. A ragged, pain-filled groan nearly tore from his chest though. She said it so easily as she stumbled against him. Just as she would have years before when she was put out with him. As though she knew, or sensed the truth.

He lifted her into his arms again and carried her up the stairs, but his throat was tight with emotion. The hollow emptiness that had filled him for so long now seemed to overflow with feelings, with emotions. With grief.

He laid her in their bed, watching as her head settled on the pillow, her lashes fluttering drowsily.

He untied her boots and set them carefully by the bed. He pulled her jeans from her, and because he knew she hated sleeping in a bra, he unhooked it and removed it from beneath her shirt.

She stared up at him. "You can take advantage of me. I promise not to get mad."

"Later," he promised her as he sat on the bed beside her.

"Would you hold me?"

Hold her? When everything inside him was screaming for so much more. But it wasn't so little to give her, when he had taken so much from her.

He pulled his boots off, moved to his side of the bed, and lay down beside her before pulling her into his arms.

"I have nightmares," she whispered as he tucked her against his chest.

"I know, baby." He undid her braid, worked her hair loose.

"I see blood," she told him. "My hands are covered in blood. And you're crouched in front of me. You are. Then Nathan is. Then you. Then Nathan is drifting away and you're still there. And suddenly I'm you, and the pain is so bad. And all I feel is you thinking about me. Begging me to save you as I dance in front of you and tempt you to take me. But it's not me. And it's so frightening, Noah."

He flinched. God, she had seen into that hell. The temptation Fuentes had brought him in the women that so resembled Sabella. He was pumped on the whore's dust, so aroused it was a clawing pain, but knowing. Knowing the women brought to him weren't his wife.

"I didn't save him," she murmured as she slipped off to sleep. "He begged me to save him, and I couldn't." Her voice thickened with tears and with sleep. "I couldn't save him."

She finally relaxed against him as he bent his head over hers and held her tight.

"You saved him," he whispered into her hair. She had no idea how she had saved him. The man he had been didn't exist any longer, but the man that loved Sabella, that ached for her, that had endured hell because of his vows to her, had survived.

He rocked her when she whimpered in her sleep, comforted her, and held her. He stared into the darkness and wished he could cry himself. Because she had suffered when he had thought she could go on. Because Grandpop had been right. He had loved her until at times he swore he could feel the beat of her heart next to his own. But he knew Grandpop had been right about the eyes. Because in the memories of the hellish existence he had lived, he had remembered seeing images that weren't there. He would be in his bedroom, staring into the mirror, staring at Sabella. And it seemed his Sabella had stared through his eyes as well. Straight into hell.

His arms tensed, tightened around her. He tilted his head back and forced himself to breathe through the pain. To hold back the agony welling inside him.

"Sabella." He whispered her name, breathed her in.

She shifted against him. Sleeping, sensual, tempting. "I missed you, Irish."

And he ignored the single tear that fell from the corner of his eye. The pain. The loss. She knew. Deep inside where she refused to see who he was, she knew, because that bond was still there, those vows were still there. By staying away from her, he had left her drifting between reality and hell. Still bound to him, yet alone, facing the nightmares without him by her side. Enduring, even when she had glimpsed the horror he had lived through.

And he had thought his wife wasn't strong enough to face what had happened to him. Hell, he had a feeling his wife was far stronger than anyone knew. Perhaps, in her heart, in her soul, she was stronger even than him.

She was warm. Sabella shifted in the bed, almost moaning at the sense of warmth that surrounded her. Noah's arms were wrapped around her, holding her close, his head tucked above hers just like Nathan used to do. It must be a male thing, she decided. Nathan had been her only lover, so of course she would notice it. One leg was thrown over hers, her head rested on his arm, the other arm was lying over her waist, holding her to his chest.

She couldn't escape him if she wanted to. And she so didn't want to. She wanted to luxuriate in this warmth. Hold on to it. But something prodded at her mind, nipped at her, wanting her to awaken.

She shifted against him, trying to escape it. She wanted to stay here, right here. No matter how much she ached for other things, she didn't want to lose this feeling of incredible peace.

Then his hand shifted, moved beneath the hem of the shirt she still wore and pressed against her stomach. Sabella stretched, moved, pressing more firmly against the warm male body behind her, her breathing hitching, half sob, half moan as she realized it wasn't a dream.

She was weak. She needed.

What had Kira said, get rid of the sexual crisis and everything else would clear itself up? It made sense to her. Right now, enfolded in his embrace, as his hand moved to the band of her panties, it made sense.

"Stay still." Hoarse, guttural, his voice rumbled in her ear as she tucked her butt closer to the iron-hard length of the heated cock pressing against her.

He was naked. Sometime during the night he had undressed and gotten under the blankets with her. She shivered at the thought. She could feel the naked length of his body behind her, powerful and hard.

Her lashes lifted. It was still dark. Dawn hadn't yet begun to lighten the room and she didn't have to face what was and what wasn't. All she had to do was feel.

Her head turned until her lips could press against his neck beneath his chin. The abrasion of his beard was erotic, sexy. She hadn't known a beard could feel so sexy.

"Kiss me," she whispered.

He stilled behind her. His hand pressed against her stomach, moved to her hip, and tightened to hold her still.

"Don't tempt me, Sabella." His voice whispered through the darkness, wrapping around her as she let it stroke her senses.

"I want you." She hadn't wanted since her husband's death. She wanted now. She wanted with a strength she knew she would have to face later, but not right now. Right now, she would experience it, revel in the pleasure of it.

She felt the tension that whipped around them, that filled the air and heated the room.

"Do you want me?" he growled then, turning her, the shadow of his broad shoulders suddenly filling her vision as he leaned over her. "Is it me you want, Sabella? Or your husband?"

Her hands lifted to his shoulders, smoothed over them. Her nails bit into his flesh, tested his muscle.

"Does it matter?" she asked him, feeling the clench of both needs suddenly filling her. She hated that confusion, that sense of being so off balance she didn't know who or what she was reaching for. "Does it matter to you?"

He was silent for so long that she wondered if he would answer her at all.

"It doesn't matter to me." A snarl filled his voice. "I would take you, Sabella, and when you cried out my name I wouldn't give a damn who you were crying out for. But if you expect me to take you as your husband would have, you're in for a sad surprise."

"You don't know how my husband took me," she told him then, lifted her head and let her tongue stroke over his chest, rubbed her face against the crinkle of chest hairs. "Take me, Noah, however you want to."

He wanted to take her hard and rough. She could feel that. She had known it, even before now. He wouldn't be an easy lover, but it wasn't an easy lover she wanted. She wanted to still that dark, furious need that had built up in her over the past years. A product of the dark, sexual dreams that mixed with nightmares and tormented her, on nights like this. Dark and indolent with the need for sex. For touch.

She was tired of fighting. She didn't want to fight him. She hadn't wanted to fight from the first day he had walked into the garage and tempted her with his wild arrogance. Her body ached for this touch. Her heart, so torn, so ragged now, wanted ease. Just a little bit of ease. Just for the time it would take to still the arousal burning through her.

"Sabella." He whispered her name as his forehead lowered to hers. "Do you know what you're asking for?"

"I want you."

She had to be asleep. Here, in Nathan's bed, in the bed where he had taken her as his wife, and she wanted another man.

"Make it go away, Noah," she whispered desperately. "Please, make it go away. The nightmares. The need. Stop torturing me. Take me or get the hell out . . ."

His lips took hers. They slanted over hers, and she was waiting, parted and desperate as she met him with a wild, hungry moan.

Noah could feel the dark need pressing at the edges of his vision, consuming his senses. He kissed her, pausing only long enough to jerk her T-shirt from over her head and to rip the panties from her body.

He was torturously hard. His cock was furious, determined, his balls tight with the need for greater release than what he had found in the past with only his hand for ease.

He was fighting for breath, his hand sliding between her thighs, finding the soft curls there wet, saturated, slick from her need. Slick and hot. Like honey.

Pressing his fingers closer, sliding between the swollen folds of flesh, he found the entrance to her pussy. It was tight, flexing around the tip of his finger as it had done the night he took her virginity so long ago.

He pushed her legs apart, lifted himself between them. Foreplay would come later, he promised himself. So many years. Ah God, so long. Nineteen months of that time spent in the horrific grip of a drug so powerful that the need to fuck nearly drove him insane.

And standing between him and the crazed need had been his wife. Her gray eyes staring at him, stark with longing, her voice whispering in his head, holding him back.

"Damn you." He jerked his head back from the kiss, stared down her, barely seeing her face in the darkness that surrounded them. "Do you know how bad I want you?" He clenched his teeth, fought back the words.

"Then take," she panted. "Take me, Noah. Take me how you need me."

How he needed her.

He shook his head. He tipped it back on his shoulders and wanted to howl in rage.

He wanted to love his wife. He wanted to touch and kiss and taste every inch of her body. He shook, shuddered. He pressed the furiously tight head of his cock against her entrance and groaned at the heat, the slick sweet essence of her.

He pressed forward. Just for a moment, he promised himself. He had waited this long to take her again. He could wait long enough to pleasure her first.

As he wanted to pleasure her the day Rick Grayson had interrupted them. As he had meant to pleasure her the day before when she took his seed and left him twisting on a rack of arousal that nearly destroyed him.

She wanted him, as he had been. All he had to give her was who and what he had been made into. He pressed inside. He caught her wrists as they slapped against his chest, pushed them to the bed as he came over her, poised at the gates of ecstasy, only the tip of his erection feeling the pleasure.

"Say no now," he bit out. "Say it now, or you'll not say it at all. Do you hear me?"

She lifted her head, her sharp little teeth nipped his lips.

"Kiss me," she whispered roughly. "Kiss me as you take me, Noah."

So she couldn't ask him to stop? So she wouldn't scream one man's name and mean another's?

"Ah Sabella," he groaned. "Ah God, baby."

He covered her lips, took them with his own, and let the hunger tear through him.

It had been too long since he had felt his wife beneath him. Too long since he had felt the fiery pleasure of her pussy stretching to take him, heard her cries beneath his lips and known she was riding the same wave of pleasure he was.

His hips jerked, his cock pushing, thrusting, plunging, working its way inside her as she tightened and arched beneath him.

His lips took her cries, his tongue filled her mouth,

thrusting inside it as he pumped his erection inside the sweet bliss between her thighs.

He was pushing, penetrating, and when he couldn't stand the torture any longer he jerked his head back, released her lips and her wrists.

His hands caught at her hips, held them to him as he straightened on his knees, lifted her ass to his thighs and began the hard, driving rhythm he needed.

He heard the sounds coming from his throat, and they didn't matter. Deep, hoarse growls of need as his eyes closed, sweat beaded his body, and the tight, hot clasp of her pussy convulsed and rippled around him.

He was driving inside her. Unable to stop, relishing, loving every stroke that damned his soul forever as he gave his wife every furious inch, every agonizing ounce of lust that raged inside him.

Sabella felt her fingers tighten in the comforter beneath her, fought to hold on to something because she was losing her mind with the pounding strokes filling her body.

She had never been so ready. Foreplay wasn't needed. His kiss, the almost brutal strokes of his erection filling her were ratcheting the pleasure, the dark, seductive call of something she had never had rising inside her.

This. She had never had this. Pure, desperate hunger. Lust in its richest form. The rapid-fire strokes digging into her, stretching her, burning her, sending racing, flaming arrows of sensation tearing through her body.

Noah took her hard, without apology. He took her like a man riding the edge of insanity, the only thought the release she could give him. Just her. No one else. Just this, taking her, melting with her until she was screaming his name. Screaming, begging, then erupting beneath him as she felt her orgasm explode in a brutal wave of sensation.

It was cataclysmic. As though the foreplay had gone on forever, when actually there had been none. As though he had teased her unmercifully, pushed her higher and higher, and she was flying. Arched tightly to him, feeling his release spurting inside her as he continued to thrust, to push for more, his hungry groan filling the air as she jerked beneath him.

"Not enough!" The snarl rent the air.

Sabella felt him jerk back, turn her to her stomach, and lift her to him. He was inside her again, jackhammer strokes arching her, jerking her upright until her arms curled behind her, catching his neck as she felt his hands over her.

All over her. He stroked her thighs as he fucked her, her stomach, cupped her breasts, and pressed her nipples between his fingers as he spread his thighs wider, balanced them both and pushed inside her with rapid strokes.

Heat flowed around them and through them, and the night became immersed with her cries.

"So tight," he groaned, pausing, his breathing rough. "Sweet and tight. Move against me, Sabella. Show me you want it."

She moved. Worked her hips against him, rotated and lifted herself, lowered herself. She rocked back against him, gasping for breath as she felt his lips at her neck, his beard rough against her skin.

"Tell me." The rough, wicked whisper caressed her ear. "What do you want?"

His hands gripped her hips again.

"Hard?" He buried himself inside her hard, deep.

"Slow?" He moved, retreating, filling her with a slow, throbbing stroke that had her crying out in protest.

"Hard. I want you hard and fast. You know what I want."

She was shaking in his arms, trembling from the need to come again as one hand lowered and the tips of his fingers began to strum against her clit.

Sabella felt the tension rising again. It was tearing into her, spikes of white-hot sensation as his hips began moving hard and fast again.

He unlooped her arms from his neck, one hard hand pushed her shoulders to the bed and he came over her. The thrusts grew faster, harder. The slap of flesh, damp and hot, melding together. The sounds of his thrusts, her moans, his desperate cry, and when release detonated inside them, it was an almost soundless clash of agonizing pleasure.

The breath tore from her. She could only arch, her eyes opening wide, dazed as a whimper left her lips, and she swore she flew free of her own body and that bodiless part of her met pure rapture.

Behind her, Noah stilled, a hard, rumbling cry filling the air that could have been her name, could have been a curse, and he was spilling inside her again. The heated rush of release spurting free, shuddering through him, drawing another surge of pleasure before receding, slow and easy, and leaving them tangled on the bed.

He lay half on her, half beside her. Still buried within her, still erect. Hearts slamming against their chests and exhaustion marking her, Sabella let herself drift. She let herself drift until she swore she heard something she knew she couldn't have heard.

"Go síoraí."

Her eyes opened. She blinked, listening, tense now, filled with fear. But it didn't come again. It was gone, just as the dreams were always gone, just as the hope had left a long, long time ago.

But Noah was still there.

He dragged himself from her, pulled her into his arms, and minutes later, she felt him slowly, so slowly, relax into sleep.

Still, she stared into the darkness, blinking back her tears as she held on to the arm that crossed over her stomach and held her to him.

"Forever," she whispered. A breath of sound. Too light for anyone to hear.

But there was no forever. A single tear fell, silent, wasted, because tears didn't heal. They didn't cleanse. Eventually, she let herself fall into a sleep she never thought she would know again. The sleep she had found once, only in her husband's arms, and now in another man's.

Behind her, Noah stayed still, silent. Unmoving. The sadness and the pain in her voice dug talons of agony inside his soul until he could barely breathe.

He held her, felt her, and inside, deep in that ragged wound that had once been his soul, he cried with her.

CHAPTER TWELVE

"No more tears for another man while you're in bed with me."

Sabella turned slowly from the coffeepot to the man who strode into the kitchen, too big, too forceful, too dominant that early in the morning.

She still didn't have a handle on what had happened last night, and had forced herself to escape from the bed and into the shower before she could allow a repeat of it.

Now, dressed in jeans and T-shirt, her boots tied firmly on her feet, she turned away and ignored him, fighting to ignore her racing heartbeat.

Something had happened last night that she couldn't quite put her finger on. Something that filled her with a sense of dread. With a nervous energy she didn't know what to do with. And there was something about him this morning that wasn't helping the situation. It wasn't just the dominance. It was something about the way he was standing, the look in his eyes. Something that had her chest tightening and her sex creaming.

He was pissing her off and turning her on, all at the same time. She didn't consider that a good combination.

"My bed. My tears." She moved away from the coffeepot and made room for him as he opened a cabinet door, and of course he opened the right one and pulled a cup free.

"You fuck me and then cry?" He snorted. "The next time it happens, Sabella, I'll ride you until you can't cry."

"How would you know I even cried?" She watched him. The shift of his shoulders, the way his muscles bunched. "You fell asleep."

"I don't sleep that deep." He poured his coffee and turned back to her, rugged and sexy, his black hair damp and falling to his shoulders, his beard and mustache darker than night when emphasized by his deep, dark blue eyes.

Dressed in the clothes he had worn the day before, he looked both rumpled and powerful. Not a good look for her peace of mind this morning.

"You won't have to worry about it." She finally shrugged. "I'm certain we have the sexual crisis out of our systems now. We can go back to sniping at each other. And you can sleep in your own bed."

She set her coffee cup on the counter and gazed at him with determination.

He made her wait. He studied her over the rim of his coffee cup as he sipped at the dark brew, his eyes turbulent, sparking with something, not anger but definitely not agreement.

"One-night stand, was it?" he asked.

A frown wrinkled her brow at the tone, the flavor of his voice.

"It was expedient," she lied. "Now you can get on with your own life and I can get on with mine."

"Get on with building that shrine to your dead husband?" he growled.

It almost hurt, the way he said it. It should have hurt, but for some reason, it didn't have the power it would have had before he arrived.

Where the hell was her mind? He hadn't been here that long. She had slept with a man, had had sex with a man she had known for less than a month. It had taken her husband at least a month to get her into bed and she had been a virgin then. But this man rode into town on his black Harley with his riding chaps and his glare and the next thing she knew she was trying to eat him alive?

She shook her head at the thought of that.

"Whatever I do is no one's business but my own. We'll pretend last night didn't happen."

Because she couldn't make sense of it. Because she couldn't still the certainty that something had happened that was going to change her life forever.

"Will we now?" He sipped at his coffee again, finally finishing it as Sabella stood there observing him, forcing herself to be calm. "Just pretend you weren't coming before I ever sank my cock fully inside you? That we both didn't come like we'd never had sex before?"

When nothing else was said he set his cup in the sink and leaned back against the counter, crossing his arms over his chest and staring back at her silently, thoughtfully.

"What?" she finally asked, the tension tightening around them like a noose.

His lips twitched. "It's not going to work, you know. You can fight this as hard as you want to, Sabella, but it's not over."

"It's over."

He shook his head. "I'm heading to the apartment. I have to change clothes. I have to run an errand this evening, but I'll be back later tonight."

"Not here, you won't be."

He gave her a look that almost had her shaking in her boots. Almost.

Sabella crossed her arms over her breasts and glared back at him, wishing she could ignore the flicker of lust in his gaze.

Finally, the corner of his lips tilted, just enough to cause her nostrils to flare and the challenge to ignite inside her.

"I'll see you this evening," he stated before striding across the kitchen, passing her, and then leaving the house.

Sabella gritted her teeth then followed him.

Rory must have returned her car sometime the night before. Rory's truck was gone and that damned Noah was heading down the small rise to the garage, long legs eating the distance as she locked the door behind her and stomped to her car.

He beat her to the garage. But so had Rory.

Smiling tightly, she strode into the office, closed both doors softly and faced her brother-in-law.

His head had lifted from the papers he had been going over. His blue eyes studied her warily, his broad, roughly hewn face smoothing out in an attempt at a neutral expression.

"You're just not as good at that as your brother was," she told him softly, remembering well how Nathan would look at her with that look of male superiority when he knew she was angry with him.

"Good at what?" He cleared his throat.

Sabella leaned against the door and watched him closely.

"That look," she told him. "The one that dares anyone to question anything you've done. Nathan had it down to a very fine art. You need to practice it a bit more."

Amusement might have flickered on his face. He reached up and scratched his cheek, the short sleeves of his work shirt stretching over his biceps.

"You're mad at me," he finally said.

He glanced to the door leading the apartment.

"He can't help you," she stated softly as she smiled back at him coolly. "Did the two of you really think you could pull over on me anything you wanted to?"

The door to the apartment opened and Noah stepped into the office. He'd changed clothes. Damned fast work he'd made of it too.

"Rory, you'll need to run into Odessa to get those parts," Noah told him, looking at Rory. "This morning."

Rory rose from his chair.

"Don't even consider it," Sabella warned him softly.

Rory grimaced, swallowed. He looked from her to Noah then eased back down in the chair. Good. He'd chosen the right side.

"Who owns this garage?" she asked him then.

Rory scratched his cheek again, cleared his throat, and glanced between her and Noah as if he were the innocent party caught in the middle. Innocent, her ass. The two of them were up to something and she knew it. "We do?"

She narrowed her eyes at him. "Did you sell your part to him?" she asked softly, jerking her head to Noah.

Rory looked at Noah. Noah didn't take his eyes off her. The look should have made her wary, nervous. It would have, long ago and far away, if her husband had looked at her like that.

"No." Rory pursed his lips, watching her carefully now.

Ignoring Noah, she walked across the room, placed her hands flat on the desk, and leaned over it.

"Do you want to buy me out? I can pack up and move back to Georgia and you can have it, without me. Is that what you want?"

Shock, surprise, filled his eyes. "No. Belle. Damn. No." He shook his head fiercely. He looked at Noah and said, furiously, "What the hell did you do to her?"

"Does he own a part of this garage?" she snapped.

Rory blew out a hard breath. "No."

"Then his opinion doesn't matter, does it?"

"Maybe I wouldn't say that." Rory winced. "Come on, Belle, he knows what he's doing."

"And I don't?" She straightened, her chin lifting. "Where was he the past six years? Did he walk in here and bust his ass to fix what went to hell when Nathan left?"

"No. He didn't." Rory's voice firmed, his expression tightening.

"Next time, Rory, the two of you can have at it," she bit out. "Don't make that mistake again. My husband left me half of this business. That means half the decisions are mine. Not a stranger's and sure as hell not some interloper who thinks he can walk in and own everything Nathan possessed. Are we clear on that?"

Rory rubbed the back of his neck. "We're clear." He finally nodded.

Sabella didn't bother to spare Noah a glance. She turned, jerked an overshirt off the nearby hook, and stalked back into the garage, satisfied that at least that obstacle had been taken care of.

Noah stared at the door, crossed his arms over his chest,

then turned back to Rory. His brother was sweating. There was a fine film of perspiration on his forehead and, frankly, his blue eyes held a gleam of fear in them.

"Who was that woman?" He nodded to the door.

Rory shook his head. "The same one who walked into this garage almost three years after her husband left her, took one look at it, and started cleaning it up."

Rory jerked to his feet and glared at Noah. "And she's right. Where the hell were you when she was dying inside and nearly losing everything that meant anything to her? You want your dirty work done here, do it yourself." He jerked his keys from the desk and headed for the door. "And stay the hell away from her, if you're smart. The last man who pissed her off like that nearly ended up with a wrench buried in the back of his head when she went after him. I have a feeling she wouldn't deliberately miss where you're concerned. I wouldn't if I were her."

Noah watched as his brother disappeared through the other door. He stared at the door to the garage, then the door Rory had left through. Through the window he watched as Toby James strode across the lot, throwing Rory a frown as he passed.

Noah leaned against the desk behind him as Toby entered the office.

"Still pissing everyone off?" the boy grunted, as though it were a given.

Noah stared back at him coolly.

"Great," Toby muttered, shook his head then moved to the desk behind Noah. "Can you move your butt for me? I need to get some work done here."

Noah turned his head, stared the boy down, and watched him slowly pale. At least he could still intimidate *someone*.

"Maybe not." Toby sat down, pulled a list of invoices from the stack at the side of the desk, and powered up the computer.

Noah moved then. He opened the garage door, revealing the sight of his wife's knees sticking out from under a car, and felt his cock go stone hard in a heartbeat. As though it hadn't been hard to start with.

Her legs were spread over the sides of the mechanic's roller; whatever the hell she was doing under that car it wasn't something she had done during their marriage.

Where was his wife? And why the hell was this woman pretending to be her making the blood surge hard and heavy through his veins?

He was furious, aroused, and intrigued. And damned determined. Tonight, he was definitely getting into his wife's pants again.

Lifting his gaze from her jean-clad legs poking beneath the car, he looked across the garage and caught sight of Nikolai Steele. Alias Nicolas Steele. The six-foot-six Russian lifted his gaze from the motor he was working on, his ice-blue eyes stone hard, staring back at Noah before nodding slightly.

Noah's jaw bunched. He had work to do tonight before he could treat himself to another taste of Sabella. But when he was finished, his wife had best watch out.

As the day progressed, the garage eventually locked up, and Noah got ready for his weekly little night on the town, he couldn't get Sabella out of his mind.

The way she had stared him and Rory down. She hadn't screamed or yelled. She hadn't cried. She simply stated hard cold facts and her intentions. If Rory made decisions that affected her livelihood again, then he could have all of it. And as she had said, she had been the one who had walked into the garage and saved it.

The last person Noah had expected to be able to run the place was Sabella, with her too pretty hair, which she had obviously had colored. How had he never known she colored her hair? It was still bemusing to watch her, those darker blond tresses longer now, running around flipping that braid over her shoulder.

She didn't do the manicures and the pedicures anymore. And he had to admit, he might miss that a little bit, but only because he'd always enjoyed knowing his "girly" wife had everything she needed to be girly.

Finding out she wasn't so girly, and that she had held back

parts of herself, both infuriated him and made him determined to learn exactly what he hadn't known about her.

As he sat in the smoky, dimly lit bar later that night and
talked to men he didn't want to talk to as he played the
friendly curious mechanic, he couldn't get over the look on
her face earlier that day.

Pure, livid determination. She hadn't shown her anger,
but there wasn't a doubt left in his or Rory's minds that she
wasn't serious. To-the-bone serious. She would sell out her
share of the garage and she would leave.

Backbone. She had backbone.

Why had she never shown that part of herself to him?
Why had she hidden herself?

Probably for the same reasons he had concealed the
darker parts of himself, he thought with an inner grimace. It
seemed he and Sabella both had held back during those first,
tempestuous years together. They'd only had two years together. Not long enough. Not nearly long enough for them to
really get to know each other.

"You know, the Black Collars, they don't like strangers in
town asking questions either," the retired ranch hand from
one of the outlying ranches commented as he and Noah
shared a beer at the end of the bar.

Jesse Bairnes was well known to Noah. A friend of Grandpop's that Noah remembered.

"They don't like a lot of people," Noah stated.

"Specially those different from them," Jesse said, his
voice pitched low. "I have a friend, pure Irish. His son has
lived in hell." Jesse shook his head at that.

In hell? Grant Malone?

"How so?" Noah asked him.

Jesse shook his head, his lined expression somber. "Lost
his whole damned family," he said, sighing. "Ever' one of
'em. The militia only leaves him alone 'cause he keeps his
head down, doesn't try to do anything more than run his
ranch, and killin' him wouldn't be enough for them. But they
got nothing else to hurt him with now." The old man
shrugged. "Shame, it was."

Noah stared down at his beer. Jesse couldn't be talking about the Malones.

"How do they get the power to do this?" he murmured. "I've not heard much about them and I've made my rounds of Texas plenty of times." Hell, he'd lived here, worked here, loved here. How hadn't he known?

"Quiet is always better." Jesse shrugged. "They're paranoid 'bout secrecy. The only ones that talk are the young dumb ones. They weed those out as they try to climb in the ranks. No one that cain't keep their traps shut makes it to those hunts I hear they do." Jesse turned back to him, his faded dark eyes somber. "They been huntin' for years and no one cared till they killed some FBI agents. Now ain't that a shame?"

Noah nodded. "That's a hell of a shame."

He finished his beer, completed his conversation with Jesse, and headed from the bar. The late-evening visits to the local watering hole were giving him a new insight into the changes that had been developing in his hometown. Or perhaps, more accurately, the underground intricacies that were finally showing themselves after decades.

He was nearly certain now that the Black Collar Militia's ranks were still small enough, here at least, that pinpointing one of them wasn't going to be easy. That or they were hiding themselves better than he could have imagined.

Though, after his search of Mike Conrad's office, he knew at least one of the members. Black masks for the members, black collars for the victims. How the hell had he managed to keep his eyes closed to what was going on in his own hometown? This wasn't a new organization. It was something that had been building, growing, for decades.

An even better question, he told himself, was, how had he managed to miss what kind of a man Mike was through the years of their friendship? He had trusted the other man. Laughed with him, drank with him, and he hadn't suspected. If someone had told him Mike was involved with a militia, he would have laughed at the thought.

The militia wasn't something new. Hell, there were plenty

of militias with varying agendas all over the west, but few that were walking in the footsteps of this one.

Late-night hunts for illegals. Kidnapping legal aliens and taking them into the canyons of the national park to torture and murder them.

Their agenda was an atrocity to humanity.

Leaving the bar, he almost paused. The second he stepped into the sultry, late-summer heat, he could feel his skin prickling.

He almost grinned. The need to expend the energy raging through him was about to find an outlet. Evidently, someone didn't like the questions he had been asking over the weeks. Or the people he was talking to. He didn't tense, he didn't do anything to overtly prepare his body for what was to come. He knew where it was, as though the pores of his skin were soaking in the danger lying in wait in the parking lot.

Bullet or gang? Gun or knife?

He couldn't feel a scope on his head, that left other means. And oh, he would feel a scope on his head. He had learned well that feeling under Fuentes's tutelage. Diego Fuentes had liked to play with his captives. The gun sighted on him, the bullet burying within inches of his head as he was chained to a wall, blindfolded, unable to avoid whatever was coming.

Yeah, Noah knew the feel of gun sights. Just as he knew the scent of violence. And he was moving closer toward it.

He was ready for the dark figure that jumped out at him. The knife barely grazed his bicep as he used his attacker's momentum to jerk him to the side, break his arm, and pull the knife from his grip.

Noah left him where he was lying and he gripped the knife, steel lying along his wrist as he lifted his arm, and braced himself.

The shadows flowed from the darkness. Black masks, knives instead of guns.

"You want to leave town, Blake," one of the shadows rasped through the darkness as half a dozen darkened figures began to surround him.

"Oh, I don't know," Noah drawled. "I think I like this

little town. Lots of excitement. I might stick around a
while."

He let them surround him. He could feel it now, the blood
surging through him, cold hard death filling him. He
wouldn't be taken again, never again. And he wouldn't be
defeated. Diego Fuentes hadn't managed to break him and
he would be damned if a few home-grown terrorists were
going to get the best of him.

"Sticking around could be bad for your health," another
informed him with a nasally accent.

"Are you boys here to chat or to give me a good time?"
He grinned back at them. "The odds are almost even. Let's
play."

"Six to one," another said with a laugh. "You're outnum-
bered, motherfucker."

And Noah chuckled. They had no idea, no clue what a
killer he could be. But he knew. He knew, because he had been
killing for far too many years before this little show-and-tell
began.

"Then come get me," he invited them with a little flicking
motion of his hands. "If you can."

They were good. The shuffle, the life-or-death dance that
ensued spiked the adrenaline always ready to pour into him.
He used it, felt the power feeding into his muscles as they
came at him.

Steel met steel. Noah kicked his attackers' feet out from
under them, jumped aside, and met the next. He didn't kill
them. He didn't want them dead. He wanted them alive and
bleeding. He wanted to know who to follow, who to suspect
when it was over, and the bandages, the injuries, couldn't be
hidden.

He wanted to leave witnesses and he wanted the bastards
to remember what the hell they were dealing with.

He buried the knife in one attacker's thigh, stole another,
and sliced across another man's midriff. Cutting them a little
here and there, relishing the feel of steel biting into flesh and
the sound of grunts, painful cries, and the snap of bones
when he could manage it.

They were down from six to two. He stared back at the one facing him and smiled at the smell of blood.

"Do you want to keep this up?" he asked the other man, staring into dark eyes, memorizing the curve of the face beneath the stretchy black mask. "Come on, asshole. I can slice and dice all night long."

He proved his point. He sliced a forearm, his knife bit through denim and cut a deep furrow across another thigh as he kicked out, brought down the bastard trying to blindside him. Noah stole his blade and buried it in the other man's shoulder.

"That's going to hurt," he said with a chuckle, jumping back and watching as the others limped away.

The last one pulled a gun.

Spinning, Noah jumped, buried his foot in the bastard's stomach, gripped his wrist and twisted until the gun dropped to the ground.

He took a blow to the kidney and grunted, his elbow slamming into the man's throat. Bastards. They should have used the gun first.

He followed the elbow to the throat with a fist to the man's gut, knocked him backward and then watched as he turned tail and ran to join his little buddies. Headlights flashed in front of him as he rolled and lifted the gun from the gravel before jumping to his feet.

Noah stepped back between several other vehicles, ducked, and watched the truck hauling his new buddies squeal out of sight.

He breathed in deeply, flexed his shoulder, and knew his own aches and pains would show up soon. Hell, he hadn't come out of the fight unscathed. He could feel the blood soaking his shoulder, arm, and side. Those knives had been razor sharp and there had been too many to avoid all at once.

He grinned at the thought of that as he pulled his keys from his jeans and found the Harley. Checking it out, he didn't take long to find the little device created to trigger a spark into the gas line. He would have been toast if that little baby had gone off.

Unlocking a saddlebag, he slid it inside along with the handgun, checked out the cycle again then watched as Nicolas eased from the shadows at the back of the bar. His eyes met Noah's for one long, telling moment.

The big Russian had watched the fight, obviously. His gaze flickered over Noah.

"You're bleeding. Do you need a ride?" His voice was low as he approached Noah.

"I'll be fine."

Nik inclined his head then and continued on to the four-wheel-drive pickup he was driving. At this point, they couldn't afford to show an association. If Noah had been in danger of losing, Nik would have stepped forward. But not until then.

Noah straddled the motorcycle and started the motor as he put it in gear and headed for the apartment.

He could feel the blood trickling beneath his clothes, dampening them, and now he wished he'd killed at least one of the sons of bitches. Because they'd definitely messed up a hell of a plan for tonight. That of visiting his wife.

That plan was about to be axed, and that just pissed him off. So maybe she could handle the sight of the blood, but she was going to demand answers. And answers weren't something Noah was ready to give.

CHAPTER THIRTEEN

Sabella waited. She watched the window, listened carefully through dinner, and by the time she heard the Harley's hard throbbing purr pulling in behind the garage, she was furious.

It was after midnight.

She paced the living room, pausing at the windows and staring down at the garage apartment. There weren't any lights on. What man didn't turn on the lights when he arrived home?

Except, her husband. Nathan hadn't needed lights either.

She was nervous and she couldn't explain why. The more she stared down at the apartment the more the impulse to go down to him filled her.

The sexual crisis was over, she told herself. She'd had him, she should be okay now. Except she wasn't, and this wasn't just about the sex. It was about the pounding in her head, pushing her to go to him, to check on him.

Hell, he was over thirty, he didn't need a keeper.

He was thirty-four.

She pressed her hands to her stomach, over the thin sleeveless T-shirt she wore. He was the same age as her husband.

Sabella shook her head. She wasn't going there and she wasn't going to go down to that apartment to have sex with him either, she told herself as she slipped her sneakers on and tied them.

Grabbing her keys from her purse, she left the house and within minutes she was pulling her little car in behind the garage.

She had the key to the apartment in her hand. She shouldn't just walk in on him, she told herself, even as she moved quickly up the back steps to the deck. After all, he could have brought a friend back with him. He could be busy. In the shower. Any number of things. But she jammed the key into the door, stepped inside, and before she could gasp found herself jerked inside, the door slamming closed as she was pushed against the wall.

Dangerous, tense. The hard arm that lay across her neck was Noah's, the almost feverish glitter in his navy blue eyes was predatory, intense.

"Do you like living dangerously?" he asked her softly, his face too close to hers, his hard body, mostly naked, pressing into hers. "I'm not to desecrate that hallowed marriage bed of yours, but you can slip in here any time you please?"

His voice was grating. It raked across her nerves, fired nerve synapses that triggered chills racing across her body as she stared up at him through the darkness.

His arm slid from across her throat, but he didn't release her. His hands gripped her hips and jerked her up to him, even as another gasp parted her lips.

He wasn't just mostly naked. He was naked. And hard. The full, pounding length of his cock pressed into her lower stomach as he watched her with heated, absorbed interest.

"We needed to talk." Her hands pressed against his shoulders, and it took only a second for awareness to seep into her brain.

She felt the slight flinch as she pressed against him, as though the flesh were tender. He was damp, he'd obviously come from the shower, she could feel the water on his flesh, and something slick, perhaps remnants of soap. His hair was wet, his shadowed expression was harsh.

"You're hurt." She pressed against his other shoulder. "Noah, what happened?"

"Not yet," he growled.

"What do you mean not—" Yet.

He stole the words with his kiss. His lips lowered to hers, took them, sipped at the curves, and a low, male groan of need rumbled in his throat.

Parted lips tugged the lower curve, his tongue flicked over it as her own parted, to breathe she told herself. Just to breathe, not so that hot, hungry tongue could flick against them, taste her.

She felt her heart rate spike.

"Noah, are you okay?"

"Later." His lips sealed hers, slanted across them, and ate into her with hungry, heated demand.

Sabella whimpered at the pleasure. She had lied to herself. She knew she had. She hadn't come down here to inform him of anything, she had come for this.

"Look at how you're dressed," he growled, his lips moving from hers to her jaw, her cheek. "Short little shorts." His hand slid down her stomach to cup the wet heat between her thighs, beneath the silky stretch material of her shorts. "Snug little shirt." And she hadn't worn a bra. She sometimes slept in these clothes. They were thin and comfortable, too thin, because the heat of his palm against her mound was making her crazy.

The heel of his hand rotated, pressed.

"You're hurt," she gasped. "What happened?"

"Nothing."

"Noah . . ."

"God, yes, say my name like that again," he growled. "Tell me you want me, Sabella. Hot and wild, all over again. Pounding inside you, stretching that sweet, hot little pussy all around me."

Her breath caught. She could feel his blood beneath her hand, his naked cock through the layer of material separating them.

"Noah, stop this. Are you bleeding?" She thought maybe she could smell a hint of blood.

"No. Trust me. Just a scratch." His teeth raked over her jaw and she shuddered at the sensation, like little tingles of electricity raking over her, through her.

"What kind of scratch?" she moaned.

"You can bandage me up." His voice throbbed, became deeper, harder. "Later."

"Noah." She breathed his name as she felt his hand move, sliding from between her thighs only to push beneath her shorts and panties to fill his hand with the swollen, wet flesh beneath.

"You're wet, Sabella." His fingers tunneled into the slit, slid through the slick cream that gathered there. "Tell me you want me. Ask me to fuck you."

She was panting for breath. Pressed against the kitchen wall, all she could think about was feeling him inside her, around her.

"I want your mouth on my dick again."

He shocked her with the blunt, naughty words. "I want to watch you going down on me, feel your mouth sucking the head of my cock again. God, it was so good, coming in your mouth like that, watching you love it."

His finger pierced inside her. One finger, sliding in deep, rasping over tender nerve endings, as the heel of his palm pressed and rotated against her clit.

She was shaking. He was bleeding, he was hurt. She should be more concerned with forcing him to let her see what kind of damage he had done than she was with his finger, pumping, inside her.

Her eyes closed, her legs shifted wider, and a tremulous cry left her lips as he used his finger to drive her crazy. Sliding in slow and deep, his fingertip reaching high inside her, finding that spot, that one spot. And rubbing.

"Noah. It's so good." She ground her head against the wall, felt her knees weakening. "It's so good."

"So damned good," he amended. "You're wet and tight around my finger, Sabella. Do you want to come for me, baby? Do you want to make those sweet little sounds in your throat that hit my senses like wildfire just before you come for me? Do you want to come for me, baby? All over my fingers? Do you want to make me go crazy for just a taste of that sweet little pussy?"

Oh God. Oh God. He shouldn't talk to her like that. She could feel her moisture flowing, soaking his fingers, her hips moving as she thrust against his stroking fingertip.

"Oh, now there's a good girl," he groaned. "Fuck my fingers, Sabella. Let me feel you come around them."

She whimpered. This was too wicked. It was too hot. She had never done anything like this, never heard words like that whispered from a man's lips as he touched her.

"Tell me," he crooned in her ear. "Talk to me, baby. Tell me you want it. Beg me to fuck you with my fingers and I'll give you another. I'll push two fingers inside you. Wouldn't you like that? Don't you want to burn for me?"

He couldn't be serious? He wouldn't be?

"I could come just like this." He nipped her ear, pressed his cock against her hip as she almost melted. "All I'd need is your sweet little voice talking me through it."

He licked the sensitive flesh beneath her ear, raked the flesh with his teeth.

"This is crazy," she moaned.

"Tell me it's hot," he demanded, his breathing heavy, harsh in the stillness of the night.

"Oh Noah, it's so hot." She felt the sensitive internal muscles clenching around him, felt the punch of sensation to her womb as the words tore from her lips.

He jerked against her, his finger pressing deeper before pumping inside her in hard, desperate strokes.

"Don't stop." She wanted to scream, but she could barely manage a broken cry when he buried deep again and stilled.

"Tell me to fuck you with my fingers." He bit her neck and she arched against him. "Tell me you want two fingers inside you. Tell me to make you burn, Sabella."

"Fuck me," she groaned, feeling the heat rising inside her. "Please, Noah, now."

"More." The harsh demand in his voice rasped over her senses. "Give me more, Sabella."

She cried out. It was too wicked. Too wicked and too hot.

"Two fingers," she gasped. "Noah, please, I want two fingers inside me."

His finger jerked back, and when it returned, there were two. Two pressing into her, spreading her further apart, stretching the muscles and sensitizing her further.

Sabella cried out as she felt the moisture that rushed through her vagina sliding over his fingers as they moved slow and easy inside her.

"I want to come," she whispered. "Let me come, Noah."

He groaned, growled. He pressed his fingers high and hard inside her and she nearly, just almost exploded around them.

"Take your shirt off." He eased back, gave her just enough room to stare up at the glittering wild fire in his eyes. "Take it off. I want to see your nipples."

"Noah."

"God, sweet hard, rosy pink little nipples. I want to suck them. Take the damned shirt off." His voice hardened, the hunger tearing from him was washing through her, sizzling through her veins and her pussy.

Shaking, her ragged breaths almost moans, she gripped the hem of her shirt and pulled it over her head before dropping it to the floor.

"Keep your arms up," he demanded as she moved to lower them. "All the way up." One hand gripped her wrists and shoved them against the wall. "That's a girl. Up like that." His gaze raked across her nipples and she swore she could almost feel the touch of them.

"Why are you doing this?" she moaned.

"Because I want to eat you alive. I want to go down on you and taste all that wild hot cream covering my fingers right now. I want to eat it from you, Sabella. Lick it with my tongue and devour you."

She jerked against him.

"When I'm done, I want to watch you go down on me. Watch my cock sink into your pretty lips and I want to fuck your mouth until I'm shooting everything I have down your throat." His fingers moved inside her, the sound of the damp caresses filling her ears, whipping through her mind.

"Do you want that, baby?"

"Yes. Oh yes." She wanted that. She wanted it so bad.

She felt her shorts easing over her hips as his head lowered. He bent his knees enough to allow his lips to catch the viciously tight nub of her nipple between them as his fingers caressed and rotated and her knees weakened with the extremity of the pleasure. She wanted him inside her so bad, filling her. She wanted his lips all over her, hers all over him. She wanted every blistering act he was whispering in her ears.

She jerked as his mouth consumed her aching nipple. Felt the surge of electric shock as it traveled through her system. She lifted against him, desperate, eager for more.

Noah was lost in a world of sensation. The earlier violence, the racing adrenaline in his system did this. For the past years, recovery had been hell. Retraining had burned his mind with the surge of lust so hard, so powerful, that no amount of jacking off could ease it. He'd been half insane more than once, for this.

Sabella. In his arms. Hot and wild for him, whispering her naughty little secrets in his ears. Demanding he take her. That he do all the wicked, carnal acts that had filled his head while under the influence of the aphrodisiac Diego Fuentes had pumped into his body.

Now here she was and he was on fire for her. Blazing. Burning out of control. Two fingers shoved inside her hot pussy, feeling the burn of her body as he sucked her hard little nipples.

Everything about his Sabella was little, compared to him. So sweetly curved and delicate, and that will of iron he was glimpsing only made him harder.

"Noah, this is killing me," she moaned at his ear, her hot breath searing his flesh. "You're teasing me to death."

Just a little more. He groaned around her nipple, licked it, rasped it. He wanted to hear more. Wanted to hear her voice broken with lust, demanding and carnal.

"Tell me how to take you." He nipped the curve of her breast. "Tell me how you want it."

She shuddered, and he almost lost it when he felt her juices flood his fingers.

"Hard," she panted. "So hard. Now. Fuck me now."

"Against the wall? Here?"

"Oh God. Anywhere," she wailed. "Damn you. Give it to me. Now."

"Are you hot enough for it yet?" He kissed her shoulder, nipped it. "I don't think you're hot enough yet."

He wanted more. He needed the words. He had never needed the words before, but he did now. He wanted her hot enough to forget herself, to forget the memories of how he used to love her, to accustom herself to the bleak, dark lust that consumed him now.

"I'm hot enough," she moaned.

"Tell me how hot you are." He wrapped his free arm around her hips and lifted her to him, stumbling to the table, ignoring her shock as he set her naked ass on the edge and knelt between her thighs. "You're not hot enough. Let me help you out with that."

He laid his lips against the swollen folds and had to grip the base of his cock to hold back his come. God, he was going to blow. He could feel it, building in his balls, throbbing at the head of his cock.

She tasted so sweet. Her thighs parted as he lifted one small foot and placed it on his shoulder, opening her further.

The light was better here, but still not good enough for her to the see the damage he had been trying to clean up. Several of the cuts were almost deep enough for stitches. He needed to be in the command center letting someone patch him up. Instead, he was here, his lips buried in his wife's pussy and loving every second of it.

He licked and lapped at the little mound. She was so sweet, the flavor of her burst against his tongue and he was ravenous. He stabbed inside the fluttering opening, feeling her clench, hearing her moan as she leaned back, allowing him greater access to the treat that was fast becoming as addictive as any drug.

Ah hell. He wanted to lick her forever. He wanted to immerse his senses in the tangy bite, the sweet soft flavor and the clean feminine scent of her. He wanted her, for breakfast, lunch, dinner, a midnight snack, and everything in between.

"Talk to me." The words were hard, brutally torn from his lips as he moved them to the hard bud of her clit. "Tell me you like it. Tell me to eat you. To suck you forever."

He couldn't wait much longer. He wanted to tear the words from her lips. He had dreamed, fantasized.

"Noah, lick my clit," she moaned. "Roll your tongue on it."

Ah God. Yes. She loved that, didn't she? The way he rolled his tongue over her clit. He gave it to her. He gripped her thigh with one hand, pressed her legs further apart and gave her what she needed.

He pumped his cock, a wild, agonizing sound of arousal falling from his lips as her hips jerked, arched, and she cried out his name again.

"Noah. Oh yes. Like that." Her voice was high and thin. "Oh God. I'm going to come for you."

"Not yet." He pulled back and she almost screamed. Her hands caught in his hair, tangled in it, and she jerked him back to the hot, humid flesh awaiting his tongue, his lips.

"Lick my pussy." She was lost now, lost in the pleasure, and he shoved his tongue inside her, fucked her with it and tasted all that hot, sweet cream flowing from her.

Ah hell. He was going to come in his hand at this rate. He didn't want to come in his hand. He wanted to be high and deep inside her. Buried as deep as a man could get in a woman, filling her, marking her.

He wanted to brand her with his seed. He wanted to be so deep inside her that she never forgot who owned her body. Never.

But first, he had to tear himself away from her taste. And ah sweet merciful heaven, her taste. Her taste was so hot on his tongue, liquid and filled with life. He didn't want to leave it. He didn't want to stop.

"Give it to me." Her voice seared his senses. "Damn you, give it to me now, Noah. Fill me with your cock. Make me scream for you. Oh God, I'll scream for you, just do me now."

Noah jerked to his feet, his hand still wrapped around his cock, his senses filled with the taste of her, the heat of her. And he pressed forward.

He watched her face, her eyes. Rolled the head of his cock against her clit and watched her pant, watched as her hand pressed against her stomach, then, as he lowered himself, pressed against her entrance, those pretty, graceful fingers moved to her clit. Shyly. Hesitantly.

During their marriage, he had never allowed her to touch herself while he was taking her. He had taken full responsibility for her pleasure as well as his own. But she wasn't waiting now, and the sight of it nearly had him erupting. With no more than the tip of his cock pressed inside her, he was losing it.

He watched her fingers as he pressed deeper, his fingers tight at the base of his shaft to hold back the furious release he could feel pounding in his skull.

"Do it." His voice was hard, thick. "Use your fingers. Show me what you like, baby. Damn you. I'm going to fuck you so hard and so deep you'll never deny me again. Do you hear me, Sabella. Never."

She had denied him that morning. Denied his place in her bed, denied what he knew was between them. Why didn't matter. He was deceiving her, he knew it. Lying to her in the most elemental of ways, and he couldn't say the words to fix that. But he wouldn't let her deny this.

He gripped her hips. Watched those pretty fingers. Ah God, so graceful, so slender, sliding into the curls at the top of her mound, opening herself.

He felt on fire. His cock was a flame and it was destroying him. He pressed in, gritting his teeth, grimacing at the complete, unadulterated pleasure in just feeling her. Seeing her. He pushed in, pumping in short, hard strokes, working inside her as her fingers slid to her clit, circled it and became wet, glistening with her juices.

His stomach clenched. His balls went so tight they were in agony.

"Stroke it," he snarled. "Finger your clit, Sabella. I'm not going to last. Ah hell." He shoved in deep, to the hilt, felt her muscles fluttering around him, gripping, clenching.

He couldn't stop. He held her tight, feeling her legs wrap around his hips, her heels pressing into his ass as he began pumping inside her. Hard and deep.

She was crying his name. *His* name. Not her husband's name. Sweet God have mercy on him, how had he stayed away from her? How had he remained separated from this woman for so many years? For even a day longer than he'd had to.

"Take me," he groaned, barely biting back the words that would betray who he was. What he was. "Take me, damn you. Take all of me. All of me."

She was arching, clenching, her pussy so tight, contracting around him as he felt her explode from the inside out.

Sabella existed in sensation. She was sensation. Pure, electric, nothing but energy and pulsing consuming pleasure as she felt herself coming apart in Noah's arms. Dying in his arms and being reborn. Screaming out his name and feeling *that* pleasure. A pleasure she had sworn could never be felt twice. Only with one man. Only with one heart.

But she felt it pulsing through her and into him. Pulsing through him and into her. His come spurted inside her, deep and hot, filling her, sinking into her and becoming a part of her.

She jerked, twisted, arched to the extremity of the orgasm racing through her, and then finally collapsed back on the table. Sweat dampened, too tired to move, to breathe, to exist without his help.

And he was still hard.

She opened her eyes as he lifted her to him, remained connected to her in the most elemental fashion and carried her through the dark apartment to the big bedroom at the end of the building.

He laid her back in the bed, and moved within her again. Blue eyes so dark it hurt to stare into them. His hands hard, his voice so rough and gravelly it was almost another sensation against her overly sensitized flesh.

"I need you." He shook his head, jaw clenching. "I need you more."

Forever.

Sabella shook the thought away. Nothing lasted forever except her love for the husband that had been taken from her. Nothing lasted forever.

But as the night deepened and dawn came closer, it felt like forever. And when he finally collapsed beside her, wet with sweat, his arms dragging her to his chest, his breathing finally easing as she slipped into exhausted sleep, she wondered if maybe, a little bit, he did feel like *her* Nathan.

CHAPTER FOURTEEN

Sabella was furious the next morning after returning to the house, showering, and dressing for work. A scratch, he had told her the night before. He wasn't hurt, he was fine.

It was more than a damned scratch. She had caught him when she awoke trying to bandage himself, thinking he could hide from her. Damn him.

There were three long slices on his upper body. One across his bicep, one at his abdomen, and again at the hip, and they were deep. Deep enough she had insisted he go to the doctor.

He had refused. When he had pinned her with the blazing determination to do it all his own way, for a second she could have sworn he had the same look in his eye, the same tense set of his face and body, the same shape of his jaw, that her husband had had when he was angry and determined in the face of her anger.

It had been frightening to see, to acknowledge. Because sometimes, she saw those little things, and she was terrified she was trying to turn Noah into the man she had lost simply to justify her need, her overhelming hunger for him.

And of course, Noah wouldn't tell her how it had happened or even what had happened. A "disagreement," he'd said.

She was so pissed that she walked to the garage later after she had returned to the house, rather than driving, simply to give herself time to cool down just a little bit more.

Entering the garage, she stared as Noah stepped from the open doors, wiping his hands on a shop towel as he lifted his hand and watched Toby as he approached on foot from the other side of the street.

Sometimes, Toby walked to work. He said it kept him in shape. She watched as Noah walked along the cracked blacktop in front of the station, eyes narrowed, body tense.

Sabella paused, looking around, wondering what had caught his attention, but she couldn't see anything. She shook her head and took another step, watching as Toby strolled to the corner of the street. He stepped off the curb and started across the wide road when she heard it. A motor gunning.

A black car, low and fast, windows tinted, squealed from its parked position and aimed for Toby.

"Toby!" She screamed his name as the car barreled toward him.

Toby's head jerked up, expressing surprise at the sound, and he turned, facing the vehicle speeding toward him.

Sabella ran. She would never reach him in time. She could see, knew the driver had every intention of running him over. She wouldn't make it to the end of the driveway, Toby wouldn't reach the sidewalk.

She saw, almost in slow motion as Toby jerked and tried to run. The car followed, heading straight for him as Sabella screamed and tried to run faster.

The morning sun beat down on her, fear and rage pumped through her. She couldn't let this happen. She couldn't let someone else she cared about be taken. Toby was a kid, just a kid.

As she screamed Toby's name again, horrified, Noah streaked across the road, seconds, oh God, seconds in front of the car, his broad, powerful arm wrapping around Toby's thin waist and threw them both across the road, rolling over the sidewalk and into the gully beside it as the car's tires hit the sidewalk seconds behind them and then roared off.

The big, white blond giant Rory had hired in place of the mechanic he had fired was across the road in a flash. He jumped into the gully as Sabella raced across the street.

Noah. Oh God. Oh God. Noah. He had to be okay. She had seen him. Hadn't she seen him roll to that gully before the car hit the sidewalk?

She didn't realize she was screaming his name until someone grabbed her from behind, holding her back as the mechanics raced into the incline.

"Noah!" she screamed, sobbing, clawing at the arms holding her back. "Noah!"

"Sabella. Stop. Enough!" Rory shook her, his voice harder than she had ever heard, his hands rough as he jerked around, glaring down at her.

"Let me go!" Her fists struck out, one landing on his jaw, knocking him back, as she tore herself away from him and stumbled over the incline.

Toby was sitting up, dazed, but Noah wasn't moving. Blood seeped down his arm, darkened his shirt at his waist, his thigh.

The big mechanic, Nik, was leaning over him, slapping his face with hard, rough hands.

"Don't you touch him!" She barreled into the bigger man, threw him off balance. "Call an ambulance!" she barked to the men standing around staring at her as though she were crazy. "Now or I'll fire every friggin' one of you!"

She was running her hands over his body. She lifted the edge of his shirt to see the blood oozing from the vicious cuts at his side and on his abdomen from the night before. His jeans were damp with blood. He was losing blood. And a lot of it from his leg. Damn him. Damn him. She knew it was worse than he had tried to convince her this morning. Knew it.

She tore her overshirt off, ripped it up the seams and packed the cotton at his waist, applying pressure to it before shoving the other cloth to the blond giant staring at her with cold, seething pale eyes, his lips parting as though to say something. "His shoulder. Or get out of the way and I'll handle it."

He was pressing it to the wound in Noah's shoulder as her hands examined Noah's body. His arms, ribs, upper legs. Nothing seemed broken.

She stared at the men around her. "Ambulance."

"No ambulance."

Her head jerked around at the sound of his voice, the seething anger burning inside her as Noah blinked up at her, dazed.

"I'm okay." He shook his head and glared past her at Nik. "Did you get the license?"

"No plates," the other man rumbled. "If she'll let me haul you up I'll take you to my place. Get you patched up if you don't want to go to the hospital."

"Like hell, he's going to a hospital." Sabella glared at both men, pain and fear raging through her, mixing with the anger.

"No hospital, Sabella." Noah pushed himself up. "Where's Toby?"

Toby was fine. He was still sitting on the incline, staring around him in shock.

"Dude. Some bitch tried to run me over," he exclaimed.

"Some bastard more likely," Noah muttered, easing himself up, his gaze pinning Sabella.

His eyes were fevered, glowing. Something not wholly natural was blazing in them, holding her speechless as the mechanics rushed around him.

"Come here." He held his arm out to her, his eyes demanding. "Come here, Sabella."

She moved to him slowly, watching his eyes, just his eyes. His arm moved around her, jerked her to him. If Nik hadn't been bracing them they would have both landed in the dirt.

He lowered his lips to her ear. "Stay steady. No ambulance. No hospital. You can't, under any circumstances, allow anyone to believe I'm not in fighting shape. Don't fight me, baby. Not yet. I'll explain everything later."

She shuddered at the sound of his grating voice but nodded. He wouldn't go to a hospital, didn't want a doctor. And she wanted to know why.

"Let's go." Rory on one side, Nik on the other. Sabella felt crushed as they moved Noah across the road, his arm so tight around her back she wondered if he even realized his own strength.

"We need to get you to my place at least," Nik stated again. "I have a friend that can patch you up if you're this determined."

Noah shook his head. "The apartment."

"I'll get him upstairs," Nik growled at Sabella, a hiss of sound no one else would have heard but her and Rory. "We'll have help en route. Rory, keep your ass down here and hold down the fort. Take care of the sheriff, you know he'll be here."

What was going on? What the hell did Nik and Noah have in common besides cars? Cars and dangerous eyes.

They dragged Noah to the back stairs, the weakness she could feel in him terrifying her. Her hand was wet with his blood, she could smell the scent of it, sharp and metallic, as Nik all but carried Noah up the stairs.

"Keys," Nik ordered.

Sabella dug into Noah's pocket for his keys, barely holding back a gasp as she encountered the steel-hard thickness of his cock on the other side of the pocket lining.

Pulling the keys free, she stared up at him again. His eyes were so hot, so bright, lust building in his gaze despite the weakness of his body. They weren't dark eyes, not the navy blue she was used to. They were bright, almost sapphire. Almost. Oh God. They were almost, just almost Irish eyes.

She forced herself to turn away, to shove the key into the lock, and would have entered the apartment if Noah hadn't jerked her back.

Leaning against the porch railing, he jerked his head to the inside of the apartment in some indication to Nik. Nik slid into the apartment, and the movement reminded Sabella of a predator, or of all those damned government documentaries where she watched federal or military agents slipping into unknown territory.

They were agents of some sort. She wasn't stupid; she had been married to a SEAL, for God's sake. What made them think she hadn't paid attention to her husband?

Even at home her husband had been careful, checking the house out, checking windows and doors, his eyes always hard, wary, until he knew beyond a shadow of a doubt everything was safe.

Sabella would sit in the hall, file her fingernails, or pretend to. She had always paid more attention to the man she loved than she had to her nails. It had been a part of being married to him. One she had accepted even as she lusted after his tight, hard body while he looked all dangerous and predatory.

"Let's get him inside." Nik stepped out no more than a minute later and helped her steady Noah.

They pulled him into the apartment and back to the bedroom. When she stripped the sheets back she stared down at them in horror.

There was so much blood. So much blood. Blood he had to have shed through the night.

She turned and stared at him, watching as Nik helped him lie back then bent and unlaced his boots before taking them off.

"Go into the living room." Noah was staring at her, hungry, fierce. "Go now, Sabella."

"Why didn't you tell me?" she whispered, her voice hoarse. "Why didn't you tell me you were bleeding like this?"

Nik looked up at her, then to the bed. "How much blood was smeared on you when you woke up?" he asked.

"I washed it off her while she slept," Noah snapped, still glaring back at her. "Go into the living room and no farther. Go now."

She shook her head, moving instead to grip the hem of his shirt and pull it off.

His hand jerked out, catching her wrist. "Do you remember what happened last night?"

She stared back at him silently, her breathing harsh, heart racing in fear.

"It will happen again. And I won't give a shit who's watching. We have company coming. Let Nik know when you hear them coming to the door. Don't open it, you understand me?"

"Ease off, Noah," Nik muttered, obviously wary, concerned.

"Answer me, Sabella," he growled. "Do you understand me?"

She tugged at her wrist, jerked it, but his hold was like iron.

"Sabella." He growled her name, an order, a hint of determination in it that seemed like a slap from the past. "Do you understand me?"

"I'll wait in the living room," she whispered hoarsely. "When I hear someone on the deck, I'll let Nik know."

He held her gaze; those eyes, they were molten, like blue fire staring back at her.

Finally, he nodded slowly and let her go, finger by finger, releasing his hold on her until she was drawing back, retreating slowly from the bedroom, walking through the hall, and standing silently in the kitchen.

She was the widow of a Navy SEAL. She knew agents from various law enforcement agencies, her father had been a detective with the Atlanta police department. She knew men like this. She knew how they moved, she knew how they looked, and she knew when she was being lied to.

She swallowed tightly and stared around the living room. It was dim. Curtains were closed, she knew the windows would be firmly locked.

What sort of government agents could they be? She searched her mind frantically then sat down on the couch, trembling. Border patrol maybe? No, they seemed too hard eyed for border patrol. The only thing she could think of were the deaths that had been reported in the park in the past year or so. Illegals that had been hunted down in the dark. And there had been that girl that went missing from the college a few months before. A pretty girl, Lisa? She had been a friend of Toby's.

FBI? Maybe CIA. She could see a CIA agent with that hard, stony gaze, with the power in every command he issued. Or a SEAL.

A shudder swept through her. A SEAL acted like that. But

SEALs wouldn't be investigating anything in Texas. They were a strike force, not an investigative agency. Noah was something similar at least. An agent of some sort. Perhaps a former SEAL. A former SEAL as tall as her husband, the same age as her husband would have been, one that held her as Nathan had and one whose eyes had bled with sapphire fire just moments before. The same color as Nathan's.

She shook her head. God, was she so messed up that she had to believe Noah was Nathan to excuse her attraction, her hunger for him? There was no other excuse. There were vague similarities, she knew. Even Duncan had seen them. But he wasn't Nathan. Nathan was dead. The man she loved was gone. Wasn't he?

She felt the tension tearing through her, fighting to find the differences between Nathan and Noah. Noah was hard-core, Nathan had always been gentle in the bed. But she had sensed that darkness in him, had known there was more coming. Noah didn't hide it.

She nibbled at her thumbnail. Her Nathan hadn't been scarred. His voice had been lyrical, a pure dark sound that caressed her senses.

Nathan had twirled his wrench just as Noah now twirled it. And chewed gum when he worked in the garage.

She shuddered and pressed her hands to her stomach. That man in there was not her husband, because her husband would have never stayed away from her for six years. He would not have left her alone and grieving for him. He couldn't have.

Noah was an agent, he was just similar to Nathan sometimes, she told herself. Perhaps had the same training. So what was he doing in Alpine?

The militia. The Black Collar Militia was rumored to have been behind the deaths in the park lately. Illegals who were hunted down. There had been murmurs about it for years. It had to be that or drugs. And there were no drugs in her garage, she made sure of it.

She rubbed her hands together before wiping them over her face, realizing tears still tracked her flesh. She went to the kitchen drawer to get a dishtowel to wash her face. She pulled the top one free and noticed the odd arrangement, the slight hump in the middle. Drawing them aside, she found the gun.

Glock. She knew the type, the model. It was the same kind her husband had preferred. It was kept in the same place. What? Was there a damned class for where warriors hid their weapons?

Nathan had never realized that she knew exactly where his guns were hidden through the two years they were married. She hadn't bothered them, had never mentioned them, but she had always known how to find them.

She was aware of every place in the house where Nathan had a weapon hidden while they were married. And every place in the apartment. And this had been one of those places.

She pushed the drawer back slowly, still gripping the dishtowel as she moved to the sink and dampened it beneath the cold water.

She wasn't going to go searching the apartment. Not yet. She could feel the panic rising inside her now, slowly, insidiously. She had to catch her breath first.

Who was the man bleeding to death in the bedroom? Had he known Nathan? Had he researched her? Was that why he had come to her garage, why he had invaded her life?

Was she a part of it, somehow? Her garage?

She put the towel over her face and fought back the need to run, to hide. She had only hidden once in her life, those first three years of hell when nightmares and pain had seared every inch of her soul. When they had eased enough for her to function, she had come out of her bed, and had fought to rejoin the living.

For what? So another man, another adrenaline junkie, could walk into her life and destroy it?

The sound of vehicles pulling in behind the garage had her head jerking up. She was on her way to the bedroom when Nik came out of the room, caught her arm and dragged her back into the living room.

"Stay!" he mouthed, his rugged face tight, his body tense as he went to the door and cracked it open.

Sabella stood back and watched the men that came in. They stopped daily for gas. She didn't know their names, but they looked a hell of a lot different with their flat, hard gazes.

There were two strangers, and bringing up the rear were Ian Richards and his wife Kira. She almost laughed. Hysteria almost bloomed inside her as she met Kira's compassionate and knowing gaze. Ian Richards was involved in this, and so was his wife. And Sabella wanted to know why.

It wasn't as bad this time. Noah gripped the straps Nik had tied to the posts at the headboard, gritted his teeth, and endured the stitches as Micah sewed his flesh together. He could feel his blood burning in his veins, churning through him and raging into his cock.

Fucking whore's dust. Fucking Diego Fuentes. The bastard was still alive and grinning, protected by Homeland Security, as Noah lay in his own sweat and blood and fought to hold on to his sanity.

The doctors had warned him that the effects of the drug his body had been filled with for so long might never be totally gone. There were still traces of it. Especially after a hard surge of adrenaline as there had been last night. Fever only made it worse. The cuts in his body had been deeper than he had wanted to admit to, and stopping the flow of blood had been an on again, off again thing.

He had to still the surging lust beating in his brain somehow. He didn't want Sabella to see him like this. Like an animal, intent on nothing but sex. Hard. Fast. Driving sex. He'd used the last of the witches' brew of antibiotics, painkillers, and lust supressors that the Navy doctors had put together for him the night before. It hadn't helped.

"You shouldn't have come," he bit out to the Israeli Mossad agent, or former agent. Dead men. They were all fucking dead men now.

"Jordan called in the order." Micah kept his voice low. "We came in Travis's car. The garage isn't being watched. Travis had been watching for any eyes. You didn't pick up notice until that fight in the bar last night. Did you inject yourself when this happened?"

Noah nodded. "Last of it last night. It didn't do much."

"You'll need a larger dose. Ian should have more here soon. The new batch was flown in last night."

"You'll be noticed leaving," Noah bit out. "I can't trust all my mechanics. Sabella's going to have questions now."

"Rory has eyes like a hawk. Jordan called him first thing. He's watching everyone, keeping the boy inside. And you were advised to inform Ms. Malone of the status of this operation to begin with. She was given clearance for partial information, it's because of your stubbornness that she'll be pissed off now. You can deal with it. Now stop worrying. You sound like my mother."

"Fuck you."

"Wrong sex, big boy," he grunted. "I've a mind for a little satin flesh, not your tough hide."

"Bastard." Noah coughed out a laugh.

"Yeah, ain't we all." Micah grinned as he mangled his hopeless Texas accent all to hell.

Noah dug his head into the pillow as a punch of lust slammed into his balls. He swore he could smell Sabella's scent. It was making him mad with the need to fuck. The fever and adrenaline, twice, this close together, was too much. He thought he'd have time to get the refill on the injections whenever he was wounded. Evidently, he'd been wrong.

"Ian has your meds, Noah," Micah told him softly. "We can't give you anything for the pain until you get that, you know what that shit does to you. But the doctors sent some new shit, they seem to think they have a nice little concoction put together for that woody of yours and the pain as well."

Noah shook his head. "No more drugs." It would go away, it would ease, until he was as close to normal as possible. He'd fought this for too many years now. He was learning to get by. Or he had thought he was, until last night.

"We have to do something for the fever, Noah," Micah warned him, his black eyes concerned, worried. "There's antibiotics in it, a mix of painkillers. Same crap they used on you when you took that bullet three months ago. It eased it then. Let's give it a chance this time, okay?"

Nothing really eased it. Sometimes, the crap the Navy doctors came up with allowed him to keep his sanity, but it didn't ease the need. The fiery, bloodcurdling lust for his woman.

Not any woman. His woman. His wife.

As he blinked back the sweat from his eyes he loosened his grip on the straps and fought back the driving insanity. It had held him in a grip like iron for months after his rescue. Incessant, burning, the furious lust was like a vicious plague burning through his system.

All he needed was Sabella. If they would just get the hell away from him he could survive it. Let his sweet little wife wash over him like rain.

A ragged groan tore from his throat at the thought of her. So tight and hot, just flowing over him, sucking him into her and taking everything he had to give.

"There's Ian." Nik moved from the doorway and headed back into the apartment, where Sabella was.

Murderous jealousy rose inside him. He'd always had to fight his jealousy. He'd never let Sabella know it, had never shown it around her, but it had been like a growling animal inside him anytime, every time another man had been close enough to touch her.

And now Nik was in the other room with her. Big, blond, gentler no doubt. Noah doubted the Russian would take her without foreplay. Or that he would sit her on a table while he bled to death and care about nothing but burying his face between her legs.

"Whoa. Hold on there, Noah." Micah pushed him back to the bed as he surged upward. "Break my stitches and I'll knock your ass out like I did with the bullet."

That pierced the haze, a little.

Noah grunted a laugh. When the doctors refused to give him a painkiller and Noah refused to pass out from the pain, Micah had taken care of it. He'd gone behind the hospital gurney, behind Noah, and the hell if Noah knew how he'd done it, but after that, there was only the dark. And no pain.

He couldn't afford to lose consciousness this time. Sabella could be in danger. If Toby was in danger, then he knew Sabella would be. It was just a matter of time. God, he should have stayed the hell away from her.

"How's he doing?" Ian stepped into the room.

His voice was rough, almost as ragged as Noah's was now.

Noah stared up at his friend. When they were ten, Noah had heard Ian's screams piercing the desert surrounding his father's ranch. He'd forced his father from his bed, harassed and screamed until Grant Malone had followed him.

And they had found Ian, cradling his mother as her life nearly slipped away. Screaming. Enraged. His voice broken by the time they reached him.

They'd been best friends from that night. And that friendship had endured, even after Noah learned that Diego Fuentes was Ian's father. Even after Fuentes had nearly destroyed Noah.

"You look like shit," Noah growled as Ian moved to the bed, his eyes dark with pain, with regret.

"I should have killed the bastard while I had the chance," Ian said heavily. "I'm sorry, man. Fuentes should be dead."

Diego Fuentes was Ian's father. The man who had tortured Nathan, who had nearly destroyed him.

"Yeah, and once for me as soon as those bastards at Homeland Security lift the ban on him." Noah breathed in roughly before glaring back at Ian. "Get Sabella out of here, Ian. Get her to Jordan in the comm bunker. Keep her safe till this is through."

He could smell her, like sweet hot rain.

"It's bad this time," Micah murmured to Ian. "Doc send him some goodies?"

"Here." Ian tossed Micah the black leather bag he carried and turned back to Noah and stated, "Belle's not stupid, Noah. You know that. You'll have to give her the mission parameters at least. She and Rory both were cleared for that. She's probably already figured you're an agent of some sort anyway."

"I hate this shit." Noah rose up in the bed, glaring at both of them, ignoring Ian's warning as Micah shoved a syringe in his shoulder.

"Come on, Noah, it made it better last time." Ian breathed out roughly.

"The hell it did. Made it better for you guys because you couldn't hear me screaming," he snarled. "I heard it in my own fucking head."

"Do you want Sabella to hear it?" Micah asked him then.

Noah shook his head. "That's the only reason you got that needle anywhere close to me."

He lay back on the bed, glared at Micah as he inserted a second syringe. "I'm going to break your fingers. You won't be able to shove that shit in me then."

Micah grinned at him. It was the norm. They cursed, insulted each other, threatened to kill each other on a daily basis. It kept them alive.

"Keep chirping at me and I'll pump you so full of this shit I'll make Fuentes look like a choirboy. You got me?"

Noah nodded shortly, licked his dry lips, and breathed out. "Bastard."

"I can't take Belle to the bunker," Ian told him then. "You know we can't do that, Noah."

He closed his eyes. God, he wanted her safe. He wanted her away from his madness and away from the danger he had brought down on her and the questions he knew she was going to ask. Where the hell had his mind been? He should have never taken this mission. He should have gone to Siberia.

"We're tracking the car that went after Toby." Ian sat down in the chair by the bed. "Some of the mechanics thought they'd seen it last night, close to the bar. I'm guessing it's one of the yokels that attacked you."

Noah nodded jerkily. "Yeah, stupid bastards. Thought they could slice and dice me and run me the hell off. Toby was a message, they'll target friends next."

"They definitely sliced and diced you." Micah snorted. "I

have you all stitched and bandaged now, little soldier. You can go back and play with all the bad boys again tomorrow."

"Bite me, you half-breed little bastard," Noah said.

"He keeps forgetting I prefer the female persuasion." Micah laughed.

"Doesn't that go against your damned religion? Don't you have to be married first or some shit?" Noah bit out.

The general insults were a game. A tension stiller. Bitch at each other to take your mind off the pain. It was a head game, because it sure as hell didn't help the pain.

"What religion?" Micah rolled his black eyes. "Since joining up with you yoohoos, all my beliefs have been shot to hell."

"Yahoos," Ian corrected him, but his eyes were on Noah.

Slow easy breaths. Noah could smell Sabella with every breath he took. He could feel his blood pounding in his dick, the need racing through him as fresh, as violent, as it had been the first time Fuentes shoved a needle in his arm.

Noah dragged himself up on the bed, the fabric of his jeans cutting into his dick. Hell, he needed to fuck. This wasn't like the past six years when taking a woman meant breaking the vows he'd made to his wife. Now it would mean burying himself inside his wife. Feeling her tight and sweet around him.

It would mean loving her, touching her. It would be stilling the fire burning in his gut and probably bleeding like a stuck pig all over her again.

He breathed in roughly, feeling his head beginning to clear marginally. As much as he hated that shit they shot into him, at least he could think now.

"Hell." He took a hard breath then looked at Ian. "Get Micah, Travis, and Nik out of here. Put Travis on Mike Conrad's ass. I want to know why I was hit last night and why they struck at Toby today. Tell Rory to keep his ass and Toby's in the office, Nik can keep an eye on them without anyone knowing. I want Micah on long-distance watch of the garage and the house, make sure no eyes caught you coming in and none catch you leaving. People would expect Ian and

Kira Richards to show up, they'd expect Nik to help his boss's lover up to the apartment. That's it. Get the rest of them out of here."

"And Belle?" Ian asked.

"Sabella stays here." It was too late for her to leave and he knew it. He would only follow her. No matter where they hid her. And the bunker was off limits to her unless she was directly targeted.

"Noah, you're in no shape for this decision," Ian said quietly. "You know where it's going to go. Those drugs haven't done anything for the lust, man. It's burning in your eyes. And that surgery might have darkened them, but right now, they're blazing almost pure sapphire. You need her out of here."

"I still have the control." He was sure of it. He knew he did. "I won't hurt her." He'd never hurt her. He'd slice his own throat first. "And the eyes are just fucking eyes. They'll dim once this eases."

"You'll have explanations to make. Tell her what the hell is going on," Ian told him harshly. "At least as far as this mission is concerned. But you're fooling yourself if you think she's not going to figure out more than that. You didn't see the look on her face when Kira and I arrived."

Noah breathed in deeply. It would kill him, but he'd take care of that too. She wouldn't suspect who he was when he was finished. After all, her husband never yelled at her, he didn't fuck her like an animal, and he sure as hell didn't put her in the middle of a dangerous assignment. No, Sabella would never suspect who he really was.

"You break open my stitches and you'll bleed like you were gutted again," Micah snarled.

He shook his head. "Get the hell out of here. Now. Leave Nik in the garage. Tell him to stay in place for cover. We can't afford to have the team here like this. When those bastards move we need to be right behind them. Until then, we won't have a break in this and we'll never catch them."

"And if you break with Belle?" Ian asked him. "If you tell her who you are, what you are. What then?"

Noah stared back at him. That wouldn't happen. Ever. He couldn't bear for his Sabella to know what had happened to the man she had loved so desperately that she came to him in hell.

"Dead men don't talk," he said, his voice bleak. "She won't know. Ever. Her husband is dead."

Ian stared back at him, his lips tightening before he turned to Micah and nodded to the door.

"He's fooling you," the Israeli snapped. "He doesn't have enough control not to hurt her."

Oh, he had control, Ian knew. More control than any of them realized.

"Get out of here," Ian ordered. "Give the others their orders. This is his play, not yours."

Micah rose to his feet, glared at both of them then lifted his lip in a sneer and headed to the door. Like the Russian, the Australian, the Englishman, their Israeli didn't always understand some of the rules they broke, and others that they made. Incorporating these men into a viable working team hadn't been easy. They were hard men. Dead men with nothing else to lose but their honor. But they were good men.

Ian turned back to Noah. He was wild with the lust, there was no doubt of it. But Ian had seen him in a hell of a lot worse shape. He'd disappeared on them more than once in worse shape, and Belle had never suffered.

The man had lived for nineteen months pumped up on a drug that the doctors still couldn't figure out entirely. Pumped so high on it that he'd been like an animal, nearly deranged with the need for sex. And he had never taken what Fuentes had offered him. He'd never broken his vows. He'd never let go of his wife.

Ian had to trust in his belief that Noah wouldn't hurt her now.

Nodding, he moved to the door, glancing back at his friend and hating himself, hating Fuentes with a strength that still had the power to fill him with bitter rage.

His father had done this. The man who sired him. And Ian

still let him live. Because he was his father or because Homeland Security needed him? And where, he wondered, was the line drawn?

He should have killed the bastard while he had the chance.

CHAPTER FIFTEEN

Sabella was standing at the narrow counter that separated the kitchen from the living room watching the hall when Ian stepped out of the bedroom. She and Kira hadn't spoken, the words were there between them, but neither of them had yet broken the silence.

The obviously Middle Eastern agent, and she knew they were agents, had stomped from the apartment with Nik and the others moments before, leaving an eerie silence between her and Kira.

The other woman watched her closely, her gray eyes thoughtful. Now, as Ian moved into the room, Sabella straightened and glanced back to the closed bedroom door.

"Is he okay?" She shoved her hands in the pockets of her jeans and stared back at the man who had been her husband's greatest friend. Strange, wasn't it, that he seemed to be Noah's friend as well.

"He will be." He stood straight and tall, though his arm went around his wife as she came to him.

Sabella held his gaze, she didn't hold her tongue.

"Who is he? What is he?"

Was that surprise that flickered in his eyes? Ian didn't speak.

She stomped to the kitchen drawer, jerking it open and practically slammed the Glock on the counter. She bent, opened the doors beneath the sink, and pulled free the weapon Velcro'd onto the cabinet frame.

She stalked over to the couch, bent, and pulled the smaller handgun from the little pocket beneath the couch and added it to her pile.

"Who the hell is he and what is he doing in my garage and in my life?" Her hand slapped the counter. "And why are you here with him? You were my husband's best friend, Ian. He said you were the same as his brother, and now you bring an agent into his wife's life."

"His widow's," Ian said softly, gently.

Sabella flinched. "And that makes it okay?" she bit out. "Damn you, Ian. You'd betray him that way?"

"I haven't betrayed Nathan, Belle." His stare was fierce and hard. "I don't order Noah Blake anywhere. Whatever the hell he's doing, he's doing on his own. I know him. We're friends. I'm your friend."

Yes, they were friends. For two years she had watched her husband and his friend together. They had been as close as brothers, maybe closer. And Ian had a particular little habit. One her father used to have. When he lied, he didn't so much as bat an eyelash. His expression didn't change, his body didn't tense, and he reacted so normally that it had always appeared abnormal to Sabella.

"Don't you lie to me." She pointed a trembling finger back at him, stabbed it in his direction. "Don't you dare lie to me. Something's wrong with him and it's more than a few knife cuts. And there's more going on here than that crap you just let slip from your mouth."

"And if he could tell you anything more, he would," Kira stated.

Sabella's gaze sliced to the other woman. What was the warning in her eyes? It was there. She could see it, feel it, and so did Ian.

"Kira, could you wait outside?" he asked her.

"No, Ian, I really can't." She smiled back at him, the obvious love she felt for her husband in her eyes, her smile. But her determination defining her stance.

He almost rolled his eyes.

"You're my friend," Sabella said harshly. "Yet you're standing here and allowing him to lie to me. You're lying to me?"

Ian breathed out roughly. "Sabella, listen to me."

"Who is he?" she asked both of them, again. "He's an agent, isn't he?" She was shaking, torn apart by that realization. "Which agency? FBI?"

Ian shook his head. "Noah isn't an agent, Belle. Not of any government agency."

"That leaves private?" she guessed. He didn't answer her. "Are you a part of it?"

"Let's say you're cleared to know only the fact that there is an operation being conducted in Alpine," he finally told her. "You and Rory were cleared for that knowledge, no one else."

And he wasn't lying. She licked her lips nervously.

"What's wrong with him?" She was still breathing roughly, the question she wanted to ask held back, from the fear of disappointment.

Ian's jaw bunched. "Nothing you need to be frightened of." He hoped. She heard what he wasn't speaking.

"Why is he here?"

"That's his story to tell, Belle," he said, sighing. "I'm here as your friend, and as his. That's all anyone else can know. I heard about the attack on Toby and received a call that Noah had been hurt as well. I wanted to check out the situation for myself."

"You're lying," she cried out. "Damn you. Damn you both to hell, you're lying to me, just as you lied to me about how my husband died." She whirled away from him, her hands covering her face before she turned back. "He wasn't just shot. Was he?" She was shaking now, so desperate for some part of the truth somewhere, that she was nearly mad for him. "Tell me, Ian, tell me what happened to my husband and then tell me what the hell that man is doing in my life." She pointed toward the hallway, watching as Noah stepped into the hallway.

"Belle." Ian shook his head.

"They wouldn't let me say goodbye to my husband," she snarled. "I couldn't see his body—"

"You didn't want to see his body, Belle," Ian snapped back. "Trust me. Remember him the way he was and let him go. Because he's dead. And I promise you, you didn't want to see what we recovered."

A sob tore from her throat. For a second, just for a second, she had almost thought . . . She shook her head. No, she had known better.

She covered her mouth with her hand but had to turn away from them all. All of them.

"Belle." Kira spoke behind her.

Sabella lifted her hand. Silence. She just needed silence. She just needed a minute to let that last flame of hope die within her.

"I want to go home," she whispered, turning back to them, her gaze going to Noah. He stared at her, his eyes flaming, his expression agonized. She wanted to go to him. She wanted to wrap her arms around him and she wanted the world to make sense just one more time.

"Do you really want to walk away from him, Sabella?" Kira asked, stepping to her, laying her hand on her shoulder as another sob shuddered through her body. She leaned close. "He may not be your husband. But do you really want to walk away from who he could be to you?"

"You're the same one who told me to fuck him and get the sexual crisis out of the way," she bit out, sniffing back the tears. "That didn't help, Kira. Not at all."

"Didn't it, Belle?" She smiled, a sad, gentle smile. "Your husband is gone. But you didn't die with him."

"Kira, tell me the truth," she whispered, so filled with pain and suspicion it was ravaging her.

"Enough."

Sabella lifted her head to see Noah walking into the living room, almost staggering. He wore the jeans he had worn earlier, snapped and zipped and obviously straining beneath an erection.

Kira sighed as Ian came to his wife and wrapped his arm around her waist. "Come on, troublemaker."

Noah eased to the counter and stared at the weapons she had managed to locate.

"How did you find them?" he asked her, his voice more grating than normal.

Sabella clenched her teeth then smiled mockingly. "You hid them exactly where my husband would have hid them."

There, she'd said it, it was out in the open and she could have sworn he barely held back a flinch.

He was silent for long moments before he finally nodded.

"I'm a contract agent for a private company," he finally said, reaching out to pick up the Glock before edging around the counter.

He replaced the first two weapons.

"An adrenaline junkie." She sneered. "Just what I needed in my life. Tell me, *Noah,* did you know my husband?"

She cocked her hip and crossed her arms over her breasts as she stared back at him, looking, searching, desperate to either confirm or disprove the suspicions rising inside her.

He paused, staring down at the counter, his hands braced on it before his eyes, just his eyes, lifted to her.

"I knew your husband. We weren't exactly friends."

"Enemies?"

His lips quirked mockingly. "No, we weren't enemies. We just knew each other."

"So is Noah your real name?"

He nodded slowly, still watching her. "It's my real name."

"And what made you decide to come to Texas to fuck Nathan Malone's wife?"

He flinched. Sabella could feel the hurt radiating through her. Betrayal. It felt like betrayal. Like deception.

"That's not what happened." He shook his head, and she knew he was lying. She could feel it. Like instinct. Like a scent that teased at her senses. Just as she had always known when her husband was lying to her.

"You knew who I was, you knew who Rory was, and you targeted us, didn't you?"

He licked his lower lip. The action wasn't nervous, it wasn't hesitant. It was sexual. The look in his eyes was sexual. Everything about him screamed hard-core sex.

"I did." At least he didn't lie to her.

"Why?" she cried painfully. "Why did you do this to me? I didn't hurt enough? Do you think I wanted another adrenaline junkie who doesn't care for anything more than he cares for his fix?"

He stared at her in surprise. "Is that what you think being a SEAL was to your husband? A fix you couldn't give him?"

"What else could it have been? Look at you." She flung her hand toward him. "Admit it. You love the adrenaline. You love how it hypes you, makes you high. It's better than sex." She sneered. "Isn't it, Noah?"

His eyes. Those eyes. They were rapacious, blazing, so hot they melted parts of her she didn't want to admit existed. They weren't navy blue, but shades lighter. Not Irish eyes, but neither were they entirely natural.

His gaze roamed her body and she swore heat licked over her flesh.

"There's nothing as good as sex with you." His voice was guttural now. "There's nothing, no high, no drug, no amount of danger as good as burying my cock inside you. And I'd give the last ounce of blood in my body to come inside you, one more time. But I'm not Nathan Malone."

She lost her breath. Sabella stumbled back a step, her chest tightening as the need for oxygen battled with the shock that seared her insides.

"You want him back until it rips your guts inside, don't you, Sabella?" He pushed himself back from the counter, moved around it. "You want him until you live and breathe the memory of a man that's never going to come back to you."

She shook her head, agony searing her heart to hear him say that. To hear the words, when that fragile flame of hope had been moving inside her. A hope she refused to even name, because she ached so desperately for it.

"They wouldn't let you see his body, so you prayed he was alive." The cruelty of his words bore down on her, the very gentleness of his tone struck inside her like the vicious lash of a whip.

"Don't." She shook her head, feeling the tears that eased from her eyes, feeling the pain that dug into her soul and tore at the last dream of ever holding her husband again. "Please don't."

His hands touched her. He pushed her hair back from her face, his thumbs eased over the tears and more fell.

"Your husband is dead." Pain echoed in his voice as well. "He's gone, Sabella."

"No." She shook her head. "No."

"He's only alive in your dreams." His lips touched hers. "But I'm here. Right here. Let me, Sabella. Let me have what Nathan Malone didn't have. Let me have all of his wild witch."

"No!" She screamed out at the rocking agony. She wanted to strike him. She wanted to tear at his hair, at his eyes, and all she could do was jerk away from him, jerk away and force her feet to the kitchen, and no further.

"You didn't give him all of yourself," he accused her, his voice grating, soft, as he followed her. His hands gripped her shoulders, fingers splaying, holding her firmly as she tensed in his grip. "You give it to me. Admit that much. You give me the woman you didn't allow him to see."

"I love him."

"You loved him." The fire in his eyes burned with pain, bleak sorrow, and lust. "Loved, Sabella. Because he's gone."

"Stop." She shook her head.

"I'm not Nathan Malone!" He yelled the words at her, striking her with them as she hunched her shoulders against the blow and the firm shake he gave her.

She shook her head, sobbing, the cries tearing from her chest.

"Get that in your head, Sabella. I am not Nathan Malone. I am not the man you loved, but by God I am the man that's going to fuck you. That's going to hold you when you cry in the night, and the man that's going to bind you to him so tight, so hard, that you'll never think to hide even a partical of who and what you are from him."

"Stop. Stop." She sobbed. Her breath was heaving, tears dimming her vision, as the words tore through her with the effect of a jagged knife.

"I won't stop." Hard hands held her to him, refused to let her go. "Look at me, Sabella."

His features were blurred, the need to lean against him, to find something to hold on to, weakened her knees.

"I'm not Nathan Malone. But I'm your lover, Sabella. And I need you. I need you like your husband had no idea how to need you. I need you until the fever burns inside me for your touch, your kiss."

He clasped her head in his hands, lowered his lips and smoothed them over hers, sipped from hers. He tasted her tears and her pain, and something inside his soul tore loose.

Ah God, how he was hurting her. Hurting her until her sobs tore through him like dull spikes and ripped at his insides. But he knew. The second he heard her questioning Ian, he knew she had begun to suspect. Somehow, some way, his too perceptive little witch had sensed the ghost of her husband inside him.

She shuddered against him. The whore's dust, those last minute amounts that infected his system, pumped through him, overshadowed everything but the feel of her. The feel of her soft lips, the taste of her pain in her tears.

"Sabella," he whispered. "Touch me. Just touch. Close your eyes and be with whoever you need to be with, but touch me."

He lifted her hands, pressed them against his hard stomach beneath the bandage that covered the knife wound. He felt her jerk, felt her response.

"I would die for your touch." He kissed her lips again, watched as her head lifted, her soft gray eyes cloudy with her tears, with the lost dreams.

She shook her head and he kissed her again. His lips caught hers this time, settled against them, and rather than devouring as he needed to, he let himself sip, let himself taste.

Because she responded. Torn between the man she loved

and the man she wanted. And he couldn't allow her to suspect both were breathing and aching for her.

"Please don't," she whispered when his head lifted and he drew her back into the living room. Drew her to the bedroom.

"Walk away then." He turned, shucked his jeans, and palmed the thick, heavy erection pounding with lust.

Her gaze flickered to him and she trembled. He could see the battle on her face. Sweet beautiful Sabella. Battling her anger, her fear, her want.

He lay back on the bed and stroked his heavy cock. And she watched. Her fingers fisted in her T-shirt now, her face flushed though tears still glittered in her eyes.

"I'll lie right here," he promised her. "I'll be a good boy and you can ride me, Sabella."

She used to love that, he remembered. She had loved rising over him, taking him, working his cock inside her at her own pace.

He watched her gaze darken, watched the hunger crawl inside her, watched as her breathing deepened, grew heavier. Her breasts lifted against her shirt, hard little nipples pressing into the fabric.

"Come here." He held his hand out to her. "Let me tell you what it feels like inside you. How your mouth feels going down on me. Your hands on my flesh."

He was dying for her hands on him. Aching. Racked by the need in ways he had never been tortured before this.

She hesitated. He watched the battle in her gaze. The battle between him and the memory she refused to let go.

Forever. Something inside him gentled as he remembered the vow she had always whispered to him. That she would love him forever. And he had sworn he would return to her forever.

Finally, after what felt like an eternity, her hands lowered to the hem of her shirt and she removed it. Slowly.

Her hair was unbound, lying past her shoulders in thick, heavy waves as she tossed the shirt aside, leaving her breasts covered only by the filmy silk of her bra.

She sat down, unlaced her boots, and pulled them free of

204 *Lora Leigh*

her small feet, then pulled off her jeans. It wasn't a seductive striptease. It was a woman finally releasing something inside herself. Or testing something. He wasn't certain, and his mind was clouded by the lust raging inside him.

"This isn't normal." She stepped to him, easing onto the bed beside him as she let her hand smooth up the inside of his thigh. "This hard. This aroused. You were bleeding bad last night, Noah. Give me this much at least. Tell me what's wrong with you."

He clenched his jaw. He could feel the sweat popping out on his flesh, dampening him as the fever nearly took his head off it spiked so hard inside him.

"Have you heard of whore's dust?"

She blinked. "It's a date rape drug. Or was."

"Was." He nodded. "We were tracking the man selling it and I was captured. Pumped up on it for a while. There are still minute amounts of it in my body. Adrenaline pumps it through me. Wounds, fevers. I get hard. I need to fuck."

"Anything? Anyone?" Her lashes lowered as her fingers eased over the torturously tight sac of his balls.

He shook his head. "No."

"How many women have you had since they did this to you?"

"Does it matter?" He wouldn't lie to her, not now, not while her fingers were caressing his balls.

His thighs shifted apart, allowing her to cup him as a ragged groan tore from his lips.

"Right now, it won't matter. Later, maybe it will." She lowered her head, and Noah felt live electricity sear his nerve endings as she tongued his balls with her damp little tongue.

She gave him a wet kiss. Cupping her lips over his balls she licked him until his hands were buried in her hair, pulling at it, then pushing her head closer. Kneading her scalp like a cat and flexing beneath her touch.

There was something different in her touch now. He couldn't pinpoint it. Not yet. He'd figure it out tomorrow. Later. After he got her mouth on his dick. But damn, those sweet lips felt so good on his balls. They were tight, they were always tight when the fever hit him, when the need for her touch was an agony, a starvation.

When nothing mattered but feeling her. Just feeling her. Just for a minute, before the hunger sharpened and he had to move.

She sucked at his balls, kissed them.

Had she ever done that when they were married? He swore she hadn't. But he hadn't exactly pushed her to be adventurous. He had always been too damned greedy just to get into her pants in the first place.

Now, now, he wanted more. He wanted that wild woman he was glimpsing. The one who liked being talked dirty to. The one who burned in his arms when he let her have her way with his body.

"Is this what you want?" Her voice was velvet soft, a rasp of pleasure so sweet he felt it lance through his body as her tongue licked up the heavy stalk of his erection.

"God yes!" He lifted to her, watching, his teeth clenched, pleasure ricocheting from nerve ending to nerve ending as her mouth finally closed over the head of his cock.

Ah hell yes. This. Her mouth sucking his cock head tight and hot, so sweet. His hips arched to her as he felt her tongue the underside, rub it, her tongue stretching against it in that hot little way she had.

He shivered at the sensation. Shit. That was good. It was too damned good because he was going to blow any second if she kept that up.

Then she changed tactics. She sucked him.

"Hell. Damn you." His hands locked in her hair at the tight, deep strokes of her mouth. "Suck me, Sabella. God, that hot mouth of yours is like heaven. Sucking me straight to ecstasy."

She took him deeper inside her mouth than he ever remembered going before. She worked his cock head against her tongue, the roof of her mouth. She stroked him with silken lips, a destructive tongue, and when he thought he was going to shatter from the pleasure, she released him.

"Pretty lips," he groaned. "Swollen from my cock fucking them. Do you know how much that turns me on?"

His witch. His sweet hot little witch. She stared back at him, her gray eyes darkening, her face flushed, her hair wild around her face and shoulders.

"A lot?" she whispered, licking her lips, then licking the underside of his cock head. "I'm guessing you like it a whole lot."

A temptress. A brazen little sexpot licking her tongue over the head of his cock and tasting the pearl of semen that beaded at the tiny slit of his cock head.

And then she moaned.

He was going to come with nothing more to spur it than the sound of that moan, hot and hungry. His cock jerked in her hands and she smiled. A sensual, confident little smile. The knowing smile. A woman that holds a man in the very palm of her hand, literally. Not just his soul, but his dick.

She held all of him. Noah knew it. He had known it since the first day he saw her, frazzled, worried about her job and her car and asking for a wrench.

Hell, if he'd known she meant the wrench itself rather than a helping hand . . .

And here she was now, her body sliding slowly up his, straddling his hips, easing over him and staying clear of his wounds.

That hot, wet pussy slid over the shaft of his cock, tucking it between his own body and her swollen flesh as her lips lowered to his.

He was waiting on her, hungry for her. Desperate. Dying in her arms and she didn't even know it. He died in her arms every time he shot his seed inside her. Every time he felt her contracting around him in release.

"Kiss me, Noah." Sweet, sensual, her voice worked his senses like a master musician with an instrument. She strummed through his heart, plucked at his ragged soul and left him reaching for her.

"You're teasing," he growled as her tongue licked over his hips.

His hand gripped her hips, moving her against him, feeling her pussy slide over his erection as her tongue tasted his lips.

"I intend to deliver." She nipped at his lips, stared down at him.

"You better deliver fast." He was this side of panting, one second from rolling her to the bed and burying the thick, tormented length of his cock inside her.

She lifted her hips as his hands slid up her torso, cupped her swollen breasts. He bent his head to her hard little nipples as she let the head of his cock tuck into her entrance.

Noah felt heat sizzle through his dick. It began at the tip, her juices kissed it, glazed it, then pure tight bliss began to enfold it.

He sucked her nipple harder, lashed it with his tongue and heard her cry out his name.

"Oh yeah. Baby, so good." He had to release her nipple, had to hold her face in his hands, stare into her eyes. "So damned tight. Sweet. Ride me, sweetheart. Ride me out of hell."

She took him deeper, rocking on him, moving against him as he lifted to her, watching her eyes, watching them as his chest tightened, exploded. She was staring at him the way she'd stared at him before he died. Before he was taken from her.

He had told her to imagine him however she needed to. To let him be whatever she needed. And this was how desperately she needed her husband. The man who had chased the adrenaline high rather than his future with her. But it had been more than that. So much more. And it ended here, in her arms, and he knew the loss hadn't been worth it. Nothing was worth losing this woman.

"Yeah. Ride me now. Fuck me hard and sweet. But later. Later I'm going to lay you down and lap that pretty pussy again. Fill my mouth with your sweet juice. I'm going to tongue your pussy, Sabella. I'm going to suck your clit until you're screaming. Begging. For me."

She shivered and arched. She took more of him, her pussy growing wetter around him, tighter around him.

He had never talked to her like that. He'd always cuddled her, tried to protect her from what he was, from what had once been just a shadow of darkness inside his sexuality.

"Yes." She hissed her pleasure, she loved it. Her head fell back as she moved on him, working herself on him, faster, slower, teasing and taking and giving until he was ready to roar with the agonizing pleasure of it.

The whore's dust made the need sharper, harder. But it hadn't changed the pleasure. She still gave him more pleasure, destroyed him with each touch, took him like a vixen in heat, and made him want to beg for more.

She rode him now, sliding up and down, watching him, her eyes narrowed, her face flushed as he watched the pleasure rising inside her as well.

He smiled. A tight hard smile. And did something he had never done as her husband. Hooking his arm around her he drew her to his chest, took her lips. The fingers of one hand slid into the syrupy juices surrounding his cock and drew them back to a place he had never touched as her husband.

A place he hadn't yet explored, dreamed of exploring, ached to take. She was jerking against him, her breathing shallow now, taking his cock harder as he slickened his fingers, tucked one at that entrance and took control from her.

His hips slammed upward, his finger eased inside her. Slow and easy. Working in and out, lubricating with her own juices just enough to allow this penetration.

She was going wild. Arching and bucking.

"Easy. Slow down, Sabella. Slow and easy." He pulled his finger back, worked more of her juices to the tiny entrance and slid in again. Slid in until he was lodged inside to the base of his finger, feeling her hot and tight there as well.

Then he moved.

"I want to take you here." He was fucking her, driving inside her, shafting her with quick hard strokes.

"I want to stretch you, ease you. I want to slide into your hot little ass and feel you go insane with the pleasure of it."

His finger moved slow and easy, sliding with the lightest strokes as he surged inside her pussy with his cock, slammed inside her until he felt the first ripples, the first warning contractions rippling through her pussy. She was getting ready to explode. He thrust harder, deeper, impaling her with his cock and with his finger and feeling his balls catch fire.

The flames rushed up his spine as she screamed against his chest, exploded around him and began jerking in his arms with the pleasure.

He heard his own yell. Her name. Just her name. Not the vow he had always given her. But it was followed by the hardest, hottest come he'd ever had in his life. Semen shot from his cock in furious, violent eruptions. It filled her, washed through her, and she cried out again, shivered and contracted around him again. Tense, tight, holding him inside her as she shuddered weakly through the pulsing pleasure then collapsed against his chest.

Later, much later, Sabella stared into the darkness. Noah slept beside her, one arm under her, one thrown over her. His head rested next to hers, the soft rhythm of his breathing flowed over her.

There were things, Sabella thought, that men just did not always consider when it came to women. Because women were smart enough not to tell them.

Women took the time to know the men they loved. The little things. Women were curious like that, where men weren't always as perceptive, even big tough SEALs and superagents.

For instance, the way a man touched a woman's body, the woman he loved. Not just the feel of his fingers, but how he did it. The strength could change, it could be gentle and firm, or it could be desperate and hungry, but still there were things that remained the same. Certain sensations, certain ways of doing it.

The way a man took a woman, hard and fast or slow and easy or anything in between, there was always a single constant. And that was the man.

Scars marred Noah's hands and his body. There were calluses her husband hadn't had and there were calluses her husband had had that were missing from Noah's hands. But the way his cock pressed into her, the nerve endings it stroked, the way he filled her, the way he stretched her, it was all too similar.

Too many things were too similar.

"Sabella. You hit my truck. It was right there, in plain view."

The memory slashed over her, around her. It seared in her memory. Nathan yelling at her. Nathan never yelled at her. He always controlled himself. But she had shocked him that day. He had gripped her shoulders to move her out of the way, but she had felt it. Felt the way his fingertips pressed, not ungently, in a distinct way. The way his fingers flared out, gripped, moved her.

She remembered his eyes. So wild, the way they went feverish with anger, arousal, and pure lust as he dragged her into the house.

It was distinctive. She remembered the exact spots his fingers had pressed into her shoulders, how it made them feel, how his eyes had changed.

She remembered where he hid his guns. How he hid his guns.

He had known where the coffee cups were in her kitchen that first morning when she had informed him he wouldn't be sharing her bed. She had distracted him, made him angry right off, and he had stalked straight to the coffee cups and pulled one free, and not once had she shown him where they were.

He slept against her as her husband once had. He held her as her husband had held her.

And that first night, between sleep and waking, she was certain, now she was certain to the soles of her feet, that she had heard him whisper "go síoraí." The words only her husband had known to whisper to her.

She turned her head to stare at him, watched how his hair fell over his brow now. Nathan had always kept his hair cut short, but the profile hadn't changed that much. Small differences, enough to fool her at first.

He was her soul. No other man could have walked into

her life and taken her over as he had. Only her husband could have done that.

And he had been lying to her all along.

He said he'd been captured. Pumped full of that horrifying drug that had been in the news a few years back. And she remembered her own nightmares. The crawling certainty that he was in danger, not dead. Hearing him scream out for her, begging her to save him, to help him. Her horror, her uncertainty. Waking in the middle of the night screaming from an agony that had no beginning and no end.

He said her husband had died. His eyes had held bleak, raging pain. And he hadn't lied to her. He truly thought the man he was had died. And perhaps in ways he had. But this was still her husband, her lover, her soul. Only his name had changed. He was still *hers*.

And he was still lying to her. He was, and Rory was. Her eyes narrowed. The son of a bitch. Rory knew. He had told Rory, but he hadn't told his own wife.

She fought back the panic, the pain at the thought that Noah hadn't told her the truth, perhaps even hadn't returned home for her. Rory was stronger. He was a man. And he knew the truth, she was certain of it. Whatever Noah was doing, did he think he would need help?

He had had to get into the garage, but why? To get to her? To do whatever he had come here to do?

She inhaled slowly. Whatever the reason, it was time her husband, as much as she loved him, adored him, as much as having him back in her arms meant to her, it was time he learned. Lying to Sabella was a very, very bad thing.

CHAPTER SIXTEEN

The next morning Toby was still shaken, but he was at work on time and determined to stay. He wasn't going to let anyone run him off, he claimed.

Sabella worked in the garage for several hours, tuning up one of the vehicles that had come in the evening before and finishing it before she looked at the clock and smiled.

She lowered the hood, her gaze going to Noah.

He was watching the computer readout on a new SUV, twirling a wrench lazily through his fingers and chewing gum. Damn, she was glad none of the old mechanics he had employed worked here anymore. They would have seen that and suspected instantly. If they had ever paid attention to it. It was something Sabella had found completely sexy the few times she had seen him do it, so many years ago.

Irish. Her heart swelled, tears threatened to rush to her eyes, and she had to turn away quickly to keep from sobbing out in joy.

Her Irish. He was back, he was here. She trembled at the knowledge and shook with the anger. Whatever had kept him away, it was obvious he had spent quite a lot of time recovering from it. She would have been there for him. She could have been there. She would have given up her life to have made a single day, a single hour, easier for him.

And he had refused to allow it. He hadn't let her come to

him, hadn't let her comfort him, and even now, he tried to hide from her.

From the corner of her eye she watched as Rory came over to him, caught the wrench, and gave his brother a warning glare.

Oh yeah, Rory knew. He knew well enough to know to watch for the little things that would give Noah away. She turned away before narrowing her eyes as a sense of betrayal filled her. He could tell his brother, but he couldn't tell her?

She turned and jerked the mechanic's rag from the counter and cleaned her hands.

"Rory, I have an appointment," she called out. "I'll be back around five."

Both Rory and Noah turned to her, their expressions wiping, becoming bland. Bastards.

"We have a lot of work piled up here, Belle." Rory cleared his throat as Noah crossed his arms over his chest and gave her a brooding stare.

"It can't be helped." She shrugged. "I'm running up to the house to shower then I have to meet Sienna and Kira."

She tossed the rag back to the counter and dug her car keys from her back pocket. She flashed them both a tight, hard smile.

"I'm sure you can survive without me."

Kira had been surprised when Sabella had called her that morning and asked if she wanted to meet her and Sienna at the spa. The other woman was wary, cautious, but game. Sabella liked that about her. Kira was no one's fool, but she was also curious as hell.

Sabella moved from the garage to her car aware of Noah following her. He caught her as she reached the little red BMW Z8 Nathan had rebuilt for her just before he had left on that last mission.

The fender was still crumpled from slamming it into the back of Nathan's truck. The truck that still sat in the garage. Unused. His pride and joy. She wondered if he had even checked on his truck. He could have done it easily without her knowing about it.

She had just reached the car when she felt his fingers curl around her upper arm, drawing her to a stop.

Sabella felt her breath catch. Her eyes closed and emotion swamped her. Joy, anger, sorrow, and so much hope. So much hope it nearly brought her to her knees. And fear. Did she want this so badly that she was seeing no more than an illusion?

No. It wasn't an illusion. It was her Irish.

"What's going on?" His voice was rough, grating. Somehow, something had happened to the voice that had sung Irish ballads to her, that whispered her name with such a lyrical quality.

But it wasn't the voice that held her soul, it was the man.

She cleared her throat and turned to him, staring at his chin.

"I told you, I have an appointment at the spa." She tugged her arm out of his grip before glancing up at his eyes, fighting to hold back the sheer awe she felt that she could hold him again. That she could love him again.

Her Irish. She wanted to throw her arms around him and cry out his name, and she couldn't.

She didn't know how dangerous it could be, to him, to all of them. But mostly to him. If he had come back to her as another man, he would have had to have a reason that risked all their lives. And her husband was incredibly protective, no matter what name he went by. He would fight to save those he loved, no matter the risk.

"Why today?" His voice hardened. He didn't want her to leave. He wanted her to stay, where he could watch her.

"Does it matter? Is there a reason why I shouldn't go?"

"Well, nothing other than the fact that one of your employees was nearly killed yesterday." His lips tightened and his eyes glowed back at her with an edge of worry and anger.

"They were striking at you, not at me." She wasn't ignoring the truth. "Whatever happened the night before is what targeted Toby, Noah. Not me. I know how to be careful. And my *husband* taught me how to watch my back," she reminded him. "I'm not an unwary teenager."

She saw him flinch.

"No, you're a stubborn little hellion determined to do things her own way," he growled.

She opened the door to her car before turning back to him.

"I'm meeting Sienna for lunch, then we have an appointment at the spa. Now that you're here and the garage is doing so well, I thought I'd take an afternoon off and be a girl rather than a grease rag for a change. Do you have a problem with that?"

Those eyes. Arousal sparked, then flamed within them.

"Manicure?" He lifted his lips in a little snarl.

"A manicure would be wasted on this place." She waved her hand to the garage. "And I'd much prefer playing with guys' motors than babying a set of nails. But a nice massage. A cut and style." She shook her hair at him. "Maybe a facial." *Maybe a wax.*

She could feel the thought hovering between them. Maybe having the curls removed from between her thighs again, feeling his beard against sensitive bare skin, feeling his tongue love the bare folds. She had her husband back, but she wasn't willing to give up her independence again. There had been a few things she enjoyed from the girly zone she and Sienna called the spa.

As he watched her, she could see what was coming. His lashes blinked over his eyes slowly, his expression became set, determined, dominant. The dominance was a new facet, or perhaps one that had been hidden in the past.

"I'd prefer you wait," he finally said. "Or let me drive you in."

"I don't need a babysitter, Noah." She shook her head. She needed away from him, just for a little while. "Stay out of knife fights at night, and maybe you won't have to worry so much."

She had checked the wounds this morning when they awoke, rebandaged them, and she was amazed he hadn't bled to death while he was taking her.

"I have to go." She slid into the car. "Don't forget Becca

Jean's car this afternoon. She has a heavy class load over the next few months and I want to make sure there's nothing more wrong with it than resetting the computer chip."

"I'll take care of it," he bit out. "Dammit, Sabella. At least be careful."

"I'm always careful." She gripped the steering wheel and stared back at him, infuriated. "You're the one that doesn't know how to stay out of trouble."

She gripped the door handle, pulled it from him, aware that she only did it because he allowed it, and started the car.

A second later she was pulling out of the parking lot and glancing in the rearview mirror to see him putting his cell phone to his ear.

She wondered who her babysitter would be.

Noah watched as the little BMW pulled into the parking lot beside the two-story brick house and Sabella went inside.

Micah Sloane and John Vincent were taking turns keeping an eye on her when she wasn't with Noah. Noah hadn't intended that she be out of his sight for long. And he didn't like her running around town without him. There were too many unknowns in this case and not enough information yet.

Shaking his head, he punched in the speed dial for Micah, let him know to watch her, because there was no doubt she would catch him tailing her, and went back to the pickup he had been working on.

Delbert Ransome was Mike Conrad's cousin. He'd brought the truck in when the other two garages in town couldn't fix the revisions he'd made to the motor to add to its power and to the traction control.

Delbert liked to take the spiffy little four-by-four into the mountains and act like a damned fool. He worked for a neighboring rancher, Gaylen Patrick, and liked to brag about how close he was to the bank president, his cousin and one of the most powerful ranchers in town.

Biting off a curse, he threw an irritated look toward the house again and grabbed a mechanic's creeper before lying back on it and rolling beneath the engine to see what the hell Delbert had done to the new motor.

It was clean. Delbert like to keep the motor power-washed and looking nice and pretty. He hadn't been beneath the motor for long when he found it. The flashlight he was using skimmed over the odd shadow, then came back. There, lit by the powerful little light, was something he knew Ransome couldn't have imagined he'd missed in washing the motor. A small clump of mud, mixed with something darker, and lodged in its underside, a clump of black hair and dried flesh.

He slid out from under the truck, checked to see if the other mechanics were watching, then levered himself up and pulled two small vials and a penknife from the toolbox along with several tools he wouldn't be needing.

He moved back under the vehicle, scraped the samples from the motor into the little plastic vials, capped them, then pushed them into his jeans pocket until he could get the vials to one of the other men to take to the bunker.

Gaylen Patrick was on their list of suspects as being involved with, or heading, the Black Collar Militia. He had the contacts and the cash. And now, one of his main ranch hands would be implicated in the deaths.

If the DNA matched any of the bodies that had been found, then they had a main player, and hopefully more information.

And the danger would rise.

Noah checked the underside of the truck again, looking for more samples and finding several lodged in various areas of the motor, tucked into places Delbert's power washer hadn't been able to reach.

Stupid bastard.

He stored the samples and let the motor go. Checking into it more deeply for the problem with the traction or power could lead to complications. If Delbert thought the garage had done no more than an overall test, then when he was arrested for those samples he wouldn't pin the blame on Sabella's head. Or Noah's.

Hiding a smug grin, he called over to the mechanic he suspected was a plant, and put him on the truck instead.

Noah knew for a fact he'd found everything incriminating in there, and what was left, the sallow-skinned little mechanic working on the truck wouldn't find. It was tucked in too deep. Just enough left to incriminate Delbert when the truck was taken apart.

Noah went upstairs to the apartment, and recorded the positioning of the remaining evidence, the areas from which he had scraped the hair and skin samples, folded the paper around the vials, and wrapped it all together with heavy rubber bands before pushing it into the pocket of his jeans again and returning to the garage.

It would be a few hours before Nik could safely leave, without being noticed, and head to the bunker. Going over to Sabella's friend's car, he looked it over carefully, while keeping the mechanic working on the truck in close view.

If he found anything, Delbert would be there fast to pick up the truck. If he didn't, the mechanic would keep doing what he was doing now, scratching his head and checking the fuel injection. Those samples weren't anywhere close to the fuel injection.

Noah saw Sabella pulling out of the driveway to the house, and a few seconds later Micah's car pulled out of a nearby street and followed behind her. She was covered, but it bit his ass that he wasn't the one covering her, protecting her.

Shaking his head, he moved back into the garage and grinned back at the mechanic watching him from Delbert's pickup. In a gesture of friendliness, the man was shaking his head and grinning.

"She's a fine one." The mechanic, Chuck Leon, grinned and pulled at the dirty blond goatee he wore. "You could do worse in these parts."

"Yeah, I could," Noah grunted. "And I could get more mechanics too if you don't want to work."

Something flickered in the other man's brown eyes. But he nodded slowly before bending to the motor and going back to work.

Noah wasn't there to make friends with militia members, he was there to identify them and get their asses behind bars. But he had to admit, Leon was a hell of a mechanic when he wanted to be.

Noah's eyes met Nik's. The Russian was bent over the hood of the third car in the bay, while the fourth man was working the counter in the convenience section. Nik wasn't the sociable type. The big Russian with his white-blond hair and icy blue eyes was more killer material than checkout.

Glancing back toward the road, Noah clenched his teeth and went back to work. There were more cars waiting in the parking lot outside. Nik seemed to be pulling in the college girls. They liked his rough looks evidently. More of Toby's friends were dropping their cars off when they had to, and more of their parents were coming, stopping by, checking to see how things were going.

There was a rhythm developing, and Noah was letting it seep into him more and more. Just as Sabella was taking a firmer hold on his very spirit than she had ever had.

Enough so that he was beginning to wonder, when it was all over and done with, how he would manage to walk away from her again. The men of the Elite Ops were dead men except the current members of the former SEAL Team he'd fought with. There was no rebirth. Nathan Malone could never return. Not to Alpine, not this family, and to Sabella.

But walking away from her was going to be impossible.

I'm convinced we need a girls' night out." Sienna stretched on the massage table as she, Sabella, and Kira Richards lay beneath the thin sheets in the massage room while talented hands worked at the kinks along their bodies.

"Girls' night out?" Sabella mumbled. "I remember those. They were hell. I always had a hangover after hanging out with you, Sienna."

Her friend snickered. "I'm sick of hanging around the house at night. Rick doesn't come in till all hours, and when he does come home, he just goes to sleep."

There was something in Sienna's voice, some note of anger that Sabella remembered hearing several times in the past few years.

"You and Rick still fighting over his schedule?" she asked.

"Same old." Sienna waved her hand indifferently. "But

now that you've rejoined the land of the living, I thought a night out would be nice."

Sabella pondered the idea for all of a second.

"My new mechanic needs supervision," she finally said mockingly. "I'm supervising."

Kira snorted. Sienna groaned. "I can't believe you're doing the nasty with your mechanic. Nathan would have had a fit, Sabella."

There was a tense silence as Sienna's comment struck a raw nerve. Sienna had been friends with her and Nathan, but she'd had more of a history with Nathan.

"Nathan would have wanted me to be happy," she finally said softly.

"With another man just like him?" Sienna asked. "Come on, you're on the rebound. The guy has eyes that remind you of your husband's and the same attitude. Second best isn't enough for a man like that. He's going to go ballistic on you soon."

"Then he can go ballistic the other way." Sabella shrugged as though it didn't matter.

But why wasn't she more inclined to want to talk to Sienna about this? To share the knowledge building in her. She had always told Sienna everything. Shared everything with her friend, until Nathan's "death."

Now, she didn't want to share this with anyone, though she admitted she had to bite her lip to keep from grilling Kira about Noah Blake, because she knew, knew to the bottom of her soul, that Kira knew everything Ian knew.

"I told you, get the sexual crisis out of the way," Kira mumbled from her massage table beside Sabella's. "Let her get the kink out of her guts, Sienna. She'll feel better for it."

That edge of amusement in the other woman's voice could have meant anything.

"One of these days I'm going to make you pay for that advice," Sabella warned her. "The man is positively possessive. He could make me crazy."

Let her make of that what she would.

"Nathan was so easygoing." Sienna sighed. "He never got jealous."

Oh, that wasn't necessarily true, Sabella admitted to herself. Nathan had been jealous, he just hid it, even from her. He'd been easygoing, filled with laughter, always polite, but there had been a core of seething emotion inside her husband that was finally free. And one of those emotions was jealousy. She had known even years before that Nathan, the man he had once been, had capped that particular emotion. He had fought it, because he trusted her. Because he had known there was no way to lock her away while he was on a mission or while he was home. But that hadn't meant he hadn't felt it, and that she hadn't felt the echoes of it.

"No. He never got jealous," Sabella agreed.

That was something else Sienna didn't know, and Sabella admitted she had no intention of telling her. Noah was hiding, obviously for a reason. She couldn't risk endangering whatever he was doing. She refused to risk his life.

"Is he anything like Nathan?" Sienna lifted her head, her gaze direct as she met Sabella's.

Sabella stared back at her friend, hating the suspicion that raged inside her. She didn't trust her best and dearest friend in the world. And that hurt.

"No," she finally said, and in some ways, it was the truth. "Nathan was easier going. Always smiling. Always loving. Noah is more intense, quieter. More dominant maybe."

"An animal." Kira pretended a shudder. "He looks like he would be wild in the sack."

"Would you shut up," Sabella said, laughing.

"Is he an animal in bed, Belle?" Sienna snickered.

"He's an animal all right. All growls and snapping and snarling around," she said. "And what he's like in bed has nothing to do with it."

Kira and Sienna both lifted their heads and stared at her in shock.

"Since when?" Kira arched a perfect brow in false surprise.

"After marriage, definitely," Sienna grunted. "It's hump hump, sleep sleep."

Kira and Sabella jerked their gazes to Sienna. She lifted

her brows, waggled them then laughed and laid her head back to the padded table.

But there was something about her statement, that laugh, that made Sabella wonder if there wasn't more to her comment than she was letting on.

Conversation eased then. The massage wrapped up, and soon after, Sabella was dressed and paying her bill. She was waxed and oiled, styled and pedicured. Her nails had been buffed and trimmed. She felt like a woman again. She hadn't felt like a woman in so many years. It felt like forever. She felt like a lover, almost like a wife, and excited, exhilarated by the emotions and the sexuality that flowed freely within her again.

She felt the excitement moving with her. Noah had an edge now, a hard-core, hungry edge that called to that part of her that she'd always kept a rein on during their previous relationship.

He talked dirty to her. He was naughty and he made her feel naughty. He made her want to push him, challenge him. He made her want things she would have never asked him for before. Because he had controlled their sexuality. Because she hadn't had him with her nearly enough in those two years. The missions he had gone on had been steady; sometimes, she had done without him for weeks at a time. When he came home, she gave her husband what her husband needed, though she had known that as the years passed, they would grow into each other. If they had had those years to share.

As she waved back to Sienna, who had managed to find a parking spot close to the entrance, Sabella and Kira walked at a slow pace, silent. The tension between them wasn't hostile, but it was there, thick and heavy.

"How's Noah doing?" Kira tucked her hands in the pockets of her shorts as they walked, glancing over at her curiously. "His wounds are doing okay?"

"So far." She nodded, swallowing deeply. Kira knew something, as did her husband Ian, and Sabella knew it. And she hated the lies, though she was trying to understand them.

"You didn't tell Sienna about the attack," Kira mentioned then. "Why not?"

Sabella paused at the back of her car and turned to meet Kira's gaze. "Because I don't know how widespread that knowledge is. If no one knows he's wounded, then they won't think he's weak and come after him again. They reported the attempted hit-and-run on Toby, but Sienna asked about that this morning. There was no sense in saying more about it."

Kira's too perceptive gaze met her own then.

"How do you feel about a few hours and a few glasses of wine?" Kira finally asked. "Ian's going to be out of the house until morning, and like for Sienna, the house gets too quiet sometimes."

Sabella doubted that. She stared around the parking lot for a long moment before turning back to the other woman.

"Why don't you come to my house instead." She turned back to her. "My husband had a nice stock of wine in the basement. We could uncork one of his favorites." Wouldn't that horrify Noah? "Get drunk and trash men."

"You're still angry with him?" Kira asked, a curious glint in her eye.

"I can always find a reason to be angry at a man that lies to me," she informed the other woman. "It's in the rule book. We're allowed."

Kira's lips quirked as she nodded. "I'll follow you," she decided. "You know, Sabella, I have a feeling you're a hell of a lot more perceptive than Ian or Noah wants to admit to. That could make our men uncomfortable."

"Serves them right." Sabella laughed, though she gritted her teeth at the thought moments later.

Finding out exactly why those two men were lying their asses off to her was her objective. And if she didn't find out on her own soon, then she was going to be bashing one dominating, overly possessive, lying Navy SEAL. And she was going to do it with the flat side of her black iron skillet.

CHAPTER SEVENTEEN

"We have trouble." Nik spoke as he eased up to Noah where he stood in the wide entrance to the garage, staring up at the house on the hill, his eyes narrowed, jaw bunched.

Kira Richards had driven in behind Sabella an hour before. The two women had carried several grocery bags into the house and he hadn't seen them since.

Sabella hadn't come down to collect the deposit for the bank. She had called and told Rory to take care of it for her, and she hadn't even asked to talk to him.

"What's the trouble?" Noah asked as he crossed his arms over his chest and glared at the house, willing Sabella to step outside.

"Micah reported in a few minutes ago. He hung around town after she left with Ian's wife. He saw Mike Conrad go into the spa, pull their masseuses and techs aside. From what Micah saw from out back, the man was questioning them pretty heavily."

Noah flicked him a look. "He didn't find out anything."

Sabella didn't know enough to be a danger to them, but it wouldn't matter what she knew, she would have never discussed it.

"Probably not," Nik agreed. "Point is, he's suspicious. It could come back on her." He nodded to the house, indicating Sabella.

"Then he'll die." Noah turned back to Nik, icy resolve burning inside him as he met the Russian's gaze.

Nik nodded slowly, his pale face as cold, as bleak as death. And Noah knew he was remembering his own lost family and the lengths he would have gone to protect them.

"I'll be at your back," Nik told him then. "No doubt, Noah Blake, I'll be at your back."

Nik turned and reentered the garage, and Noah stayed in place, and watched the house. Wondered what the hell Sabella and Kira were up to.

"Toby, Nik will drive you home," he yelled back to the office. "Get ready to roll."

He looked at the clock. It was nearly seven, almost closing time. And Sabella had been to the spa. For hours. He remembered those all-day spa trips. And he damned sure remembered what awaited him that night when he crawled between the loveliest pair of thighs he had ever known.

Bare, slick flesh. Sheened with her juices. Luscious, tasty, a hint of almond oil on her flesh, nothing between him and tasting her.

"Belle thought we should start keeping the convenience store and gas pumps open longer now that we have more help," Rory announced as he stepped out to Noah minutes later. "You working tonight's shift?" Smug amusement filled his brother's tone.

"Only if you're dead." He turned back to Rory slowly. "You look like you're breathing to me. Should we see about giving you an excuse not to work it? But death is the only one that will work."

Rory grimaced as he shoved his hands in his dark gray work pants and glared back at Noah. "I had a date."

"So do I," Noah informed him.

"My date is more important," Rory growled. "I've been after this woman for months. Pretty little phys-ed major." He sighed. "She's built, Noah."

"She's doomed to disappointment tonight. Unless you want to go ahead and close on time."

Rory glanced up at the house. "Do you think she'll notice?"

"Probably."

Rory turned back to him, narrowed his eyes, and got that calculating look on his face that Noah knew well.

"I'll close up early, and you keep her busy so she doesn't figure it out," he suggested. "And when Sabella finally figures out what a prick you are, I'll take up for you."

"You close up early, you face Sabella's wrath. And if she ever figures out what a prick I am, then we're all in a hell of a lot more trouble than you ever imagined," Noah told him, his voice low, intent. "So you better pray that one doesn't happen."

He left it at that before striding through the garage, into the office, to the door of the apartment. Locking it behind him, he took the stairs two at a time until he was at the second door. There, he pulled the narrow sliver of the toothpick he had pushed into the lock free and stepped slowly inside.

He could see the glimmer of Scotch tape on the door across the room that led to the deck. It was still in place. The door hadn't been opened.

He was still cautious as he moved through the apartment though and locked the heavy door to the bathroom behind him. Sabella had been to the spa, and he couldn't wait, he was damned near shaking in anticipation of what could be awaiting him.

A bottle of wine sat empty on the bar and Sabella stared morosely at her half-empty glass. Unfortunately, she had drunk most of it.

"I'm turning into a lush," she said as she lifted her gaze and glanced at the other woman.

Kira was relaxed into the high-backed bar stool, one slim leg crossed over the opposite knee and staring at her own glass.

"It's damned good wine. Good thing your husband isn't here. He might have spanked you otherwise. It's very old wine, I do believe."

Sabella grinned at the thought of it, and at Kira's particular phrasing. Her deliberate phrasing. This wasn't a woman

who messed up. She was too much like her husband. Too deliberate, too comfortable in her own skin, in who and what
she was.

"Lucky, ain't I?"

Kira's brow arched. "You must be getting along very well
with your mechanic then."

"I haven't thrown a glass at him yet." Sabella sat back in
her bar stool and regarded the other woman curiously. "My
husband and I were barely married a year before I threw a
glass at him. He was a damned good man, but I believe he
might have thought I needed 'guidance.'"

"Guidance in what?"

Amusement glittered in her gray eyes. Sabella sipped her
wine and watched the other woman. There was an air of confidence, of sheer daring, in Kira Richards that Sabella envied but wouldn't wish for herself.

"In being a SEAL wife." Sabella's lips quirked in a grin.
"He could come home busted up, wounded, bruised to hell
and back, and just say 'bad mission,' and I wasn't to worry. I
wasn't to check the bruises or kiss his boo-boos. That was
the reason I threw the first glass. I thought it would help. He
can let the bad guys beat up on him, but I can't worry about
him?" She arched her brows. "Fine, he could carry bruises
from me as well."

"You just said 'can,' not 'could,'" Kira stated.

It reminded her of the way Nathan used to watch the
world, and still did in some cases. With knowing suspicion.

"Slip of the tongue." Sabella shrugged, and they both knew
better.

"So, your mechanic doesn't attempt to guide you?" Kira
asked her.

"I've matured." Sabella sipped at her wine. "I don't throw
glasses anymore."

Kira's brow arched. "What do you do now?"

Sabella stared down at her wine before lifting the glass and
finishing it. "I do as I please," she finally answered. "I won't
build my life around a man again." She met Kira's gaze once
more. "And I don't accept lies any longer, Kira. From anyone."

"I haven't lied to you," Kira pointed out with a smile.

Sabella nodded. "And for that, you got to share my husband's prize wine with me." She grinned. "I'll imagine it's him spanking me if my mechanic ever decides to get around to getting that brave."

Not a flicker betrayed the howl of laughter Kira was holding inside. Damn, Sabella had grown on her over the years, but in the past weeks, she had seen the true measure of strength this woman had.

"Ian retired from the SEALs just before Jordan did, didn't he?" Sabella asked.

"He did," Kira affirmed. "He'd had enough."

"So what's he doing now?"

"Not a lot." Kira smiled. "He consults every now and then with a few places. Security matters." She waved her hand as if she didn't have a clue.

Bullshit. Sabella inhaled slowly. Half-truths, but enough to understand Ian and Noah were working together. This woman was working with her husband and with Noah. It was why she had befriended Sienna and it was the reason she had made certain she met Sabella.

"Kira." She leaned forward. "If you knew anything about what Noah is doing here, or any information about my husband's last mission or specifically the recovery of his body, would you tell me?"

Kira eyed her thoughtfully for long moments before her lips pursed and she said softly, "No. I wouldn't be able to tell you that." Then she leaned forward as well. "I like you, Sabella. You're a very dear friend of mine, and because you are, between you and me, I'll tell you one thing."

Sabella leaned back, knowing she wasn't going to get what she wanted, but listening anyway.

"You're intuitive. You told me once your dad was a detective, and he taught you to use those instincts."

"He did." Her father had been her life until his and her mother's death. He had taught her so much.

"Then trust those instincts. I believe your father loved you. He taught you how to protect yourself, how to watch people and how to know them. Believe in what your father taught you. In what your husband taught you."

"I think I need coffee rather more than more wine." Sabella set the glass aside and she let it go. She'd found out what she needed to know. She wouldn't push this friendship further. She and Kira knew the truth, they couldn't speak it, neither of them could acknowledge it. But they knew. "How long are you and Ian going to be in town this time?"

"I'm not certain." Kira put her glass on the counter as Sabella moved to the coffee maker. "Ian hasn't set a time limit, and we're still rather enjoying our time together."

Sabella nodded. In other words, however long the mission here took, she guessed.

She wondered what Noah would do when the mission here was over. Would he tell his wife, then, who he was and what had happened to him?

"Are you having problems stepping into a relationship with Noah?" Kira asked her suddenly. "I would imagine it's hard. Sienna mentioned you've not been involved with anyone since your husband died."

"Just as she suggested it was a rebound relationship?" Sabella snorted. "No. I'm not having any problems at all."

She tucked her hands into the back pocket of her short jeans skirt and moved to the wide kitchen window.

She could see the back of the garage. Noah's Harley sat close to the cement building, gleaming black in the waning summer sunlight.

"You and Sienna have been friends for a long time," Kira stated. "Still, I'd have hesitated to say that to a friend of mine."

Sabella shrugged. "Sienna can be blunt sometimes, especially when she and Rick are going head to head over something."

"They don't get along well then?"

Sabella turned back to her. "They get along fine. She just hates his schedule. And Rick is pretty intense about his job."

"Most men that work in a protective capacity are rather intense." Kira nodded. "Ian mentioned that Admiral Holloran said you had called Rissa Clay a few days ago. That was very kind of you."

Sabella frowned and pushed her fingers through her hair worriedly.

Her husband's last mission had been the rescue of Rissa Clay and two other young girls. She hadn't called to ask Rissa anything, she remembered very little of that night, Sabella had been told. But she called occasionally, because she knew Rissa. Cared for her. Thankfully the other girl seemed to be doing well.

"I knew Rissa before she was kidnapped," she said softly. "Nathan and I sometimes flew into Washington to visit with his uncle Jordan. Rissa was around a lot. She lived close by with her father so we were invited to several of the parties. She was a sweet girl."

She hadn't deserved what had happened to her.

"Rissa is a very sweet young woman." Kira nodded. "I saw her a few weeks ago. She's recovered well from the horror of the kidnapping. Six years has given her some distance, some resolution I believe."

Sabella was silent, the thought of what Rissa had gone through weighing heavily on her. Nathan had supposedly died during the mission to rescue Rissa Clay and two other senator's daughters. One of the young women had died, the other, Emily Stanton, had married another of Nathan's friends and a fellow SEAL, Kell Krieger.

Before she could say anything more, Sabella swung around at the sound of Noah's Harley purring to life behind the garage.

God. He was dressed in snug jeans and riding chaps. A snug dark T-shirt covered his upper body, conformed to it. And he was riding her way.

"Is there anything sexier than a man in riding chaps riding a Harley?" Kira asked behind her. "It makes a woman simply want to melt."

And Sabella was melting. She watched as he pulled around the side of the garage then took the gravel road that led to the back of the house. The sound of the Harley purred closer, throbbing, building the excitement inside her.

"I think it's time for me to leave," Kira said with a light laugh. "Don't bother to see me out."

Sabella didn't. She listened as the Harley drew into the graveled lot behind the house and moved to the back door. She opened it, stepping out on the back deck as he swung his leg over the cycle and strode toward her.

That long-legged lean walk. It made her mouth water. Made her heart throb in her throat as hunger began to race through her.

"The spa treated you well," he announced as he paused at the bottom of the steps and stared back at her. "Feel like messing your hair up and going out this evening? We could have dinner in town. Ride around a little bit."

She hadn't ridden on a motorcycle since she was a teenager. She glanced at the cycle, then back to Noah.

"I'd need to change clothes."

His gaze flickered over her short jeans skirt, her T-shirt.

"That would be a damned shame too," he stated. "I have to say, Ms. Malone, you have some beautiful legs there."

No one had ever been as charming as Nathan. She remembered when they were dating, how he would just show up, out of the blue, driving that monster pickup of his and grinning like a rogue when he picked her up. He'd been the epitome of a bad boy, and he had been all hers. He was still all hers.

"Bare legs and motorcycles don't exactly go together," she pointed out.

He nodded soberly, though his eyes had a wicked glint to them. "This is a fact, beautiful. And pretty legs like that, we wouldn't want to risk."

She leaned against the porch post and stared back at him. "I have a pickup, you know." She propped one hand on her hip and stared back at him.

"Really?" Was that avarice she saw glinting in his eyes, or for just the slightest second, pure, unadulterated joy at the mention of that damned pickup?

He looked around. "I haven't seen a pickup."

"It's in the garage," she told him carelessly. "A big black monster with bench seats. Four-by-four gas-guzzling alpha-male steel and chrome."

He grinned. He was so proud of that damned pickup.

"Where did something so little come up with a truck that big?" he teased her then.

She shrugged. "It belonged to my husband. Now, it belongs to me." That last statement had his gaze sharpening.

"You drive it?"

"All the time," she lied, tormenting him. "I don't have to worry about pinging it now that my husband is gone. He didn't like pings."

Did he swallow tighter?

"It's pinged then?"

She snorted. "Not hardly. Do you want to drive the monster or question me about it? Or I could change into jeans and we could ride your cycle. Which is it?"

Which was it? Noah stared back at her, barely able to contain his shock that she had kept the pickup. He knew for a fact there were times the payments on the house and garage had gone unpaid—his "death" benefits hadn't been nearly enough—almost risking her loss of both during those first months of his "death." Knowing she had held on to that damned truck filled him with more pleasure than he could express. Knowing she was going to let someone who wasn't her husband drive it filled him with horror.

The contradictory feelings clashed inside him, and he promised himself he was going to spank her for this.

"You're being awful generous with your late husband's possessions," he told her.

She grinned back at him. "You've loosened me up maybe? Besides, you've already slept with his wife, why not drive his truck? Kira drank his 1925 Chateau Feytit Clinet red wine today."

Did he look pale? Noah swore he could feel himself blanch. His 1925 Chateau Feytit Clinet? No. She hadn't shared that with Kira Richards. The one person in the world besides Sabella who knew exactly how horrified he'd be to hear that Sabella had dipped into his treasure trove of wines?

"He had a 1925 Feytit Clinet?" He almost wheezed. How he kept his voice calm and level he didn't know. Hell, his training had just been shot to hell. "And you shared it with Ian Richards's wife?"

"He had lots of wine." She turned and shot him a look over her shoulder. "Maybe one of these nights I'll share the other one with you. Do you want me to meet you at the garage with the pickup? It won't take me long."

Let her drive his pickup? Had she lost her damned mind?

"I can leave the cycle here." He nodded to the back drive as he stepped to the porch. "I'll just help you lock up."

"Okay." There was a swing to her hips that almost had his tongue hanging out of his mouth. And he almost—only almost—forgot about the wine and the truck.

She drank his wine? Drove his truck? And Rory hadn't warned him ahead of time?

He locked the back door, checked the house, as she gathered her purse and grabbed a light denim jacket from her bedroom. They met at the bottom of the stairs where she held up the keys to the truck. He almost sighed with pleasure as he took them and followed Sabella into the garage.

He knew the minute he looked at the black and chrome Ford four-by-four that she hadn't driven it since the day she brought it back from the garage. After she had slammed her little BMW into it and claimed it was all his fault.

Because he was cutting the grass without a shirt and she had been looking at him instead of the truck.

That had been the day he had realized just how much he did love his spritely little wife. Because instead of raging, instead of babying his truck, he had picked his wife up, carried her into the house, and fucked her on the stairs because he couldn't make it to the bedroom.

"Nice." He patted the side of the hood, ran his hand along the curved frame.

"Yeah. It was Nathan's baby." There was an edge of amused indulgence in her voice.

"You weren't?" He looked up at her, staring at her across the hood of the truck. Because he knew she had been his life. She was still his life.

Hadn't he loved her well enough that she knew she was the most important thing to him?

"I was his wife." She moved to the door and opened it before climbing onto the running board and stepping into the passenger side.

Noah pulled the driver's side door open and moved in beneath the steering wheel aware that her answer wasn't enough to satisfy him. Yes, she had been his wife, but she had been so much more as well. His heart. His soul. And for nineteen months, she had been his sanity.

"How long since you started it?"

She stared out the windshield. "A while."

The odd note in her voice had him pausing as he pushed the key into the ignition.

"I start it every few weeks." She shrugged.

She lowered her head to where her fingers were twining together in her lap and shook her head. She pulled the seat belt across her, buckled in, and propped her elbow on the window before turning to look at him.

"I used to sleep in the truck when I couldn't sleep in the bed."

"You missed him." He was glad for the darkness in the garage, the shadows between them.

"I missed him," she agreed, before reaching out her hand and pressing a button in the dash. "Garage door opener. I had it installed while he was on that last mission. It was supposed to be a surprise."

The garage doors eased open, sliding up, revealing the lengthening shadows outside.

"Come over here." He unlocked her seat belt, caught her wrist and pulled her to his side. He latched the middle belt before locking his own and sliding the truck in reverse.

He pulled out of the garage, hit the button for the garage door, and watched it close and lock as easily as it had unlocked and opened. He'd wanted the damned thing so badly he could taste the need before that last mission. But he'd been saving for something else. Something for Sabella.

She'd done it for him, and he found his chest expanding, his heart breaking. Every minute he spent with her, he saw more and more things he hadn't taken the time to notice when he had been "alive." Things he wished he had taken the time to discover.

"Sure you want me to drive your husband's truck?" he asked. He was pushing her, and he didn't know why.

Six years she had grieved for him, and in the space of a few short weeks, she'd become his lover, she was letting him drive her husband's truck, had let him fuck her husband's wife, had let him sleep in his bed.

The fact that he was her husband was beside the point. Sort of.

"Yeah." She nodded slowly. "I think it's time."

"Time for what?"

She turned her head and stared back at him, her expression composed, calm. Almost cool.

"I think it's time to let my husband go. Don't you, Noah?"

And what the hell was he supposed to say to that? He clenched his jaw, slid the truck into drive, and pulled away from the house.

Let her husband go, his ass. She had a hold on him so damned tight he didn't know if he was coming or going, and the chance to tell her the damned truth was long gone.

There was no way she would understand now, so many years after his rescue, why he hadn't sent for her. Why he hadn't wanted her with him. She would never know the demons that ravaged his mind then, and he thanked God for that. She would never know the nights he spent thinking of her, aching for her. She would never know how hard it had been not to come to her, to take her, to love her as he was doing now.

And still he was holding back parts of the sexual needs that raged at him, that filled his mind, that filled him with dark fantasies. Needs he was afraid Sabella wouldn't be able to understand if she had any idea who he was, or who he had been to her.

As the silence lengthened in the truck and they drove closer to town, he realized mistakes, too long past, that he had made. Both in his marriage, and later, after his rescue.

She had held on to every aspect of their lives together. And though she didn't know who he was, still she had moved back into his arms, his dreams, his life, as though she had been born to be there.

"Your husband was a fool," he finally told her.

She didn't say anything for long moments before she glanced up at him, her eyes somber, sad. "Why do you say that?"

"Because only a fool would have risked losing his life, and losing you, as he did." That mission. He had been so certain it would be a piece of cake, though a part of him had known better. A part of him that he no longer ignored. But he had ignored it that time.

She turned her head and stared through the windshield. She didn't answer him. She studied her fingers in a gesture that he knew was both sad, and lonely. Whatever emotions were twisting inside her, she kept them to herself. And perhaps it was better that way. This was better for her, letting him go, getting on with her life, choosing a lover, letting go of the past.

When the time came that he had . . . That this mission was over. He couldn't even let himself think of losing her again.

Noah Blake didn't have to die. Noah Blake could claim Sabella Malone. He could hold her, keep her, he could marry her and move into that house on the hill.

He stopped himself. Noah Blake didn't even belong to himself anymore. He belonged to the Elite Ops. He had signed the papers. He had given them what he should have given his wife.

His future. And as he had been warned, once he signed those papers he was the property of whatever shadowy organization had paid for his rebirth. The advanced surgeries, the repairs to bone and muscle that no amount of money could have paid for otherwise.

Had he returned to Sabella then, he would have been partially disabled, he wouldn't have been a SEAL, he would have been a husk of the man he had been.

He had signed away his life as Nathan Malone and resignation wasn't an option. The only question was, could Noah Blake have a life instead?

CHAPTER EIGHTEEN

The restaurant Noah chose was a new one. The Steak House and Grill was owned by another resident Nathan had known from school. Sally Bruckmeyer and her husband Tom.

Their kids, five in all, worked with them. Sally, two of her girls, and the oldest boy worked the dining room, while Tom and the next oldest boy and girl worked the kitchen along with a cousin or two Sabella remembered.

As they walked into the restaurant, it seemed all eyes watched them. Sabella had maintained a very low profile for the six years she had been without her husband; now she was running around town with a bad boy who wore motorcycle chaps and drove Nathan Malone's pickup. She could hear the gossip now and she didn't give a damn. She had never cared about the gossip, and being with Noah made it feel right.

A secret they shared, but didn't. It made the night seem more intimate.

"Sabella Malone, if it ain't good to see you out and about." Sally Bruckmeyer was tall, wide, and wreathed with smiles as she came around the checkout and enveloped her in a hug. "And who's this handsome devil running around with you?"

She was sharply aware of Noah's hand on her back, his fingers splayed wide.

"Sally, this is a friend of Rory's and mine, Noah Blake."

Noah, this a friend of mine, Sally Bruckmeyer. Her and her husband own the restaurant." As though Sally didn't know his name. She bet everyone in town knew who he was and all the drivel Rory had spilled about meeting him in a bar in Odessa.

Her ass!

"Ms. Bruckmeyer." He extended his hand for a hand-shake, causing Sally's eyes to twinkle as she accepted the gesture and looked back at Sabella teasingly.

"A bad boy, Belle." Sally wagged her finger good-naturedly, her brown eyes twinkling in her dark face. "You better watch out for this one. He's a heartbreaker."

"I figured that one out for myself, Sally." Sabella laughed as she looked around the nearly full dining room. "Do you have room for us tonight?"

"If you're willing to sit out on the patio, we have tables out there. Nice candlelight." She leaned forward and whispered, "A few less eyes bugging out at you."

Sabella's grin widened. "That sounds perfect."

"Come on then." Sally grabbed two menus and silverware and led them across the room. "I have the perfect table for you."

Sabella could feel the stares. Noah, with his long, shaggy black hair falling to his shoulders and framing his savage, bearded face. His hard, corded body, snug jeans, T-shirt and chaps. He was dangerous, exuded danger. Screamed it and owned it. And she loved every minute of it.

There wasn't a man or a woman in the room that would ever mistake him for her husband. He was safe from that, if that safety was what he needed.

Sally led them to the open glass doors onto a wood patio. The lighting was low here. Umbrella tables with candle lanterns hanging beneath the umbrellas. It set a romantic, charming mood.

There were fewer guests outside. The music was lower, the sense of intimacy thicker, while inside, there was a feeling of togetherness.

"Here's your menus, and I'll send Katy out to get your drinks and your order. You two enjoy." Sally leaned to Sabella.

"And dinner is on the house, sugar. A welcome back present, how's that?"

Sabella blinked at the offer. "I haven't been gone, Sally," she teased, though moisture filled her eyes.

"Yeah, sugar, you left us the same time our boy Nathan did, no matter how many times you were seen with that Sykes boy." Sally hugged her, hard. "At least you're still with us. And bringin' in some damned fine eye candy." She winked at Noah.

She moved away then and Sabella stared down at the tablecloth and swallowed tightly. She hadn't realized she had been missed. She had been here, in Alpine, but she hadn't been. She had been immersed in the past, in her loss, in rebuilding the business her husband had been so proud of. It was as though she hadn't lived at all while he had been gone and that had been frightening.

"Sorry about that," she whispered, opening her menu as she glanced at the patio doors. "Sally and her husband Tom were good friends of my husband's."

"Not a problem." Noah leaned back in his chair and stared around the patio as she glanced back at him.

"Sabella Malone. I thought that was you." The rough, masculine voice had Sabella tensing as she looked up.

Gaylen Patrick, one of the larger ranch owners in Alpine was waddling from the doorway. At forty-five, Gaylen was still a powerful-looking man, though much of the power was the paunch of his stomach, and wide thighs. He waddled, almost like a duck. But she had seen him wrestling steers, she knew there was power in those heavy arms despite the decadence beginning to show in his lined face.

He was bald, with hazel eyes and bushy dark brows. He talked too loud and laughed too hard. And for some reason he had thought Sabella should be willing to sleep with him no more than weeks after Nathan's death.

"Yes, it appears it's me," she answered as he stopped at the table and stared hard at Noah.

"And who's your friend? Stranger in town, ain't he?" He shoved his hand out to Noah. "Gaylen Patrick. I hear you're saving Malone's garage. That's right good of you, son."

"Noah Blake." Noah took his handshake, but his gaze was cool, his expression closed. "And there was no saving needed. Sabella had it all under control."

"That Rory, he was helpin' her some." Gaylen nodded. "Poor little thing. Bein' a widow and all, we've worried about her."

Sabella bit her tongue. Worried so much that the son of a bitch had pulled his gas account from the station the minute she had thrown him out of her house after his ridiculous proposal. He'd wanted the business, and as he had stated, he wouldn't mind marrying the widow to get it. And for some reason, he'd thought she should be willing to consider it. That nothing but the money should matter.

"She was doing fine," Noah said. "She just needed a few more mechanics willing to do their job."

Sabella almost winced. Timmy, the mechanic Rory had fired, was a distant cousin to Gaylen's ranch foreman.

"Of course she did," Gaylen boomed, gazing down at Sabella with barely veiled malice. "Too bad about her husband dyin' on her. Nathan was a hell of a boy. Everyone loved him. Why, Belle almost up and died on us when he did."

Sabella's lips tightened. Gaylen was striking where he thought it would hurt the most.

"She looks very much alive to me, Mr. Patrick," Noah drawled in that gravelly voice of his. "It's been six years since her husband's death. I don't think you need to worry any longer."

"How long did you say you were stayin' in these parts?" Gaylen hitched the band of his jeans over his girth and glared down at Noah in a pale mimicry of friendliness.

"I didn't." Noah smiled. "I haven't decided yet." He glanced at Sabella. "Leaving isn't exactly on my mind right now."

"Of course not." Gaylen laughed again, the sound strained. "Well." He wiped his hand over his jowls. "Guess I'll get back to my table." He looked at Sabella. "Your father-in-law is having dinner with us tonight, Belle. You should stop by and say hi."

Sabella clenched her fists in her lap. She stared up at Gaylen, the strike going deep.

"I think Grant Malone can do without my greetings to-night," she told him firmly.

"Family, Belle." Gaylen shook his head. "Making amends wouldn't be that hard."

"In this case, no amends are needed." Her smile was tight. "It was good talking to you again, Gaylen. Thank you for stopping by." But please get the hell away from me.

"Come out and see us sometime, girl," he boomed, his laughter so false it grated on her senses. "Take care of her, boy." The look he shot Noah was filled with dislike.

"Of course I will." Noah smiled. All teeth. "It's upper-most in my mind."

Gaylen nodded then and waddled back to the door.

"Grant Malone?" Noah's voice was perfectly bland. "Your husband's father?"

She nodded.

"So you're estranged from your in-laws?"

"They're in-laws," she whispered. "Rory stayed around, but you know how it is. We didn't have children. In-laws don't stay close in those cases."

"Rory's grandfather comes to the garage," he reminded her.

Sabella smiled at the thought. "Grandpop Rory. He's a sweetie. Rory and I don't stress him out over things. I still visit sometimes. Sometimes he stops by the house or garage. He still calls me his 'girl' whenever he sees me."

She loved Grandpop. She wondered if Noah had been to see him since Grandpop had shown up at the garage, if he had told the old man he was alive. He had told Rory, why wouldn't he tell Grandpop?

She was saved from answering any more questions when Sally's daughter Katy stepped out to take their order. Con-versation was slower after that. Sabella sipped her wine and fought against the need to ask him, to beg him for answers.

She watched everyone that came onto the patio. A few stopped to chat, to say hello. Most were just curious, others, like Gaylen, sliced where they could.

It made dinner a nerve-racking experience and she wished she had directed him to Odessa instead. That was where she and Nathan had normally gone to eat. They didn't have to socialize in Odessa. Here, in his hometown, Nathan had been popular. Dinner out meant too many other couples gathering around their table when they just wanted to eat, enjoy an evening out.

"Are you ready?" Noah asked as she played with her wine after dinner and frowned down at her glass.

"Whenever you are." She slid the glass back as he rose from his chair and tossed a tip on the table. A rather large one, she noticed. She liked that he was generous with the tip, considering Sally had given them their meals on the house.

He guided her out of the restaurant, and she noticed that not even once had he glanced at Gaylen's table where his father was staring after them.

Sometimes, she actually felt sorry for Grant Malone. There were times during the two years she'd had with Nathan that she had sensed more feelings from the other man than he showed his son. Things he held back. Nathan had been convinced his father felt nothing for him, that nothing mattered to Grant but his ranch. And after Nathan had "died," he'd been determined to acquire what Nathan owned as well, though Sabella had never understood why. He'd been as determined to acquire it as Gaylen Patrick and Mike Conrad had been. As though it were a symbol of something. She'd never understood it, had wondered if she even wanted to understand it.

There had been so many times over the past years that she had wondered why the hell she had stayed here. Why she had fought, why she had tried to continue on without Nathan.

Now she knew why, and the knowledge had the power to shake her to her core. She'd stayed because she knew he would be back.

The truck was parked close to the entrance to the restaurant. They were quiet as he helped her in then moved around to the driver's side.

Getting in, he started the motor then stared at the restaurant for long, silent moments. It took her a second, but Sabella finally saw what he was looking at.

Grant Malone had followed them out. He stood on the porch of the restaurant, arms at his sides, his blue eyes narrowed and staring at the truck.

"Your father-in-law?" he asked carefully.

Sabella nodded, her gaze connecting with Grant's for long moments. What she saw in his eyes was confusing. She could have sworn she saw grief.

Noah backed the truck out of its parking space before shifting into drive and easing out of the parking area. He didn't say anything, he didn't look back. There didn't seem to be an ounce of regret in his expression or his attitude. But she felt the regret. She felt it filling him, eating at him.

That was his father and she knew Nathan had always hoped that the day would come that he and his parent could find common ground.

"Why did you stay here after your husband died?" he finally asked her as he turned onto the main road and headed back toward the house. "You could have moved. Gone anywhere."

She shrugged. "My husband was here."

"Your husband was dead," he bit out. "You hold on to him like a talisman, Sabella. As though he still exists, and he doesn't."

She shook her head. "He did. And as long as I was here, with the things he loved, then I still held a part of him." She stared back at him, feeling the pain that welled between them now.

"Do you think this is what he would have wanted for you?" he argued furiously. "To stay here grieving for him? To put up with the petty damned bullshit I've seen you put up with from these damned people? Did he love you that little?"

"How he loved me is beside the point," she told him. "I loved him that much. And why do you care, Noah?"

His hands clenched on the steering wheel. "Then you were a fool," he finally snarled. "Or too damned young to know any better. How old were you when he died? Twenty? He married a fucking baby."

She was quiet for long seconds. She watched the night go by and grew angrier by the second.

"I spent nineteen months living the nightmare of every way my husband could have died," she finally stated coldly. "I was twenty when he left on that last mission. Almost six years ago. I would wake up in so much pain I swore I'd been beaten. I woke up screaming, praying, I watched him die so many ways I could barely function." She had seen his hell, and she knew that now. "Don't tell me what a fool I was, Noah. I loved him. That isn't up for debate, and it's most certainly not up for discussion. You might sleep in his bed sometimes, or drive his truck and fuck his wife, but you don't carry the papers that could give you the right to attempt to have an opinion on it."

She was goading him and she knew it.

He shot her a glare from the corner of his eyes. "What the hell does that mean?"

"No marriage license, Noah. You're not my husband, my father, or my brother. You have no right to that opinion."

"I'm your lover," he growled furiously. "That gives me the right. And I'm sick of hearing about Nathan. Sick to my back teeth of having him shoved down my throat."

"In my eyes, you don't have that right," she informed him. "And my eyes are the ones that count. And by the way, you just passed the house."

"I know I just passed the damned house." His fingers were wrapped tight around the steering wheel. "I meant to pass the house."

She shot him a wary look. "That's good to know."

He turned his head, glared at her, then turned back to the road. "You have a habit of being mildly sarcastic, Sabella."

And she hadn't before, she knew that. Sabella managed to restrain her smile.

"Just mildly? Damn, and here I was trying for completely sarcastic. I must need to practice."

His expression was set in tight, furious lines as he stared broodingly at the road stretching out before them.

"Bastards," he finally cursed. "They treat you like a simpleton and it pisses me off."

She laughed at that. "My husband thought I was a sweet little thing. The classic dumb blonde. He was tall and muscular, and he loved it when I was helpless."

It was the truth and he didn't like it. He hated it. It showed him a side of the man he had been that he simply didn't like. He'd wanted Sabella dependent on him. He'd never realized how much it was the opposite. He'd been dependent on her. Depended on her to bring the laughter and the warmth back to him when he returned from a mission. Depended on her laughter and her love to keep him human.

"And you tolerated that?" he asked her.

"I loved being helpless for him. Then. I've grown up, Noah. I'm not a doll. I'm not dumb. And I can survive without a big strong man to lean on. I've proved it. To myself and to anyone else who thought I was no more than the dumb blonde I let them see. Hell, I was eighteen when I married Nathan. Twenty when he was lost on that last mission. I loved him with all my soul, but I'm a woman now and games aren't a part of who or what I am. And you may as well get used to it, because I won't play the simpleton for you."

"Your husband didn't deserve you." His jaw was so tight it looked ready to crack.

"He deserved all of me," she said softly. "The fact that he didn't have it was my own fault. That and my youth. But we would have grown into each other, I believe. We would have learned all those things neither of us had shown the other at that point."

She watched curiously as he made a turn onto a dirt road rather than continuing to Odessa as she thought he was doing. The truck lights speared into the darkness, picking up the pine and piñon, lighting their way as he cut into a small canyon, turned the truck around, and cut the lights.

"We're here why?" She looked around in the darkness.

"For this." He turned, unclipped her seat belt, and a second later, the back of her seat met the back seat of the dual cab, creating a bed, of sorts.

"I didn't know it did that," she exclaimed nervously as he lifted her, pushing her until her head rested on that back seat and his hands gripped her waist.

His breathing was hard. Deep. She could see the wild glitter of his eyes, the hunger in his face.

"You had no business staying here," he bit out again. "No business putting up with the bastards that stare at you as though you should be in their beds while they sweat over you. As though you're a toy for their amusement."

Jealousy, it poured from him. It glittered in his eyes and struck an independent nerve she didn't know she had.

"Am I more than that to you?" Her hands lay by her head. She didn't push him away. She didn't fight against the arousal building inside her. "You're bitching over something you want yourself, Noah. Possession."

He parted his lips as though to speak. To answer her. A second later his head lowered and he caught her lips in a kiss instead.

Like a match to gasoline, the hunger and the need exploded inside them just that fast.

Noah could explain, but not fully, the need to fuck her in that pickup truck. The fact she had let him drive it, thinking he was another man. That she had sat next to him, that the irrational jealousy was eating him alive. He wanted to imprint himself on the truck and on the woman. He wanted to make damned sure no other man ever drove this truck, ever fucked this woman.

His.

Possessiveness bit into his guts like a demon. The unfairness of it was uppermost in his mind, but the need overpowered the thought and left him helpless to fight it. He had known, before he left her, during his capture and after, that there were plenty of men willing to fill Sabella's bed. He'd assumed that after three years, she would have had a lover. At times he had wished she had so he could have walked away and never had to look back.

But as her kiss filled him, as he took it with a desperation, a hunger, that only continued to build inside him, he knew it wouldn't have mattered. They would have still ended up here, one way or the other. The clock had been ticking, each second drawing him back; his hunger for her would have eventually proved to be too much.

Tonight, though, he might have gone too far. Only Rory knew that Nathan had readjusted the lever on the seats in the truck that would allow it to create a small bed within the dual cab. To make the front seats lower all the way back to meet the edge of the back seats and hold their position there.

The head rests folded back once the seat was lowered automatically, creating a wedge between the seat and the floor to keep it sturdy.

It had been done with every intention of eventually doing this. Taking Sabella parking. He'd never gotten around to it. But now, that obsession he had always fought with his wife rose inside him, ripping at his mind.

She thought her husband dead. Gone. And she had allowed another man to touch her, hold her, to drive his damned truck.

After tonight, no matter what the future brought, no other man would have what was his.

His hands tightened on her hips as he growled against her lips. His tongue stroked inside her mouth, licked over hers, and the pulsing awareness of need flowed around them like bands of flames, tightening on them.

He didn't feel the stretch and pull at the tender healing flesh of his wounds. He didn't give a damn. All he felt was Sabella, her hands gripping the leather of the back seat as he kissed her, craved her.

Jerking his head back, he stared down at her. Moonlight flowed into the cab of the truck, caressed her face, her dove-gray eyes, and swollen lips. Beneath the thin silky blouse her breasts rose and fell as she panted for air. Noah had to clench his teeth to keep from tearing the blouse from her body.

Levering himself over her, he stared down at her body. The skirt had ridden up her thighs, nearly showing her panties, kicking a punch of reaction in his gut that stole his breath.

Her thighs shimmered in the moonlight, like satin, like sweet, soft magic. Sabella had always been magic to him.

Loving her had been his salvation and his greatest torment. His fiercest hunger.

"You're perfect." He laid his hand against her thigh, watched the lightly toned muscle ripple around his touch, felt her response against his palm.

"Not hardly," she whispered, the throaty sound slicing through his senses with a surge of lust he could barely contain.

He smoothed his hand over her thigh, petting, caressing. The feel of her was like a narcotic, going to his head faster than any drug.

"I want you naked." He wanted it until it filled his head with nothing but the remembered sight and feel of her. "Keep your hands up there." He pushed them to the back of the seat, watching as her fingers curled beneath the shallow indent between seat and cushioned back. "That's a good girl. Just let me touch you."

"But I like touching you too." She arched as his fingers went to the little buttons of her blouse. They were almost too tiny, his fingers almost too clumsy. God, he wanted her until he was shaking with it.

Adrenaline spiked through him. He could feel it. He could feel the advanced lust that surged inside him, just at the thought of having her naked.

No other woman would do. No woman but Sabella had the power to do this to him. Even during his stay in hell, when the erection throbbing between his thighs had been in agony, he couldn't bear the thought of touching another woman.

He always knew. No matter how dazed the lust and the drug made him. No matter how much the women they brought to him looked like Sabella, the second he touched their skin, he knew. Knew it wasn't his wife, his life, he was touching.

"I dream of you," he murmured as the edges of her shirt parted, flashing pretty, pale flesh. "Dream." Had dreamed. "Of touching you. Tasting you."

"Why dream?" She watched him with shadowed, dark eyes, her lashes feathering her cheeks. "You don't have to dream, Noah. I'm right here."

He smoothed the shirt aside, stared down at her breasts, covered in nothing but the thinnest lace, her nipples hard, pointed. He knew the shape of them. The color of them. How they felt beneath his tongue, in his mouth. He knew and he hungered for more.

No woman should have the power over a man that this woman held over him. But he'd accepted the power she had long ago. He had accepted it. Loved it. Relished the heat and the need that flowed between them.

He pulled her hands from where she gripped the bottom of the seat back, lifted her and drew the shirt over her shoulders, his hands stroking her flesh.

He had to clench his teeth as her lips found his neck. She licked his flesh, her lips smoothed over it. He wanted to howl with the need striking hard and deep at his balls.

He pushed the shirt from her arms then flicked open the little hooks on her bra and drew it from her as well.

God, her breasts. What was it about a woman's breasts that so fascinated a man? Hard tight nipples. Smooth luscious mounds. A woman's response showed in her breasts. They became swollen, flushed. Nipples darkened, lengthened, and tasted like pure, sweet desire.

His hands flattened on her back, holding her in a half-reclined position as his head lowered to the tight points of her nipples.

He curled his tongue around one and her moan raced over his senses like a caress.

"I love your nipples," he sighed, pursing his lips and kissing one tight point with a soft suckling motion. "So sweet and tight. So hot and hard."

She tensed, arched.

Noah slid her to the middle of the seat, straddled her legs, holding her, laying her back, and lowered his head again.

"I'm going to suck your nipples, Sabella. Suck them so sweet and deep that you come from that alone."

He had done that for her, once. Long ago. In those months before they married. He'd had her so hot, so wet, teased her perfect body with merciless hunger until the suction at one sweet nipple caused her to come.

He wanted that again. He wanted her wild and waiting for his lips against her pussy. Her juices thick and slick, clinging to his lips. He wanted her so wet, so hot, the imprint of their lust so deep inside this vehicle that she never, never allowed another man inside it with her.

She writhed beneath him as his head lowered again. He licked around her nipple. Kissed beneath the swollen mound. His teeth raked close to her nipple, he nipped at the creamy flesh and left a soft, reddened mark as he drew it into his mouth.

Branded her. The little love bite would darken, mark her as his.

"So sweet and lush." He drew his shirt over his head as he watched her and tossed it aside.

"I want to touch you." Her voice was thick with desire now, dazed, hungry. "Let me touch you, Noah."

"Not yet." He ran his palms over her arms, pressed her hands deeper between the seat bottom and back. "Hold on right there. Don't move your hands, or we'll stop."

The hell they would. If she touched him he was going to go up in flames and slam inside her so hard and fast that neither of them would know what hit them.

"Stay right there, Sabella. Stay there, and let me love you."

CHAPTER NINETEEN

What was he doing to her? There were aspects of him that bore no resemblance to the husband she remembered, that drew parts of herself free that she knew Nathan had never possessed. Just as he gave her the parts of himself that she hadn't known during their marriage

She arched as his hands cupped her breasts, just rough enough to spike an air of danger and overwhelming hunger. Pressing the mounds together as he licked around her nipples, stroked his fingers over them, then his tongue.

Nathan had always been a thorough lover, but now, it was as though the hunger that raged inside him raged for everything. Every part of her. Even her soul.

And her breasts were so sensitive. Her nipples were hard points of pure sensation. His short, closely cropped beard rasped against her flesh. His lips smoothed and nipped, and his tongue. She arched, twisted, and tried to get closer to that diabolical tongue as each lick around the tight points sent rapturous spikes of sensation tearing into her pussy.

She was so wet. So sensitive. She needed so bad that the moans falling from her lips were more pleas, begging need, than anything else.

"You like this." Confidence, pleasure, filled his gravelly voice.

"I hate it," she panted, lying, knowing better.

Noah chuckled, and for a moment she was thrown back in time. That chuckle, rough, velvety, was a sound from the past and nearly threw her into orgasm as he chose that moment to swipe his lips over a hard nipple.

"I bet you're so wet," he crooned roughly. "If I stroked my tongue through your pussy, your juices would cling to it. Caress my lips and make me high with the taste of your need."

That tone, it was almost lyrical, despite the rough pitch of his voice. Sabella shivered at the sound, and felt more of her juices easing past her intimate lips, coating her bare flesh.

"Once I get down there, your curls are going to be soaked, aren't they, Sabella?"

She smiled up at him. "I'd have to have curls there for that, Noah."

He froze. His eyes glowed. His expression contorted with so much lust, so much hunger, that the sight of it sent a hard convulsion of sensation straight to her womb.

Oh yes, her Nathan loved her bare. He had loved sucking at the curl-free lips, licking them, kissing them.

His breathing roughened, rasping from his throat as his jaw tightened.

"Bare?" The muscles in his chest and biceps tightened, bulged.

"All bare, Noah." She smiled, a slow, knowing smile. "All soft and silky. Nothing but flesh."

He jerked as though a lash had been laid to him.

One hand moved to his jeans, pulled his belt loose, tore open his jeans. His head lowered to her breasts again and she nearly screamed as his lips covered her nipple.

He was releasing himself. Stroking himself. Sabella knew he was and she wanted to touch. She wanted to taste. But his lips were consuming her, the pleasure driving hard, brutal lashes of pleasure into her womb, her pussy, until she felt an eruption.

Not a hard orgasm. A rush of fiery ecstasy detonated her womb and washed through her vagina. She cried out, shuddering and jerking against the pleasure as his tongue flickered over her nipple and a groan tore from his chest.

He jerked up, then shifted, one hand burying in her hair, lifting her head and giving her exactly what she wanted.

The thick knob of his cock pierced her lips and she sucked it in greedily. One hand pulled at the front snap of her skirt. Jerked at the zipper and pushed the material to her thighs.

Sabella lifted, using one hand to help him divest her of the skirt, leaving only her panties covering her hips. Silk thongs that did nothing to hold back the moisture glazing her now.

She swallowed the head of his erection into her mouth, licked the underside, sucked and moaned around the taste of the precum that had spilled from the tiny slit at the tip.

"Yes," he hissed with brutal pleasure. "God, your mouth is good. So hot and wet. Suck me deeper, Sabella. Suck it deeper, baby. Just a little bit deeper."

She took him deeper, flattening her tongue as he slid in and back, slow, deliberate strokes that filled her mouth and her senses with his taste.

Noah stared down at her, watching her as she watched him, her mouth moving over the torturously hard knob of his cock. Her mouth was so hot. So brutally good. God, sucking him like she loved it. Loved the taste of him, the feel of him in her mouth.

And he loved his dick in her mouth. Loved watching her, that little edge of innocence in her expression making him harder, hungrier, if possible. As though she were almost a virgin. Almost as innocent as the first time he took her.

Noah gripped the base of his cock, his thighs tightening, as she slid one hand up his thigh, cupped his balls.

He snarled at the ecstasy of her touch. The firm, liquid hot suction of her mouth.

He ran his hand down her flexing abdomen, pushed his fingers beneath her panties, and paused. Not yet. If he let his fingers feel the slick moisture now, he'd lose it. He'd pulse between her lips, fill her hot mouth with his come and all hope of control would be shot to hell.

"Look how bad you are." He let a tight, approving grin curl his lips as she teased him with her lips and tongue.

She pulled back, curled her tongue over the lip, flickered against it as a groan tore from his chest.

He pulled his fingers back from beneath her panties, stared down at her with wicked promise, then laid a light, sensual little tap against her pussy, over the wet silk of her panties.

She froze. Her gray eyes nearly went black then her mouth covered the head of his cock and she was sucking with hungry, aroused demand.

"Like that, baby?" he whispered. "Should I spank that pretty pussy for you?"

She jerked, the sweet suction of her mouth deepened, drawing his balls impossibly tighter as he laid another heavy caress to the silk-covered mound and nearly blew every ounce of come tightening through his cock.

Sabella tried to scream as she sucked him deep. The heavy caresses, not really smacks but a deep, fiery impact against her sensitive flesh, were flashing through her nerve endings, ripping through the rest of her body.

It was nothing gentle. She didn't want gentle. For each fiery caress she sucked him deeper, firmer, lashed her tongue over the sensitive crest and told him with more than words the pleasure tearing through her.

"You love it." He cupped her pussy, rotated the pad of his palm over her clit. "You like it just a little rough, don't you, baby? Just a little bit. Enough to make it burn."

She loved the burn.

She couldn't believe he was doing this, here in his truck. He'd never done anything this extreme in the whole time she had known him before his disappearance. He had never loved her like this, taken her with such lust and hunger.

Holy hell. Noah felt the need exploding his brain. Adrenaline punched through his system. Lust sliced through his senses. He wasn't going to be able to hold back. If he didn't get her sweet mouth off his cock he was going to explode.

He pulled back. Smoothed his palm over her wet panties and heard her sharp intake of breath. He laid another heated caress. It wasn't a slap, it was a heavy pat, enough to make her burn, to make her clit pulse and throb, but not enough to make her come. Not yet. He wanted her to come on his lips, against his tongue. He wanted to feel her pussy clenching, creaming, tightening for him.

He pulled back, lifted her, moved her until her head was in the corner across from the steering wheel. He spread her legs wide, stared down at the pale peach wet silk that covered her mound.

He drew her panties over her thighs, pressed her legs together, her knees back, lifting her legs as he drew the silk off her legs and then stared down at the pretty pink folds and the curve of her ass.

Smoothing his hand over the pretty rise of her butt he lifted it, then tapped it. Just a little smack.

The light of the moon gleamed over the pale flesh as his fingers slid to the narrow cleft, caressed, felt her juices coating the little entrance there, below her pussy.

"Do you need, baby?"

"Noah." She moaned his name, her voice dazed, her fingers clawing at the leather seats behind her, marking them forever.

The abuse to the leather filled him with a sharp surge of satisfaction. Marked. Branded by her passion. Just as he was.

He lowered her legs, spread them again, and stared at the pretty, shadowed folds of her pussy. His jaw clenched. He wanted to see more.

He flipped on the dim floor lights, his jaw clenching, teeth grinding at the sight of the silky moisture glazing her pussy.

"I'm goin' down on you," he bit out, moved back until one knee braced on the floor and his head lowered to the sweet, pretty flesh of her pussy.

His Sabella.

Wet.

Hot.

"God. Noah. Yes." Her hips arched to him.

"What do you want, Sabella?" He breathed over the wet flesh. "Tell me, baby. Tell me how you want it. Slow and sweet?" He licked through the swollen folds, gathered her juices, and groaned at the fresh, sweet taste of her.

"Or hard? Fast?" He lifted her, shoved his tongue inside her as a thin, ragged scream left her lips.

He felt the delicate, feminine muscles clamping on his tongue, milking it. His cock jerked in response. The engorged crown throbbed, pulsed. Hell. If he didn't touch her, taste her, take her, he was going to die. If he didn't have her one more time he was going to expire.

He wanted all of her. Every touch, every taste.

Her hands moved to her side. Her nails dug into the folded back of the seat. Long scores, ripping the surface of the leather. Another brand. Another mark. She would never forget. Never lose the memory of who she belonged to.

To him.

He flicked his tongue inside her again. Licked at the sweet softness meeting his tongue, flickered over hidden nerve endings and felt her rising, lifting.

She was shuddering in his grip as he pulled back. Kissed the swollen folds. Sucked at them, licked at them, his lips moving ever closer to the swollen bud of her clit.

He let his fingers part the folds. As his lips pursed over her clit, he slid one finger into the heat of her sex, the other, he worked slowly, gently, until the tip penetrated the little entrance of her ass.

"Noah." Her hands tangled in his hair. Her hips lifted, pressing her clit deeper between his lips. "Oh God. Noah. Please. Please suck me. Suck my clit. Make me come. Oh God. Make me come."

He sucked her inside, flicked his tongue around, around, sucked her sweet and easy, then harder, filled his senses with the taste of her and felt the explosion rip through her.

Noah jerked back. He gripped the hardened shaft of his cock with one hand as he came over her, felt her arms curving around his shoulders as he tucked the crown against the slick, hot folds of her beautiful sweet little cunt.

"I want to take you slow." He could barely push the words from his lips for the sheer pleasure enveloping the blunt head of his cock. "Slow and deep."

She lifted against him, her nipples stroking over his chest, burying in the mat of hair covering it. He could feel them, like little hot pebbles burrowing against him.

"You're so tight, Sabella."

She stared back at him, her expression tight with pleasure, her eyes heavy lidded, her face flushed with arousal.

God, he loved looking at her while he took her. Loved watching her face, the expressions that flickered across it, the almost painful need that filled it.

He worked the thick crown inside her, watched her breath catch, and felt his muscles tighten as he fought to hold back. He had to hold back. Just a little bit. Just a few more minutes of sheer overwhelming pleasure.

Sabella's gaze dimmed as she felt Noah begin to push inside her. The thick crest pierced her, worked inside her, spreading and stretching her until she could feel the burn beginning to blaze inside her.

His eyes held hers, the blue candleglow, flickering with emotion, brighter, darker than they had ever been for the emotions raging through them. His eyes were shadowed, but the lust filling them wasn't.

He burrowed inside her, his long hair falling over his face, touching hers, as a grimace contorted his face.

"I can feel you." His voice was a hard, delicious rasp. "Tightening on me."

She could feel the muscles inside, flexing, milking him as her juices built and flowed against the heavy width invading her.

"It's . . ." she gasped. "It's so good, Noah."

"Tight and hot," he crooned, lowering his lips to hers as her lashes fluttered closed. He brushed his lips over hers, licked the parted curves. "Like a hot little mouth sucking me deep and tight. Do you feel it, Sabella? Your pussy sucking me in? Loving my dick?"

She jerked, cried out at the stab of pleasure that struck her womb.

"You like that, don't you, sweetheart? Just a little bit nasty, just a little bit rough. Just a little bit dangerous."

She loved him like this. She ached for this. Realized as her lashes lifted that this was what had been missing, what he had been holding back from her during their marriage.

"You're a whole lot dangerous," she groaned, lifting to him, feeling her lips brush his as she spoke.

"Hold on tight, sugar. We're gonna make you burn brighter."

Her hands tightened in his hair.

His hips jerked, pushed forward with a hard, deep stroke, and a thin ragged wail tore from her lips.

"Fuck, yes. Scream for me."

One hand gripping her hip, he tugged his cock back, the crest only poised inside her as he gave a hard, fast thrust inside her again.

Sabella nearly exploded. She felt the vibrations slam inside her before he stopped, not quite filling her yet, a ragged snarl falling from his lips as she screamed his name.

"Again. Scream for me again, Sabella. Scream my name." He pulled back. "Who's fucking you, Sabella?"

The hard penetration filled her with him. Her hips jerked, writhed. "Noah," she screamed his name. "Oh God. Noah."

"Yeah. Oh yeah." He ground against her, his pubic bone rotating against her clit as he thrashed, her legs lifting, wrapping around his hips as she fought for that last bit of pressure that would send her hurtling into release.

"Yeah, baby. Scream my name. Noah's fucking you. Taking you." He pulled back. "Who does this sweet hot pussy belong to?"

He impaled her, pressed hard and fast inside her, and she screamed his name again.

"Damn right. Noah. Noah's fucking you."

Sabella opened her eyes, staring up at him in dazed need, watching his expression contort, his eyes burn brighter, darker. Then he was pushing inside her hard and fast again, and he didn't stop.

The sound of flesh slapping, deep wet penetration, and her own screams filled her ears. Each slamming thrust ground him against her clit, threw her higher, harder, until she was crying out, beginning, and then exploding into such rapturous, perfect pleasure that she could feel herself becoming lost within the sensations ripping through her.

She heard him. He cried out her name, his ruined voice agonized as two more thrusts buried him deeper, harder, and then he was jerking inside her, against her, filling her with the heated hard pulses of his release.

He filled the interior of the truck with the scent of sex and satisfaction. His scent. Her scent. They mingled, marked them, marked the seats and the vehicle and marked her soul.

When he collapsed over her, his arms wrapping around her, folding her in his powerful hold, Sabella had to fight to hold back her tears, her need for explanations.

She had her husband's body, held all the dark passion she had only glimpsed in him before, but she didn't have his trust.

It was a hard blow, the realization that he didn't trust her, that he trusted his brother, but not her.

Her arms tightened around him and a single tear slid from her eye before she could battle the rest back.

For whatever reason, he was here now. Here, and hungry for her. He was still hard inside her, moving slow and easy against her, filling her ears with his ragged breaths and his gentleness.

"One more time." He nipped at her ear, then kissed her neck, and his hips moved, pulling his erection, still thick and hard, back, until only the crown was poised inside her, before pushing inside her again.

Slow and easy. He took her slow and easy. His lips whispered over hers, sipped at them. His tongue tasted them and slid against hers like rough velvet.

And his gaze held hers. Fierce. So bright. Agonized and filled with emotions she was certain he didn't know he was showing.

His jaw was locked tight. He wasn't speaking now. He was forcing the words back. Forcing back that guttural vow he had always given her in Gaelic. The promise he had always made with his heart and with his body.

"Don't stop," she whispered, lifting her hand to his rough cheek, holding him to her, relishing the feel of his body sliding against hers. "Never, Noah. Never stop."

Their breathing was rough in the steamy heat of the truck cab. Their flesh slipped and slid against each other, against the leather seats. He groaned and his pace increased. His jaw tightened.

"Never stop," she cried out as she felt the ribbons of pleasure snapping inside her again, jerking her against him as she cried out his name. "Oh God, Noah. Never stop."

Noah pumped inside her, his release spurting with agonized pleasure inside her as he felt the final assault to his senses easing.

She had always done this to him. Always made him insane to take her, as many times as he could take her. But now, that need was like a steady flame inside him. Having her enough would never happen.

He pulled her into his arms as they fought for breath, his body curled around hers on the makeshift bed of the truck cab, the leather wet beneath them.

He let his hands stroke over her, ease her. Her back was to his chest, his hips spooned against her, and he should have been uncomfortable. He wasn't. He was holding her, brushing her hair back from her face before kissing her brow gently.

"Okay?" he whispered as he felt her breathing finally steady.

Her little laugh was thready, almost tearful.

"Does alive count?" Her voice was hushed, as soft as his. As though to speak any louder would somehow damage the intimacy enfolding them.

"I definitely want you alive." He smiled at her, his fingers stroking down her bare arm as her head lay on the pillow of his other arm.

She was relaxed, soft against him. Like a lazy little cat. All that was missing was the purr.

"This is nice," she murmured, turning to stare up at him, flowing against him like silk. "You're very hard-core, aren't you, Noah?"

He grunted at that. "You call that hard-core? Baby, that was just a little snack. Playtime."

He grinned as her eyes widened in playful surprise.

"I might not survive it if you get serious then." Her lips pursed at the thought. "Maybe I should double up on my vitamins?"

He nipped the tip of her nose, almost laughing at her expression as he stroked his fingers along her hip.

"Very bad girl," he warned her. "You could end up getting spanked."

"But I like getting spanked." She looked up at him from the corners of her eyes. "You're all threat, I—" She broke off.

God! She pushed her fingers roughly through her hair. She had almost called him "Irish." Almost let her knowledge of who he was slip past her lips.

"You what?" Noah grinned, pulling back.

Her expression seemed to even out, a rueful smile pulling at her lips. "I think you're all talk."

His eyes narrowed. "I could say different."

"Tonight?" She laughed, a low, lazy sound. "Let's go home first. The bed is more comfortable."

Home. He paused as he stared down at her.

"Home, huh?"

Her gaze flickered as though some uncomfortable thought had suddenly invaded her mind. A reminder that it wasn't his home maybe?

He was the other man. The man holding her, fucking her, while her heart belonged to the man he had been. Fuck, he was going to have to stop this. He could finish the long, slow slide into insanity if he continued to let himself be jealous of . . . himself.

"Back to the house." She finally shrugged. "Home is only where you want to be, I guess. If you prefer the bed at the apartment, then that's your choice."

She lifted away from him, gathered her clothes from the floor of the truck, and began dressing.

"I hurt you. I didn't mean to." He frowned at her back. Shit. He needed to get a handle on himself.

"How long do you intend to stick around, Noah?"

The question surprised him. Noah narrowed his eyes at her, aware that she was deliberately keeping her back to him.

"Do you want me to leave?"

An irritated little sniff sounded through the cab of the truck. Feminine. Filled with ire.

"Did I ask you to leave? Perhaps I'm just curious if you intend to stick around or if you have other plans anytime soon." There was a tension in her voice that had his body tightening.

"Other plans, such as what?"

"Such as leaving." She shrugged. "You blew into town from nowhere. Took over my life and my bed. Perhaps I'd just like to know if you're considering more than a few one-night stands?"

She wanted commitment. Sabella wasn't a easy lay, he had known that when he first met her. Yet, here he was, knowing when this mission finished it would be time to leave.

"There are some things I have to leave to take care of soon," he finally warned her. He couldn't promise her anything yet, not yet. He couldn't promise her forever until he knew if signing his life away to the Elite Ops meant signing everything away.

Sabella closed her eyes and fought the pain. Which was worse? she wondered. Losing him to a supposed death, or having him walk away voluntarily?

The latter would hurt worse, but at least she wouldn't wonder. She would know he was safe. Know he was alive.

But that didn't keep the anger from burning inside her like an inferno that only seemed to grow.

"I see." She buttoned her blouse in hard, jerky movements before reaching for her panties and skirt.

"What do you see?" He seemed genuinely curious.

"You're not future material, just a quick lay wherever you happen to be." She shrugged as though it didn't matter.

Damn him. Damn him to hell. Fuck it. Screw it. She'd had enough of this. Enough, as of now.

She jerked her skirt on.

"Get dressed. I need to get home. I have things to do tomorrow and they don't include lying around all day. I've wasted enough of my life as it is."

"What the hell does that mean?" His voice turned cold. Stony.

She turned back to him, watching as he levered up, glaring back at her with narrowed eyes.

"Exactly what I said. I've spent too many years grieving for a man who didn't love me enough to keep his ass alive and come back home to me." She let her gaze flick disdainfully over him. "I'll be damned if I'll waste so much as another day on a man who doesn't even care enough to let me know if he intends to stick around for a while."

"Promises are for fools, Sabella," he rasped. "You should have learned that with your husband."

"You're damned right. I should have." She threw his pants at him. "There are a lot of lessons I should have learned with my husband. Starting with the fact that he was a son a bitch who obviously didn't know how to love anything but himself and his fucking job. Lesson learned. I won't make that same mistake with you."

His shirt hit him in the face. "Get dressed. I'm fucked out and ready to sleep now. In my bed. Alone."

"Like hell."

"Hell describes it," she muttered. "But it beats sleeping with a no-commitment asshole who doesn't mind a bit to fuck and run. Now, take me home."

Her eyes were dry. There were no tears. She watched as

he dressed, and the bastard, he didn't even struggle or contort to do it. He watched her with narrowed, fierce eyes.

"I'll be sleeping in that bed with you," he promised her. "I might be a no-commitment asshole, and a luckless son of a bitch, but don't forget, while I'm here, you're mine."

She stared back at him. "Keep dreaming, Noah Blake. Because my bed is the last damned place you belong."

CHAPTER TWENTY

Noah twirled the wrench between his fingers and chewed thoughtfully at his gum as he watched Sabella two days later.

She hadn't been joking. She'd kicked him right out of her bed, and apparently, out of her life. For now at least.

He watched her from beneath lowered lashes as he pretended to stare into the guts of the SUV he was supposed to be working on.

"You're hard at work, huh?" Nik leaned against the fender and peered into the motor. "Need some help?"

"Sure," Noah murmured absently. "Any word?"

Word on the DNA samples they had slipped to the bunker and Jordan had shipped out for testing. Delbert had picked up his pickup that morning. The sneering smug little turd. He'd looked at Noah as though he had crawled out of the dumb pit when Noah had informed him there was no way to juice up his motor.

Let him juice his own motor. By time the feds were finished taking that son of a bitch apart searching for the evidence Noah had left, good ole Delbert was going to be too busy to be worrying about juice.

"No word," Nik answered. "I could use some help this evening though, if you are not busy." They both glanced at Sabella in the office then.

She was frowning over something Toby had said.

She hadn't braided her hair this morning. She hadn't worked on one of the cars this morning. She'd worked in the office, done the filing, made Toby crazy as she butted in and did his job.

"I don't appear to be busy," he drawled, twirled the wrench and stared at the waves of dark hair framing Sabella's face as she turned her frown to the papers on the desk.

"How did you screw up?" Nik asked then.

The wrench paused then moved deliberately through his fingers.

"Who says I screwed up?"

His wife had said it. His wife, and she'd thrown him out of his truck. Even worse, she'd thrown him out of their bed. Threatened to call the sheriff if he didn't leave. Son of a bitch, could anybody be more tangled than he was right now?

She was right. He was slime. A bastard. A no-commitment son of a bitch who didn't deserve to be anywhere close to her.

He threw the wrench in the toolbox at his side, hearing the clank and clatter as he jerked a greasy rag from the fender and wiped his hands quickly.

"What kind of help do you need?"

Nik scratched his jaw and looked at where Noah had thrown the wrench.

"I need to go see a friend," Nik stated, the code smooth, rueful.

A meeting had obviously been called at the bunker.

"Hell!" Noah plowed his fingers through his hair and grimaced.

He'd have to tag Rory, put him with Sabella. After the attempt on Toby, Noah was terrified to leave her alone.

"Sorry, dude. You promised." Nik slapped him on the shoulder. "But you know, it's not like you can't have your cake and eat it too. She's a fine woman. She'd make any man an even finer wife. I'd consider that if I were you. Walk away, and someone else will step in eventually. Is that what you want?"

Noah felt his lip twitch as fury began to burn inside him. He shot the big Russian a hard look and only got a cold smile in return.

Yeah. He'd promised. It had been his fucking hand that signed the papers, giving his soul to the Elite Ops rather than returning to his wife. He'd been warned then, he could never return to his old life. There was no resignation, there was no opting out unless he was dead.

And there was no revealing who and what he was, but there was no clause that hadn't said Noah Blake couldn't marry or fall in love. But could he keep his Bella and remain here, in his hometown, and maintain the illusion of who he was forever?

The Elite Ops wasn't a prison, but the consequences of breaking contract weren't pretty. Gitmo wasn't a place Noah wanted to be. If he revealed who he was, what he was, and it was learned, he could be shipped out as an enemy combatant and never be seen again.

The question was, could he remain with Sabella and never tell her he was the husband she had lost? Could he live with hating one part of himself because his wife still longed for something she thought could never return?

The jealousy was like an acrid burn in his soul, and despite his determination to keep her, Noah wondered how long he could actually stay and have that life with her while maintaining his secrets.

The wife who wasn't a damn thing like the pretty little thing he'd left six years ago. The Sabella who had stared back at him, dry-eyed and furious, two nights before was nothing like the tender, softhearted young woman he had left when he went on that last, fateful mission.

The woman he remembered shedding tears when she saw new wounds on his body after a mission. He'd seen the horror in her eyes over a shallow knife cut. He'd seen the nightmares in her eyes when he returned, exhausted, from six to eight weeks, sometimes longer, deployed into areas he could barely pronounce the name of.

The Sabella he had known would have broken at the sight of his face, destroyed from so many beatings. His back, chest, and thighs lashed to ribbons from a whip. Starved down and so desperate to fuck he was like an animal.

He'd been like an animal for three years. Jacking off until his dick felt raw, and on the retraining missions, he'd been the demon of death. He didn't ask questions. He didn't pull punches. He didn't give anyone the chance to strike at him, capture him.

He'd thought his life with Sabella was over. The woman he had thought he had known couldn't accept the man he had become.

And he'd learned he'd never known the woman he had loved. Not all the way to the bone. He'd only known what he'd wanted to see. The helpless little blonde Southern baby. Sexy and vulnerable. And so young.

It was what he had wanted to see, because seeing the strength in the core of her would have given him a clue into the future, into a woman who would have stood by him no matter how broken he had been. And his damned pride, that was it, his pride, hadn't been able to consider the thought of Sabella ever seeing him as less than what he wanted to be in her eyes.

Invincible. But he hadn't been invincible. It had taken Fuentes almost two years, but before his rescue, Noah had known it wouldn't be long before he lost the will to live or to fight. And Sabella had been there with him. In the darkest nights, the bleakest days, she had been there through it all, holding on to his soul.

That damned woman had a spine like steel and a look that could flay a man's flesh at a hundred paces. If she deigned to look at him. She was the woman who had held him through hell, through her dreams. And he had thought she wasn't strong enough to hold him broken and in pain.

He'd been a fool. And now, walking away from her just might kill him. But staying, what if staying could kill her?

"What time do we need to leave?" he finally asked Nik, forcing his gaze away from Sabella.

"Just after the garage shuts down." At dark.

They would enter the bunker under the cover of night, lights off and on stealth mode.

He nodded slowly.

"I'll let my friend know we'll be there," Nik murmured as Noah rubbed the back of his neck and moved from the garage to the convenience store where Rory was taking his turn manning the counter.

The convenience store was empty. One of those lulls that came every few hours.

Rory watched him approach, his blue eyes flat, his expression set. Rory had been watching him like that for a week now.

"What do you need?" His brother crossed his arms over his chest as he glanced at the closed door between the store and the office.

"I have to go out this evening." Noah stared back at Rory curiously.

Someone else had changed in the past years. Maybe Rory had grown up. Noah felt his chest clench at the knowledge that he had missed it. His baby brother. Their father had cast him and his mother off, refused to acknowledge the black-haired, red-faced infant he'd created with the dark-haired shop clerk from Odessa.

Grandpop had taken him instead. The squalling little scrap of flesh that no one wanted but an old man and a ten-year-old boy.

Noah had helped raise Rory, and he'd missed whatever moment Rory had faced that turned him from a lazy, reckless young man to the man facing him now.

"Fine. You go out, I'll watch her. It's what I've been doing all along anyway." Rory shrugged, that thread of anger warning Noah exactly what the problem was. The same problem Sabella was having.

He breathed out roughly and glanced at the door.

"She doesn't need to know," he finally said, his voice hard as he turned back to Rory. "She still has her memories of what was. She doesn't need to know what it became."

"I said I'd watch her." Rory grunted. "I didn't ask for your excuses."

"What the hell do you want to ask me for then, kid?" Noah bit out. "Spit it out before it eats you alive."

"Before it eats you alive." Rory smiled mockingly. "Don't worry, man. I got nothin' to bitch at you about. You're free and easy, right? Go be free and easy. I have work to do."

Noah glanced at the door again. In the past two days, he could have sworn he felt her tears. Her pain.

"Get off that attitude, Rory," he told his brother warningly. "This thing is getting too close. I have to be able to trust you to handle the fallout."

When things went to hell, Rory had to get Sabella out of town. He wanted her out of it, away from it.

"I know my responsibilities," Rory assured him, a snap in his voice. "Damn good thing one of us remembers."

Before Noah could stop the reaction, his hand snapped out, his fingers gripping Rory's neck. His brother's eyes widened as Noah gritted his teeth and pulled back. Slowly.

"Don't forget them." He was aware of Sabella standing in the doorway, the doorknob gripped in her hand, as she stared between Noah and Rory.

She was pale. There were dark shadows under her eyes. His cock jerked, already erect, he swore it only hardened impossibly further at the sight of her.

"Do you two have a problem I need to know about?"

Rory's jaw clenched. "No problem, Belle," he answered for both of them. "He just grates on the nerves sometimes, I guess."

"Do tell?" She arched her brow as she stepped from the office. "I'm going out for a while. Toby has the office and I'm getting on his nerves."

"There are cars in the bay," Noah gritted out.

"And you're so handy with them," she stated coolly as she moved from the office and closed the door behind her. "I'll see the two of you in the morning."

"Where the hell are you going?" The words were out of his mouth before he could hold them back.

Noah could feel the tension brewing in him, between them. She wanted promises. She should have learned how easily promises could be broken. He knew. He knew and it ravaged his soul, tore at his guts minute by minute, knowing, at any moment, any promise he made to her could be like dust. Like death. Simply gone.

"It's none of your business where I'm going, Mr. Blake," she told him. "But if you must know, I thought I'd go clean house." Her eyes met his and he felt something constrict in his soul. "See ya'll tomorrow."

She moved to the cooler, grabbed a cold water, and left the store. Noah watched her walk across the asphalt of the station lot and take the walkway up to the house.

She moved slow and easy, her hips shifting, ass bunching. His hands clenched at the remembered feel of those curves under his hands. Two days without her and it felt like another six years.

"You're killing her," Rory said then. "You fly back in here, make her live again, and then suddenly, she's hollow eyed and quiet. I hate you for that, Noah."

And Noah nodded slowly. Yeah, he understood that. Related. Felt it. He hated himself. He shook his head and moved from the store, back to the garage. He had vehicles to fix, a mission to finish. Things were better this way. She wasn't hiding in the house, burrowed in the bed, grieving for a man who no longer existed.

She was pissed. Probably hurt. But this one she could survive, he told himself.

He picked up the wrench and braced his hands on the frame of the SUV and wondered if he would survive it. Because he could feel the pain fracturing inside him, spreading through him until the ache was like an open wound.

Until the need for her touch, her laughter, her smile, sliced at his soul.

Sabella walked into the house and slammed the door closed. She was met by pictures. Dozens and dozens of pictures that filled the living room. Pictures of Nathan, of her and Nathan, Nathan and Grandpop, and Rory and Nathan.

They stared at her, mocking her.

She moved to the fireplace, to the mantel, and lifted the

trifold frame. And she smiled. Their wedding picture. How young she had been. How stupid. She let her finger trace over Nathan's strong jaw. It wasn't as blunt now, it was sharper, leaner.

She'd been on the computer that morning, researching what kind of damage could have caused that. Shattered bones had been the most likely cause. Or broken bones that had rehealed improperly.

She closed her eyes and swallowed tight. Repairing it would have been almost as painful as the cause. His lower lip wasn't as full as it had been, and there was a fine web of barely detectable scarring at one side.

She leaned her head against the picture of the man she had been married to.

"I love you," she whispered. "I love you, Noah." Because he was Noah now, and she knew it. Nathan still lived inside him, but she had a feeling Noah was the man Nathan had never given her.

She replaced the picture before she trudged up the stairs and moved to the shower. She'd promised Sienna and Kira she would meet them at one of the bars in town later. One of the few Rick didn't fight Sienna over going to.

Rick was as protective of his wife as Nathan had been over her, long ago and far away. She shook her head at that thought.

She had several hours before she needed to get ready for that little girls' night out.

She walked into the bedroom, stared at the bed. She started by stripping off the comforter then the sheets. The pillowcases that still held his scent.

She changed the bed, packed the sheets downstairs to the washer, and poured the detergent and bleach to them.

She walked to the basement, pulled free one of the most expensive bottles of his wine and brought it upstairs. Hell, it wasn't as though he needed it. He wasn't sticking around and she damned sure wasn't packing it up for him.

She cleaned house and drank the wine. She dusted and scrubbed. She cleaned the scent of him out of her home. She changed her comforter, pulled the pillows from the guest room and placed those on her bed. They definitely didn't smell like Noah.

She turned the music up loud. Godsmack, Nine Inch Nails. All the those pesky hard rock bands Noah had always hated. And she hadn't played them when he was home. She finished the wine and let the glow suffuse her.

She filed and painted her finger- and toenails. She showered, lotioned her body, fixed her hair, and put on the makeup she hadn't worn in three years.

The dainty little ankle bracelet he had bought her while they were dating graced her ankle. She smiled with a mocking little twist of her lips as she clasped a silver necklace around her neck, and attached the silver armband to her upper arm that he had bought her just before the son of a bitch "died."

"Bastard," she muttered. "Has to leave to sort some things out, does he? Screw it."

It wasn't like she had asked him for the truth. She'd asked if he was staying. That wasn't uncalled-for. It wasn't wrong and it sure as hell wasn't pressure. He was *her husband.*

She stared at the gold wedding band she had taken off only months before. She had to blink back her tears as she picked it up, stared at it. Inside, *go síoraí* had been engraved. Celtic for "forever." She had finally looked it up. It meant "forever." His vow to her.

"Forever didn't last long enough." But she slid the ring on the ring finger of her right hand.

She was a widow, right? That's where widows wore their rings. Her husband was indeed dead. Because her husband would have never told her he had to leave, to "sort some things out."

She inhaled roughly, trying to ignore the sense of comfort the ring brought her, even on the wrong finger.

Pulling on snug jean shorts and a sleeveless blouse, she clenched her teeth, forcing herself to go through with this little girls' night out Sienna was so determined to have. She tucked the shirt into her shorts and threaded the leather belt through the loops.

She slid a toe ring on. Something else he had bought her. She wiggled her toes, eyeing the cherry-red polish critically before sliding her feet into stylish leather sandals.

She spritzed herself with the softly scented cologne she had always favored then headed back downstairs. Striding into the kitchen, she heard the Harley and went to the window to watch as its headlight cut through the darkness and sped away from the garage.

Where was he going? Another fight?

He was here for a mission, she reminded herself. She knew he was, she just hadn't figured out what it was. And she hadn't asked. That was dumb of her. Because she hadn't wanted the inevitable question to come up. What happened when the mission or assignment was over? What happened when he no longer had a reason to be in Alpine?

And now she knew. He'd have to leave. To sort some things out.

She shook her head, picked up the phone, and called a cab. She didn't want to drive tonight. She intended to enjoy this little outing Sienna had guilted her into. She intended to dull her senses just enough to laugh with her friends, to be a girl again.

It had been a damned long time since she had been a woman, just for the sake of being a woman. Too many years since she had felt a sense of—freedom. And that freedom hurt. It hurt like hell.

She shoved a credit card and her house keys in the back pocket of her jeans and went out to the front porch to await her ride.

Sabella knew she was too damned pissed to be leaving the house. Too hurt. She should face Noah with what she knew, scream and demand the truth, but pride held her back. Who wanted a man who stayed simply because a woman reminded him that he was married?

As the cab drew into the driveway, she watched Rory step out of the convenience store, staring up at the drive.

"Pull down to the garage first," she told Art Strickman, the young man driving the cab that night. His daddy owned three cabs, and they all kept up a steady business. Especially on a Friday night.

"Yes, Ms. Malone." He flashed her a smile before turning and driving to the front of the convenience store.

Rory was waiting on her. "Where the hell are you going?"

Rory took one look at her and barely managed to keep his mouth from dropping open. Holy hell. Noah was going to explode.

This was the Sabella *he* knew. This woman standing in front him of looking like a damned goddess. Her hair all fluffed around her face, her eyes smoky in the dim light, legs a mile long, and nails painted cherry red.

"Girls' night out." She wagged her brows. "I'll be back late, so make sure you lock up tight and take the bank bag with you. I'll get it in the morning."

"Hell, umm, Belle." He swallowed tightly. "Hang around a bit. I'll go with you. I close up in an hour."

"Girls' night out, Rory." She patted his cheek with a mocking little laugh. "Sienna and Kira Richards are waiting on me. I've just put away a bottle of Nathan's eighteen hundred and something French wine, and I'm heading out to have a little fun. You can survive without me."

Shit. Shit. He pushed his fingers through his hair and stared around the lot as he heard the door open behind him.

"Ms. Malone. Wow. You're hot," Toby almost cackled. "You're going out tonight?"

"Ain't he sweet?" Belle wrinkled her nose back at him. "Girls' night out, Toby. Make sure you get a ride home, no walking. Promise?"

"You betcha." Toby laughed. "Tell me where you're going. Maybe we'll join you."

Sabella shot him a sharp look. "Do I look like I need a babysitter?" She waved her hand down her body as she cocked her hip with feminine arrogance. Rory and Toby both nearly swallowed their tongues at the look. Rory swore Noah was going to detonate like a nuclear bomb when he caught sight of this. And oh boy, Rory did intend to make damned certain his brother knew his wife was out on the town looking like a sex goddess visiting for a little down-and-dirty pleasure.

Not that Belle looked sluttish. She looked damned good. Too damned good. Too damned hot dressed like the female she was, and too innocent to know what the hell she was letting all those Friday-night cowboys get a glimpse of.

One pissed-off, hurting woman.

"No, ma'am." Toby was the first to speak. "I just want to see the fireworks later."

Rory shot Toby a silencing look. One the boy ignored.

"What fireworks?"

"The ones that are going to hit Alpine when Mr. Blake finds you," Toby said, laughing. "Talk about a Friday night free-for-all."

"Yeah. Mr. No-commitment-has-things-to-sort-out-Blake. Don't worry. I have a feeling he couldn't give a damn one way or the other."

And she believed it.

Rory saw it in her face, in her eyes. She believed to the bottom of her heart that Noah didn't give a damn. Hell. Someone was going to end up hurt tonight, and he just prayed it wasn't Sabella. Or Noah. Or God forbid, him.

With his luck, Noah would rip his head off just for letting her go.

But he let her go. Watched the cab pull out and breathed out roughly.

"How old are you, Toby?"

"Nineteen. But I got friends," Toby told him. "I can get in any bar in town."

Rory ran his gaze critically over Toby. Yeah, he could pass for twenty-one.

"We are such dead meat. Noah will kill us both!" he snarled.

"Man, you can't let her go by herself if there's shit goin' on. And I'm not stupid. I've watched you and Noah enough to know there's definitely shit going on," Toby snapped. "We

have to follow her. Call Noah, man. This is bad. It's Friday
night, Rory. You know how many men are going to be hitting
on her? It's like setting a baby lamb loose in a pen of wolves."

Rory glanced at his watch and bit back a curse. Noah
wouldn't even have cell coverage for another two hours.
He'd warned Rory of that. Only Uncle Jordan had access.
Shit. This was bad.

"Lock up."

They turned and rushed inside. Pumps were shut down,
lights turned out, and they ignored the car that pulled in, its
horn blowing imperiously in front of the pumps.

"Start calling your friends. Find out which bar she's at,"
Rory ordered half an hour later as they jumped into his car.
"I'll get hold of a contact and see if they can catch Mr. Noah
asshole Blake. How stupid can a man get?"

"As stupid as Blake?" Toby asked.

"That was rhetorical, kid," Rory groaned. "It was supposed to be rhetorical."

Jordan listened to Rory's frantic voice mail, lifted his brows,
and stared through the window into the briefing room
where the agents of the Elite Ops had gathered.

"Man. Get hold of Noah. Fast. Don't know what he did to
piss off Belle. She's got girls' night out and looks like something that just stepped outta every man's fantasy. She's
headed to the Borderline. Kira Richards and Sienna Grayson
are meeting her. Get me some backup before that psychotic
bastard you have with you goes nuclear and blames me for
this. He grabs my neck one more time, and I swear to God.
To God, Jordan, and I'm telling Grandpop. Your name will be
in it. You don't want that. And I'll tell on you." The message
cut off.

Jordan clicked the button to continue to the next frantic
message and almost smiled. Rory was losing his mind, and
Noah would be next.

"I'm telling you. I have to tell Grandpop, and we're all
gonna pay. All of us. Tell him that one for me. He does it

again and we're all screwed 'cause I'm squealin' like a pig to the old man and savin' my own ass first. You tell him that."

The message cut off.

Rory was threatening to tell Grandpop on all of them. Hell, he almost felt young again. Rory was always telling Grandpop on them when he thought they were getting his ass in trouble.

What Rory had never known was that Grandpop had usually already guessed. But having the kid trust him, love him enough, always made the old man proud as hell. Unfortunately, this time, telling Grandpop wasn't an option.

Jordan leaned back in his chair, stared at his nephew, and he almost smiled. Almost. Because Noah chose that moment to stare back at him, as though he knew something was up, and Jordan knew exactly what that something was.

Damn, he loved that boy. A part of him had died when he'd thought his nephew had, and he swore his soul had lightened when he found out Nathan was alive.

And he'd worried. Worried like hell, especially when Nathan refused to let them call Belle.

But this might be working out better. He rose from his seat and strode into the briefing room. Yeah, things just might be coming together for his nephew. And when they did . . . He nodded to himself. When they did, then all the conniving and manipulation he'd used against his nephew would have been worth it. Every second of it.

If Noah didn't kill him first.

"Okay, boys, here's your files." He tossed the files to the table. "We have DNA verification. Order will go out to the sheriff and the state police first thing in the morning to haul Delbert Ransome's ass in. Let's be prepared."

CHAPTER TWENTY-ONE

Micah had photos. Late-night recon had observed several midnight hunting parties in the past week that had thankfully not resulted in prey being located. But they had the pictures, taken at long range, one of which showed Delbert Ransome's pickup.

"We have Kira and Tehya running matches on the other vehicles but we haven't identified them yet." Jordan was still outlining the files an hour later.

Noah's head lifted from the pictures to stare at his uncle.

"Everyone, Tehya will be working communications and logistics for us." He nodded to the door and the small redhead who stood leaning against the frame, arms crossed over a snug T-shirt, her jeans-clad legs crossed at the ankles.

"What happened?" Noah asked then. "The orphan turned heiress has decided to stay"

Teyha's lips lifted with an edge of amusement. "I never claimed the Fitzhugh estate. My name was wiped from the reports of the mission that Joseph Fitzhugh was killed in. His estate went to cover debts and to secure the future of the young woman he was still holding on his estate."

Who would want the world to know she was the daughter of a terrorist and white slaver so vile that a cartel drug lord had been promised protection to secure the terrorist's identity and capture.

Her long red hair was pulled back into a low ponytail, her green eyes stared cynically into the meeting room.

"We also have reports of a newborn showing up with the housekeeper of Gaylen Patrick." Jordan turned back to the file. "One of the kidnapped legal aliens had a child. An infant, mere months old. The baby's body was never found. The DNA found beneath Ransome's truck matched that of the father, but not the mother."

"The feds can get him on both deaths though, correct?" Micah spoke up, his eyes gleaming like black ice in his hard features.

"That's what they're working on." Jordan nodded. "Federal, state, and county law enforcement will converge on the Patrick ranch in the morning. Sheriff Grayson, not Alpine's small police force, will be aware of the arrest warrant before the FBI arrives with it. There will be agents ready to catch Ransome if he tries to run, or ditch the truck. They're going for complete secrecy, and there's a good chance they can contain any calls outgoing to the Patrick ranch with the plan they have in place."

"What basis are they using for suspicion?" Noah asked.

"Anonymous tip." Jordan smiled mockingly. "Seems someone thinks they saw Ransome's truck possibly chasing someone through the valley that night. A lone hiker."

Noah nodded. It was imperative that they keep suspicion off the garage.

"We've had John on the daughter of Coalton James, the owner of the bank Mike Conrad is manager of. Katy James works in accounts there. It seems some of Conrad's accounts appear a little off to her." He nodded to the Australian then.

John Vincent flicked Jordan a rather sarcastic look before he spoke.

"Katy seems to think there are a few too many inconsistencies in some of the larger accounts. Namely the fact that several of the corporate accounts he manages have signs of being used to launder large amounts of money."

"And she told you this why?" Noah asked him. "I know Katy, she doesn't run her mouth about bank accounts."

Lora Leigh

John's lips twisted mockingly. "No, she doesn't. But she does keep a rather detailed journal. She's looking at getting her very delectable little rear in quite a bit of trouble if she isn't careful."

Noah shook his head. Didn't it just figure. He wondered if Sabella kept a journal. Hell. He realized he had no idea if she did or not.

"The evidence found in Conrad's library along with the suspected laundering and Ransome's involvement puts Gaylen Patrick right in the thick of it," John continued. "One of those very lucrative accounts that Katy has found suspicious ties into Patrick. His ranch borders the park, and it would be easy for him to offset any suspicion."

"Patrick employs legal aliens," Noah pointed out. "What about the program we got into Conrad's laptop? Have we found anything through it?"

"Nothing yet," Tehya answered. "We're still working on the encryption on some of the files, but other than that, we've not been able to track any information through it."

"John, I want you and Micah in town tomorrow." Jordan cut through the comment hovering on Noah's tongue. "John, stay on Miss James. See if you can get her to talk. Micah, make certain you report to your job at the local police station a bit early. See what you can hear." He turned to Travis Caine. "Set up in the hills above the Patrick ranch. See what you can see. Make certain to stay out of sight."

Travis nodded sharply, his aristocratic features cool and composed.

"Nik, you're with Noah at the garage. We know the gossip that flows through there. You two keep your ears open, and be ready for any fallout."

Nik nodded while Noah watched his uncle carefully.

"Are you expecting fallout?" Noah asked then.

"I always expect fallout," Jordan informed him. "Go through your file. Gossip attained throughout the county points to the BCM's interest in acquiring that garage. Belle was considered an easy mark to take out, but they couldn't kill her. That would have roused too much interest from me personally. I would have investigated the murder of my nephew's wife and they knew it. After her little venture into the night life tonight, I'd expect to see a few interested parties coming around though. Let's see who takes up that interest."

Noah froze. He stared at his uncle, feeling a tight ball of carefully controlled fury beginning to slip its leash.

"Now, let's move on to the rest of our suspected hunting parties. If you'll turn to page—"

"What did you just say?" Noah asked carefully, aware of the edge to his voice and the tension that filled the room as Jordan paused and looked back at him in surprise.

"I said, turn to page—"

"What venture into what night life?" His teeth clenched, he swore he felt something explode in his head.

Jordan arched his brow coolly. "Does it matter? Our only interest in her at this point is the location of her business and the militia's interest in it."

Noah rose slowly to his feet, his fingertips pressing into the wood with enough force to turn the tips white.

"What venture? What night life?"

"Agent Blake, are you forgetting something? The mission is our objective here, not the bar where one lone citizen is having a girls' night out. Agreed?"

Something exploded. Detonated. Noah felt the implosion in his brain.

Friday night. In Alpine. In a bar.

Girls' night out, his ass. Sabella had known better than that shit even six years before. She knew what the weekends were like in those bars. She knew being a single woman out on the town on a Friday night was like throwing fresh meat to wolves.

"Like fucking hell." The guttural force of the curse cut through the room before he jerked back from the table, slamming his chair and the wall and striding from the meeting room.

He ignored the sharp command in Jordan's voice as he called him back.

He'd signed on for the mission. He'd accepted his death

and let his wife go. That was what he had told himself since walking back into her life. He was doing her a favor. He was teaching her to live again, not to love again. He was going to walk out of her life the same way he had walked into it. With no fanfare, no heartbreak. Simple. To the point.

God. Loving her was killing him. Destroying him. And the thought, the knowledge, that she had taken him at his word, no strings, no commitment, was burning inside his head like a supernova as he tore down the metal steps leading to the cement parking area. He hit the security button, releasing the lock on the heavy doors, and listened to them slide open as he straddled the Harley and twisted the key in the ignition.

With no more than an inch to spare on the door, he was speeding out, lights off, his gaze narrowed against the darkness as he shot through the canyon and hit the dirt road beyond.

As he hit the main road, he flipped the lights on and laid the gas to the Harley.

A venture into the night life on a Friday night in Alpine? Like hell.

He jerked his cell phone from his belt as he rode out of the blackout surrounding the bunker. The message indicator was flashing. Hitting the button, he held it to his ear and listened to Rory's threats.

Tell Grandpop, would he? He was going to strangle that little bastard. What the hell was he thinking, letting Sabella go out like that? Dammit to hell, all shit was about to hit the fan and Sabella was out partying? A girls' night out with Kira Richards and Sienna Grayson.

God help them all.

God help him. Because he knew what he was doing. What he was going to do. He was going to drag her ass out of that bar, stake his ownership on her, and destroy them both when he was forced to leave.

Because he couldn't stay. And if he tried, then sooner or later he'd trip himself up. He wouldn't be able to hide the truth from her forever and he knew it. And once she knew, once she understood what had become of her husband, how could she forgive him? She wouldn't forgive him. He'd left her alone for over four years after he'd been rescued. He hadn't let her come to him, he'd given his life to the Elite Ops rather than her. How could she forgive him for that? A contract he couldn't break, missions he couldn't refuse, and the chances would increase with each one that he wouldn't return.

She was attached to Noah Blake. A rebound lover. She'd realized that in time, he had told himself. Tried to convince himself of it. Convince her of it.

But as he hit town, possessiveness, arousal, and sheer male fury burned through his mind, and he knew better. There was no convincing him, because he knew the truth.

No matter who or what he was, Sabella owned him. She always had, and she always would. And that left a decision he had to make soon. If he walked away, he'd have to walk away forever. If he stayed, eventually, he'd have to tell her the truth and he knew it. Because he knew his Sabella. Eventually, she would figure it out.

Friday night at the Borderline was no place for a woman to be without her husband or significant other, Sabella thought with an edge of mockery as she sipped at her wine and watched the cowboys eyeing their table.

A half dozen had already asked her, Kira, and Sienna to dance. Sienna danced. She loved to dance and she wasn't particular about who she danced with.

Ian had joined Kira not long after they arrived. He sat in a chair behind his wife, his expression amused, his chin propped on his wife's shoulder as she talked to him during the louder portions of the live band belting out a facsimile of country music's current hits.

"You're not dancing, Sabella." Kira watched the dance floor with a gleam of laughter in her gray eyes. "I thought you'd enjoy it as much as Sienna does."

Sabella looked out to where Sienna was dancing with two cowboys.

She used to enjoy dancing, but not with a bunch of cowboys. A smile tugged at her lips. Nathan had always made dancing fun rather than making her feel she was being interviewed as a possible one-night stand.

Her lips thinned at the thought. No, she was his one-night stand now.

"Come on, Belle. Dance with me."

Her head lifted and she had to laugh. Martin Sloes was a friend of Rory's. Young. His hazel eyes were filled with laughter and he was just a little bit tipsy. He held a bottle of beer in one hand.

He was swinging his hips, his snug Wranglers a little too tight in the crotch and his western shirt unbuttoned halfway down his smooth chest. His dark brown hair was close-cut, a little goatee tried to grow at his chin.

She shook her head as his gaze roved over her bare legs and he gave her a lecherous waggle of his brows.

They were the same age, but she felt years older.

"Not tonight, Martin. Maybe next time."

"You're a coldhearted woman," he said, pouting, but he moved off to the next table and the little coeds sitting there.

Sabella laughed at the pout. Martin was a charmer, or wanted to be. An overgrown kid with more money in his pocket than good sense in his head. And she knew on his pay he wasn't overrun with money.

"This is a friendly little town." Kira leaned forward, her expression filled with laughter over the exchange.

Sabella glanced back at Ian. His gaze, for just a second, was hard, cold as he looked out over the dance floor. He was working. She just wondered what the hell Kira was doing.

"It has its moments," she agreed as Sienna plopped into her chair and waved her hand over her flushed face.

"Damn, those cowboys are wearing me out," she said, laughing.

For a moment, Sabella wondered at the changes she saw in her friend. Not that Sienna hadn't always loved to dance, but she did it more vigorously now, and flirted a hell of a lot more than she used to.

As the music slid into a slower tune, Sienna was back on her feet, this time with Martin, and Kira and Ian moved from the table to the dance floor as well.

Sabella shook her head at the three offers she was given and turned her attention to the crowd filling the Borderline Bar instead.

She pretended she didn't see Rory and Toby sitting in the back, along the side of the room she was on. Rory was nursing a beer and glowering, while Toby had what looked like a soda and was glowering at Rory. Evidently, Rory wasn't letting him have the beer.

What the hell were they doing following her? Babysitting her?

She let her nail tap against the table as she considered that. No doubt Noah would be worrying that whatever he was up to would slap back at her, as it nearly had Toby. Which didn't make sense, because as far as she could tell, Noah wasn't actually doing anything. He worked on cars. Spent his evenings torturing her, and other than a few nights a week that he disappeared with Nik, she couldn't find a single clue that he was anything other than what he pretended to be. A mechanic. One that liked to get into knife fights, obviously.

She lifted her beer and sipped at it, almost grimacing at the bitter taste. Maybe tomorrow, she'd crack open another of those vintage heirloom wines Nathan had once been so fond of. Not that he had ever drunk the damned things. He'd just collected them.

Like he had collected his truck and his wife.

"Hey, Belle. Dance with me." Jason Dugall, one of the Malone cowboys, stepped up to her as the music picked up its beat again. "Come on. You don't wanna just sit here all night."

His brown eyes sparkled with fun, his blond hair was sweat dampened and falling over his brow.

"One dance." She picked up her beer, took a large drink, then rose to her feet and let him take her hand and lead her out to the dance floor.

She hadn't danced in years, but the steps came back to her naturally. Within minutes she was laughing, twisting. Jason was a good dancer. A fun dancer. He didn't touch below the waist, they laughed when she screwed up the steps and he would swing her around to get her back in step.

They finished the song and moved into another, then another. She let her mind drift, remembering the nights she and Nathan had spent dancing here when they went out with friends. And it was fun. It was something she hadn't done since she and Nathan had been married, for one reason or another.

Finally, her legs weak and her mouth dry, she waved off another dance and headed for the table. From the corner of her eye she saw movement and turned.

A path opened to the door and Noah Blake came striding in like the biker bad boy from hell. Leather chaps over snug jeans. Kick-ass boots on his feet. A leather jacket over a black T-shirt. His blue eyes blazed like hell on fire in his dark face and his black hair was windblown, mussed, and lying to his shoulders in erotic disarray. As though the wind had loved his hair as he rode. Combed invisible fingers through it and left it lying in just the right way to reveal the rugged savagery of the re-formed bones and angles of his face.

And he was heading straight for her.

The music drifted away, a slow sensual tune heated up the dance floor, and she felt her breathing become harder, deeper.

Two days. She had been without him for two days. And it had been hell. How was she going to make it without him when he left to sort-things-out?

He strode to her, that loose-hipped dangerous swagger that made her mouth dry and her pulse pound. And before she realized his intention, his arms went around her and he pulled her into the softly swaying crowd.

It was like making love. Like long, slow sex.

His hands gripped her hips, hers pressed against his chest, fingers curling beneath the vest as they moved to the music.

"Having fun?" His eyes raged, his voice deepened, darkened.

"Of course." She let her hands slide up his chest to his shoulders, moved in closer, and let herself feel him.

Oh God, how was she supposed to do without him again? How was she supposed to go on when he went off to sort his little things out?

She was married. She wasn't a widow, she wasn't a divorcee. She was married and she still loved her husband, even if somehow, somewhere, his love for her had died.

She let her head fall against his chest, her eyes close. A memory, she told herself. Something to hold on to when he was gone again. And his arms folded around her, held her close until her bare legs were sliding against the leather chaps, reminding her of the leather seats of the pickup and the scent of sex that infused it now.

She could feel her body warming, her breasts and clit swelling. Flesh became overly sensitized, and when his hands dipped beneath the short hem of her blouse and touched the bare flesh of her back, she drew in a hard, deep breath.

"I've missed you," he breathed against her ear and she felt herself flinch at the admission.

Eyes closed, her face buried against him, she didn't worry about anyone seeing the pain in her face, or her eyes. He hid her, sheltered her.

"There's nothing to miss," she finally answered, forcing herself to remember that he was going to leave her, walk away from her again.

He caressed the side of her head with his jaw.

"I want you, Sabella. I want back in that big bed with you. I want to feel you hot and wet beneath me."

"For how long?" She shook her head against his chest. "How long, Noah? A night? Two? A week? What do you want from me? What makes you think you can just breeze into town, breeze into my bed, and then ride into the sunset and I'm just going to accept it?"

Noah could hear the hurt in her voice, he could feel it. Jealousy over the memory of the man who had spoiled her into seeing exactly how much she was worth, and the knowledge of what he was now, tearing through him.

She deserved so much better. Deserved a man who didn't face those nights that, for whatever reason, pumped the remnants of the damned drug back into his senses. When the lust and the hunger consumed him to the point that he was terrified to be around any woman. Especially his Sabella.

And he couldn't tell her that. He couldn't tell her about the animal that raged inside him. He couldn't tell her his agreement with Elite Ops, and he couldn't forget that for eighteen months he had refused to let her know her husband was alive.

The truth would destroy her as surely as the lie eventually would. And at least with the lie, she would have that memory of her husband and what she had meant to him.

"There's so much you don't know," he finally sighed against the shell of her ear. "Why I'm here. What has to be done."

"Then tell me, Noah." She lifted her head and stared back at him, her gray eyes dove soft, filled with anger and with need. "I'm not a child. I'm not some little ditz that can't understand or handle the realities of life."

Noah stared back at her, feeling the wild pulse of hunger tightening between them, and the need for answers blazing in her eyes.

"I already know part of it," she said softly. "You can sleep with me? Torture me with everything I can't have, but you can't tell me the truth?"

Only so much of it, and he knew it. But parts of it, considering what was coming tomorrow, parts of it she had to understand. When this operation started moving, it would move fast. He needed to know she could protect herself, she had to know she needed to stay safe. For him. For his sanity.

"Ride with me," he invited her, knowing that the partial truths would have to come tonight. Who he was, what he had been, would have to remain a secret, forever.

"I wore shorts."

He shook his head. "I'll be careful. Come on." He pulled back as the music stopped. "We'll ride."

Sabella took his hand, her heart thudding in her chest, a

feeling of hope rising inside her, though a part of her knew, a part of her accepted, he wasn't going to tell her who he was.

But she couldn't stop hoping.

She was aware of the eyes watching them as they left that bar. Rory and Toby stood as they passed. She took a second to shoot Rory a narrow-eyed look. The day was going to come when they were going to talk. Hard and deep. And that day wasn't far off.

She didn't confront him now, wouldn't confront him until Noah left, because she needed to *know*. She had to know what had happened to her husband, why he hadn't come back to her as he should have. But even more, she needed to know that he wasn't leaving her. That no matter the *things* he needed to sort out, that he intended to stay. That he intended to claim her again.

"Rory called you, didn't he?" she asked as he helped her on the back of the Harley before straddling the machine himself.

"Rory called." His voice was harder now. Cool. "How do you feel about a ride to the city park?"

He pulled off his jacket before turning and helping her into it.

She nodded slowly. "The park sounds fine."

The Harley throbbed to life. The motor vibrated with throttled power before Noah kicked up the stand, kicked it in gear, and pulled out of the parking lot.

The summer air whipped through her hair. The remembered sense of freedom that overcame her brought a smile to her face as she wrapped her arms around Noah's lean waist and held on as he headed to the small park.

Medina Park was small, beautifully kept. Noah pulled into the deserted parking lot and helped her off the motorcycle.

Holding her hand, he led her along a narrow walkway until they turned into a small sheltered picnic area. A lone table sat in the shadowed area, together with the dim outline of an iron barbecue grill.

Sabella shoved her hands into the pockets of the jacket as she stepped up on the seat of the table and sat on the wide bench of the table itself.

"Why here?"

"No ears to listen," he said, sighing. "And if there were, I'd know it."

His head turned as though probing the shadows.

"You can see that well in the dark then?" Nathan had always had exceptional sight, even in the dark.

"You know I'm here for a reason, Sabella," he finally bit out, moving until he was sitting behind her, his powerful legs bracketing hers, his arms looping around her as he pulled her back against his chest.

"Have you heard about the bodies they found in the national park?" he asked her then.

Sabella nodded carefully.

"Legals and illegal aliens alike, as well as three FBI agents, have died over the past year or so, victims of a vicious hunt. I'm trying to track the men who did this, get the evidence needed, and turn it over to the federal agents working the case."

"You're not an agent?" Something inside her tightened into a hard knot of pain.

"I'm independent. Contracted," he told her, brushing his lips against her ear. "It doesn't stop here, Sabella. The link to this goes much further than this little county. It's growing, and it's a security threat to the nation. I don't have a choice about where I go from here."

She nodded jerkily. "So you really won't be staying?"

She was shaking on the inside. She couldn't understand how she was managing to stay calm, collected, on the outside.

She felt him behind her then, the question hanging between them, filling the heated air with tension and with regret.

"You're the best thing that ever happened to me," he finally said. "In my life, touching you, holding you, is the best thing I've ever done. But shit happens, baby. And shit blew up in my face a long damned time ago."

She felt the first tear fall, and made sure it was the last.

She could feel the pain inside her though. It was clawing, vicious, digging out her heart as she fought against the sobs that wanted to tear through her. Her lips trembled, but she held them back. She didn't know how she held them back.

"I want you safe," he continued. "From here on out, I want you to stay out of the bars, out of town. Stay where I can keep an eye on you, where I can keep you safe in the event that anyone has managed to suspect why I'm here, or what I'm doing."

"Something's going to happen then?"

"Something could happen at any time," he said. "But this case is moving now. Once it blows to hell and back, I don't want the fallout at your doorstep."

She nodded, then froze, her eyes closing tight as his lips took a slow, gentle sip of her bare neck. How could she have not known those lips the first time they touched her, the first time sensation had slammed into her. Only her husband, the man she had given her soul to, could do this to her.

Before Sabella could help herself, she leaned her head to the side, inviting more, needing more. God help her, he was going to leave her again. She should be screaming. Kicking. She should be crying. But the hope wouldn't still inside her ragged heart.

He had told her this much. He was just waiting, just preparing her for what could happen. Noah wouldn't actually walk away from her again. Not her Noah. Not the man whose hands were tightening on her now, whose breath was growing ragged, and whose hunger was flaming over her.

Her Noah would never walk out of her life like that. Never by choice. Not her *husband*.

CHAPTER TWENTY-TWO

"Who are you chasing, Noah?"

She asked the question he was hoping she wouldn't ask.

"You're as safe as I can make you right now." He let his lips feather over her jawline. "The less you know, the safer I can keep you."

"Knowledge is power." She tilted her head for him, letting his lips and tongue caress the sensitive little path down the side of her neck.

"Not in this case." He nipped at her neck. "In this case, for you, innocence is your best weapon. And I'll keep it that way, Sabella."

He felt her soften then. As though he had given her something she needed. What could it have been other than an assurance that he cared for her, wanted her safe?

God in heaven knew he wanted her safe. He could live without sex. He could living without Sabella in his life. But he couldn't live without Sabella living. His heart would stop beating. All will to live would flow out of his body.

He had known that before he ever married her. The night he had realized that his heart beat for this one tiny little woman, Nathan had known he would give up the free and easy lifestyle he had held on to for so long, and marry her.

And now, letting go of her again, it would rip his soul out.

It would tear him into so many pieces he was certain he would only be a living shell of what he was tonight.

"I missed you in the bed with me." He pulled the jacket from her shoulders and laid it beside them before caressing her bare shoulders, her arms.

His hands smoothed over the silver armband he had bought her. Damn, she looked good in that. Like a savage princess decked out for a sensual battle.

"This isn't going to solve anything." Her voice was weak, filled with hurt and with desire.

That vein of hurt in her voice broke his heart. It tore something in his chest and left him burying his face in her neck, fighting to hold back the pain ravaging him.

And he couldn't stop touching her. Having her against him, in his arms, he couldn't help it. It was like an addiction, a craving he couldn't control. He needed this, needed her. When the time came to walk away, he wanted as many memories as possible to take with him. Enough to help him survive the lost, lonely nights he knew he was going to face.

"You deserve so much more," he whispered, his hands sliding beneath her blouse, cupping her side, caressing over silken flesh to the heavy weight of her breasts. "A man that's whole. That's what you deserve, Sabella. And I'm not whole any longer. I haven't been in a long time."

Her breath hitched and he knew it was a sob that shuddered through her body.

"My Sabella." He turned her to him, pulling her legs over his thigh and cradling her in his arms as he stared down at the tear tracks on her face. "I won't lie to you. I can't do that. I can't tell you I'm going to stay and that we're going to fulfill the dreams we each have." He touched the tears on her face. "We can't do that to each other, or for each other. I'm not your husband, Sabella. And we both know no one else is going to fill your heart but your husband."

He pushed her, he had to push her. She had to realize what could happen. She had to face it.

Her eyes flashed.

He caught the hand that aimed at his face as surprise stuttered through him.

He stared at the hand, then at the anger flushing her face.

"Sabella, did you just try to smack me?" he asked her carefully.

It had been one of their rules during their marriage. She could throw anything she pleased, she could scream, cuss, she could call him a dirty son of a bitch, but she was never to try to hit him. Or to surprise him. No running up to goose him, or jumping out from corners.

His reflexes were too well honed, that survival instinct inside him too well developed to allow her to know any fear of him.

He wouldn't hurt her, but he'd be damned if he wanted her afraid he would hurt her when he had his hand around her neck and had her on the floor before either of them thought.

"You're lucky I don't try to shoot you!" She scrambled off his lap, stumbled on the bench below, and would have fallen if he hadn't caught her.

He stared back at her in surprise. One second she was sweet and soft in his arms, now she was spitting at him like a little cat.

"Where the hell are you going?" He grabbed his jacket and followed after her as she began striding, almost running, along the path back to the parking lot. "Dammit, Sabella."

"Go to hell!"

"I've been there, thank you," he retorted. "I opt not to return, if you don't mind."

"Then go wherever the hell you go when you drive off in the evenings." She waved a hand back at him, her expression, the set of her body, flat furious. "I told you the other night, Noah Blake. I've had enough."

"Well, maybe I haven't," he muttered.

He hadn't had enough of her sweet touch and he sure as hell hadn't had enough of her laughter, her kisses, or her presence next to him.

"Well, maybe that's too damned bad. Because I don't like

your rules and I don't like the game you're playing with me."
She turned in the middle of the parking lot then, turned to
face him, and Noah came to a hard stop.

If he hadn't seen the determination in her eyes the other
night, he saw it now. Naked pain, anger, and self-confidence.

He asked himself again, Where was the woman he had
married? This wasn't the helpless little blonde, but damned
if she didn't turn him on more than she ever had.

"I'm trying damned hard not to play games with you." He
propped his fists on his hips and glared back at her.
"Dammit, Sabella, I'm trying to be honest here. I don't want
to hurt you."

She stood beneath the parking lot lights, her hair falling
around her face and shoulders in thick waves, her slender
hips cocked, one hand propped on one hip, the other hand
hanging loose and ready at her side.

"I don't want your honesty." She sneered at him. "Shove
it. It sucks."

She turned and started walking.

"Where the hell are you going?" He strode after her,
caught her arm, and pulled her to a stop. "Back to that damned
bar where those cowboys can sniff around you like wolves after fresh meat? The hell you are."

"Oh my, Mr. No-commitment. Are we jealous?" The sarcasm in her voice was doing things to him. He could feel it.
Like that fucking fever rising inside him, filled with lust,
dominance, and a dark, hungry need. "You're right. You're
not my husband. My husband had better sense than to tell
me when I could or couldn't do something."

She had never confronted him like this during their marriage. Sarcastic and defiant. She had always spoiled him, and
he saw that now. And the love that rose inside him threatened
to strangle him. As did the pride. And fuck it, the fear.

He wasn't the man she had loved six years ago. The man
who crooned Irish lullabyes to her, or the man who would
whisper "forever" in Gaelic because it made her shiver with
pleasure.

He was scarred, changed. Inside, the man he was had been

scarred forever, and admitting it to her would kill him. She would want answers. This Sabella would demand answers. And when she learned that for four years he had refused to let anyone come for her, she would hate him. Hate him because she would realize that he'd thought her weak. Weak and unable to handle the monster he was. And that would destroy *her* pride.

He'd weaved a web so damned tangled that now he had no idea how to get out of it.

"What do you want from me, Noah?" she cried, causing him to jerk his gaze back to her, to see the tears on her cheeks.

"Don't you dare cry!" he snarled. "Don't you use tears on me, Sabella."

He couldn't handle her tears. Silent tears. She had never sobbed, but he heard a sob in her voice now.

She shook her head, pushed her fingers through her hair, and turned and walked away.

It took him long seconds to realize exactly what she was doing. She was walking. Walking past the motorcycle, walking away from him.

"Sabella, no." He covered the distance, gripping her arm and pulling her to a stop as he placed himself in front of her. "We can talk about this."

"There's nothing to talk about," she snapped. "You can't just blow into whatever town, find yourself something to fuck for a few weeks, and then blow right out." She jerked her arm out of his grip. "God, Noah. You're breaking my heart and you don't even care."

"How can I break something that belongs to another man?" he yelled in jealous frustration. "That damned house with pictures of him spread through every damned room. The bedroom you shared with him, you still have his clothes in the closet. And look at this." He jerked her hand up, the gold wedding band gleaming beneath the lights, ripping through his heart because she wore it on her right hand, not her left. "Look at that ring, Sabella. You still wear his ring."

His ring, the ring she had slid on to his finger, burned a hole against his thigh. It was tucked in his pocket, always with him, always a part of him.

She was crying now. Her breath was hitching on her sobs and her gray eyes were washed with diamond-bright pain. It sliced through his soul.

Her lips parted. Her hand lifted as though to say something. At that moment, the clash of sirens sounded for the briefest second.

Sabella swung around as the sheriff's cruiser pulled up, stopped, and Rick Grayson eased out of the cruiser. He took one look at Sabella then sliced a hard glare at Noah.

"Get in the car, Belle." Rick nodded to the passenger side.

"Sabella. Don't." Noah stood still, every instinct inside him demanding that he not let her go with the sheriff. The sheriff was no longer a suspect, but Sabella was still Noah's wife.

He stared back at her intently, willing her to remember the danger. "Please, Sabella."

She looked from Rick to Noah. He could see the indecision in her face, her eyes.

Rick stood silently, watching them, his face creased into a scowl as he kept one hand carefully on the butt of his weapon.

"Let me take you home," Noah said then. "I'll just take you home. I swear it."

A sob caught at her throat. "You're killing me."

"I know, baby." And he did know. He was ripping them both apart and she had no idea how it was killing him too.

She ducked her head, shook it, then walked past him toward the motorcycle. Noah looked back at the sheriff intently, seeing the worry and the concern on his face as Grayson watched Sabella, then turned his gaze back to Noah. He was silent for a long moment. Finally, his hand lifted from the butt of his gun and he laid his forearms over the open frame of the door.

There was something knowing in the other man's gaze. Something suspicious that had Noah tensing.

"You know," Grayson finally said. "I've seen some real losers pass through this town in my day."

"Really?" Noah drawled. Like he gave a damn.

"Really." Rick nodded. "But I have to say I think you're the biggest loser I've met to date. And for some reason, I just didn't expect that of you."

"I needed your opinion," Noah grunted as he glanced back at where Sabella was wiping her cheeks and staring into the park.

"You need a bullet in the ass," Rick growled, shaking his head. "Stay out of trouble, Mr. Blake. Otherwise, we're going to talk."

Noah arched his brows before deliberately turning his back on the sheriff and moving to where Sabella waited on the Harley.

He wrapped his jacket around her, pulling it over her arms before tipping her head up to him and staring into her tear-drenched eyes. His hands framed her face, his thumbs smoothed over her trembling lips.

"One more night, Sabella," he whispered, so hard, so desperate for her, he wondered if he could survive it. "Give us one more night."

Sabella stared back at him. Anger and hurt and fear all clashing inside her, raging inside her. And mixed with it was the need. The fiery hunger she wondered how she had lived without for six years.

"You bastard!" she sobbed.

"The worst bastard," he whispered, and kissed her lips, the tears from her eyes.

She sniffed, her hands lifting to grip his wrists as her lips softened, felt his kiss, and needed more. She needed so much more.

"Take me home, Noah," she whispered. "Please, just take me home."

She wasn't going to cry any more.

Holding on to Noah as they rode to the house, her head buried against his back, his heartbeat against her cheek, she tried to sort out the future. The near future. The far future.

She tried to sort out her emotions. They weren't that damned far from the house.

She lifted her head as they pulled up to the house and waited until he helped her off the Harley then swung free himself.

"Where's your key?"

Her husband.

He'd always made certain he checked her small apartment after bringing her home while they were dating. After they married, he always went into a room or the house first. He'd always been protective.

She handed him the key and watched as he opened the door, going inside cautiously before turning back to her. She walked into the house and waited in the large entryway and living room while he went through the place.

She pulled his jacket tighter around her, breathed in his scent, and promised herself again, no more tears.

Was she going to throw him out, hang on to her anger, or give him one more night? And every other night she could steal before he left? Because the next time he left—she stared around the house. The next time he left, she knew exactly what she was going to do.

It was the only way to survive the loss.

She was standing in the living room, staring at the mantel, at the pictures. Their wedding picture. Their faces close, his wild blue eyes dominating the picture. His dark skin against her paler cheek, his expression quiet, confident.

She walked over to that picture, her fingers playing with the wedding band that she slid back onto her left hand. She wasn't a widow. She was a wife. She would always be his wife, no matter what name he used. And wasn't that pathetic? No wonder he hadn't wanted to come home. He'd had a wife who presented no challenge, no defiance. A wife who only knew how to love him.

Noah stepped into the bedroom, checked the closets that still held his clothes, the large bathroom he and Sabella had planned together.

When he went back to the bedroom he stood in front of the small table by her bed and stared down at the picture of them together.

Sienna Grayson had taken that picture just after they married. He was touching her cheek, the broad gold band of his wedding ring bright and new on his finger.

Reaching into his jeans, he pulled the ring free, rolled it between his fingers then stared down at it. It wasn't new anymore, but it was still bright, and warm.

He gripped it and pushed it on his finger, his fist clenching as a furious, agonized grimace twisted his lips and he fought the raging need to tell her. To own her. To be the man he knew she missed. The man she loved. Because the man who had come from the ravages of hell wasn't the same man. And the life he would lead now, after signing on with the Elite Ops, wasn't a life she would want to be a part of. A life he couldn't resign from. Nathan Malone could have left the SEALs. If Noah Blake tried to leave the Elite Ops, then he would simply disappear and never return.

It was a life of always lying. Always hiding. Hell, he'd thought he could do it. He'd thought it would be best this way. But with his wedding band branding the flesh of his finger, he wondered how things could have been different. Tried to imagine something different, and he couldn't. Because he was still the man he had been turned into. And though Sabella was different from the woman he remembered, she would never accept anything but the man she had loved.

She was stubborn. Determined. She thought she knew what he was, who he was, and she was wrong.

He slid the ring from his finger, stared down at it, then shoved it back into his jeans. It was his talisman. His lifeline. His lifetime reminder of what could have been.

Sabella turned away from the mantel as Noah came down the stairs, his gaze finding her instantly before his eyes slipped to the pictures behind her.

She watched him pause, saw the somber sadness that flickered in his eyes for just a second.

"You made a beautiful bride," he said softly, standing before her, his legs braced solidly beneath him, those black riding chaps emphasizing the heavy bulge in his jeans.

God, he was so thick and hard. And she ached. Ached as though it had been years since he had touched her rather than mere days.

"He would have made any woman look beautiful in a picture with him," she stated ruefully. "Cameras loved him."

"And he loved you." It wasn't a question.

"He did love me." She knew he did. "I wonder sometimes if he would love me now."

He tilted his head, looked at the pictures for a long moment, his expression almost softening as he nodded slowly. "He would have." He met her gaze once more. "The man in that picture knew how to love. And he knew how to live. You can see it in his face."

But he didn't any longer. He didn't love, and he didn't live for that love. She could accept that. She had no choice but to accept that.

She moved to him, letting all the hunger, all the need, that had tormented her for two days rise inside her. He had stripped her bare at the park, jerked all the illusions from her eyes, and showed her what she was dealing with. No more dreams, no more pretty, flowery memories.

His eyes narrowed on her as she let his jacket slide from her arms to the floor, her gaze gliding over his jeans.

"One more night?" she asked then.

"As many nights as you're willing to give me," he stated.

"Until you have to leave?"

His tongue touched his lower lip and she felt everything inside her tighten.

"Until I have to leave," he agreed.

She let a small laugh slip free. Bitter. Taunting.

"Who says I'm even going to care when you leave?" She edged up to him, looked up at him from the corner of her eyes. "You know what, Noah?"

"What, Sabella?" The careful tone of his voice warned her, and she didn't give a damn.

She was doing something that was going to get her spanked, and she wanted spanked.

She took her finger and ran it across his chest. "Perhaps your leaving is for the best."

"You don't say?" Beneath the rough, gravelly tone of his voice was a hint of that sexy, lyrical brogue she had always loved.

She smiled, licked her upper lip, and cast him a look from beneath her lashes.

"Just think. You helped me pull my head out of my ass where my husband was concerned. Getting over your leaving should be a breeze. It's not like you're going to be here long. Right?"

Did his eyes just darken? Grow wilder?

"You don't want to push this, baby," he warned her softly.

She smiled. A slow, easy smile before catching her bottom lip between her teeth and taunting him with her look.

"What, you don't want to hear the truth?"

His hands gripped her hips as something wilder, something hungrier, suddenly lit those supercharged eyes.

"That's not the truth," he growled.

She reached up, caressed his lower lip with her tongue, then nipped it. Hard.

He jerked back, his eyes narrowing as his tongue swiped over the little wound a second before he jerked her closer, his erection burying against her stomach.

"But you'll be gone, Noah," she taunted him. "Like the wind," she stated mockingly. "Goodbye, so long. Just like my husband." She looked back at the pictures.

Nathan's loving smile mocked her from the frames, his blue eyes, so full of love, so soft with desire, lied to her every time she looked at them.

That was the hardest part to accept. It made her wish she had never known who Noah Blake was; it would have been easier. She wouldn't have loved him, this deep she wouldn't have hurt with the ragged desperation that she hurt with now. She could have let Noah go without a whimper, because she would have hated him for stealing anything that belonged to her Nathan. But how could she hate the man Nathan had become?

"Say goodbye, Noah," she told him. "You have tonight to do it. Because if you intend to walk out of my life, then it may as well be goodbye. I won't wait on another man. And I'll be damned if I'll become a living shrine to another."

CHAPTER TWENTY-THREE

It rose inside him.

He could feel the dominance fueled by her challenge, her defiance, her intention that tonight was going to be their last night.

He let his gaze flicker over her face, the slight throb on his lower lip reminding him that she was pushing him deliberately.

Those soft gray eyes roiled with shadows, light and dark clashing together as emotions tore inside them both. He wanted to be tender. He wanted her last memory of being his woman to be one of tenderness. But it wasn't tenderness she wanted. It wasn't tenderness rising inside him.

The lust wasn't tempered, but neither was it mindless. Like the death that filled him when he hunted, this lust that rose inside him for this woman was patient, determined.

She smiled tauntingly. As though she didn't believe he could do it. Couldn't master her. Couldn't fight the memory of the man she had become a living shrine for.

His gaze flickered to the pictures behind her, and agony, sharp and red-hot, lanced his soul. He wasn't that man anymore. A part of him wanted to be. A part of him needed to be. But that man really had died, leaving only what had risen from his ashes.

He stepped back from her. He didn't touch the chaps, he

unzipped his jeans and released the thick, heavy length of
his cock. He stroked his hand from shaft to tip as his hand
struck out, tangling in her hair as she moved to jerk back
from him.

"Do you want it all, Sabella?" he drawled then, smiling
back at her, daring her. "Do you want it, or do you just want
to play games and talk the talk, baby?"

She glared back at him, her lips parting, teeth clenched.

"You came to the bar this evening because of me, didn't
you?"

"I did." He lowered his head, bared his teeth. "You're
mine. Right here. Right now. As long as that tight, sweet little pussy gets wet for me then you belong to me. Not those
jackin' assed cowboys puffin' around you like a bunch of
damned stud horses butting around after a favorite mare."
Indignation ripped through him. "You were dancing with
them."

"Where were you?" she asked deliberately, her lips pouting back at him mockingly. "Where were you, Noah? Were
you here? Were you keeping your mare satisfied, or turning
her loose to pasture?"

His eyes widened. "You little witch," he growled.

His fingers tightened in her hair. "Did you find my replacement?"

"I haven't started looking yet. Should I let you know before I do?"

He had to grip the base of his cock to keep from blasting
his come. She was more than challenging tonight. She was
standing before him daring him, fucking daring that dark,
deliberate hunger inside him.

"Just waiting on me to leave?" he growled, tipping her
head back, feeling her hands against the leather vest he wore
over his shirt.

She was peeling it back from his shoulders, tugging at the
hold he had on her hair to rid him of it.

"Do you think one of those jackasses on that dance floor
can even come close to this, baby?" He shed the vest, releasing her and his cock just long enough to let it drop to the floor.

Before she could duck away from him he had her again.
One hand in her hair, the other at her hip, pushing her
against the side of the stairs as she stared up at him, lips
parted and curled mockingly. But he saw the pain in her
eyes, the tears that were so close.

What was he doing to her? To himself?

Holding her in place, he lifted his hands and jerked his
T-shirt off. Her eyes flicked to his chest and her breathing
grew heavier.

My heart beats for yours.
My soul lives for yours.
My body, my hands, my lips.
They love only you.

The words sang through his mind. His vow to her. The
night they had married, lost in the pleasure, the exhaustion
of each other's bodies, he had whispered those words to her,
and they surged in his soul now.

They trembled, hovered on his lips.

Noah snarled back a curse, jerked her to him, and his lips
burrowed against her, kissing with the desperation of a man
trembling too close to the edge.

Dominance surged and tightened inside him.

Hunger was like a beast, clawing at his balls.

And love, love was a double-edged sword ripping through
his soul, reminding him with brutal efficiency of everything
he had lost.

He kissed her like a man who knew it would be the last
kiss he ever knew from any woman's lips. It would be the
last stroke of tongues, the last hungry moan, the last time he
ever knew a woman's softness.

She was imprinted into his very spirit. Before the night was
over, he would imprint himself, as he was now, not as he had
been, into hers. He would take the memory of Nathan Malone
and replace it forever with the memory of Noah Blake.

And then, he would leave.

He was a bastard. The worst sort of son of a bitch and there was no way out of it. No way to fix what had been broken, no way to remove his name from the papers he had signed or to overcome the fears that he knew, knew, she couldn't accept him as he was, rather than the man she had lost.

So he took what was his now. Here, amid the pictures of all she had lost, his lips bore down on hers, nipping, sipping, kissing until he felt immersed inside her.

His cock pressed against her stomach, full and thick, the heavy blunt crown throbbed, spilling a minute amount of come against her bare flesh where her shirt had risen.

Noah jerked back, staring down at her fiercely before he simply gripped the edges of the shirt and ripped it loose from the buttons.

Damn her!

She should have shown fear. She should have gasped in alarm.

Did she? Hell no. Her eyes lit up like Christmas and the arousal that flooded her face almost, just almost, matched his lust.

"Like that, baby?" He jerked the pieces over her shoulders and watched the flush that climbed the rounded flesh of her breasts that the bra she wore didn't quite cover.

"Hated it," she mocked him, but her eyes said otherwise. Her hard, spiked nipples proved otherwise.

"You're hot," he drawled, unclipping the bra between her breasts and dragging it off her shoulders. "I bet you're so wet I could drown in your juices."

"As wet as you are hard."

His breath jerked in his chest as her fingers curled around his cock. Not all the way. He looked down, seeing the space where her fingers wouldn't meet, then glanced up at her and grinned.

"I'm hard, baby. Real hard."

"You are, aren't you?" She stroked the length as his hand tangled in her hair again.

"You're going to find out how hard," he growled. "Go down on me, Sabella. Suck me. Show me how bad you want to be fucked."

Her eyes flashed back at him. Hunger and defiance. But the hunger won out. She wanted him in her mouth just as damned bad as he wanted to be there.

"Fuck, yeah," he groaned, almost shaking from the need as she began to kiss her way down his chest, his hard abs. Son of a bitch, he was going to explode before her lips ever touched him. "God, Sabella. Sweet baby. Your lips."

He jerked. He felt as though liquid fire were enveloping the crest of his cock, stroking over him, vibrating with a moan.

He looked down at her, watched his flesh stretch her pink lips, watched the head sink inside her suckling mouth, and felt himself break apart.

Sabella watched his face. She watched the emotion that suddenly contorted it, and felt the pain that struck inside her. Pain and hunger, twisted hopes and shadowed fears that she couldn't hang on to.

Oh God. Like before. A part of her. She sucked him deeper, eagerly, watching the wild fire in his eyes, watching his face, the dark lust that filled it, the agony that creased it, and she fought to fill him with pleasure. He loved this. He loved the total dominance he was releasing against her, he loved her need to buck against it, her need to feel that power, that force inside him that urged her to fight it, as well as to submit to it.

Conflicting pleasures and urges that she knew would leave the memories of his past dominance a pale shadow. He was going to take her tonight. Tonight, she would have everything he had ever held back from her. Tonight she would know, finally, the man she had held but whose dark core she had never been given a glimpse into.

And she loved it. She loved the sense of struggle between them, of being able to assert and to submit.

And he was making sure of the submit part. Both hands dug into her hair, clenched and held her still as his cock pushed past her lips in short, hard strokes.

"Fuck. You love it." He held her head still, dragged his cock back slowly before pressing back in in a series of short, hard strokes. "You love it, baby. Your mouth filled with my cock, your body burning for me."

She gripped his thighs, her nails digging into the chaps, so turned on by the sight of his cock jutting out from leather and denim that she was creaming furiously. She could feel her juices washing to her panties, slick and hot, tormenting her clit as the folds of her pussy became saturated with the heat of her moisture.

She clenched her thighs together, her vision dazing as his head tipped back, long hair rippling around his face, and his hips moved. He fucked her mouth as she tightened around his cock. Rippled her tongue over the underside and moaned at the taste of him.

Could anything be sexier? Hotter? Total and complete dominance. He was going to push her, and she knew it. He was going to crawl so deep inside her that she didn't have to worry about being free of him.

"Damn you," he panted, staring down at her again, pausing, then pulling back slow and easy, seeing the moisture of her mouth glistening on his cock before he pushed back, lost control for fragile seconds, and fucked her lips like a man dying for the sensation.

Ragged pleasure, sensations sharp and hot, wrapped around the head of his cock, struck his balls, and then raced up his spine to sizzle in the base of his brain.

Damn, he had never known pleasure like this. Never before Sabella.

He forced himself to pause, his breathing harsh, heavy.

He jerked back, pulling his cock from her lips before he could spill his come in her mouth. Pulling her to her feet, he spun her around, gripping her wrists and forcing her to wrap her hands around the cherry spindles of the stair railing.

"Stay there." He nipped her shoulder as she arched her back, her denim-clad ass rubbing against his cock.

Reaching around in front of her, he jerked her belt loose, unsnapped and unzipped the shorts and pushed them over her thighs.

Sliding his hand between her thighs, he cupped the humid

heat of her pussy through her panties, felt the damp need, the roll of her hips as his fingers played over her clit.

The fingers of his other hand cupped her breast, rolled her nipple.

"God, your nipples are so hard. So tight." He raked his lips over her shoulder, glimpsed her profile.

Closed eyes, lashes feathering her cheeks, her face flushed and dazed with pleasure. Her lips were parted, reddened, swollen from his dick shuttling between them.

He groaned against her shoulder as he shoved her panties down her legs and palmed her bare sex.

"So slick and wet." He let his teeth rasp over her shoulder, moving to her neck.

Sabella was lost in the pleasure. She held tight to the spindles, feeling it washing through her body like a tidal wave. Swamping her with sensation.

"Such a pretty sweet pussy." He cupped her again, his fingers caressing around her clit, never close enough to send her rocking into orgasm. "It's so pretty and tiny. So tight and hot it's all I can do not to come just thinking about it."

She felt her juices flood her channel, spread her legs further, and trembled with the need to come.

"You like it when I get nasty, don't you, Sabella?" He licked her neck, one hand gripping the front of her neck and tilting it back. "Look at me, baby. Tell me how much you like being nasty with me."

Her lashes lifted and she stared into the navy blue fire raging in his eyes.

She wasn't ready to submit to him.

She smiled tauntingly. "You're so bad," she drawled, letting her Southern accent free, tempting him with it, reminding him of everything they had once had. "Maybe I'm just going along with you."

His hand landed against the curve of her ass in a light little slap. The feel of it streaked across her nerve endings, a light little fire that she needed. She needed that racing pleasure-pain, the intensity of the sensation burning through her mind.

"Should I beg you?" she gasped, pressing her ass back as his palm shaped it, cupped it. "Don't have the nerve to go through with it?"

She watched the smile that curved his lips. Rakish. Dangerous. Confident.

"Wrong words, baby," he growled.

"Yeah. I'm scared."

His hand landed again and she rose on her tiptoes, her fingers tightening on the spindles as a gasping cry fell from her lips.

Before she could recover, another fell. Two. One on each cheek.

One hand gripped her hip, holding her in place. With the other he laid the fiery little caresses along her ass, making her burn with the pleasure. She could feel it echoing in her sex, her clit. Oh God, in her nipples.

She writhed, tried to twist out of his hold, to press back closer to each heavy tap on her butt. Her head thrashed against his chest, perspiration dampening her skin, as she whimpered and bit her lip to keep from begging for more.

"Had enough?" He bit her ear.

"Getting tired?" Her voice was part sob.

"Sabella, baby, you don't know what you're tempting here." His hand smoothed between her thighs again, fingers dragging through the thick juices, easing them back to the tender opening between her rear cheeks. "We keep on this path, and you'll go places you've never gone before."

She opened her eyes and smiled tauntingly. "How do you know where I've gone before, Noah? Maybe you're just scared of going there with me."

His eyes locked with hers. They narrowed, his expression tightened.

His finger slid fully inside her rear entrance and she swore she almost climaxed. Her eyes rolled back, closed, and she shook, shuddered.

"Do you think you get to come that easy, sugar?" he whispered against her ear. "Oh baby. Not hardly."

With his finger lodged inside her, just penetrating her, he

held her in place as the other hand landed on the curve of her butt again. The little smack, his finger stretching inside her, not really moving, just kind of flexing, and she felt fire streak through her senses.

She was gasping his name, almost pleading as she tried to bear down on the impalement, to make him go deeper.

Another slap and she was crying out his name, lost in the sweet burn and dying for more. Just a little bit more. Each heavy caress, each tiny slap, heated her flesh and sent fingers of that heat racing to wrap around her clit, to tighten around it.

She was so close. So close she could feel the edge of madness burning inside her.

"Do you want to come, baby?" He kissed her neck, her shoulders. He bit, licked, sucked at her flesh until each touch was an agony of pleasure. "Tell me, Sabella, sweet little lover. Do you want to come for me?"

So bad. Oh God, she wanted to come so bad.

"I'll consider it," she gasped hoarsely and heard his surprised chuckle.

"Oh baby, you're going to do more than consider it. You're going to beg for it."

His finger slid free of her and she had to bite her lip to keep from crying out in disappointment. Until he went to his knees.

Sabella froze and swallowed tightly. Oh Lord, what had she done?

"God, I love your ass." He kissed one cheek, licked it, lightly smacked the other and she swore she nearly lost strength in her legs. She almost melted in front of him. She almost went up in a shower of flames.

"I'm going to fuck this pretty ass." His fingers parted her, and a little scream left her lips as she felt his tongue lick down the cleft before rimming the tiny entrance he had penetrated with a quick, hard lick.

"Hold on to the rails, Sabella." He spanked her again as her legs turned to jelly and she nearly went to the floor from the pleasure. "Hold on tight, sugar. I'm not finished here yet."

He pushed her thighs farther apart, turned, and before she

could process the change in position, his head was between her thighs, his mouth on her pussy.

Long, callused fingers parted the bare flesh as he licked through the sensitive, drenched slit. His tongue slid inside her, worked her, drove her crazy with the need racing through her, burning her with pleasure.

"You taste like sunshine," he growled at her clit. "The sweetest pussy I've ever tasted in my life. Like fucking ambrosia." He licked around her clit as his fingers drew more of her juices back, back, penetrating her rear again while one finger on the other hand slid inside the tormented depths of her.

"So tight. So hot." Two fingers penetrated her dually, working inside her as Sabella laid her head against the stair rail and sobbed in pleasure.

"Tell me you like it," he demanded then kissed her clit. A pursed-lipped kiss with the added lick of his tongue, just above it.

"Oh God. Noah!" She screamed his name, sobbed it.

"You're so fucking wet you're drenching me. So hot and wild, Sabella. Get wild for me, baby. Give it to me. Give it all to me."

Both fingers slid deep, impaled and stroked, and still he kept her on the edge. Just enough that her body flooded with the excess of her need, and he was there, lapping at it. Fucking her with his fingers, licking her with his tongue.

"Are you ready to come for me, Sabella?" His fingers slid back, returned, thrusting inside her slow and easy and making her insane for fast and hard. "I could get that pretty little clit off for you? Or do you need to think about it a while longer? I could give you a few more minutes. I could tie your hands to those rails and give you a few more hours."

Hours? Sabella blinked in dazed tormented pleasure. She could feel the perspiration on her skin, the slick need that coated her thighs. She stared at her hands, locked on the spindles, and knew she couldn't last. She could never last hours.

"Sabella." Lyrical, hoarse, deep, his voice was another

caress. "Tell me, baby. Do I need to tie you and let you think about it a while longer?"

"Noah." Her voice was ragged, her breathing heavy, labored. "Oh God. Let me come. Please let me come."

"Such a good girl."

And he rewarded her. His finger slid back from her pussy, another joined it, pressed forward as the one in her rear thrust deep again. He drew her clit between his lips, sucked and licked, and Sabella saw fireworks.

She screamed at the pleasure, racing explosions fractured through her nervous system and left her shuddering, trembling, as she rode the pleasure for every fiery wave she could get from it. Her wail echoed inside her head. Her legs shook and only the hands that suddenly gripped her thighs held her on her feet.

She was sobbing from the need now. The pleasure was still racing through her, and still, she needed more. That need had crawled under her flesh and seared her with a hunger as desperate as the one she glimpsed in Noah's eyes.

"Wildcat." He moved behind her, peeled her fingers from the rails, and pulled her to him. "Sweet, sexy little wildcat."

His lips came over hers, tasting of her, and of him and of wild need. Sabella moaned in pleasure, trying to crawl up his body, to force the thick stalk of his cock inside her where it belonged. If she didn't get him inside her she was going to die. She ached. Needed.

"So beautiful." His voice was hoarse now, as wild as his eyes. "Come on, baby. I have another treat for you."

Her fingers wrapped as far around his cock as they could, stroked, and she nearly came again at the sight of him, so thick and hard, rising from between the material of his jeans and the chaps covering them. Like a damned sex god. And she was melting like a slavish little pet.

He pulled her fingers from him, turned her and headed her up the stairs. She moved up the first two steps, desperate to get to their bedroom.

Until he stopped her, pulled her to her knees, and a second later his cock was pressing into her.

"I can't wait." His hands gripped her hips, flexed at them. "Ah God, Sabella, I can't wait."

He surged inside her, hard and deep, thick and heavy, the ropy veins caressing and stroking hidden nerve endings as she arched her back and cried out his name.

How was he supposed to survive this? Noah blinked back the sweat from his eyes, his breathing harsh, heavy as he felt the tight, gripping muscles of Sabella's pussy wrap around his cock.

He was lost in her. That dark lust he had always capped was driving inside him now, released, freed. So wild, so hungry, there was no way to control it. He didn't want to control it.

He pumped inside her, staring down, watching as his thick flesh pulled free of her, dripping with her juices, only to sink into the tightest, hottest flesh he had ever known.

He was supposed to survive without this now?

He was supposed to walk away? To give her up?

He shook his head as he pumped harder, deeper, groaning as he felt the slick, desperate clutch of her pussy along the hard shaft.

Pressing high and deep he heard her wail. His name, a plea. Her pussy milked him, devoured him. The slap of flesh against flesh filled his ears, the liquid grip of her muscles, the feel of her beneath him, giving to him, taking him.

He shook his head. He groaned her name. He couldn't think, couldn't speak. He could only take her. Take her hard and deep.

"Fuck. Yes. Damn you." He was rocking inside her, every inch of his erection stroked and clenched inside every inch of her pussy. "Damn you, milk me. Milk my cock, baby. Ah hell. Yeah. Ah yes, come around me. Come around me, baby."

She was coming, milking, rippling, crying his name. Crying his name in a voice filled with ragged emotion, with more than lust, more than need as he pumped his seed inside her, filled her, and collapsed over her, fighting for breath.

If he had to move right now, he might shatter. Noah could feel so much rising inside him, devouring him. What the hell was he going to do? Because he didn't know now, if he could walk away from her, no matter the risk.

CHAPTER TWENTY-FOUR

Her bed smelled like him again. Sabella woke up the next morning, Noah was curled around her back like a living blanket, and she sighed at the realization that she wasn't going to be free of him. Ever. And God only knew what was going to end up happening on this mission of his.

She let her hand smooth over his arm, feeling the rasp of dark hairs, and let herself just luxuriate in the feel of him for a moment.

He was wild. After taking her on the stairs, he had taken her once more in the bed. As though he couldn't get enough of her. Just as she couldn't get enough of him.

"Go back to sleep," he mumbled behind her, and the husky sleep-worn sound of his voice reminded her so much of their marriage.

"But I'm awake." She kept her voice soft, almost at a whisper.

"It's not daylight yet."

No, it wasn't. But she didn't want to miss a second of being with him.

"Do you ever watch the sun rise?" she asked, turning on her back and staring at his face.

Thick long lashes lay on his cheeks. His cheekbones weren't as high as they had once been. She could see where his nose had been broken.

God, the hell he must have endured. Alone. How had he borne it?

"Sometimes," he mumbled.

"I love the sunrise." She looked over at her window. An eastern view, where she could watch the first light coming into the house. "It's warm, even in the winter. It's like seeing a new beginning. A new reason to get out of bed. If the sun can rise every morning, then there's a reason to hope."

His lashes lifted. For once, his eyes weren't wild. The color wasn't as dark. It was all she could do to hold back her shock, her cry. They were Nathan's eyes. Irish eyes. Like gems flickering with laughter and love in his dark face.

"You're strange," he muttered before closing his eyes and dragging her closer to rest his head against her neck.

She stroked the arm over her waist. Caressed his shoulder. She smiled at the drowsy little groan he gave before opening his eyes again and peeking over at the clock.

Noah had put off waking up as long as he could. It was six, two more hours and the warrant against Delbert Ransome would be served. He needed to be ready.

He rose from the bed and stared down at her. "I need to get to the apartment."

She looked away from him, her lips thinning, staring at the window. And he could tell he was hurting her again. It struck against his heart, hurting her like this, making her feel she wasn't wanted. Wasn't loved. When it was anything but.

"Fine. Go." She waved toward the door. "I'll take a shower by myself."

He came back down on her, keeping the sheet between them, clasping her head in his hands. He stared at her face, at the eyes, the gray so soft, so filled with vulnerability. As if with each word out of his mouth she was praying for something more. Praying for a dream that wasn't going to happen. And he couldn't give her that dream, but damned if he had to hurt her any further. He couldn't do it. Hurting her was ripping apart pieces of him that he thought had died in that cell Fuentes kept him in.

"Wildcat." He nipped at her lips. Kissed them. Let himself love them, for just a moment. "If I stay, I'll never be ready on time. And your safety is more important, baby. More than you know."

She stared up at him, softer now, a strange little smile on her lips, her arms curling around his shoulders.

"Would you miss me if something happened to me, Noah?"

He felt his guts clench at the thought of anything happening to her. At so much as scratch marring her flesh.

"I'd rain hell on someone if anything happened to you, Sabella," he whispered, staring down at her, feeling a surge of emotion escaping that tight hold he'd tried to keep on it before. It was building inside him, threatening to tear free, and he couldn't let it. Couldn't allow it. "I'd lose the final shreds of sanity I've managed to hold on to, sweetheart. And neither of us wants that."

Her fingers tangled in his hair as she softened beneath him, and he couldn't help but taste her lips. Lips so sweet and swollen from his kisses throughout the night. Lips that melted beneath his and burned him with passion. Lips that nearly drove every thought from his mind but the erection pulsing between his legs.

"God, you burn my brains." He moved back from her, plowing his fingers through his hair as he jerked his boxers and jeans from the floor.

He dragged them over his legs as she sat up and watched him with hot, slumberous gray eyes. He tucked the unruly flesh beneath the cotton and denim and eased the zipper up slowly as she grinned.

"Seems a shame to waste it," she said as she slipped from the bed, proudly naked.

Noah swore he lost all the spit in his mouth as she strode from the bed. The curve of her ass tempted him. The bare pink flesh between her thighs, those high, proud breasts and tight, flushed nipples. Damn. He needed to fuck her just as bad as he had the first time he took her.

"I'm going to shower," she stated.

He groaned. "I'm getting my ass down to the apartment. Call me before you come down, so I can watch for you."

"I'll call." She closed the door behind him as he forced himself to finish dressing.

Grabbing the cell phone, he hit Nik's number and waited.

"Yeah." Nik sounded wide awake.

"Where are you?"

"The apartment. Waited on your ass all night and you never showed up."

Noah grunted at the amused statement. "I'm heading that way. I need you to stand watch on the house while I shower. Then we'll talk."

"Gotcha." Nik disconnected, as did Noah.

He dragged his boots on, then slung his chaps over his shoulder with a grin as he remembered the look on her face when she had sucked him, his cock spearing out from his jeans, his legs in those chaps. She'd damned near melted for him.

He gave his head a hard shake as he moved down the stairs and grabbed his shirt from the floor, pulling it on. He found his jacket, his vest, and laid them with the chaps on the chair by the door.

He checked the house out just to be on the safe side. Moved back upstairs, checked the spare room and bathroom then returned to the front door.

He grabbed his leathers and stepped out, locking the door carefully behind him before moving to the Harley. He checked it out, then checked out Sabella's little BMW, to be sure.

Everything was clean.

He stared around the area and breathed out roughly. Delbert Ransome was a rat, he'd squeal high and hard once the feds put the screws to his ass, and they'd have the members of the Black Collar Militia, and the wild card. The man providing them information on the investigations that had come through.

They had suspected Rick Grayson for a while, but the information Noah had glimpsed in that file said otherwise. What he knew about Rick told Noah otherwise. The man had dreamed of being the local sheriff when he was a teenager. He wouldn't have turned on his badge.

That left someone in the local police department. Someone had revealed the three federal agents, especially the young woman posing as a local college student. No one should have known about her. No one.

As he pulled the Harley behind the garage Nik was coming down the stairs. He positioned himself in a hidden corner at the side of the building where he'd have a clear view of the house, but the cottonwood tree and the tall yucca plants almost hid him from view.

Damned Russian Viking. He was too fucking big to try to hide much of anywhere.

Shaking his head Noah strode quickly up the stairs and headed for the shower. Delbert's truck wasn't at the garage, but the second word hit on the arrest, the gossip would start. It would build like a damned bonfire. It was the fallout Noah had to watch for. The fallout that could possibly ricochet back to Sabella. And that he couldn't allow.

That afternoon, Sabella walked down to the garage. Dressed in jeans and a sleeveless T-shirt, another of Nathan's old work shirts as an overshirt, she strode into the garage and pulled the roster from the mechanics' table.

Her gaze found Noah where he was bent beneath the hood of a late-model sedan. He wasn't as interested in the motor though as he was in the vehicles pulling into the gas pumps and the citizens moving into the convenience center.

Rory was manning pumps, laughing and chatting as he pumped gas. Toby was in the convenience center, and by all appearances keeping steady business.

News had hit of the arrest of Delbert Ransome in the gruesome deaths of a young Mexican couple. DNA taken from his truck was reputed to be suspected as matching that of the husband of the couple. According to the news report droning on the television, Ransome would have had to have run over the body several times for the physical evidence to have lodged where it was reported to have been found.

The arrest had come from an anonymous tip, a hiker that had been in the area and recognized Ransome's truck and Ransome running a man down.

The sheriff, Rick Grayson, had served the warrant, federal agents had been waiting at the impound yard, and within hours had managed to find the physical evidence.

Noah turned back to look at her, eyes narrowed as she listened to the report, and she knew damned good and well who had found that evidence, and where. He had found it while Ransome's truck had been in *her* garage.

She inhaled slowly before letting her gaze wander over the garage and noticing one of her mechanics missing. Chuck Leon wasn't much of a talker, but he'd never missed a day either.

"Where's Chuck?" She moved over to Noah and asked the question quietly.

"Don't know yet," he answered softly.

Sabella leaned closer. "He worked on Ransome's truck while it was here. Didn't he?"

"Uh-huh." Noah nodded before reaching in to test one of the connections on the wiring harness of the sedan. "He did."

"Did you call him?" She lowered her voice further.

"Toby called. No answer." Noah's voice carried no further than her. "Go work on the car, Sabella. Stay low and don't worry."

His gaze lifted at the sound of another vehicle pulling into the lot outside.

Sabella looked around the car and grimaced at the growing crowd. Nathan's garage had always been a focal point for gossip. It was on the edge of town, but the front lot was large enough that customers didn't have to worry about being blocked or how long they stayed. Old men stood outside the door with coffee in hand muttering to one another. Customers met in various areas, stopped, chatted, lingered to add to the gossip.

"Stay where I can see you," he muttered to Sabella, slicing a hard glance her way. "Every minute."

She looked outside then nodded shortly before returning to the sports car.

Noah watched the crowd ebb and flow outside, catching bits of the conversation and adding it to the mental notes he was taking.

Ransome liked to run with several other men, names that hadn't come up during the investigation, but names the unit would be running now.

There were reports coming in from the impound yard, via Jordan and Tehya, as well. The fact that a federal marshal had poked his nose into the investigation. A man known as an associate of Gaylen Patrick's. Jordan was running his background now.

And Delbert Ransome wasn't talking.

Added to that, Chuck Leon, the plant Noah suspected in the garage, was missing. When Micah had checked out his small apartment in town, there had been signs of a struggle, and his cell phone had been left lying beneath the couch, open, the last call to an unknown number. Coded.

He was starting to suspect Chuck was in a shitload of trouble and that perhaps one of the abc agencies in Washington hadn't been up front with the Elite Ops contact about any agents in place.

Something was going to hell in a handbasket, Noah could feel it.

Shaking his head, he moved from the car he was working on into the convenience center. He walked to the back of the small store as the bell jangled again over the entrance door and he caught a glimpse of the man stalking into the garage during a lull in customers.

Grant Malone.

Noah stared through the glass over the cooler, watching as Grant zeroed in on Rory as he grabbed a soda from another cooler.

"What the hell is going on, Rory?" Grant seized his son's arm and jerked him around before Rory could pull his arm out of his grasp.

"What the hell are you doing here?" Rory muttered. "Slumming?"

"Talking to an idiot," Grant hissed. "When are you going to get the hell out of this place? How many times do I have to warn you you're going to end up getting yourself in trouble?"

"Piss off," Rory snapped, and Noah could see the anger beginning to spew from both men. "Just jack right out of town, huh? Forget the promises we gave Nathan before he went on that mission, and just turn our backs on his wife?"

Noah clenched his hand around the water bottle as he stared at Grant Malone's back. At fifty-five, he was still in peak condition. His hair was nearly fully gray, but his skin was swarthy, his shoulders broad. Malone men didn't go down easy, and Grant was proving it.

"She won't listen to reason any more than you will," Grant snapped. "And you're endangering yourself here. Everyone's talking about that Ransome boy, and everyone knows that truck was here, in this garage. What the hell did you find?"

Rory's expression was suitably shocked. "Have you lost your fucking mind?" He pushed his father back. "If I'd found anything I'd taken Delbert apart myself. Damn you, is this how you're going to destroy Sabella? Start this trashy little story so someone slips in and slices her fucking throat?"

Enough was enough.

"Rory." Noah turned, snapped out his brother's name.

Both men turned to him. Grant's eyes narrowed, his fists clenched, as Noah walked toward them slowly.

"You should be on the pumps." Noah nodded outside. "Toby can't handle those alone."

Rory wiped his hand over his face in irritation. "Hell. Just what the hell I need. You poking your nose in this."

"What?" Grant looked over at Noah, his gaze hooded, brooding. "He's just sleeping with her. What the hell does he care if she dies?" A second later, he was choking.

Noah ignored the nails digging at his wrists as he snapped his fingers around Grant's throat and put him against the cooler, holding him in place with the sheer force of the rage transferring to his hand.

"One of these days, someone's gonna cut that hand off," Rory muttered before stalking off angrily.

Noah stared into his father's eyes. Flecks of green glittered in the Irish blue that stood out against suddenly pale cheeks.

"You want to leave," Noah told him carefully. "You want to leave, and you don't want to come back here."

Grant stared back at him, there was no fear in his eyes, but there was a hint of knowledge that Noah didn't want to see.

"That's enough." It was Sabella's voice that drew his attention.

He turned his head slowly, staring back at her.

"Let him go," she ordered between pale lips. "Now."

"Sabella, go finish that car," Noah suggested easily. "Mr. Malone and I are just having a friendly little conversation."

Sabella looked outside the store. "You're about to have an audience. Let him go. Now."

Noah released him, slowly, watching as Grant stared back at him in something akin to horror. He lifted his hand, rubbed at his neck. He started to speak, then clamped his lips closed.

"That's right," Noah said softly. "You don't want to say anything else. You want to walk right out of here. You want to drive away. Because we don't want your business here. You got me?"

Grant blinked back at him.

"You didn't answer me." Noah smiled slowly. "Do we want to discuss this later? Maybe around midnight." His voice went lower. "When you're in your bed, tucked in nice and tight. I could be there. I could slip right inside your nightmares, and we could chat about it then."

"You don't have it in you," Grant said softly. "Do you?"

Noah grinned. "Watch for me. If you have the nerve."

"Let him go, Noah. Now." Sabella's voice was inflexible. That tone that warned she could get mad without much more provocation.

He let him go, watching as Grant slipped past him, and unhurriedly left the building.

He turned and stared at Sabella. Glared at her.

"Don't interfere again," he warned her.

He turned and strode past her, moving back to the garage as rage pumped fast and furious inside him.

His father. That son of a bitch was his father, and he could barely keep from hating him, wanting to kill him as he heard him encouraging Rory to desert Sabella. To take away the last link to family that she could have. It didn't matter that he knew Rory would never do it. What pissed him off was that Grant was still pushing for it. And he didn't know why. He couldn't figure out why. He jerked the cap of the water off, tilted it up, and tried to drink enough to still the rage burning in him. It didn't work, and before he could control the impulse the half bottle of liquid was slamming into the wall of the garage. A torpedo that smacked and burst against the cement wall before falling to the floor.

Nik lifted his head from the truck he was working on, stared at the bottle, then Noah, before his gaze moved to the office doorway.

Noah jerked around and she stood there, staring at him, her gray eyes bleak and filled with pain.

This was one of the reasons why he couldn't stay. This. This burning need to rip apart anyone who had hurt her. The rage that blazed inside him, that tore away logic and control, that left him either tasting blood or tasting lust. Sometimes, he swore he could taste the need for both. At the same time.

She licked her lips slowly and moved from the doorway, coming toward him. Her face was pale, her eyes dark gray diamonds at they glittered with tears.

She stopped in front of him and simply leaned her head against his chest. That quickly the rage burned out. His arms came around her, and behind the hood of the car sheltering them, he jerked her to him, holding her. Holding her, and screaming inside. Because honest to God, he didn't know if he could let her go.

"Back to work." He stepped back.

Noah pushed his fingers through his hair and fought to get a hold on the feeling of betrayal he felt at hearing Grant's opinion of Sabella.

He'd asked only one thing of his father. In more than a decade, only one thing. If anything happened to him, protect Sabella. Take care of her. And Grant had sworn he would. He had lied. He had let Sabella suffer. He'd done everything he could to run her out of her home and out of the business Nathan had left to her.

He shook his head and went back to his job. He pushed thoughts of Grant Malone to the back of his mind, to deal with later. And he would be dealing with his father later, there was no doubt.

CHAPTER TWENTY-FIVE

Two hours later Noah stood in the closed office, his jaw clenching in rage as he held the secured cell phone to his ear and listened to Jordan's report.

"Delbert Ransome was released on order of Federal Judge Carl Clifford, Houston, Texas," Jordan reported. "Federal Marshal Kevin Lyle arrived at the airport an hour ago on a private flight, carrying the orders. He's taken over the investigation on the feds' end."

"And what do the feds think of this?" Noah asked carefully.

"My contacts are screaming," Jordan bit out. "Judge Clifford released Ransome on the fly-by-night excuse that Ransome's truck had been stolen and missing for several days around the time of the death. Good ole Delbert just didn't report it because he was drunk at the time, and by the time he sobered up, they found the truck parked in one of the pastures. He thought maybe he'd just parked it in the wrong place."

Noah snorted at that.

"No shit. My opinion too," Jordan grunted. "We have the leads we need though. We don't have to play by the rules here, Noah. Our orders are to stop this, no matter what we have to do."

No matter who they had to kill. Noah didn't balk at killing

when it was needed, but he'd like to have a little bit of proof before he pulled the trigger or wielded the knife.

"We'll set up watch," he told Jordan quietly. "I'll put Travis back in place. We'll get what we need."

"I'm running background on the names you gave me and Tehya's running probables and pulling in satellite time for the area. Watch your ass. When it hits, we'll have to move fast."

They were watching. Waiting. The next hunting party that went out would have a few surprises waiting for them.

"Did they get anything during interrogation?" Noah asked, watching through the wide square window of the door into the garage where Sabella was running a computer diagnostic on the sports car she was working on.

She was sweaty, greasy, her hair was escaping her ponytail, and she was the sexiest damned thing he had ever seen in his life.

"Nada. He didn't say shit. Didn't even ask for a lawyer. Just sat there and stared at the interrogators until the order came through on his release. Then, the bastard smiled."

He'd known he was covered. Whoever operated in those hunting parties knew their asses were covered. Noah nodded slowly, plotting.

"We'll cover high cards of interest," he told Jordan, letting him know someone would be on the federal marshal in town.

"Someone needs to get that sheriff out of the game while they're at it." Jordan said. "I hear he almost threw a punch at the marshal. He left the office in a rage. Apparently, there was a leak in information. Word came down the line that physical evidence was collected before the arrest. And it seems it might have come through his office, and back out of it. He threw his deputy out the door, sent his secretary home, and locked up the office. No one's seen him since."

Noah's eyes narrowed. It might be time to talk to the sheriff.

"I'll lay out the deck," he told Jordan, indicating he would place the members of the team where they needed to be. "I have priority here, and we're searching for the missing." For

Chuck Leon, who Noah was beginning to suspect was more than a mechanic, or even a militia plant.

"We're tracking for the leak," Jordan promised him. "We should have it soon and you can bet the sheriff is searching as well. I'll update you as I have more."

Noah closed the cell phone slowly and continued to stare at Sabella.

She brushed back a wisp of hair and left a smear of grease at her temple.

She was damned good in that garage. She didn't do auto body work, but she was mean as hell on a car motor. He'd seen the auto manuals at the house, knew she kept up with the latest reports, standards, and trends. She had even signed herself and Rory up for classes in Odessa on the new crossover vehicles.

His perky little wife was a tomboy and he had never known it. She was strong, resilient, and she was slowly moving away from the memory of the man that had loved her with every part of his soul.

She had taken a lover. It didn't matter that her lover had also been her husband, and she didn't know. She had exorcised her husband's ghost in her bedroom, in her home, and in his pickup truck.

He lowered his head and stared at his oil-stained work boots. She'd moved on. He didn't have the right to change that. Once he left this time, she might shed a few tears, but she'd pull herself up, and she would find someone who deserved her. Someone whole. Without demons. Without a past to hide or hell burning just behind his back.

His head jerked up as Rory stalked into the office and closed the door. The boy was still pissed off. Closed, set expression. His eyes burning in pure anger, he tossed Noah a half sneer before he glanced out the window into the shop.

Sabella was watching Noah. Noah had felt that look, had kept his head down, almost afraid to meet her eyes.

Rory turned back from the door and glared at Noah. "If you leave her again, don't come back."

Noah rubbed at his jaw before shaking his head slowly. "Do your job, Rory. Stop bitching at me."

"I'll tell you the same thing I told the old man, piss off," he retorted. "And wrap those damned fingers around my neck again and I'm going to Grandpop."

"You sound like a ten-year-old," Noah snorted.

"If it works use it," Rory muttered, grabbed a clipboard, and headed back into the convenience store.

Noah wanted to grin. Rory wasn't above tattling and Noah knew it. He'd have to kill him to keep his mouth shut if the boy was determined to go to Grandpop.

Damn. Grandpop. Sabella. Rory. He shook his head. What the fuck was he doing? What the hell made him think he could do this and still survive walking away?

Because he was a fucking fool.

They closed the garage at seven. Business had been steady through most of the day, with only occasional lulls. The gossip running through town and hitting every business was high. Most of it made it to the garage; what didn't, had been picked up in town as Nik and Micah made their way through it. Travis was watching the Patrick ranch house, where, surprise surprise, Federal Marshal Kevin Lyle had arrived late that afternoon with Delbert Ransome.

Chuck Leon was still missing and Rick Grayson was locked in his office going through files and on the phone yelling, it was rumored, and demanding answers about the leaked information.

Noah could feel the mission brewing now, a sixth sense warning him that something was getting ready to hit.

As he walked into the house ahead of Sabella, his senses seemed ultraalert, each speck of dust, each crack in the hardwood floors remembered, as he went through the house, checking it out.

As he returned downstairs it was to find Sabella sitting in the chair by the door. Like she used to do. But she wasn't filing her nails or watching television. She was staring at the floor and twisting the wedding band she had slid back to her marriage finger.

She was frowning at it, glaring at it. Twisting it on her finger as though trying to figure out exactly what it was doing there.

"Everything's clear." He stepped from the stairs before turning and heading into the kitchen. "I could use some dinner. How do you feel about pizza?"

He stepped into the kitchen, his gaze caught again by that damned bottle of what used to be a hundred-year-old wine. Hell, he had been saving that for the day they paid off the mortgage on the house and garage. He'd gotten it for a song. Traded it for a '57 Chevy he'd rebuilt for a collector for next to nothing.

Beside it was the bottle of wine she and Kira had polished off. He didn't wince, but at one time, he probably would have pulled his hair out. His lips quirked at the thought of it as he felt Sabella step into the kitchen behind him.

"Making awful free use of my house now, aren't you?" she asked him as he grabbed the cordless up from the kitchen handset and punched in the number taped to the wall beside it. Evidently, Sabella ordered pizza often.

"What do you want on your pizza?" He paused before hitting the button to dial it in.

The look she shot him was mocking. "Anything including the kitchen sink." She shrugged.

At least that hadn't changed over the years.

He hit the dial button, gave the order, and then disconnected. He lifted one of the bottles and turned back to her.

"Have more of these?"

She glanced at the bottle, then back at him. "Plenty. My husband collected them."

"We could share one with the pizza," he suggested.

She frowned at the bottle as he set it back on the counter.

"They're in the basement." She pointed to the door. "Pick out whatever you like."

There was one in particular he wanted to sip from her body. A light-bodied, priced-out-the-ass vintage he'd been saving for something extraspecial. Their twentieth anniversary. Their first child. But he'd always meant to share it with *her*. He fully intended to share it with her.

"Don't open the door," he warned her.

She rolled her eyes. "I had no intention of it."

He nodded and moved to the basement, opening the door and stepping down the wooden stairs he had built himself.

He looked around the open, well-lit basement. There were few things stored there. The cover over his pool table was dusty, the heavy wooden wine shelves were shadowed, the bottles covered with a layer of dust as well.

It was obvious Sabella didn't get down here very often. Not that he had expected her to. This had been his area, a place she'd seemed to understand he needed to get things in perspective sometimes.

He chose the bottle of wine, stared at the label, and felt that slicing pain in his chest again. There were nearly two dozen bottles of vintage wines. He'd started collecting them before he was old enough to be legal. He'd traded for them, bargained for them, lucked into a few. And each one had significance. Each one he'd planned the date or event to open.

He turned around and took another good look at the basement, watching as Sabella stepped into the doorway and stared down at him.

Her face was in shadow, but he could feel the worry that seemed to wrap around her.

"I haven't cleaned it," she said softly as he moved back up the stairs. "The basement, that is."

He strode up the steps as she backed up into the kitchen, her expression thoughtful. "Perhaps I should."

"It's a basement. Doesn't look like you use it much."

"No," she answered. "I don't use it much." She shook her head before turning away from him. "I need to shower."

Sabella moved upstairs quickly, her hand pressed to her stomach as she fought back the tears threatening to spill from her eyes.

She could do this, she told herself. She could handle this, and she could live through whatever happened if he left her.

If. She was holding on to the prayer that he wouldn't. It was the only thing keeping her sane at this point.

The pizza was good, the half bottle of wine they consumed with it was ambrosia. Despite the fact it was the middle of summer, Sabella lowered the air conditioner, and lit a small fire in the fireplace.

They ate the pizza in front of the fire, the chill of the AC whispering around them while the warmth of the fire heated them.

After eating, they dragged the heavy pillows from the back of the couch and stretched out on the floor. It was quiet, easy. And she wasn't surprised that Noah's head ended up in her lap. It was normal. This was how they had always ended up on cold winter nights. His head in her lap, her fingers playing through his hair.

Did he remember? she wondered. As he stared into the fire, his hands folded on his stomach, did he remember the nights they had shared, doing just this?

And other things.

She grinned at that thought. The fires they had built in that fireplace had seen a lot of loveplay. Nights they had spent just touching, just holding. Nights they had spent consuming each other, devouring sighs, kisses, and passion.

She stared down at him, watching his eyes, the flames reflecting in the wild blue, his lashes lowered slumberously. Her gaze drifted down his body and felt the familiar flexing of her womb at the sight of the heavy bulge beneath his jeans.

"Do you stay aroused?" Her voice was quiet, almost amused as she asked the question.

His head turned, his eyes staring into hers. "If you're around, I'm hard," he admitted ruefully. "I think you're a bad influence on me, Sabella. You encourage wild, wicked thoughts."

"Really? What kind of wild, wicked thoughts?"

He shifted, sat up, and turned to her.

"Thoughts of how sweet and wet you get for me." His hand cupped her cheek, his fingers threading through the hair at the side of her face. "Thoughts of taking you, fucking you until you're screaming my name, over and over again."

"Been there," she whispered, leaning back against the pillow behind her. "You've already done that."

"Hm, I have, haven't I?" He lowered his head, touched his lips to hers. "Maybe it bears repeating."

His kiss. She moaned against his lips, felt him sinking into her with that kiss, making love to her lips, her mouth, tasting her, drawing her inside him.

Sabella wrapped her arms around his shoulders, her nails digging into them as he came over her.

It was another memory, another moment in time to hold on to. She felt his hand caress up her thigh, beneath the light summer lounging dress she had worn.

The silky material slid up her thighs easily, pooling just below her hips as he drew back from her.

Firelight flickered over his body as he rose to his feet. He'd showered earlier, dressed in clean jeans and shirt. Those were disposed of quickly, leaving him naked, his bronzed flesh shimmering with the soft light of the flames, his cock jutting out from his body, heavily veined, the crown dark.

"Your turn." He knelt beside her, gripped the hem of her dress, and drew it off her body.

She wore panties, no bra. She wore her ankle bracelet and her wedding band.

She was married. Fuck him. Screw whatever reasons he had for hiding who he was from her, she was still his wife. For now. For now, she was Sabella Malone, and he, he was Nathan Malone. A ghost. A vision from the past with another face, another name, but still the man she loved.

"Kiss me." She stretched out against the thick, incredibly soft rug that covered the floor in front of the fireplace.

Pushing the pillows out of the way, she arched her back and saw the surprise that flickered in his eyes.

"Where?" His lips tilted with wicked eroticism.

"Right here." She tapped her lips with a finger. "We'll discuss other areas as we go."

His brows arched, and the temerity she showed obviously pleased him. He came down beside her, one hand gripping her hip, turning her to him.

"I won't break," she told him with a light laugh. "Kiss me, Noah. Kiss me right."

His eyes flared, darker, wilder.

"And what is right?" His voice was rougher, more guttural.

"Have you ever dreamed of a kiss? Dreamed of it, and ached to live that dream?"

"Every time I've dreamed of kissing you." His thumb brushed over her lips.

"Kiss me like that. Like you dream."

His hand tightened on her hip. Some emotion raged in his eyes, and then he was kissing her as he had never kissed her before. He braced himself over her, touching her with nothing but his lips, his tongue. Deep kisses. His lips slanted over her, and he kissed her with a desperation and a hunger that tore straight through her soul.

All the pent-up dreams, lonely nights aching for him, the nightmares that left her gasping, screaming for him, all of it went into the kiss she returned to him.

She didn't touch him any other way. Her nails dug into the rug beneath her, she felt his body tensing above her. They made love with their mouths. With their tongues. They licked and stroked and desperate moans filled the air as the need rose, blazed inside them.

When they came up for air, it wasn't oxygen that drew them. Sabella's arms lifted, wrapped around his back, and drew him to her. Her nipples brushed his chest as his lips scoured her neck.

Hunger pounded inside them. It filled the air around them, brushed them with a sheen of perspiration from the flames that licked inside them, over them.

"I need you," she breathed against his neck, nipping, licking, leaving small reddened marks beneath his closely cropped beard as she fought to get closer. "I need all of you, Noah."

"God. You have me, Sabella." His lips moved down, down. His tongue licked over the upper curves of her breasts, and a second later she was arching, crying out as he sucked the hard tip of her nipple into his mouth.

Electric sensation shot through her. She arched. She moaned. She was dying inside with the need to hold him, hold all of him within her forever. Or whatever small part he would allow her to keep if he left her.

If. She couldn't allow herself to believe he would leave. She refused to. Love alone would hold him, she promised herself. It had to.

"You taste like summer," he groaned as his lips moved from her breasts, down her stomach. "Spread your legs, Sabella. Let me see if you need me."

She bent her knees, spread her thighs. She watched him as he sat back on his knees, his hands pressing her legs farther apart, his eyes glowing as he stared at the swollen folds between her thighs.

"Damn, you're wet," he whispered. "Always so wet for me. So sweet."

Her juices glistened on her flesh. In a bold, daring move, Sabella ran her fingers down her stomach, dipped her fingers into the narrow slit, and let one caress gently around the straining bud of her clit.

His cock jerked. She watched a droplet of creamy liquid pearl at the tiny slit at the crown as he watched her.

"Is that how you like it?" he growled. "Slow and easy?"

She let her lips curl invitingly. "Is that how you like giving it?"

His tongue touched his lower lip as he glanced back at her. "I want to take you like an animal," he rasped. "So hard and deep you don't know anything but the fact that you're being taken."

She lowered her fingers as he watched, parted the wet lips, and let him watch. Watched her hands as she dipped her finger into her pussy and drew it back. It glistened with her juices. And then she lifted them to his lips.

A ragged moan filled the room as his lips parted and he

sucked her fingers inside. At the same time, his hand lowered and Sabella arched, a tortured cry falling from her lips, as two fingers filled her.

He pushed inside her, strong and deep, a shock of penetration, of pleasure, as he reached deep and with the tips of his fingers caressed that hidden spot of exquisite sensation inside her.

Sabella's hips arched, her gaze followed his. It was the most erotic sight she could have imagined, seeing his fingers penetrating her, pulling back, then pushing inside her again as his head lowered.

"I'm going to eat you like candy, baby," he told her, the sexual, erotic sound of his voice spearing into her womb. "Like the sweetest candy."

His tongue licked around her clit and he watched her, held her eyes. The tip flickered over the tight, straining bud before he went beneath it and lapped at it. Long, slow licks as his fingers shifted and shafted inside her.

"You're going to tease me to death," she panted.

"Fuck us both to death," he growled before sucking the tender knot of nerves into his mouth and creating the most exquisite sensation. He drew on her, let his tongue rub against the ultrasensitive flesh as she cried out his name.

"Not fair," she cried out.

"Hmm. So sweet." He kissed the little bud gently.

"I want to touch you."

"You make me crazy when you touch me." He nipped her thigh. "You make me lose my mind with hunger."

"Yes," she hissed, lifting until she rested on her elbows, staring back at him. "Like you make me. Lie back for me, Noah. Let me touch you. Let me ride you." She grinned back at him. "Afraid you can't handle me?"

Hell, he knew he couldn't handle it. But it was a dare, a challenge, and Sabella had never challenged him quite like this.

He pulled his fingers back from her tight grip, grinned, and sucked her juices from them. Her face flushed, her eyes darkened, and it was the prettiest damned sight he had ever seen.

Then he pulled back and lay down for her. Watching her, his body tensing, tightening as she moved between his thighs as he had hers.

"Oh, I think I like this." Her hands smoothed up the bunched muscles of his thighs, coming close, so close but not touching the tortured sac of his balls.

"You're playing a dangerous game, baby," he told her, his voice rougher than normal, the blood pumping harder, faster through his body.

He linked his hands beneath his head, otherwise he was going to jerk her over him and take what he knew she would give him anyway.

"I like living dangerously." Her lips lowered, lowered.

"Ah fuck!"

Her lips were on his balls, open, drawing one side into her mouth, her tongue flickering playfully, licking at the tight sac as his hips jerked, arched involuntarily.

The whisper of her moan filled his head as he watched her. He had to watch her. This was another side of his wife that he had never known. Catlike, seductive. Licking and stroking until she was licking up the ropy veined shaft of his cock and finally, teasingly, mouthing the head of his cock.

He watched her lick the crest. Watched her suck him into her mouth. Watched her love every inch of his massively hard erection.

He could feel the sweat beading on his forehead. Felt the arousal like an ecstatic, rapacious bite tear through his system.

She moaned and sucked the crown deeper. Tongued it. Consumed it, until he thought he was going to die from the need to fuck her. To have her. To pound into her until she was screaming his name.

Finally, her lips lifted. She shifted, moved, stood. Noah stared up at the juices that had built on her pretty, bare pussy. He licked his lips. Wanting to taste. Knowing he needed to fuck her more.

He pulled his hands from beneath his head, gripped his cock with one hand, spearing it up to her as his hand lightly circled her ankle.

"I want to watch," he growled. "Let me watch you take me, Sabella."

With her feet flat on the floor she bent her knees, keeping her thighs wide, and she lowered herself to him. Noah let his hand caress up her leg, grip her hip. Watched, watching in agonizing pleasure as the engorged crest parted the swollen folds.

He watched the lips of her pussy embrace the blunt tip of his erection, felt the fiery heat of her, the slick, wet desire that rained from her. And he watched as she lowered herself, felt as he began to impale her.

She took only the head, then lifted, let him see the juices coating the tip of his cock before she lowered further. Took more, lifted.

Smooth pale thighs tensed. Swollen, hard-tipped breasts glistened in firelight. And he watched as she took him. A little. Then pulled back. And watched with each downward stoke, then saw the slick, heated syrup clinging to his cock as she lifted.

She took him slowly. Relishing every penetration, every stretch as her tight pussy enfolded him. Released him.

He could feel the sweat beading his body, feel her nails digging into his chest. And he felt her take him to the hilt on a long, slow downward motion of her body.

He felt the moment she lost herself in the pleasure, because he lost himself with her. He pulled her to him, easing her onto him as she straddled him fully now, her knees on the floor, her back arching.

His hands gripped her ass as she moved. Each thrust pushed him deep inside her as she did just as she had promised. Rode him. With quick hard motions of her hips. Long slow shifts and slides, then quick and hard again. His hips lifted to her, his hands covered her breasts, palmed them, then as he felt her building, climbing to her pleasure, he let his fingers grip the hard little points and apply just enough pressure to send her rocketing over the edge.

Noah felt himself unraveling. Staring at her face, the exquisite ecstasy, the sweat running in rivulets down her neck, her breasts, he lost that last hold on reality. He poured himself into her, pumping hard and deep, feeling his come spurting, jetting from the head of his cock as he groaned her name and pulled her to him.

His lips on hers. His tongue licking her, tasting her, loving her.

Until the pleasure left her limp, exhausted. A drowsy little kitten against his chest. His Sabella.

When he could breathe again, when he could think, he turned, laid her back on the floor, and pulled from her. She mumbled a protest as he grinned and lifted her into his arms.

He carried her to their bed, tucked her in then moved downstairs to smother the fire and close the glass doors to the fireplace.

Naked, ravaged by her loving, he watched the glowing embers for long moments before returning to her. She was sleeping. One arm thrown over her head, her left hand lying on her stomach, atop the blanket. The wedding band winked back at him, mocking him.

She belonged to Nathan Malone. That wedding band reminded her of that. He knew why she had put it back on again, to remind her where her heart belonged, even if another man did touch her body.

He lay down, sliding beneath the blankets, watched her sleeping face and knew she was lost in slumber.

He lifted her hand, kissed the ring he had slid on her finger eight years ago, and closed his eyes against the pain rising inside him.

"Go síoraí." He whispered the vow against that little gold band, and felt the helpless, gaping pain in his soul. "Forever, Sabella. Always yours. Forever."

He held her hand in his as he laid his head on the pillow beside her, and let sleep have him as well.

He didn't see the tear that fell from the corner of her eye. He didn't see her lips move, see the word "forever" pass the trembling curves. And he didn't understand, Sabella knew, that no matter where he went, how hard he ran, that vow would always follow them both.

CHAPTER TWENTY-SIX

By Monday morning information was amassing. The team was called to the apartment over the garage for a before-dawn meeting after Noah received another call from Jordan. Jordan was in attendance with pictures transferred from the field laptop Travis was using above the ranch, as well as satellite images obtained through a commercial satellite Tehya had managed to hijack during the night.

There was definitely something going on at the Patrick ranch.

"We have Federal Judge Carl Clifford as well as Marshal Kevin Lyle in attendance." Jordan pointed out the pictures Travis Caine had taken from his vantage point above the Patrick ranch house. "We also have several other ranch owners in attendance." Several other pictures snapped into view. Grant Malone wasn't one of those ranch owners.

Noah didn't let himself feel a sense of relief that Grant wasn't there. At this point, he was finished with the man who should have been his father.

"We also have this."

This was a picture of a black van parked behind the house. A figure was being dragged from the vehicle by two cowboys. The face was covered by black material, hands bound.

"Chuck Leon," Noah stated. "Our missing mechanic."

"Try our missing undercover FBI agent," Jordan snorted.

"He was a lower-level member of the militia, working his way up the ranks. He's been in the area for over six years. Kept a low profile, worked a few of the ranches. His cover was blown two days ago and no one knows how. We have a leak between here and Washington, and we can't tap it, we can't find it. It's like a disease, and it's starting to piss me off."

Jordan's expression was brutal.

"Four FBI agents, all using completely different under-cover identities," John Vincent pointed out, his steely gray eyes flickering between the men in the team. "It's not a leak you have, it's a rather good eye."

Noah slid the other man a curious look.

Dressed in camo pants and an olive green T-shirt, Vincent leaned forward in his chair and tapped at the pictures of the four agents. "College student, car salesman, pharmacist, and mechanic. Those were their covers. They were all in different areas, in different jobs, but all those jobs were public related in some manner. Now, I don't know 'bout you blokes, but I can smell an agent, foreign or otherwise, a mile off. Your mechanic was better than most." He nodded to Noah. "But we all suspected him as a plant. He had that feel, that air of an agent that only another agent or trained eye would recognize." He tilted his sandy blond hair and stared at the pictures. "Are we certain the sheriff's clean?"

"The sheriff is clean. We know it." Jordan nodded. "Then you have someone else. An officer on the police force, a deputy or other law enforcement agent with the training that would allow him to identify your agents. It takes a special eye, you know that. Grayson has that eye. I know damned well he does because every time he sees one of us he gets that cop look in his eye and starts trying to figure out the puzzle."

Noah scratched at his beard as he rose from the couch and paced the living room. "Grayson's clear, so who does that leave us with?"

He turned back to the other men. There were no answers.

"It has to be a resident. Someone who's come in contact with these agents between here and Houston."

"A needle in a haystack," Nik quipped before turning to

Jordan. "Are we rescuing Mr. Leon?" Anticipation filled the Russian's large face.

"At this time, we're watching." Jordan's expression cleared, his eyes went hard. "They don't just kill, they hunt. Let's see if they take him out to hunt."

Months of training in preparation just for this tightened Noah's body. They had practiced being the hunted. All of them. Playing intricate games of cat and mouse, flee and evade, working together to give the illusion of one target as they circled around the SEAL members playing the hunters to take them out. Not that taking out Reno Chavez's SEAL team had been easy. Their success rate with those men had been dismal.

But Gaylen Patrick and his little hunting party weren't a SEAL team prepared for them.

"Stay on alert." Jordan began gathering his equipment together and storing it in the leather case he had carried with him. "When they move with Leon, we move."

Noah crossed his arms over his chest as he paced into the kitchen, his mind working through probables. He couldn't get the information out of his head now. Something wasn't sliding into its proper slot, and he couldn't figure out why.

"We're certain Grayson is clean?" He turned back to Jordan with the question.

"As certain as we can be." Jordan nodded. "We have his office bugged, Tehya's been running through the tapes. The man is ready to pull his own head off trying to figure this out. He knows there's someone, somewhere, leaking information. He just can't tag the leak or where it's coming from."

"It's someone close," Noah growled. "The wild card in this little setup has to be someone we're overlooking. Someone the mechanic was in contact with as well."

"If you figure it out, we're ready to roll." Jordan shrugged. "Until then, all we can do is play what we have."

Jordan looked outside to the faint rays of light edging through the darkness. "We better clear out and get in position."

The last thing they needed was for all of them to be in the

apartment at the same time. As Jordan, John, and Micah slipped from the garage, Noah turned back to Nik.

The Russian was slumped back in his chair, his icy eyes narrowed as he watched Noah pace.

"You feel it, don't you?" Nik growled. "Shit's going to explode."

Noah heaved a hard sigh. "Yeah, shit's going to fly when it hits. Do you have everything laid in place?"

Nik nodded to that. It was their own plan. A series of weapons and equipment placed in strategic locations in the mountains where they had known several hunts had taken place.

They were both carrying deactivated trackers in the buckles of their belts, and the technologically advanced night vision contacts they had procured from another source. That particular toy hadn't even made it into military testing in the three years they had been in research.

"And your woman?" Nik asked.

Noah looked at him from the corner of his eye. "I have her covered."

Rory was all the backup he had, but Nik didn't have to know that.

Nik grinned at his answer but nodded as he rose from his seat. Noah went to the door of the apartment, stepped outside, and checked the area before heading down the steps and making his way back to the house.

The lights were on in the kitchen. Sabella would have coffee waiting. As he entered through the back door, the past flooded him like a tidal wave, momentarily washing away everything but the memories.

Sabella, wrapped in nothing but a robe, making biscuits. Bacon was frying on the stove, water was boiling for the grits. Eggs were set out on the counter and her smile was still tinged with sleep as she looked at him.

She was rumpled, sexy, and cooking breakfast. Here was one of the few glimpses he had been given of the woman who had shared his life. The woman who held his soul.

"You already showered." She pouted back at him. "I guess that means you intend to work?"

Noah let a smile curve his lips as he advanced toward to her. He turned off the bacon, jerked his belt loose as he turned to her, and pushed the bowl of flour out of the way.

Surprise widened her eyes as he gripped her waist, lifted her to the little work island, and stepped between her thighs then unzipped his jeans and drew his raging erection from the opening.

"Noah, are you crazy?" She laughed, aroused and excited. He could smell the excitement on her. As he spread her thighs and glimpsed the shimmering sweetness between them, he could see her excitement.

He lowered his head and ran his tongue through her pussy. She tasted like a lazy summer morning. Like a fire in winter. Like all the dreams he told himself could never be. She was his oasis in the middle of hell, and he needed her again. Right now.

He circled the straining bud of her clit, wrapped his lips around it, and stared up at her face as she leaned back, propping her tiny feet easily on his shoulders and arching into his intimate kiss.

He circled the straining bud with his tongue, rasped it, sucked it and watched her, heard her as she arched to him and came undone.

As the little orgasm rushed through her, trembled through her pussy, he straightened, gripped the base of his cock in his hand, and positioned himself before plunging inside her.

"Noah." She screamed his name.

Sabella felt the incredible pleasure stealing through her again. It worked over her nerve endings, the burning stretch between her thighs echoing through her body as she fought to hold on to her senses.

She gripped the edge of the work center, her legs falling over his arms as he held her hips and pulled her closer.

There were few preliminaries, and she didn't need them.

She had been ready for him when she awoke alone, missing him. Desperate for one more touch, one more kiss, before she had to face whatever she could feel coming.

"Damn you. You're tight as a vise around me," he groaned, leaning to her, his lips feathering over hers. "Like fire and ecstasy together."

She panted as her body adjusted to the invasion. Taking him, all at once, was pleasure and pain, it was an inferno of sensations she couldn't grasp or make sense of as she felt herself flying to the edge of release. Her hands tunneled into his hair, holding his lips to hers as they made love with their mouths, their tongues. As they moved and thrust against each other, pleasure tearing through them, almost violent, tinged with desperation as she moaned into his kiss and fought for more.

Then he was giving her more. Moving between her thighs, plunging into her, taking her over that edge and filling her mind with a rainbow of colors as their release exploded into and around each other.

His seed pumped inside her. His groan was a harsh, rasping sound of completion and need, and he was holding her. His arms wrapped around her, holding her to him as he buried his face at her shoulder and they both shook, trembled, in the wake of the pleasure.

She couldn't imagine being without him now. She wouldn't let herself imagine being without him.

His kiss was long and slow now. His eyes open as she stared back at him.

"Hmm. That was a surprise." She smiled as he moved back from her, her breath catching at the feel of his cock sliding from her body, tugging at the oversensitive tissue, before he lifted her and set her back on her feet. "I'm supposed to walk now?"

She smoothed her hand over his chest as he bent his head and stole another kiss.

He flashed her a grin as he finally pulled back and readjusted his jeans.

Sabella made a quick trip to the bathroom, and when she returned it was to find him sipping his coffee and staring down at the garage from the wide kitchen window.

"You were up early this morning," she said as she turned the stove back on and went back to her biscuits.

"Needed to shower and get some clean clothes." His voice was distant now. "I didn't expect you to be up yet." There was a question in his voice.

Sabella grimaced. "Doctor's appointment I forgot about this morning. And I can't miss it." She turned back to him with a frown. "If I don't make that appointment then you don't get to have any fun."

His lips tugged into a rueful smile. "I'll send Rory with you. I don't want you going alone."

"Sienna usually goes with me." She shrugged at his demand. "But you can send Rory. I'll just meet her there."

The flu that had kept her in bed for nearly two weeks the month before had had her doctor worried. She hadn't bounced back as she should have. At least not before Noah returned. But the follow-up coincided with the birth control shots she needed to keep her system regular.

"I'll send Rory too. He can drive you."

She nodded at that. "Everything going okay?" she finally asked, knowing Delbert Ransome's release yesterday worried him.

"So far." He swiped his hand through his hair, feathering the long, thick raven-black strands around his roguish face.

God, he made her heart beat faster. She'd just had him, and she wanted nothing more than to take him again.

She nodded when he didn't say anything more. Conversation after that was quiet. They talked about the garage, parts needed, and the business that was now flowing back to them.

They argued over new equipment she wanted to buy. Advanced computers for the new chips coming out and the classes she had signed up for in Odessa. The pros and cons to each move she wanted to make in the business.

As they talked, Noah realized in one heart-stopping moment just how perfect Sabella had been for him all along. The fact that he hadn't realized that six years before still had the power to rip into his guts.

The mistakes he had made since his rescue piled atop him, one after the other. He should never have hid from her, what the hell had he been thinking? As long as he didn't face her, didn't face the consequences of his decision, then he'd been able to remain strong.

It had been all about his stupid fucking pride though. Not being the man he had been, fearing her rejection in the face of it. He'd been a fucking fool and now there was no way out.

He could just imagine her face if he said, oh yeah, by the way, baby, I'm your husband. You know, the one that died? The one that wouldn't come back to you for six fucking years. Yeah, she'd accept that easily enough.

Bullshit.

This Sabella would rip his eyes out of his sockets and shoot him with his own gun. Before she divorced him. Because she couldn't forget the man he had been. The one whose ring she was wearing, even now, on her marriage finger. The one whose pictures graced damned near every surface of the living room.

Shit. The anger tore through him as she showered and dressed for that damned doctor's appointment. He didn't want to let her out of his sight.

He strode furiously to the phone and called Rory, pulling him in to take her to the doctor when Noah wanted to go with her himself.

He couldn't risk being off site when this mission went nuclear. And if they acted out of habit, then suspicion would rise against Bella. Rory had taken her to the doctor before, Noah knew. She rarely went alone. Sabella hated doctors and she hated waiting in the doctor's office alone. She and Sienna had often gone with each other, then gone shopping for lunch afterward. After Nathan's "death," he knew Rory had tagged along many times, often bullying her gently into doing the things she used to do with Sienna.

"There's my babysitter." Sabella grinned as she stepped

into the kitchen later to find Rory with Noah. "Who's watching my garage?"

"Toby and Nik," Rory grunted. "That kid is turning into a damned maniac. Thinks he owns part of it or something."

"He's learning." She shrugged as she adjusted the low-rise band of her jeans and slid her feet into a pair of sandals. "Toby has a good head on his shoulders, and if we manage to keep him another year, we'll be lucky."

Rory grimaced. It was something Noah had acknowledged as well. Toby would move on. The little shit would probably end up taking over the world before he was done.

"Okay, let's go. I called Sienna. She's meeting us at the doctor's office." She eyed Rory with a grin. "Are you going into the office or waiting in the car?"

Rory grimaced. "Damned women in that waiting room, you'd think they never saw a man the way they act when I walk in there."

Noah felt a curl of anger burning inside him. For six years Rory had watched over her, taken care of her. He had gone to the doctor with her, held her when she cried, he had stepped in and made certain Sabella wasn't alone. That she survived. He should be thanking his brother rather than questioning his motives.

"Come on, stud," Sabella teased Rory then. "Give the girls a smile and a wink and they'll swoon for you."

"I'd end up raped," Rory muttered, but it was good-natured.

They left the house, but before he let Sabella get in Rory's pickup, he pulled her to him, his lips covering hers, staking his claim on her senses before he let her go.

"What was that for?" She gripped his shoulders, her nails digging into his shirt like a little cat's, kneading his flesh with primitive hunger.

"To remind you," he growled.

"Of what?" Something flashed in her eyes then, a flare of anger, of determination.

"Of who you belong to," he bit out. "Don't forget it, Sabella."

She tilted her head as though staring at some strange, unknown creature and attempting to make sense of it.

"You're leaving," she reminded him gently. "You've warned me of that all along, Noah. You can't stake a claim on someone you have no intention of keeping."

The hell he couldn't. His head dipped again and he stole her defiance with another kiss. He pushed his tongue in her mouth, claimed it, just as he had claimed her body each time he fucked her into a screaming orgasm. His hands pulled her closer, pressing his erection against her stomach through the material of his jeans and fought to get a handle on the possessiveness tearing through his gut.

He couldn't control the need. He couldn't stop the fury of dominance, the instinct to make damned sure she never forgot. Never forgot who she belonged to. Whose soul she held in the palm of her hand.

He pulled back and glared down at her. "Remember."

He stalked away from her then, refusing to acknowledge the tears that had shimmered in her eyes, because to acknowledge them would break him. He was riding a line so fine now that sometimes it didn't make sense, even to him. He knew, though, if this operation didn't end soon, if he didn't manage to pull back just a little bit, then he was never going to be able to walk away from her. And that just might kill both of them.

CHAPTER TWENTY-SEVEN

"You're gettin' pretty close to him, huh?"

Sabella turned her head and stared at Rory. God, he looked so much like Nathan used to look. Rugged features, the perfection of male beauty paired with wicked blue eyes, thick heavy lashes, and long black hair.

He was almost Nathan's twin. So close to him in looks that for nearly two years Sabella had been unable to look him in the face.

"Shouldn't I be?" She knew Rory was aware of who Noah was. She could feel it to the marrow of her bones and it hurt.

She was past mad. It just hurt now that Noah had trusted his brother rather than his wife. The woman he had sworn his heart to. He'd dared to whisper those words in their bed, after he thought she slept. Dared, dared to whisper that vow in Gaelic, in their bed, while he was lying to her. Lying to her with every touch, every kiss, every rasping word from his lying lips.

Rory finally shrugged. "Do you think he's going to stay?"

She would have gotten angry at that point if she hadn't heard the regret, the somber realization in his voice, and seen it in his face.

Sabella turned and stared out the window. She watched as the town passed by, as everything familiar to her suddenly seemed alien and strange.

"No." She finally whispered the truth, to him, and to herself. "I don't think he'll be here much longer."

She looked down at her hands, touched the wedding band, and slid it slowly from her finger before tucking it into her purse. Sienna would ask too many questions if she saw it. It could raise too much suspicion.

"You know, Belle." He cleared his throat, his hands tightening on the steering wheel. "I love you like a sister. You know that."

"No advice, Rory." She could feel it coming. As he pulled in to the doctor's office parking lot and parked beside Sienna's car, she realized her control wasn't strong enough to endure even Rory's well-meaning advice.

He nodded as Sienna jumped from her car, stylish in gray capris and a sleeveless T-shirt. Her long nut-brown hair fell past her shoulders in carefully styled waves, her green eyes sparkled with the same excitement and love of life she had always known.

"There you are." Sienna laughed, hugging Sabella as she stepped out of Rory's truck. "And there's one of the handsomest men in town." She sighed, her expression creasing in sudden somber realization. "He looks just like Nathan, Belle."

She mirrored Sabella's earlier thoughts.

Sabella looked to Rory and saw the flash of pain on his face.

"No, Rory looks just like himself," she said softly. Close. He was close. But not just like Noah. Not anymore.

"I can't believe you nearly forgot about your follow-up appointment," Sienna grumped at her then. "You were too sick, Belle. You need to take better care of yourself."

She had been sick. That last flu bug had been a vicious one.

"I'm working on it, Sienna," Sabella promised with a smile as they entered the doctor's lobby, signed in, and took their seats.

She wondered if that bug was coming back. She hadn't felt her best the last few days. She felt off. Out of sorts. But emotionally she was on a roller-coaster ride that threatened to drive her insane.

"They're looking at me," Rory muttered as she took a seat beside him.

She smiled, shaking her head. " 'Cause you're cute."

He grimaced. Then grinned. "I am, ain't I?"

And she just shook her head at that Malone grin, the twinkle in his blue eyes. He was a heartbreaker. Her friend. Her brother.

"I'll protect you," she whispered.

Then he stared back at her in surprise. "I want to be protected?"

And Sabella could only laugh.

She wasn't laughing over an hour later though, she was close to sobbing, to screaming in joy. And in fear.

"I'd venture a week, perhaps a little longer," Dr. Amy Aiken said softly as she sat on the stool in front of the exam table. "The shot was low dose to begin with, because you stated you weren't involved in any sexual activity. You're over a week late returning for the shot, and with the antibiotics . . ." The doctor shrugged. "It happens, Sabella."

She was pregnant.

Sabella pressed her hand against her stomach. This time. This time, God had heard her prayers, he had given her a part of Noah to hold on to, a part of everything she loved to see her through the pain.

She swallowed tightly. "Could you not tell your nurses?" she finally said. "Could we keep this between us? For a while?"

The nurses were notorious gossips. Sabella had always suspected it was one of the reasons Dr. Aiken often ran many of the less complicated tests herself. The blood test had been done in the exam room while Sabella waited. Dr. Aiken was conscientious, she was personal. She was a friend to the women who came to her. And she knew her nurses.

"Is there a problem, Belle?" the doctor asked her gently.

Sabella shook her head. "I want a chance to believe it myself," she said softly. "Before anyone else knows."

Dr. Aiken sighed at that. "It's a very small town." She rose and collected the data on the test before folding it and pushing it into her lab coat. "I can wait a few weeks before I add it to your file." She winked. "I forget these things sometimes."

She sat back down on the stool. "Do you want this baby, Sabella?" she asked gently.

Sabella's head snapped up. "More than anything," she breathed out roughly. "I didn't consider." She paused and shook her head. "I didn't think. I'd forgotten about the antibiotics. Things have been crazy at the garage." In her life. The shock of having Nathan back had dulled her senses.

Dr. Aiken smiled, her serious hazel- and blue-flecked eyes somber. Concerned. "I want you back in three weeks. I'll rerun the blood tests then and we'll do a full workup. You weren't pregnant when you were in here last month, you're no more than a few weeks along."

Sabella shook her head. No more than weeks. But she knew. She knew she carried Noah's baby. She knew it was growing inside her. She swore she could feel it now. That unknown feeling that had plagued her the last few days, the sense of being off balance, not entirely certain why. It wasn't just because of Noah. It was their child, letting her know he was there.

"You can get dressed now." Amy rose to her feet. She paused again and looked at her. "If you need to talk, you know you can call me anytime. Or come by the house. We'll have coffee." She smiled suddenly. "Though it's decaf for you."

Decaf worked for her. She was already planning revised menus. She would have to eat better. Eat more often. No more caffeine and she didn't even give a damn.

She was carrying Noah's baby.

She dressed quickly, floating, feeling as though a surge of euphoria had taken hold of her mind and refused to release it. She stopped as she buttoned and zipped her jeans, and touched her stomach again. Just felt it. Needing to feel the life growing inside her.

She and Nathan had talked about starting a family after he returned from that last mission. They had wanted children, but they had wanted a stable environment to bring one into. They were going to pay off some of the bills. They were going to talk about it when he got home. But he hadn't come home, until now.

Her lips curled softly, though sadly. She could keep him, she thought. She could tell him about the baby, he would never leave her . . . She shook her head. No. She wouldn't hold him. If he left, he would leave without knowing. And then she would have to leave as well, because Rory and Jordan would make certain he knew. They would never keep that information from him. And she would be back where she started, with a man who had returned, not for her, but because of their child.

Besides, if he knew about the baby, and he left anyway? It would destroy the love she felt for him, and that she couldn't bear. Noah was the best thing that had ever happened to her. Loving him had been the greatest fulfillment of her life. Until now.

She finished dressing, then left the exam room, and went back to the lobby.

"Everything okay?" Rory came to his feet as she stepped back into the lobby and moved to the counter to pay her bill.

"Everything's fine." She smiled back at him, forcing herself to keep the curve of her lips restrained. "I'll be ready in a minute."

The nurse took her check. She was busy inputting information into the computer and, thank God, didn't ask about the shot Sabella hadn't received.

"I thought you would be in there forever," Sienna teased as they left the doctor's office and emerged in the parking lot. "She never takes that long."

"She wanted to make certain I was over that flu bug." Sabella shrugged.

She was dying to tell someone. Why wasn't she telling Sienna? Rory? Why wasn't she shouting it from the rooftops? She was pregnant. Finally pregnant and it was her husband's baby.

She inhaled slowly as they turned the corner of the building and headed across the back lot to Rory's truck. She was lost in the happiness, trying to hide it from Rory and Sienna. She kept her head down, and she didn't see the van.

"Sabella!" Rory's yell had her head jerking up as he tried to grab her, to pull her back from the black van that suddenly stopped beside them.

Sienna was jostled into her, throwing her closer to the wide door that was flung open. Black masks. Black clothes. A gun aimed at Rory, a muffled report sounding as Sabella tried to scream over the hand that covered her mouth, tried to fight the ruthless force that tossed her into van.

Her last sight of Rory was the horror in his face and the blood pouring from his shoulder as he went down. Then the doors slammed closed, locking her and Sienna into the back of the van as it squealed out of the parking lot and accelerated as it headed out of town.

Horrified, terrified, she fought against the hands holding her. Her arms were jerked behind her back. Oh God. Her stomach was undefended. She couldn't cushion it, couldn't protect her baby like this.

Cuffs were snapped on her wrists and tape slapped over her mouth as she stared at her friend, her best friend, in shock.

Sienna wasn't being cuffed or gagged. She was settling herself into the lap of one of the masked abductors, a smile curving her lips as she tilted her head and regarded Sabella like a distasteful chore.

Sienna stared at her for long moments then she got up, braced her hand on the ceiling of the van, and before Sabella could process it, Sienna backhanded her with enough force to send her head bouncing against the side of the van, stars exploding in front of her eyes as she crumpled to the floor.

Sabella didn't bother lifting herself from the floor. She blinked, felt the blood trickling from her nose, and stared back at the woman who smiled with cool, calm arrogance.

"You stupid fucking bitch," Sienna drawled. "That's for all the years I've had to put up with babying your whining ass because Rick insisted I should worry about you. And for

marrying Nathan. Whore. You should have left the hometown boys to the hometown girls." She settled back on the
lap of the man who had held her moments before.

Brown eyes glared at her from behind the mask. Mike
Conrad's brown eyes. His gaze was malicious, satisfaction
filling them, hatred glittering in them.

Sabella curled herself in a ball, her knees lifting to protect Noah's child. And she stared at Mike and Sienna in disbelief.

Mike she could believe. But Sienna? Sienna who had
been there when Nathan's casket was buried. Who rocked
her when she cried, who had forced her out of the house over
the years and had played the part of the loving friend so con-
vincingly.

"Look at her." Sienna laughed. "Didn't I tell you, lover?
I'm the best. No one ever suspected."

Sabella hadn't suspected, but she knew in that moment,
that a part of her had known, unconsciously, that this woman
wasn't her friend. Just as she knew, beyond a shadow of a
doubt, that Sienna intended to see her dead.

But she knew no matter how hard they tried to hide, no
matter how deep they might bury her body, Noah would find
them. And when he did, he wouldn't let the fact that Sienna
was a woman save her. Mike Conrad's past friendship with
Nathan wouldn't even be a memory.

He'd kill them both. And he would make it hurt.

She just prayed he found her before they managed to kill
her.

Noah stepped from the garage as they heard the sirens in
the distance and the squeal of tires, the sharp blasts of a
horn.

He was aware of Nik moving behind him, the other mechanics as well as Toby stepping out to the parking lot. He
was aware of a cold core of ice freezing inside him when
Rory's truck slid around a corner and raced to the garage,
the sheriff, lights blazing, riding on his ass.

He stood stiff, still, as Nik cursed behind him. He heard

the Russian cursing, felt the tension suddenly building in the air as Rory barreled into the parking lot, the truck fishtailing as he put on the brakes, slamming to a stop.

He wasn't aware of moving. He wrenched the door open and caught his brother as he fell into his arms, blood staining his shirt, tears washing his face.

"Noah!" Rory screamed out, hysteria brightening his eyes. "Ah God. Ah God, Noah, I'm so sorry. I'm so sorry."

Noah held his brother, dragging him into the garage and then the office as Rick rushed in behind them. He could feel Rory's blood soaking his shirt, his skin.

"Where's Sabella, Rory?" He put his brother in a chair before grabbing a handful of clean mechanic's rags and pressing them to Rory's shoulder. "Tell me where Sabella is."

Rory sobbed. His head fell back on the chair and he howled in rage. "They took her! Took her and Sienna. Noah, I tried to grab her, but Sienna stumbled. And they took Sabella."

Noah stared at him. Something beyond rage took hold of him.

"What the hell do you mean, they took them?" Rick tried to push past Noah, rage echoing in his voice. "What the fuck is going on here?"

Nik hauled him back, jerked the handgun from his hand, and snarled down at him. Noah didn't pay attention. He didn't give a fuck about Rick.

"Who has her, Rory?" His voice was calm. "Did you recognize anyone?"

"Masks." Rory shook his head furiously. "They were wearing masks. When I tried to grab for Sabella, one of the bastards pulled a gun. It was silenced. I jerked to the side and kept trying to get to her." He held his shoulder and rocked forward. "Ah Christ. I'm sorry, Noah. I'm sorry."

"Nik, get on it," Noah ordered quietly.

"Calling now."

"Rory." He gripped Rory's jaw. "Rory, look at me. Tell me what you saw."

Rory stared back at him, dazed with pain and blood loss. His shirt was soaked with blood.

"Tan van." He shook his head, tears still filling his eyes. "Black masks. Black clothes. Pulled to a stop beside us and Sienna stumbled." He shook his head again. "I don't know why. She knocked into Belle and they both fell toward the door while I was trying to grab Belle. They jerked her inside. Mud on the tires, on the frame. It looked fresh. No plates, I checked. They were gone. Brown eyes." He stared up at Noah. "The guy that took Belle. He had brown eyes. Really dark eyes. I know those eyes."

Conrad's eyes.

"Nik, ambulance," Noah said softly. Rory was going to need help. He turned back to his brother. "Did they say anything? Tell me, Rory, did any of them say anything?"

Rory was panting now, shock taking over. He stared back at Noah, dazed, fighting back unconsciousness.

"Said. Said something about good hunting. As the doors closed. Someone laughed, and said it would be good hunting."

"Teams moving," Nik reported. "ETA is twenty minutes."

"How long ago, Rory?" Noah questioned him then. "When did it happen?"

Rory was shaking now. He looked at his wrist. Blood coated the face of his watch. Noah wiped it off, watching his brother carefully. The false calm that filled him was just a prelude. The ice was coming. Noah could feel it coming.

Rory sobbed. "An hour," he whispered. "Christ, Noah. An hour. I blacked out, and the lot was nearly empty. No one saw. I'm sorry. I'm so sorry."

"Nik. What's Travis reporting?"

"Movement on Leon," Nik stated. "There was a pullout five minutes ago. He's trying to track but T lost signal."

T. Tehya.

Noah turned and stared at a silent Rick. He was watching Rory, watching Noah.

"You're supposed to be dead," Rick said faintly. "I watched them bury you."

A man ran a risk when returning to his hometown, pretending to be someone he wasn't, and claiming the wife he had left.

"I still am. Dead." He bared his teeth at Rick. "You're in. But God help you if you're a part of this."

Rory shuddered as Noah turned back to him.

"Noah, she called him 'baby.'"

Noah sharpened his focus on Rory. "Who?"

Rory frowned. "When the door closed. Sienna. Brown eyes jerked her inside. She said 'baby.'"

"You misheard," Rick objected behind them. "You had to have misheard, Rory." But the objection was faint and filled with bitter pain.

When Noah turned back to the sheriff, he was staring at Rory in horror, in knowledge.

Rick shook his head as though clearing a fog and stared back at Noah, his tobacco-brown eyes filled with anguish. "He misheard."

Rory hadn't misheard. There was a leak in the Alpine sheriff's force. That leak was Sienna, not Rick as they had first assumed.

"Nik, what do we have?"

"Ambulance pulling in."

Noah jerked around, pinning him with his gaze as Nik grimaced. "We got nothing yet, man. The team's pulling in. Trav is tracking and T is working comm. That's all we have."

"Who the hell are you?" Rick grabbed Noah's arm.

Slowly, more to control the impulse to rip the sheriff's throat out than for any other reason, Noah turned back to him. Then he smiled.

He could feel the blood pumping through his veins, his muscles hardening, tightening. His vision edged with red, with blood, and the monster was free.

"I'm the BCM's worst fucking nightmare," he said softly. "I'm a dead man walking, and I'll take every damned one of them to hell with me."

CHAPTER TWENTY-EIGHT

Rory had been transported to the hospital under duress. He hadn't wanted to go. He had begged Noah not to make him go. The team was assembled, quietly, in the apartment after that. No one had seen them enter, no one knew they were there.

Rick stood at the back door, staring through the narrow window, tense, prepared, as he listened to the team assemble the gear the other Elite Ops agents had brought in. Trackers. Communications. Weapons.

Noah was listening to Travis Caine's report from his attempts to track the van that had transported the FBI agent Chuck Leon, when his cell phone rang.

Silence filled the apartment when Noah pulled it free of its holder, and mouthed, *Sabella's cell.*

He attached the electronic GPS tracker into his phone, then flipped it open.

"Blake."

"I'm sorry," Sabella whispered.

She was crying. Noah could hear the huskiness in her voice, the tears.

"It's okay, baby," he told her gently. "Are they there?"

"They want to talk—" Her voice cut off, and if he wasn't mistaken, he heard her cry out.

His nostrils flared, the need for blood exploding, pounding in his head.

"The sheriff is with you, we know that." A mechanical voice came over the line.

"He is."

The thin, distorted chuckle did nothing to disguise the glee in the abductor's voice.

"Tell him to stay there. If he leaves, they both die."

"Very well."

There was silence. "You're being agreeable. That's very good."

He remained silent.

"You went over the truck, didn't you, Blake?" the voice drawled. "You found the evidence and turned it in. Didn't you?"

"I did."

They knew. He knew. He would give them that much.

"Yeah, that putz agent we questioned just didn't convince us that he found it. He's still alive, by the way. Do you care?"

"Not particularly."

Another chuckle. "You're not an agent, are you? What are you then?"

"Let's say, a concerned bystander," he drawled. "My mother was Mexican. She wouldn't have liked you very much."

It was a lie. His mother had been pure blue blood.

"Then your mother was a whore. We kill whores."

Noah waited. A heartbeat. Two. Three.

"What do you want?" He kept his voice calm, cool. It was icy. There was no burning rage. There was no impatience. He had known they would call.

"Belle is a beautiful little whore too." The voice was smug, taunting. "She'll make a nice play thing when you're dead."

"You have to kill me first," Noah pointed out.

He didn't look at the men in the room. He stared at the single picture that Sabella had kept in the apartment. A picture of them before they married.

His arms were around her shoulders as they stared into the camera, her expression soft, vulnerable. Loving. He could almost smell that day. The scent of her perfume, the scent of sex still clinging to them.

"Yes, we do get to kill you first." Laughter trickled over the connection. "It's good that you're alone except for the sheriff. All your mechanics in place as they should be. Everyone just busy little beavers, aren't they, Mr. Blake?" We're watching, you know.

"That's their job," he agreed.

No emotion. He felt nothing. He kept staring at the picture of him and Sabella. No, the picture of Sabella and her husband. The man he was then didn't resemble the man he was now. There was no fear, no worry. There was a sense of death, a knowledge that no matter the outcome, blood was going to spill and it wouldn't be all his. None of it would be Sabella's.

"You'll make an interesting hunt," the abductor said to torment him. "A nice little addition to my trophies. That wasn't nice of you, poking your nose in where it wasn't wanted"

He nodded slowly. Here it came. Finally. The end of the road.

"Here's what you're going to do, Mr. Blake. And you're going to do it alone. If we see anyone else leave the garage, then the girls die. If you don't follow directions exactly, they die. If you're late, they die."

Melodrama. Fuck, he hated the wait.

"Yeah, I breathe the wrong way and they die. I got it."

He was aware of Jordan wincing, the looks the other men gave him.

Another chuckle. "Do you know the national park?"

Like the back of his hand. "Not very well. I haven't had time to do much sightseeing."

There was silence. Noah waited it out. He let it flow over him, refused to consider the risks. He was a nobody here. They didn't suspect anything. He was a mechanic, nothing more.

"Do you know where they found the little female FBI agent? I know you been in town long enough for that."

The canyon was about an hour away.

"I know."

"You'll be met. You have an hour after this call disconnects to get there. Would you like to tell your little girlfriend bye?"

"If you want your hunt, I'll see her alive before it begins. She's of no use to me dead."

Laughter again, grating, knowing.

"Sure. You can say your goodbyes in person. You'll be met. You have one hour."

Noah disconnected. He dragged his jacket from the back of a chair. He was already outfitted in the chaps. The butter-soft leather conformed and moved easily with him. Hiking boots. Skin tag locator on both shoulders. Belt buckle equipped with a locator as well. All deactivated until needed.

"You'll have to slip out with the others," he told Rick as he moved for the door.

"Like hell. If she's in on this, then I'll take care of it." The sheriff's eyes burned with anger as he caught Noah's arm.

"Grip my arm again and your throat comes out." He peeled the sheriff's hand from his arm. "You'll come in with the others. And she's the only way they could have taken Sabella so easily. You know it, as well as I do."

Rick's jaw clenched, a muscle ticking furiously at the side.

"We need someone to prosecute, Noah," Jordan reminded him. "Remember that when the hunt starts. We'll be in place and ready to move. T will track you from the rendezvous."

Noah nodded and left the apartment, slamming the door behind him.

He could feel the eyes on him. By time he made the rendezvous, it would be nearing dark. The others could slip into place then. Getting them out of the garage wouldn't be a problem.

Noah had been a SEAL. He believed in escape routes to hell and back. And Jordan knew them all.

He straddled the Harley and set the motor to throbbing before kicking into gear and tearing out of the parking lot.

The wind whipped through his hair, and he heard Sabella's light laughter, her passion moans. The sound of tears in her voice when she called.

She was frightened. He could hear the fear. But he heard something else too. He had heard trust. There hadn't been hysteria. She hadn't begged him to save her. She had known he would come for her. He had heard that in her voice. Her knowledge, her trust.

She was a woman any man could be proud to call his own. But Sabella was still tender, still vulnerable. She was a woman who loved with everything inside her. And that was how she loved the man he had been.

With everything inside her.

He kicked the gas to the Harley and let it tear down the road. He knew exactly where he was going. He'd tracked the area after the unit moved in and canvassed every inch of it. The female FBI agent's body had been found at the base of one of the small rises, her body dug up by scavengers. The area had been widely publicized.

For a second, just a second, an image of Sabella flashed in his mind, eyes wide in death, her face white, lips bloodless. He twisted the gas and let the Harley tear down the road. Rage bit at him, hard, fast, before he countered it, before the icy hunger for blood overrode it once again.

He wasn't a husband. He wasn't a lover. He was a dead man. And he was about to have company in hell. It was that simple. That was how he had survived for the past six years and. It was how he had rehabilitated, it was how he rebuilt himself.

He was a husband. A lover. And what belonged to him had been threatened. Taken. It wouldn't happen again.

Dusk was settling as Noah pulled in, only feet from where the dead agent's body had been found. Three black-masked shadows waited on four-wheelers at the base of the rise.

Noah kicked the stand on the Harley, turned it off, and dismounted slowly. He stared back at them. None of them were Mike Conrad. But there was Delbert Ransome, those watery brown eyes gleamed like a rat's. The other two men he identified by the shape of their faces and the color of their eyes. One was a ranch hand from the Malone ranch. The other was the sheriff's deputy, Hershel Jenkins. Damn. Rory was going to be pissed. He and Hershel had been drinking buddies at one time.

Hershel moved from his four-wheeler and pointed to the small rack behind him. In his hand he carried plastic restraints.

Noah moved to the back of the ATV, slid on, and let the son of a bitch cuff his wrists to the edge of the rack. Seconds later, they were tearing off through the night.

He felt the first electronic skin tag tracker on his left shoulder heat up. It had a five-minute range. Eyes were already watching. He could feel them. The SEALs would be in place. Reno, Clint, Kell, Macey, and Ian. They would have been deployed from the bunker the minute they knew the rendezvous point and they'd be tracking.

Satellite would be trained on the ATVs' progress. The ATVs' headlights cut through the darkness, but Noah knew there were others watching as well. Militia members, to make certain there was no backup.

There was plenty of backup.

They'd thought Noah would be taken, not Sabella. The outsider coming in and taking over something it was rumored the militia wanted. That being the garage. He had controlled it, controlled its owner. They hadn't expected Sabella to be taken.

Noah held on to the rack, braced himself, and flowed with the hard thumps, the deliberately rough ride. These boys thought they knew how to hurt. They didn't know anything about pain. About madness. About death.

Noah knew. And he knew they had no idea what monster they were bringing into their midst.

The night vision contacts were working, though not as well as goggles would have. The faded green aura of the landscape was clearly visible. He could see another of Gaylen Patrick's ranch hands in a pickup as they passed it, tucked into the shelter of a small grove of pines.

He saw the shadow behind it and smiled. Yeah, there were a lot of shadows moving in these mountains tonight.

Ten minutes. Fifteen. Twenty minutes.

Finally, the ATVs turned off into a small canyon and pulled in front of an opening into the base of a nearly sheer cliff.

They hadn't known about this one. It was perfectly hidden by the brush and bramble in front of it and the ledge of the cliff over it. There was a faint light coming from inside.

The restraints were cut and a rifle shoved in his face as he was pointed to the opening.

How easy it would be to shove the barrel of the weapon up the deputy's ass while he took out the other two. Silently. It could be done so silently.

He grinned instead and turned, walking into the entrance and waiting for the contacts to adjust as the light deepened. Sabella's abductors' precautions against the light showing from the outside allowed the contacts time to adjust until his vision was clear when he turned into the main cavern.

He stepped in, his gaze finding Sabella immediately.

Someone had hit her. Her cheek was bruised, blood still marred her nose. Her gray eyes were dark with anger. And fear.

The cavern was large enough. She was tied to a small cot, her wrists cuffed to the metal frame, though she had been left sitting.

Across the room Mike Conrad grinned back at him. He hadn't bothered to cover his face. Sienna sat between his splayed legs, playing with the ends of her hair as she stared back at him maliciously.

"All that leather just looks hot," she drawled. "Come on, Mike, let me make him fuck me before you go hunting. That illegal ass you kidnapped last month did it. His wife cried so pitifully. I want to see Belle cry while her lover fucks me. Just like her husband did."

Noah had never touched her. There had always been something about Sienna that just put him off. There had been no challenge. No sense of depth.

"Strip." He shrugged, staring back at her. "I have time if you do."

Head games. He knew head games.

She pouted and sniffed. "Not on your life. You're probably diseased after fucking that heifer." She nodded to Sabella.

He lifted his shoulder negligently and turned to Mike.

This had once been his friend. Strange, he'd never seen the bloodthirstiness in Mike's eyes before now. What had changed? What had changed him?

Mike grinned. "As you can see, she's alive. She's not very talkative though."

He glanced over at her as he felt the tracker on his right shoulder heat. He shook his head at the setup, looking around again.

Mike and Sienna watched him, obviously less than pleased at his reaction.

"I told you the bastard wasn't as easy to intimidate as you thought he was."

Noah didn't tense. He didn't turn. He stood still, relaxed. Yeah, he knew that voice. Gaylen Patrick. He waited long seconds before turning just enough to see the other man.

He waddled in, his thick lips creasing into a smile, followed by the shorter, trimmer form of Federal Judge Carl Clifford and the paunchy Marshal Kevin Lyle.

"Quite a little group," Noah drawled.

Smug satisfaction filled Patrick's beady hazel eyes.

"Yeah, we have some pretty good boys that like to play." He walked over to Mike and Sienna. When he reached out and twisted one of her hard nipples she moaned like a bitch in heat and leaned into him.

Camp whore. Damn, he just hadn't seen this one coming.

"I want a minute with Sabella alone." He stared at Patrick, aware of who was running this show.

"Why would I do that?" Patrick stared back at him in amusement.

Noah smiled. The smile of a man with more confidence, more ability, than those around him suspected. And Patrick's eyes gleamed at the challenge.

"This is a hunt?"

"Boy, we're gonna be hunting you." Gaylen laughed. "If

you can keep your ass alive until dawn, then we'll just put a bullet in your heads. We won't rape her and we won't make you watch if you're still alive. Real simple. You get caught before dawn, or dead. Then she's a nice little plaything, just like that female agent was."

Noah nodded and held his smile. "You'll want a real challenge then."

"We love a challenge," he chortled.

"Give me a minute alone with her. I'll give you your challenge." He let his voice lower, let the monster inside him echo in his voice.

Sienna shivered as though in arousal. "If you catch him before dawn, do I get to rape her first?"

Gaylen stared at her, rather like a man stared at his favorite pet.

"We'll hold her for you," he promised before turning back to Noah.

"You think you're a challenge, do you?"

His brow arched. "You'll never catch me."

Gaylen grinned. "Other men have made that promise."

"I'm not other men." He was already a dead man, and he knew who was going to die tonight.

Gaylen's fat lips widened before he nodded shortly. "You have three minutes. I'm gonna be nice about it. Let you kiss her real sweet before she gets to listen to you die."

He nodded to the radio set up in the corner of the cavern. "She'll get to listen to you scream like a pig."

Noah just stared back at him.

The old bastard laughed before wrapping his arm around Sienna's shoulders. "Come on, sugar. You can blow me before we head out."

She giggled like the damned cheerleader she had been in school.

Noah moved to Sabella. Knees bending, he hunched down in front of her and cupped her cheeks. Tears filled her eyes. And for just a second Noah allowed himself to feel.

He went past the rage that threatened to overwhelm his control. He went past the murderous fury at the thought of how frightened she was. And there, tucked into his soul, was the love he had felt for Sabella since the moment he had seen her.

She had strode into his garage, her smile flashing in the sunlight, her eyes mysterious and watchful. He'd had eyes for no other woman since that day.

He leaned close, his forehead against hers, and smiled back at her confidently.

"They'll die," he promised her, every one one of them.

Her lips trembled and more tears rolled down her cheeks.

"Be ready." He kept his voice low, for her ears only. "Stay low. Don't anger them."

She nodded jerkily, her eyes locked on his, fear, fear for him, filling them.

"It's going to be okay, baby."

She nodded again and when her lips trembled this time, he wanted to kiss them. He wanted to cover them, to ease her past that fear for just a moment. It was a need he couldn't afford. Kissing Sabella would strip him down to that final, darkened core where hunger pulsed in an eternal need. Just for her.

"Noah—" He put his finger over her lips.

"Nothing will happen to you. I swear it on what little is left of my soul, Sabella. Nothing will happen to you."

"Rory?"

"Safe."

She nodded again.

Noah smoothed a tear from beneath her eye then brought his thumb to his lips and let the salty taste of her pain and her fear harden the icy core of rage.

"Who hit you?" He wanted to know who to kill first.

"Sienna."

And he nodded. He touched her lips with his thumb, touched her hair then drew back slowly as Mike stepped back into the room.

He rose to his feet, the sound of her muffled sob raking over the ice inside him. Hardening it. Colder. Icier. There was no flame. Nothing hot or fierce burning inside him. This was death.

He turned back to Mike.

"So, are we gonna go play, or are you too busy getting blown next?"

Mike's eyes narrowed before his gaze flicked to Sabella. "When you die, I'm going to stretch her out and come in her mouth. She'll die swallowing me."

Noah grunted. "Let's cut the shit here, Conrad. Let's get moving."

He headed to the entrance. He left Sabella behind him. For now. Just for now. And the look he gave Mike was a promise. He would be one of the first to die.

Killing him would be incredibly easy. He'd known that when he first arrived back and saw the drunken abuse the other man had heaped on her. He had trusted his family, his friends, to watch out for the woman who was his life.

As they entered the narrow entrance Noah watched as Gaylen Patrick moved from deeper inside the cavern. His face was flushed. Expression smug.

"Doesn't take you long to blow, does it?" he observed mockingly.

Patrick glared back at him. "Boy, I'm going to enjoy killing you."

The monster lifted its head inside him. Icy, murderous determination infused him. It wasn't a surge of adrenaline. It was a surge of intent. A hard, brutal core of calculated deliberation.

Noah grinned. "Funny. I was thinking the same thing about you."

Sabella lowered her head and fought her tears. Her body ached from the abuse she had suffered. Her shoulders, her legs and hips, her upper back. So far, Sienna hadn't gone for her stomach.

Was the pregnancy too early for a blow to her stomach to hurt her child? God help her if Sienna learned she was carrying Noah's child.

The other woman was insane.

Sabella stared across the room as the psychotic imitation

of her best friend played with Mike Conrad. Rubbing at his crotch, letting him bury his head in her cleavage. They were all but fucking in front of her. And they had no idea what they had unleashed when they had taken her.

Sabella had seen it though. In his eyes. The flecks of green in the blue were artificial. There was no green in Noah's eyes. But the blue. The blue had been like ice lit from inside with a cold, brutal flame.

There had been no rage, no fury. Just calculated death.

Those weren't her husband's eyes. Whatever had happened to him during his imprisonment with Diego Fuentes *had* changed him. Changed him in ways that sent a shiver up her spine. Six years ago, her husband hadn't had that hard core of icy rage inside him. It was there now. There was death in his eyes now.

Sweet Jesus, he was going to kill tonight. She knew it. She had seen it in his eyes. Not that every damned one of the bastards involved in this didn't deserve to die. They were so confident. They had killed for so long that they didn't even care if they let their victims see their faces. They were that certain of themselves and had succeeded for so long in these hunts they conducted.

"Poor little Belle," Sienna crooned in a mimicry of compassion as she moved across the room.

The other woman gripped Sabella's jaw and jerked her head up. Her green eyes glittered with excitement, with almost maniacal pleasure.

"Poor Rick," Sabella whispered. "He loved you, Sienna."

Not that Sienna appeared to care. She rolled her eyes.

"Bastard hasn't touched me in over two years," she huffed, her lips thinning. "The only reason he even still lives in the house with me is because I have just enough on him to make him wary."

She released Sabella's jaw and plopped down on the cot beside her. Sienna leaned back as Sabella shifted, protecting her side and her stomach by pushing herself farther into the corner of the wall.

"I've so wanted to tell you what a weak-kneed little bitch

you are." Sienna giggled. "Crying for your lost Nathan. Haunting that house of his like a damned ghost." She lifted her nails and checked them carefully before looking up at Sabella. "I fucked him in your bed, you know."

No. She hadn't. Nathan would have never fucked another woman, especially Sienna. And Sabella would have known if he had.

But she lowered her head, let the other woman think she had gotten her jibe in.

"You are so fucking boring," Sienna breathed out in irritation. "Come on, Belle. Admit it. You're sick because you know I fucked your husband. I'd have fucked your little punk biker, but I bet he doesn't even have a dick."

Mike chuckled across the room as he moved to the equipment on the table in the corner.

"I want him to watch while I rape you," Sienna breathed as Sabella glared back at her from beneath the cover of her lashes. "I'm going to love raping you, Sabella. I'll laugh and bite you." Sienna shivered in longing. "I'll make you scream and beg your Noah to save you."

"You won't have the chance," Sabella told her softly. "He's going to kill you, Sienna."

Sienna licked her lips lustfully. "No one has survived a hunt, Belle. Your biker won't last an hour. Then." She leaned forward, gripping Sabella's chin with enough force to bruise. "I'm going to strap on my dildo, and they're going to hold you down while I gut you. I'm going to rip into that pussy Nathan and that biker thought was so damned good and let him watch while you scream."

Sabella shook her head. "No, Sienna. You won't have the chance to hurt me in front of him. You won't even know when he returns. All you'll know is death."

She had seen death in Noah's eyes. Whatever had happened to him, whatever group he was a part of, they were ready for this, and she knew it.

Sienna smirked, then before Sabella could jerk back, smashed her lips onto hers.

Gagging, furious, Sabella jerked back, and before she could

stop herself, she slammed her head into the other woman's face.

Sienna's shriek of rage was followed by another blow to Sabella's face.

Lights exploded in front of her eyes again, the agony of the other woman's fist to her cheek sending screaming, white-hot pain lancing through her body.

But Sienna jumped from the bed and flounced off to Mike. He was laughing. He pulled the other woman to him and stroked her hair, kissing her abused cheek.

"My poor little slut," he crooned. "It's okay. When we're done with her, you can blow all of us. Suck her blood right from our dicks."

And Sabella saw the little shudder of pleasure that whipped through Sienna. God. She was insane. Somewhere, somehow, Sabella had missed the fact that the woman pretending to be her best friend was certifiable. It was no wonder Nathan had never seemed to like the idea of their friendship.

She inhaled roughly, tasted the blood in her mouth again, and forced back the sickness rising inside her. Noah would come back. And when he did, he'd make certain tonight was no more than an unpleasant memory.

CHAPTER TWENTY-NINE

They didn't take him far from the canyon for the hunt to start. The militia members were masked, and they brought him a running buddy. How nice of them.

Chuck Leon had seen better days, no doubt. His face was swollen, his leg had a tourniquet tied around it. Hell, he'd have to take care of this before he returned to the canyon.

"What kind of shape are you in?" he asked the other man as they stood in the middle of a small valley.

Noah looked around. It was bisected by a stream and several deep gullies. He hadn't seen the other members of the team yet, but with the militia wearing night vision, he knew he wouldn't.

Cottonwood and pines grew strategically, thick in areas, thin in others.

"Bad shape." Chuck shifted on his good leg. "They always hunt more than one. They like a quick kill and a challenge. I guess I'm the quick kill, huh?"

There was fight left in him though. His hazel eyes glittered with anger.

"Piece of advice," Noah told him quietly. "Get rid of the mad. Use your head and watch your ass."

Chuck shook his head. "We're going to be sitting ducks out here."

Noah didn't say anything more. He watched as other vehi-

cles moved in. There were a dozen vehicles, more than double
that in men. A small group. They hadn't branched out to let
anyone into their little pack that they didn't implicitly trust.

"Do you have a plan?" Chuck grimaced as Noah bent and
checked the tourniquet on the other man's leg.

"I always have a plan."

"Mind letting me in on it?"

Noah grunted. He didn't trust anyone with Sabella's life,
especially an unknown agent.

"Head for the gully, jump in, and run north." One of the
team would be close enough to pull him out. "You might
live."

The agent stared at him in disbelief. "You're kidding,
right?"

He stared back at Chuck coldly. "Do I look like I'm kidding?"

"Jesus." Chuck tunneled his hands through his hair.
"Okay. Hit the gully and go north."

"And don't stop. This gully runs into another gully and
then heads to the main road. If you're not stopped, just keep
truckin'."

The team might let him pass and head to town for help. Hell
if Noah knew what they would do. But he had seen the brush
moving, waving a little too hard for the wind blowing through
the valley, at the edge of the ravine. There was another sign of
the Elite unit in the gully that headed back toward the canyon
Sabella was being held in.

That was where Noah intended to head. Let the bastards
think he and Chuck were going to make it easy for them. The
team would play with them until Noah could get to Sabella
and get her out of there. Once she was safe, Noah was going
hunting himself.

"Looks like they're all here." Chuck's voice was resigned,
but it vibrated with determination now.

He was young, but he was game. Noah nodded as Gaylen
Patrick got out of the powerful four-by-four he was in.
Night-vision goggles covered his eyes. High-tech rednecks,
he thought mockingly.

"Ready, boys?" Patrick chuckled, his thick lips stretched wide, like a maniacal clown as he waddled over to them.

Noah slipped his thumbs beneath his belt and activated the tracker there. He'd waited. He'd been searched, his chaps and jacket removed, but that was okay. He could function without them just as well as he could function with them.

He stared back at Gaylen, the green aura that transposed over the other man from the contacts he wore didn't take away from the pure evil glittering in the man's eyes.

"You have a ten-minute head start. Run wherever the hell you want to." He chuckled. "We like to make things interesting. We'll give you ten minutes then head out for you."

Ten minutes. Noah felt the amusement welling within him. Stupid motherfuckers. They were giving him ten minutes?

"We usually give our prey a little longer," Gaylen announced amid the laughter that echoed around him. "But we just plain don't like you. So we're going to make it harder for you."

Noah looked out over the valley. Half an hour wouldn't seem like much, unless a man knew the area as well as Noah did. He'd played in the national park, camped in it, hunted in it. He knew it like the back of his hand. Half an hour would have seen him well on his way to the Malone ranch. Ten minutes would see him almost back to Sabella's location.

"You don't talk much, do you, boy?" Gaylen observed in amusement. "Savin' your breath, are you?"

Noah smiled. It wasn't in amusement, and for the first time, Gaylen was beginning to look just a little nervous.

Gaylen grunted, irritated now as he looked at the face of the watch he wore. "Ten minutes, cocksuckers. Get moving."

Chuck hobbled at a near run for the gully. Noah stood and stared back at Gaylen as the other man lifted his brow and laughed in his face.

"Watch your back," he told Gaylen. "Watch it close. Because I'll be there."

Gaylen laughed as Noah turned, stared around at the unlit vehicles, and hoped to hell Tehya was able to track some of the bastards with the satellite. They needed proof. Just in case he let one of them live.

Then he ran. Less than ten minutes. He needed to get to the gully and prayed to God the team had had time to get in place.

He could feel the sights on his back. Someone wasn't going to wait. He could feel it. He dug his feet into the hard clay dirt and pushed harder, running for the gully and throwing himself into it as the first shot rang out.

The bullet sliced across his bicep and stung like hell. The flesh wound was going to bleed like a son of a bitch. He hit the rocky gully hard, the heavy stones that filled the dry ravine bit into his ribs, a barely noticeable pain before he was on his feet and moving along the shallow crease in the land.

He could hear the laughter behind him, engines gunning, the roar of a dirt bike or two. They were fully loaded, technologically advanced, and well planned. They had done this time and time again. This would be their last time.

"Gotcha."

Nik caught him as he rounded the ravine five minutes later.

"Hold in place. Clint is moving ahead and jumping the gully into the trees as they start moving. Reno is imitating Leon and Macey is pulling him out of harm's way. We have you covered."

"I have to get back to the cavern." He flicked an irritated glance to where Nik was tying off the wound with camo bandaging.

"Weapons."

A rifle was shoved in his hand then a handgun. He tucked the smaller weapon into his belt and cradled the large one.

"Knife." Motors were revving as Nik handed over his own Russian-made military dagger.

"They put more guards on the canyon," Nik told him. "You have five to take out. I can't cover you there but Jordan and the sheriff are moving on that position. They're a little behind schedule. Seems there were some added eyes posted at the road leading out here. They had to slip around them."

"Get that fucking agent out of here." Noah accepted the information as he heard a horn sound behind them.

Whoops sounded and vehicles were moving out.

"Comm." Nik shoved an earpiece in his ear, leaving Noah to adjust it.

He could hear the team now.

"Wild card in place," he said carefully.

His code name, the mission code name, and the source they were after. That source was Sienna, and killing a woman wasn't a preferred action, but what he had seen in that cavern wasn't a woman. It was a disease.

"Wild card move and secure ladybird." Reno's command came through the earpiece. "All sources in place and pulling from your position."

"Go." Nik slapped him on the back, picked up his own weapon and moved out.

Staying under cover wouldn't be easy. He had to work his way through the shallow gully back to the canyon and then along the cliff wall without being seen. The point was to keep the majority of the militia in the field as a few took out the command center.

Jordan and Noah were the few, and Jordan was running behind.

"Wild card, eye in the sky has you," Tehya said into the link. "You have two bogies coming up, thirty-five meters to your left, twenty-two to your right. Proceed with caution."

Noah stayed down, using the vocal directions Tehya laid out as the background chatter and directions given by Reno and Clint pounded in his brain.

"Cycle one down," Clint reported, his voice filled with glee despite the quiet nature of his voice.

Noah slid out of the ravine under cover of the pine and juniper growing along the bank. The bogies were behind him. On his stomach, he crawled the distance to the next pass, making certain to keep covered.

Once he reached the cliff face he was on his feet, crouched and working his way behind the cover of boulders, trees.

"Bogie in the cliff," Tehya reported. "I have heat across

the canyon, positioned to spy your direction. Use extreme prejudice if needed."

Kill if needed.

Not yet. He wanted everyone in that cave nice and complacent.

"I need distraction," he murmured.

There was silence on the line.

"Distraction coming in." Micah's voice came across the line. "Be ready to move."

There was a flash of movement at the mouth of the canyon.

Noah watched as the sentry turned, shifting position and allowing Noah to slip into the mouth of the cave.

"Insertion achieved." Tehya reported his position to the group.

"Clint, twelve meters to your left, duck and cover," Kira directed. "Ian, slide that hot ass of yours out of the way, you have a bogie moving in."

"Hot ass?" Reno's voice was muffled amusement. "New code name?"

There was muffled laughter in his ear as Noah edged through the narrow entrance and into the natural hall that had been carved through the inside of the cliff.

The contacts adjusted slowly as he made his way toward the command center. He could hear the radio squawking, reports coming in. Like the team Noah was with, each man in the militia hunting party was wearing a personal communications device.

They were tracking two "prey." Whooping and yelling when they disappeared then cackling in glee as they reappeared.

"They're giving us a run, boys," the judge yelled in fanatical pleasure. "Woo-wee. We're gonna run their asses down."

"This is taking too long," Sienna bitched, her voice strident and filled with displeasure. "Gaylen said it would go fast and we could have fun."

Mike laughed at her statement, but Noah could hear the nervousness in it.

"They usually catch one of them by now," Sienna snapped.

"Come on, Mike. Just hold her down. I won't hurt her too bad, I promise. I'll just show her how good I can be."

There was a whine in Sienna's voice.

"She doesn't look so agreeable." But there was lust in Mike's voice. "If I do that, Sienna, you gotta help me hold her mouth open while I come in it."

"Oh yes," Sienna hissed.

Sabella was silent. He could hear her breathing, hard, rough.

"Oh, I wish that Noah Blake could hear her once we start making her scream," Sienna drawled.

Noah palmed the dagger Nik had given him with one hand, cradled the rifle in the other arm.

"Jordan and Sheriff Grayson are moving in. Be advised, wild card, you have friendlies coming in," Tehya reported.

"Sienna, don't do this. Don't make Noah kill you."

He heard her voice then. It struck through his soul with the fear in it.

"Keep begging me," Sienna panted then. "Oh yeah, Bella, I want you to beg while I eat your pussy and Mike comes down your throat."

Noah didn't think so.

He stepped into the cave.

Mike had a single second to whip around with the gun he was holding. Noah let the knife fly, burying it in his shoulder as Sienna screeched and came flying at him.

Sienna was easy. He didn't even have to put any power in the punch to her jaw and she went down. But when she fell she tangled in his feet and Mike came roaring at him.

He'd torn the dagger from his shoulder, rage burned in his brown eyes, flushed his face. And he could fight. He and Nathan had always sparred together. The other man might have gained some paunch, but he was maddened, enraged. Noah felt the gun at his back slip out to the floor in a distant part of his mind.

Mike's arms wrapped around Noah, threw him into the cavern wall as he heard Sabella's cry echo through the stone room.

He took the first blow to his kidney, let Mike land another in his stomach, then he moved. He threw his elbow into the other man's throat, knocked him back. Mike's gutter-fighting abilities had improved. He threw a kick back that Noah dodged, but the pure rage in Mike was nothing compared to the cold brutal ice that filled Noah.

He ducked, rolled, gripped the fallen knife in his hand, and as Mike came back at him, Noah wrapped one arm around the other man's shoulders and felt the crunch, the slice of the blade as it pierced Mike's chest and ripped into the heart.

Mike froze. His eyes widened as he stared back at Noah.

"Nathan Malone," Noah whispered back, just loud enough for Mike. "I warned you, years ago. Don't touch what's mine."

Something flickered in Mike's eyes then. Regret. Fear. He wasn't certain. Mike's hand lifted, his lips formed his name as blood dribbled from the corners and he slid slowly to the floor.

Where Noah faced Sienna and the gun she held on him.

"I've killed before." Her nose was bleeding, her green eyes were deranged.

Drugs. He could see it now, saw the evidence of it. Fucking junkie.

"I don't want to kill you, Sienna." He was aware of Sabella, pressed into the corner of the wall, watching the scene in fear and pain.

What he had put her through, no woman should have to experience. His death. His return as another man. Seeing everything that she believed was safe and secure in her world falling apart around her.

"But I want to kill you, Noah Blake." She sneered, sniffed as tears fell from her eyes. "You killed Mike." She grimaced then screamed. "Where the fuck will I get my coke from now, you son of a bitch?"

He shook his head. "Prison beats dead, Sienna."

She sneered at that. "And wouldn't the high-and-mighty fuck-turd Rick just love seeing me in prison. That son of a bitch. He's going to be next and he just doesn't know it. You won't get out of here." She waved the gun for emphasis.

Noah heard the comm activate at his ear. "Deck be appraised, command center compromised. Take out objects."

Noah's lips tightened.

From the radio at the corner the first gunshot sounded.

Sienna's eyes widened.

"Fuck! Fuck! Where did they come from? Where did they come from?"

Terror filled her face. The gun shook in her hand.

"I'll kill you!" she screamed back at Noah.

"You have a one-shot chance," he told her, opening his arms. "Go for it."

She smiled, coke-bright eyes glittering as she turned the gun on Sabella. Sabella's fear raged through the room, silent, filled with the rasps of her breath, the terror she was holding inside.

Noah tensed, jumped as the shot rang out and Sabella screamed. And Noah cried out, "Bella."

He landed against her, driving her back against the wall, tightening in preparation for the bullet that didn't come.

He jerked around to see Jordan and Rick Grayson in the entrance. Rick's weapon was drawn, and Sienna lay stretched out on the floor, blood massing beneath her neck.

The sheriff stared down at his wife, his face expressionless, his eyes dead, as he bent and picked up the rifle Noah had dropped. He turned and left the cavern as Noah quickly cut Sabella's bonds.

"Noah. Oh God. Noah."

His arms were around her, holding her to his heart.

"I knew you'd be here," she whispered, her fingers digging into his chest, holding on to him as he closed his eyes against the hard core of agony that resonated inside him. "I knew, Noah. I knew you'd be here."

He kissed the top of her head as Jordan stepped forward.

"Take her home," he told his uncle.

Jordan nodded. "Rory's there too, and Grandpop. I'll stay with her."

"No!" She jerked back, stared up at him.

Her eyes were like thunderclouds. He'd never seen them like that. Shock and fear filled them. Her face was paper white. Her body shuddering.

"Don't you leave me!" She gripped his shirt and tried to shake him, tears falling from her eyes. "Don't you leave me, Noah."

His head lowered. He touched her lips with his and knew this woman held the best part of him. The memories of the husband he had been, the man he had been. He couldn't destroy that. He refused to.

He pushed her to Jordan slowly, loath to let her go. To release her. Knowing that releasing her was the only way to save the memories she held.

"Don't you leave me!" She screamed the order, eyes blazing, her lips trembling as tears fell and hysteria threatened to overwhelm her. "If you leave me, Noah Blake. If you don't come back when this is over, don't bother coming back at all."

He touched her cheek. Ran his thumb over her lips. "You're the best part of me," he whispered. "Always remember that, Sabella. The very best part of me."

Before she could grab him, hold him to her, he pulled away, grabbed one of the rifles Mike had laid on the table across the room, and left.

Nik was wounded and the militia members were scattering like rats on a sinking ship. It was time to contain them. It was time for death to take its toll, and Noah was the hand that would deal the devil's deck.

He strode from the cavern, her sobs in his head. He shouldn't have had to hear her crying for him. It sliced through his senses, through his control, but not the ice that filled him. Every man in the militia Gaylen had brought together had threatened his wife. Risked her life. Risked her world. They wouldn't have the chance to do it again.

Sabella let the tears stop. She pulled out of Jordan's arms and stared at Mike Conrad's and Sienna's dead bodies.

The cave stank of death, of blood. She pressed her hand to her stomach, to her child.

"Take me home."

Noah had left and a part of her knew he wasn't coming back. She wanted out of here. She didn't want her child exposed to this scent, to the atrocities that had been committed in this cave, any longer. She swore she could hear the screams of the innocent people who had died here recently.

Sienna lay in her own blood. Her slender body was stretched out on her stomach, her long hair covering her face. Sabella knew she would have to deal with the fallout on this one soon. She had loved Sienna like a sister. Trusted her.

"Sabella." Jordan said her name softly. "You can't talk about this."

She held her hand up, silencing him. "I know the line. I was married to a SEAL. Remember?"

Jordan nodded slowly.

"I don't know shit," she whispered tearfully. "Not a damned thing. Now take me home, Jordan. Take me home before I lose my mind."

From the radio the screams of the dying could be heard. Orders to run, to ambush, curses and cries echoed through the cave as Jordan gripped her arm and they made their way out.

Outside, firelight flickered in the distance. Gunfire. The echo of shots sounded, overly loud, causing her to flinch as Jordan helped her into the black SUV he and Rick must have arrived in.

She stared into the night as she buckled up. She held on and rocked with the vehicle as Jordan raced from the canyon. He was barking commands, though she couldn't see a radio. She glimpsed an insert at his ear though.

"Nik, get your ass out of there," Jordan was ordering. "I don't give a shit if you're a reincarnated berserker. Haul ass!" Then he cursed.

Nik. Her mechanic. She crossed her arms over her stomach and turned her face to the window beside her. And she cried. As they hit the small dirt road that led back to the main interstate, she let her tears fall, and she let the past go.

Her husband was dead. The man in his place wasn't coming back. She had seen it in his eyes, felt it in his touch. But this time, Sabella wasn't alone.

She touched her stomach, closed her eyes. This time, she had a part of that love to hold on to. Their child.

CHAPTER THIRTY

Jordan took her home.

Sabella waited in the living room, curled up in the same chair she had sat in the day Jordan and Reno had arrived to tell her of Nathan's death.

She wasn't crying. Her head was pillowed in the corner of the wingback, Grandpop Rory had wrapped a quilt around her then pulled his chair close to her and held her hand.

For hours he just sat there. Until Jordan and Rory went into the kitchen and the silence stretched between them.

Finally, Grandpop sighed deeply. His age-ravaged face was filled with sadness, with grief, as he patted her hand.

She lifted her eyes to him. Blue eyes. Wild Irish blue eyes. She wondered if she would ever be free of them.

"He loves you," he said softly. "He always loved you, girl. From the day you showed up here, till the day he came back."

Her lips parted in shock as he made a little shushing motion. "We'll not tell them." He nodded to the other room. "They know, but what we know is between us. Right?"

She blinked back her tears.

"When I lost my Erin, I couldn't go with her." His voice became hoarse, tear filled. "I felt her death in every corner of my soul. But I had Nathan and Rory, and Grant, well, he changed over the years, I guess. Someone had to watch over my boys."

A sob caught and locked in her voice. "He's not coming back." And it hurt. It hurt until she was a mass of pain, worse than it had been when she thought he was dead. More all consuming. Ravaging her insides.

He lowered his head. Shook it. Then stared back at her. "He loves you with all his soul. If he's not coming back, then it's for you, Bella. Not for him." He looked to her stomach. "And he left you life. Don't be bitter, girl. Don't convince yourself he doesn't love you. You know better."

The sob tore free. Grandpop did the same thing he'd done when he came to the house after the notice of Nathan's death. He rocked her. Wrapped his arms around her and rocked her against the pain before she drew back and shook her head.

She wiped her tears. She had cried for him the first time. She wasn't crying for him again. Grandpop, in some ways perhaps, was right. Nathan had always had a sharp, very narrow vision of honor. He would leave her to protect her. She had known that ever since she had realized who he was, that he was hiding, pretending to be dead. If it meant her life, or her sadness, he'd take her sadness gladly. Just as she would have.

But she couldn't pull herself out of the chair. She waited. She waited until the sun rose high overhead. The phone rang and no one answered it. Finally, Rick arrived.

He looked haggard. Years older. Blood stained his clothes and grief etched his face, but his eyes were hollow.

"State and federal agents are on scene rounding everyone up," he told Jordan. "They're covering the judge's involvement in it. He was hustled out of there by the first two agents on scene. The marshal's dead. They found Gaylen Patrick in a gully, gutted like a fish, and son of a bitch if they didn't catch Mayor Silbert in the group. Most of the militia is dead. What's left alive won't live long. Otherwise there were no other bodies to collect."

Noah was alive.

"And you?" Jordan asked him. "How much of this will you keep to yourself?"

Rick's lips tightened. "Sienna and Sabella were kidnapped. Sienna was killed in a rescue attempt. That's the orders from the feds." His lips tightened. "What the fuck-ever. Kent doesn't need to know his mother was a fuckin' murdering junkie. And I'll be damned if I can find it in me to give a shit right now."

Jordan nodded.

Rick turned back to look at her, his shoulders straight, his gaze direct. "I'm damned sorry, Belle. If I'd suspected . . ."

She shook her head. "None of us did, Rick. It's over. Let's let it stay over."

But it wasn't over. She turned to the mantel and saw the pictures and felt something wither inside her.

"Grandpop. Rory. I want to speak to Jordan alone."

"Belle." Grandpop started toward her.

He was stooped and aging, and it broke her heart how he accepted the man his son was, and the deceit of his grandson. Noah, Nathan, he hadn't told grandpop either. They were losing him all over again.

"Alone, Grandpop," she whispered. "Just for a minute."

Rory shook his head as Grandpop sighed. They moved out the front door with Rick. She watched from the wide window as they walked the sheriff to his car.

Sabella turned back to Jordan and walked toward him slowly.

"Where. Is. My. Husband." She made it simple for him. Said it clearly. Even a simpleton couldn't mistake the question.

Jordan inhaled roughly. His lips tightened but he stared her in the eyes and he lied to her. "Nathan's dead, Belle."

She wasn't aware of her own clenched fists until she delivered a right hook her father would have been damned proud of.

"Fuck!" Jordan stepped back, shock, disbelief filling his eyes. "Damn, Belle. You hit me."

"Do I need to ask you again?"

He stared back at her, keeping plenty of distance between

them now. He watched her carefully, that edge of Malone calculation in his gaze.

"It won't change my answer, Belle."

Her smile was tight. Hard. "Go home. You're not needed here."

"Belle." His protest was low, rough.

He was a damned handsome man, she thought. He resembled Nathan. Just as Rory did. The Malone men were quite simply male perfection. In looks anyway. And he had been her friend. Once.

"My husband has been dead for six years," she told him. "And he was never the man I thought he was anyway. I don't need your compassion or your sympathy over another man that never cared enough to stick around either. So leave."

He started to say something more.

"Get out!" she screamed. "Just go."

He left.

It took longer to convince Rory and Grandpop to leave. It hurt more to make them go. But finally, the house was silent. She turned the phones off, she locked the doors, and she walked to the mantel. The pictures.

She stared at them, seeing the stranger who had held her and the stranger she had married. They had loved, but they had never known each other, not fully. She had sensed all that darkness roiling in her husband, but he had never shown it to her. And she—she touched his brow in the closest picture. She had been what she thought he needed her to be. She wouldn't ever be that woman again. Not for him. Not for the man he was now.

As she stared, the fury rose inside her. It bit inside her mind, dug vicious claws into her soul, until she screamed with the rage and the pain that exploded through her.

In one long hard swipe of her arm they crashed to the floor. Glass shattered, flew around her. She pressed her fists to her stomach and let the first sob free. It ripped out of her. It tore through her. It was a howl of agony that echoed through the house and caused the man standing in the doorway to flinch.

Noah felt the ragged pain inside him as though it were his own. Sharper, brighter than any pain Diego Fuentes had ever dealt him.

He watched as she knelt in the middle of that broken glass, lifted the broken frame of their wedding picture, and held it to her breasts as she curled over it.

The sobs were wrenching, torn, desperate, and he couldn't handle it. He hadn't been able to handle the pain since the moment he walked from those caves.

He had lost it. Lost control. Lost that icy edge. He had slashed through the militia in a rage so brilliant, so white hot, it had terrified him.

He moved across the room now, still bloodstained. He hadn't changed clothes. Dirt and blood were caked on him. He smelled of death. Reeked of it. But he hadn't been able to stay away from her. He hadn't forgotten the knowledge in her eyes as he walked away from her. Heard her last desperate cry in his ears.

She had known. All along, his Bella had known who he was. And still, she had loved him. She had waited. She had cried and she had fought for him in every way that she knew how.

He bent his knees and crouched down in front of her, staring at the past, destroyed in front of his eyes.

Her head lifted, tears streaked her pale face, fury burned inside her.

"Six years," she sobbed accusingly. "Six fucking years. Where were you?"

He stared at her, at the pictures, and he knew the truth for himself. "Nathan truly died, Sabella. The only part left living was his love for you."

Not he was dead. Or her husband was dead.

Sabella heard the quiet acceptance in his voice, the resignation. And in part, he was right. The man he had been had changed. Changed drastically, but he was still the man she loved.

"But that part of him is here," she whispered. "Has always been here."

She couldn't stop the sobs, the tears, the agony. "And that part was alive inside me. No matter the name, Noah, no matter who or what you want to call yourself, that part of you has always been with me."

His hands hung between his bent knees, his hair was tangled, dusty, and fell over the savage angles of his face like a fall of worn silk.

His eyes were wilder, darker than they had been before he disappeared. His face sharper. His brows were the same. His lower lip a little thinner. But he was still her Irish. He was still her husband.

He looked at the pictures and finally lifted another of them together. He held it out to her. "This man," he said gently. "Nathan Malone didn't know the darkness, Sabella. He didn't know the hell other men could inflict. He didn't know the monster that lived under his own skin."

She shook her head.

"Listen to me, baby. The man you married didn't kill first. He didn't go after blood on a mission. He pulled his punches, he tried to be fair. Until he was forced to spend nineteen months pumped up on hell's own mix of drugs. All he had to do was break his marriage vows to find death. To escape it. All he had to do was fuck whatever they brought him, and he would have known peace."

Shock and disbelief brought her mind to a stop.

Noah sighed heavily. "I was a SEAL, but I was also one of the few used for extreme high clearance missions. I knew things. They thought if they could force me to break my vows, then the rest of my honor would fall by the wayside." He shook his head at the thought. "They brought women that looked like you. That could mimic your pretty Southern accent. But I always knew. I knew; I would look at them and in my head, I'd come here." He looked around the room, his expression heavy, filled with pain. "I saw through your eyes. I felt your pain. Your love. And went mad from the agony. But you were seeing through me too, weren't you, Bella?"

Bella. He called her Bella. Not Sabella, rife with hunger and pain. But Bella, as he had called her before.

"I knew," she whispered tearfully. "I called Jordan, and he lied to me." Her lips trembled. "And you lied to me, Noah."

He shook his head. "I never lied to you."

"You told me you were dead," she cried out furiously. "Stared me in the eye, and lied to me."

"Bella. Nathan Malone *is* dead." He caught her shoulders, shook her.

"No!" she screamed back. And she couldn't hit him. She wanted to, and she couldn't.

"Look at me," he yelled. "Look at me, Bella. What happened killed the man you loved. All that's left is this. The man you see now. The name I carry now. Anything else is not possible."

"No!" She pulled away from him, stumbled to her feet, and shook with the rage pounding through her. "The name might be dead, but you are not dead. You weren't just a SEAL," she cried. "You weren't just a friend, or just a son or a grandson or brother. You weren't just a warrior." She clenched her fists, pressed them to her stomach as the agony welled through every cell of her body. "You are my husband. My lover. And you hid that from me, Noah. I had the dark passion you hid from me while we were married, and I saw the ferocity of the man who would protect me in those mountains. It doesn't matter if your name is Nathan, Noah, or Hey Fucking You, you are my lover. My soul. My heart. And by God, you are not dead. Because if you were." Her lips trembled. "If you were, then I'd be dead. Don't you know that? Don't you see that? If the man that loved me was gone, then I'd be ashes now. Not standing here screaming at a moron with more pride than good sense."

Noah felt his heart unclench. He felt something dark, something nearly rabid in his soul, finally shudder as it eased. He rose slowly to his feet and stared back at his wife, seeing all that strength. Seeing the woman who had always watched him with what he knew now was a touch of amusement. Because she had known, he had no idea that she was so much more than he realized. But she had always known him. Had always sensed the darkness. Had always sensed the pride that he had in overabundance.

"You always knew," he said then. "Didn't you?"

"I always knew you," she cried angrily, swiping the tears from her face and staring at him scathingly. "Big tough SEAL. You would walk into this house as though nothing existed in it until you entered the door. Lord of your domain. The big warrior who could fix everything." She sniffed. "How often did you have to fix anything?"

He never had. Sometimes, he swore she had to think of things to do, and he had accused her more than once of hiring people to fix things he was certain should have needed fixing.

"Bella." He shook his head. "You were always my soul."

"Except for eighteen months." She sneered. "Where were you?"

"Recovering. Retraining."

"Alone." Her finger poked into his chest, dug in. "Without me."

Without her.

God, his hands were shaking. He was staring into her face and he wasn't looking at a woman willing to forgive and forget.

Noah swallowed tightly. Had he waited too long? Christ, no. He couldn't consider that. He hadn't waited too long. Made mistakes, yes. She would forgive mistakes. She would have to.

"I love you, Bella," he whispered.

The look she gave him caused him to wince. Feminine fury, disbelief, and intolerance. Fuck.

"Why?" she snapped. "Why did you wait?"

"Because I was a mess," he said simply. "A hard-on-packing, ignorant fool too fucking scared to have his wife see him weak," he snarled. "Is that so fucking hard for you understand?"

"Weak, my ass," she yelled back. "You were probably a son of a bitch railing and growling at everyone and everything in sight."

His lips almost twitched and he should have been raging now.

"You think I wanted to rage at you?" he bit out instead.

"It was my right." She was back in his face. "Do you hear me, Noah? My fucking right to put up with it. And to do it gladly. You bastard!" He caught her fist, stared at it. His eyes narrowed.

"Sabella, you're not allowed to hit," he reminded her carefully, staring into her bruised little face, her thunderous gaze.

God, he loved her. Wanted to go to his knees and thank God for her.

"Are you staying?" Her chin lifted. "If not, get the hell out now."

"Yes!" They were nose to nose now, anger flipping and flaring around them rather than contained as it had always been in their marriage. "By God, you're not getting rid of me."

Nose to nose. He'd never gone nose to nose with her. He had brooded, hid in the basement. But maybe he liked this better. Because the arousal was suddenly bursting, burning, whipping through him like the storm raging in her eyes.

"Did I say I wanted to be rid of you?" Hoarse, furious, her voice caressed his senses as nothing else ever had.

"It wouldn't do you any damned good if you did," he bit out. "But Malone stays dead, Bella. It's Blake. Period."

Her eyes narrowed. "The team you're a part of? Is that why?"

"We'll talk why later." He gripped her arms, jerked her to him. "This is us, Bella. Me and you. He stays dead. Do you hear me?"

She knew her husband. She knew that look in his eyes. This was for their safety, not for his pride.

"The name stays dead," she amended. "But the man." Her lips trembled. "The man you are is my soul."

Two tears ran down her bruised face again. Sienna had died for those bruises. Man or woman, nothing, no one, would risk what was his again.

He cupped her tender cheeks and felt the pressure behind his eyes, the lump in his throat.

"My Bella," he whispered. "My heart died for you. Every

day, every minute. Every second that I thought you believed I was another man. Every second you believed I was dead."

And her smile lit him, from the inside out. A tremulous, vulnerable smile. "I always knew who touched me," she whispered. "Only you, Noah. Only you can touch me." Then she touched his cheek, her fingertips touched his lips. "But you really need a shower first, sailor boy. You reek."

The laugh that tore from him shouldn't have surprised him. The surge of love, of pure joy that ripped through him, should have been uncertain, should have been rife with the fears he knew had consumed him for so long. That Sabella couldn't accept the man he was. That she might regret. That she might see him without those rose-colored glasses he thought she wore.

He realized now, she had never worn the glasses. He had. Deliberately. Because of pride. Because of that fear inside him that he'd lose her. And losing her was his greatest fear.

"Shower with me." He picked her up, cradled her in his arms. "I'll wash your back."

He moved through the broken glass, took the stairs easily, held her to his heart.

"We'll talk terms later." She snuggled against him.

"What terms?"

"Marriage terms, Mr. Blake," she informed him. "Our baby isn't being born without a marriage. Don't even consider it."

Smug satisfaction filled her as he came to a blinding stop in their bedroom. He could feel his eyes widening, feel the panic that bit at his chest.

"What did you say?"

Her smile was female, triumphant. Loving.

"Our baby, Noah. When I went to the doctor yesterday, she told me. Antibiotics and birth control don't mix, and I just didn't think."

He shook his head. "A baby?"

Their baby? Jesus. She was pregnant?

She cupped his jaw, kissed his lips, and whispered, "Our baby, Noah. I'm pregnant, with our baby."

He set her slowly on her feet.

"I can't wait to shower." His cock was pounding. So hard it was brutal. The engorged length felt bruised. Desperate.

"Shower," she whispered, caught his hand, and led him to the bathroom.

Mindless, in shock, he could only follow. He'd follow her, no matter where she led him.

CHAPTER THIRTY-ONE

He was alive. And he was hers.

Sabella stood beneath the shower, staring up at him. She couldn't stop touching him. His face, his wet hair, his scarred chest, his powerful thighs. The heavy, thick erection that bobbed out from his body. Luscious and wide, dark and delectable.

She let him wash her hair. It was something he had always done years ago. Washed it slow and easy, threading his fingers through it as he conditioned it, kissing her brow, holding her to him. Then he washed her body.

She almost cried as he kissed the bruises on her cheek, whispered how sorry he was. Didn't he know? It was worth it. It was all worth it to have him with her, to have him alive and touching her.

"I dreamed of you," he whispered against her lips, holding her face between his hands as the water fell around them. "Every time I closed my eyes, Bella, I saw you as you were the day I left. Teasing me. Laughing at me. I saw you tempting me to take you, one more time, and I ached until the ache nearly destroyed me."

"I touched you in my dreams." She touched his lips, caressed his beard. "I kissed you, I held you."

"You saved me." His head lowered and the kiss he gave her was more than lust this time, it was more than hunger. It was a homecoming, and her breath caught at the sweet heat of it.

His lips loved hers, made love to them. They stroked and caressed as his tongue licked and slid over hers, tasting her, sinking into her, until Sabella felt lost in the wonder of it.

This was her husband. He hadn't died. He had been wounded. Perhaps hiding. But the man who loved Sabella Malone was still there, and he was still living proud.

"Bella, if I don't do you soon, my brain is going to explode."

His hands were clenched at her waist, his expression tight, honed with the lust he did nothing to hide now.

Well, the dirty talk was new, but she liked that. And she had a feeling that like the naked lust that slipped out of control, the vocalization of it had just been hidden before as well.

Her hand slid down his chest until she could curve her fingers over the thick, iron-hard shaft.

"Hmm. How are you going to do me?" She looked up at him from beneath lowered lashes. "All those threats you've made over the past weeks, maybe I should be wary?"

His gaze flared, blue back lit by a fiery blue flame.

"I don't make threats. I make promises," he warned her, watching her now with a sensual intent that had her body humming.

He shut off the water before reaching outside the shower and dragging one of the large bath sheets from the towel rack.

"I think you're all talk," she breathed out before rasping her teeth over her lower lip and giving him a look that promised she belonged to him. As long as he belonged to her.

He didn't say a word. He dried them both off. The look in his eyes warned her though. Warned her that the promises that had slipped past his lips over the past weeks were going to be kept.

Her rear clenched at the thought, her juices spilled from between her thighs, creating a hot, sensual, sexy feeling that she couldn't escape. Didn't want to escape.

Her husband had always made her feel this way. Like a

woman, desirable, earthy, willing to be pleasured. Waiting to be pleasured. But so eager to pleasure in return.

She watched as he dried her. Watched as he knelt in front of her. For just a second, the barest second, his fingers splayed over her lower stomach and his lashes flickered over his eyes.

She wished she could see his eyes. Wished she could see the same hopes and the wellspring of paternal pride she knew he would be feeling. They had always wanted children. But they had always wanted to wait until he would be home more to see their baby grow.

Those thoughts became swamped then. Pleasure whipped through her like lightning gone wild. It sizzled over her nerve endings, attacked her fingertips, her toes, her hard nipples, and the burgeoning knot of her clit.

And he was just kissing her. Kissing the rise of her mound, just above her clit, feathering his breath over her clit and sending erratic, ecstatic impulses of pleasure racing over her flesh.

Her fingers dug into his wet hair as his hands pressed against the inside of her thighs, parting them. Callused hands caressed the flesh there, tested the muscles, came so close to the weeping center of her body that her breath caught. Though he didn't actually touch her with his hands.

"You're teasing me to death," she breathed out roughly.

His only response was a muttered "mmm" as he kissed her clit and nearly threw her into climax. And oh, she needed her climax.

"I love your bare little pussy." He lifted his head and stared up at her with wicked dark blue eyes. "It gets so wet, your flesh so silky."

She shivered at the sound of his rough voice.

"I could come real easy too," she panted, parting her legs further and flushing furiously as he parted the folds of her pussy and just looked at her.

His gaze was almost a physical caress as he stared at her pussy then licked his lips hungrily.

"I'm gonna eat you first," he growled. "Eat you like candy, Bella. Lick all that sweet, wet sugar and listen to your cries fill my head."

She was going to melt all over him just like hot, wet sugar if he wasn't careful. His voice, so rough, so ruined, but that hint of lyrical Irish lurked just beneath the surface.

He straightened, his hands running over the curves of her butt, up her back, curled around her until the tips of her breasts rasped against his chest hair.

She loved that thin sexy growth of curls. Loved the heat and the caress of it against her skin. She shivered, a moan passing her lips at the need that welled inside her. Tipping her head back, she luxuriated in the stroke of his lips over her neck, against the bruises on her face.

"I love you, Bella," he whispered at her ear, and wrung a cry from her throat as she held on to him, tried to pull him beneath her skin, or burrow beneath his. Which she wasn't certain.

"My husband." Her arms wrapped around his neck as his lips took the kiss they both craved.

It was intense, driving, primal, and hungry as he lifted her and carried her to the bedroom. It was a kiss that wiped the past away and left only the future, the present. It was a kiss that tore past boundaries. It was a kiss that opened them both to all the emotions that swirled unchecked between them.

The darkness. Hungers as yet untapped. Eighteen months of brutal memories and dark fantasies. Years of aching loss, and the memory of tender love.

It swirled between them, rocked them, fed the lust surging and gripping until they were eating at each other as Noah fell to the bed with her. Lips and tongues, teeth and hands, they were consuming, hungry, desperate.

They needed. The stark, vicious pain that had consumed her when she thought he wasn't returning to her still blazed through her soul. The thankfulness, love, the sheer brutal desperation for this one man, back in her arms, drove her.

Drove her until she was sobbing. Until she was holding him, passion edging into such an intensity of emotion that she could let it free. Sob against his chest as she kissed him, loved him, whispered her need.

"Ah Bella." And he held her. His voice was thick with the

same emotion as his arms tightened around her. "Never again, my love. I swear it. Never again. I won't let you go again."

She hit his chest. His shoulder. Struck out first in rage, then in need.

"Baby, you gotta stop hitting me." He gripped her wrists and stretched them above her head as he came over her. "Hitting's against the rules."

"So is dying," she cried. "If you can die on me, then I can hit you when you come back."

His lips quirked. "If you won't hit any more, I won't die any more."

"Don't joke about it," she gasped, fear almost paralyzing her. "Don't you dare joke about it."

He kissed her chin.

"I'll make you forget about it."

His lips moved over her collarbone, like rough silk, a caress that shouldn't have stolen her mind, but it did. It moved through her. It sent flames racing across her flesh and had her stretching, arching closer, as his lips lowered.

His lips covered a nipple. Sucked it inside his mouth and electric heat shot to her clit. Sabella gasped, arched. She felt his moan vibrate on the tender peak, and her gaze shimmered from the waves of excessive heat rising inside her.

"Oh. I like that." She strained against the hold he had on her wrists. "Oh yes, Noah. Just like that. It feels so good. So good."

He was working her nipple in his mouth, his tongue rasping, his teeth scraping around it as he consumed her, devoured her.

"I want to taste your candy, Sabella," he breathed, moving down her abdomen. "All that sweet sugar building on your pussy. I love your pussy. I could eat you for hours. Make a fucking meal of you."

He released her wrists and his head moved between her thighs, his tongue raking through the narrow slit and gathering her juices to it.

He licked, sucked, probed with his tongue and filled her with his fingers. She writhed beneath him, twisted, hungry, desperate as he moved again.

"Stay there."

She stayed, watching as he went to the leather bag he had brought here days ago and left beneath the side table.

He grinned as he picked it up, opened it, and withdrew a small bottle of lubrication.

Sabella's breathing picked up. She knew what was coming. She could feel it. Her butt clenched in anticipation and in excitement.

"Roll over," he ordered her.

She turned slowly as she heard the bag thump back to the floor.

"Raise your ass for me."

She lifted to her knees, her fingers curling into the comforter as he moved behind her, one hand stroking over her butt cheeks as a murmur of approval passed his lips.

"This is the prettiest ass in the world."

Sabella moaned as he pressed a kiss at the top of the cleft. His fingers moved between her thighs, eased through the thick, heavy juices that had collected there.

When he touched the hidden entrance beyond, she lost her breath. Nathan had never taken her there before, during their marriage. He had playfully threatened but had never actually gone this far.

He was tired of waiting. She was tired of waiting.

As he caressed her, prepared her, she felt the wildness of hunger building inside her. As if this act would finish something, complete something. As though the submissive position, the need he was building in her, connected them as she had never imagined possible.

He eased her slow and easy. Lay beneath her and licked at the drenched folds of her pussy as his fingers parted her rear, stretched it, prepared it, send a blazing heat burrowing through her body.

Sabella became lost in the hunger.

Pleasure swelled through her as he licked, sucked at her clit then plunged his tongue inside the clenching muscles of her pussy. His fingers worked inside her rear, easing, lubricating her heavily as his other hand caressed, patted, then began landing on the cheeks of her ass in a series of subtle little slaps that had the flesh heating wickedly, erotically.

Sabella never imagined she could enjoy this. Never imagined she could let herself be immersed in her sexuality, in Nathan's, to the point that she forgot everything. That she needed nothing but the increasingly lustful caresses that her husband gave her.

She was clawing at the blankets when he moved from between her spread thighs. Perspiration dripped from her, dampened her body as sexual tension sang through her system in a rising clash of impulses.

"Christ, I fucking love eating your pussy." He came over her. "I love fucking that tight pussy, Sabella. But this. This is going to blow us out the roof."

The head of his cock tucked at her ass.

The gentle strokes of his fingers inside her ass moments before, easing the muscles there as he built the lust burning in her pussy, had relaxed her. Tension whipped through her body, but the tiny opening flared open over the heavy crown of his cock.

Pleasure-pain tore through her as he eased back and forth. He worked the thick length inside her as one arm curled over her hips and his fingers moved over her clit.

Feathery strokes that had her crying out, pushing back.

"There, baby. Take that dick," he whispered. "All the way inside you, Sabella. I'm dying for you, baby. Dying for this. Give me all of it. All of you." His voice broke. "All of you, Bella. My sweet Bella."

She screamed as the head of his cock passed the tight, tense ring of muscles inside her rear. The blinding flash of pleasure bordering on pain nearly had her coming. She creamed instead, covering his fingers with more of her juices as she felt his cock slide in, all the way, filling her, stretching her.

It was primal. Primitive. Sabella couldn't understand the sensations, the emotions whipping through her, but the acceptance as well as the penetration opened something inside her.

She had always trusted her husband. But until now, she

hadn't realized that trust hadn't gone soul deep. He hadn't known her as she knew him. Until now. Now, he would know her. In life. In death. She would never hide from him.

Noah laid his head against Sabella's, fighting to breathe. Just to breathe. He couldn't move yet, if he did, he would lose it. He'd pump inside her and lose his soul to her before he ever had a chance to chain hers as well.

God, it was fucking beautiful. He closed his eyes, feeling her muscles flex around him, but he felt something more. Intimacy on a scale he had never known with her before. A knowledge, a certainty, that this one woman was everything, every part of him. The bond he felt inside his own soul all these years had never been complete, and he had been too damned man-stupid to realize it. Until now.

Until this. Until she gave him an entrance inside her that was more than physical. This.

He shifted, moved, and heard her cry of pleasure. This was total acceptance. Total trust. And knowledge.

They were both stripped to the bare bones now, his cock moving inside the sensitive, nerve-rich depths of her rear, and she was taking him, open for him and begging for more.

"Beautiful Bella," he sighed, lowering his head to kiss her shoulder, her neck. "My Bella." His voice broke again.

Fuck. He was dying for her. Broken and being reborn inside as he filled her. As she filled his heart, his soul. He could feel the emotions pouring into him, easing the ragged wounds, his fierce pride, his hidden fears.

He moved inside her, easy at first. So easy.

Leaning back, he spread her rear cheeks apart to watch. To watch as he took her, sinking inside her pink flesh and delving into fiery bliss.

"More. More," she begged, she pleaded. She was screaming out for him and the sound of her pleasure tore through the need for slow and easy. It tore past control, slammed through hidden fears, and he took them both to places he knew they had never reached before.

He rubbed around the hard, swollen bud of her clit. Sweat dripped from his hair, his face, as his hips thrust, stroking his erection deep, hard and she pressed back, crying for him. Crying for more.

"More. Oh God. Noah. Yes. Yes. Take all of me."

"My Bella." He groaned her name, shafting harder, his hips pounding against her ass, his balls slapping against her wet flesh as he felt the need to come clenching around his testicles, whipping up his spine.

Sabella exploded first. She tightened, surprised cries, curses, prayers falling from her lips as he felt her fly head-long into ecstasy. And he followed her. He plunged deep, shoved two fingers inside her pussy and set her off again as he felt his cock explode.

His semen filled her. Fierce, shuddering jets of cum spurting inside her, tearing from his soul rather than his balls as he cried out her name.

"My Bella!" His head fell back on his shoulders. One hand clenched her hips, and he didn't lose himself inside her. He gave himself to her. All of her. Spilling and groaning her name until he collapsed over her.

She was asleep when he came to himself. Lying next to her, wrapped around her, he saw her hand, her left hand, ringless against his chest. His left hand was wrapped around her, and he could feel the missing weight of the bond that burned inside him.

He slid from her slowly, grinning as she grouched and flopped on her back, her hand on her stomach almost protective as she continued to sleep.

He strode through bedroom and bathroom first, looking for her wedding band. She had been wearing it the day before when she left with Rory. He remembered her wearing it. But she hadn't had it on at the caves.

He walked to the kitchen and checked her purse. Organized little Sabella. There it was, tucked into a zippered compartment, the little ring shining bright as a band tightened around his head.

He moved back upstairs, picked up his pants, and pulled his wedding band free before fitting it back on his finger.

The outside of the bands were plain. Just gold bands. Sabella hadn't wanted frills for them. Inside was the Celtic vow, "forever." Go síoraí.

Inside his were the words "Forever, my soul." Matching vows. Matching hearts.

He lifted her hand and slid her ring back in place.

His wife.

He tangled his fingers with hers, staring at the sight of her pale, creamy flesh against his own.

His wife.

His gaze drifted to her flat stomach.

His wife and his child.

His hands were shaking as he touched her stomach. Shaking so hard the shudders worked through him, making it hard to breathe, to think.

Jesus. They made a baby!

He stared in shock at her stomach. Then in awe.

He spread his hand over her stomach and felt the tightness in his chest fill his throat, lock behind his eyes.

Then he watched in disbelief the little bead of moisture that dropped to her stomach, shimmered against it.

Tears?

He blinked and another fell.

He felt the slam of emotion. Love, regret, pure blinding God-thanked reverence filling him as he lifted his eyes to his wife's face, to see her watching him, tears sliding down her darkened cheeks.

The bruises would fade, but this moment in time would always fill his memories.

"Go síoraí," he whispered, the old lilt to his voice almost, almost, normal as he reaffirmed his vow to her.

"Forever, Noah," she whispered tearfully, her hand covering his on her stomach, her breath hitching in joy. Not in pain. "Forever, my love."

EPILOGUE

Four months later, on a blazing September day, Noah pulled his pickup into the graveled driveway of his grandpop's cabin and stared at the vehicles gathered there with a sense of throttled fury. Grant Malone was there.

"This wasn't our agreement," he said coolly, glancing over at her.

The bruises were long gone, but his memory of how close he had come to losing her wasn't. She sat beside him, her hand on the tiny mound of her stomach as she stared out the windshield thoughtfully.

She finally turned to him, and he saw the determination in her gray eyes. "It's time, Noah. Grandpop called this meeting, Noah. There's things he wants us to hear. And we're going to hear them."

"With him there?" He stabbed his finger to his father's ranch truck. "No, Bella. No way. No how."

He hadn't visited his father, hadn't made good on his threat to reach out and enter his nightmares, and he would be damned if he would hold a civilized conversation with him now. He'd asked one thing of him. Protect Sabella. His wife had spent six years with only Rory standing between her and the world. And her own stubborn strength. He wouldn't forget that.

It was all he could do to bite back his curse. He couldn't

curse in front of the baby when it came so he might as well start practicing now. Right?

Something softened inside of him as he looked down at her stomach again. She was barely showing, but their baby was there. His guts shook at the thought again and everything inside him seemed to explode in a riot of sensation. Even now. Four months later.

He blew out a hard breath and stared back at the vehicles. Rory was there, and Jordan, Grandpop, and Grant. Grant, not Father, and sure as damned hell not Dad.

"This wasn't part of the marriage rules," he gritted out, thinking about the page-long list they had fucking negotiated before she would marry him.

Negotiated, like a damned lawyer squabbling over pennies. She'd made him so fucking hot he'd had her right there on the kitchen table. Hell, he was hard again just thinking about it.

"Yes it was," she answered calmly.

"Where?" He turned on her, his hands clenching on the steering wheel, no longer afraid she would run away crying if he raised his voice a little bit. "Where the hell was it?"

"The part that stated Sabella was always right."

He snapped his teeth together and turned back. Fuck. He'd forgot about that one. The last one. He was going to negotiate the hell out of it at the time, but he'd been too busy trying to get under that silky skirt she was wearing.

"You cheat." He turned on her, nose to nose now. "We renegotiate."

"Too late, you signed it and you sealed it with marriage vows. You're stuck, Mr. Noah Blake." Her lips curled in satisfaction, but her eyes were dark, her expression assuring him she was very well aware of how difficult it would be to face his father now.

She laid her hand on his arm. "Grandpop is old, Noah. Whatever's waiting on us in there means a lot to him. Give it a chance. Maybe you'll have some answers instead of the questions I know burn inside you."

Why had he deserted Sabella? Not why hadn't he been a

fucking father to him. Why had he cheated on his mother? Why hadn't he claimed Rory and given him a home? God, why had he turned his back on Grandpop and stolen everything the old man tried to work for?

So many questions that he had actually put behind him the day he faced Grant Malone in the convenience center four months before.

"Fine." He gave his head a hard shake. "It won't change anything."

"All I ask is that you hear Grandpop out. Not Grant," she promised him. "I love you, Noah. Some things, we need closure on. If not for us, then for our child."

Closure. He blew out a hard breath before he got out of the truck and strode around to the other side. He lifted Sabella from the high cab, setting her easily on her feet as she leaned her head against his chest for just a second.

"You owe me for this," he muttered. "That's definitely one of the rules. If I have to give in to Sabella knows best, then Sabella gives me head. Period."

"I always give you head," she said, laughing.

"Yeah, but I want special head."

"There's a special way to do it?" Her eyes lit up.

He loved that about her. She was always ready to play or get down and dirty.

"We'll discuss it," he grunted. He'd tease her until she begged to suck his cock. That was special to him.

He kept his hand at her back as they moved to the rough boards of the porch. He loved touching her. He touched her every chance he had, because he could, because she was his.

Jordan had made it easy on him. And whoever the hell backed the Elite Ops seemingly hadn't even blinked at the situation. Noah was on backup on the few missions they had gone out on in recent months. They were still waiting for information to see where the fallout on the militia had gone. But even then, Noah would pull back. The name Malone might be dead to him, but he was a husband, a father, and he wasn't risking that again. Not like he had before. Another of Sabella's rules.

His job wasn't low risk, but it was lower than it could have been. And maybe he should have read the whole Elite Ops contract. There was no resignation, there was no opting out, but there was a stated waiver once the operative reached what they considered noncombatant age or was deemed unable to effectively complete or conduct missions. They were then moved to backup or technical ops.

Elite Ops would always own whatever job he did, but they didn't own his soul. Sabella owned his soul.

Grandpop was waiting. The door opened and they stepped into the small living room. Grant was sitting on the couch. Jordan and Rory in chairs that faced it. There were two more chairs to the side that Noah knew had been pulled from the bedrooms.

Grant sat with his head down, his hands clasped between his knees. Jordan's expression was somber, Rory's eyes gleamed with fury.

"What's up, Grandpop?" Sabella asked, kissing the old man's cheek as Noah moved in behind her.

Grandpop held Noah's gaze. Noah had gone to him the day after he returned to his wife. They'd held each other as Grandpop cried, slapped his shoulder, and then they had walked to the grave and Noah had seen the truth there.

The gravestone had simply said "Nathan." Nothing more. Grandpop had never believed he was dead.

"Grant has something to tell his son."

Noah's gaze moved to Rory.

Grant lifted his head as Noah glanced at him, and a shock of disbelief filled him. Tears filled Grant's eyes, and knowledge. He knew. The same expression Grant had had the day Noah had held him pinned to the cooler in the convenience store. Grant Malone had known who he was.

"Who told?" he growled.

"I knew," Grant whispered. "I knew the minute I saw you." He shook his head and a tear slipped free. "I knew when Dad didn't have your stone engraved. I knew when I heard Sabella had a lover." He shook his head. "I knew."

"Doesn't change anything." He held Sabella to him, trying to harden himself. Trying to tell him it didn't matter.

Grant shook his head. "It has to matter." He looked at Sabella's small abdomen and another tear slipped. "It has to matter, Noah."

He lifted his eyes back to Noah. "Thirty-five years ago, I married a woman I didn't love. She married me for the money I could bring to the ranch. You know that. I married her because I wanted to build a legacy for the sons I intended to have. I got the ranch, but by the time my first son came, I knew the danger we all faced."

Nathan knew about the loveless marriage. Before Tammy Malone's death, she hadn't exactly been silent about the fact that she only married an "Irish cur," as she called him, to save the ranch her father was losing.

"We had you," Grant whispered. "The militia started targeting me then, Noah. I was Irish. They didn't want me here, but they couldn't kill me either. Killing me would break the agreement I had with Tammy's father. And he was one of them. But they could hurt you. Dad." He looked at Rory. "My other son."

Noah stilled.

"I made sure they knew I didn't have anything that they could destroy me with." He swallowed tightly. "Dad knew." He nodded to Grandpop. "We both made sure you and Rory, and Belle, were protected. You know he did, Noah."

"You took everything he had!" Noah snarled. "Don't lie to me now."

"No." Grant shook his graying head. "We made it look that way. We let everyone believe that." He swallowed tightly. "Rory's mother died because they thought, rightfully, that she mattered to me. I had to pretend she didn't." He shook his head. "Even your mother didn't know because she was best friends with some of their wives and I couldn't risk my son. Neither of my sons." He swallowed tightly. "I let them think I didn't care. I let them think there was no way to hurt me, and I skated by. I stayed quiet. I ran my ranch and looked for ways to hurt them that wouldn't come back on me." He rubbed at his face with his hands. "I sent pictures of the hunts to the FBI. And those agents died. Finally, I went to Jordan."

Noah turned to his uncle. Jordan nodded slowly. "This is why we brought together a team no one could tie to an agency. We had more than four dead agents. There have been six total. Every time we sent someone they were identified. We couldn't figure out how. Until Sienna."

Because she had hacked her husband's computer files. Because she knew how to watch, how to listen, and how to deceive.

"Between her and the federal marshal and judge, no agency could get anyone in close enough for proof."

"That was eight years ago. You were engaged to Belle," Grant whispered. "I did my best, Noah, to protect her. Grandpop would make the mortgage payments when we had to do something. He would let his buddies know I was being a bastard that refused to help. It nearly broke him."

"You should have sold out when I wanted you to," Grandpop argued.

"We would have lost everything, Pop, you know that. Everything I tried to build for my boys. For my grandchildren. Everything we saved all those years would have gone down the drain."

"Poor and happy ain't that bad, boy."

It was obviously an argument they had had often.

Grant could only shake his head as Noah let himself ease into a chair, pulling Sabella to his lap. He couldn't let go of her. A lifetime of what he thought he knew was exploding in front of his face.

He hadn't known his wife. He hadn't seen what was evolving in the town and with his father. His vision had been so narrow, his focus on the SEALs, his career, on loving Sabella, and little else.

His "death" had shown him how little he had lived, how little he had known.

"You didn't tell me," he whispered.

"You were one of the things I was trying to protect," Grant bit out. "For that." He pointed to Sabella's stomach. "Your future. Your wife and your children. Nothing else mattered to me, Noah. I loved you, and I loved Rory, and I did my best. Not good enough, I admit, but my best. And I prayed Dad could do the rest."

And Grandpop had.

Noah shook his head.

"I'm not asking for forgiveness, or for acceptance," Grant whispered. "But I want to know that baby, Noah. I want to be called Grandpop. I haven't been called Dad since you were a boy, and I've lived with that. But I want to be a grandfather, just as bad as I wanted to be your father."

Silence filled the room then. Grandpop stood behind him, his hand settling on Noah's shoulder.

"The world is never what we think it is, Noah." He repeated the words Noah had heard so many times. "There are layers, son. And layers. This is just another."

"But it's always love," Sabella whispered and pressed her hand against his where it rested over their child.

"Nathan Malone doesn't exist anymore," he told his father, thinking of him as a father, despite the practiced determination not to.

"But Noah Blake does," Grant stated. "And Sabella Blake is a gentle, compassionate woman. Everyone knows that. If Grant Malone needs to pretend, hell." He shook his head. "Everyone knows he's damned strange anyway. And I've been inconsistent enough over the years that it won't be remarked on too much. I'm getting old. Rory is close to Noah Blake and his wife. No one will question it."

And that was the truth.

Noah's lips kicked up at the corners.

"Rules," he murmured, and Sabella gave a rude little amused sniff.

"There's always rules." Grant nodded.

Noah frowned as everyone watched him expectantly.

"Noah," Sabella's voice was warning, knowing.

Noah cleared his throat. "I'm always right."

Grant frowned in confusion. Sabella shook. He had a feeling it was silent laughter.

"Noah is always right," he stated. "That's the rule."

"Right about what?" Grant's frown deepened.

"Whatever I want to be right about, dammit," he growled. "Hell. Noah Blake doesn't have a damned father. He's an orphan." Grant winced, paled before he could continue. "But if Nathan Malone's father needs a surrogate son." He shrugged. "I married his wife. I drive his truck. Hell, I guess I can claim his dad."

At that moment, feathery soft, he felt it. His gaze jerked down to where Sabella held his hand to her stomach, then to her eyes.

He felt it.

She smiled. Her eyes filled with love, with the future. With forever.

Their baby had moved. Right there, against his hand, as though in agreement. So soft he hadn't been certain, not really sure until he looked in her eyes.

"Forever," he whispered.

And her eyes shimmered with tears. "Forever."

When he turned back to his father, he thought, maybe, just maybe, there were a few less flecks of green in his eyes. A bit more of the sapphire Irish eyes that were his legacy. He thought, maybe, he could get to know the father he had never known.

He held his hand out to his father, watched the other man blink back his tears, and they shook on the rule, and the future.

Finally, a future. Six years late. A lot of stubborn pride and too damned much time lost. Noah Blake wasn't a stupid man. He wasn't losing more time. He wasn't losing more love. Noah Blake would snatch back everything Nathan Malone had lost and give it everything he had.

The future.

BITTER
RECOIL

ALSO BY STEVEN F. HAVILL

Heartshot

BITTER
RECOIL
Steven F. Havill

St. Martin's Press   New York

Design by Judy Christensen

Library of Congress Cataloging-in-Publication Data
Havill, Steven.
      Bitter recoil / Steven F. Havill.
          p. cm.
      "A Thomas Dunne book."
      ISBN 0-312-07656-8
      I. Title.
PS3558.A785B5   1992
813'.54—dc20   92-1011
                                              CIP

First Edition: July 1992

10 9 8 7 6 5 4 3 2 1

For Kathleen

Acknowledgments

I am grateful to several people for providing technical information that I used in this novel. I would like to thank in particular Fidel Duenas, Rick Jones, and Paul Pierce.

'Revenge, at first though sweet, bitter ere long back on itself recoils.'

John Milton

1

I S T O P P E D at the top of the saddleback and looked down through the pines. The campgrounds were still a mile below me, hidden behind the fat swell of Steamboat Rock. I took a deep breath, found a big granite boulder, and sat down. This walking was worse medicine than pills or needles.

Walk, the damn doctors had said. Walk. I hated walking. That's what cars are for. Or elevators.

Nevertheless, the heart surgeon had convinced me that if I walked, gave up smoking, and shed my considerable girth, I might live a couple more years. I fumbled in my shirt pocket and pulled out a cigarette. Hell, I was walking. That was one out of three.

From where I sat, I could see all the way down Isidro Valley. The sky was a blank, merciless blue, and the sun beat down on my back, roasting right through my shirt. It burned out the kinks.

I had walked up a trail from the Steamboat Rock campground and had worked my way through the thick ponderosa pines for almost two miles. At first, the notion of a hike had seemed like a pleasant idea. . . . I had a long afternoon to kill before I tried cooking supper over the little gas grill stowed in the back of my Blazer.

After the first ten minutes, the hike had been nothing but sweaty, grinding work. And the Smokey Bear signs down along the highway hadn't been joking. The mountain was dry. The needles under my feet crackled like little shards of glass, and I probably shouldn't have even thought about a cigarette. I lit one and relaxed on the rock.

It was peaceful. Maybe wilderness hikers had something. Get away from it all; leave worries behind. I'd been working up a sweat and hadn't thought about Posadas County for nearly half an hour.

Here I was, basking in the sun like a fat toad, 300 miles north of my own New Mexico border town. For two hours I hadn't thought of the past winter, when I'd spent the valuable hours of my life dealing with an unpleasant and mixed bag of drunks, punks, child abusers, drug runners . . . or even simple, wacko souls like Vinnie Jaramillo, who'd arrived home one night in May to find his wife cheating on him. He'd taken a shotgun to his wife and her boyfriend while his three small children watched. Then he'd called the sheriff's department.

I hadn't gotten there first, but it wouldn't have mattered anyway. He'd waited until the first deputy arrived, and then, when he was sure he had an official witness, Vinnie sat down on the living room sofa and blew his own skull to pieces. It had been a hell of a mess.

I guess we were lucky Vinnie had kept his targets within the walls of his own home. And that's how it happened in Posadas County most of the time. Someone went off the deep end and made news. Maybe there's a natural tendency to think one's own community isn't as nuts as the rest of the world, where the loonies try to change the lives of complete strangers.

Hell, I still had a two-week-old copy of the Albuquerque newspaper tucked in my Blazer with headlines about the assassination of Washington State's governor, along with a Department of Corrections warden. According to the article, the governor had been fishing by himself, sitting peacefully in a canoe on some remote Washington lake, and a high-powered rifle bullet fired from hundreds of yards away had exploded his

2

skull. And the prison warden had been shot later that same day when he stepped out of his station wagon to unlock the garage door of his suburban Tacoma home.

Real freaks running loose . . . the paper said the resulting manhunt was the largest Washington had ever had. We'd even gotten a teletype from Washington in our office, for God's sakes . . . probably because we sat right on the border with Mexico.

I took another drag on the cigarette and wished that I could keep my mind off work for more than a few seconds at a time. But replay, replay.

In Vinnie Jaramillo's case, for months afterward the scene still flogged my brain, unwanted but tenacious. The faces of the children left behind were the worst.

What do you do with a three-, four-, and six-year-old who've seen their parents splattered all over the wallpaper? The deputy and I had made some awkward motions and then with relief had watched my chief detective, Estelle Reyes, take the three traumatized and orphaned children under her wing.

She didn't try to stop their sobs, didn't try to distract them. Instead, she was just there, hugging them all close and giving them a spot safe from all the strangers. Later, she wouldn't let the relatives take the children until she was convinced the children understood what was happening to them.

I watched her teach the children, including the youngest one, her telephone number, the four of them playing with the telephone like it was one of those Kmart toys for tots. What a wonderful mind for law enforcement that woman had developed. And two weeks after that incident, her letter of resignation was on my desk, and I was plunged into the deepest funk I'd wallowed in for years.

I sighed. I admit it. I missed her damn near as much as I missed my own daughters. As undersheriff of Posadas County, I'd watched Estelle Reyes work for six years, moving from dispatcher to road patrol to detective—our only detective.

She'd come to us as a part-timer, a college student who

3

showed a flair for common sense and organization. Stunning-looking, too. I know the lawyers who make their living from discrimination cases would be after me for saying so, but she brightened up our drab little office just with her presence. She'd even won the confidence of our sheriff, who viewed anything in skirts as either a sex object or a nuisance.

Shortly after the Jaramillo tragedy, she married a young physician, he as handsome as she was lovely. It was a hell of a wedding, and the department attended in full force . . . and we behaved ourselves throughout. The young couple's plans meshed nicely. Dr. Francis Guzman took a residency with the Public Health Service, running a clinic in San Estevan, 300 miles north of Posadas County and 6 miles down-canyon from where I now sat. Estelle had applied for a job with that county sheriff's department, and Sheriff Pat Tate had jumped at the chance.

His turf was a long, narrow county that was awkward to administer from the county seat far to the southeast, a county that was split down the center by a single state highway, with the rest dirt roads. Towns and villages were scattered far and wide. An Indian pueblo in the north end of the county made jurisdictional matters there even more interesting, especially since the pueblo had only a couple of law officers of its own.

Tate had had the good sense to assign Estelle to what he euphemistically called the San Estevan substation so she could avoid the forty-mile daily commute from the county seat to her new home. The "substation" turned out to be nothing more than a spare room in the highway department's district headquarters.

When I decided to take a short vacation late that summer—an escape from doctors who wouldn't mind their own busi-ness—I found myself traveling north. I didn't mean to pry, mind you, but I wanted to cruise through another county and see what Estelle Reyes-Guzman had won for herself. And if I had to walk, it might as well be in spectacular mountains that should be cooler than the summer blast furnace of Posadas.

I crushed out the cigarette and tucked the remains in my

4

shirt pocket. I lay back on the rock with a groan of aching muscles, hat over my eyes. I had a dinner invitation from Estelle and Francis for Saturday . . . I hadn't told them I was coming up the day before. That gave me a good stretch to loaf and play outdoorsman. I knew me pretty well and twenty-four hours was about my limit for recreation. I even had grand plans to sleep in my Blazer, figuring if I parked clear in the back of the Steamboat Rock campground, I'd have peace and quiet.

The granite wasn't comfortable for long and I sat up. Another hour would see me down to the campground, if I didn't take the short side trail out to the promontory of Steamboat Rock. I'd briefly imagined that I might walk up there, come the cool of the evening. Briefly.

I was sixty-two and fat, fully recovered from a quadruple bypass the winter before, but inclined to lie down and rest whenever someone mentioned serious exercise. I would do well to stumble my way back down to the campground, much less anything more strenuous. Even the grilled dinner was improbable. I knew damn well that when the time came, I'd settle for a couple of pieces of bologna on a hamburger bun, washed down with a beer or two.

And that's exactly what happened. I made it off the mountain without falling on my face or even having another cigarette. The last hundred yards were easiest, following a well-packed trail with no grade.

Back at the campground I unlocked the Blazer, stowed my daypack, and popped a beer. The sun was already filtering through the trees, ready to drop behind the rugged mesa rim. I unfolded an aluminum lounge chair and settled back to watch the mountain colors fade and blend.

The campground was quiet for a Friday night . . . for about five minutes. Then a big Winnebago pulled in, one of those things with the canvas awning that folds down from one tall, slab side. Two elderly folks made home away from home in that monster . . . all thirty feet of it. In minutes they had a

5

covered patio with a gas-fired barbecue grill sending up plumes of cooking chicken.

Two slots down was a Volkswagen bus, crammed to the gills with two young couples and an endless supply of noisy, scrapping children. They should have hijacked the Winnebago and had some room. Another Blazer, a couple years newer than mine, pulled in, and the first creature to emerge was a Dalmatian, nose to the ground and on a beeline for my peaceful corner. He snuffled up, tail wagging, expecting me to pat his wide, empty head.

"Get out of here, brute," I said and waved a hand.

"Pokie, come!" his owner called and Pokie angled off to bother someone else. I opened another beer, just about ready to start sulking. Hell, I could have parked just as easily in a convenience store lot and had more privacy. I needed to find a rough old Forest Service road leading out to nowhere so I could vegetate in peace.

I scowled and looked across the large campground toward the highway. Several of the children from the Volkswagen were barefoot, and I wondered if their parents realized how much broken glass littered the place.

"Jesus, Gastner," I muttered aloud. How the hell had I gotten so adept at minding other people's business? Occupational hazard, I guess. By 8:30 I stopped fighting the fatigue that kept me from making any effort to move to a more secluded spot. I crawled into the back of the Blazer where the mattress was soft and cool. With windows cracked for air I was asleep in half a minute, despite the shrieks of playing children and the endless slamming of car doors.

And it seemed no more than half a minute before the first siren jerked me awake in the deep pitch of that mountain night.

2

I S A T upright in the Blazer and cracked my head on the roll-bar brace. I cursed and flopped back down, one hand clamped to my skull and the other scrabbling for my glasses.

The siren that had awakened me was just down-canyon, coming hard up the winding mountain highway. I heard the vehicle enter the sweeping curve just before the turnoff to the campground. The tires squawled on the pavement. The engine bellowed and then the car was past us.

I sat up more carefully this time and could see the red lights winking through the thick timber. Almost immediately the emergency vehicle slowed. They had reached the call, whatever it was. At the same time, far in the distance, another siren note floated up from the valley below.

After some more searching I found my flashlight and looked at my watch. I was surprised to see 3:18.

If there had been a collision, I hadn't heard it. I snapped off the light and peered outside. No one else in the campground was stirring. Maybe someone had sailed their car off into the canyon . . . the road was ripe for it at any of dozens of places. If they had, they'd done it quietly since I hadn't heard a thing.

I lay back down, listening as the second siren note pulsed and wailed. I didn't have this county's frequency on my radio, or my curiosity would have been easily satisfied.

But hell, it wasn't any of my business. I had an invitation for dinner in another fifteen hours, and over the frijoles Estelle Reyes-Guzman could tell me all about whatever had happened. Maybe it was the state cops anyway.

"The hell with it," I muttered and threw my sleeping bag open. I was wide awake now and would remain so. My biological clock didn't take much monkeying with to be screwed up completely. In country like this somebody might need a hand.

I pulled on my boots, buttoned my shirt, and ran a hand through my hair before pulling on my cap. That would have to do. Mindful of the damn roll bar, I climbed into the driver's seat of the Blazer, fumbled the keys, and started the vehicle. The fat tires crunched gravel as I backed out. I didn't turn on the headlights until I reached the bridge across the creek, ready to climb the upgrade to the highway.

An ambulance roared around the corner of the state highway, and I waited until he'd shot past before I pulled out to follow northbound. The highway jogged left around a buttress of jutting rock, then eased along the river gorge with only a set of stubby guardrails keeping vehicles from zinging off into the void.

In another quarter of a mile I was greeted by a psychedelic display of colored lights bouncing off rocks, trees, and the tight walls of the canyon. A county sheriff's car was pulled diagonally across the highway, blocking my northbound lane. The ambulance had pulled around that car and parked on up ahead, blocking the lane from the other direction.

I slowed to a crawl, obeying the flashlight signals of a man standing near the highway's center yellow lines. Behind him, parked on the southbound lane's shoulder and snugged right up against the rocks that formed the near-vertical embankment, was a dark-colored pickup. My headlights reflected off the white front license plate, and I guessed Forest Service even before the man stepped up to my Blazer.

I rolled down the window, held up my badge, and said, "I'll park up ahead, behind the ambulance."

The young man frowned and rested a hand on the door of

8

my Blazer as if he were going to hold it in place with five fingers. I knew exactly what he was thinking. There were at least a million ambulance chasers in the country, many of them with Special Deputy commissions and pot-metal badges. They showed up like the goon squads at every serious accident or fire, making pests of themselves.

I held the wallet still until he'd focused the flashlight on it and read enough to be satisfied. "That would be fine, sir," he said. "And we sure need someone up at the other end, catching cars coming down that way. There's just a civilian up there."

"You got it." I drove around the patrol car, avoided the orange cones that straddled the centerline, swung past the ambulance, and parked in the center of the highway. I turned on the red grill lights. Their light pulsed on the anxious face of a middle-aged man who walked toward me from up the road. A Buick was pulled off on the shoulder fifty yards ahead. I took my red-head flashlight from the glove compartment and climbed out.

"Use this," I said and handed the man the red light. "There's not going to be much traffic this time of night, but if there is, we want 'em at a crawl. I'll be back to give you a hand in just a minute."

"Oh. Okay," he said, then hesitated. He looked at the light as if it were about to bite him.

"Just wave 'em down. Another officer will probably be here in a minute or two anyway."

I walked back down the highway, past the ambulance. The harsh spotlights from the patrol car converged on a spot near the guardrails where the ambulance attendants and the officer worked over a single figure crumpled on the ground. The victim was lying facedown. I could see one leg extended under the guardrail.

"Let's immobilize her just the way she is," one of the attendants said. "I think we can do that."

I kept out of the way. I don't think the emergency crew even knew I was there. I recognized the deputy sheriff even in the

9

tricky light of the spots and flashlights. But it was no time for a reunion with Estelle Reyes-Guzman.

I took the opportunity to step to the rail and beam my own flashlight down into the rocks. There was no vehicle in sight. Maybe the victim had been a pedestrian, maybe drunk. They had said "she." Maybe she'd staggered into the path of a car and been clipped. If so, it had to have been hit-and-run. If the man up the road with the Buick had been involved, they sure as hell wouldn't have left him up there by himself, directing traffic.

I turned away from the rail and took a closer look. The victim was female and appeared to be young, perhaps in her twenties. I didn't have much of a view but she looked vaguely familiar to me.

The attendants transferred her to the gurney with a minimum of movement, and I could see from the extent of their emergency field dressings that she was hurt in a dozen places. One leg was bent near the hip at an impossible angle.

With a coordinated effort the two paramedics picked up the gurney and carried the victim to the ambulance. I felt a hand on my arm and turned.

"You're just in time," Estelle Reyes-Guzman said. "I saw you drive up."

Miss Sharp Eyes hadn't missed me after all. "Yeah," I said. "I was camping out and you woke me up. What have you got here?"

"I don't know."

"Pedestrian?"

Estelle played her flashlight over the area where the victim's body had been. "Let me show you." We walked to the guardrail. "We have a single victim, as far as we can tell right now. Haven't found anyone else. The gentleman who owns the Buick up where you parked saw her first and used his CB radio. The owner of the all-night convenience store up at the head of the canyon heard him and called me. She was lying right here when I arrived. Les Cook with the Forest Service had stopped before I got here. He's over there working traffic.

He said the same thing. She was lying here, part under the rail."

"Sounds like she got hit pretty hard," I said. "A little more and she'd have been down in the rocks and probably wouldn't have been found for days."

"I think that's where she was," Estelle said. "Look here." She motioned for me to bend over the steel guardrail. "Don't step over yet, though," she added as she saw me make a move to do just that. "See right here?" She pointed and held the light close. On the back flange of the rail were bloody fingerprints. "I think she grabbed here to help pull herself up to the rail."

"Is there blood on the bottom of the flange?" I asked. "If she grabbed ahold, her thumbprint would be on the bottom."

Estelle crouched down low and ducked her head. The bottom of the rail was about eighteen inches off the ground, and she played the beam of the flashlight along the steel surface. "There's blood opposite," she said. "Look here."

"I'll take your word for it." If I had scrunched down in that position, I'd never have gotten up. I turned the light to shine on the slope. The rocky incline was just highway fill, and the scuff marks that might be made by someone crawling up the slope would be hard to see . . . especially by flashlight. Undaunted, Estelle stepped over the rail and examined the ground.

"Lots of blood," she said, and she worked her way carefully down the steep slope, keeping her own feet off to one side of the track she was following. "I think she crawled up here. See the dislodged rocks?"

"You need to look at it in daylight."

"I'll take a set of pictures now. Can I get you to hold the light so I can focus?"

"Of course." I knew Estelle's affinity for photography. When she worked for my county, our film-processing bill had been astronomical. But her results were equally so.

Before she went to work, we made the highway a little safer. I walked south and stabbed a flare in the centerline, and then we repositioned the cones, Estelle's county car, and my Blazer.

11

After taking down what information we needed from the man in the Buick, we let him go. He didn't waste any time. The timber cop agreed to stay for a while and manage traffic . . . I think two cars had gone by since I had arrived.

Estelle set up her 35mm camera and took a series of photos of the slope, each picture downhill from the last, while I held the flashlight so she could focus. The electronic flash was like a lightning bolt in the narrow canyon.

When she was satisfied, she said, "We can take a close look come dawn, but this way, if it rains or something, we're covered a little. Look here."

I did and could see that the blood trail turned at the base of the steepest part of the embankment and then angled away to the south.

"The way she was broken up, moving that far took some set of nerves," I said.

Estelle took more pictures. Together we followed the trail. The girl had crawled, apparently pulling herself forward with only her hands and sheer will, for fifty yards along the base of the embankment before trying to climb it. The trail led back through a thick stand of grass, and we saw the crushed stems left by the girl's passing. The grass gave way to a jumble of boulders, and a smear of blood on one of them showed us where the girl had slid off the rock into the grass.

"Christ," I said. Estelle muttered something and reloaded her camera. She started up on the rocks, and I said quickly, "Watch for the goddamned snakes." She ignored the warning.

"I think this is it," Estelle said.

" 'It' what?"

Estelle played the flashlight on the rocks. From where she stood, the highway embankment up to the guardrails was a seventy- or eighty-degree slope. "The blood ends here," she said. "At least I can't see any more."

"Nothing coming down from the roadway?"

"Not that I can see. Shine your light right up here." She indicated the slope. I did so, and she snapped more pictures. "I don't see any scuff marks," she added and then climbed

12

down to where I stood. "I want to climb up the embankment over there, where we won't be apt to obliterate anything. Maybe there are marks up by the highway."

We made the climb, with me huffing and puffing. There were no marks on the highway shoulder, nothing on the steel rail. The only marks on the highway's road surface itself were two short skid marks, about twenty yards south of where Estelle's patrol car was parked. The marks were straight and centered in the lane, as if someone had spiked the brakes without swerving. The marks were short—the vehicle hadn't been traveling fast.

"They might not even be related," I said.

"And probably aren't," Estelle said. She took pictures anyway.

"So what do you think?" I asked as she put the camera gear back in the trunk of her car.

"I just don't know, sir. I really don't. It looks like she was struck and knocked over the rail back there, maybe hit so hard she flew over it, and landed on the rocks. Then she crawled to where we found her. That's all I can imagine." She frowned.

"Maybe," I said. "But if someone gets nailed by a car hard enough to toss 'em down a goddamned cliff onto rocks, I can't believe they'd survive, much less be able to crawl so far."

"That's what bothers me," Estelle said. "Maybe we'll be able to piece something together when we have the medical report."

"She didn't have any identification?"

"None."

"Terrific." I looked at my watch. It was already quarter of five. "What now?"

"I want to walk down along the road and see if I come up with anything. And then up the other way. By then it'll be dawn and we can see what we missed."

"What do you want me to do?"

"You're on vacation, sir."

"Pretend I'm not. I had a couple hours of vacation yesterday. That was probably enough."

13

Estelle smiled and shook her head. "Maybe you'd go down to San Estevan, where they took the girl. She'll go to the clinic there first and no doubt be transferred to Albuquerque. You might be able to find something out there."

I nodded. "Invitation for dinner still on for tonight?"

"Of course." She slammed the trunk closed. "By then this'll be all wrapped up."

Estelle Reyes-Guzman wasn't wrong too often.

3

B Y   T H E time I reached the public health clinic in San Estevan, the victim had been airlifted to Albuquerque. The EMTs in the ambulance had been quick-witted and efficient. They knew that the extent of the girl's injuries was more than the clinic could handle. The helicopter air ambulance, a Bell Jet Ranger, had been dispatched from the city and made the roundtrip flight before I left the mountain.

As I drove into the village at six in the morning, San Estevan was beginning the rooster and barking dog stage of awakening. I drove past the Catholic retreat complex north of the village and caught sight of one friar or monk or whatever he was, as he crossed from one white adobe building to another, toiletry kit in hand.

A hundred yards beyond and on the opposite side of the road was a National Park Service historic site, the restoration of Gualate Ruin, a two-story stone structure that I'd heard was one of the dozens of outliers for the major ruin at Chaco Canyon to the west.

None of the feds were up yet, nor was there life stirring at the Forest Service District Office, a low, flat building tucked in the cottonwoods where the state highway turned away from the river and into the village.

No more than two dozen houses, scattered here and there across the narrow valley, made up the ancient village of San Estevan. Originally, the town had sprung up on the edge of the Indian pueblo, a mixture of clergy, traders, and farmers.

A few of the houses were massive, with adobe walls a yard thick and large courtyards—architecture that said there'd been some rich times in the valley.

But the inevitable was happening. The village was just outside the pueblo's reservation, and so the valley was salted now with crackerbox shacks and trailers, bright aluminum mobile homes insulting the stolid, ancient adobes as city folk established their weekend camps and "ranchettes," as the realtors say.

If I drove a thousand yards south of the village's gas station, south of the modern clutter and detritus of seasonal residents, I could imagine that a century had been peeled away.

The pueblo, one of the state's smallest, was neat and uniformly reddish-brown. Burnt sienna adobes with mud ovens in every yard, neat stacks of piñon and juniper firewood behind every dwelling, narrow brown lanes packed hard as cement between the houses, all leading down to the brown-trunked cottonwoods that screened the river from view.

The demarcation between pueblo land and private land beginning with the village of San Estevan was as obvious as if there were a solid wall between the two.

I passed the Texaco station and, where the highway jogged another right angle turn, the combination of Dairy Queen and general store. Just beyond, a group of three trailers was parked willy-nilly to form a compound filled with wrecked car and truck carcasses, and beyond those was a fenced pasture where two horses grazed themselves fat.

Remembering Estelle's directions, I looked for the sign and found it nearly camouflaged by purple bee-weed. Below the sign for the San Estevan Clinic, United States Public Health Service, an arrow pointed to a graveled lane.

I pulled into the clinic's driveway and parked beside a blue Isuzu Trooper with Posadas County plates. No matter where

16

they moved in the state, Estelle and Francis Guzman would carry that tag until it rusted to pieces . . . a gentle reminder of their home to the south.

Only one other vehicle was in the lot, an older model GMC pickup—maybe a '55 or '56. It was no collector's item, though, just an aging, battered work truck.

I crushed out my cigarette and walked inside the building. The clinic was cramped, with a twelve-by-twelve waiting room, a tiny cell for the receptionist, and a narrow hallway that led back to the treatment rooms. I guessed there were two of those at the most. I heard a metal pan clatter and voices, and then an Indian woman stuck her head out of one of the examining room doors. She saw me and held up a hand with one finger raised.

"I'll be right out," she said and disappeared again. I turned, looked around the waiting room, and saw universal doctor's office decorations . . . aging magazines, a few children's books. A large Ojo de Dios woven out of gaudy yarn hung on one wall and a sand painting of an Indian dancer in an awkward pose on another.

Across the room on the west wall was a framed state map with a large water stain rumpling all of Colfax, Mora, San Miguel, and Guadalupe counties. Beside the map was a framed aerial photograph of a mountain in fall colors, aspens aflame. It was no local mountain, of course . . . probably one from Colorado or Wyoming—wherever the postcard artist had been able to find a nice, conical, generic mountain with no towns, powerlines, or highways to mar the picture.

I stepped to the window and looked out at chamiso, cactus, and rocks.

"May I help you?"

I turned quickly. The nurse had a pencil and metal clipboard poised at the ready. She was older than I had first thought. Steel gray was beginning to temper her ebony hair, tied back tightly in a bun. Her black eyes regarded me calmly from a broad, flat face whose flawless skin was like burnished walnut. I read the name tag on her white blouse and wondered

17

how long Mary Vallo had been an R.N. She might have been forty years old or sixty-five.

"Good morning, Mrs. Vallo," I said. "I'm Bill Gastner, undersheriff of Posadas County, down in the southern part of the state. I've been assisting Deputy Guzman with an accident investigation this morning." I started the standard smoker's fumble for a cigarette and thought better of it. "I wondered if I could talk with Dr. Guzman for a minute, if he's not tied up."

"Surely," Mary Vallo said. "Come on back." She led the way down the hall, and in one small cubbyhole I saw a coffee maker just beginning to drip. Sharp-eyed Mary saw my glance and said, "I just started it. I'll get you a cup as soon as it's ready."

"Wonderful," I said, feeling about three hours overdue for my first morning caffeine buzz.

The examining room we entered was small and the scene of considerable recent action. Mary Vallo resumed her labors, at that moment cleaning the spatters from the front of the portable X ray unit. Francis Guzman was sitting at a table by the window awash with paperwork. His white smock was white in small spots only. He glanced up, not eager to move.

"Well, I'll be damned!" the young physician exclaimed, and he pushed himself away from the table, extending a hand to me at the same time. "You're about the last person I expected to see at this hour. How have you been, Sheriff?"

"Just fine, except that wife of yours has been putting me to work." At his puzzled expression, I added, "The accident this morning with the girl pedestrian happened just above where I was camping. And you know the way old cops are. I couldn't help snooping."

"Up at Steamboat, you mean?"

"Yes. And how is the girl?"

Guzman shook his head and sat down again. He was six inches taller than my five-eight and built like an athlete, but now he looked like he'd just finished the pentathlon.

"I don't think she's going to make it, Sheriff. She has about

18

eight broken bones, including her skull. She's hemorrhaging internally as well as suffering a dozen gashes and lacerations. She was out there a while, you know, before anybody found her. I was surprised she hadn't bled to death."

"And with all that, she still managed to crawl almost a hundred yards," I said and accepted a Styrofoam cup of coffee from Mary Vallo.

"You're kidding."

I shook my head. "The last few yards were up a steep embankment, back up to the highway shoulder. It looked like after she was hit, she ended up on a pile of boulders down by the river. At that point the highway embankment is almost vertical. Since she couldn't crawl up there, she apparently moved in the only direction she could, along the stream in the grass until she reached a spot where she could try for the road again."

"I don't see how that would have been possible," Guzman said. "I really don't." He stood up. "Look at this." He had a set of small X rays and he handed the top one to me.

"We don't have very good equipment, but even so, look at that hip." He traced the fracture with his index finger.

Even I could see the damage. The head of the femur looked like it had been pried off the shaft, taking a chip of the hip socket with it.

"And her right arm was broken in three places. Her left ankle was snapped. There are what look like compressed fractures of two lower vertebrae. And a comminuted fracture of the right parietal."

"What's that?"

He tapped the side of his skull above his ear. "With all that and the bleeding, I can't believe she crawled."

"No one was there to help her that we know of," I said. "Not as far as we've been able to determine. Of course, it's hard to tell. But Estelle's still there and might turn up something."

Francis Guzman leaned forward, hands clasped and forearms resting on his knees. He remained silent, deep in thought.

19

Finally he said, "The other thing that bothers me about her injuries—and I'm no great expert, you understand—what bothers me is that they're not really consistent with being smacked by a car or truck. I know that's what the ambulance attendants told me, but still . . ."

"Meaning?" I sat back, my chair leaning against the wall. I wanted a cigarette, but the "Thank You For Not Smoking" sign was staring me in the face.

"If a car hits you hard enough to do serious damage, to fling you right over a guardrail, there's usually some clue that that's what happened."

"Well, sure." I'd seen hundreds of accident victims in twenty years.

"But there were no paint chips, Sheriff. No chrome. Nothing."

I shrugged. "That happens all the time."

"Maybe. But there were no sharp lacerations, the sort of injury we'd expect from headlights and rims and bumpers or grill parts. And we'd see those in relationship with traumatic fractures and deep tissue bruising."

He paused, then added, "And look at the fractures. Her right hip, Sheriff. The sort of fracture you get in football, when the joint is yanked and wrenched the wrong way. No compression injuries related with the fracture, except minor scrapes. Now, the major lacerations on her broken right arm were contaminated with rocks and dirt. The same thing is true of her broken left ankle."

Guzman was warming up and I let him continue without interruption.

"And see here, on her skull. She took a hell of a rap there. You know what I found in her hair? Besides dirt? Lichen. The stuff that grows on rocks. Flakes of it right in the wound. Her head hit a rock, Sheriff, and hit it hard."

"Well, we know that. That's likely where the other fractures came from . . . or some of them. When she landed on the rocks. She was walking along the highway and got clipped. The impact threw her over the embankment. She tumbled ass over

20

teakettle down into the rocks, breaking who knows what on the way."

Francis Guzman shook his head. "Where did the car hit her?" He stood up and pretended to be walking along the road. "Right hip? She turns and it's her left hip that's facing traffic, not right."

I grimaced. The young doctor had a hell of an imagination. "Come on, Francis. She could have just as easily turned the other way."

"Not likely. And that leg was yanked out of its socket, not impacted."

"So what are you saying happened?"

"I'm not sure, but I'm willing to bet she was never hit by a vehicle of any kind."

"What, then?"

Francis Guzman hesitated. "I think she was thrown over the embankment."

"Oh, you do."

He nodded. "The rest fits that way, too."

"The rest?"

"There was an attempt at rape, Sheriff. I'm sure of that. And what I'd say were deep fingernail gouges on her back, near the base of her neck. Her hands were busted up pretty badly, and I didn't have a chance to check under her fingernails. The M.E. in Albuquerque will do that. And it looks like she was punched hard in the mouth. Right here." He touched the left corner of his own mouth. "Not the sort of injury caused by sharp rocks. But a fist, yes."

I toyed with my empty and crumpled coffee cup. "It's hard to believe the other injuries were caused by sliding down an embankment like that."

"Not if she were thrown from a moving vehicle it's not."

I stared at Guzman incredulously. "Tossed out of the back of a moving pickup truck, you mean? Something like that? Jesus. A hit-and-run I can imagine. But the other?"

Guzman nodded and glanced at his watch. "That's what I

21

think. You've got at least one murder on your hands. I'd bet on it."

"She's not dead yet, Doc."

Guzman looked pained. "No, but her baby is. The young lady was four months pregnant."

4

I STARED at Francis Guzman. He misunderstood my silence and said again, "She was pregnant. Lost the fetus, of course."

"I heard you," I murmured. "Did you know her? Was she from around here?"

"I think that she's been living in the village for about six months to a year." Guzman had gotten to his feet wearily, like a man a decade older than I. With a grunt, he opened the window beside the desk. The air that washed into the room was fresh and tinted with sage.

"Her name's Cecilia Burgess. She didn't have any identification on her when she was brought in last night, but both my nurse and I knew her. I met her about . . . well, four months ago. She came in for a prenatal checkup." Guzman stepped out of the room and then reappeared with the coffeepot. "More?"

"No, thanks. And then you saw her off and on after that?"

"That's right." He smiled but without much humor. "Estelle's got you drawn right into this mess, hasn't she?"

I realized I was grilling the doc as if he were a witness—which he probably would be sooner or later—and as if it were my own investigation, which it certainly wasn't. "Sorry," I said. "Occupational hazard."

"Can't help but be curious," Guzman said and sat down, long legs stretched out in front of him. "There are a lot of answers I'd like, but I'm so damn tired I can't think straight." He grinned. "Estelle's going to bust in here in a few minutes and give me the third degree, so I might as well warm up with you, right?"

"Might as well. I can't help being a nosy old bastard. Who was the girl's husband?"

"She was single."

"Boyfriend, then?"

Guzman shrugged. "I didn't know her that well. I didn't ask, either. She worked some of the time in Garcia's. That's the trading post on the south end of the village. You probably saw it when you drove up."

"The place with all the Indian drums and pottery in the window?" Guzman nodded. I patted myself on the back. Now I knew where I'd seen the girl before. Up on the mountain where Cecilia Burgess had been knocked over the guardrail, the light had been poor—just the spotlights and flashlights. And when the girl had been placed on the gurney, her profile had been visible to me only briefly. But it was enough to stir a memory.

Earlier in the day, before I'd started my outdoorsman's hiking act, I'd stopped at Garcia's Trading Post, thinking I might find a birthday present for my oldest daughter, Camile. Odds were good I'd find something that she hadn't seen already in ten department stores near her home in Flint, Michigan.

The polite young lady who'd let me browse without interference through blankets, beads, and jewelry had been Cecilia Burgess. I was sure of it.

"What I mean is that she had the opportunity to see all sorts of people," Guzman continued. "San Estevan is pretty small, but there's still plenty of the young and willing. My nurse said she'd heard Burgess had been seeing a guy from on up the canyon."

Guzman turned and called Mary Vallo, who'd gone back

out front. When she appeared in the doorway, Guzman asked, "Who was that kid you said Cecilia Burgess was seeing up north?"

"I don't know his name," Mary Vallo said, keeping her voice and facial expression that wonderful stone neutral that serves Indians as such a perfect barrier when they don't want their minds read.

"Yeah, but wasn't he the one who was living up at the hot springs?"

"I heard that he was," Mary said.

Guzman turned to me. "There's a little group of leftover hippies who camp out about nine months of the year in the National Forest, up behind the hot springs. They drift in and out of town, work a little, panhandle a little, and generally make the tourists nervous. I heard Cecilia Burgess was hanging around with one of them. I never saw him."

"He didn't wash much," Mary Vallo said evenly, and when I glanced up, surprised at her opinionating, all I saw was her back as she retreated back down the hall to the front office.

I chuckled. "Terrific. And hippies? I thought they were twenty years extinct."

Guzman grinned. "Maybe that's the wrong word. But whatever you want to call 'em, then. Squatters. My father used to call them *greñudos hediondos,* but then anyone who drove a van without being a plumber was suspect to him."

"Is there a colony of them up there?"

"No," Guzman said. "Not as far as I know. Just a few individuals, kids who like to spend the summer sacked out under the stars. Some of them live in tents . . . some just throw a bedroll under the overhang of a rock." He spread his hands. "It's just some place to stay where they aren't harassed. The only time I've ever heard that the Forest Service forced anyone out of there was when the fire danger got too high."

"Like now?" I asked, remembering the crunch of the needles under my feet.

"This is wet compared to six years ago, according to some of the locals. Ask Mary. I've heard that back then the state cops wouldn't even let you park along the shoulder of the highway."

I fell silent for a moment, deep in thought. "That's quite a hike, from town up there."

"About six miles," Guzman said.

I shrugged. "If you're young, I guess that isn't so bad. Maybe that's what she was doing . . . hoofing it on up there for a little midnight nookey. Did she hang around with anyone else?"

"No, but as I said, I don't keep a census. You might find some other answers if you check with the Department of Social Services. The girl might have filed for child assistance. And I don't know where the other child is or even *if* it is."

"What other child?"

Guzman frowned and grimaced. "I keep forgetting." He flipped open the manila folder on his desk, and I wondered what else he'd forgotten. After a minute he said, "This isn't the first child she's had." He held up his hands. "I don't know what the story is. Or even if the child, assuming it lived, is here in San Estevan."

"But she did have one."

"Yes, she did."

"Could you tell how long ago? How old the child would be?"

Guzman shook his head. "I'd guess it wasn't more than four years or so."

I started to fiddle for another cigarette and then changed my mind. "So it's possible there's a little kid roaming around somewhere wondering what the hell's happened to his life."

"Possible," Guzman said, and he held up his hands again in surrender. I was about to shoot another question at the tired young physician when I heard the front door open and then the sound of enough boots on the tiles to herald an invasion.

Estelle Reyes-Guzman appeared in the doorway, and behind her were two other uniformed deputies, a state trooper, the same Forest Service employee I'd seen up on the mountain, and one other man in plainclothes. It was that man who

26

pushed his way past all the elbows and gun butts and crossed the office to pump my hand.

"Goddamn, look what crawled in!" Castillo County Sheriff Pat Tate bellowed, and I stood up, hand still locked in his beefy paw. I'd tipped more than a few brews with Pat at law confabs all over the state through the years. "Estelle said you was up this way. How the hell have you been?"

"Not bad," I said.

"No, really," Pat said, squinting at me like I was lying to him. "The heart and all? That's fixed up now?"

"All fixed up. And you?"

"Fine, until I got jerked out of bed. Hell of a note. Let me introduce you, here." He jerked a thumb at first one deputy and then the other. "Paul Garcia and Al Martinez. I think you know Al, don't you?"

I nodded and shook hands. "It's been a while," I said, and Martinez grinned. About six years before, he and I had been involved in a particularly messy prisoner extradition and transfer from my county to Castillo. I was surprised Martinez could still smile when he saw me. As I remember, he'd ended up having to drive the prisoner home in a patrol car that reeked of vomit and it was a six-hour trip. And that was about the best part of the whole deal.

I didn't know the state policeman, a hatchet-faced man of thirty-five or so with eyes like ice chips. The trooper, Bobby Padgett, shook my hand impassively, since Sheriff Tate hadn't told him who I was yet. I didn't figure him for the sort of man who shed any warmth until he had to.

"And you met Les Cook up on the mountain," Tate said, and I shook hands with the pine tree warden. "Gentlemen, this is Bill Gastner, undersheriff of Posadas County, about a thousand miles south of here, down in the frijole district."

Tate looked pleased with himself, stepped back, and put his hands on his hips. He was not a particularly big man, maybe five feet seven and 170 pounds. But he managed to look aggressive with his close-cropped and thinning hair, bulbous

27

nose, and stout jaw. "So, you got this goddamned awful affair solved for us?"

I shook my head and sat down again. Estelle had been using her husband's shoulder as a leaning post, but now she was no longer in the room. I assumed she had slipped out front, either for coffee or maybe to talk with nurse Mary Vallo.

Knowing Estelle, she had thoroughly briefed Sheriff Tate. But she'd still know ten times more than he did. As politic as she was, she'd let him lead the way because he was the boss. She'd done the same with me in previous years, making me and the department look good.

"This is a goddamned mess," Tate said and found himself a chair. He looked sideways at Guzman. "Did the transfer to Presbyterian go without a hitch?"

Guzman nodded. "She was losing it, though. Dr. Bailey rode down in the ambulance with her."

"The girl's not gonna make it?"

"No, I don't think so. Short of a miracle."

"That's what Estelle said up on the hill." Tate sat forward on the very edge of the chair, one hand on each knee. He lifted one hand to rub his whiskers. "Estelle said she thinks it was murder."

I looked at Francis Guzman and wondered how Estelle had jumped to that conclusion without the medical evidence her husband had gathered.

"That's why she called me up here before the roosters. Hell, otherwise it's just another car-pedestrian accident, and in Indian country they're every other day."

"Had Burgess been drinking?" I asked Guzman.

"Not enough to smell," he said. "I'm sure the medical examiner will order a full workup, though."

"Well then," I said, "the deputy isn't alone in seeing this one as murder. So does the doc here. Tell them what you told me."

Guzman ran through his findings without wasting a word, and Tate listened without interruption.

When Guzman finished, Tate asked to see the X rays. "Huh," he said, standing in front of the lighted viewer.

"That's the sort of damage you'd get in a car wreck, where your knee is slammed up against the dashboard, isn't it? The big leg bone drives backward and smashes the hip joint all to hell."

"Exactly," Guzman said. He shot Tate a look that said he was impressed as hell at the sheriff's acumen. "Or from a very bad fall. Rock climbers, for instance."

"Estelle!" Tate called. He turned to one of the deputies. "She's out front. Get her in here, will you?" He turned back to the X ray. "Knee damage?"

Guzman traced a faint line with his finger. "Fractured patella. Some torsion injury. Lacerations."

"That's consistent, then."

"With a fall," I said. "Not with being hit by a car."

"Right."

Estelle came in, coffee in one hand, cookie in the other. "These are out front if you want some," she said, but Tate's mind wasn't on breakfast yet. "Look at this X ray," he said. "Look at that leg."

Estelle did so, then turned to her husband. "Were the neck scratches consistent with fingernails?"

"Yes. I'd say so."

"And I started thinking about the way her clothing was torn," Estelle said.

"What do you mean?" Tate asked.

"A fall down a slope doesn't tear underclothing or the neck of a blouse. Not like that."

"All the girl's clothing went to Albuquerque?" Tate asked Guzman, and the young doctor nodded. To Estelle, Tate said, "You might give the M.E. a buzz and put him on the alert. It might help him find what you need. Make sure he doesn't miss anything." Tate looked out the door.

I could see the other officers clustered around the coffeepot. The trooper was standing in the hall, his back to us.

Tate said, "This mess happened on Forest Service turf, so you keep them informed." He took a deep breath and narrowed his eyes at Estelle. "I'm going to dump this one in your lap, for a couple reasons. Most important, I'm not sure a small, closemouthed community like this one is going to react positively if a whole brigade of lawmen descends on them, tearing the place up and sticking their noses where they maybe don't belong. It's a hell of a lot easier just to shrug and say, 'No se,' than to cooperate with the government. Do you see it that way, Bill?"

"Every time," I said. "And if you get about four agencies trying to work together, forget it."

Tate grunted agreement. "If you need anything, just call. I'm going to assign Paul Garcia to you for a few days. He needs experience, and you can work in plainclothes." He pointed a stubby finger directly between Estelle Reyes-Guzman's dark eyes and added, "And don't you decide to get heroic on me. When it comes time for an arrest, you call me first. Do you hear me?"

"Of course, sir," Estelle said quietly.

"Good." Tate turned around and grinned at me. "How long are you staying up in these parts?"

"I'll probably drive back tomorrow or the next day."

"You mean you're not going to stick around and see the action?"

I grimaced. "Come on, Sheriff. Estelle doesn't need any help from me. And I'm on vacation, remember? The last thing I need is a busman's holiday. There's already been too much excitement around here for me. All I want is the home-cooked dinner I was promised, and then I'm on my way."

Tate glanced at Estelle as if to say, "You cook, too?" but had the good grace not to. Instead he turned, extended a hand to Guzman, and said, "Doc, can we buy you some breakfast?"

Guzman shook his head. "No, thanks."

Tate then took me by the arm like a comrade of old and ushered me toward the door. "Let's give the man his office back and find us some breakfast burritos. Then I need to get back to the city. Estelle, you need to show Paul your plush office and get him set up."

I should have been flattered that Pat Tate wanted my com-

30

pany, but I knew damn well that breakfast with the sheriff was going to be reminiscing—one war story after another until we'd both drunk enough coffee to ruin a kidney. By then half the morning would be shot.

That was an agonizing thought, because I'd been watching Estelle Reyes-Guzman's face during the past few minutes and wanted more than anything else to hear what was on her mind.

5

"DO YOU feel like taking a short walk?" Estelle Reyes-Guzman asked and I groaned.

"Sure. Why not." There were several good reasons why not. Sheriff Pat Tate had finally taken leave around 10:30 that morning, and I was still bloated from the coffee and raw-mouthed from too many cigarettes. When Tate left, I had remained at Bobby's Cafe.

Earlier I had made arrangements to meet Estelle there when she'd finished her errands. The cramped, dimly lighted eatery was across the street from Garcia's Trading Post, and it had been interesting to watch the traffic come and go. In a common enough display of poor sense, when noon rolled around I'd ordered a "Burrito Grande" special for lunch.

I had just finished eating when Estelle's county car swung into the cafe's parking lot and pulled to a stop beside my Blazer.

As she entered the small dining room, I waved her to a seat. That's when she hit me with the invitation for exercise.

"Where are we walking to?" I asked.

Estelle looked at the big plate in front of me and the scattered remains of the lunch. "What was that?"

"It was too much, that's what it was. Burrito Grande I think they call it. And you're as evasive as ever. Where are we walking to?"

"I'd like to hike up to the hot springs camp."

"To talk with Cecilia Burgess's boyfriend?"

"You heard about him?"

I nodded and looked at the bill for lunch. If food that good had been that cheap down in Posadas, I would have weighed 700 pounds. I fished out a tip. "Your hubby knew about him. I asked Francis if the Burgess girl had any other romantic flames besides the hippie. He didn't know."

Estelle nodded vigorously. "She does. Or did. I talked with Mary Vallo . . . Francis's nurse?"

"I met her." I tucked the tip under the plate and stood up. "Tell me on the way. If I sit here any longer, I'll go sound asleep."

"Mary's born and raised here. She knows every living soul, I think. Anyway, there were some rumors going around that really upset some of the older folks. They'd talk with Mary at the clinic. Apparently Cecilia Burgess was spending some time with Father Nolan Parris. That's what the *solteronas* told Mary."

"Who's Parris?" I paid the bill, and we stepped outside into the bright sunshine.

"He's in retreat. At the Servants of the Paraclete. You might have noticed the enclave just north of the Forest Service office?" I nodded and she added, "Parris and Burgess were seen together on several occasions."

"Whoopee, Holmes," I said dryly. "Maybe they're cousins. Maybe a thousand other possibilities. Maybe Cecilia Burgess went to the good father for confession. Are the little old lady gossips assuming that there's an affair going on? That's pretty thin, Estelle."

"I'm just telling you what Mary Vallo told me. It's another angle." She nodded at my Blazer. "Let's drop that off at my house."

I followed her car north until, just beyond the gas station, she turned off on a lane between two irrigated cornfields. A

33

quarter-mile farther on, tucked under two massive ancient cottonwoods, was a tiny adobe. Estelle pulled into the driveway and gestured for me to park close to the wire fence. Judging from the outside, the house had four rooms at most. But it was neat and clean, and the nearest noisy railroad or interstate was seventy-five miles away. It would be peaceful as a tomb at night.

"Cute place," I said as I settled into the county car.

"It's cheap," Estelle said. "Until Francis and I decide what we want to do this fall."

"Do?"

Estelle shrugged. "We might not want to spend the winter here. The house has just a couple of those little wall heaters . . . and they're not much good."

"I don't imagine either one of you is home much."

"No. Especially not this week. But he's always said he wanted to practice in a tiny village."

"He got his wish. This is hardly Denver." We rode silently for a few minutes, and I watched civilization thin as we drew away from the village. "How do you like it here?"

"Interesting," she said. "It's quite an experience being the only cop in town. You wouldn't believe some of the domestic disputes I've been called to."

"I think I would. What do the *solteronas* think?"

Estelle grinned. "About me, you mean?"

"Uh huh. If the old maids are upset at the idea of a woman talking to a priest, what must they think about a female deputy sheriff?" She didn't answer right away, and I added, "Has there ever been one around here?"

She shook her head. "I don't think so."

"I imagine that takes some adjustment." I stretched to ease the seat belt tension on my full stomach. "They'll get used to it, like anything else. And in time, they'll all wonder how the hell they ever did without."

"I don't know," she said. "My mother isn't used to the idea yet."

I knew Felipina Reyes pretty well. The old woman, a widow

34

for twenty years, lived alone in Tres Santos, a tiny village thirty miles south of the U.S.–Mexican border.

When Estelle had worked for me in Posadas, she was only an hour's drive north from her mother, but to Felipina Reyes, her daughter might as well have worked on the moon.

And ay! To be carrying around a revolver as an *agente del Alguacil Mayor de un contado en los Estados Unidos!* Double ay.

"So what else did you find out this morning?" I asked.

"Well, I talked with Orlando Garcia."

"Who's he?"

"He owns Garcia's Trading Post, right across from where you were eating."

"Son of a gun. I never saw your car over there."

Estelle grinned briefly and left me hanging. Maybe she could go invisible; I don't know. "Garcia had a lot to say about Cecilia's boyfriend up at the springs. Not much of it good."

Before she had time to elaborate on all the juicy particulars, we reached the turnoff. She swung the patrol car into the campground below Steamboat Rock and then drove to the far end of the parking lot. A grove of runty Douglas firs would provide enough shade to keep the Ford from turning into an oven.

The trail east to the hot springs followed a small stream that ran into Isidro Creek. We walked slowly in deference to the discomfort in my gut. After a couple of minutes, I felt better. Maybe there was something to this exercise business. I even had enough breath for a question.

"What's the boyfriend's name? Did Garcia know that? Mary Vallo never said."

Estelle nodded. "H. T. Finn."

"H.T.? I wonder if his mother named him Huck and he couldn't stand it."

"Maybe. Garcia didn't know what the H.T. stood for."

"How old a guy is this Finn?"

"Orlando wasn't sure. Older than thirty, though. And that sort of surprised me."

I took a deep breath. "Hiking this trail will keep him in shape, that's for sure."

We skirted the buttress of Steamboat, a massive volcanic plug that rose vertically from the canyon and towered upward for nearly 300 feet. The trail was well worn and marked further with a considerable collection of refuse. Beer and pop cans, gum wrappers, cigarette packs, diapers . . . you name it.

After a hundred yards the trail forked and the Forest Service sign announced that the hot springs were three-quarters of a mile to the left, with Quebrada Mesa a mile and a half to the right. Of course I noticed morosely that the trail to the hot springs angled steeply uphill.

We trudged a hundred yards and I stopped to catch my breath. "Are you all right?" Estelle asked.

"I'm fine," I gasped. "Just fat. And I smoke too much."

Estelle grinned. She gestured ahead and said sympathetically, "I think it levels out just up ahead." It did, but not nearly enough.

The first sign of human encampment was a site tucked under a limestone overhang, with the recess sheltered on either end of the overhang by mixed oak and aspen. Smoke from camp fires had blackened the overhanging rock, and I guessed that if a scientist could find a way to section that smoke residue, there'd be traces dating back hundreds, maybe thousands of years.

It would have been a favored spot for any hunter passing through, from yesterday's hippie back to Pueblo Indians before him and then back to whoever came before the ice age.

A sleeping bag was rolled up tightly and stuffed well back under the rock. Estelle crouched down and pulled out the bag. A quick examination produced only a well-worn flashlight and a half roll of toilet paper.

"They travel light," I said. Estelle pushed the bag back where it had been. "Are there other sites on up ahead?"

"Yes," she said. "That's where most of them are. Right by the springs."

Another fifteen minutes answered my question. The hot springs formed a series of stair-stepped pools, nestled in a grassy swale. The overflow burbled downhill, forming a tiny rivulet not more than two feet wide. Thickly timbered saddlebacks rose steeply on either side of the swale. Any wind would have to do some serious corkscrewing to reach campers down in that protected place.

A gigantic boulder rested like a granite house near the first pool. And I would have missed him had Estelle not stopped suddenly. I followed her gaze and saw the young man sitting on top of that boulder.

He was sitting Buddha-fashion, legs crossed, and wearing only a pair of cutoff jeans. As we stepped closer, I saw he had a book open in his lap. He watched us approach without any obvious interest or movement. When we were a dozen feet away, we stopped. I had to crane my neck back to look up at him and felt foolish.

"Good afternoon," I said.

"Hello," he replied. He was so scrawny his ribs looked like they might pop through his skin. Long snow-colored hair hung down to his shoulders, and even if he'd given up most of society's conventions, he certainly hadn't lost his comb. His hair was placed just so . . . like he'd finished giving it the hundred strokes with the comb moments before.

"Beautiful afternoon, isn't it?" Estelle said, but the boy's only reply was a slight toss of his head to move a fall of hair farther from his eyes. "Are you H. T. Finn?"

"No."

"Is he still camping up here?"

The boy's eyes darted off to one side, to glance at the big tent that was pitched up at the head of the swale. He was a miserable sentry, and I figured that he'd lie, too. He did. "Nope."

"Do you know where he went?"

The boy shook his head.

At that moment we both heard the voices, first that of a small child, then the faint mumble of an adult's reply. I turned and looked north, past the tent and on up the saddleback. Two figures were walking slowly down through the timber, and by squinting I could make out a man and a small child, hand in hand.

"That's maybe him?" I said, ignoring the boy on the rock.

"Could be," Estelle said quietly. "Or maybe just hikers."

"She's a little small to hike so far from the parking lot," I muttered when I could see the child more clearly.

Estelle turned and looked intently at the boy up on the rock. He'd closed the book at least. "Is that Finn?" she asked, and her voice carried some authority. The boy finally nodded, and Estelle turned back to me. "Well, technically, Finn isn't camping at the moment, just as his friend here said. He's hiking. Let's go have a chat with him."

6

H . T . F I N N nodded at me without much interest, but for him Estelle Reyes-Guzman was another story. He eyed her as if he were choosing another member for his harem.

Normal interest was certainly excusable, since she wasn't wearing the starched and quasi-military duds that sheriffs' departments favor . . . and those, along with a wide Sam Browne belt loaded with hardware, take most of the sex out of the figure.

But Finn's gaze started at Estelle's running shoes and drifted slowly upward, pausing here and there until I was ready to slug him.

Finn was no kid. I guessed him to be within shouting distance of forty. He wore blue jeans torn at each knee and a gray T-shirt. On the T-shirt was one of those fish symbols with the words JESUS CARES stenciled underneath.

He was fit. The T-shirt stretched over a wide chest and powerful shoulders, with no bulge at the waistline. And he was either tough or heavily into pain, because he was barefoot. I winced at the thought of walking over the limestone-studded forest floor without something to protect my soles.

I glanced at the child . . . a toddler, almost. She was a pretty tyke with golden hair parted down the center and pulled back into a thick ponytail. Big, trusting blue eyes watched Estelle without blinking.

Her red jumper needed a washing, but at least she was wearing shoes. Her hand was tightly clutched in his. She edged closer to his leg and started to back around behind him when she saw me looking at her.

"Mr. Finn?" Estelle asked.

"Who are you?" Finn grinned, still letting his eyes drift.

"I'm Deputy Estelle Reyes-Guzman, Castillo County Sheriff's Department. This is Undersheriff Bill Gastner."

I didn't bother to correct Estelle's implication that I was on home turf. Finn wasn't impressed anyway. "You have some identification, I assume?" he asked, still grinning. At least he had enough control over his hormones to raise his eyes from Estelle's chest to her face. The grin was only from the nose down—his gray eyes were void.

"Yes." Estelle pulled out her wallet and held it up so he could see her badge and commission. He glanced at it briefly, then looked at me. He raised an eyebrow.

"Pretend that I'm a civilian," I said. If I had to arrest this son of a bitch, that would be soon enough to show him anything. His eyes narrowed.

"Mr. Finn, we'd like to talk with you for a few minutes," Estelle said.

"So talk," Finn replied. "This is National Forest land. They let anyone in." He flashed that humorless grin again.

"I understand that you knew Cecilia Burgess?"

Finn hesitated only a second before nodding. "Yes. I knew her."

"She came up here from time to time?"

"Of course." He said that as if he thought us both simple.

"When was the last time you saw her?"

Finn pursed his lips. "Alive, you mean?" His bald-faced response startled me. "Before last night?"

"You knew that she was involved in a pedestrian accident last night?" Estelle asked.

"Yes."

40

I glanced down at the little girl. She had transferred her grip to the seam of Finn's jeans. And she had given up on us as something interesting to watch. The thumb of her other hand was jammed in her mouth as she watched a stinkbug make its way through the pine needles. All the adult talk was lost on her.

When I looked back up, Finn had clasped his hands together, resting them lightly on his chest like a priest.

"She's still alive, Mr. Finn. At least she was this morning, when she was transferred to Albuquerque." Finn accepted that with a slight nod and spread his hands apart slightly as if to say, "So you say."

"How did you hear about the accident?" I asked.

Finn lifted only one hand this time and pointed downhill at the youth on the rock. He did it slowly and gracefully, again reminding me of a priest, maybe extending the consecrated bread during Eucharist. "Robert was in the village this morning."

"How did he hear about it?"

"You'd have to ask him," Finn said. "But in a village so small news travels rapidly, doesn't it?"

Estelle nodded as if she hadn't thought of that on her own. "How long had you known Burgess, Mr. Finn?"

Finn took a deep breath and gazed off into the distance. "Several months," he said finally. "What's today?"

"August 5."

"Well then, let's see. I first met her just before Christmas. So I guess that's seven or eight months."

"Do you know who else she associated with? On a regular basis?"

Finn looked irritated for the first time. "I have no idea. What she did down in the village was her business."

"And when she was up here?" I asked.

"What do you mean?"

"You and she were close?"

Finn glanced down at the little girl. The tyke had squatted and was nudging the stink beetle with a tiny index finger. The

41

beetle thrust its hind end up in empty threat. "Of course," Finn said after some hesitation. "Otherwise she wouldn't have come up here."

I decided to try a long shot, based on my conversation with Francis Guzman. "Is this her other child?"

"I beg your pardon?"

I knew damn well that Finn had heard me just fine, but I repeated anyway. "Is this child her daughter?"

"No," Finn said immediately. "Ruth is my niece. She spends the summer with me." He smiled faintly. "The city is no place for a child."

I had no argument with that logic. Estelle Reyes-Guzman turned slightly so she could see Robert of the Rock. "Did your friend say anything to you about hearing how the accident happened?"

The smug expression returned to Finn's face. "You'd have to ask him."

This time Estelle came as close to snapping as she ever did. "No, Mr. Finn. I asked what he said to you, sir."

"Nothing, Deputy," Finn said, one eyebrow raised. "If you want to find out what he knows, talk to him."

"We'll do that on the way down. And by the way, do you have some kind of identification with you?"

"Identification?"

"That's right."

"Certainly." He pulled a wallet from his right hip pocket, rummaged for a moment, and then held out a New Mexico driver's license. Estelle took it, pulled out a small notebook from her hip pocket, and jotted down information. Finn waited patiently until she had finished and handed the document back. "If there's nothing else?"

"Thank you for your time," Estelle said pleasantly. Finn reached down and took the little girl's hand, turning to go back toward the tent.

Before the child could turn, Estelle knelt down so she was looking at her squarely in the eye. "What's your name, honey?" Estelle asked quietly.

42

The tyke hesitated, then responded to Estelle's warm smile. "Daisy," she said with a faint lisp.

"That's a pretty name," Estelle said. She tousled the child's hair and stood up. She smiled at Finn. He frowned, then nodded curtly and led the child back uphill toward the big tent.

"Sweetheart, isn't she?" I said as we strolled down toward the rock. "Finn says her name is Ruth, and she says it's Daisy. And you know something you're not telling me."

"She is a sweetheart," Estelle said. "And I'll bet you twenty bucks that she's Burgess's child. Orlando Garcia knew Cecilia had a child . . . he'd seen her many times. The child used to play in the back room of the store when Cecilia worked there."

"And her name was Daisy," I said. Estelle nodded, and I continued, "So Daisy is her nickname. And maybe Finn's lying, and maybe he's not. How is it your husband never had occasion to meet the child? Here we are wondering about Burgess's other kid and she's right under our noses."

"She was never sick maybe? I don't know."

"You just found about her today? When you talked with Garcia?"

"Yes."

"Then I feel a little better."

"We still have a problem though," Estelle said, then dropped the subject as we approached the rock. Robert had started to move when we were fifty yards away. He pulled on a T-shirt, gathered up the book, and dropped off the backside of the rock as agile as a cat.

"Robert," Estelle said as he appeared on the uphill side of the boulder, "did you either witness yourself, or talk to anyone who did, the accident last night down on the state highway?"

"No."

"You just heard about it in town this morning?"

Robert hesitated for just a fraction of a second. "Yes."

Estelle nodded and glanced at me. "Thanks," she said, and Robert almost said another word but thought better of it. "I think we're finished here," she told me, more for Robert's benefit than mine.

When we were out of earshot, she added, "Blabby kid, isn't he?"

"Yes."

Estelle grinned at my imitation. "I'd be willing to bet another twenty bucks he knows lots more than he lets on."

"He'd have to. And did you happen to notice what else was interesting?"

Estelle frowned, and I felt an unprofessional twinge of pride that I had seen something she hadn't. "What do you mean?"

I stopped and looked back up the trail. "He was wearing a gun."

"Oh, that. Yes, I saw the bulge under his T-shirt when he came around the rock." She twisted around and put a hand on the small of her back, where the gun had been.

"When you asked him if he'd seen the accident, he turned a little to face you. That's when I saw it," I said.

Estelle shrugged. "Probably half the people in New Mexico carry guns." She looked back up the trail. "That's kind of interesting, though. A gun in one hand, a Bible in the other."

"Is that what the book was?"

"Uh huh."

"Couldn't read the title," I said lamely. I concentrated on where I put my feet. It was easier going downhill, but I was top-heavy and needed to watch my step.

"If the child is Cecilia's daughter, it's going to be a mess trying to work through the social services department to get that kid out of the woods," Estelle said. "Paul Garcia is working on finding Burgess's relatives, if there are any. He should have turned something up by the time we get back."

"And if there aren't any?"

"Then we'll have to work a court order of some sort."

I nodded. "You're running on a lot of assumptions."

Estelle held a branch so it wouldn't whip me in the face. "You think she should be living up here? Without her mother?"

44

"She didn't seem to mind."

"No, maybe not. I do though." She stopped and stood for a minute with her hands on her hips, staring off into space. "Do you think that either Finn or Robert knows who tossed Cecilia Burgess?"

"No, I don't. They would have said something if they did."

"That's what I was thinking."

"And by the way," I said, "I hate to tell you your job, but you didn't I.D. Robert of the Rock. It might have been handy to know who the hell he is."

"I know who he is," Estelle replied and started off on the trail once more. I had to puff a little to catch up.

7

THE sun rolled down the edge of Chuparrosa Mesa west of San Estevan, and the wash of evening light blushed the sandstone layers below the rimrock into a dozen hues. The ceramic chimes beside the Guzmans' front door hung motionless.

I exhaled and watched the plume of smoke curl through the chimes, to fan out and then disappear into the *savinos,* the peeled and smooth juniper poles that lay diagonally across the vigas to form the small porch roof. I closed the file folder and tipped my chair back until I could lean against the adobe wall.

"Robert Arajanian," I said and tapped my index finger on the cover of the folder. "And you say that the guy who owns the trading post—Orlando Garcia—he knows him?"

Estelle Reyes-Guzman returned from the kitchen and handed me a mug of coffee. "Yes, he knew him by name. He'd had the opportunity to cash a couple of checks for the kid."

"What kind of checks?"

"The only one he remembered for sure was one made out to Cecilia Burgess. It was her tax refund check. For just a few dollars, as far as Garcia remembers. Burgess had signed it over to Arajanian. Orlando Garcia didn't seem to approve much. I got the impression that he thought Cecilia Burgess was wasting her time with both Arajanian and Finn."

I opened the folder once more. "That seems to be a generally held view around here. Odd that she signed the check to the kid instead of her boyfriend Finn. Maybe the trio shares everything." I read the file. "And Arajanian has quite a record."

The folder had been delivered from Albuquerque earlier that afternoon by a deputy. It had been on Estelle's desk when we returned from the hot springs, and it made interesting reading.

Robert Arajanian had experimented with the law when he was just fourteen . . . an assault charge filed by the parents of another high school student. I noticed the other youngster involved had been seventeen—either he'd been small for his age or a complete wimp. Or young Robert had been spectacularly aggressive. Less than a year later a charge of vehicular homicide had landed Robert Arajanian in a youth detention home for two years.

"Interesting that he wasn't drunk for the vehicular charge . . . or at least there's no mention here that he was," I said. "The implication is that he used the damn car as a weapon."

"He was drag racing and bumped the competition into a grove of pine trees."

"Where's it say that?"

"It doesn't. I called Albuquerque while you were in the shower."

"You don't waste a second, do you?" I looked at the file again. "So he gets just two years for what is essentially murder."

Estelle moved her Kennedy rocker so that she could put her feet up on a big planter that supported one sorry-looking beaver-tail cactus. She shrugged at my comment. Under New Mexico law two years was the most detention any kid got, no matter what the crime, as long as he wasn't tried as an adult. I grunted with disgust. Murder could come pretty cheap.

After his release from the detention home, Robert Arajanian had remained clear of the law for four years. Two days before his nineteenth birthday, and eight months previous to his playing lookout on the hot springs rock, the kid had been charged with misdeameanor possession of marijuana and attempted burglary of an apartment in the Northeast Heights of Albuquerque. He'd pulled six months probation for the marijuana. The attempted burglary charge never went to court.

"Well, that's neat," I said. "He must be a slick talker, too, when the spirit moves him. The burglary complaint was withdrawn. His first chance at a good, solid felony as an adult and someone wimps out. So now he can possess a firearm legally. Otherwise, as a felon, he'd be in violation."

"There probably wasn't enough evidence to make the burglary charge stick. Who knows?"

"So," I said. "All very interesting, but nothing yet on H. T. Finn."

"Albuquerque didn't have anything on him. It's going to take a while to track him down, I suspect." Estelle sounded disappointed—as always, hating unanswered questions.

"What do you think the odds are that either Arajanian or Finn or both pitched Cecilia Burgess over the embankment?"

Estelle grimaced impatiently. "Zero."

"Really? Finn didn't seem awash in grief at the news of the accident. In fact, he seemed to assume that she was already dead."

She shrugged. "And he didn't say anything about going into the city to visit her either, but what does that prove?"

"That he doesn't like talking to strangers, especially the law, or that he doesn't have a car."

"He could hitchhike. The Indians do it all the time. Do you need more coffee?"

"No, thanks." I sat silently as she got up and went inside. I heard the coffeepot clank against the stove burner, and she started talking before she was out of the kitchen.

"I don't know why we're even worrying about Finn and Arajanian anyway. What we need—" She was interrupted by the telephone. I heard her monosyllabic side of the conversation but what I heard was enough. When she hung up and returned to the porch, her face was sober.

"She died?"

Estelle nodded. "At six-sixteen P.M." She glanced at her watch. "Twenty-two minutes ago."

"What's your next step then?"

She sat down in the rocker and gazed off toward Chuparrosa Mesa. "Someone must have seen her shortly before she was struck. Did someone pick her up in the village? Was she walking up to the hot springs?"

"Late at night?"

"Who knows. And we don't know what time she was hit either. She could have been lying there for some time. It had to have taken her some time to crawl up to the highway."

"It's hard to imagine, the way she was hurt."

"Sheriff Tate said that they're still in the process of running a complete background on her. He'll let me know." She made a face of frustration and leaned forward in the chair. "Not a single piece of evidence to tie in a vehicle of any kind, Tate said. No paint chips, no nothing. And . . ."

"And what?"

"And that's not what really bothers me."

"What does, then?"

"Daisy bothers me, sir."

I said nothing and watched Estelle's face as her agile brain sifted the facts.

She shook her head after a minute. "I hate to think of her up there with those two creeps."

"We don't know anything about Finn, Estelle. He says he's the girl's uncle. If he really is, the Department of Social Services will never give you a court order unless you can prove abuse or neglect or something like that. And if Finn's lying to us, it'll still take a while for a court order. And there's one other possibility, too."

"What's that?"

"We don't know for certain that the child is Cecilia Burgess's daughter. We're making an assumption just because her name is Daisy."

"Come on, sir," Estelle said in a rare display of contention. "Who else would she be? Coincidence is one thing, but that would be ridiculous. She even looks like Cecilia."

I held up my hands in surrender. "I couldn't tell you. And little kids all look alike to me. I'm just tossing it out as another possibility, that's all. Farfetched, but a possibility. And maybe Finn is telling the truth. But trust Tate to dig it out. He's a ferret." I sighed deeply and stretched. "I'm glad it's not my worry."

Estelle looked at me over the top of her coffee cup. "Give me another dozen hours, and you'll be so tied up in this case you won't be able to sleep at night, let alone go home." She grinned. *"Como dos y dos son quatro, as mi madre* would say. And besides, I need your help."

"Yeah," I laughed. "Another hike like today's and you'll be attending my funeral. You've got Deputy Garcia. Walk his young legs off."

"Exactly," Estelle said. "We're going to find an eyewitness if we have to talk with every soul in this valley. Everybody. I asked Paul to talk with as many folks as he could, to see if anyone remembers catching a glimpse of a vehicle late last night. Especially a pickup."

"There's thousands of pickups around here."

"We have to start somewhere."

I nodded and listened to a long, plaintive growl from my stomach. "And when do we eat?"

"As soon as Francis comes home."

I groaned. "My God! We have to wait on a country doctor? It's apt to be midnight. I'll be dead by then."

Estelle laughed. "I'll get you a beer, some chips, and salsa. That'll tide you over. Really, he won't be long."

She got up and said over her shoulder as she disappeared into the house, "And I need to ask you a favor."

"What's that?"

"Just a second." After a bit she returned and set the promised snacks on the porch floor beside my chair. She handed me the beer. "I need you to talk with somebody for me."

"Who?"

"Father Nolan Parris. At the retreat house."

I regarded Estelle with interest. "He's the monk or friar or whatever you call 'em who was hanging out with Cecilia?"

"According to rumor."

"He might know something. I wonder if he drives a truck."

"A priest? No, I don't think so."

"Well," I sighed, "it's a place to start."

Estelle grinned. "It'll give you something to do."

I shrugged, convinced for about thirty seconds that the reason Estelle Reyes-Guzman was asking me to talk with Parris was because of the vast years of experience I had under my belt. And then, looking across the porch in the failing light and seeing the last bits of summer sunshine play around the planes of her face, I realized Estelle's request was astute. If she arrived at the Catholic retreat complex in uniform, there'd be talk. If she strolled in to visit in civvies, there'd be even more talk, all of the wrong kind. What could be more innocent than one old man visiting another?

"It'll cost you several beers," I said. I expected jocular agreement, but Estelle shook her head.

"We need to talk with Parris tonight." She pulled a small photograph from her blouse pocket. It was a picture of Cecilia Burgess, the posed kind with the misty background that college yearbooks favor. "Make sure he looks at this." She handed the picture to me. "See if you can get him to hold it just the way you are right now."

I frowned. "Where'd you get this?"

"She lived in one of the small back rooms at the trading post when she wasn't up at the springs with Finn. Garcia let me in. There wasn't much there. Just some clothes and things. The picture was being used as a page marker in a children's book."

"And you want Parris's prints?"

"I want a thumbprint."

"Parris doesn't have any kind of record where his prints were taken? Passport, anything like that?"

Estelle shook her head. "Not that we can find."

"And what good will his prints do, anyway?"

"Remember the guardrail? The bloody prints, top and bottom? We assumed Cecilia Burgess somehow pulled herself over or under the rail."

"You're telling me the prints we saw aren't hers. . . . she had help?"

"That's right. The prints aren't hers. That's what Sheriff Tate told me over the phone when he called to tell me Burgess died."

"What about that guy who stopped and called on the CB radio? Maybe he tried to help her."

"He said he didn't. And he's a state employee. Works in the Department of Revenue and Taxation. His prints were easy to doublecheck. He's clean."

"And no luck on what's his name, with the Forest Service? He was there before you were."

"Les Cook? He's a cop. Not a chance."

"Then someone else was there and split," I said. Estelle nodded. "Might have been the driver of the vehicle, maybe someone else." I cleaned off the photo with my handkerchief and carefully slid it in my pocket. "I'll get Parris's prints for you. And I suppose this means we're going to have to walk all the way back up to the hot springs, too."

"The prints don't match Arajanian's. Tate already checked for me. We don't know about Finn. So yes, we need to go back." I groaned at the thought of this exercise business becoming a habit.

ESTELLE and I ate dinner without her hubby. Francis called from the clinic just about the time Estelle had to turn on some lights so we wouldn't trip over the furniture. He'd been about to leave for home when an Indian woman walked through the door with a sick youngster.

The stoic little kid had been flinching from a middle ear infection for several days, and the infection had bloomed. When his temperature spiked through 104 degrees, the mother decided herbs weren't enough. The kid had himself a fine case of infectious meningitis.

Estelle sighed with resignation when Francis told her he wouldn't be home much before midnight. After the youngster was transferred to Albuquerque, Francis wanted to follow up with a visit to the pueblo to see with whom the kid had come in contact.

The two chatted for a few minutes, and when Estelle hung up I smiled. "Marry a doctor and you starve to death."

"Usually, it's me who gets called out at all hours," Estelle replied.

I leaned against the refrigerator and watched her cook. The kitchen was as tiny and cramped as the rest of the house, and I took it in at a glance. The row of bottles on the narrow windowsill above the sink surprised me—a whole alphabet of vitamins, minerals, and human fuel treatments. I reached over and picked up the largest, a collection of vitamin E capsules.

"I thought you always said that green chili cured all," I said. She glanced my way and I put the bottle back.

"Francis wants to make sure the baby gets everything he needs," she replied as offhandedly as if she'd remarked on the weather.

She laughed at the blank look on my face and went back to chopping onions.

"Well, congratulations," I said. "When?"

"When what?"

"When's it due?"

She took a deep breath. "February 10."

I laughed. She even had that event pegged to the day. "That's great. Does Sheriff Tate know?"

Estelle shook her head. "Francis and I agreed that I'd go on leave in October. That's soon enough."

"Then what?"

"We're not sure. I don't think I want to work." She grinned widely. "I don't think I want to face the wrath of *mi madre.* She'd never speak to me again if I left her grandson in a day-care center."

"You two will work it out I'm sure," I said. I picked up a loaded plate and carried it over to the table. She'd called it frijoles con something, and the food was so damn hot I accused her of serving it with a sauce of lit gasoline. But the spices—and the news about the pending kid—perked me up.

As we ate, our conversation kept circling back around to Cecilia Burgess and her boyfriends. Estelle wanted me to visit Father Nolan Parris, and there was no better time than that evening.

Shortly before nine, feeling fat from too much high-octane dinner, I arrived at the retreat complex just north of the village. As the crow flies the place was less than a mile from Estelle's home.

The center included several small buildings clustered

around a large three-story house. Monstrous cottonwoods shaded the complex and blocked out what little light there might have been from passing traffic, the moon, or even star-shine.

Estelle hadn't needed to worry about being seen by the wrong folks if she visited Parris. It was too dark for starting rumors. I parked the Blazer behind an older model Fairlane station wagon. A single bulb beside the double front door of the main house illuminated enough of the siding and porch to show that the facility was well maintained. I opened the door of the Blazer and listened. The compound was stone quiet. Maybe the clergy were in the middle of their late evening services.

The three raps of the brass knocker were loud enough to make me flinch. I formed a mental picture of a row of bowed, maybe even shaved, heads snapping up at the sound and nervous hands clutching rosaries.

The retreat was for clergy who had strayed from the straight and narrow. Some may have nipped the bottle too often . . . maybe a few dallied with members of the fair sex—or even with their own sex. "I think it's sort of a second chance house," Estelle had said and that made sense. If a priest couldn't concentrate on his prayers here, he was probably out of luck.

The right-hand side of the double doors opened and an elderly cleric peered out at me. I shouldn't say elderly . . . hell, he was about my age, maybe a year or two younger. He wore basic black, without the Roman collar.

"Good evening," I said and held my identification up so he could see it through the screen door. I adopted my most accommodating tone. "I wonder if it would be convenient for me to visit with Father Parris?" The priest squinted at the badge and commission card, and I wondered if he could read it well enough to see the county name.

His watery gray eyes flicked from the identification to my face, and I put the wallet away. "Well," he said and placed one hand on the screen door like he was preparing to push it open for me, "this isn't the best of times."

"I won't need much of his time," I said. "And it would really be a help."

He started to push open the door, then asked, "You may have to wait a moment or two. May I tell him who's calling?"

The doorkeeper had just flunked the reading test. I could just as easily have held up my Sears card. "Undersheriff Bill Gastner." He'd forgive a minor sin of omission. I opened the screen the rest of the way and stepped inside.

"If you'd care to wait here, in the front room?" the priest said, indicating a small parlor crowded with overstuffed furniture and a small upright piano. "I'll fetch Father Parris." He touched my elbow lightly as he guided me into the room and then left.

I thrust my hands in my pockets and gazed around. I stepped over and perused the titles in the single bookcase. Most were Reader's Digest chopped editions. If the good fathers had a theological library, this wasn't it. I turned at the sound of footsteps.

"Father Parris will be down in a few minutes," the priest said and smiled. "Can I get you a cup of tea or coffee or something?"

"No thanks. Appreciate it though."

He nodded and left. I sat down in one of the chairs and found that it supported me in all the wrong places. I perched forward on the edge of the cushion, clasped my hands together, rested my forearms on my knees, and waited. After about two minutes, I noticed that there were no ashtrays in the room. I took a deep breath and occupied my mind by trying to imagine what Parris looked like. In another minute, I had my answer. My guess hadn't been close.

Nolan Parris stepped into the doorway of the parlor and stopped. He rested a hand on the jamb. He was short, no more than five feet five and handsome in a well-oiled sort of way. His black hair was carefully trimmed with the part just off-center, and he kept the sideburns short. He wore gold wire-rimmed glasses, and his brown eyes glanced around the room when he first came in as if I might have company hiding behind the furniture.

I guessed that he was no more than thirty-five, just beginning to soften around the edges and expand at the gut. And he was pale, like a man just risen from bed after two weeks with the flu.

"Good evening," he said cautiously.

I rose and extended my hand. "Father Parris?"

"Nolan Parris, yes." He entered the room and limped to the center of the carpet, where I met him. His perfunctory handshake expended two pumps. "Do I know you?"

Once again I pulled out my identification. Parris looked at it and a muscle in his jaw twitched. He nodded and gestured toward a chair. "Please."

"Father Parris, I'm assisting Deputy Guzman with an investigation of a pedestrian accident earlier today up the canyon." A pained look swept briefly across his face. He was wearing slippers, and his right sock was bulging around what was probably an elastic bandage. I didn't know if the grimace was because of the ankle or my announcement. "Perhaps you heard about it."

He nodded. Something was interesting in the pile of the old purple carpeting in that room, because that's all Parris was looking at. "I heard about it, yes."

"Would you take a look at this, please?" I held out the picture of Cecilia Burgess, and Parris took it. With satisfaction I saw his thumb clamp down on the bottom margin of the photo. "Do you know the young lady?"

"Yes, of course. Cecilia Burgess. I've known her and her family for years." He took a deep breath, held it, and slowly let it out with a slight shake of his head. He handed the photograph back.

"Her family? She has relatives in the area?"

Parris shook his head. "No longer. Her parents died when she was quite young. For a time she was living with her brother in Albuquerque."

57

"Where's her brother now?"

"Richard's dead. About five years ago."

"How did that happen?"

Parris took his time collecting his thoughts before he said, "He was riding his motorcycle on Central Avenue in Albuquerque. A pickup truck ran the red light at Washington. Richard wasn't wearing a helmet. It probably wouldn't have done any good even if he had been."

I grimaced. "Hard luck family. And he was her only brother? No others? Sisters?" Parris shook his head. "What did the brother do?" Parris glanced up at me, puzzled. "His line of work?" I added patiently.

"He was a priest." Parris hesitated and watched me pull a small notebook out of my hip pocket. When my ballpoint was ready, he added, "We attended seminary together."

"He was older than Cecilia?"

"Yes. By about twelve years."

"What was your relationship with Cecilia?"

Parris eyed the carpet again. "We were good friends. As I said, we'd known each other for years."

I paused and stuck the pen in my mouth. "Father Parris, are you aware of what happened last night?" Parris nodded. His eyes were closed. I waited until he opened them and looked at me. "Would you tell me how you found out?"

Parris slumped back in the chair, and his left hand strayed to his pectoral cross. He toyed with it for a minute, then clasped his hands together. "I heard all the sirens, of course. And then this morning I had occasion to drive into the village. I sprained my ankle last night, and I needed an elastic support. Orlando Garcia, at the trading post, saw me and asked if I'd heard."

"And what did you do then?"

"I called the clinic immediately."

"Do you remember what time that was?"

Parris pursed his lips and glanced at his wristwatch, as if the hands might have stopped at the moment in question. "Mid-morning. It was shortly after I'd finished mass here."

"And then?"

"They told me that Cecilia had been transferred to Albuquerque. To Presbyterian. I drove into the city immediately."

"So you were aware of the extent of her injuries?"

Nolan Parris stood up with a grunt and limped across to the bookcase. He rested both hands on the top shelf for support. I waited. Finally he said, "I administered last rites. I was there when she died." He turned and looked at me without releasing his grip on the bookcase. "I made arrangements. A friend of mine at Sacred Heart will say rosary and mass, probably tomorrow. I did all I could. And then I drove back here."

"Father, are you aware that Cecilia was pregnant?"

"Yes." His lack of hesitation surprised me.

"Do you know who the father was?"

"I'm not sure I understand how that is relevant to the investigation of the accident," Parris said without much conviction.

"Do you know?"

He pushed away from the bookcase and sat down on the only straight-backed chair in the room. "I can't imagine what good these explorations into Cecilia's private life can do now."

"Father Parris, a hit-and-run is homicide." Parris's face flushed, and his shoulders sagged a little. "So you see, information of any kind might be helpful to us."

Parris bowed his head, and for a moment I was afraid he'd sunken into one of those hour-long prayers. Eventually, he looked up at me. "Yes, I know who the father was. Or I should say, I know who she said he was."

"And who's that?"

"A fellow by the name of Finn."

"First name?"

"I'm not sure. They're just initials I think. H.P. maybe. Something like that."

"Are you aware of where Mr. Finn lives?"

"Oh, he lives around here, all right." Parris almost chuckled, the sound coming out like more of a snort. "Up at the hot springs. He and a *friend* camp out there." He stressed the word *friend*.

"Do you know the friend?"

"No. But I've seen him once or twice. And Cecilia mentioned him now and again. A younger man, I believe."

"And so you think Finn is the father?"

"Cecilia said he was. She said he paid one or two of her bills at the health clinic."

"Did Cecilia Burgess have any other children?"

The question seemed to catch Parris off-guard. He watched the rug patterns for a long minute, then settled for a simple shake of the head. A very small shake.

"So the little girl who's staying with Finn—Daisy, I think her name is—isn't Cecilia Burgess's child?"

"No, not as far . . ." Parris stopped abruptly. His face was anguished. "No, I'm not going to do that." He was speaking more to himself than to me, and I remained silent. His features twisted with some internal struggle, and I thought for a moment that the young priest was going to weep.

He closed his eyes again for a while, then got out of the chair, limped to the door, and gently closed it.

"I'm sorry," he said quietly. "Forgive me. This is hard." He made his way slowly to the chair nearest mine. I said nothing, letting him take his time. He surprised me with a faint grin. "I feel as if I'm in the confessional."

"Some different laws apply," I said gently.

He nodded sad agreement with that. "The girl living with Finn is my daughter."

"And Cecilia's?" I prompted.

"Yes," Father Nolan Parris said. He looked relieved.

9

O V E R the years, I've had lots of practice at not looking as surprised as I felt. This was one of those times. I leaned back in the chair and regarded Parris with interest. Then, trying to sound fatherly instead of intimidating, I said, "So tell me."

He shrugged. "It's no long story. As I said, Cecilia's brother was a close friend of mine. My best friend. We'd known each other since we were two. We went to school together, all the way from kindergarten through college and seminary." He stopped, arranging his mental cards.

"I wish some of his willpower and discipline had rubbed off on me. I drink too much, Sheriff. Or at least, I did." He clasped his hands tightly together. "I guess that I was an alcoholic by the time Richard Burgess was killed. That's what they tell me. Anyway, his death . . . the stupidity of it . . . the waste . . . was all the excuse I needed.

"I don't remember all the grim details, and I don't think I ever want to. The next eighteen months were my own private hell. They say a drunk has to hit rock bottom before he'll admit to being in trouble." He shook his head. "Do you know where they found me, finally?"

I shook my head and Parris said, "I was living in a card-board box under an Albuquerque overpass—downtown, where the old railroad station used to be. And *living* is probably the wrong word. A rookie cop happened by and he thought I was dead. Next best thing. They took me to St. Joseph's, and one of the nurses recognized me . . . she remembered when Richard Burgess and I hung out together. We used to be on rotation together as police department chaplains. *Los dos padres,* they called us. But that was a long time ago." He hesitated, lost in his memories. My back hurt from sitting so long.

"I didn't have any close relatives. Just one cousin back east somewhere. The nurse knew about Cecilia Burgess and called her. That was the big mistake, I guess. That's when it started. I held onto her like a damn leech. I guess I put her through more hell than even last night."

"I doubt that."

"Anyway, one thing led to another. I was an accomplished liar. Always have been. I could lie to myself as easily as to anyone else. I made up some of the most wonderfully creative stories . . . personal sob stories that suckered that poor girl right into my world. I guess it was one of those nights when she was trying to keep me from tearing the apartment apart . . . that's when we started."

"You had sex with her, you mean?"

"Stripped of all the niceties and excuses, that's the gist of it."

"And that guilt really set you off?"

Nolan Parris looked up sharply at my tone. He moved his jaw sideways, assessing me. "Maybe you don't understand, Sheriff. You impress me as the kind of man who's always known exactly where he stood, who always knows exactly what he believes."

"I've had my moments. Anyone does. But that's not what's at issue now. I gather the two of you didn't stay together long?"

"No. I can remember having long discussions with her about my leaving the clergy, after finding out she was pregnant. But I . . . I just couldn't."

"Why not?"

Again Parris looked at me critically, but he wasn't in a hurry to answer. To let him off the hook a little I asked, "How did the two of you end up here, in San Estevan?"

"She took some courses at the university, and one of them involved a field trip to the mountains around here . . . geology, I think it was. She fell in love with the village and had dreams of raising Daisy here, away from the city."

"Daisy's the girl's name?"

"Yes."

"When did Cecilia move up here?"

"About a year ago."

"And you?"

"Me? I received the ultimatum from my bishop last August. Dry out or get out." Parris smiled faintly. "Bishop Sanchez didn't use those exact words." He shrugged. "I've been here ever since. I could have left long before, but I'm serving as a resident counselor."

"And you've stayed dry?"

Parris nodded slightly. There wasn't any pride in his voice when he said, "Dry."

"Good for you. Even today?"

He covered his face with two smooth hands and then cupped them under his chin. "Even today. Falling off the wagon wouldn't have done Cecilia any tribute."

How noble, I thought. "What's Daisy doing up at the hot springs with Finn?"

I couldn't imagine leaving a kid of mine on the mountain with a long-haired freak while her mother expired in a hospital a hundred miles away . . . even if I were a priest and inordinately sensitive about appearances.

Parris's face hardened, and I noticed the tick in his cheek again. "You have to understand, Sheriff, that even though we live in the same village, Cecilia and I see little of each other. We saw little of each other. For very obvious reasons." He stopped in case I had to ask what the reasons were. I didn't. "And she had been living with Finn, off and on. And was to

63

have his child." He held up his hands helplessly. "Now you have to believe I was going to—"

We were interrupted by the sound of a powerful car's engine as the vehicle slowed and then lunged down into the retreat's driveway. The flash of headlights stabbed through the window and then I saw the wink of blue and red.

"What the hell . . ." I said, rising to my feet. I peered out through the window and saw Estelle Reyes-Guzman's county car as it nearly climbed the steps. "Excuse me." I yanked the parlor door open, then the front door, and met Estelle just as she reached the porch.

She immediately turned around and headed back for the car, saying over her shoulder, "Come on, we need to get up the canyon."

I turned to Parris, who'd limped to the door and was standing behind me. "Don't go away," I said and then made for the car. Estelle had already yanked the Ford into gear, and as soon as my ass dropped into the seat, she slipped her foot from brake to accelerator. The cruiser kicked gravel all the way out to the highway.

"What's up?" I said as she got the car straightened out and howling on the pavement.

"Paul Garcia thinks he's found the pickup truck." Estelle Reyes-Guzman's voice was charged with excitement. She was riding the cop's high that comes when a burst of new information cracks a case wide open and makes the adrenaline flow. I stayed quiet, not wanting to distract her. I didn't want the county car plunging into the canyon. Besides, I was feeling a little let down. Here I had spent an evening pumping gossip out of a priest, and a rookie deputy sheriff had gone and solved a murder case.

10

I DIDN'T need to see the speedometer to know that the county cruiser was rocketing up Isidro Creek canyon fast enough to turn us both into jelly if we ran off the pavement.

If we didn't wipe out a tourist family just as they pulled out of a campground, it would be a deer standing stupidly in the middle of the road just after a corner, blinded by the lights and spellbound by the noise.

Estelle held the steering wheel tightly in one hand, and with the other she played the powerful spotlight along the sides of the highway far ahead of us. Her jaw was set in determination. I reached back and groped for the seat belt, then pulled it around my girth and snapped it tight.

We entered a long straight stretch and I asked, "How does Garcia know it's the truck?"

"He spent the afternoon dogging after someone who might have seen something . . . anything. I guess he hit paydirt. Pat Waquie said he'd seen a blue over white Ford half-ton cruising around the village last night."

"Who the hell is Pat Waquie?"

Estelle didn't answer for a moment as she paid attention to a series of S-curves. Then, as calmly as if she were selling stamps, Estelle said, "Pat lives in that rambling adobe just beyond where the pueblo land starts. He has the orchard where the trees practically hang out over the highway." She glanced at me to see if I was following her description.

I gestured at the highway. The white lines, what few there were between long strips of double yellow, blended together into one racing stripe.

"So how does it figure to be the truck we're after?" I asked.

"Garcia's hunch. Waquie remembered it because one of the guys in it tossed a beer can in the old man's front yard. Waquie was sitting on his front step enjoying the evening when the Ford drove by. They were really whooping it up."

"Living by the highway, he must get lots of that."

"This time, it was his own nephew."

"And how . . ." I stopped as the Ford blasted toward a sign that announced a tight switchback. The yellow sign called for fifteen miles an hour. I tried to push both feet through the floorboards, and one hand reached for the dashboard.

Estelle hung the big car out wide, braked hard, slapped the gear selector down to first, and when the rear end howled and broke loose punched the gas. We exited the corner as pretty as you please, straight in our own lane and accelerating hard.

". . . how does that connect with Burgess?"

"Garcia said the old man told him that he'd seen the nephew drive by a couple of times, each time a little faster and noisier . . . and the kid had picked up some passengers. The last time, well after dark and just before the old man went inside, he saw his nephew go by with at least five in the truck . . . three inside and two in the back."

"The old man notices the fine details," I said, skeptical.

"That's what he said he remembered. And the boy's been in a couple good scrapes before. His folks let him run wild. The uncle doesn't like it much, but what can he do?"

"So based on the old man's tale, Garcia thinks that maybe Cecilia Burgess got herself picked up by a bunch of drunks and ended up raped and in the rocks."

"It's possible."

"It's as good as anything else you've got." We hit a straight

66

stretch for a few hundred yards, and I tried to relax. "Where's Waquie's nephew now?"

"He's with the truck."

"And Garcia's sitting on him somewhere up here? He's got him staked out?"

"Right. So to speak." We had reached the head of the canyon, and the stop sign at the T-intersection shot past as we swerved out onto the main state highway that ran east–west through the mountains. The convenience store off to the left faded behind us as we headed east.

Estelle said, "A group of Girl Scouts found the truck. They're camping out on the backside of Quebrada Mesa. As the crow flies, it's only a mile or less to the scout camp over on Forest Road 87."

"What do you mean, 'found the truck'? Crashed, you mean?" Estelle nodded. "And let me guess. The kid's inside it."

"Apparently." Estelle suddenly stood on the brakes, and we skidded to a stop in the middle of the highway. "I missed the turn," she said, and we backed up so fast my forehead almost hit the dashboard.

"Christ," I gasped. "If your kid ever wants to be a damn racing driver, you'll know where he got the notion." My neck snapped back as she braked our backward plunge.

Off to the right, a small Forest Service sign announced: QUEBRADA MESA CAMPGROUND, 7 MI., and SNAKE RUN TRAIL, 4 MI. Below that, it said: PRIMITIVE ROAD—NOT MAINTAINED. We jolted onto the forest two-track, and if I'd worn dentures, they would have been in my lap.

"We're not going to the campground," Estelle said as if that made everything hunky-dory. "The scouts are a couple of miles this side of it, where the mesa edge is right next to the old logging clearing."

She was already assuming that I knew the country as well as she did. I let it ride and concentrated on keeping my head from being driven through the roof of the Ford. In a couple places, the road would have been narrow for a three-wheeler, and the low-hanging ponderosa pine branches wiped scratches the full length of the patrol car. A limb as thick as my thumb whacked the mirror on my side askew and screeched across my window.

"Guzman, this is Garcia." The radio message cracked loud despite the bouncing car, and I reached for the mike. I wasn't about to give Estelle an excuse to take her hands off the steering wheel.

"Go ahead, Garcia."

We hit another rut and I almost dropped the mike. Garcia's voice was loud and clear. "I can hear you coming up the two-track. Estelle, stop where the scouts are. There's a washout or two farther on. You'll break an axle if you're not careful."

"Ten-four. Appreciate the thought," I said, and to Estelle, I added, "I wonder if he broke his."

For another five minutes we crashed along the path. Then Estelle swung the Ford around a corner and slewed the car to a stop. Four Girl Scouts stood in the middle of the lane, terrified. The lights from the roof rack pulsed across their faces.

The oldest kid couldn't have been fourteen, and I wondered where their counselor was. "We can park right here," Estelle said. She switched off the car and the lights. ". . . if you don't mind hoofing it for a few yards."

"No, no. I don't mind," I said and popped my seat belt before she changed her mind.

"The other officer told us to meet you out here," the oldest scout said as Estelle got out of the car.

"Good girls," Estelle said. She snapped on her flashlight. I was still rummaging, and Estelle called, "In the glove compartment." I found the other flashlight and grunted my way out of the car. It felt good to plant both feet on unmoving ground.

"Where's the other deputy?" Estelle asked, and the scout pointed off to the west.

"It's shortest this way," the girl said. "Part of the road farther on is washed out pretty bad. We can cut straight across." There were six of us and six flashlights, and still the timber was dark as tar. I brought up the rear, hoping that the five young ones in front of me would kick all the obstructions out of the trail. They left enough to keep me paying attention.

This particular portion of Quebrada Mesa was a narrow spit of land where the two sides of the mesa tucked in tight before fanning out to blend with the swell of the mountain behind it. The Forest Service two-track was an access road to an old timber sale area. Campers used it and maybe serious lovers who didn't want to be disturbed. I couldn't imagine casual drinkers jolting their innards just to quaff a brew under the moon.

We reached the edge and as we paused for a minute, I could hear the faint shush of wind through the pines below us. "Where's Garcia?" I asked.

"Down this way," the brave scout said, and we walked along the edge single file. A hundred yards ahead I saw several lights gathered at the edge and then, when the timber thinned some more, I saw a single flashlight down below, fifty, maybe sixty yards away. It had to be a hell of a drop-off.

Four more scouts and two counselors waited for us. The counselors—two gals of maybe eighteen or twenty—looked as scared as the little ones. Estelle looked down and then asked, "Is there an easy way down there?"

"It's all pretty steep," one of the counselors said. "The other deputy just slid down from here."

Estelle sighed, and I knew what was going through her mind. She didn't like someone skidding willy-nilly through the middle of her evidence. She pulled the hand-held radio from her belt and keyed the button.

"Paul? You copy?"

"Ten-four."

"We're up on the edge above you."

"I see the lights." His flashlight swept an arc for us.

"What have you got down there?"

"One nineteen-seventy-six Ford half-ton, blue over white. As far as I can tell, there were just the two occupants."

69

"All right. I called Dr. Bailey from Jemez. He's covering for Dr. Guzman tonight. He's our closest. It'll be a half hour at best."

"Ten-four."

Estelle turned to me. "I called for ambulance and coroner before I picked you up. But it's going to be a while. Do you want to go down or stay here?"

"Should you be doing stuff like this?" I asked and knew right away my concern was a waste of breath.

"Come on, Padrino," Estelle said. She grinned. "The kid may want to be a mountain climber someday."

I grunted disapproval, at the same time swelling a little with pride that when Estelle had finally called me something other than "sir" it had been the Mexican equivalent of "godfather."

"Let's do it," I said. Skinnying down into that black void wasn't my idea of a good time, but what the hell. When her child was born, I didn't want him looking up at me from his cradle and saying *wimp* as his first word.

Estelle swept the ground with the flashlight. "Paul," she said into the hand-held radio, "did you locate exactly where the truck went over?"

"About fifty feet south of you. To your left."

"Ten-four. We're going to look around up here a little; then we'll be down."

"We ain't going anywhere."

Estelle included all the scouts in her flashlight arc. "Maybe you girls would go on back out to where I parked the car. An ambulance and other personnel will be following us in, and we don't want them going any further than we did." That would be a real trick, since the fat rump of her patrol car was blocking the two-track. The girls started to move off, and Estelle added, "And we'll want to talk with you all, so don't go anywhere else."

I heard a "Yes, ma'am," from one of them, and then we could see their flashlights bobbing as they made their way back through the big pines.

"Hell of a way to spend a campout," I said. "Imagine the ghost stories you could tell 'em now."

"And you'd have wet sleeping bags for sure," Estelle muttered. "Let's see where it went over."

I took a deep breath, suddenly and deeply feeling fatigue as it snuck up and clubbed me. Being an insomniac is one thing, but I'd been on my feet, one way or another, since the accident sirens had awakened me at the campground. And this was the second time I'd been stumbling around in the dark, peering at evidence with the feeble light of flashlights.

"I wish to hell you'd learn to work during the daylight hours," I said as Estelle made her way along the rim to the south, her light sweeping the ground.

"No time like the present," she said cheerfully. "And here we go." The tracks she had found were faint impressions in the soft duff. Estelle followed them with the light. The tracks came from off to the left, from the old two-track.

Her flashlight beam reflected off the white of Garcia's four-wheel-drive Suburban. The road he had driven wound down through the trees from where we had parked, then looped over toward the mesa rim forming a turnaround that the logging trucks had used years before.

The driver of the pickup had driven straight across the turnaround and held course for the vertical drop-off . . . and as tired as I was, even I could see that not once had he spiked the brakes before going over.

71

11

T H E pickup truck lay on its side at what we later measured as sixty-three yards below the mesa rim. I pictured the Ford crunching almost lazily off the precipice. The undercarriage had scraped the rocks as the truck tipped over, so it certainly hadn't vaulted off like something driven by a Hollywood stuntman.

Fifteen feet into the plunge, the truck had hit a small juniper and twisted sideways, beginning the first of several rolls. On the second roll, the windshield had smashed against a large limestone boulder.

The trail of glass followed the truck's course downward from when first the back and then the side windows had shattered. Forty-one yards from the rim, the truck had flopped on its back on an outcropping that almost stopped the trip.

But inertia won, and the Ford had tipped on over, dropping eighteen feet straight down. It landed on its left side, rolled twice more, and finally wedged to a stop against a collection of house-sized boulders.

It wasn't so clear what had happened to the occupants. The first was lying where he'd been crushed when the truck smashed into the outcropping.

The kid . . . he wasn't much more than that . . . had been

sieved through the space between the collapsing cab roof and the dashboard on the driver's side. The blood, tissue, and clothing fragments on the rocks told a familiar story. The truck had held onto him for one full roll and then tumbled on, leaving the crushed and torn rag doll behind.

"What I.D. did you find?" Estelle asked Paul Garcia.

"I haven't touched anything yet. I didn't look."

Estelle nodded, and I held the light for her while she pulled out the kid's wallet. She handled it carefully, just with the very tips of her fingers. "Robert Waquie," she said and looked up at me. I snapped open her briefcase and handed her a plastic evidence bag, and she dropped license and wallet inside.

"So the old man called it right," I said.

"Yes, it appears so. Paul, where's the other one?"

Garcia twisted and pointed downhill, off to the south. "Over there about twenty yards, almost on a line with the truck."

"You're kidding," Estelle said and stood up. "There's no way he could have been thrown that far, and certainly not in that direction."

I was the only one who took time to find an easy way around the outcropping . . . Estelle and Garcia went straight down the rocks like goddamn mountain goats.

The second victim was as dead as his companion. From what we could tell, his injuries were consistent with being bashed around inside a crushed cab.

"He was extruded out through the back window," I said. I held my light close and pointed at the crescent-shaped piece of Plexiglas that was driven into the small of the victim's back three inches above the belt. I swept my light back to the truck, pointing it at where the custom sliding camper window had been installed in place of the solid glass window. Most of the window's aluminum frame had been torn from the cab.

His I.D. said Kelly Grider, and he had lived long enough to pull himself a few yards away from the wreckage, and then he'd bled to death.

Estelle stood near the corpse. Several times she flicked the light from Grider to the truck, as if trying to outline the path crawled by the victim. "What do you think?"

"You sure pick 'em," I said. "They had to have been drunk to pull a stunt like this."

"They were drunk all right," Estelle said. "I can smell it on both of them."

"And the truck's loaded," Paul Garcia offered. "Empty cans, a couple of empty bottles. A couple of six-packs waiting to be opened. They had to be so stoned that they just idled right over the edge."

"Easy enough to do if you're not paying attention," I said. "But why were they up there in the first place?"

"Scout hunting, probably," Estelle said.

"Then the scouts are goddamned lucky," I muttered. To Garcia, I said, "Did you take a good swing around the area? No other surprises?"

Garcia shook his head. "No, sir. I spent an hour down here, and I spent it looking. Not a thing. Just the two."

"How did the scouts come across this in the first place?" Estelle asked.

"They're on a campout just down the mesa. They said about a mile or so."

"Then they probably heard this."

"They said no. Apparently, they were taking a night hike up the canyon bottom."

"A night hike?"

"Scouts do that," Estelle said. "So they were down this slope even farther than we are now."

"That's what the counselor said. They were following the watercourse, and one of them flashed her light up here on the slope. That's when they saw the truck."

"Damn strange place to hike," I said.

"Not really, sir," Estelle said. "The watercourse follows the bottom of the ravine and gradually slopes up until it joins the mesa almost at the two-track where we came in. So you can hike it and know right where you are when you surface. Good for orienteering."

74

"And they didn't think the wreck was just a leftover from the logging days?"

"It was steaming," Paul Garcia said.

"Steaming?"

"Yes, sir. That's what they said."

"What did they do then?"

"A couple of them climbed up to the wreck, saw what it was, and then the whole squad beat a trail back to the main camp . . . straight east as the crow flies. There's a good trail the scouts have made. They use this mesa all summer. So it's not bad hiking, even at night."

"Especially when you're in a panic," Estelle observed. "And they called you from the camp."

"That's right. They gave me directions to find the two-track turnoff from the main road, and they met me right where I'm parked now."

"I'd think half the camp would be out here," I said.

"The head counselor of this group said the camp director and assistant director are in town for something. She thought it best to keep it kind of quiet until we had a chance to see what's what. She didn't want to upset the kids any more than she had to. So she kept her group together and kept a lid on things."

"Make sure she gets a medal," I told Estelle. "Her kind's rare."

"That's for sure." Estelle pinned the truck with her flashlight beam again, then swept the light up the steep slope. "Let's get some pictures and measurements before the coroner gets here."

I left the legwork to the youngsters . . . Garcia didn't even breathe hard as he worked the idiot end of the tape measure up and down the rock- and stump-strewn path down which the truck had plunged.

I concentrated on the truck. And I thought about Cecilia Burgess. If she had ridden in this vehicle earlier, who had pitched her over the side . . . Grider? Waquie? Old Man Waquie had said there'd been five kids in the truck when it disturbed his peace . . . where the hell were the others? Had they ridden up here on this remote mesa, too? Or had they ditched from the joyride sometime earlier?

For many minutes I just sat on a rock, my light beam playing around the inside of the bent, twisted truck bed. Plenty of blood smeared the remains of the rear window and the top rails of the bed . . . but that could be—and probably was—Kelly Grider's. With better light we could establish blood tracks. We'd see exactly where he crawled and be able to estimate just about how long it took before he collapsed and died.

Far in the distance a coyote yipped. It was a lonely place to die, and I felt a touch of sorrow for Waquie and Grider. But as drunk as they had been, maybe there'd been no chance for reflection.

I grunted to my feet. Estelle was starting her photography, and I let Garcia work the lights for her.

"I'm going to work my way back up to the car," I said. "Our traffic is due and they might want to talk with us on the radio. The hand-helds don't reach out so good."

"The scouts could use a little company, too," Estelle said, then added, "Are you all right?"

"I'm fine. Just tired. I need to sit on something soft and think for a while."

Sixty yards is not all that far, but I had to stop half a dozen times for breath. By the time I reached the mesa rim, my heart was pounding in my ears. I was so tired I almost turned the wrong way, but caught myself with a start.

I didn't try the short cross-country route through the trees but stuck instead to the two-track. I skirted Garcia's Suburban, saw that there was enough starlight, and flicked off the flash. I sauntered along the Forest Service road until I reached Estelle's patrol car.

The scouts were seated in a group under a huge ponderosa, and they stopped their quiet discussion when they saw my dark figure loom out of the darkness.

"Who's the head counselor?" I said, keeping my light off.

"I am," she said quietly and held her flashlight up so that the beam just nicked her face.

"You did good," I said. "We appreciate all your help."

"It's awful, isn't it?"

"Yes, it is. But you did all you could."

"When will we be free to go back to our camp?"

"You're still going to spend the night out here?"

The girl—I couldn't tell much about her in the faint light— almost chuckled. "Nobody's going to get much sleep tonight, so we might as well not get any out here as back at base."

"Well, the young woman detective is going to want to talk with all of you, but as long as we know where you are, I don't see any problem."

"You just follow this road another mile beyond the turn-around," she said. "That's where we'll be, then."

I opened the door of the patrol car, rolled the window down, and sat down. As the scouts filed out, I said to the counselor who brought up the rear, "You kids stay together tonight. Don't anyone go wandering off."

"No fear of that," she said quickly.

The scouts stuck so close together they looked like a single shadow, moving on twenty legs down the two-track. Exhausted, I leaned back against the seat. I must have dozed off, because I startled when the red lights of the ambulance bounced off the rearview mirror and winked across my face.

12

D R. E L L I O T Bailey was a man after my own heart. He stood on the edge of the mesa and looked down into the black void where flashlight beams zapped this way and that, punctuated periodically by the fireball of Estelle's electronic strobe.

"If you think I'm going to jump down there, you're nuts," he said. Both he and Francis Guzman had arrived on the heels of the ambulance, and on the short hike to the mesa edge from where they'd parked Bailey complained to me about every stick and root underfoot. Maybe he figured none of the young pups would listen.

Guzman and Bailey were opposites. The older doctor was a little gnome of a man, not much more than five feet tall. He wore one of those canvas fishermen's hats, and when he swept it off to rub his forehead, I saw that he was bald as an egg.

"What do you think, Francis? Go ahead and bring the bodies up?" He patted his belly, not eager to risk that investment on the sharp rocks below. That's what ambulance attendants were paid for.

I interrupted before Francis could answer. "I think Estelle wanted one of you to answer some questions down there before they're moved. Francis, I'll show you the way if you want."

"You sure you want to go back down there?"

"Hell, it's easy going down," I said with more confidence than I felt.

"If I break my neck, I'm going to sue the county for every penny it's got," Bailey said, but he followed us. The ambulance crew, four of them, lugged the body boards and other paraphernalia. They discussed using ropes but agreed finally that the darkness made the slope look worse than it was.

We skirted the rocks that formed the vertical drop-off.

"I don't believe this," Francis said. He spotted Estelle and shook his head. "You sure pick the spots, Officer."

"I was afraid you'd still be busy at the pueblo."

"Oh, I wouldn't have missed this for the world." He pointed his flashlight downhill and sucked in a breath. "Wow."

"How's the little boy?"

"Meningitis is the pits, that's for sure. But he'll be all right. What have we got here?" Francis knelt beside Robert Waquie's corpse. "Did you I.D. this one?"

"Robert Waquie. From the pueblo."

"I know his family," Guzman said as he examined Waquie's face. He pointed to a recent scar over Waquie's left eyebrow. "He did that earlier this summer when he put his dad's truck into a wash south of San Estevan." He twisted and played his flashlight back up the rocks, then down the hill at the tangled pickup. "From what I can see, Estelle, his position is pretty consistent with this kind of incident."

"He's not the one that concerns me," Estelle said quietly.

"Oh." Francis let that pass and continued his examination. Bailey bent over and assisted, the two of them reeling off all the gruesome medical details of what the Ford had done to Waquie.

"So he would have died instantly," Estelle said when they paused.

"Absolutely," Bailey said. "He might as well have been lying in front of a steamroller. Same results."

Francis Guzman motioned to the attendants, and while we

79

started down to the truck, they prepared Waquie's corpse for the rugged trip up to the ambulance.

Estelle let her husband and Bailey examine Kelly Grider's remains without interruption for a few minutes, but I could see by the intent expression on her face that she was eager for them to reach the same conclusion she obviously had . . . whatever that was. They left the piece of Plexiglas in place for the M.E. Bailey lifted the corpse carefully at the hips when they rolled Grider over so the glass spear wouldn't be damaged or moved.

Francis Guzman held the light close and examined the corpse's upper extremities, working his way to the head. He checked the pupils, then moved the corpse's skull carefully. "Huh," Francis said finally. "Go ahead and put him down," he told Bailey. He squatted back on his haunches and looked at the other doctor. "What do you think?"

"I think he was bleeding to death when he crawled out of the truck," Bailey said. "He was about exsanguinated by the time he got here. What surprises me is that he made it this far."

Estelle stepped closer. "I don't understand why he crawled over here, though."

"What do you mean?"

"I'd think someone hurt that badly might try to make it out of the vehicle, but why crawl off in a random direction? The only way there's help is up the hill."

Bailey frowned at her. "Come on. When a person's hurt that bad, they don't think. They're crawling away from the pain, is all. Just motion. You ever see a dog get his legs busted by a car and then drag himself sideways? Where's he going? Nowhere. Just away from the pain. And this kid didn't crawl through the window. He was thrown out . . . or most of the way out, anyway."

"His neck's broken though," Francis Guzman said. He touched the base of Grider's skull with his index finger. "Feel right there." Bailey frowned and placed his hands gently on either side of Grider's neck as Guzman moved the skull.

"Son of a bitch," Bailey said. "You're right." He looked up

at Estelle. "Third or fourth cervical. The autopsy will tell us for sure. But if the fracture is as complete as it feels, then he didn't crawl an inch after it happened."

"Now wait a minute," I said. "You're saying an injury like that is instantly fatal?"

"No, I'm saying that it's probably instantly and completely paralytic," Bailey said.

"Then if it happened in the wreck, we should have found him immediately beside the truck."

"Or half in and half out," Estelle observed. "But the blood trail clearly shows he crawled over here. You can see the bloodstains on his clothing . . . the bleeding is spread all the way to his shoes, and to me that's consistent with crawling and hemorrhaging."

"You can't crawl with a broken neck," Bailey shrugged.

"If you want a best guess, I'd say someone caught up with him . . . just about here. And finished him off." Francis Guzman hesitated before continuing. "There's no other visible neck trauma associated with this fracture. It's done neatly, like someone knelt on the victim's shoulders, took his head in hand, and pop." He stood up. "And that takes a lot of strength."

"Is there any other way it could have happened?" Estelle asked.

Francis shook his head. "If there is, it's beyond my imagination. It's too bad this didn't happen in the middle of a nice mud flat. Then you'd have some footprints to help out." He looked first at Estelle and then at me. "But there was a third person around here. Bet on it."

"You might want to be real thorough when you dust that truck for prints," I said to Estelle. "If that Ford didn't go over by accident, then something has to show up. It's too heavy to push, but maybe on the gear knob or door handle. Something."

Estelle took a deep breath. "It wasn't an accident." She examined her flashlight as if the answer were printed on the aluminum tube. "I want the autopsy report on these two the minute it's finished." She looked up at me. "And the doors are locked."

"Locked?"

She motioned with her hands. "The lock buttons on the pickup are punched down."

"I know what locked means, Estelle," I snapped. "What I meant was so what?"

"Can you picture a couple drunks, out on a lark in the middle of the forest, being so safety conscious that they lock their doors? If they did that, they would have worn their seat belts, too . . . and that's absurd. And doors don't lock themselves."

"You're saying that someone didn't want these two popping open a door when they started over . . . assuming they were sober enough to think of that. But those locks could have been punched down when those kids were flailing around inside, on the way down."

"Maybe. Maybe. But I don't think so. A warm summer night, no wind . . . why were the windows rolled up, too? Why would they do that?"

She had a point. "It wasn't because of mosquitoes." I looked up the hill and my fingers fumbled for a cigarette. I snapped my lighter and then a thought brewed in my mind that must have been a holdover from my Marine Corps days. I snapped the lighter shut, wondering if the son of a bitch was out there in the dark somewhere, standing behind a tree, watching us.

13

"'THEY heard a cough?" Sheriff Pat Tate frowned at Paul Garcia. The Girl Scouts had been chauffeured off the mesa and their camp director told to keep all the youngsters on camp property until our investigation was finished.

Deputy Garcia consulted the notes he'd made during an hour spent with the youngsters. "Yes, sir. That's what the counselor said. They were on a night hike, right up the watercourse. They'd been singing to chase away the bears, she said."

"Jesus," Tate muttered. He stood by the tailgate of the pickup truck, trying to make sense of the surrealistic scene. Off to one side a gasoline generator he'd heisted from the highway department chugged away, and the big flood-lamps washed the mesa side in white light.

"Girl Scouts do things like that," Estelle said.

"So what's with the cough?"

Garcia continued, "They heard the noise, and one or two of them turned their lights up the hill. That's when they saw the truck. One of them said she could see a wisp of steam coming from it."

"So they went up to investigate?"

"Yes, sir. The counselor said they could hear the engine

pinging, like it was cooling. And then they saw Waquie's body. They took one look and lit out to camp."

"I bet they did," Tate said. "So it could have been Grider, still alive."

"I don't think so," Estelle said. "The scouts climbed right up here after they saw the truck. I don't think Grider would have coughed after his neck was broken . . . I think they heard the killer."

Tate thrust his hands in his pockets and said to Francis, "I told downtown that I want the preliminary autopsy report on Grider sent up by courier just as soon as they have something. But you think it was murder?"

"Yes."

Tate nodded absently. "No other possibility?"

Francis had been in the middle of a yawn, but he stifled it and shook his head. "None that I can think of." We were all too tired to be creative. Old Doc Bailey had been the only smart one, going back to town with the ambulance and the two corpses.

"Stranger things have happened," Tate said. He looked across at me as I lit a cigarette. "Gimme one of those." I handed him one, and he took his time. "Hell, textbooks are full of incidents when a soldier suffered some hellacious wound that was bound to kill him, but he kept right on . . . maybe hundreds of yards."

"Anything except a broken neck," Francis said. "If the spinal cord is torn, no amount of desire or wishful thinking is going to make it possible to crawl anywhere."

"So assuming all that's true, how did the killer get up here, and how did he get away without being seen by the scouts?"

"We don't know," Estelle said.

"And what the hell's the motive? Hell, these two were nothing but a couple wild-hare kids. Who'd kill them?"

"We don't know that either."

Tate crushed out the cigarette in exasperation. "But you think this is the same truck involved in the girl's death last night?"

84

"Yes, sir."

He turned and regarded the truck. "Then the connection is there somewhere. Somewhere. Make sure you don't miss one square inch on that thing. We want prints, and we want good ones. If there was a third person up here, maybe he touched something. Maybe we'll get lucky."

The deputies didn't miss. Five of us swarmed over that truck and used enough print dust to powder a thousand faces. I worked as long as I could, but after a while my eyes refused to focus.

I sat on a rock off to the side and watched. Francis Guzman had stayed with us, and as the clock ticked toward three in the morning he finally lost his patience. I saw him escort Estelle away from the truck, and for several minutes the two were in animated conversation. I didn't want to eavesdrop, but I found myself watching like some damn Peeping Tom.

Estelle stared at the ground as Francis talked, and at one point she looked up at him and shook her head. That set off another long session of lecture, and finally she nodded. Francis didn't look pleased. Their faces were only inches apart, and after a minute Francis put one hand under her chin, lifted her head, and kissed her lightly.

The young physician started up the hill, and Estelle walked slowly over to join me.

"Francis is going back to town if you want a ride," she said.

"No. I may go up and grab the backseat of your car for a few minutes after a bit. But how about yourself? You're pushing pretty hard."

That earned me a raised eyebrow, and I guessed that Francis had said much the same thing. Estelle changed the subject.

"Tell me what Parris said." She sat down beside my rock.

"Cecilia Burgess's little girl is his daughter."

Estelle's mouth opened slightly, her lips forming a silent whistle. "He said that?"

"Yes." I told her about Parris's friendship with Richard Burgess and the priest's sorry affair with the girl after Richard's death.

85

She looked back over at the truck, lost in thought. "Maybe he'll try for custody now." She turned back to me. "He's got to understand that Daisy is ultimately his responsibility. He can't just give her away. He can't just leave her out in the woods with Finn. Not with her mother dead."

"The kid's the least of your worries right now," I said. "She's happy chasing toads and beetles." I gestured at the truck. "You need a motive. And my first question is simple. If this is the truck involved in Cecilia Burgess's death, what's the connection to this mess? Neither Parris nor Finn had the time or motivation to act out of revenge . . . assuming that somehow either of them knew who drove the truck."

"You don't think so?"

"No, I don't. Finn didn't appear to give a shit, one way or another. I don't know what his trip is, but he didn't seem too concerned when we talked to him. His focus seemed to be the little girl."

"That's what worries me," Estelle muttered.

"Trust the child's judgment, Estelle. You saw the way she clung to him." She wasn't convinced, but I continued, "And Parris is a marshmallow. It takes a special kind of monster to break a hurt kid's neck in cold blood. Nolan Parris certainly isn't the one." I realized how silly that sounded as soon as I said it. The history of crime was full of innocuous-looking little schmoes who turned butcher.

"We need time to process the prints," Estelle said. "There's got to be an answer here." She stood up. "And I still think you're wrong about Daisy, sir. She doesn't belong in a tent out in the middle of the woods with a couple of Jesus freaks who probably aren't even related to her."

The vehemence of her remark took me by surprise.

14

WE ABANDONED that damn mesa at seven in the morning. I'd had so much coffee I couldn't go ten minutes between visits to the bushes. My eyes were open all right, but behind them my brain was comatose.

It felt good when the tires of Estelle Reyes-Guzman's patrol car finally turned onto the pavement and we drove back to San Estevan.

She had a briefcase full of fingerprint cards and not much else. We sure as hell weren't dealing with one of those nut cases who hangs signs all over his murder saying, "Catch me, catch me."

Sheriff Pat Tate wanted us all to meet for breakfast and a strategy session, but as we rolled through the village I could see Estelle had other plans. We passed the lane that led down to their adobe. Without slowing the car, she glanced at me and asked, "Do you want me to drop you off at the house?"

I should have said yes just to see if she'd really turn around. Instead I said, "That depends on what you're going to do."

"Francis has a low-power stereo microscope at the clinic that I want to use. For a preliminary print comparison."

"Are you going to eat?"

"I'm not hungry. Maybe after a little bit."

I sighed with resignation but had enough sense to keep my mouth shut. "I'll tag along. If I go with Tate, I'll eat another of those breakfast burritos, and it'll sure as hell kill me."

We drove through the village, and I noticed the parking lot of the San Estevan Catholic church was full. "Wedding, do you suppose?"

Estelle laughed quietly. "You *are* tired, sir. This is Sunday morning."

"Oh." I looked at the date window of my watch. "Son of a gun. Is the clinic going to be open?"

"I have a key. And Francis might be there."

Francis wasn't there. If he had any sense at all, he was home in bed. To keep myself awake, I made a pot of coffee while Estelle set up in the examining room.

The viewer was designed for counting bacteria colonies growing in petri dishes but worked just fine for ogling fingerprints. She pulled out the card with Cecilia Burgess's prints and then selected through the prints lifted from the truck.

For a long minute she focused and arranged until she had the two sets side by side. Then she just sat and looked. I waited patiently and found it was more comfortable to wait with eyes closed.

"Take a look," she said. Her voice startled me, and I realized I'd been asleep. She got up to give me room.

I'm glad the scope had two eyepieces . . . that way, it supported my head when I leaned over to look. If I had had to close one eye, the other would have followed suit.

In the forty-one years I had been in law enforcement—twenty in the marines and twenty-one for Posadas County—I had looked at thousands of impressions left by human fingers, some of them in unlikely places. When I looked at fingerprints long enough and often enough I found that it was very much like looking at human faces.

They're all unique, yes, but there are family portraits where similarities show up. All that's required is a clear print—smudge it, and the personality vanishes.

The prints on the left had been provided by the Office of the

Medical Examiner. They'd been lifted from Cecilia Burgess's corpse. All ten digits were clear, the prints marred on three fingers by trauma associated with the crime.

I shifted the cards and looked at the prints Estelle had taken from the top right bed rail of the truck. My pulse picked up a few beats. "Huh," I said and shifted the cards. Estelle remained silent and then I heard her leave the room. I could smell the coffee, but what I was looking at was even more interesting.

"The coffee's at your left elbow," she said when she returned.

"Thanks. This is remarkable, you know that?"

"They're clear. It's a good thing the top edge of the truck's bed was clean."

"It usually is. That's where everybody leans when they're standing beside the vehicle yakking. It rubs off the dirt. Now if I had to read a story into these, I'd say that I can imagine a match. We've got a right index, ring, and middle finger and a smudged fragment of the little finger."

"With no trauma."

"That's right. I can't swear to any of the others, but the comparison of the two index fingers would stand up in court. The laceration cut deeply, but just above the center most characteristic swirl."

"That's what I thought."

I looked up from the scope. "She grabbed the side of the truck . . . and the print position shows she had to be facing forward at the time. Sometime after that, she was assaulted and pitched out. The fingers were cut in the process."

Estelle pushed the coffee cup toward me and indicated a brown bag. "Some of Mary Vallo's cookies left over from yesterday." Cookies weren't my idea of breakfast.

"So she was in that truck for sure," Estelle added. "That's one square of the puzzle that fits." I moved and let her rearrange the evidence under the stereo scope.

"I'm most interested in the prints along the truck bed," she said as she worked. "That's what's going to tell us who was in the back with her."

"Or who killed Waquie and Grider," I added. I looked inside the paper bag. The cookies were those big oatmeal creations that kids hate . . . and that mothers make so that the cookie supply will last more than a single day. I took one and tried to pretend that it was a bowl of hot oatmeal with brown sugar.

For fifteen minutes I watched Estelle work, trying this card and that. I was just crushing out a cigarette when she sat back, frowning.

"What's the matter?"

She groaned. "Maybe I'm wrong." She leaned forward and concentrated on the scope, but now she had my full attention.

"Wrong how?"

"You look."

I played musical chairs again and found myself comparing the top half of a perfect print on the left with a full but slightly smudged version on the right. The smudges weren't so bad that I couldn't extrapolate how the lines continued. "I'd bet they're the same. I could be wrong, but I'd bet they are."

I straightened up and rubbed my eyes. " 'Course, two of almost anything would look the same to me right now."

"I think it's a match."

"Fine. Who do they belong to?"

"The half print is from the graduation photograph of Cecilia Burgess. It's the one that they brought up from the lab early this morning."

My brain was slow to digest that. "You handed the picture to Nolan Parris," Estelle continued, "and that's his thumbprint. Only the top half . . . like anyone does when they want to pick up a piece of paper carefully by the edge."

"And the other one?"

"From the truck. The right side. Two feet behind Cecilia's."

"Son of a bitch."

"It was oriented the way it would be if Parris had taken hold of the truck side when he was standing beside it. Four fingers inside, thumb outside and pointed to the left and slightly downward." She walked to the sink and grabbed the side, her thumb on the outside. "Like this."

"Son of a bitch," I said again. We looked at each other for a long minute. "That leaves a big question."

"Yes, sir. It does."

"When did the good Father Nolan Parris grab the side of that truck? Here in town? On the state highway? Or up on Quebrada Mesa."

Estelle nodded. "Let's go ask him."

"On a Sunday morning a priest shouldn't be hard to find." I stood up slowly and said more to myself than to Estelle, "And maybe I can find out how he actually sprained his ankle."

"I beg your pardon, sir?"

I waved a hand wearily. "I'll tell you on the way."

15

W H E N we started to pull out of the clinic's parking lot, Estelle radioed the county dispatcher to let the office know she was bound for the Catholic retreat north of the village. The radio cracked the burst of static that was characteristic of the signal hitting a repeater tower somewhere, and almost immediately the dispatcher was back on the air.

"Four-o-two, ten-nineteen San Estevan."

"Tate's waiting for you at the office," I said. "He's going to want to be briefed on what you've got."

"I was going to stop," Estelle said. "Either there or the restaurant, whichever."

I laughed. "Sure you were."

"I was." She glanced at me, mock hurt. Only a state police cruiser was parked in front of Bobby's Cafe, so Tate wasn't lingering over breakfast. The party was at the highway department building. I counted six vehicles that belonged either to Castillo County or the Forest Service.

Inside Estelle's closet-sized office, the air was thick with smoke. She propped the door open. I lit a cigarette in self-defense.

Pat Tate was looking at a wall map with two of the deputies, tree warden Les Cook, and another serious-looking young man in pine-tree green. Deputy Paul Garcia was sitting at the single desk, frowning over paperwork.

"We wondered where you went," Tate said when he turned around and saw us. "You missed breakfast."

"No, I didn't. I had a wonderful cookie while she matched prints. The clinic has a good viewer."

"What did you find out?" he asked Estelle.

She put her briefcase on the desk where Garcia worked. "First of all, it is the truck that was involved with Cecila Burgess's death. We lifted a perfect print of hers from the truck bed."

"She might have touched it some other time," Tate said.

Estelle grimaced. "No. I think she was picked up, probably here in town. Maybe she was hitching up to the springs. It's the truck. I know it is."

Tate held up a hand to slow her down. "All right. What else?"

"Second, one thumbprint from the truck bed belongs to Nolan Parris."

"The priest?"

Estelle nodded. "It was on the outside, consistent with gripping the truck side while standing on the ground. We have no evidence that shows he was actually up in the truck bed."

"I'll be damned," Tate muttered. "What would he have to do with all this?"

"He's the father of Cecila Burgess's daughter."

Tate ducked his head with surprise. "You shitting me?"

"No."

Tate looked at me. "Is this the kid you told me about last night? The one who's staying with the hippies at the hot springs?"

"Yes."

"And the priest is the father? You didn't tell me that part."

I was about to say something like there were lots of things I didn't tell lots of people, but Estelle saved me from my tired temper. "That was an angle we were just starting to work on when Paul found the truck."

Tate crushed out one cigarette and lit another that he bummed from Al Martinez. "So what's the connection?"

When he said that, every pair of eyes in the room was locked on Estelle. They were expecting a grand pronouncement, I guess.

"I don't know," she said.

Tate held up his hands, prompting. "Is Parris a suspect? In your mind? Did he kill the girl?"

Estelle shook her head immediately. "No. That doesn't make any sense."

"Did he kill the two young men up on the mesa? Revenge, maybe?"

"We thought about that," Estelle said and looked at me. "I'm not sure he's capable of it. And you, sir?"

"Stranger things have happened." I was no longer so eager to make assumptions.

"You're going to talk with him today?" Tate asked.

"Yes, sir."

The sheriff took a deep breath and looked around for a chair. "We're going to have to get you some furniture." He settled for sucking in his gut and sliding his hands down behind his belt, like he had gas. If he ate at Bobby's too many more times, he would. "I need to go back to the city, or I'd go with you. Bill, are you staying with us for a while?"

I shrugged. "I'm kinda curious now. Besides, I need about thirty-six hours of sleep before I tackle an eight-hour drive home."

"All right. Estelle, I'm leaving both Paul Garcia and Al Martinez here. Whatever you need, holler."

Estelle nodded. "If we keep this kind of quiet for a while, it might be easier," she said. "If the killer is still in the county, I'd rather not spook him."

"In that you're lucky," Tate said. "If this was the city, you'd have thirty-five media types crawling down your neck. Hell, nobody outside of San Estevan knows we're here unless we tell 'em."

He stood up. "Go talk to the priest who's strayed into

94

fatherhood and let me know." He grinned at his own dumb joke, then turned to the two deputies. "Paul and Al, are you all set? Anything you need?"

Both shook their heads, and Tate prompted Martinez by adding, "Give your wife a call, Al. Tell her you'll probably be home tomorrow. Maybe Tuesday."

He picked up his baseball cap and snugged it down on his head. "It's my granddaughter's birthday today, and I'll be at my son's house most of the afternoon if you need me. The dispatcher will know. Bill, you take care. Don't push so hard. You look like hell."

Tate thrust out his jaw like a master sergeant who's just given his troops their marching orders and was now going to retire back to the comfort of his quarters.

"Thanks," I said. "That's going to be my epitaph."

Estelle sent Deputy Martinez north to orbit Quebrada Mesa. Paul Garcia pulled a sleeping bag out of his Suburban and spread it out on the office floor. "Wonderful," he said and was asleep in ten seconds at most.

I envied that kind of metabolism. But what the hell. I'd had insomnia for so long I had developed the skill of falling asleep with my eyes open, in the middle of a conversation. If I actually were to lie down to rest, I'd end up staring at the ceiling.

Estelle ran on her own private, inexhaustible power pack. Her ancient mother would have had biting words to say about her daughter's apparent disregard for her own *condicion,* but I knew better than to say anything. I knew damn well that the hours were going to catch up with both of us, sooner rather than later.

As we drove out of the highway department yard, Estelle glanced at her watch. "It's almost ten. Do you think we'll catch Parris between services?"

"Maybe. Or you might wait until later this afternoon. Catch yourself a few hours rest."

"I'm not tired."

I stretched and groaned. "I bet." I could see the determination set into the muscles of her face. "Estelle, trust me. Parris isn't going anywhere. And if he makes a break, a radio's faster."

"That's not what worries me."

"Yeah, I know it isn't. Daisy's been up there with H. T. Finn for a couple of days. She's enjoying the hell out of life in the woods. Her father knows she's there. It's a beautiful day. It isn't going to rain and give anyone pneumonia." I looked over at her. "Your mothering instinct is in overdrive."

"Do you want to go home?"

"To Posadas? No. I want you to get some rest so you don't make a mistake that you'll regret. And yes, I want some rest. If we go and see Parris, the next thing you'll want to do is walk up to the hot springs again." I shook my head. "The old snowball effect is going to get you."

Estelle looked like she wanted to say something, to argue. But old habits are hard to break. She knew I didn't lean on her unless there was a reason.

"Look at it this way," I said. "Al Martinez seems bright enough. He's got his eyes open. And every road up there is covered, either by the Forest Service or some of the sheriff's department reservists that Tate called in."

She gave in finally and told the dispatcher that we would be ten-seven.

We heard: "Four-o-six, do you copy?" Al Martinez acknowledged. We reached the adobe, and Francis Guzman's Isuzu was in the driveway. I stepped out and level ground felt good. What felt even better was the cool, dark interior of the adobe.

Estelle walked quietly to the bedroom, looked inside, and then turned to me, holding her hands up on her cheek, like a kid sleeping. Francis was home and zonked. She showed me the tiny guest room—about the size of an Amtrak sleeping berth.

"Don't go anywhere without letting me know," I ordered, and Estelle grinned.

"No, sir."

Then I surprised myself. My head hit the pillow, my nose enjoyed the faint aroma of clean cotton for a few seconds, and I fell asleep. My dreams were a restless jumble at first, but then I dreamed that Nolan Parris was helping Daisy Burgess build stinkbug traps.

16

I SLEPT soundly until about four that afternoon. A car door slammed and I opened one eye and looked at my watch. Other than that I didn't move.

What the hell. Nothing was going to happen up on Quebrada Mesa. That sorry patch of ground was sealed tight. Sheriff Tate's staff had notified the victims' next of kin. The medical examiner in the city would release the bodies to the families when every last *t* was crossed and *i* dotted. And Estelle didn't need to worry about Nolan Parris . . . he wasn't going anywhere.

I stretched and found a new ache. In the distance I heard a telephone ring and then quiet voices. I rolled onto my back and covered my eyes with one arm. Maybe we'd have a quiet dinner and go to bed early. We'd see Parris in the morning.

By then the Social Services office would be open and Estelle could turn Daisy's case over to them if Parris balked about custody. That sounded pretty good. I enjoyed the illusion for another two minutes.

At six minutes after four a knuckle rapped on my bedroom door.

"Yo!" I called. I put my hand behind my neck and raised my head a little. The door opened and Estelle looked in. I was surprised to see she was in uniform. "What's up?"

"There's been a hunting accident over on the west side of the pueblo. The pueblo police asked us to assist. You want to come?"

"Sure," I answered with more enthusiasm than I felt. I swung my feet off the bed and pulled on my boots, shoved the clip of the slip-on holster over my belt, and wondered for a minute where the hell I'd put my hat. I got up and walked out into the living room.

"Here," Estelle said, holding the Stetson out to me.

"This means no dinner again, doesn't it?"

"We'll catch something," she said cheerfully. "Anyway, we won't be long. It's not our case. We're just assisting Buddy Vallo."

I got into the car and noticed that Francis Guzman's Isuzu was gone.

"Is Francis already out there?"

Estelle nodded.

"Who was it? Do you know?"

"No. Paul Garcia called dispatch and asked for me. That's all I know."

"You get tangled up in reservation jurisdiction, and you'll be there forever," I muttered.

"Well, they have only two officers," Estelle said. "Buddy is chief . . . he's Mary Vallo's husband . . . Francis's nurse? And Buddy has one assistant who works nights. Sometimes that's not enough."

I didn't bother to remind her that there was only one of her for the entire northwest end of the county.

We skirted what looked like the main residential area of Isidro Pueblo. There wasn't an extra square inch of packed dust to spare. Low, brown adobes that had been settling into the hard earth for centuries lined the single-track roadway.

Estelle slowed down. There were lots of children and they watched us go by with eyes wide. We headed for the river.

The crossing was one of those upside-down bridges where the engineers make a concrete dip through the riverbed. When the river is rolling, nobody crosses. It's that simple. I could have jumped across the trickle of water that day.

The road turned south, following the river for a quarter of a mile before turning west again around a series of rolling hills that formed the base of Chuparrosa Mesa.

I relaxed as we poked along at forty miles an hour on a road designed for ten. The road forked again, one path going up through the hills. Estelle took the other, keeping to the flatland. We angled away from the river toward the vast, open country that stretched virtually unblemished to the Arizona border. The patrol car crested an abrupt rise and bounced down hard enough to scrape the undercarriage.

The road ran along the rim of a deep arroyo, and up ahead I saw Guzman's Isuzu, Paul Garcia's Suburban, and a white Chevy Blazer with government plates. Well off the road, its wheels less than a yard from the arroyo edge, was another vehicle, an old and battered International Scout.

We slid to a stop. So deep was this erosion cut that I couldn't see the bottom until I stepped out of the car. Fifty yards up the arroyo I saw the officers. Estelle's hand-held radio crackled.

"Estelle, there's a spot behind you guys where you can get down into the arroyo. If you walk up the far side, you won't disturb anything."

Estelle waved a hand. We found where both Paul, Francis, and the Indian cop had slid down through the loose sand, and we followed their tracks up the arroyo bed.

The body was lying facedown, close to the arroyo side, with fresh sand from the edge both under and on top of the corpse. He was an Indian, maybe eighteen or twenty, broad-shouldered, and husky bordering on fat.

Estelle stood on the opposite side of the arroyo and looked first at the body, then at the area. I know she would have preferred that everyone had stayed well away until she had arrived, but the damage had been done. The Indian policeman watched us but made no move to walk over to meet us.

"Hello, Buddy," Estelle called, and he nodded a greeting.

He was of indeterminant age, moon-faced, and short. My first impression was one of great patience. I guess he'd have to be patient, working law enforcement in an area the size of an average cattle ranch. I'd have been bored to pudding in a month. He stood with his hands in his pockets, leaning against the arroyo bank, watching the doctor.

Francis Guzman knelt just beyond the corpse's feet, waiting for Estelle's undivided attention.

"What killed him?" I asked, walking across the arroyo.

"A single gunshot wound under the chin," Guzman said. When he saw Estelle step closer, he stood up and gently pulled the corpse's shoulder, rolling the body just enough so that we could see the weapon underneath. It was one of those stubby little .22 auto-loaders.

"See the hand?" Francis asked. The man's index finger was still in the trigger guard and was twisted awkwardly.

When the victim had fallen, he'd clenched onto that rifle out of reflex. He'd have been better off to drop it. Sometime during the fall, probably when he'd crashed to the arroyo bottom, he'd jerked the trigger.

The small bullet had torn into his throat on the right side of the Adam's apple. He'd bled profusely from the mouth, and Guzman added, "It angled up . . . almost straight up. Through the roof of his mouth and into the brain."

"It looks like he fell when the edge of the arroyo caved in," Estelle said.

"That's what I guessed," Buddy said. I squinted at his name tag and read Rupert Vallo.

"Who called it in?"

"I found him myself," Paul Garcia said. He was on quite a roll.

Estelle looked sharply at him. "What were you doing over here?"

When she said that, the corner of Buddy Vallo's mouth twitched just a little. Indian pueblos were sovereign, each with its own police department. We were careful not to trespass on their turf unless asked. Their lead agency for the serious stuff

101

was the Federal Bureau of Investigation—and who the hell wanted to mess with *their* paperwork.

Garcia said, "I left the station and was going to patrol south, since Deputy Martinez was up on the mesa. One of the things on my list was to talk with Chief Vallo here and find out what I could about Robert Waquie. Maybe find out who he hung around with. Maybe get a lead on who was with him Friday night in the truck."

He took a breath and continued as if he were reading from a report.

"Then I heard on the scanner that the Forest Service had a little brush fire off to the west somewhere. They were reporting smoke but hadn't found the source yet. And you know how they've been talkin' that one little smoker could spread and take out the whole mountain. So I thought, what the hell. I was already headed this way.

"I got to the pueblo and saw that this dirt road crossed the river. So I decided to follow it and see if it went far enough to reach the National Forest over on the mesa. Maybe I could see the smoke better from over here. Three point two miles later, I see this Scout parked by the road. Just out of habit, I checked the plate. I saw that the tag was expired so I called it in. Then I got out to look around." He shrugged.

"That's when I saw the fresh crumbled sand along the arroyo lip. I got to lookin', went downstream a ways, and then I saw him."

"How'd the plate come back?"

"The Scout's registered to a Cecil Lucero. From here."

"That's Cecil," Buddy Vallo said. "I know him real good." A long pause followed. "I warned him about the license plate last week. Him and Robert Waquie, I spend more time chasin' their tails than anybody else in the pueblo."

Estelle glanced at Vallo. I saw a flicker of what might have been annoyance. She knelt down as Francis handed her the man's wallet. The corpse's driver's license said that Cecil Lucero had turned twenty-one three days before.

"Are there any other injuries?" I asked Francis.

"A broken index finger on his right hand."

"Caught in the trigger guard when he fell?" Estelle asked. Francis nodded. "Probably."

"How long's he been here?"

"I'm no expert on postmortem lividity," Francis said, "but if I had to guess, I'd say no more than a couple hours . . . five or six at the outside."

Estelle straightened up and craned her neck to see the top of the arroyo. The sides were steep and twelve feet high . . . enough that we couldn't see the truck unless we stepped to nearly the center of the arroyo.

More to herself than any of us, she said, "So he maybe saw a rabbit or something, stopped, got out, and got excited. Stepped too close. The arroyo is a little undercut here. It caved in and he fell. Pop."

"That's what I thought," Paul Garcia said.

"I don't see any other obvious tracks," I said. The bottom of the arroyo was a mass of hoofprints where rambling cattle had mixed the gravelly sand.

"Did you see any tracks when you climbed down here?" Estelle asked Buddy Vallo.

"No."

She looked at Paul Garcia. "And he was dead when you found him?"

"Yes. He sure was."

Estelle methodically pressed on. "Was the Scout idling when you came by or switched off?"

"Off. The keys were in the ignition."

"And the driver's door was closed?"

"Yes."

"And the window?"

"Closed."

"Was the door locked?"

"I didn't check."

Estelle frowned. I said to Estelle, "You're wondering about the window, aren't you?"

"That's what I was wondering."

"People do drive with their windows closed, Estelle."

"When it's ninety out and they're hunting?"

I exhaled wearily. "Estelle, maybe he was planning to do some hiking. He got out and buttoned the thing up."

"Then he locked his keys in the car."

"That's happened before."

We heard another vehicle and Francis Guzman said, "That's probably the ambulance. One unit was tied up with a transfer, and they had to get the second one out of the garage."

Estelle turned to her briefcase and began to unpack the camera equipment. She was still frowning and thinking hard, and I knew it was best just to let her stew until she was ready to put the pieces together.

But this time if she was trying to tie Lucero's accident to the murders up on Quebrada Mesa, she was daydreaming. She had the murder jitters. Vallo had mentioned Lucero and Waquie in the same breath, but what the hell did that mean? The pueblo was tiny. The odds were nearly a hundred percent that two victims from the same village would know each other.

What had happened here was obvious to me. Accidents where the hunter shot himself almost always involved a fence, a fall, or a dropped weapon . . . one or more of the three. This one fit the pattern.

I looked around for some shade. Even in the late afternoon, the arroyo was an oven. It was going to stay that way until sunset, too, since the arroyo's general orientation was east–west. And when Estelle began her unpacking, I knew I had time to spare.

My bladder began to send signals. The only tree in sight was a sorry little scrub juniper that was about to fall out of the arroyo bank fifty yards upstream. At that point, the arroyo veered to the right.

"I'm going around the corner," I said and thrust my hands in my pockets as I walked slowly through the soft sand. It was almost as much work as trudging up a mountainside.

I reached the juniper and stopped. What looked like a single boot print was pressed into the sand. It was hard to be sure, since the sand was so coarse and dry that it refused to hold any positive definition. I stood and looked at the mark, then up at the slope where the juniper was hanging on.

If someone wanted to climb up out of the arroyo, this was a good spot. The bank was sloped, and cattle had beaten an obvious trail down from the top.

With the lack of rain the boot print—if indeed it was one—could have been made any time in the past month. I decided to walk around the next "S" in the arroyo for some privacy. I took about twenty steps.

"Well, son of a bitch," I said aloud and stopped in my tracks. My right hand drifted around behind my back to where the stubby .357 nestled. I didn't move for a good three minutes, looking and listening.

With my hand still on the magnum, I stepped forward to take a closer look at the corpse. No hunting accident had dropped this one.

17

T H E corpse lay on his face, arms and legs outstretched like he'd been bashed to the ground by a giant club.

A bloodstain the size of a dinner plate soaked his denim work shirt. The shirt was old and faded, with plenty of rips here and there, the kind barbed wire would tear when a man's a little careless ducking through fences.

I stepped closer. The seven small holes in the center of his back weren't from barbs . . . and they were grouped tightly enough that I could have covered them with my hand.

Without moving my feet I twisted around looking for spent shell casings. There were none. I walked backward the way I had come, trying not to disturb the arroyo bottom. A half dozen times I thought I had found a shell casing, but it was only the sun winking from the quartz-loaded stream gravel.

At the juniper I turned around. Downsteam, the ambulance crew was just making preparations to load Cecil Lucero's body on the gurney. I whistled sharply. Estelle Reyes-Guzman must have read the urgency on my face, because she got off her knees where she'd been photographing the .22 rifle and walked up the arroyo to meet me.

"I don't think this is a simple hunting accident," I said.

"Why? What did you find?"

"There's another corpse, just around the corner. And he didn't fall on his own gun."

"Shot?"

"Yes."

"For sure murder?"

"No doubt. Seven times in the back. That's tough to do by accident."

"Son of a bitch," Estelle breathed. It was the first time I'd ever heard her curse. She touched my elbow. "Lead me up there. I'll walk in your tracks."

"That's Kenneth Lucero," Buddy Vallo said.

"Cecil's brother?" Estelle asked.

Vallo nodded. "Younger brother." Buddy pointed, holding his arm out straight like he was pointing a rifle. "You can see their truck from here."

I stepped over to where he was standing, just where the arroyo turned south. Sure enough, for several feet the banks didn't block the view.

"Maybe seventy yards," I said. "Any kid with a scoped rifle could do that or better." I looked at Estelle. "Hell, even I could shoot like that."

Francis Guzman pulled up Kenneth Lucero's shirt. The bullet holes were small and dimpled inward. "Right through the spine, at heart level," Francis said, pointing at two of the small holes.

"That explains why he dropped in a heap," I said. "Just like tagging a rabbit in midhop." I knelt down. "Twenty-two caliber, you think?"

Guzman nodded. "Not much bleeding. No through-and-through. That's what I would guess."

"And the rifle downstream is a semiautomatic," I said.

"There's still one bullet in the clip of the rifle and one in the chamber," Estelle said. "The clip's capacity is ten." She turned to Buddy Vallo. "It could have happened that way. Cecil could have shot his brother and then fell and shot himself by accident. That would account for all the rounds."

"If the gun was fully loaded in the first place," I reminded her.

She squinted against the sun and harsh sand. "We need to find those shell casings."

I asked Vallo, "Was there any animosity between the two brothers? Anything that might have led to this?"

He pushed out his lower lip and frowned. "Maybe. Brothers fight sometimes." I was about to add that a fight between siblings usually didn't result in murder, but Vallo added, "And they were both chasin' the same girl."

He half grinned at the irony of it. "I don't think she was interested in either one of 'em. She was a white girl." He said it as if that explained everything. He hadn't spent much time in society outside Isidro Pueblo, where you never could be sure who—or even what—was going to experiment with matrimony.

Estelle asked, "Who's the girl?"

"Lucy Grider. She lives on that ranch on the way to Encinas."

"Where the hell is that?" I asked. The girl's name hadn't registered.

"About six miles. Where the state road forks, south of the pueblo? You go east. It's a little village up that valley. She's the sister to one of the boys you pulled off the mesa yesterday."

I turned and looked with surprise at Estelle. She'd sat down abruptly on a hummock of sand. She took off her Stetson and dropped it crown down beside her. "Kelly Grider's sister," she said. "I don't believe this." She looked up at me. "Waquie and Grider were killed together. Now these two. They both chased Grider's sister."

"They hung out together off and on," Vallo said.

"The four of them?"

"I've seen them together."

"I would have liked to have known that," Estelle said, more to herself than anyone else. But she knew as well as I that the information would have come out in due time. None of us had

108

been at leisure the past thirty-six hours to survey the county, picking up leads. "Have you seen anyone else with them?" Estelle asked, and Vallo shook his head. Old man Waquie had said five in the truck . . . maybe he'd miscounted. Or maybe the fifth one had been Cecilia Burgess.

Estelle took a deep breath. "All right. We've got the daylight. I want this arroyo swept clean. I want those shell casings. And anything else. Paul, go back the way we came, start at the truck, and, really carefully, work along the top edge of the arroyo to this spot and even beyond. Then do the same on the other side, just in case. Buddy and I will work the body and this area."

She turned to me. "Sir, would you dust Lucero's truck? The print kit is in the trunk of the car."

"You bet. Are you going to call Pat Tate?"

"After a bit. We're on the reservation, and it's Buddy's case. It's up to him." She raised an eyebrow at Vallo.

"Let's see what we find," he said. "Maybe this is as far as it goes."

Stranger things had happened, of course. But I think the same scenario was going through my mind as Estelle's. That little International Scout was small enough that a man could hide it pretty easily . . . especially on a mesa as thickly timbered as Quebrada Mesa. And if there'd been friction between the Luceros and Grider over the latter's sister, who the hell knew.

If Cecil Lucero was cold-blooded enough to use his own brother for target practice, he'd have had no trouble arranging a trip for two friends over a cliff—and then snapping a neck afterward.

18

◆◆◆

L U C Y Grider might have been able to provide some answers. I was surprised when Estelle sent Paul Garcia to Encinas to interview her. I had to agree that Paul was as diligent a rookie as I'd ever seen—it was hard to be irritated at him for chasing brushfire smoke when, in the process, he'd stumbled onto a murder.

Estelle coached him on what questions to ask and then we headed home shortly after eight that evening. This snowball of events was leaving us miles behind in its wake.

"I want to talk with Nolan Parris," she said as we turned into the dirt lane that led to the Guzman adobe. "And I want to talk with him tonight."

I should have guessed that was coming. She pulled into her driveway and asked, "Will you go with me?"

"Of course," I said. "If you feed me first." Francis pulled into the driveway before we reached the front step. He hadn't slammed the Isuzu's door before Estelle met him. The two kids embraced for a long time.

"Seems like a couple of days since I've seen you," she said, and Francis laughed and removed her Stetson so the brim wouldn't hit him in the mouth when she hugged him. Their nap that afternoon had done some good.

"You don't like clandestine meetings out in hidden arroyos?" he asked. I went inside so they'd have a minute together without a chaperone. I tossed my hat on the two-cushion sofa and pulled the holstered revolver off my belt.

The telephone was on the wall by the doorway to the kitchen. I dialed zero and then Martin Holman's home number in Posadas. The call went through after I gave the mechanical-sounding operator the billing. It rang twice, and then another robotic voice said, "I'm sorry, that number is temporarily out of service. If you need assistance, please stay on the line and an operator will help you."

I hung up, perplexed. Holman didn't earn a bundle as sheriff of Posadas County, but he sure as hell earned enough to pay his phone bill. Maybe his four-year-old had jerked the cord out of the wall. The little bastard was capable of that and worse.

Estelle and Francis came in the house just as I was dialing the Posadas County Sheriff's Department. Gayle Sedillos was working the desk. She was the best dispatcher we had. Estelle had started that way. But unlike Estelle, Gayle had no aspirations beyond the desk. She answered the phone after the first ring.

"Where's Holman?" I asked the instant she said she'd accept the call.

"He hasn't gotten hold of you, sir?"

"No. What's he want?" Holman always wanted something, and most of the time it could wait.

There was a pause at the other end, and I could hear voices. Then Gayle said, "Sir, Bob Torrez just came in. Let me have you talk with him."

I glanced at Estelle and looked heavenward. She grinned. Deputy Bob Torrez picked up the phone. His voice was usually so soft I had a hard time hearing him.

"Sir?"

"What's up, Bob?"

"Sheriff Holman was trying to get hold of you earlier today," Torrez said.

I glanced down at the unchecked answering machine where his message no doubt awaited. "We were out," I said. "What's he want?"

"His house burned down last night."

"His house burned down?"

"Yes, sir."

"Anyone hurt?"

"No, sir. But the house was a complete loss. And his two dogs."

"How'd the fire happen?"

"We don't know, sir. But we've sealed the place off. The sheriff's out there. And the investigators from the fire department are still out there."

"Are they going to need an assist?" Sheriff Holman had lived in the village of Posadas and the volunteer fire department was eager and generally efficient. But the two men who called themselves investigators were good-intentioned amateurs.

"They haven't said," Torrez answered.

"Call the state office and get somebody over from Cruces," I suggested. "And you're sure everyone's all right?"

"Yes, sir. Sheriff Holman sent the family to Deming to stay with relatives. And he's staying at the Essex Motel."

I groaned. "Christ, nobody wants to live in a motel, Bob. Holman knows where the key to my house is. Tell him to use it."

"I'll pass the message along, sir. He wanted to know when you were planning to head home."

"It's going to be a day or two. We've got a little action up here, and I'm giving Estelle the benefit of my vast wisdom."

Torrez took that seriously as he did most things. "Yes, sir. Sheriff Holman wanted to know if you were coming back tomorrow."

"I'll see. It's unlikely though. Just tell him to use my house and call the state fire marshal's office, if he hasn't already."

"Yes, sir."

"Let me talk with Gayle now."

"Yes, sir."

When the dispatcher came on the phone, I said, "Gayle, is there anything the Holmans need that you know of?"

"I don't think so, sir. But I'll ask. They sure lost everything, though."

"Well, tell him to use my house instead of camping out at the damn motel."

"I'll do that. How's Estelle doing?"

"Fine. You want to talk with her?" She said yes, and I held the phone out to Estelle. They talked for ten minutes. Maybe Holman would have enough on his mind that he wouldn't rant about the phone bill.

Estelle finally hung up and for the first time since I'd set foot in San Estevan, the three of us had dinner together.

I damn near drooled a puddle as I watched the enchiladas sink in a sea of fresh green chili. Francis handed me what I hoped would be the first of several cold beers. He poured a glass of red wine for Estelle. Estelle must have read something on my face, because she said, "Vitamin W. It goes with Mexican food better than that stuff you guys drink."

The fire of her chili was undiminished . . . it made even the cafe's burrito grande seem like a bland milk shake. I wiped my forehead, blew my nose, and panted. "God, this is good. Destructive, but good."

"Destructive, hell," Francis said. "Did you know it's been proven in the lab that green chili kills bacteria?"

"I don't doubt it," I said. "Does the kid start kicking when you eat this stuff?"

Estelle laughed. "Not at two months, sir."

"What are you going to name him?"

"Or her," Francis said and handed me another beer.

"Ask me again in seven months," Estelle replied.

"Is your mother going to come up here?"

"For the grand event, you mean?" Estelle shook her head. "We're going to Tres Santos."

"You're kidding."

"They've got a pretty good clinic there," Francis said.

I frowned and said, "Huh," for want of anything better.

"My mother is too frail to travel up here," Estelle said. "This probably will be the only grandchild she lives to meet. There are worse things than being born in that big adobe house in Mexico."

"Huh," I said again. I shrugged. "What do the Guzmans think of that idea?"

"They're going to be there, too."

Estelle offered seconds and like a fool I accepted. "El Padrino should be present, too," she said.

"I'm flattered. But I've had so many days off that Holman's not going to let me take another one for five years."

"Are you going back tomorrow?"

"Probably I should." I glanced at my watch. It was night shift time again. "You'll wrap this up this evening, after we talk with Parris. . . . I'm interested in what he has to say about his prints being on the truck."

"Do you think that Cecil Lucero shot his brother?"

"Don't you?"

She toyed with the remains of the enchilada on her plate. "I don't know. Usually, when I'm sure of how something happened, I can picture it in my mind."

"The two of them got out of the Scout and walked a ways up along the arroyo," Francis said. "Kenneth went down into the arroyo. Cecil shot him from up above."

"Maybe."

"That's where Paul found the seven shell casings this afternoon, Estelle," I said.

"The M.E. will tell you for sure about the angle of the bullets," Francis said. "After the shooting, Cecil walks back toward the Scout. He's nervous. So like most of us would, he turns around to look back up the arroyo. He can't see his brother's body, so he steps closer to the edge to try another view." He shrugged.

"What's the problem with that?" I asked.

"I'd feel better if we'd found the last casing," Estelle said. "I'd feel better if I had that."

114

"There are any number of ways it could have happened that make sense," I said. Estelle nodded, but I knew she wasn't convinced. I pushed my plate away and stood up. I said what she really wanted to hear. "Let's go see Parris."

19

◆ ◆ ◆

F A T H E R Nolan Parris greeted us at the door, and it seemed as if he had expected us—and more than that . . . he was somehow relieved we'd returned.

"I think you know Deputy Reyes-Guzman?" I said as Parris showed us into the front room.

"Our paths have crossed once or twice," Parris said. He and Estelle shook hands. "Would you folks like some coffee or tea or something?"

We declined, and Parris closed the door. His limp hadn't improved. He gestured to chairs and we sat. Estelle pulled out her notebook and pen and said, "Father Parris, I want to talk with you about Friday night."

Parris nodded and folded his hands, waiting.

Estelle leafed through the notebook, stopping to read here and there. "Father, as you may have heard, we're investigating the deaths of two young men. Their truck somehow went over the edge of Quebrada Mesa, probably sometime early yesterday evening."

Parris again nodded. "A tragic thing," he said quietly.

"Father, we have reason to believe that the truck in question was also involved somehow in the death of Cecilia Burgess on Friday night."

Parris sat back in the chair. His right hand drifted up to touch his pectoral cross. He watched Estelle. It may have been my imagination, but I sensed an inner calm that hadn't been there the day before.

Estelle looked up from her notes and cocked her head, giving Parris an opportunity. The priest held up his left hand, palm up, as if he were going to beckon for more information. His right hand remained on the cross. "And you feel that I have information about that night?"

"Yes, sir, I do."

Parris looked at me. "Since we talked yesterday, I've had time for considerable counsel." I didn't ask if it was counsel with someone else or with his own soul. It didn't matter as long as he had the right answers.

Nolan Parris took a deep breath, held it, and then released it the way a smoker might jet out a long, thin plume of smoke.

"On Friday evening I was out in the garden. Perhaps you've seen it, beyond the driveway. It's not far from the highway. I'm not a gardener but it's a quiet spot for reflection. There's an old wooden bench under one of the apricot trees that's a favorite of mine. I like to sit there and watch the stars.

"Anyway, shortly after ten . . . in fact, I was just about to go inside . . . I glanced up as several cars passed. In the light of their headlights I noticed Cecilia Burgess. She was walking along the highway."

"Northbound?" I asked.

"Yes. But on the other side of the highway, facing traffic." He hesitated. "I saw the moment as an opportunity, I suppose. I called to her. Now you must understand that we haven't been on the best of terms . . . at least from her point of view. I thought that she was going to ignore me and so I called again. She crossed the highway. I wanted to talk with her about Daisy . . . about where the child might go to preschool in the fall, where the two of them were planning to stay. I was uneasy that she might not have made plans."

"Were you able to settle anything?" Estelle asked.

Parris shook his head. "No. In fact, I made matters worse,

117

I suppose. She asked me how much I was willing to pay, and I hesitated. She interpreted that as reluctance on my part to provide for the child. I tried to explain to her that I simply have no funds of my own—nothing significant anyway. She didn't accept that. I tried to explain that there might be some sort of diocesan help . . . scholarships, housing, maybe that sort of thing. She took offense at that, perhaps thinking that I wanted the child in someone else's custody other than her own."

"Did you?" I asked.

"No, of course not. A child should be with its mother if at all possible. But Cecilia became angry. We'd had this same conversation before, I suppose. I tried to reason with her, and she became angrier still. She could be a most vocal young woman." Parris looked rueful. "As her voice raised, I tried to calm her, and that made her even angrier."

He held up both hands. "I'm afraid I made a stupid mistake. Thinking that she might react positively to a show of strength on my part, I reached out and held her by the elbow. I told her that if she really cared about the child, she wouldn't leave Daisy out in the forest while she walks here and there late at night along a busy highway.

"I offered to drive her up to the hot springs. She retorted that I was last person she wanted to be seen with and that she'd walk wherever and whenever she pleased." Parris shrugged. "It was one of those verbal fights that just . . . well, nobody wins."

Estelle asked, "Did it end there?"

"No," Parris said. "By this time, we had moved from the garden where I'd first suggested that we talk out to the shoulder of the highway. There were several oncoming cars, and as if to spite me, she stuck out her thumb to hitch a ride. None of the traffic stopped, of course." He looked down. "I wanted nothing more than to jump into the underbrush along the road and hide." He looked at me and smiled slightly. "I'm not much of a hero, am I?"

An appropriate philosophical reply didn't materialize in my head, so I just shrugged.

Parris looked pained. "The next vehicle came around the corner almost immediately, and it did stop. It was the Ford pickup truck. I don't think I've ever felt such panic because I could see, perfectly clearly, what would happen." He stopped and both hands clutched the crucifix.

"A blue and white truck?" Estelle asked.

"Yes. I've seen it in the neighborhood on a number of occasions."

"How many occupants?"

"There were at least four. Maybe five." He hesitated. "Let me think." After a moment he said, "Five. Two in the bed and three up in the cab. I knew from their behavior that they had been drinking."

"What did they do?"

"They were loud and when the two in the back stood up to see why the truck had stopped, they could hardly keep their balance. The passenger on the window side held out a can toward Cecilia."

"And she accepted a ride from them," Estelle said, and I could see that she had finished the story for herself.

"I tried to prevent it; I really did. Cecilia stepped up on the back bumper, then over the tailgate, before I could reach her. She almost lost her balance, but one of the drunks helped her to the front of the truck bed. I reached the side of the truck and grabbed ahold, pleading with her to show some sense. The driver stepped on the gas hard just as one of them pushed me away. I thought for a moment I was going to be hit by the rear tire."

"That's when you sprained your ankle?" I asked, but Parris shook his head.

"No. They drove off, and I could see the truck weave this way and that. I was furious with myself and petrified for Cecilia. I pictured every tragedy that might happen except the one that did.

"I pictured the truck weaving off the highway and into the

119

river. Or crashing head-on into someone else. The more I thought about it the worse I felt.

"Finally the obvious solution was the easiest one. I took the retreat's station wagon and drove up the highway. I reached the campground and stopped. If they had let Cecilia off there, she would be walking up the trail to Finn's campsite. So I parked and tried to find the trail. My flashlight wasn't very good, but eventually I found the path and the Forest Service signs."

I reflected that while Parris was stumbling around among the ponderosas, I had been snoring away in the Blazer, right there in the parking lot. He would have had to walk within a dozen paces of me. That was another reason to give up on the damn exercise routine. If I hadn't taken the hike earlier, I would probably have been lying in the Blazer, eyes open like a lemur, insomnia in control. I'd missed a chance.

"I found the camp," Parris said. "And Cecilia wasn't there. Both Finn and the boy who stays with him were. Finn told me that Daisy was asleep in the tent. I told him what had happened."

"What was his reaction?" Estelle asked.

"I'm not sure. It was dark and other than the camp fire and my flashlight, there wasn't much light to see by. He told me that she probably was up the canyon, maybe at one of the other campgrounds, partying . . . that she'd be all right . . . that she could take care of herself."

"Did you give Finn a description of the truck?"

Parris frowned. "Not a description. Not like you would. But I told him who I thought it was."

"Who do you think owns the truck?" I asked.

"I don't know who owns it. But I've seen one of the Waquie boys driving it on occasion. And his father. The family are parish members."

"And you mentioned the name to Finn?" Estelle asked.

"Yes."

"Then what?"

"Finn offered me a cup of coffee. He had a pot on the fire."

"That's it?"

"Yes."

"You didn't discuss Daisy with him?" I asked.

"No. I have to admit, Sheriff, that Finn makes me uneasy. Cecilia had mentioned at one time that Finn was a minister of some sort. I've only met him twice—that night was the second time. Both times, he looked at me . . . and my Roman collar . . . as if I were something of a joke." Parris managed a wan smile. "I know I've got an active imagination. But that's the impression I got."

He looked up at the ceiling, using a dramatic pause like a good storyteller does when he's organizing his thoughts.

"But I found myself thinking that if I accepted a cup of coffee, that might somehow bring the two of us—Finn and me—a little closer, and I'd be able to talk with him."

"But that wasn't the case," I said.

"No. In fact, he handed me the cup and then went into the tent. So did the boy. Without a word. I stayed by the fire a few minutes, and when it was obvious that our conversation was over I left. Just a moment or two after the boy did."

"Arajanian left?"

"Is that his name? Yes. He and Finn talked a little when they came out of the tent, and then the boy left. He went down the hill. Finn went back in the tent."

"You didn't go with him?"

Parris shook his head. "No. And I could never have kept up with him anyway. He ran." Parris shook his head. "Like a ghost. He didn't even use a light."

I could feel Estelle looking at me and when I glanced at her, I could see that her face was set like stone.

When she spoke, her voice was so low I could hardly hear her. "When you left, Finn was still in camp?"

Parris nodded.

"And then you walked back to your station wagon in the campground."

"Yes. It took me nearly an hour. I fell hard, just above the

121

fork in the trail. I thought I had broken my ankle." He rubbed his sock. "But it's just a bad sprain."

"And then you drove back here," Estelle asked. "What did you do between that time and when you heard about Cecilia?"

"Prayed, I suppose," Parris said. He looked at me thoughtfully. "I lied to you earlier, Sheriff. I told you I found out about Cecilia the next morning at Garcia's Trading Post. That's not the case."

He turned to Estelle as if he wanted to make sure she got it right in her notes. "I heard all the sirens. I'm sure everyone in the valley did. I knew right away that whatever it was, the emergency somehow involved Cecilia. I knew it in my heart. I got up, got dressed, and took the station wagon."

"With that bad ankle?"

"Yes. And I drove north until I came to the accident site. I saw all the red lights, the ambulance . . . I saw that they were just loading the gurney. I'm ashamed to say that I rationalized myself out of it at that point."

"Meaning what?" I asked.

"Meaning that I should have stopped. I saw her face, knew it was her. I should have talked with you on the spot. But I decided that I couldn't help Cecilia any more just then. She was in good hands. There was nothing I could do. So I drove back to the retreat, and when I learned she'd been transferred to the city, I drove to Albuquerque."

"And you were at the hospital when she died?"

"Yes. The rest of my story, as I told you yesterday, is the truth."

"Did you ever have your ankle looked at by a physician?"

"No."

"Why not?" I asked.

"It's just a bad sprain. There's nothing a doctor could do for it that I can't."

"Did anyone else here at the retreat look at it?"

Parris frowned at my question. "Well, yes. Father Sandoval examined it shortly after I returned home. I had planned to ask him to look at it in the morning, but apparently he'd been

122

awakened by the station wagon pulling into the driveway. He said he looked out the window and saw me limp to the front steps." Parris turned and gestured at the door. "He met me in the entranceway and insisted that he look at the ankle then and there."

"Is this Father Sandoval here now?" I asked.

"Of course."

"We'll need to talk to him."

Parris looked at his watch. "It's quite late. Can't it wait?"

"No, it can't," Estelle said, her tone flat.

Parris turned from her to me, his eyes searching my face. "There's something you don't believe?"

I didn't see any point in sugarcoating it. "You lied to me once, Father. We have no way of knowing if you're lying now. If we talk with Father Sandoval and he confirms when he treated your ankle, that gives us something to go on."

"I'm telling you the truth."

"Perhaps. Is Sandoval here?"

Parris fell silent for a minute, then said as he stood up, "This is going to be a very public case after a while, isn't it?"

"What do you mean by that?"

"I mean it will all come out in the end . . . about Cecilia and me, about Daisy . . . all of it."

"I suppose it will," I said. I wasn't feeling kindly at the moment. It didn't bother me much that Parris might have to wallow for a while in his own mess. "I'll go with you to fetch Father Sandoval." Parris didn't argue.

We left Estelle in the front room and went upstairs. It was obvious that Parris's ankle really did hurt. Father Sandoval must have been waiting at his door because he answered Parris's light knock immediately.

Sandoval was the same priest who had greeted me on my first visit. He joined us downstairs and we made it brief. The older priest verified Parris's story, and my instincts told me that Father Mateo Sandoval was telling the absolute truth.

After Sandoval left the room, Parris looked relieved. Estelle snapped her notebook closed and stood up. "There's one more thing," she said. "Finn has no legitimate custody claim on Daisy."

"No, I suppose he doesn't," Parris said. I grimaced, because his tone said clearly to me, "I wish he did." Estelle read the same message on his face. She didn't raise her voice, but the words came out clipped and hard.

"Father Parris, I want Daisy out of the woods. And I want her out tomorrow."

The priest started to waffle. "I was going to talk with you about that," he said.

"I'm listening."

The man didn't know what to say. Maybe he couldn't face H. T. Finn eye to eye . . . or maybe he was still unwilling to admit that his uncomplicated life at the retreat was over. I didn't know what the Catholic Church did to one of its priests who became a parent . . . and right then, that wasn't our concern.

"You're her father," Estelle said. "You can go up there with us tomorrow morning and take custody of the child. It's that simple. You are her father."

"I wish it were that simple," Parris said, and Estelle locked him with an icy glare.

"It *is* that simple," she said. "And between now and seven tomorrow morning when we pick you up, you might give some thought to the form your child support is going to take." She stood up and turned to me. "I have all I need."

As I stepped by him, I patted Parris on the shoulder. It was the sort of fatherly pat I might have given one of my sons after an ultimatum he didn't like. "Seven o'clock, Father," I said.

On the drive back home Estelle didn't say a word until we turned into the lane to the adobe. And then, so quietly I almost didn't hear, she said, "The fifth one."

"In the truck, you mean?"

She nodded. "If we find the fifth kid who was riding in that pickup truck, maybe we'll find the answers."

"Paul Garcia's been talking with Lucy Grider. Maybe he turned up something."

"I hope so. Otherwise, unless number five comes forward, we're going to have to sift through this community one person at a time."

"That won't be the first time we've done that." I glanced over at Estelle. She was chewing the corner of her lower lip, her forehead wrinkled in thought. I could have counted on one hand the number of times I'd heard Estelle express doubts when she'd been working on a case. She had an excuse this time. We hadn't enjoyed an extra minute to think things through or hunt for answers.

But this evening, as it turned out, the doubts weren't necessary. We didn't have to hunt. Kyle Osuna came to us.

20

T H E light was on over the front door at eleven that night. The good doc was working late, called to the clinic to set a broken arm. The arm belonged to one of the Girl Scouts over at Camp Tracy, who'd done nothing more spectacular than fall off the top bunk during a pillow fight.

Francis promised that he wouldn't take long—a quick cast, a handful of aspirin, and the little girl would be back in business. In a couple days she'd feel good enough to use the heavy cast as a weapon and inflict some real damage.

Estelle turned the light on after Francis left. I was reading the Albuquerque afternoon paper and Estelle was poring through her notes. She had talked for almost a half hour with Sheriff Tate on the telephone, and Tate was just as frustrated as we were. He told Estelle that all she had to do was say the word and she'd have reinforcements, but she nixed the idea. In fact, leaving men up on Quebrada Mesa was a waste of time. She was sure that what had happened there was finished. Tate didn't argue. If you put an army in the field, it costs lots of bucks.

"All you can do is keep scratchin'," Tate had said.

"We're close," Estelle had told him. Close to what, I wondered. The wave of murders was three-pronged . . . Cecilia

Burgess pitched out of the truck, Waquie and Grider crushed in that same truck, with a neck snapped for good measure, and now the Lucero brothers.

Estelle was the only one who doubted that Cecil Lucero had pulled the trigger on his brother. I thought she was fishing and told her so. True, the entire scenario was based on assumptions. It was even an assumption—a grand one—that the Luceros had been in the truck with Waquie and Grider. Who the hell knew.

"You don't think Cecil Lucero is the key?" I asked, laying down the newspaper. Estelle shook her head. "You don't think he killed his brother?"

"No. It doesn't make sense, sir. The shots were fired from the lip of the arroyo, approximately twenty yards from where we found Kenneth Lucero's body. That's where Paul found the shell casings. Now why would Kenneth Lucero be walking or running up the arroyo bed?"

"He was being chased."

"By his brother? If his brother took him out there with the intention of killing him, what ruse did he use? That they would go hunting? If that was the case, why didn't Kenneth have a gun of his own?"

"Maybe he forced him out there."

"Come on, sir. Cecil would have had to make Kenneth drive and hold a rifle on him in the car. That's difficult to do. Why didn't Kenneth try to get away before they got out that far?" She stopped for breath. "You see? It's got so many holes . . ."

"Do you think the Luceros were involved in Waquie's and Grider's deaths then?"

"Maybe. I don't see someone who'd push a truck over a cliff, then snap a neck for good measure, using a rifle the next day."

"That's what we're missing," I said. "There's no pattern to any of this. You think someone aced the Lucero brothers. All right. Suppose that's true. If that same person was the one who killed the two in the truck, he was a creative son of a bitch . . . and he didn't leave much of a trail. If the incidents are unrelated, it makes even less sense." As I saw it, our problem was time. Cops like to work methodically, but we'd been chasing one fire after another, without a moment to sit and reflect.

Earlier in the evening, Deputy Paul Garcia had stopped by and summarized his interview with Lucy Grider. The girl had given him a list of a dozen people who might have been hanging out with Robert Waquie or the Lucero brothers that night, assuming that they all had been together in the first place. None of the names stood off the page for Estelle.

"Talk to each one of them," I had said. The idea of overtime didn't bother either Garcia or Al Martinez, and Estelle had sent them off together.

From out of the blue Estelle announced, "Finn had all the information." I put down the newspaper. She was staring into the open briefcase, not focusing on any of the papers. "Parris told him about Cecilia Burgess in the truck. He even told Finn that the truck belonged to Robert Waquie. How much work would it be to find out who was involved?"

"Not much, I suppose," I said. "Although we seem to be having problems."

"Just suppose Finn is involved," Estelle persisted. "Just suppose. The priest goes to his camp that night, and Finn learns about the truck. Now, he's got all the next day . . . we're working the case without Parris's information. Finn finds out that it's Waquie's truck. When he catches up with them, Waquie and Grider are together. And maybe he finds out from the two of them who the others were."

"Maybe, maybe, maybe. Come on, Estelle. You saw Finn. He couldn't care less."

"It could have happened that way."

"He'd have to be one fast worker, Estelle. In the first place, we were up at his camp on Saturday, right after the accident with Cecilia Burgess."

"He may have found Waquie that morning . . . or later in the afternoon."

"He would have had to. And then you're suggesting he finds

128

the Lucero brothers and murders them. Nice theory but no evidence."

"And he's got Arajanian to help him."

"Sure. You don't have a scrap of evidence to support that."

"No, but there's possible motive," she said doggedly. "And that's enough for a start." I was about to question that when we heard the thumping at the back door.

I said, "You got a dog that wants in?"

"Sure don't." She got up and went into the kitchen. She pulled the curtain back a little and looked out. There was no outside light over that door, and she couldn't have seen a train if it had been parked on the step. She pulled the door open and I heard her suck in breath with surprise.

"Sir," she called and I sprang to my feet, dumping the newspaper on the floor.

A hunched figure was sitting on the single wooden step. He leaned sideways against the screen door, head down. He whimpered a little, then lifted his head and said, "Please."

My first thought had been that we'd collected a wandering drunk, but there was no inebriation in that voice . . . just hurt. "Now what the hell." I pushed past Estelle and tried to open the door, but he was blocking it. From the hunch of his shoulders and the hang of his head, he wasn't up to moving.

"Let me go around front," Estelle said, and she darted off, grabbing her flashlight from the kitchen counter. In seconds she appeared in the darkness. When the beam of the flashlight hit him in the face, the man cringed against the door. "No," he murmured.

"It's all right," Estelle said. "We're here." She saw the blood at the same time I did. A puddle was forming on the gray wood of the step.

"Move him away from the door so we can get him inside," I said. I slapped on the overhead kitchen light.

Estelle put her arm around the man's shoulder and tried to scrunch him sideways to the edge of the step. His head tipped back, and I saw that he was biting his lower lip so hard that he'd drawn blood.

With a grunt of agony he pushed himself to his feet, supported by Estelle on one side and stiff-arming the side of the house with his free hand. I held open the door, and the two of them careened into the kitchen. He dropped to his knees, taking Estelle with him, and then slumped over to curl on the floor in a fetal position.

"The door," he whispered. "Close the door." I did so. Now that he was in the light, I could see that he wasn't more than a kid, maybe twenty at the most. And he was wearing the universal kid's summer uniform—running shoes, faded blue jeans, and T-shirt. And if he bled much more, he wouldn't live to be older than a kid. His left side was soaked with blood from lower ribs to knee. And what wasn't bloody was dripping wet, caked here and there with fresh mud.

I knelt down. "You hold the flashlight," I said. The overhead light fixture held one of those useless sixty-watt bulbs that threw just enough light so you didn't bark your shins on the table and chairs.

The kid lay with his head on the cool linoleum, eyes closed, breath rapid and shallow. I pulled up the blood-soaked T-shirt. "Jesus Christ," I said. "Hold the light over here." I pried his right hand loose from where it was clamped to his side.

He was leaking from two places. The entry wound was a pencil-sized, punched hole a hand's width from his spine, right on the second floating rib from the bottom.

The projectile had blown right through him, exiting by taking out the front end of the same rib. The exit wound wasn't neat and was as big as a quarter. It bled copiously, and I guessed the bullet had nicked either the kid's stomach or kidney or both. I yanked a dish towel off the side rack by the sink and made a large pad.

"Make sure Francis is still at the clinic," I said, but Estelle was already moving. "Can you hold that in place?" I asked, and the kid nodded slightly. His hand drifted back and rested on the towel. "I'll be right back," I added. He wasn't going anywhere, but the last thing someone wants who's hurt badly is to go solo.

On the way out through the living room, I jerked the old army blanket off the sofa. It only took a minute to arrange the back of the Blazer so he'd have a place to lie, and by the time I trotted back into the house, Estelle was back in the kitchen, kneeling by the kid. She looked up and said, "He's there."

"There's no time to wait for an ambulance. We'll take mine. There's some room in the back." Estelle helped me pick him up and I carried him out to the Blazer, ducking sideways so I didn't whack his skull on the doorjambs. It was a good thing for him and me both that he was slightly built.

Estelle rode in the back with him, keeping the pressure on the dressing. In less than three minutes we were swinging into the parking lot of the clinic. I saw Mary Vallo's old pickup truck and murmured thanks. I wasn't much of a nurse.

Francis Guzman was organized and waiting. He had already called the ambulance for a transfer to Albuquerque. He and Mary Vallo worked quickly to stabilize the kid. Before I had time to catch my breath, he was stuck with needles in both arms, with chemicals going in from one side and whole blood from the other. Guzman debrided the exit wound enough so that he could see what was what.

At one point he said, "Well, that's good," and continued working. I leaned against the wall and watched. Mary Vallo was damned close to a mind reader. Only once or twice did Francis Guzman have to verbalize what he needed.

"Sir?"

I turned and looked down the hall. Estelle had the contents of the kid's wallet spread on the coffee table in the waiting room. It wasn't much of a display.

I walked out and sat down beside her. "Who is he?"

She held up the driver's license. "Kyle Osuna. San Estevan. He's nineteen."

"I wonder who the hell he crossed," I said.

Estelle tossed the license down. It fell on three one-dollar bills. The license and the money were it.

"Estelle?" Francis beckoned his wife, and I followed her back into the examining room. The young doctor spoke with confidence. "The ambulance will be here any minute and we'll want to transport. But he's conscious and lucid so you might take your best shot now. He'll go into surgery, and it'll be tomorrow morning before you can talk with him again."

"How is he doing, Francis?" I asked.

Guzman put his hands on his hips and regarded the still form on the table. One of the kid's hands twitched, and Mary Vallo rested her hand on his forearm. "He'll be fine. It's not as bad as it probably looked when he was bleeding all over the kitchen floor." He flashed a grin at me as if this sort of thing happened all the time. "What's the story?"

"I don't know," I said. "That's what Whiz Kid needs to find out." Estelle stood beside Ozuna's shoulder with Mary Vallo on the other side. Two faces like those would have been enough to convince any patient that he'd died and gone to heaven. I stood at the foot of the bed and took notes in shorthand.

"Can you tell me your name?" Estelle asked.

"Kyle Osuna." The kid's eyes focused on Estelle's face.

"Kyle, do you know who shot you?"

"No." He took a shallow breath.

"Did you see the person who shot you?"

"Yes." He frowned, probably trying to think straight as the intravenous Valium fogged more than the pain.

"Can you describe him for me?"

"He was . . . he had long white hair."

"White hair? He was an old man?"

"No." Kyle closed his eyes, and his right hand lifted and started to drift over toward the dressing covering the wound. Mary intercepted and held his hand in hers, careful that she didn't dislodge the I.V. "He was young."

"Do you mean blond hair? Very light?" I heard the crunch of tires pulling into the clinic's driveway, and Francis went out to meet the ambulance crew.

"Yes," Kyle Osuna said. "Very light." He took a deep

132

breath, very slowly. "He's about my age. Thin, not too tall. About my size. I've seen him around some."

"But you don't know his name?"

"No."

"Do you know where he lives? Does he live around here?"

Osuna nodded slightly. "I've seen him a few times. I don't know where he lives."

"Can you tell me what happened? Why he shot you?"

"I was walking up the highway from my house. I was going to come talk to you. He was walking the other way, just about by the trading post. He knew my name. He asked if I had a cigarette. I said no and kept walking. That's when . . ." He paused and looked over at me. "That's when I heard this noise. Like a metal latch or something. I turned and saw that he was just standing on the shoulder of the road. And right away I saw that he had a gun of some kind. I freaked, man. So I ran."

"You could see the gun in the dark?"

"There's that light by the trading post parking lot."

"And he chased you?"

"No. He shot me. I didn't hear the gun. But it knocked me down. At first I thought maybe he'd chased me and hit me with his fist. But then I looked back and he was still standing there. He hadn't moved none. Just standing there. And then he started to walk up the road toward me. Real slow."

The ambulance attendants brought the gurney down the hall into the examining room. If we wanted to know more, we'd have to ride the ambulance to Albuquerque.

"What happened then?" Estelle persisted.

"I got up and ran into the orchard there and made it over toward the river. That's when it started to hurt. It hurt so bad and I was scared. I thought that maybe with all the brush he couldn't follow me. There's a hundred places to hide. After a few minutes I thought I heard him running up the highway. I'm not sure."

The attendants moved into position and Estelle held up a hand, gaining a few seconds.

"Do you know why he shot you, Kyle?"

"Yes."

"Why?"

"Because I was in the truck when the girl was killed, just like them." He closed his eyes tightly and bit his already bloody lip. "That's why I was coming to see you. The other four, they got murdered. I heard about Kenny and Cecil . . . I got so scared."

Estelle's eyes locked on mine, and I could see the triumph on her face. "Arajanian," she said and headed for the door. I should have shared her excitement, but it was dread that twisted my gut. I knew Estelle, and I already knew exactly what mistake she was going to make.

21

E S T E L L E Reyes-Guzman's first move couldn't have been more logical. If Kyle Osuna survived, and Dr. Guzman assured us that he would, then he would be charged either with the murder of Cecilia Burgess or as an accessory to murder, depending on how his story developed. Either felony would go a long way toward making Osuna's convalescence painful.

Estelle used the telephone in the clinic to call her county dispatch and made sure that two deputies would meet the ambulance when it arrived in Albuquerque.

We'd been caught unaware, but Tate wouldn't be. In Albuquerque, the deputies would have a file photo of Arajanian. If Osuna was lucid before he went to surgery, they'd make sure he saw the photograph. *If.* I knew the odds of that were small, with his system battered by shock and painkillers.

Estelle wasn't willing to wait. Her mind was made up, set in concrete.

By the time we pulled into the driveway of the house, I was ready to yell at her as if she were a wayward teenager.

I parked the Blazer and she sat in the passenger seat, making no move toward the door handle.

"In the first place," she said, "no judge is going to give me an arrest warrant for Robert Arajanian unless Osuna I.D.'s him from a photo. Not on the evidence we have." She ticked off on her fingers the meager points. "One, we suspect him. Two, Kyle Osuna says his assailant had blond hair and was skinny. That could be Arajanian, or it could just as easily be someone else."

"Yeah, there are dozens of blondies in this valley," I said with heavy sarcasm. "Whole tribes of 'em."

She ignored that and plunged on. "We know Arajanian has a gun but not what kind. And we don't know what caliber weapon was used to shoot Osuna."

"It wasn't a .22."

"No, it obviously wasn't." She opened the door of the Blazer and stepped out. "The only way we're going to get anywhere is to go up there and confront Arajanian. And Finn. You can bet that he's behind it . . . that Arajanian does just what Finn tells him to."

I slammed the steering wheel with the base of my hand. "Damn it, Estelle. What's wrong with you? If we left right now, it'd be two in the morning before we could get there."

"That's what I mean. The darkness would be to our advantage. They'd never expect it."

"For Christ's sake," I muttered and got out. I followed her into the house. "Think a little. Think about this: If Finn and Arajanian are guilty—and I say *if*—look at their track record. They managed to lure two healthy young toughs over the edge of Quebrada Mesa. We don't know how the hell they did that, but it's a fact. And then, cool as a snake, one or both break Grider's neck. That's cold-blooded and they did it under cover of darkness."

Estelle raised an eyebrow as if to say, "So what?"

"And then, if they're the guilty parties, they somehow managed to bushwhack the Lucero brothers . . . and neither one of those boys looked like your basic wimp. We don't know when that happened, but it wouldn't surprise me if it happened at night. And notice that seven shots were placed in a saucer-sized target at more than twenty yards . . . so fast that the victim didn't have time to twist and vary the wound paths.

136

"And then, finally," I held up a hand to stave off her rejoinder, "if he's guilty, like you're sure he is, Arajanian shot Kyle Osuna in the middle of San Estevan . . . at night, with a silencer-equipped handgun. Hit him pretty solidly, too. But no one can bat a thousand all the time. So the killer screws up just a tad. The bullet is an inch too low and wide. He doesn't get a chance for another because Kyle Osuna is spooked into being jackrabbit-fast on his feet."

"If we wait until dawn," Estelle said with great patience, "then both you and I know that they'll be gone. And Daisy will be gone right along with them."

"We don't know that. And I share your concern for the kid. But you're letting your emotions rule. There's nothing to be gained by rushing in half-cocked."

"Sir," she said as if I'd added two and two and gotten five. All the time I had been talking, Estelle had been buttoning on her bullet-proof vest.

"Arajanian knows the boy got away," she said. "Now maybe he's stupid enough to think Kyle Osuna crawled off into the bushes and died, but I don't think so. It's logical to assume that someone who is fit enough to jump up after being knocked flat by a bullet can maybe make it to help. It's a good chance. Would you just sit up there in the woods, waiting for us to come and arrest you?"

"I might. If I knew there was no direct evidence against me, I might think that it was better to wait and keep my eyes and ears open for movement of the troops."

"And all this time Daisy is up there. You know who she's with, don't you? She's with two freaks who have managed to kill five people. I'm not about to wait a minute longer than I have to. If I'm wrong, then I'll be the first to apologize to Finn and Arajanian, face to face."

"No, Estelle. If you're wrong, you'll probably get us both killed. And maybe Daisy, too." I snapped my lighter, touched the flame to the cigarette, and promptly coughed so hard my eyes swam with tears.

137

Estelle waited until the spasm passed before saying, "I'm not asking you to go up there with me, sir."

"I'm charmed," I managed to say, and when I caught my breath I held up a hand. "Will you at least grant me a condition or two?"

That stubborn eyebrow went up, saying, "Let me hear it first."

"First, let's be a little smart and have some backup. Call Garcia and Martinez. Leave Martinez with the vehicles in the campground so we've got radio communication with dispatch if we need it. We can reach Martinez with the hand-held."

Estelle nodded. "And?"

"Listen to an old marine, Estelle. If Finn and Arajanian have done what we think they have, we're going against two cold hands. Unless we can take them completely by surprise, it won't work. Remember that ridge that runs along the creek, up above the campsite on the west side?"

"Sure."

"All right. If we follow that instead of the creek bed, we'll have some protection and the opportunity to see the camp before we approach it. We're going to want to make damn sure that we know what's what before we go in there."

Estelle frowned. "That's all?"

"All?" I said. "No. . . . Most important, we aren't going there at all until dawn, with about thirty-five state police and deputies behind us . . . and maybe a helicopter or two."

"The more people are involved, the more chance there is for Daisy to get hurt. Remember when we busted the gold diggers down in Posadas?"

I remembered that well. We'd been part of a grand night-time embarrassment that included, among other things, a customs agent holding a cocked magnum on his spread-eagled prisoner . . . and then finding out when someone swung a flashlight around that he was guarding nothing but an empty down jacket, crumpled around the base of a cactus. Everybody had been so nervous that if a trigger had been pulled, twenty lawmen would have been plugged by their own compadres.

"We can slip in and out and use the darkness as a cover," Estelle said. "It's safer at night with just a few of us." She added, "I've got another vest at the office you can use."

I stared at her in disbelief. "I suppose the other alternative is to handcuff you to the bedpost," I said, and Estelle gave me that fetching smile that lighted her face.

"You could try, sir." She could melt ice at absolute zero.

"You and your unborn child . . . who by the way has nothing to gain from any of this." As I said that, Estelle's smile faded and she regarded me evenly.

"I'm not helpless, sir."

"I know you're not. And sometimes I wish you goddamn were, that's all."

That earned me a fleeting grin, but she was determined. I could call Pat Tate and have him try to order some sense into her head, but her car would be kicking dust before the call was completed.

I took a deep breath. "That vest had better be size triple X," I said. Hell, I couldn't let her go alone. Paul Garcia was a rookie. Martinez had a wife, two kids, and another baby on the way, so he'd stay with the car . . . at least I could make damn sure of that.

We walked out to the patrol car. I made sure that the plastic ammo wallet I carried in my hip pocket had all eighteen rounds and that the magnum held its six. I got in, muttering all the while.

"What did you say, sir?"

"I said I don't even work for this county. This is ridiculous."

"Yes, sir." Estelle backed out of the driveway and I tried one last card.

"If Francis hadn't gone to Albuquerque with the ambulance, would he have let you do this?"

"Probably not, sir."

139

"But you would have done it anyway."

"Yes, sir." Her jaw had that stubborn, resolute set. I knew that she intended to rescue little Daisy, just like in the fairy tales. I didn't like the only ending I could imagine.

22

T H E moon was huge and bright. It shone into Steamboat Rock Canyon like a gigantic spotlight. When I stepped out of Estelle's patrol car in the campground parking lot, I could see my shadow. Garcia and Martinez waited.

The moon-washed air was dead. I hitched my gun a little higher under the overhang of my gut. Not a stir through the pine needles, not a whisper down the halls of the canyon. Nothing. I sighed.

"They better be sound sleepers," I muttered and watched Paul Garcia thumb five fat cartridges into his shotgun. He was nervous and that would keep him alert. Martinez fidgeted. He didn't much like staying behind.

Except for the three vehicles and Al Martinez, the campground was deserted as we started up the trail through the silent forest. We reached the fork of the trail, and then we veered even farther to the north, cutting away from the trail and following the granite spine of the ridge that paralleled the creek. I tried to breathe quietly, but after a few yards I was rasping like an old steam engine. Estelle slowed some, and when we reached a rock outcropping fifty yards above the trail fork she stopped.

I sat down on one of the ledges with a grunt. My pulse

slammed in my ears, and out of habit I counted it for a minute.

"This is crazy," I whispered.

"We'll take it easy," Estelle murmured.

"It's still crazy." I took a deep breath. The banging in my ears receded a little. The smells were rich, floating up from where our boots crushed the pine needles, grasses, and herbs. "When we reach the top of this ridge, it's going to be rough. If one of us kicks a single pebble, the sound's going to carry."

Estelle nodded and repeated herself. "We'll take it easy."

I stood up and looked ahead. "I'm ready." We faced perhaps a hundred yards of open rock slide and then the timber capped the granite ridge.

One rock at a time was my pace. I made sure of my footing before trusting my weight to wobbly ankles.

I reached the trees, and both Estelle and Paul made motions as if they were ready to move on. I held up a hand. Tour guides were all alike. They rushed ahead to the next attraction and waited for the old tourists who were poking along behind. When everyone caught up, it was time to be off again. The guys bringing up the rear, gasping because of bad hearts or recent hernias, never got to stop and rest. "We should have called for a helicopter," I said.

"Are you all right?" Estelle asked, and I waved a hand.

"Just fine. I love hiking, don't you? Especially in the middle of the goddamn night when I can't see where to put my goddamn feet." I turned and surveyed the hillside. The terrain swept up steadily, curving off slightly toward the east.

Estelle whispered, "If we just stay on the highest line, we should be just right."

"Let me lead," I said. I was under no illusions that I was the most competent woodsman of the group or even that I had the best nose for direction. But I hated being there more than the other two did, and because of that I might make fewer mistakes.

Hell, Estelle had time to take up knitting lessons while she waited for me to select steps. But we made progress. I passed a big, mistletoe-twisted ponderosa and saw rocks jutting out to the right toward the canyon.

I turned and held a finger over my lips. Both Estelle and Paul stopped. I made my way in slow motion out on the outcropping. I could see, off to the south, where the two canyons joined down by the creek. If my distance judgment was correct, the hot springs were less than a quarter mile away.

I remembered . . . it seemed a year now rather than a day . . . seeing Finn and little Daisy walk down through the timber. The slope hadn't been extreme. That was the route we should take, coming in from the north behind the tent site.

I grunted up from my squatting position and waved for Estelle and Paul to follow. As we drew away from the terminus of the ridge and worked toward its root where it joined the mesa top, the pines were widely spaced, a park stand that would have been lovely to a Forest Service timber cruiser.

The ridge's spine curved to the right, and I knew it circled behind the campsites below. I stopped. Estelle stepped so close I could smell the faint aroma of the shampoo she'd used.

"We'll come in right behind them," I whispered. She nodded. I motioned to Paul Garcia and laid a hand on his shoulder. "We don't want to go down the hill as a group. Spread out and watch your footing. You on the left, Paul, with Estelle over on the right. Don't get ahead of me. Don't rush."

His head bobbed with excitement, but I didn't release my grip on his shoulder. "When we're about a hundred feet from the camp, I want to stop and listen. You watch for my signal. And we'll stay there for a while, so don't get in a hurry."

The footing was easy. I kept the inchworm pace, giving each boot toe plenty of time to find twigs or sticks that waited to let out rifle-shot cracks. Like three ghosts, we moved down through the timber.

The moonlight was broken into soft patches by the forest canopy, but before long I could make out Finn's tent. The black rectangle was a geometry out of place in the tapestry of irregular shapes.

I held up a hand and stopped. To my right, I could see

143

Estelle. She stood at the base of a ponderosa that was thick enough to hide three of her. With the authority of her uniform stripped away by the night, her figure was almost that of a child. The outline of her Stetson reminded me of the flat brim of an Easter bonnet worn by a girl a century ago.

I twisted at the waist and for a moment Paul Garcia remained invisible. Almost all the images in the nighttime forest were vertical . . . everything else disappeared.

My eyes clicked from tree to tree until I found him. He was leaning against a pine as if he were taking a breather during a Sunday afternoon stroll. He must have taken off his Stetson, because I could see the curved outline of the top of his head.

He pushed away from the tree and took a half step forward. I stopped breathing as I saw the moonlight touch the blond hair that swept down to his shoulders.

23

W H E N I realized the ghost off to my left was Robert Arajanian and not Deputy Paul Garcia, I took an involuntary step forward.

The object in his right hand wasn't a flashlight. He held the heavy automatic pistol with its muzzle pointing up. I could see the bulbous silencer.

Maybe Arajanian had deliberately chosen the young deputy as his first target. Garcia was carrying the shotgun and would appear to pose the most obvious threat. Maybe Arajanian had been padding along behind us, just keeping tabs. I had my answer soon enough.

When he knew I'd seen him, Arajanian twisted at the waist. The silenced automatic pistol swung toward me. I didn't have time to shout at him or plead or reason.

Arajanian's mistake was shooting at me. I was the least threat. I'd been on the planet long enough to be cautious . . . and that was coupled with reactions and physical abilities far from athletic. But my instincts were honed, even if the old body didn't provide much backup.

The blond-haired killer wasn't there to talk. I knew Arajanian was going to shoot before he pulled the trigger, and I threw myself sideways toward the nearest ponderosa. The bullet gouged pine and spat bark in my face.

The automatic didn't make much noise . . . just a nasty little sneeze with some clattering as the slide jarred backward to fling out the empty case and ram another cartridge into the chamber. But in the silence of the pines Robert Arajanian might as well have fired a howitzer.

Deputy Paul Garcia's nerves were wired. He was less than six months out of the academy, where instructors teach the rookies all the right moves. He was young and athletic.

Robert Arajanian wasn't allowed a second mistake. Garcia crouched and pivoted in one fluid motion. One knee hit the ground as support even as the twelve-gauge came up. He had enough moonlight and a clear target. Arajanian's arm was outstretched, the big automatic and its silencer flashing moonbeams. I scrambled for cover.

I heard the shotgun's pump action only as an extension of the explosion. The muzzle flash of the big gun lit up the hillside. Instinctively I ducked my head. Off to the left I heard a thump as Arajanian's pistol flew out of his hand, and then an awful gurgling and choking.

"Christ, no!" I gasped. My intake of breath was so violent I sucked pine duff and choked. I spat and panted for breath, at the same time trying to draw my own magnum. I lay motionless. Arajanian might not be alone, and I didn't know which way to turn. To make matters worse, I knew Garcia's finger was still tense on the trigger of the shotgun.

I moved my head a fraction. I could see only Arajanian's legs from the knees down.

"Paul," I said, keeping my voice low and even, "hold your fire. Nobody move." I pulled myself up beside the pine trunk. Garcia was crouched thirty feet downhill.

Beyond, the tent was dark and quiet. Where the hell was Finn? I cursed eloquently. What a goddamn mess. Any hope of surprise was gone. But maybe the camp was empty. The hairs stood up on the back of my neck, and I ducked and looked uphill, scanning the hillside. Nothing.

"Paul, are you all right?" I said quietly.

"Yes, sir."

"Estelle, stay put," I said, a little louder. I glanced over my shoulder at the spot where I'd last seen her. She hadn't moved, but I could see moonlight glint on her service revolver.

"Paul," I said, "hold position."

"Yes, sir." There was a little tremor in his voice, but he wasn't going to do anything stupid.

I pulled the small flashlight out of my coat pocket. With the revolver in my right hand and the light held well away from my body with the other, I crouched and stepped toward Robert Arajanian.

My light caught the glint of the automatic, and I detoured cautiously to pick it up, then shove it into my belt. It was a heavy frame Beretta . . . no kid's gun.

Arajanian lay on his back. His heart was still beating, but he'd stopped struggling and he'd stopped breathing.

The blast of double zero buckshot had hit him a terrible, slashing blow at the base of the throat. Even as I knelt with the light I saw the pulse subside in the torn left carotid artery. His left hand lifted, opened wide, and then slowly drifted down to rest lightly on his blood-soaked chest. His eyes stared up into the night.

The kid wasn't going to give us any answers. That left H. T. Finn.

I straightened up. There was still no sign of life in the tent. Would the son of a bitch just let us walk into camp? Was he waiting in the musty darkness of the tent, weapon ready, with one hand clamped over Daisy's mouth to stifle whimpers? Or was he waiting for us, hidden behind a black tree trunk, invisible and deadly?

I whispered a withering curse at my own overactive imagination. In all likelihood, Finn was long gone with Daisy pulled along for the ride.

I took a deep breath. I blinked the light at Estelle quickly, then held it so that it illuminated my own right hand. I beckoned her over, then turned the light off. I moved off to the side a little and waited.

Garcia hesitated, then crept slowly up the hill. He wasn't in a hurry to see what he'd done. When he was within whispering distance, I reached out and touched his shoulder.

"You did the right thing," I said. He stared down at Arajanian, then looked away. I could hear Estelle's quick breathing.

"Is he dead?" she asked.

"Yes. It's Arajanian."

"Was he going to shoot?"

"He did shoot," I whispered. "Once at me. That's all he had time for."

She looked downhill at the dark blob of the tent.

"I want you two to stay up here for a minute," I said. "Arajanian knew we were coming . . . there's no way of telling how long he was on our heels. Maybe all the way from the parking lot. But if he knew, then that means Finn does, too."

Estelle shook her head. "Listen," she said and her whisper was almost harsh. I couldn't see her face under the brim of the Stetson, but I knew her black eyes were drilling mine. "If he's down there, then there's a better chance with the three of us. We stay spread out, just the way we were."

Garcia's whisper was filled with tension. "And the more Finn knows that he doesn't have a chance, the better the odds are that he'll give it up."

I might have agreed with the deputy almost any other time. But Finn was no panic-stricken teenager cornered in an alley after hitting a convenience store. That sort of mentality I could understand. But Finn? He was an unknown.

I thought of another chilling possibility.

"Maybe Arajanian killed Finn," I said.

"No," Estelle said. "Arajanian did as he was told. I could see that. And nothing else makes sense."

I hesitated. I wanted a plan without risk. There wasn't one, except to wait until dawn and ring the place with troops. And then the only person who'd suffer would be Daisy . . . if she hadn't suffered already. "We're wasting time," I muttered.

Estelle motioned Paul Garcia into position. In the moonlight I could see that his face was as pale as Arajanian's. His

148

forehead was shiny with sweat, but he clutched the shotgun at high port, trigger finger out of the guard. He'd be all right. We turned and started down through the trees.

The three of us were spooked . . . but probably still thinking we could control events if we were careful enough. We reached the bottom of the slope where it splayed out into the narrow swale. I held up my hand and we stopped. The tent was twenty feet in front of me, the entry flaps on the opposite side, facing downhill.

I listened, my head cocked slightly. Nothing. No wisp of smoke rose from the ashes in the stone fire circle. A slight breeze was stirring the tops of the ponderosas, a signal that dawn wasn't many hours away. I turned and caught Paul Garcia's eye. I pointed to a spot between me and the tent. He nodded. I moved slowly to the side, toward Estelle. I wanted her off to the side of the door flaps. If I angled in from the other side, that would give us the best coverage.

With infinite care and listening so hard my ears hurt, I circled the tent until I was looking directly at the front flap. Again, I stopped. The silence was so deep that the normal ringing of my ears was a scream of head-noise.

I narrowed my eyes as if that would help me see through the tightly woven nylon. Just about the time when I had decided the place was deserted, I heard the noise. It wasn't a cry, nor a whimper. Just the faintest sniffle, like a person would make when his nose is tickling. Estelle heard it, too, because she immediately took a step toward the tent.

I held up my hand sharply, and she stopped. We waited, and after a minute Estelle shifted position restlessly. As if that motion were a signal, we heard the noise again. Someone was in the tent. And whoever it was hadn't been as patient as we were.

Estelle Reyes made her decision before I had a chance to move. She took three quick steps to the tent. She held her flashlight to one side and jerked the tent flap, hard. A frightened whimper greeted her. And this time I recognized the voice as a child's.

149

"It's Daisy," Estelle said, turning toward me so that I would hear.

I took a step forward. The first rifle shot came from behind me, so loud that it numbed like a dynamite blast. Paul Garcia's shotgun pinwheeled through the air, hit the side of the tent, and bounced to the ground. If the deputy made a sound, I didn't hear it. He disappeared behind the tent.

"Get down!" I shouted. Estelle was crouched in the doorway of the tent with nowhere to go. I was out in the open, without a target. I thumbed the hammer of my revolver back, turned, and saw motion downstream by the boulders. I snapped off a single shot and then tried to sprint off to the right to draw fire away from Estelle and the child.

My right ankle collapsed, and I staggered sideways, fighting for balance. The rifle blasted again, and this time I saw the flash out of the corner of my eye. Something tugged hard at the back of my vest. I fell awkwardly and lost my grip on the revolver. Three rapid shots cracked out from my left, and I heard one of the slugs from Estelle's revolver ricochet off the boulder and whine into the timber like a demented insect.

I was looking at the rock when the rifle fired, and I saw the massive corona of muzzle blast. The front corner of the tent collapsed, and it took an awful eternity for me to realize that it had been Estelle Reyes's body spinning into the rope and support rods that brought the tent down.

24

I SCREAMED something—I don't remember what—
then lunged for my revolver, snapped it up, and yanked the
trigger. I fired twice, so blinded by the muzzle flash from the
two-inch barrel that I lost the target.

I tried to stand, lost my balance, and fell to my hands and
knees, the revolver digging into the dirt. I heard the scuffle of
feet on pebbles. I straightened up and held the revolver in both
hands. I saw the ghost of motion and fired twice. The rifle
crashed out again, and this time the blast corona was perfectly
symmetrical, with me in the focus.

The rifle bullet jerked me backward. The revolver flew off
into the night. I landed hard on my back and felt an agonizing
stab of pain as the automatic pistol I'd picked up and shoved
into my belt dug into my spine.

I heard scuffling in the rocks down by the first of the springs.
I tried to inch my right hand around to the automatic, but that
arm wouldn't work. Someone cleared his throat and I froze,
waiting.

His feet on the pine duff didn't make much noise. A circle
of light poured over me.

I heard a "tsk," like a man sucking on a toothpick as he
surveys the remains of a big feast.

"Ah, you people," H. T. Finn said passively. He "tsked" again. The light moved out of my eyes, and I could make out the rifle that he now rested on his shoulder as a deer hunter might. Both my hands were in sight and they both were empty.

He bent down and picked up my handgun, then flung it so hard I heard it clatter on rocks on the other side of the swale. "Such a waste, isn't it?" he murmured and then moved off. I was able to twist my head a fraction and grimaced against the pain. He walked to the tent. He looked down at Estelle Reyes for a brief moment, then nudged her out of the way. He bent down, picked up something, and threw it off into the darkness.

"Ruth?" he called softly. "Ruth, it's all right. You're safe now." He knelt at the door of the tent, holding up the sagging nylon and broken support rod. The little girl emerged. It was too dark to see her face. She wrapped her arms around Finn's neck. He stood up, lifting the girl effortlessly. "That's my girl," he said. "So brave." He ran a hand through her hair. "So brave."

She whispered something and Finn said, "I know. I know. But let's finish here." He moved away from the tent and bent to let Daisy stand on her own. He took her by the hand and they walked down the swale toward the boulders. He said something else to her that my fuzzed brain didn't understand and then returned alone.

I managed to find my right arm . . . it felt detached and jointless . . . and pulled it across my stomach for support. I rolled to my left side. Finn stood quietly for a minute, watching me. "Perhaps a little struggle will be good for your soul," he said, hefting the rifle.

"You son of a bitch," I mumbled, but he wasn't interested in conversation. And maybe when it came to face-to-face bloodletting he couldn't stomach being as efficient as Arajanian.

He walked quickly past the tent, his flashlight beam darting far ahead. He headed up the slope and reached the kid's corpse. I saw his light moving this way and that on the ground. I had the pistol and silencer he was looking for and had to figure a way to pull it out of my belt. My right arm was useless, and I was lying on my left.

I started to push myself up by levering my forehead against the ground. That didn't work, and I collapsed back. Finn returned to the tent. He was no longer carrying the rifle. Maybe he was planning to return for it another day.

In a moment he emerged from the tent with two gallon cans, the kind that contain white gas for camp stoves and lanterns. With a can in each hand, he walked down the swale toward Daisy and the big boulder where Estelle and I had first met Robert Arajanian. I couldn't see him after that.

There was only one reason for taking the gasoline. I drove my head hard into the ground, humped my back, and pushed with my left hand. Balanced on my knees and my left knuckles like an old, crippled gorilla, I looked uphill. I shook my head to clear my vision. Estelle Reyes's dark form still lay at the corner of the collapsed tent.

I crawled forward, first moving my left hand and then scrunching my knees. I had no flashlight, but the moonlight was peaceful on the side of her face.

Balancing carefully, I rested my fingers against her throat. "Oh, Christ, Estelle." There was a pulse and a strong one. I put my hand under her cheek, turning her head slightly so I could see her face. Her eyes were ground shut, closed so tightly her forehead was creased with a thousand wrinkles.

I hunkered closer. Her hair on the right side was heavy with blood, and it had begun to pool on the ground under her. I swore and groped for my handkerchief. It was in my right hip pocket. I rocked backward and reached behind my back, grabbing my belt.

Using that as purchase, I walked my left hand around my waist until my fingers found the pocket. I pulled out the handkerchief and made a mess of folding it against my thigh. I changed position again and crunched my knee down on Estelle's flashlight. I breathed a sigh of relief, dropped the handkerchief, and grabbed the light.

Her thick hair made it impossible to see her scalp, especially

153

in the uncertain light. But it appeared that the bullet had hit near the crown of her head on the right side, nearly a hand's spread behind and above the tip of her ear. I had no way of knowing what damage the rifle bullet had done, but she was breathing and had a strong pulse.

I curled my arm and tucked the light in my armpit. The wadded handkerchief was a lousy bandage, but it might stop some of the bleeding. I gently pressed it against her skull. Estelle groaned faintly.

"Come on, hardhead," I whispered. "You can do it."

Estelle made a small whimpering noise, and one of her hands started to crab up toward her skull.

"Can you hold it in place?" I asked as her hand found mine. I hoped my voice was soft enough that it wouldn't crash around inside her already busted skull.

"Eh," she whispered, and I felt her fingers close on the cotton.

"I've got to help Paul," I said urgently. I eased her head down, leaned back, and, using the flashlight as a short cane, pried myself to my feet. I swayed like a drunk, but my ankle was too numb to care. I turned carefully, playing the light past the tent. Paul Garcia hadn't moved.

There was nothing that I or anyone else could do for the deputy. The rifle bullet had struck Paul Garcia high on the left cheek, just under his eye. Most of the back of his skull was missing.

I straightened up, sick at heart. The radio. A small part of my brain that was still working remembered the hand-held radio. I staggered back to Estelle and saw that the radio holster on her belt was empty—the hand-held was what Finn had tossed so negligently off into the trees.

"Run," I thought aloud, trying to will my words downhill and into Deputy Al Martinez's mind. "Run the other way." But he wouldn't do that. He would have heard the shots. Maybe he would have radioed for backup—radioed to a dispatcher seventy miles away. But he wouldn't wait. He'd immediately charge up the trail, right into Finn's gun. I swore, feeling helpless, checkmated.

I desperately wanted that radio and swung the light this way and that, trying to remember how Finn had been standing when he pulled it out of Estelle's belt holster. It was impossible. I saw Estelle's magnum and made my way over to it. By collapsing back down to my knees, I could pick it up. What the hell good it was I didn't know.

It would take us a week to crawl down to the parking lot—by the time help arrived from Albuquerque, the vultures would have us. Maybe Al Martinez would play it smart. Like hell he would. I swore again—about all the expertise I could offer.

And then I sucked in my breath as another sound caught my attention. Behind me the pine forest was alive with a symphony of cracks, snaps, and a background beat that was a pulsing, loud, ominous roar. I turned and saw the light through the trees and at the same time felt the air fleeing uphill, nudging my cheeks. I don't know why I was surprised. Maybe I'd been hoping H. T. Finn would change his mind. Maybe I'd been hoping he was a human being. But he hadn't changed his mind. He'd probably even talked little Daisy into lending a hand.

The Smokey Bear signs along the highway warned about a careless match or cigarette. Smokey hadn't met H. T. Finn. The bastard had used two gallons of white gasoline to set the mountain on fire.

25

T H E fire hugged the ground, bright enough to highlight the smoke clouds. The blaze generated its own breeze, which mixed with the morning updraft in the swale. Neither Estelle nor I could run up the mountain ahead of it.

Garcia's shotgun lay beside the back of the tent, and I grabbed it to use as a crutch. Estelle hadn't changed position, and her face was still frozen in that awful grimace.

"You have to help me, babe," I said, resting my left hand on her forehead. One eyelid flickered a little, and she nodded slightly. "Can you understand me?"

Again she nodded just enough that I felt the motion of her head in my hand.

"I can't carry you unless you can sit up some." This time she opened her left eye just a crack. It was a terrible imitation of one of her favorite expressions of doubt, that wonderful raised eyebrow that I'd earned a thousand times over the years.

"We have to make it to the pool down by the spring," I said. "The son of a bitch set the woods on fire." I put my hand under her, at the base of her neck, trying to support both her head and shoulders with one hand. She pushed against the ground with both hands. Her teeth ground together with the effort. A sigh of pain escaped as she leaned on my shoulder.

I paused to regain my breath. She was now sitting, her feet straight out in front of her. I was kneeling beside her, my arm around her shoulders.

"Do you think you can walk?" I asked.

"Uh," she said.

The fire was now so loud that I had to shout. "Can you stand?"

"Uh-uh."

"Shit," I said. I looked over my shoulder, hoping to see a couple of ambulance attendants with a gurney. All I saw were bright flames, arching high into the sky, reaching to the very tops of the ponderosa pines. Smoke rolled in rich, thundering billows, obscuring the stars and moon. We didn't have to worry about light. The fire would give us plenty—until it roasted us.

I could have easily picked her up if I'd had two good arms. If she weighed more than a hundred pounds, it was only because of the cop junk strapped to her waist and the bullet-proof vest that hadn't done her head a bit of good.

"Hold onto my neck," I said loudly. There was no immediate response. She'd drifted off into some other, less painful world.

I rolled Estelle onto her stomach. With the shotgun crutch jammed under my ruined right arm, I bent down just enough to grab the center of her Sam Browne belt.

If nothing else, my arms had gained some strength over the years with the constant exercise of pushing my own bulk up and out of chairs. I hauled Estelle up at the waist, the way an angry father might grab the belt of a three-year-old who'd been dashing for cover. She felt like a sack of grain, folded in the middle.

There wasn't time to worry about prenatal care. If her pregnancy survived this night, the kid would be one tough hombre.

The effort brought her back to consciousness. She tried to balance, then fell backward against me. I knelt on my right knee, her weight resting on my left leg. I released her belt and flung my arm around her before she had a chance to fall on her face, then hugged her close.

"Now we're both going to stand up," I said after I caught my breath. Her left hand came up and held the top of her head. She turned slightly so that she could curl the other arm around my neck. My handkerchief was still glued to her skull. We both stood up, shaky and gasping. Any other time we would have collapsed with laughter.

Like two drunks tied together in a three-legged race, we lurched down the swale toward the fire. The wind was picking up as the fire generated its own vortices.

We passed the boulder that had been the gateway to the campsite. The first spring, high in the rocks to the right, dribbled a trickle of sweet sulfur water down into a puddle the size of a kitchen sink.

Farther on through thick, rank grasses, ferns, and mosses, the water collected. Fed by other springs, it spread and mingled with the pebbly granite and limestone. In one spot campers had dug out around several boulders, enlarging the natural pool.

On the downhill side of the pool, one of the rocks had seen duty as a wash slab. The remains of a bar of soap were glued to the rock near the waterline. I headed for that pool. I couldn't have heard Estelle if she'd been screaming in my ear. The fire was seeking out heavy fuel, roaring up the hillsides on either side of the campsite and heading toward the massive stands of pine and fir up the slope.

We sank into the water. Compared to the blast of heat from the fire, the water was almost cool. The pool was eighteen inches deep where we snuggled next to the rock. The swale formed a natural chimney, and it would take the smoke and the fire quickly past us and up the hill. That's what I hoped.

Finn had miscalculated. He'd started the fire too close to the campsite. If he'd been a better arsonist, he'd have waited until he was near the highway, so the blaze would have had time to reach fire-storm proportions by the time it got to us.

As it was, there wasn't much fuel in the campsite other than

158

grass and limb wood. The fire raced upward, seeking the timber. I pulled my right arm up across my chest, wincing as the water touched the wound in my shoulder. I breathed through the soaked cloth of my shirt sleeve. My left arm was around Estelle, and I made sure my wet uniform sleeve covered her nose and mouth.

Like two forlorn trolls, we rested in the small pool. I had never felt so goddamned helpless. The smoke swirled around us and I coughed, pressing my head down into the wet cloth and squirming back against the rock. Estelle was quiet. She'd passed out again. That was all right. She'd miss the show.

A juniper tree exploded a hundred feet away, and I flinched. I cracked open one eye. The surface of the pool was turning light gray. I splashed water on us and pulled Estelle close, trying to find a pocket of half-clean air under the slight overhang of the rock. I focused my mind on H. T. Finn.

"Just breathe in," the voice said. The bedroom light was a uniform gray. The face in front of me a blur. He was trying to jam something over my nose and mouth. "Easy now, sir."

The rich smell of woodsmoke brought a moment of panic. At first I imagined I'd been pulled from my burning house.

Someone else shouted something, much too loud. I tried to suck my head in, like a hurt turtle. Nothing worked. Nothing was in order.

"We need to bring her out first," the voice said, and another mumbled something unintelligible. I closed my eyes and somewhere deep inside my skull a switch clicked. I jarred to consciousness and coughed violently. "Easy now. Just hold still."

I felt the mask repositioned on my face and opened my eyes. Like a long lens on a television camera, they focused first far away, on the smoking hillside.

The blaze had moved up the mountain, and its steady roar was like a freight train in the distance. I struggled to distinguish the face in front of me. There were several now and eager hands reaching down into our little pool of gray water.

"Be careful," I tried to say. I pushed the oxygen mask away.

"Be careful," I said again, and this time I think he understood me.

"Looks like a head injury on this one," he said. Hands far more expert than mine cradled Estelle Reye's head—her hair now gray from ash, the strands caked and thick like fresh cement. She was lifted from the pool and placed on the backboard.

Someone wiped my face and with the curtain of ash removed I recognized faces. Sheriff Pat Tate was kneeling in the goddamned pool of water. A shout from up-canyon pulled him to his feet before I had a chance to say a word.

"Just take it easy," Tate said to me, and he charged away. I turned in panic. Estelle Reyes was already gone, her stretcher headed downhill. I flailed wildly, and what seemed like half a dozen hands provided support.

"I can stand," I croaked, knowing damn well that I couldn't. It must have been a hell of a sight as a gray ash-man rose from the pool. The EMTs weren't much interested in what I had to say about my own rescue. Someone messed with my right shoulder even as other hands arranged my bulk on the backboard.

I was strapped down like a crazy man trussed in a strait-jacket. I couldn't do anything but relax and enjoy the trip. That gave me some time to think, to try to put some of the pieces together.

The helicopter rested at the east end of the parking lot, a stone's throw from the highway. My nerves tensed. The canyon was narrow and the air currents would be squirrelly.

"Maybe just a ride to town in an ambulance would be safer," I muttered, but no one listened to me. My stretcher was secured in the Jet Ranger even as the turbines increased their whine and the rotors flashed.

Estelle's stretcher was on the opposite side of the machine, and I wanted the damn mask off so I could ask about her.

I tensed as the helicopter lifted, ducked its nose, rotated in place, and then sped south, thumping up and out of the canyon. I caught a glimpse of the pall of smoke that hung on the southwest side of Quebrada Mesa and extended up the face of the mountain to the north.

It banked smoothly away from the valley. We had already gained enough altitude to establish a direct course to Albuquerque, skimming the mesas and foothills.

I shifted position, trying to see who else was in the helicopter with us. It was impossible to see, impossible to hear or even sit up. I settled back, wondering if Francis Guzman was with Estelle. I was going to have a hell of a time trying to explain this mess to him.

26

'' H O W are we?'' the nurse asked. I'd been staring at the ceiling of the ICU recovery room and hadn't heard her pad in. She smiled at me, a little bit predatory.

I cleared my throat. "We're okay," I said. "What time is it?"

She glanced at her watch. "A little after eight."

There were no tubes stuck in me, no clicking machines. That was a plus. "In the morning?"

"Yes," the nurse said. She was maybe forty-five, plain as a post, and looked like she had more important things to do elsewhere.

I raised a hand and rubbed my face. My skin felt thin and fragile. "I need to know about the injured deputy who came in on the same helicopter as me." I was about to give her the name, and my mind went blank. "Christ," I muttered and rubbed my eyes again. "Estelle," I said suddenly. "Estelle Reyes." I looked at the nurse. I couldn't read her name tag. "I need to know. I'd appreciate anything you can do."

She nodded. "I'll see what I can find out." She left the room, and I twisted in bed just a little. My right shoulder felt heavy and dull, but when I bent the arm at the elbow everything worked. I looked at my fingers. Other than some minor nicks and cuts, every finger was in place and worked on command. Hell, this wasn't too bad, then.

I flexed my right leg. I couldn't see it over my belly, but it felt like all parts were in place. My right ankle twanged a bolt of lightning when I tried to point my toes.

In a few minutes the nurse returned. "The young lady is still in surgery," she said without preamble. My spirits sank.

"Is Dr. Francis Guzman in the building?"

"He may be in surgery, sir."

"I need to see him as soon as he's free."

"I'll see what I can do." She left again. The room was insulated from the normal sounds of the hospital, and I had only my thoughts for company. The door of the recovery room opened, and a uniformed sheriff's deputy poked his head in.

"Come on in."

"You're awake," he said. I saw by his uniform that he was one of Pat Tate's troops.

"I think so," I said.

"I've been assigned down here," he said, not altogether happy about it. "Sheriff Tate said that if there was anything you needed to let me know."

"There's a whole list of things I need," I said, eager to rejoin the world. "What's your name, Officer?"

"Perry Olguin, sir." He hadn't crossed thirty yet and was shorter than the nurse—slender, dark-skinned, and hawk-featured. He was cultivating a pencil-line mustache that looked ridiculous.

"Perry, catch me up. What the hell is happening up in San Estevan?"

Olguin frowned. "It's a mess, sir."

"Did they get Finn?"

"No, sir."

I took a deep breath. "So what happened? What about Al Martinez?"

"All I heard was that Finn took Al's car."

"Took his car? What about Al?"

"He'll be all right. His room's just down the hall. Finn

163

somehow got the drop on him and shot him point-blank five times."

"And he's all right?"

"Well, he's sure sore. He had on his vest and I guess Finn didn't notice . . . or see it. Al's bruised up pretty bad. He can't breathe so good. He's lucky."

"Christ. Did he manage to get a radio call off?"

Olguin nodded. "He radioed in that shots were fired. He told me a few minutes ago that it sounded like a damn war."

"Worse," I said flatly. "Does Tate know what direction Finn went? How he went?"

Olguin frowned again. Maybe he had to do that in order to think. "They got a roadblock on State 46, sir. They're sure he didn't make it that far."

"What makes them think he's going to drive right down the state highway for Christ's sake?"

"Well . . . they've got every other road blocked, too. And the last word I had was that they were using two helicopters. It's kind of tough working north and east, though, because of the fire."

"He's not going north or east," I said. "That wouldn't make any sense."

"Yes, sir."

"How long did it take after Martinez' call before the next officers arrived?"

"Just a few minutes . . . maybe forty or so. Deputy Polk was at the southern end of State 46. He sailed on up there pretty fast. And he didn't see any southbound traffic."

And after the deputy went through it was an open road until they knew what the hell was going on and set up the roadblock. Whatever the screwup had been, it was more our fault than Tate's.

"And he switched cars, so he's not going to outrun anybody."

"They found Martinez' patrol car, you mean?"

"Yes, sir."

"Where was it? Where'd he dump it?"

Olguin paused and frowned even deeper. "They didn't say, sir. They're not talkin' about that on the radio."

"Shit," I said. It was after eight. In three or four hours Finn could easily be out of the state if he headed west or swung back around north. Or he could follow the labyrinth of dirt roads, gradually working his way south toward the Mexican border. "And Estelle Reyes is still in surgery?"

"Yes, sir."

"They recovered Paul Garcia's body?"

"Yes, sir."

"And nobody else is hurt? Other than Martinez, I mean?"

Olguin shook his head. Finn—that slimy son of a bitch—was loose and running, and none of us knew where he was.

"Is the fire under control?"

Olguin shook his head again. "That's going to be a bad one, sir. I heard on the radio that the wind's picking up. And the fire's in heavy timber, movin' up the mountain. They got crews from all around the state, tryin' to stop it before it jumps across into the wilderness area on the north side."

I nodded, but it wasn't the forest fire I cared about. "Is Tate still at the hot springs?"

"Yes, sir."

"Get hold of him on the goddamn radio and tell him I need to talk to him."

"You can reach one of the deputies down at the campground parking lot. The repeater reaches in there. They can patch through on hand-held to the sheriff up the canyon."

"I know how radios work, Deputy," I snapped and immediately waved a hand in apology. "Look, I need to talk with Tate on a telephone, not the radio. Get through to him and have him find a phone. By the time he does that, I'll be out of here."

"Yes, sir."

Olguin left, and I reached for the buzzer to call a nurse. There was no buzzer. I swore loudly. The nurse showed up on the third curse.

"Is there something I can get for you?"

"Damn right," I said. "I need a telephone."

"There's no phone in here," she said, and I looked at her in disbelief.

"I know that, Nurse."

"I'll see one of the doctors. They may be ready to move you now."

"That would be nice." I smiled encouragement and then let my head fall back on the pillow. Estelle was in surgery, I was stuck in bed, and it sounded like Tate's men were either still mining the campsite or helping fight fires.

I hoped somebody was left to hound H. T. Finn's tail before little Daisy had to learn to speak Mexican.

27

◆◆◆

" ' H E did what?" I stared at Pat Tate.

The sheriff regarded me as if I'd given Finn the keys myself. Maybe that's why Tate had driven to the city instead of prolonging our phone conversation. "The son of a bitch parked Al Martinez's car right in Estelle's driveway. Then he broke a wing window of your Blazer and that was that."

"What the hell is that simple bastard up to?" I walked to the window. To the north, the plume of smoke towered like a summer thunderstorm's anvil—hell, airline pilots were probably smelling the pine smoke at 30,000 feet. "He won't be hard to find."

"No. There are probably only a thousand beat-up '84 Chevy Blazers in the state. But we got every road covered . . . one agency or another."

"And he's got Daisy with him."

"For sure," Tate said. "We saw the tracks of her little sneakers in the dirt of the driveway." He sat on the edge of the bed. His fingers twined together and he said quietly, "I don't believe we lost Paul. Twenty-two years old, for Christ's sake." He looked over at me, knowing there was nothing I could say that would make any difference. "We don't have any background on this guy yet, you know that?"

I nodded. Tate continued, "We're trying for a print match. What we need is one of those big computers that does that. We have the rifle and it might turn some prints. I think we recovered all the weapons, including that automatic of Arajanian's. It doesn't make sense that a punk kid like him can just plunk down a thousand bucks for a fancy gun and a goddamn silencer."

Tate looked at his watch. "I've got two investigators with Kyle Osuna right now," he said and then added with no sympathy, "That's one scared kid."

"He has reason to be."

"I was there for a few minutes and heard some of the preliminaries. You know why he wanted to talk with us so bad?"

"He was scared shitless, that's why."

"Partly. He was in the truck, all right, with the other four. He was up in the cab with Waquie and Kelly Grider. The Lucero brothers were in the back and he says they started the ruckus with the girl, almost the minute she climbed into the truck."

"They raped her?"

"Eventually, I guess. Osuna says they drove all the way to the head of the canyon to get some more beer at that little store . . . Chuga's. Then he says they went to one of the campgrounds up that way. Had themselves a party. By that time Cecilia Burgess was trying to get away—Osuna says she tried to run up into the woods and Kenneth Lucero caught her. Osuna says he tried to stop him, but Lucero was too much to handle."

"And after the party?"

"They drove south and Osuna said the girl was pleading with them to let her go, to drop her off when they got to the hot springs. He says they got to fighting in the back, with Waquie and Grider yelling encouragement from the front. Osuna says they were swerving all over the road."

"And he was lily-white innocent, of course."

"Sure. So he says. Somewhere north of the campgrounds,

push came to shove. Osuna says that Kenneth Lucero lost his temper and hit the girl pretty hard. The truck swerved across the road, since Waquie was both drunk and enjoying the fight, not paying much attention to the road. He jerked the wheel at the wrong time and over she went."

"Osuna says the truck was southbound on the highway?"

"So he says. In the wrong lane."

"She gets tossed into the rocks and they drive on home."

Tate nodded. "More or less. But I have trouble with part of that punk's story. Osuna told the detectives that he went back up the canyon after a while in his own truck, found the girl, and helped her up to the highway. He says he would have done more, but then traffic came along and he spooked. He says he thought that since someone else was going to stop and take care of the girl, he could slip away."

"There's evidence that says that might be true, Pat. Both Estelle and I sure as hell thought it looked like someone had helped her up to the road. Maybe Osuna really did."

It was the first time during our conversation that Estelle's name had been mentioned, and Sheriff Pat Tate flinched perceptibly. He looked like he was ten years older than he was . . . physically tired and emotionally wrung out. He stood up and pushed one hand into his pocket, moving toward the door. He stopped and rested the other hand on the door pull, looking down at it thoughtfully.

"Al Martinez is fine. He's sore as hell, but fine. But we're not going to know anything about Estelle's condition until probably late this afternoon . . . maybe even tomorrow."

"I heard."

"If she pulls out of it, she's going to be one lucky girl."

I nodded and looked out the window. I wasn't sure I wanted Estelle to pull out of anything if she was going to face the rest of her life as a vegetable. No one had put that fear in words, but like a black cloud it hung over our thoughts.

Pat Tate turned and waited until I looked back at him. "Finn isn't going to get away with this, Bill." His heavy-lidded eyes didn't blink. "I wouldn't say this to anyone but you, but those punks in the truck had it coming. You and I both know they did. And that priest . . . Parris? He didn't know what the hell he was doing when he tipped off Finn." He shook his head in disgust. "But it's gnawing at me, what a cold, calculating bastard this Finn is. Hell, his girl got raped and smeared on the rocks. He flips out . . . I can almost understand that. I'd want to kill somebody myself. If he just walked up to each one of them and blew them away, that would be one thing. But the way he did it, Jesus. And he sure as hell didn't give you, Estelle, and Paul any notice. He just cut loose."

He stopped and rubbed the door pull with his thumb, idly polishing the chrome finish. "I'm surprised he gave you a second chance, Bill. When it comes to killing, he's no beginner."

"He used Arajanian," I said. "I'm sure of it. The boy did exactly as he was told. Cold-blooded as a goddamn lizard. I'm beginning to think that it's when Finn had to act on his own that he started making mistakes."

"I want to know what other connections he's had," Tate said. He pulled open the door. "We're going to find out who Finn is, Bill. And when we catch him, I'd straddle him over an anthill and let him take about three weeks to die, if the law would let me."

"Keep me posted," I said. He nodded and had almost closed the door behind him when my memory played a tape I didn't even know I had. "Pat!"

He peered back in the room and lifted his chin in question.

"When Finn came back to the tent, he picked up the little girl, Daisy."

"And?"

"He called her Ruth."

"Ruth?"

I nodded. "His pet name for her. I don't know why. The first time we talked with him at the springs, he called her that. Ruth. We didn't think it was important then. But now . . . it's something . . . it might lead somewhere."

Pat Tate frowned and I could see the wheels turning. No

170

easy answer held up its hand. "When I find the son of a bitch, I'll ask him," he said.

"I want to be there when you do." He nodded and I took that as a promise.

28

♦♦♦

BY LATE afternoon of the next day I was stir-crazy. Worse, I hadn't seen Francis Guzman, hadn't heard about Estelle . . . I was goddamned marooned in that stupid little room. There was nothing wrong with me other than a few stitches. "Admitted for observation" might be a nice way of saying that I'd been sidelined on purpose.

The manhunt for H. T. Finn was centering on the western half of the state . . . it was top-of-the-hour news on both radio and television and splattered a headline across both the evening and morning papers. No reporter had sought me out. Sheriff Pat Tate had hidden me away.

Shortly after 3:00 P.M., I was sitting in the hard vinyl chair by the window of my hospital room. I'd had a fitful night's sleep and, for want of anything better to do, a short morning nap. The only medication they forced on me was a mild pain-killer and I took that gladly. My back hurt worse than my shoulder.

The first rifle bullet had blown through my vest and skinned across my back just below my shoulder blades. The projectile had never broken the skin, but the bruise and burn on my back was two inches wide and nine inches long.

I'd been lucky with that one. The other bullet had done

more damage, ripping first through the edge of my vest and then through the muscle over my right upper arm bone. The bullet hadn't actually hit the bone, although the shock wave had caused all kinds of "neurological confusion," as one of the doctors put it. An hour in surgery had put stitches in all the right places. One of the doctors told me that in two weeks I wouldn't even know I'd been nicked. Two weeks was forever.

There I sat, newspaper folded on my lap, looking ninety years old, when the door opened. Dr. Francis Guzman looked about as old as I did. And now that we were face-to-face, I wasn't sure I wanted to see him. He closed the door behind himself and leaned against it. He may have needed to. The bags under his eyes were black and deep.

I rose and he waved a hand at me. "No, don't. Sit."

"I've been doing nothing but sitting all day, Francis."

He pushed himself away from the door, walked slowly across the room, and shook my hand. His grip was firm and he hung onto my hand for just a moment. "How's the shoulder?"

"Fine. What's the word?"

He grinned—barely that . . . just a weary twitch of the lips and a little dance of light in his eyes.

"I'm sorry I haven't had a chance to get up here more often to see you," he said. "I looked in on you a couple times yesterday, but you were either under the anesthetic or asleep. Sheriff Tate told me last night you were getting antsy." He grinned. "I dropped in this morning and you were sleeping in that chair."

"Yeah. The hell with that. How's Estelle?"

"She's doing as well as we could hope."

He started to say something else, but he was sounding just like a goddamned doctor. I interrupted him. "That doesn't mean a damn thing to me, Francis. Just tell me in simple English."

"She's going to live, barring complications."

"Complications?" Francis looked around the room for something to sit on. "Take the bed," I said. He flopped down

173

and fell back, arms over his head. After a moment he pulled himself up to a sitting position.

"Whenever the brain is injured, there's all kinds of problems," he said. "It's a hell of a lot harder making sure all the bleeders behave themselves." He pointed his finger as if it were a pistol. "Apparently the bullet hit the point of her skull right here." He tapped the rear crown of his head. "A glancing blow, but . . ." He took a deep breath. "With a high-powered rifle there's just so damn much force involved. She has a serious skull fracture."

I waited while he decided what he wanted to say. "At first they thought that some skull fragments might have penetrated the dura, maybe damaged the brain tissue itself."

"And?"

"She was in surgery a long time. She's strong, and the docs did a fine job. The wound is clean. No chips. Hell of a lot of bruising, and that's always worrisome with the brain. But they did a fine job." He grinned with a little more energy. "I was there to make sure they did."

"Any paralysis?" I said, and my voice was husky.

He shook his head. "Not that we can tell yet."

"Is she conscious?"

"In and out, but that's to be expected for a couple days."

"I'd like to see her."

Francis Guzman nodded but held up a hand. "It'd be best for both of you to let it wait until tomorrow." He stood up and rolled his head around, trying to loosen the neck kinks. "Give her a few more hours of rest. We'll know more then, anyway."

"Francis . . ."

He looked at me, one eyebrow cocked—just like his wife.

"What about the baby?"

The young physician smiled, and my relief was like ocean surf. "She told you, huh, Padrino?"

"Yeah, she told me. She didn't lose it, did she?"

"No. She'll be fine. Tough stuff. She really is."

"I'm sorry this happened," I said, sounding lame and dumb.

174

"Hindsight is a wonderful thing," he said. He stuck out his hand again, and I got up. "We'd all be geniuses if our foresight was as good. Who knows what might have happened if you'd waited. But she'll be fine. So will you. And the next time you have a vacation, we're all going to go to Lake Tahoe or somewhere where neither one of you can get into trouble."

"It's a deal." His spirits sounded upbeat, but I knew he was working at it. I followed him to the door, my shuffle just about as fast as his.

"And by the way . . . remember Nolan Parris?" Francis asked.

"Uh-huh."

"He's downstairs in one of the reading rooms. They won't let him up. He spent the night, I guess. But Tate set some tight rules on this one. Takes an act of Congress to see anyone or find out anything. You want to see him?"

"I don't know if I do or not."

"As I said, he spent the night. He must be pretty worried. Nobody's talking and he's concerned about the little girl. He means well, I think."

"Yeah," I said. "Finally, he's worried. We all are. But I don't know what it would accomplish to see him or . . ." and I stopped. My brain was beginning to work. I shrugged like I was making a hell of a concession. "Yeah. Send him up. No, wait. Forget it. I'll take care of it. I've got a phone."

Francis nodded. "I'll try to drop in on you later this evening. Behave yourself." He smiled.

"And you get some rest, kid. You look like shit." It felt good to be able to tell someone else that for a change.

Dr. Francis Guzman left, and I called the hospital gestapo to ask them if they'd let Father Nolan Parris enter the "R" zone. I had no desire to hash over his problems or his guilt that was no doubt rampaging after what had happened. It was simpler than that. I needed wheels, and Parris had access to a station wagon.

Age sixty-two is too late to worry about growing up and following the rules. There wasn't anything wrong with me that

175

wouldn't heal as well elsewhere . . . where I might be more useful.

Nolan Parris hadn't found his way through the multilevel labyrinth to my room when the telephone rang. I grabbed it. It was Tate. The old bastard must have been a mind reader.

"Bill, are you dressed?"

"Hell, no. I'm sitting here in a goddamn robe pretending I'm a nursing home patient. What's up?"

"We got a break. A private pilot who was going to fly over and look at the forest fire says he saw Finn's Blazer on one of the back roads of the reservation."

"It's not Finn's goddamned Blazer and where was this? Which reservation?"

"Northwest of Grants somewhere . . . over by Haystack Mesa, they called it. He's cornered at an old wildcat uranium mine. There's dozens of them out that way. We've got it pinpointed on the map. A chopper is going to pick me up here in a minute."

I was about to interrupt him and tell him that if I got left out of this one I'd curse his firstborn for generations. But there was a light knock on my door, and Nolan Parris stepped into the room. He was wearing his clerical suit, complete with white collar. I turned my attention back to the telephone.

"You have to pick me up, Pat."

"That's why I called. I cleared it with the hospital already. You need to get your old ass in gear, get dressed, and be at the helipad on the roof in about thirty minutes."

"You got it."

"And, Bill . . ."

"Yep?" I was already impatient to be off the phone.

"I'm not doing this as a favor to you. I want you to know that from the start. If it was up to me, you'd be locked in that hospital room for a week or so. I'm doing it because I was told to do it."

I slammed on the brakes. I couldn't imagine Pat Tate taking orders from anyone. "This is your case, Pat."

"Damn right it's my case. And it's going to stay that way.

176

But he's got the child and this may be our only chance." I heard the steady whup-whup of a helicopter in the background, and someone shouted at Tate. "I'll talk with you in a few minutes. Finn must know he's not going to slip through the net. He's cornered, Bill. And he knows it. Now he wants to talk to you."

"Finn wants to talk to . . ."

"Thirty minutes, Bill. Don't make us wait." Tate hung up and I stared out the window, the phone still in my hand. If the media had pried enough information out of Tate to know that the hospital was treating two survivors from the war on the mountain, Finn would have heard the news on any radio station. He knew my face. If he'd rifled through the glove compartment of the Blazer, he knew my name. The bastard wanted to negotiate.

I had forgotten that anyone else was in the room. Nolan Parris had heard enough though.

"Sheriff," he said, and I turned around to look at him.

"You have to let me go along." Parris limped across the room and touched my arm. He repeated his request, and I hung up the phone and pushed myself out of the chair.

"Why the hell not," I said. If another passenger on the helicopter was all right with Pat Tate, it was fine with me. I didn't know how they'd managed to corner the son of a bitch, but the rules had changed. Maybe the services of a priest would be useful.

29

◆◆◆

F L O Y D ' S Number Two was a vertical shaft sunk into the bleak, tan desert just off one corner of the Navajo reservation. The boneyard around the mine was littered with three decades of rusting hardware and trash.

By the time our helicopter arrived, there were five cops for every lizard.

H. T. Finn had taken the wrong turn. The two-track had swerved around an abrupt rise and then dead-ended at the mine headframe. My Blazer had been spotted earlier by a private pilot as the truck kicked up a plume of dust, heading west. The pilot had called the cops. A customs helicopter had given chase then ran out of fuel. They'd skipped back to Gallup, figuring it was either that or walk. If they'd stuck on Finn's ass another minute, they'd have had him.

"In a day and a half, Finn could have been deep in Mexico, if he'd dodged all the right roadblocks!" I shouted at Tate over the noise of the chopper. "This is only a hundred miles from San Estevan, as the crow flies!"

Tate pointed at my Blazer and I had my answer. A long, jagged rent tore the bodywork from the driver's door back to the bumper. From where I stood I could see that Finn had had to mount the spare tire, a ratty summer tread two sizes smaller than the rest.

He'd tangled with something. Too bad it hadn't ripped his goddamn arms off. If Daisy had been hurt, I'd rip his arms off.

We made our way through the flying dirt and dust to the old headframe. I ignored all the curious faces except one.

I knew Sheriff Edwin Sterns from days gone by—felons rarely bother to observe county lines, and over the years a cop meets his compadres from other agencies. This county was Sterns's—and it fitted him, big, lazy, and all but empty.

He was a tall, gangly man with a potbelly that looked like he was carrying a bedpan under his shirt. He'd been a state trooper years before but had found their military bearing too much trouble to imitate.

"How'd you rope this one, Gastner?" he asked as we shook hands. "And what the hell brings you all the way north into God's country?"

"Just lucky."

Tate said, "He's on vacation."

Sterns shook his head in wonder. "Hell of a vacation." He turned and motioned us over to the headframe.

The mine shaft gaped, the opening ten feet square. The damn hole went straight down into the earth. The shaft's edges were heavily timbered, and a thin grating of woven steel like the troops used to make runways over soggy ground in Vietnam covered the opening. The mesh rested on an H-frame of two-inch angle iron. At one time a barbed-wire fence had enclosed the area, but now that was broken and scattered. I shuffled carefully to the edge and looked down. The shaft was bottomless black.

Directly across from where I stood, a corner of the mesh had been pried up. Below the torn mesh, a steel ladder disappeared into the depths. The ladder hugged the wall of the shaft, the rungs no more than four inches from the timbers to which the ladder frame was bolted. There was no safety cage around the ladder. Once a man was on his way down, there was no other support if his hands should slip from the rust-covered, half-inch-diameter rungs . . . just a lot of empty space. It gave me the willies.

"And he's down in there? With the child?"

"Sure as hell," Sterns said.

I wasn't a bit surprised that no one had followed Finn down inside that hole.

"We've got to get Daisy out of there," Parris said. His eyes were wild, and I took him by the arm. He looked like he wanted to step out on the mesh.

"Shit," I said and looked westward. "If it was me, I'd rather take my chances walking out across the desert than sliding down in that hole. And he had my Blazer, for God's sakes. He could have kept going, road or no road."

"Maybe he figured he was cornered," Tate said. "Maybe he didn't know the chopper had to call it off."

Sterns shoved his hands in his pockets. "He asked for you, Gastner. My guess is that he thinks you're his ticket. And while he waits, he's sure as hell safe here. Nobody's going to sneak up behind him."

I turned away from the hole. I kept my grip on Parris's arm, pulling him with me like a wayward child. "How the hell deep is that thing?"

Sterns stepped right to the edge and looked down through the wire mesh. "I'd guess five, six hundred feet. Maybe more. We're lookin' to find Stubby Begay. He's a Navajo who lives in these parts. He used to work for Simon-Yates, and one of the deputies said he thinks Begay was on the crew that used to work this hole."

Chances were nil anyone would have a blueprint of the mine . . . and if they did, it'd take a week to get it. "Let's check the truck," I said. "See what the son of a bitch took. Maybe he took the hand-held radio down into the shaft with him." I turned to one of the deputies. "Stay with this man," I told him and hauled Parris around within reach of the deputy.

The Blazer wasn't locked and the keys were in the ignition. I glanced in the back. "The bastard went camping," I said. "He took my sleeping bag." I peered under the driver's seat. "And the radio." I rummaged some more. "And a .45 automatic I kept stowed here."

180

I straightened up and rested my forearms on the seat cushion. Lying on the passenger seat was the wad of newspaper that had been under the seat, serving as a cushion for the radio. I frowned. I was not an overly neat individual when it came to housekeeping—but now the newspapers had been folded with care. The two-week-old Albuquerque paper was on top, with a quarter of the front page torn off. The tear went through the middle of some notes I'd scribbled in the margin.

I remained motionless, lost in thought. What the son of a bitch was up to was a mystery to me. Hell, I had no idea whether a hand-held radio even worked underground . . . or for that matter if the batteries in mine were charged.

I reached over and snapped open the glove compartment. I couldn't tell if my mess in there had been rearranged, but nothing appeared to be missing. I shook my head.

The Blazer's two-way radio was an old-fashioned Motorola, and when I turned on the ignition I saw it still worked. So did the gas gauge. The needle rested below "E."

The Motorola was set on channel one, car-to-car. I hefted the mike. "Finn, do you hear me?" Pat Tate had walked around to the other side of the Blazer, and he leaned against the door. I repeated the call. A short burst of static crackled over the speaker, sounding faint. A try on the other channels produced nothing.

"He either don't have the radio on or it don't work underground," Tate said.

"I've never been down in a mine. I don't know." I hung up the microphone and switched off the ignition. "Finn doesn't know me from a hole in the head," I said. "He met me that first time Estelle and I walked up to the camp." That seemed years before. "If he drove your deputy's car to the Guzman's house and took my truck, then he was planning ahead. How the hell did he know about the Blazer?"

A deputy started to walk toward us and Tate waved him off. "Maybe he didn't. He knew who Estelle was and without a doubt knew who Francis was . . . especially if the Burgess girl had occasion to visit the clinic. Hell, if you live in a dinky town like San Estevan, you know everybody sooner or later. Maybe he knew about Dr. Guzman's Isuzu four by four and was after that. Guzman wasn't home so he settles for yours. And you got to figure, the way things went down, yours was about the only one he'd be able to take without worrying about the owner showing up."

"Maybe."

"Another possibility is that the night Osuna was shot Arajanian followed him to the Guzmans', hoping for another try. He sees you and spooks." He shrugged. "So he tells Finn about it when he gets back. He had the time. If Arajanian watched you load Osuna into the Blazer, it makes sense he'd tell Finn about that, too."

I didn't much like the notion that while Estelle and I had been helping the wounded Osuna the creep with the silenced Beretta had been lounging around outside the adobe house, watching our every move—with his finger itching on the trigger.

If that had been the case, he could have taken us all out, then and there. Whatever he'd been, maybe he hadn't been a creative little bastard. He'd needed instructions from his boss.

As we walked back toward the shaft, I saw that the crowd was growing. I gestured at Sterns, and he broke away from a powwow he was having with a couple of men in business suits.

"You have a bullhorn? A hailer?" I asked.

"Sure. I mean, I'm sure somebody does." Sterns turned and shouted at one of his deputies. The kid produced one of those little battery-powered amplifiers that track coaches love. I took it and walked to the shaft. Another helicopter roared overhead, and I glanced up. It was one of the television stations.

"Sheriff, you need to rope this place off before the crowd gets so thick someone knocks me into the mine shaft," I told Sterns, and the sheriff assigned that project to three of the deputies who were underfoot.

They charged off, one of them with his M-16 at high port like he'd been ordered to take a hill.

182

I took my time. I dug the bell of the bullhorn into the sand and lowered myself to my knees. I could smell the stale air of the mine as I leaned over the mesh. I knew my head and shoulders were silhouetted against the sky if Finn should be down in the shaft looking up.

I switched on the horn and pressed the trigger.

"Finn . . . are you listening?"

"I have to talk with Daisy," Parris said, again at my elbow. I ignored him, trying to hear some response from down under.

"Finn!" I yelled. My words bounced around the guts of the mine shaft. He was going to have to shout to be heard over the cars, helicopters, and yakking that was going on behind me, but I was sure there'd been no response.

I was lifting the bullhorn for a third try when I heard his voice, distant but clear as crystal.

"Send Gastner."

I glanced at Tate then triggered the hailer. "This is Gastner. I'm listening."

"I want to talk to you."

"So talk."

I didn't understand what he said next and I turned to Sterns and snapped, "If those sons a bitches can't keep quiet, arrest 'em, goddamn it. We're trying to conduct some business here."

"Finn, I didn't understand you."

He exaggerated each word with a pause between each. "Face . . . to . . . face."

"Come on up and we'll do that."

"Down . . . here."

"Oh, sure," I said without turning on the bullhorn. I triggered it and added, "That's not possible."

"Make . . . it . . . possible."

Parris was fidgeting and I said, "Do you have the little girl with you?"

"And . . . she . . . will . . . remain . . . with . . . me."

"He can't do that," Parris said and his voice shook.

"Be quiet," I said and then keyed the hailer. "Is she safe?"

183

"Yes."

"Then let us bring her up. You won't be harmed."

A sound that could have been a laugh floated up. "There
. . . is . . . only . . . one . . . choice. You . . . meet . . . me
. . . face . . . to . . . face . . . down . . . here."

"Don't be a fool. I can't climb down the ladder."

Tate leaned over a little, looking down. He said quietly, "If
he gets on that ladder with the kid, there's no way he can
defend himself."

I had visions of Daisy pinwheeling like a broken doll down
into the depths of the old mine. "He'll use the girl as a shield."

"Sure," Sterns said. "And when he gets up here and steps
away from the edge, one rifle bullet through the head, he's
dead, and the girl's safe."

I didn't like the sound of that either. I hefted the hailer
again. "Finn—you have to let the girl go. Let us send an
unarmed deputy down to bring her up."

"No. Ruth . . . is . . . the . . . answer. She . . . remains
. . . with . . . me."

"What the hell is he talking about?"

"I don't know. He calls her Ruth. Who the hell knows
why." I hefted the bullhorn. "Finn, nobody is going to hurt
either you or the girl if you give yourself up."

"Tell . . . Robert . . . that."

"He means Arajanian," I said to Tate. "That's over, Finn.
Come on up."

"No. Face . . . to . . . face . . . with . . . you." There was a
pause. "And . . . you . . . know . . . why."

I looked at Tate and said, "I do?"

The sheriff shrugged. "This guy's a fruitcake."

Apparently we hadn't responded promptly enough, because
Finn's voice floated up.

"Don't . . . play . . . games . . . Mister . . . Sheriff."

"Finn, if you don't send the girl up, we're going to have to
come down and get her. You know what that means."

He knew I was bluffing. There wasn't a drop of concern in
his tone when he said, "Don't . . . be . . . a . . . fool." That calm,

184

detached voice floating up out of the ground was enough to raise goosebumps. I sat back on my haunches. My shoulder hurt. My right ankle throbbed. I eyed the ladder. There was no way I could climb down that with only one good arm. Hell, if nothing else, my belly would throw me off balance and there I'd go.

"Any ideas?" I asked Tate.

"You want to go down?"

"Don't be ridiculous. There's no way I can climb down there."

Sterns was eager. "We can lower you somehow. Use one of those ass slings like the search and rescue uses. One of my deputies is up on that stuff."

"Um," I said. I glanced at the hole. One of the deputies trotted toward us, his boots raising dust. Everyone else had been herded well away, behind the yellow plastic banner that ran from car bumper to bumper.

"Sir," he said, "they found Mr. Begay. They'll be here in just a few minutes."

"All right," I said. "Let's find out what this hole looks like before we jump in it. See if we have any options." I raised the bullhorn and said, "Finn, we're going to find a way to get me down there. Give us some time."

"Nothing . . . but . . . time," he replied.

"That goddamned cocky son of a bitch," I said. "Find me an elevator," I said to Sterns, "and you're probably going to need about a mile of 2,000-pound test rope. By the time you find that, we'll have Begay . . . and one more thing. I want a small automatic with a good silencer." Sterns looked puzzled.

"Bill's right," Tate said. "If you had to fire a gun down in that mine, the whole thing's apt to collapse."

"I'm going with you," Parris said. I regarded him for a second. His face was covered with sweat and he looked like he was ready to faint.

"No," I said flatly. I didn't have either time or inclination to baby-sit. I motioned to one of the deputies. "Find him some shade somewhere." I turned back to Sterns. "I'm not going down there unarmed," I said. "Finn's a master of one-way deals. And it's not going to happen again."

"We've got Arajanian's Beretta in Albuquerque," Tate said. "It's in the evidence locker. You kept a hold on that through thick and thin."

"Too big. I want something small . . . something that I can hide. I won't use it unless I can get close enough to shove it up his ass."

"Well, I'll work on that," Sterns said. He walked off, scratching his head.

Tate glanced at me. He didn't have much faith in Edwin Sterns. "I know someone in Albuquerque who can get us anything we need. We'll send one of the choppers in for it."

I nodded and he gestured to his detective. For a moment I was alone at the rim of the shaft. I looked down into the hole and felt a chill.

30

S T U B B Y Begay arrived about six-thirty—a short, scrawny man with badly bowed legs, a narrow, hawk-nosed face, and stone-black eyes. He had two teeth left, one snaggled right in front of his tongue so that he lisped. He talked so softly that in order to hear him I had to hunker down with him, his face no more than a foot from mine as he drew pictures in the dust.

According to Begay the vertical shaft of Floyd's Number Two sank 785 feet below the headframe. We tested the depth with dinner.

Earlier Finn had agreed that we could send food down for the little girl. We considered spiking the food to put them both out, but I knew damn well that Finn wouldn't fall for something that simple. And we had no way of knowing who might eat what . . . a dose necessary to knock out Finn would kill Daisy. So we played it straight. The small plastic cooler of sandwiches, fruit, and milk sank out of sight. The hundred yards of chalk line that we knotted to the cooler's handle ran out and was tied to another ball of brown twine, and that reeled off for what seemed forever. Every inch of that 785 feet paid out before the cooler touched bottom.

We waited several minutes and then we heard Finn shout, "Pull . . . it . . . out!" We did so. There was no way we could touch the son of a bitch.

Begay enlarged his drawing in the dirt. "You got a drift on that side at 300 feet," Begay said. "It's an old pump station. And here, at 430, and another here, at 785. Right on the bottom."

"Side tunnels, you mean?"

"They call 'em drifts." His eyes twinkled.

"That's where he must be then," I said, tapping the bottom.

"I'd be right here," Begay said and gouged his stick into the sand where he'd sketched the first side tunnel, or drift, 300 feet down.

"Why's that?"

" 'Cause the ladder goes right by it. No need to go to the bottom."

"The food went all the way down."

Stubby Begay grinned. His gums looked like plastic. "So you think he's on the bottom." He grinned even wider. "He takes the string and . . ." He made hand-over-hand motions as if he were pulling a bundle up. "He fake you out good that way."

I frowned. "What about the other drifts? The deeper ones?"

He shrugged.

"There's no way to reach them other than the ladder?"

Begay shook his head. "If it ain't come loose."

I looked up at Tate and Sterns. "Maybe that explains why we can hear him so well when he shouts," I said. "If he's only a hundred yards down in that first drift."

"Only," Tate said. He turned and watched two of the deputies unloading gear from the trunk of one of the patrol cars.

"So, Stubby, how about this. If I was lowered down in a sling seat, right along the ladder, I'd fetch up at this drift." I tapped the dirt. "Where you say he's got to be."

"That's what I say."

"There's nowhere else he might be?" Begay shrugged. "I mean except maybe the other side tunnels." He shook his head.

I looked over at the climbing harness that one of the deputies was shaking loose. "There's enough rope there?"

"Plenty," Sterns said. He sounded confident. It wasn't his ass in the sling.

As we made final preparations, the sun set. Spotlights from three cars converged on the shaft entrance, bathing it in harsh white light. Two big four-wheel-drive pickups had been recruited and parked thirty feet away, facing the shaft. Their floodlights added to the artificial daylight. The deputies attached the ropes to both front axles. They knew their job and took their time. When everything was finally ready, it was dark outside the circle of spotlights.

I looked down into the shaft, skeptical. The rope had to let me down right along the ladder so I could keep my feet planted and be able to use my one good arm. Otherwise, I'd just dangle and spin in the shaft, nothing more than a target on a string. The two deputies repositioned one of the trucks and were confident. I wasn't.

"Sir?" The deputy, Gareth Burns, gestured for me. "Can you step into this?" He held up a bright blue nylon harness that looked like a big athletic supporter.

With several sets of hands assisting, I was trussed up tight enough to choke. Then two big steel rings were clipped into the nylon loops in front.

"Can you work these with one hand?" the deputy asked. He gave me a demonstration of how the carabiner worked and then watched me diddle with the lock ring. I pressed in the release and the ring came off. "Good. Although you might just want to leave it hooked up. We can pay out all the rope you'll need."

"Terrific."

He nodded, mistaking my grimace for enthusiasm. "And I'll just clip these two other harnesses to the belt here, so when it comes time to bring everybody up, we can do it right." He had different plans than I did.

They pushed a plastic hard hat with a miner's light on my head and pulled the chinstrap tight.

At one point during the preparations, Pat Tate handed me a tiny Colt .380 automatic. The silencer looked like a six-ounce juice can. I handed it back to him. "Put a round in the chamber."

"You sure?"

"Yes, I'm sure." After he did so, I pointed the muzzle of the gun off into the desert. The tiny safety catch was awkward to use with my left hand. I practiced snapping it on and off, then slid the little pistol inside my shirt, sticking its snout under the bandages that bound my right shoulder, arm, and ribs.

"Is that going to work?" Pat Tate asked.

"It's going to have to," I said. Pat didn't ask what my plans were. The deputy snapped another large flashlight to my belt. It hung from a nylon loop.

"Slide this in your hip pocket," Tate said and held out a slender black penlight.

The deputy saw my expression at the third light. "Rule of threes," he said. "It's dark down there." I didn't argue. Tate adjusted the hand-held radio in its holster and made sure the microphone cord was free. The mike was clipped to my collar. I felt like a goddamned hardware store, but we were as ready as we could be.

Sterns jerked a thumb in the direction of the crowd. "The television station sure would like to be able to bring their cameras on over," he said.

"Sure," I said. He looked hopeful. "On one condition."

"What's that?"

"That you be the one to go down there."

He didn't like that much, but he didn't mention the news hounds again.

I picked up the hailer. "Finn! I coming down now."

"Take . . . your . . . time."

I handed the hailer to Tate. "Polite bastard, isn't he?"

The deputies handled me like glass. The iron mesh and its frame had been pulled completely off the shaft opening, and the hole gaped ominously. I stood with my back to the hole, the ladder's top rung behind me.

"Now just lean a little against the rope so your weight is diggin' in your heels," the deputy said. "And remember with this Z-haul, you're goin' down in five- or six-foot bites. We'll keep 'er just as smooth as we can. Now just edge on back until you got your feet on the ladder."

The deputy had his hand on my left elbow while another adjusted a set of heavy edge rollers to guide the rope. I waited patiently, my pulse pounding in my ears.

"Just trust the rope," Burns said.

"Do I have a choice?" I replied.

"Really, it works easy as can be. Now, just step down. Real easy. Leave it up to the rope." I did so while he orchestrated. The ladder flexed and I stopped. "Go on down until you can hang onto the top rung," he said.

One awkward step at a time, I backed down the ladder. After four rungs, I grabbed the ancient rust of the top rung in my hand.

"Now just relax for a minute and sit in the sling."

He switched his light back and forth, checking ropes. The weight was off my feet, and with a twitch of the hand I could have spun around like a kid on one of those swings made out of an old tire. I kept my feet on the ladder rungs and my hand in place.

I twisted my head and looked down. The pencil beam from my helmet light shot down into the darkness. I looked up and squinted against the glare of the spotlights. Pat Tate was standing close by, as was Sterns. Both of them had that look on their faces that said, "Better you than me, kid."

I took a deep breath. "All right," I said. "Let's get this over with."

31

S I X feet at a time, I sank into the earth. I kept my feet free of the ladder, learning to trust the sit-harness. The ladder's iron side rail slid through my left hand. That small contact was my anchor.

The vertical sides of the shaft were timbered, and in more than one spot water dripped down the face of the wood. The timbers smelled musty. I wondered what pockets of gases waited down below, trapped by the years of stagnation. I'd heard stories about miners walking into shafts where they took a breath and keeled over before they had time to turn around. That couldn't be the case here . . . Finn had no shortage of breath.

As the bright light of the entrance drifted up and away, the shaft seemed to narrow with me at its focus. My mind played games with the perspective. When I was fifty feet down, the deputy touched me with the beam of his flashlight.

"Any problems?" he asked. He didn't bother with the radio.

"No," I said. The rope played out again. The next time I looked up, I flinched. I could have covered the opening of the mine with the palm of my hand. Looking down, I saw the beam from my helmet light stab into nothing. No bottom. Just wooden timbers and old iron.

I avoided looking at the rope. What on the surface had looked stout and unbreakable in its coil now stretched out above me thin and gossamer. Every time the deputies reached the end of a pulley bite and the drop stopped, the rope twanged from side to side slightly.

On impulse I reached up and turned off my helmet light. The blackness of the mine was complete, the entrance above nothing but an insignificant postage stamp of artificial light. I caught my breath as the rope descended again. The light had been my lifeline to equilibrium and I turned it back on.

The side tunnel, what Stubby Begay had called a drift, took me by surprise. The side of the shaft had been passing by my left shoulder as I descended, a steady, unchanging parade of old wood timbers, dripping water, and abandoned iron fittings. I hadn't used the side of the shaft for support. Nevertheless, when it suddenly shelved inward, away from me, my stomach tightened. The rope dropped me far enough that my light shot into the tunnel.

The drift was nearly as large as the main shaft. I breathed in relief at seeing something substantial and horizontal.

I turned my head slightly, keyed with my left hand, and spoke into the hand-held radio's mike that was clipped to my shirt collar.

"Stop," I said. "I'm at the drift."

"Affirmative."

I pushed away from the ladder, rotating to face the drift. The floor of the tunnel was littered with junk—old sections of pipe, fittings, various lengths of wire and cable. The light illuminated heavy timbers and a series of three small concrete pads, each two feet high. Rusted bolts thrust up from the concrete where at one time machines had been secured.

Stubby Begay had called it a pump station. The miners hadn't left much behind . . . just enough scars and litter to puzzle archaeologists in another thousand years.

For the first thirty feet the drift was as securely timbered as the main shaft. But forty feet back the drift elbowed to the left and the timber supports ended. I couldn't see around the bend. The place made my skin crawl.

Rotten and water-soaked as the timbers were, they gave the illusion of strength and support. In the drift they gave way to something that looked like monstrous cobwebs, with patches of the material hanging down from a ceiling of jagged rock. It was some sort of fabric, bolted right to the face of the shaft.

In dozens of places rock fragments littered the floor of the drift where the old fabric had pulled loose, and off to the left, just visible before the drift turned out of sight, an entire section of wall and ceiling had slumped, filling nearly a third of the tunnel.

I swept the light carefully, looking for movement.

"Finn?" I said. My voice echoed down the shaft. The dust of the years had padded the floor, and the fresh tracks were as clear as if they had been painted on a sidewalk with Day-Glo paint. And the prints came in two sizes.

"Finn, are you in there?" Again my words rattled around and died with no response. I ducked my head and looked down the main shaft. Ten feet below the drift, the iron supports that held the ladder had pulled loose . . . or rusted through. The section of ladder was twisted away from the wall and hung off at an angle. Finn had to be in the drift.

I reached for the second flashlight, adding its beam to that of my helmet. I saw that with just a slight stretch I could plant my feet on the lip of the drift's shaft and grab one of the wall timbers with my left hand. With some slack in the rope I could pull myself into the tunnel.

If I slipped and fell, it would hurt like hell, but the rope could be trusted. That's what the deputy had said.

"Turn off your light," Finn said. His voice was quiet and conversational.

Out of reflex I swung the lights toward the sound of his voice. Nothing. I snapped off the flashlight and let it hang, then reached up and turned off my helmet. The blackness was oppressive . . . the spotlights above at the shaft mouth served only as a beacon in the distance. I reached up and touched the small, reassuring pistol grip of the Colt under my arm sling. I waited.

"Sheriff, you copy?" The crackle of the damn radio sounded like a string of firecrackers.

I keyed the mike and snapped, "Stay off the air."

"Ten-four."

I took a deep breath, my fingers still covering the lump that was the automatic. "All right, Finn. What do you want?"

Unless Finn had developed sonar, he could see no more than I. His light exploded out of the darkness, and I jerked my head back in surprise.

"Get that goddamned thing out of my eyes," I snapped, but he took his time. Finally the light slipped away and I cracked an eyelid. The beam was centered on the thick bandage that bound my right arm and shoulder. My right hand stuck out of the linen and lay flat against my belly, useless. Finn played the light this way and that, examining me and my equipment.

"Turn around," he said and watched as I touched the shaft wall with my fingers and gently pushed myself so that I rotated on the rope. The wash of his light cast a fat shadow of me on the opposite wall of the vertical shaft. As I rotated back around, he turned off the light. I blinked my eyes, trying to put out the yellow sunbursts that remained.

"So," he said.

"Are you through playing games? Where's the child?"

"She's asleep. And you've managed to make quite a name for yourself, haven't you? I underestimated your tenacity."

I was in no mood to exchange compliments. "You have to let us bring her up. Nobody's going to hurt her . . . or you."

Finn chuckled. "I can imagine." The harness dug into my crotch and belly, and my right leg was falling asleep. Finn knew he had all the time in the world. I didn't if I was going to be worth anything.

"I was surprised that you had put it all together, Sheriff," he said. I tried to picture where he might be standing.

"Sometimes I get lucky."

"Yes," he said. "Had your truck not let me down, we wouldn't be having this conversation now."

"What do you want, Finn? What do you think I can do for you?" I was tired of hanging like a goddamned potted plant.

"I saw the newspapers under the seat. You're a clever man, to make the association. I'm curious why you didn't call in any of the other authorities earlier."

I frowned and said, "What do . . . " when what he'd said hit me like a sledge, smashing open the doors of my rusty memory. The newspapers. My notes. Until this day, I'd last seen the papers Friday night when I parked at the campground. The two-week-old papers, one of them with the front page headline . . . my notes in the margin.

I breathed a silent curse. We'd received the bulletin from Washington State along with a thousand other law enforcement agencies. We were close to the border. It made sense.

H. T. Finn had seen the newspaper when he'd stolen the radio—the headline and my notes. He had assumed that I'd made the connection, knew who he was, what he'd done.

"Arajanian did those hits for you, too," I said, trying to keep my voice calm and hoping that he didn't recognize the guess.

"He learned well," Finn said. "He would have been of great use to me."

My mind raced. "No, he did just what you wanted," I said. "It worked out better the way it was . . . you left the rifle with him for the police to find. It's probably the same rifle you had him use on the governor of Washington and the prison warden, isn't it? If there was a matchup, it'd tie those shootings to the kid, and you'd be long gone. No witnesses to say otherwise after you shot us . . . and set the mountain on fire."

"Cleansing fire," Finn said softly, and his voice drifted off as he recited, " 'And the fire shall cleanse the evil from the earth and . . .' " His voice became indistinct.

"And they don't know you as Finn in Washington, do they?" I said, but he refused the bait.

Finally he said, "You will make arrangements, Sheriff. Lis-

196

ten carefully." I wasn't in a position to do otherwise, but I wanted answers to a flood of questions. Finn continued, "I want a fully fueled helicopter. The television station has one. The helicopter, one reporter, and a pilot. That's all. It will land immediately beside the mouth of the shaft, close enough that I can see the flash of its blades over the opening."

I sighed. Why was an aircraft always such magic to these fruitcakes? Where would he go, other than Mexico? And what made him think Mexico would want him? He wanted a reporter, and that meant he thought the world would be interested in hearing his sorry tale.

My eyes ached with the strain of trying to see him in the darkness, and my finger itched to reach for the Colt automatic. But he had the girl, and we would play his game until the time was right.

"That's all?"

"As a beginning, yes."

"You'll let them send down two more ropes, one for the girl and one for you?"

"No!" he said sharply. "Ruth and I will use the ladder. We will go out the way we came in." He laughed softly. "You'd like me in harness, helpless. You'd like that, wouldn't you. Oh no. That's how they killed my Ruth. It won't happen again. Never again."

Another Ruth. But now it was the little girl I worried about. "It's a long climb. I was just trying to make it safe for Daisy."

"You don't need to be concerned. Just do as I say."

"All right."

"Talk to the ones on the surface now," he commanded.

I keyed the mike. "Gastner here."

"Go ahead, Gastner."

"Listen carefully, and get this right the first time. Finn wants Channel 8's Jet Ranger, fully fueled, with a pilot and a reporter on board. He wants it to set down immediately beside the mine shaft. We have to be able to see the blades flash, or he won't go for it. No one else in the way. The three of us will

197

come up. The three of us will board the chopper. Is that understood?"

After a pause, I heard Pat Tate's voice. "Understand: Channel 8's chopper, one pilot, one reporter. They might not agree to that."

"Don't waste time, Pat." The television crew would leap at the chance to be evening news. "And nothing else. Tell everyone to keep their fingers off the damn triggers. I don't want the girl hurt."

"Ten four. Search and rescue wants the girl in a harness, on a rope."

"No," Finn said loudly.

"Look," I said. "It's for her own safety, Finn. Use your head. You could slip. Without a harness, there's nothing between you and 400 feet of shaft."

His voice regained its original composure. "If you and your men do as I say, there won't be any slips, will there?"

"Gastner, did you copy?"

I keyed the mike. "Negative on the rope," I said. My brain raced. There was no way a four-year-old child was going to be carried up 300 feet of rusted, slippery ladder.

"We'll see what we can do," Tate said, and the shaft fell silent. I shifted in the harness, trying to let some blood down my right leg.

"Finn, listen to me. Turn your light on." To my surprise he did so, keeping the beam centered on my torso. "Are you wearing a heavy belt?"

He didn't answer.

"Look, if you are, use this." I turned and groped with my left hand for the small harness that the deputy had clipped to my own. "They gave me this. Put it on Daisy, and clip her to your belt. At least do that."

"No." He turned off the light.

"Damn it, she'll be clipped to you. She'll be safe that way. What can we do if she's clipped to you? No one can make a move to grab her. And it keeps your arms free. It will be even better."

198

Finn was silent, and I hoped he was weighing his options. "All right," he said. "Throw the harness into the tunnel." He turned on the light. I breathed a sigh or relief. For several minutes I fumbled with the carabiner before the big steel ring snapped open. I tossed the smaller of the two extra harnesses into the drift.

The beam always fastened on me, Finn made his way through the scattered junk. He stopped when the line of pump foundations separated us. I couldn't tell if he held a weapon in his other hand. "Tell them to pull you up ten feet."

The bastard was shrewd. I keyed the mike and repeated his order. I had no sense of moving. Rather, the entrance of the drift sank, as if the wall itself slid downward. My feet were just above the top of the tunnel mouth when the pull stopped.

"Finn, do you know how to hook up that harness? Do it properly now." I shouted, suddenly frantic at not being able to see inside the drift.

He didn't respond, but I heard his footfalls as he advanced and picked up the harness. I tried to picture him bending down, then straightening up, and then retreating back down the shaft. I counted eight footfalls, then lost him. There was no other time to take the gamble. I reached up and gently keyed the mike. I kept my voice a husky whisper.

"Don't answer," I whispered. "Give me five bites down."

Their response was immediate. In the darkness I felt the wall slide by, felt the breath of air as the drift yawned in front of me. I'd have one chance. I stretched out my feet, my toes reaching for rock. The floor of the drift touched my left foot and I grabbed with my left hand, my teeth clenched.

I felt wood, slipped, and grabbed a rough crack in the timber. I yanked with all my strength, pulling the rope in after me. As the downward bite continued, I let my weight carry me into the drift until I was resting on my left hand and both knees. My right leg, until then sound asleep, tingled sharply with the new movement.

Above they would continue to pay out the rope, giving me three more bites of slack . . . about eighteen feet of line. I hoped they wouldn't ask questions when the weight left the line. I straightened up slightly and pulled out the Colt automatic.

The murmurings of soft voices reached me. I tried to judge the distance, but the sound bounced and echoed. I recognized Daisy's little voice, high-pitched and confused.

Finn hadn't heard me. I kept my mouth closed, forcing my breathing quiet. My heart hammered in my ears. Slowly I shuffled forward five feet, a third of the distance to the pump foundations.

In minutes Finn would return with Daisy. I knew I'd have the time and the strength for only one try.

32

I EDGED my way toward the old pump foundation. When I thought I was close, I reared up on my knees like an old dinosaur, hand outstretched and groping.

The edge of my hand touched cold, damp concrete. With infinite care I palmed the small automatic, held it against my chest, and pushed off the safety. I took a deep breath and braced my forearm on the concrete. The darkness in front of me was a solid door.

Finn would have to use the light to walk Daisy out. I strained to hear. Nothing.

"Keep your eyes on your feet, Ruth," he said. The voice took me completely by surprise. I crouched as low as my belly would allow. Their feet made soft shuffling sounds with an occasional tinkle as some small piece of mining detritus was kicked from their path.

The light cut the darkness over my head, darting out into the shaft. I kept my head down. My hand on the automatic was wet with sweat. The sounds stopped. Had the son of a bitch seen the rope?

"Gastner!" His voice was strong . . . and close. The beam of light twitched, swinging from one side to the other. "I've got the girl with me."

I could hear her breathing, little chirpy breaths of raw fright. He took another step, and I watched the flashlight beam.

His voice was a soft whisper. "Stay close, Ruth." She wasn't linked. I gritted my teeth and slipped my index finger in the trigger guard of the Colt.

The flashlight beam was narrow and intense. He was close. Another step, you bastard, I thought. I saw the shadow of his hand behind the light, counted three, and moved.

Six feet away, the target for my automatic was just a murky figure behind the light. I saw Finn's trick almost soon enough. The images registered just as I squeezed the trigger. The smaller of the two figures was holding the flashlight.

I pulled the shot, but too late. The little Colt coughed and spat. The bullet sang past the side of Daisy's head, whined off the ceiling, and richocheted down the drift.

Finn was already in motion, but he was a big target. I squeezed the trigger twice, and this time Finn yelped and spun sideways. In two staggering backward steps he crashed into the wall of the shaft.

Instinctively Daisy turned, and the beam turned with her. For a moment Finn was illuminated. He scrambled to his feet. In his right hand was my .45 automatic, and there was no silencer on the muzzle.

I pointed quickly and fired twice. Each time the little pellets struck him, he flinched and staggered back. But he didn't go down. For a moment he stood motionless, his face looking up at the roof of the drift, as if he were lost and searching for direction from the rocks.

The little girl dropped the light. It clattered, rolled a couple of feet toward me, and lay against a length of rusted pipe. Its beam pointed back into the drift. She whimpered and sat down, a tiny, frightened ball.

I slapped the automatic down on the concrete foundation, lunged toward her, and grabbed the harness. I pulled the little girl to me. I saw motion and looked up to see Finn staggering like a drunk. He raised the .45 and held it in both hands.

"Don't do it!" I shouted. Releasing my hold on Daisy, I made a wild grab at the little Colt. Finn swung toward me and pulled the trigger. The .45 bellowed, the explosion mind-numbing in the drift. The bullet passed harmlessly two feet over my head, crossed the main shaft, and thudded into a timber.

I locked my arm against the damp concrete, pointed the .380 toward the center of the shadow that was Finn's torso, and pulled the trigger twice.

Finn staggered backward. The drift was filled with the crashes of the .45 as his finger jerked the trigger spasmodically. I cringed low, hugging Daisy to me. One of the fat, hollow-point bullets of the .45 glanced off an iron bracket and sang over our heads like a wasp. Finn had already lost his balance, the recoil of the gun adding to his backward dance.

Another sound became harmony to the big automatic. With a loud "whump," a section of the wall just behind the timbers caved in, the mass striking Finn and carrying him to the other side of the drift. He screamed and went down. The dust billowed toward me.

I slapped the light switch on my helmet. In one desperate motion I stood up, pulled Daisy off her feet, and plunged the carabiner through the loop of my own harness. The spring snapped shut.

With the little girl hanging from my waist like a rag doll, I turned and waddled toward the vertical shaft.

Behind me, Finn screamed. "No! Listen to me!" he shrieked. The son of a bitch would have to talk to himself.

I fumbled with the mike switch on my collar. "Pull me up!" I bellowed into the mike.

Behind me, Finn continued to shriek and then he found the .45 again. Its last cartridge exploded. The flash illuminated the back of the drift, and the slug danced off the rock and dug into the dust. Even as the clip emptied, the rumble of the earth's guts built, low and ominous.

A puff of air hit my face and with it came the acrid smell of fresh rock dust. A timber nearby cracked loudly and a shower of rocks clattered around my feet. I grabbed a fistful of Daisy's jacket and reached the mouth of the drift just as the last of the rope's slack snaked past. The rotten timbers above the pump station collapsed inward.

Something heavy struck my right foot and I spun sideways. "Son of a bitch!" I shouted and jumped into space.

The jolt of the rope damn near cut me in half. Daisy was a small child, but her weight pulled the harness off-sides.

Like a twisting, turning pendulum, we snapped out away from the drift and then crashed back against the side of the shaft, the iron of the ladder cracking my helmet. If Daisy screamed, I never heard it.

The rumble of the collapse died away in the drift even as we were lifted toward the surface. I hung limp, head back and eyes locked on the patch of light above me.

It was almost a relief to hang in the quiet shaft.

"Gastner, you copy?"

In order to key the mike, I would have had to release my hold on Daisy. That would have been a hell of a way to test whether or not the carabiner still locked her harness to mine. I didn't have the strength to yell. Let 'em wait, I thought.

33

A THOUSAND hands hoisted us out of the shaft. The ground under my feet was hard and firm—with nothing hanging over my head but the night sky.

"Be careful with the child," someone said. Her eyes were tightly closed, with her arms drawn up tightly to her chest and her fists balled under her chin.

I struggled to my feet and saw Nolan Parris. The priest was trying to reach the child, trying to push his way past the medical team and the assisting cops. His face was as white as his Roman collar and his eyes wide with concern for the child . . . but he was heading for disaster.

"Parris!" I shouted at him. He jerked up and saw me. I wrenched my arm away from someone and staggered toward the priest. I caught him by the shirtfront and for a minute we both executed a slow, clumsy dance as I tried to keep my balance.

I shook Parris until he was looking me in the eye.

"Listen!" I shouted at him and then I lowered my voice. "Listen to me. Now's not the time. You're a stranger to her, just like the rest of us."

"But I . . ."

I shook him, but it was a damn feeble shake. "Stay out of

their way. She's in good hands. And you're not going to be able to just walk back into her life. She doesn't know you. You'll make matters worse." He turned in my grip and watched the medics bundle the little girl toward the medivac helicopter.

Hell, I knew what he wanted. He'd made up his mind and now wanted to make up for four lost years. But he had no idea how tough that road was going to be. The little girl wasn't going to run into his arms, shouting, "Daddy, Daddy!" I figured she'd had her fill of adults for a while. If I'd been her, I'd have wanted to stay catatonic for about a month until I sorted life out.

Camera lights bathed the helicopter as the reporters got what they had come for. A little, helpless, battered child made damn good copy.

I could see Nolan Parris wasn't going to do anything stupid, and I released my hold on him. "Help me over to the chopper. We'll ride into the hospital with her."

Twenty hours later Pat Tate answered the telephone for me. I was standing in front of the small mirror that hung over the nightstand in my hospital room, trying to manipulate the electric shaver so I didn't hack my chin wattles to pieces. Even over the buzz of the razor, I heard the caller's ranting and knew right away who it was.

"You betcha," Sheriff Tate said. He nodded and repeated himself, then added, "Here he is." He held out the receiver, and I set the razor down.

"Holman?"

"Himself."

Posadas County Sheriff Martin Holman was pissed. I got in the first word.

"Yup," I said into the phone and the tirade began.

"What the *hell* is going on up there with you?" he shouted, and I held the receiver away from my ear. Tate grinned, tapped his watch, and mouthed that he'd be back in a few minutes. Holman was still barking, and I let him roll on until he lost some momentum.

"My God, all I see in the papers and on television is your mug, and for Christ's sakes you don't even work for them."

"Those are the breaks," I said.

Holman almost choked, and I listened to him cough for a minute before he got control. "Do you know how many times I've called?"

"No, sir," I said. He was twenty years my junior, but what the hell. He signed my paychecks. "No one told me you'd called."

"Three times yesterday," Holman barked. He really was angry. "Three goddamned times. And shit . . . four times today, at least."

"Sorry about that. Things were hectic though." Pat Tate must have been having fun. And the son of a gun never had told me.

"They said you were asleep."

"The docs wouldn't let anyone in to see me. They were worried about me combining exhaustion with coronary stress."

"Coronary stress, hell. You've got the next best thing to a new one. No one can kill you." His tone modulated a little. "They could have at least told you I called."

"I'm sure they were planning on it." I saw an opening and took it. "And Estelle is doing well. I thought you might like to hear that."

"I know that," Holman said. "I talked with her husband. More than once," he added pointedly. "He says she's going to recover fully."

"Yes."

"So how the hell did you piece together that this character was wanted in Washington? Talk about grandstanding heroics. Jesus."

"I didn't piece it together. He saw an old newspaper I'd kept after we got the APB earlier this month. He thought I had nailed him."

"You mean you hadn't made the connection?"

"Nope. I was as stupid as everyone else."

"Everyone is saying you did."

"Nope. Dumb luck."

"Well, I'll be damned. And he was in New Mexico when the murders took place in Washington . . . that's what Tate said earlier."

"That's right. He sent a friend back to Washington . . . a kid that lived with him. Slipped in, shot the governor and warden, slipped back out."

"Hell, he could as easily have ended up down here in Posadas, Bill. Right in our backyard."

"They have to end up somewhere. Pat Tate got lucky."

"And he was a nut case? That's what Tate said."

"In and out. We haven't had a chance to really sort everything out with the cops from Washington State, but from what they told us over the phone, Finn was treated at one of the state hospitals there about five years before. And he was treated as an outpatient on occasion before and after that. He and his younger sister used to run a fundamentalist church of sorts."

"He was a preacher?"

"Sort of. Fire-and-brimstone stuff. Eye for an eye. He was arrested once for assault, but that was tossed out. Apparently he managed to keep the lid on until his little sister was killed in a women's correctional facility a year ago."

"His sister?"

"Yes. A young woman named Ruth Tolever. She was arrested for something Finn contended she never did. She was killed during an altercation before she could be sprung on bail. The fight had nothing to do with her, they're telling us . . . she just got caught in it. That set Finn off. He blamed the whole system."

"He took his time, if revenge was what he had in mind."

"A planner," I said. "And the son of a bitch wasn't one of those nuts who wants to be caught. He moved down here, planning all the time what he was going to do. Hooked up with his young friend and found Arajanian was an apt pupil."

"And the little girl? The TV men sure had a field day with that story."

"As near as we can figure from what Washington tells us, Finn probably saw the little girl as a replacement for his sister . . . that's my guess. Maybe he really did love Cecilia Burgess. She was going to have his kid. Maybe he just kept her around so he could keep Daisy. We may never know for sure."

"One cold bastard." Holman fell silent for a minute. "He had his pal kill all those kids in the truck."

"That's the way it looks. The one kid lived, and from what he's told Pat Tate, that's what happened. Since revenge worked in Washington State he probably figured it'd work here, too."

Holman grunted. "So, how are you?"

"All right. Bruised and tired."

"When are you heading back?"

I chuckled. "By the end of the week, I guess. Not before. I want to stick around to make sure Estelle's on the mend and doesn't need anything. And they haven't brought my Blazer back yet either."

"My house burned down, you know."

"I know. Bob Torrez told me. Did you find the key to my place all right?"

"We're staying at the Essex Motel."

"For God's sakes, Martin, what for? Get the goddamned key and use my house."

Sheriff Pat Tate had stepped into the room. I grinned at him and looked heavenward. Holman said, "Well, I don't know . . . and it was arson. To cover up a robbery."

"No shit? Bob didn't say anything about that."

"Hell no. We didn't know until yesterday. I was going to tell you, but they'd never put me through to you. How could I?"

"What was taken?"

"The usual stuff. My stereo, some guns, pottery, a couple rugs. Stuff like that."

"Any leads?"

"None yet. I was kinda hoping you'd be back so I could go over some things with you."

"End of the week for sure. Any other messages?"

"No. Well, wait a minute." He shuffled papers. "Your daughter in Flint called. But she said it wasn't important. You're supposed to call her when you can. I think she saw something on television and got worried."

"Fine. Anything else?"

Holman laughed, his usual good mood returning. "I feel like I'm being dismissed."

"I didn't mean it that way," I said, although I had. "I got company, is all, and we got a meeting with about eight different law agencies from Washington . . . and the feds."

"Better you than me," Holman said. "End of the week, then. Give my best to Estelle and Francis. And tell Tate that you don't work for him."

"I'll do that." We hung up and I repeated Holman's message to Tate.

"By the time we're through with all the paperwork and all the meetings, you'll think that you do, kid," Tate said.

210

34

I T W A S good to walk out of that hospital room. We took the elevator down one floor, then wound through enough hallways to disorient the most die-hard Boy Scout. The door of 467 was ajar.

Estelle Reyes-Guzman's bed was partially elevated. The bandages around her head, the white gown, and the white bedding made it look like her dark face was floating in a sea of cotton. Her hands were folded on her stomach and she looked peaceful.

Even as Pat and I started across toward the bed, she opened her eyes. It took her eyes a minute to adjust. She saw me and a slow grin spread across her face. Even in a hospital bed, stuck with tubes and wired to machines, she was lovely.

"Hey, sir," she said, and her voice was soft but clear. I took her right hand in my left. She looked at the new wad of bandages and sling that trussed my right shoulder and arm. "You're almost in one piece."

"Piece of cake," I said.

"You're going back to Posadas now?"

I shrugged. "Maybe by the end of the week. No hurry."

"You're going to keep house for Francis until you leave?"

I nodded. "I'm too cheap to pay for a motel, you know

that." She grinned again. "I'll stick around until you're out of this hole."

"This hole is costing the county about a grand a day," Tate said, but he wasn't complaining.

Estelle frowned and reached across with her left hand, patting the top of mine. "Have you seen Daisy?"

I took a deep breath. "No. But she's doing all right."

"She wasn't hurt?" I was sure Pat had told her the entire story, but she needed the reassurance.

"Just bruises. Physically, she's all right."

Estelle heard that correctly and her dark eyes searched mine. I shrugged. "It's going to be a long, maybe tough road for her, Estelle. We have no way of knowing what sort of crap Finn put in her head. Now she doesn't have anybody except Nolan Parris. He's decided to try for legal custody. And he wants to remain with the order."

"That'll never work," she whispered. Her grip on my hand tightened.

"Give him a chance. It might. There aren't too many other alternatives. Who knows? He might start a fashionable trend." She smiled faintly, closed her eyes, and released my hand. "She'll be fine, Estelle."

"Will you do me a favor?" she said without opening her eyes.

"Sure. Name it."

She turned her head slightly so that when she opened her eyes she was looking directly at me. "When you think she's ready, would you bring her up to see me?"

I hesitated, then nodded. "I'll see what I can do."

She visibly relaxed and looked at Pat Tate. "You take care of him, all right? Make sure he behaves himself."

Tate threw an exaggerated shrug and thrust his hands in his pockets. "He's too old to learn anything, Estelle. You get yourself better and maybe he'll go home." He shrugged again. "That's our only chance."

We stepped out into the hall and damn near collided with

212

Francis Guzman. The young physician looked like maybe he'd gotten an hour's sleep. "She's doing great, isn't she?"

"You bet," Tate said.

Francis turned to me. "You've got a key to the house?"

"Sure do."

He nodded. "See you for dinner then. Around six." He grinned and pushed open the door to Estelle's room.

"Around six," I said in mock disgust as we walked down the hall toward the elevator. "That's what they promised before all this started. And I'm still waiting."

1337 1751